HONOR AND OBLIGATION

A Hunter's Universe Novel by David Michael Martin

This book is a work of fiction. Names, characters, businesses, organizations, places, events and incidents either are the product of the author's imagination or are used fictitiously. Any resemblance to actual persons, living or dead, events, or locales is entirely coincidental.

For information contact:

Bent Briar Publishing L.L.L.P.
Sahuarita, AZ 85629
www.bentbriarbooks.com

Book Design by Freelance Creative Support Services

978-1-942665-07-6 SC
978-1-942665-06-9 HC
978-1-942665-08-3 eBook

First Edition: September 2018

10 9 8 7 6 5 4 3 2 1

Dedication

This book is dedicated to the concept of a seamless and natural gender equality, an equality so obvious that it never calls attention to itself or causes controversy. Without it, the Eyloni could not survive.

Acknowledgements

I want to thank Dr. Anne Goiran-Bevelhimer for encouraging me to become a writer. I want to thank my editor Wendie Thomas for her hours of work and my agent Laura Kathleen Sutton for the time and effort she spent in getting Honor and Obligation published. I also thank BetteRose Ryan and everyone at Bent Briar Publishing for all their efforts. Their work is greatly appreciated.

Other Titles by David Michael Martin

Hunter's Moon

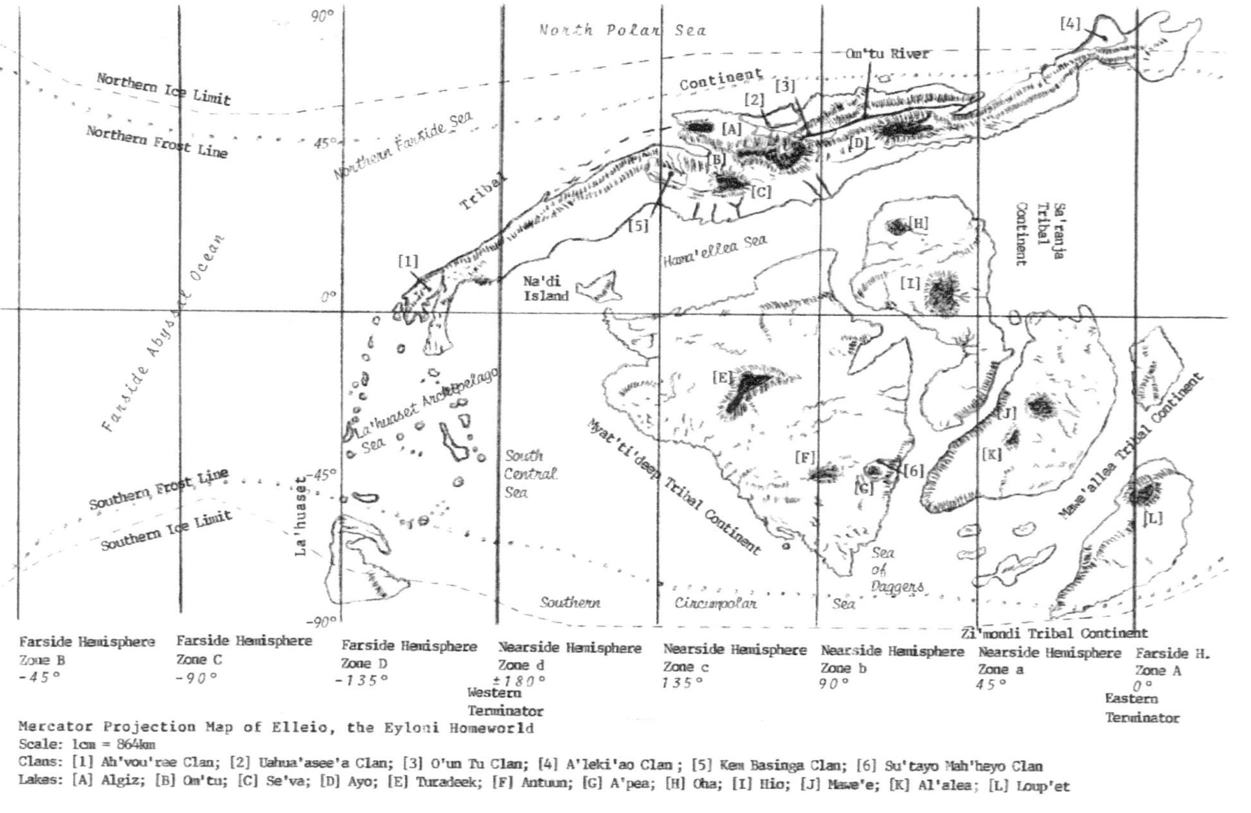

Mercator Projection Map of Elleio, the Eyloni Homeworld
Scale: 1cm = 864km
Clans: [1] Ah'vou'ree Clan; [2] Uahua'asee'a Clan; [3] O'un Tu Clan; [4] A'leki'ao Clan ; [5] Kem Basinga Clan; [6] Su'tayo Mah'heyo Clan
Lakes: [A] Algiz; [B] Om'tu; [C] Se'va; [D] Ayo; [E] Turadeek; [F] Antuun; [G] A'pea; [H] Oha; [I] Hio; [J] Mawe'e; [K] Al'alea; [L] Loup'et

Table of Contents

PROLOGUE
BASIC INSTINCTS

Hervorallin scowled at her daughter.

"She's not supposed to do this, I take it?" Warleader Delwyn asked.

"No," the Hunter female trilled ominously and scowled at Princess again.

"I wonder what she's thinking about," Delwyn said.

"She is one thousand Elleio Standard Time days old. She, as with all Eyloni, was born with sophisticated instincts. She will act within those instincts for the next two and a half years before her brain grows large enough for her to begin learning. Right now her mental processes are wired for two things: her scent-linked empathy and her preoccupation with male safety."

Delwyn smiled at his near-daughter, the Eyloni infant who had empathically bonded with him at her birth. She was no bigger than a human child's doll. She was barely sixty Earth days old, but she had better control over her body than a circus acrobat. She had no language skills at all, but she expected him to understand her by smelling her scent and getting mental pictures from her. Being human, he didn't have her empathic sense.

He caught glimpses of her mood though. He had a good sense of smell, and he had a high intuitive sense. He picked up ghostly impressions from Princess, but nothing near what Eyloni communicated to one another solely through body odor.

Delwyn popped the *malutha* berry into his mouth. The berry tasted like a concentrated maraschino cherry. He thought about the taste and the pleasure it brought him.

Princess trilled as she smelled his feelings.

"Where do you suppose she found it?" Delwyn asked.

"The berry?" Hervorallin asked. "She prowled down into the hydroponics center in the engineering hull."

Delwyn frowned. "Why there? That's a straight line three-hundred-meter trek one way. More when you consider all the weaving and turning through the rainforest simulations in the ship. Why not just go to the nutrition center? It's here in the command hull."

Hervorallin shook her head. "That would be too easy. I can smell her determination. She wanted to get something for you that was special."

"Yeah, but how did she get through the aftstation? Wouldn't the security personnel have caught her between the command hull and the engineering hull?"

"There are small vents and chases that connect the hulls. The force field encapsulated holographic flora would look like hollow branches to her. She would have used them to evade Cailindreda, the aftstation security mistress."

"Wouldn't she smell Princess?"

"I'm sure she or one of her security personnel noticed her."

Princess trilled a negative not hard even for Delwyn to understand.

"She's learning words fast."

Hervorallin looped her tail in a 'no' gesture. "She does not understand our words and will not understand them as words for some time to come. She smells our feelings, and the empathy triggered gives her a translation. That translation is emotive. This empathy is how we learned your language."

"I remember."

Hervorallin sent another empathic scold to her daughter. A warship was no place for an infant to wander about. Princess had a stubborn streak, and she used Delwyn's presence as a shield for her behavior.

He did not help matters much, either. His almost total nose-blindness to Eyloni pheromones meant he could not smell the emotions riding on her daughter's scent. No doubt Princess took his acceptance as permission for her antics.

Phelindra, the Eldest Huntress of the warship, grunted.

"What?" Hervorallin asked.

"His scent tells us more than he intends to," Phelindra murmured.

Delwyn sighed. Here they go again, talking to each other as if he wasn't there. They were in his quarters, his abode. He had been asleep, both females curled up around him. Phelindra was his Protectress, and her duties required her to never leave his side. Hervorallin was here because she knew Princess would end up here: even in newborns the instinct to protect the rare male was uppermost in her mind.

"You should go back to sleep," Phelindra told him.

"Yes, Delwyn. Go to sleep. You have many lessons in Eyloni culture and tradition you must master before we arrive in home space," Hervorallin added.

Delwyn groaned. "I'm not sleepy. I got a couple of hours in, surprise, surprise. At least security hasn't burst in on me again."

Phelindra scowled at him. "They make regular stops and look into the bole, see me, cock their ears, and then leave."

"They should not bother you," Hervorallin added. "Go back to sleep. You will need the rest."

"I have all the time I need," he protested. "We have over a month, well, one of my months anyway, before we reach Elleio. Anailiatha won't risk further damage to our jump drive by going any faster."

"You do not learn like we do," Hervorallin chastised. "We have a scent memory that acts as a mnemonic device for us. You do not associate scent with learned knowledge."

"I do sometimes. Every so often smell recalls a memorable event," he objected.

Phelindra trilled a rhythmic chanting laughter. "That is the barest scent reflex for us, and we do it consciously. Your scent tells me that you are talking about an involuntary scent reflex. From our point of view, you are going to have to 'brute force' learn it all."

"You mean how Anlann and Seralin learned the Coalition standard language before becoming co-ambassadors?"

"Yes. They had no human to sample pheromones from as they heard your Coalition tongue. They could not learn the emotional meaning of the words. It had to be told to them. Hearing about a thing is not the same as feeling a thing."

"But rote learning is the way most humans learn, rote learning and repetition. I've done it all my life. Do you know how many things I had to memorize and practice in my career as a special operations group commander while I was a senior chief warrant officer in the Coalition? Learning Eyloni customs will be like learning how to walk the paths here in *Hunter's Moon.*"

He yawned, the sudden desire to fall back to sleep was overpowering.

Both Hunters smirked at one another acknowledging their part in making Delwyn sleepy, and as they wrapped tails around their favorite male, Princess curled between her mother and his shoulder.

Hervorallin and Phelindra looked at each other over his shoulder and softly sang the universal female maxim: *males are strange.*

1

16 LIGHT-YEARS OUT OF NIKKIOLO, ABOARD THE COMPACT WARSHIP HUNTER'S MOON

Clearing his throat, Delwyn met Melkorka's eyes as he entered the command center and took up his position in the Warleader's Watch. She commanded the warship, yet his orders superseded hers. But not always—he had yet to figure that out.

He tried clearing his throat again, hoping no one—more likely a squad of no ones for that matter—would come running. The ship's combat address system sent his soft deep voice everywhere whether he wanted it to or not. Every soul aboard could hear him. The audio pickups had been programmed to track and relay his voice alone, and the crew refused to even consider disabling it!

Delwyn, a human and the only male aboard, stood out among the over twenty-six hundred alien female crew. They insisted on hearing his voice day and night as a reminder that a male walked among them and needed their support and protection.

Humans, it turned out muttered, mumbled, murmured, cleared throats, sighed, swore, ground their teeth, whistled, and talked to themselves. The crew had made that quite clear within a few hours after the first faster-than-light jump back to Elleio, the Eyloni homeworld.

Humming and whistling, any rhythmic sound, delighted them. The Eyloni had always been a musical people. Descended from upright-walking lemuroids, they sang from birth. Even their language contained musical elements. Delwyn's deep resonating voice attracted them because it had many of the Eyloni male qualities they empathized with. They loved to sing with him.

Singing with a male-reinforced mysterious cultural ties between females and the male they associated with. Since male births didn't occur often, and females outnumbered males by about twenty to one, females always protected males in Eyloni society. This protective drive kicked into high gear when a warleader sang during combat. His singing improved female morale and focused their deadly fighting powers making them extremely fierce in combat to keep their male safe from harm. In non-combat situations, any note they heard out of him was taken as an invitation to come and sing with him, and once they started singing, they resisted any attempt at stopping before the tenth or eleventh song, at least.

The crew learned his language every time he sang with them. As pheromone-linked empaths, they smelled his scent and compared the empathic visions it gave them with his words. A person from one clan could learn the language of a person from any of the thousands of clans within the Ten Tribes of Elleio by comparing pheromones and words. An Eyloni identified with the feelings she smelled in a person's scent, but scent suffered a handicap as an immediate-vicinity communication medium. The combat address system couldn't transmit scent throughout the ship. Without scent to translate his human mutters, the crew sometimes misunderstood what his sounds meant and at times they even wondered whether they meant anything at all.

Not willing to take any chances, they reacted. Lately Delwyn often found himself surrounded by his Protectress, Eldest Huntress Phelindra, and ten or more of the Hunter-phenotype females. All of them but Phelindra had a green web woven into their military rank earrings. The earrings reminded him of dreamcatchers dangling from gold wire braids in their left earfolds. Golden hoops the size of a circle made by touching fingertip to thumb were filled with different colored interwoven webs. Few Hunters aboard wore the green web identifying them as Warleader Special Security. That they reported to Phelindra the Mistress of the Watch and not to him had been obvious. When he pressed her for details, she ignored him.

Typical.

One moment they treated him like he was their captain, and the next moment they treated him like he was an invalid.

The green-webbed Hunters had burst in on him while sleeping—several times. Eyloni were incapable of snoring, and they thought his snarls signified choking or some threat. They rushed him once as he listened to Melkorka's cultural lessons after he grumbled aloud at her confusing words, and they had hunted him down once in the simulated orange-hued jungle trails running throughout the ship when he muttered an expletive aloud while backtracking to a missed trail.

Phelindra, much older than any of the Hunters with her, complemented them on their vigilance every time they arrived before excusing them. Although dismissed, they always hesitated a moment just to see him, to remain with him, and to smell his scent.

Their green dreamcatcher webs reminded Delwyn that green wasn't a popular color on Elleio. Parasitic plants looked bright green, dying plants turned dull green, and hours-dead bodies took on a greenish hue there.

Nine Earth days after leaving Iota Horologii, the star system Compact star charts called Nikkiolo, Delwyn wondered if he had enough time to learn about his crew and their culture. Had Mistress of Sails Anailiatha, the chief engineer, not recommended a slow thirty-hour recharge rate to accommodate their battle-damaged FTL drive, their ETA would have been in another 13 days and not 34.

Dammit! He was doing it again, thinking in decimal numbers and in Earth time. A ship in space kept time in the Tyreniioroneo standard, TST, because warships were given male identities. Their ETA to Elleio orbit was 310 TST days.

Melkorka, the Mistress of the Ship, a Warrior female, would have sung an angry rhythmic fit if she had smelled his lapse in thought especially after all the hours she had spent drilling him on time standards and numbers.

She had arranged for Delwyn to have lessons to acquaint him with important facts, teaching songs, governmental structure, social customs, and tribal relationships that he would need to know so as not to give offense to people he came in contact with once they reached the homeworld. Even though the Eyloni valued forgiveness, some offenses could be fatal.

The cultural lessons didn't follow any timetable or set order. Everyone had duties to perform on the naval vessel. Lessons were unpredictable depending on who was free to sing to him. That irregularity and the lulls between jumps gave Delwyn time enough for wandering the ship; meeting and talking with crew members wherever he found them.

Often Hervorallin found him. A Hunter female, Hervorallin was a gravimetric engineer. She was also the mother of Princess. Because Hervorallin's labor had been complicated by a breech birth, Delwyn had helped her with the delivery, and the baby had made an empathic bond with him when he unknowingly named her by calling her Princess. This bond, according to Eyloni cultural standards, made her Delwyn's newborn near-daughter. It also allowed the O'un Tu Clan to claim him as a clan male by adoption. But no one told Delwyn that there could be other demands made of him before that happened.

Hervorallin had assumed the responsibility of teaching him the rules and customs of the La'huaset tribe common to all clans living on the La'huaset Tribal continent and the quasi-municipal and familial ones specific to the

O'un Tu Clan. Just thinking about her called to mind a lesson she had sung in her haunting, sibilant voice about how the heart is a drum:

It beats, and in all Eyloni, male and female, the heart is the drum of male identity.

For every female, Hunter, Warrior, or Comara, her heart is a he.

Weeks ago, Kidahin, the youngest, lowest-ranked Hunter aboard, told him that music played an important role in Eyloni social life, but one of Hervorallin's recent lessons claimed that the first ancient songs formed the cornerstone of her culture. She sang a story about how the spirits had given the Eyloni those songs, telling them to use the music to call the spirits back at any time, to sing together to call strength or to push despair back into the abyss. Music, the compassionate gift, allowed the People to call archetypal forces into clan life. Singing with the spirit voice called upon deep artistic truths and created a communal consciousness—a group awareness binding the members of the clan together creating an even stronger empathic whole.

Hervorallin had also sung about the Steps to Adulthood, the Law of the Clan, and the songs of Life's Lessons. More recently, she had sung about the consequences of social debt. Eyloni society was regulated by ritualized behavior and when offenses occurred, forgiveness for all but the direst assaults against personal honor was sought.

The most important lesson on social debt issues surprised Delwyn given what he thought he knew about Eyloni warrior and territorial ethics. The Rite of Forgiveness required everyone to set offending matters aside for a time, withhold punishment, forget the offense, and abandon the social debt. Once completed, an offense ceased to exist from both personal and social perspectives. Delwyn couldn't imagine humans doing the same under any circumstances.

The Rite of Forgiveness never applied to any person who, without honorable excuse, caused the death of any male or planned to cause great bodily harm or death to any male. That crime was to be avenged as soon as possible, without appeal, by any female hierarchy having knowledge of the offense and the offender. Many of the lessons Delwyn felt he'd never need, but he had dutifully learned the songs in preparation for meeting the clan elders. He did not know what they might ask him before adopting him into Clan O'un Tu.

Delwyn sighed and shook his head, banishing the memory of Hervorallin's singing voice, and considered the current military situation. They traveled through interstellar space between FTL jump seven and eight—twelve and thirteen, dammit!—at the high relativistic velocity of 0.69 cee, sixty-nine percent of light speed. Before Melkorka had declared Delwyn warleader, he had been Senior Chief Warrant Officer Delwyn Marsch of the

Coalition of Earth Colonies carrier *Henri Edda*. That ship could achieve a maximum apparent velocity of 1,412.696 cee.

Although the Coalition carrier could achieve a faster apparent FTL velocity than *Hunter's Moon*'s 1,375.49 cee maximum, it mattered less than a footnote in a technical manual did. The carrier often had to decelerate when passing through hyperspace gravity-wave anomalies. A ship in hyperspace still used its sublight drive for propulsion, and no prudent Coalition captain ever gunned ship engines at full throttle through potential hazards.

Compact FTL technology quantum jumped a warship in 30 billionths of a second from one physical point in normal space to another point within a displacement radius of up to a maximum 2.332 light-years, 3.043 Compact light-years. A Compact ship did not travel through hyperspace during FTL jumps. He teleported, translated was the technical term, from point to point. An undamaged jump drive needed about 15 Coalition standard hours to recharge before the ship could jump again, giving an outside observer the illusion of a warship travelling at a constant 1,375.49 cee. That gave his ship about a 3.77 light-year per day actual rate compared to *Henri Edda's* 3.87 light-year per day theoretical maximum.

Still, the hours-long delay between jumps gave Delwyn an unreasonable, persistent feeling that they wasted time while in normal space. The distance gained over the recommended thirty-hour recharge rate seemed trivial next to a 2.332 light-year jump and why bother risking a high-velocity particle impact in the first place? Why not jump into normal space at zero relative velocity, recharge, and then jump another 2.332 light-years?

When he asked this question to Mistress of Sails Anailiatha, she just looked at him and said, "Because, the jump drive computer must crunch through physical quantities such as mass, charge, spin, vector, acceleration, gravitation, and velocity to arrive at an entanglement solution. Traveling at high relativistic velocities and accelerations relaxes these two variables and simplifies the jump calculation."

Oh.

So they poked along at 0.69 cee under maximum navigation shields while the gravity lensing system built up the power signature necessary to create a quantum singularity capable of translating their particle-entanglement set 2.332 light-years farther away from Nikkiolo, or closer to Elle depending on the point of view.

At least the recharge delay gave him time to appreciate the lessons his adopted people sang about their customs.

A wry smile flitted across Delwyn's face every time he thought about them.

They never left him alone for long. Eyloni took comfort in casual, momentary physical contact. They touched each other, favoring brushing their nearly two-meter-long tails against each other. They brushed him and expected him to, lacking a tail himself, caress or pet them in return.

It wasn't romantic, it wasn't sexual. Refusing to touch or be touched in this culture was foreign and signaled a psychological defect with root causes in either traumatic brain injury or congenital amusia, tone-deafness. Both led to antisocial and psychotic behavior.

And Delwyn couldn't help but touch them. The casual physical contact that passed for normal and expected here would bring harassment charges in human society. Something in their pheromones, the biochemical in their body odor, encouraged such touching, and they insisted on it. He had caught himself petting them often enough already before realizing what he was doing.

And if he petted one of them in the presence of others, then all of them insisted he pet them too. Fussy about rank and precedence, they demanded that he touch them in a specific order. That order did not match the rank-significant complexity of their military rank earring webs. The ordering reflected their standings within the shadowy female hierarchies governing Eyloni society.

Their ideas about what 'society' meant baffled him, too. Societies functioned like intracultural and intersocial membership organizations. The crew made up a society. All the females belonging to a specific female gender phenotype—Hunters, Warriors, or Comara—belonged to societies representing their phenotypes. At the same time, all females regardless of phenotype also belonged to a society.

Societies also extended down into vocational specialties. All the females serving aboard every Compact warship were a society. Even specific jobs formed societies. That meant, say, all the navigators aboard all those warships belonged to the society of navigators.

Societies formed social networks that stressed the intertwined nature of interacting groups in a physical manifestation of the metaphysical webs that made up the Oyya of the spirits. The Oyya Web represented the metaphysical and spiritual underpinnings of Eyloni culture. That Web touched all aspects of Eyloni tribal and clan life and united a people whose clans had fought each other in the ancient past. Armies of females long ago had been willing to die to provide for and protect their rare males.

"Delwyn?" a voice sang over the combat address system.

"Yes Hervorallin?"

"Come to Power Systems and Propulsion for your next session," she sang.

"Aren't you busy now? What will Anailiatha say?"

"I am able to sing the histories and monitor the gravity lensing systems at the same time," Hervorallin snapped.

"On my way!"

2

ABOARD THE COMPACT WARSHIP HUNTER'S MOON

The Huntress Hervorallin paused and cocked her ears in inquiry. Patiently she watched him consider the history lesson she had just sung. Twitching her tail, she pricked her ears forward. This song was serious. Lessons about the past always were.

Her nose twitched, catching his scent. His pheromones told her what meaning he took from the lesson.

He thought she sang a fireside tale!

"This is no tale, Delwyn!" she hissed, outraged. "This song recounts the valor of Hlorrithin the sixth and last Hero of Home, an O'un Tu Clan male. He is buried with the other Heroes of Home on Na'di, the Be'atika Senge's island home. This lesson recalls our struggle with nah'tle ke'ne's'tu, industrial pollution. Emergent industry on any scale soon became a disaster for entire territories of the La'huaset Tribal continent…all those male deaths. The clans united and destroyed those that refused to comply with the environmental edicts passed by the Be'atika Senge."

"A civil war then," Delwyn said, nodding.

"Not quite like the images your scent suggests," she corrected. "The industrial clans had all sickened, but they felt certain their science could develop cures for the toxins affecting their people. They refused to shut down their factories, all the while hoping to find a cure for their dying males and still retain their technology. But it was already far too late. Nothing they did could save them. They were soon to become dead clans, and in blind panic they continued using filthy industry as they tried to find a way to save their males, making the sicknesses even worse."

"So Hlorrithin led forces against them?" Delwyn asked.

"Yes. The Compact Counsel placed a moratorium on industrial and technological processing until the strict edicts could take full effect. Throughout the Ten Tribes of Elleio the clans united in the fight to develop clean power sources and safe manufacturing methods. The technology then existing was restricted and industrial output was placed under severe rationing to advance only those goals."

"All done to save the forests," Delwyn said.

"No," Hervorallin corrected. "To save our males and to restore our natural environment."

Delwyn nodded. His head hurt. He needed a break. Thanking Hervorallin for her time and the lesson he excused himself so he could get back to his other duties.

Those duties included receiving reports from Melkorka in the command center, making rounds throughout the ship, and making himself available for every crewmember. A warleader, Delwyn had discovered soon enough, spent a lot of time hiking the trails and pathways and making himself accessible to the crew.

Unlike human chains-of-command, his crew followed a multi-tiered command structure that juggled female military, hierarchy, and social ranking systems at once. They considered the solitary male, him, a special case, and everyone had an equal right to speak with him regardless of any chain-of-command. Any female may approach a warleader on any matter. Oh, the others might chide her for wasting his time as soon as he left, but it was still her right to approach him on any matter.

So far he'd already met several solitary stalking Hunters and prowling Warrior trios today. All of them had paused in their patrols to practice their fluency in Coalition standard, by chatting about themselves, by asking if he was enjoying his time with them, or by making polite and curious inquiries after his health.

They took their responsibility for his safety seriously. They always made that quite clear.

Delwyn entered the forward third of the warship, called the combat hull. During the battle with the Ni'zakhonii that had wrecked the ship, Kalinn, the previous warleader, had rammed a destroyer, driving his bow into the enemy ship. The heavy structural damage caused by the ramming maneuver, by point blank firing, and by taking return fire had rendered several compartments, uninhabitable. Many bulkheads and pathways had been patch-sealed with metal plates, but other structural failures were blanketed by local force fields. Damage had been heavy in spaces where critical structures or systems did not permit wholesale cutting and patching. The force fields adapted to the tangled wreckage, sealing breaches, reinforcing weakened bulkheads, and preserving life support integrity at nominal levels.

But force fields also made travel through the bow dangerous. A glitch in field power could at any time cause a deck to either collapse, or explosively decompress.

Persistent Hunters always arrived every time Delwyn ventured too close to the heavy damage areas. They didn't enjoy being reminded about the damage done to their ship, their home. They also didn't like him anywhere near areas the damage control parties had labeled hazardous, either.

Shipwide simulated jungle landscapes had failed on several decks, giving Delwyn a rare glance at the ship's bare decks. Duranium, depleted uranium, hull plating covered the outer hull. Layered titanium alloys and carbon composites fleshed out the irregular interior compartments. Corridors ran in broad wandering paths. He hadn't found any stairs, ladders, or lifts outside of the machinery and ordnance bays, those places where, by their nature, they made such structures necessary eyesores.

The paths and trails running through each deck had been built up to give the ground the rise of jungle trails. The textured uneven walls and ceilings, painted in light pastel ochers, resembled thickets and those thickets became even more lifelike when the projected forest simulation enveloped them.

"No Delwyn! Danger!" a Hunter called out as she stepped out from under the holographic forest cover and onto the trail next to him.

Delwyn flinched despite himself, "I know danger lurks here, Melakia," he said patiently.

The Hunter stopped, frowning. Her tail twisting in circles behind her, she pressed her delicate mobile ears flat against her head's bright orange ringlets and wondered.

Did I say it wrong? The warleader's language baffled her sometimes with the difficult monotonic syllabic constructions, although she continued to learn more of his words every time he sang with her.

Melakia smelled the pheromones in the air, and she pricked her ears forward as she considered what his scent was telling her.

No, she knew she had spoken the words most correctly. He understood her. Pleasure and pride filled her with confidence.

"This place… unsettled," Melakia warned.

"I know. I'm looking for the forward railgun station," Delwyn said.

The primary kinetic weapon system was a massive railgun. It fired passenger vehicle-sized ordnance at hypervelocities, and he wanted to see it.

The Hunter shook her head, a defiant jerk she had learned just for his benefit. The warleader smelled Eyloni pheromones hardly at all, and the ship's society had adopted the exaggerated head and body signs they used on the comm to express feelings normally conveyed by scent when in person. Remembering to use them when in his personal space, where scent always reached everyone, was hard.

"No!" Melakia said. "Mass driver barrel open to vacuum. Weapon breech jammed open in loading position. Weapon ordnance bay autoloading sequencer and fire control near unsafe bulkhead. Ahead is force field only separating you from open space."

Compact force fields stood out about as much as transparent nonreflecting glass. They made no noise at all, unlike Coalition force fields with their loud power hums that warned Delwyn when he was near a field.

"What force field?" Delwyn asked. He looked around and saw nothing but blackened, twisted wreckage. Under poor auxiliary lighting the place resembled blasted rocky embankments covered with scorched moss.

Looking further down the deck he saw, not ten meters away, a glowing hard green pencil-thin line running across the warped path. The hair on the back of his neck prickled.

Green signaled danger here just as red did on Coalition vessels.

Green lines outlined a force field's perimeter and identified the field type. Pale green lines marked structural fields solid as brick walls, but hard green lines warned of active hull breach seals. They kept atmosphere in to maintain life support integrity on the deck, but anyone could walk through an atmospheric seal with ease.

If Delwyn had remained on the path, he'd have walked right into cold vacuum before the force field's tingling brush even registered in his brain.

"Maybe you're right," he said.

"Of course I am right," Melakia agreed. "Come, review combat hull damage from forward combat operations center. Interior and exterior views on holodisplay, as are all current damage assessments."

He hesitated, yearning to explore.

"Come," Melakia insisted.

Delwyn sighed. He could click through damage reports in complete safety while in forward combat operations, but he preferred making personal battle damage assessments. Sometimes he couldn't get the feel for a place unless he went there. Once there he relied on a gut instinct seldom ever wrong.

He also wanted to see the Power Systems and Propulsion spaces located aft. Curiosity about how the gravity lensing system and the FTL jump drive itself worked drove his interest. Going there meant a long five-hundred-meter hike through a forested combat hull, forestation, command hull, aftstation, and halfway through the engineering hull.

Walking became easier as they retraced a path back through the combat hull's undamaged compartments between the bow and the forestation. Once there, Melakia aimed him down an amber jungle trail leading to the forward combat operations center and shoved before vanishing with a wave of her tail and an impish smile on her black lips.

Delwyn stood there, seemingly abandoned on a trail in the middle of an alien rainforest. Which choice sounded more exciting: review the railgun damage from the FCOC or continue through the ship to FTL propulsion engineering?

He'd see Hervorallin in Power Systems and Propulsion too, somewhere in gravity systems engineering, and he did have another lesson with her soon.

Watching the engine systems operate won out over looking at pictures on a display.

Entry into the command hull brought Delwyn into the deep vibrant orange northeastern upper latitude temperate rainforest of the La'huaset Tribal continent. About a minute passed before he ran into three Warriors rustling through low crimson growth as they prowled the trail ahead.

"Where are you going, Delwyn?" one of them asked.

"To the engineering hull and Power Systems and Propulsion, to see Anailiatha."

"The Mistress of Sails is in the command center lecturing the Mistress of the Ship," she said.

"Why is Anailiatha lecturing Melkorka?" Delwyn asked.

"You!"

"Me? Why me? What'd I do?"

"Nothing. Mistress Anailiatha saw you on the damage control monitors at her command station and ran to command center, growling and snarling the whole way."

"Why didn't she just call Melkorka on the comm?"

"Because Anailiatha wanted to give Melkorka the full impact of her scent, lest she miss the full force of her complaint. The scent on the air says you have more important things to do than wander through damaged compartments."

"Oh?" Delwyn raised an eyebrow, his way of copying the Warrior's cocked ear gesture. *Scent on the air* meant scuttlebutt in Eyloni phraseology. It wasn't hard for him to read between the lines, either. They didn't want him near damaged compartments, not alone, and not even with escorts chafing at the risks they felt he was taking.

"Well, I'm going to Power Systems and Propulsion. I want to watch the jump drive spooling up."

"Good," the Warrior said, hesitated, and then added, "Propulsion command center has good shields and negligible structural damage. We will accompany you there."

Delwyn groaned. Kalinn had been killed in the battle that crippled the ship, and they were determined to keep him far from any threat of harm.

"Don't take time away from your duties on my account," he protested.

The three Warriors glared at him.

"Our duty is clear," the lead female said. "We prowl our ship. We will prowl him as we accompany you to Power Systems and Propulsion. Anailiatha will meet us there."

"How? I've just now decided to go there myself!"

Smiling crafty smiles, snapping their tails, and pricking their ears at him, they waited as he got the punchline of their obvious joke.

The joke, of course, was on him. They had tricked him into charting his course aloud, and the combat address system had relayed his intent. The propulsion command center knew he was on his way, as did everyone else.

"I have a song for you!" One Warrior blurted out. "Do you want to hear it?"

Delwyn smiled. Eyloni sang given any opportunity. They sang to themselves, with others, and with him. Often they teased him with a song, trying to lure him into singing with them.

"Of course…Aheila…I want to hear it. I love hearing you sing."

Aheila preened in obvious pleasure and began singing as they pushed through overgrown jungle trails. She sang haunting, beautiful lyrics self-accompanied by her fluting notes, and Delwyn felt vigor summoned to him through the mood set by the young Warrior's music.

"There are two years of Elleio Standard Time allotted to one of Tyreniioroneo's orbital periods. One year for spring and summer, one year for fall and winter. In four seasons live one hundred and two times spanning one hundred months.

"I will begin with the season of spring. I see the north frosts thaw and all life brighten as the chill wanes. The winter retreats into its solitary home in the icy north, and the ground turns deep orange with renewed vigor. The little brothers and sisters return again to their northern territories and sing to us about ancient kinship……"

That Aheila and her prowling partners could sing three notes at the same time made the impromptu treat even more beautiful, and the delicate harmony in which they sang struck an inconsistent pose next to the formidable presence the three muscular young Warriors carried with them. Aheila's song taught him something, too: the seasonal times of the year.

Aheila's hidden purposed had not been to teach but to goad the warleader into singing along with them. The combat system did not carry their voices throughout the warship, but it did carry his and that was all that mattered.

Delwyn surrendered to their manipulations and sang with them, slowing his pace as they pushed through jungle undergrowth on uneven trails.

Delwyn's one-sided conversation had already warned Anailiatha, and she ran from the command center in the command hull aft to the engineering hull intent on intercepting him and his escort. People jumped into the undergrowth as she darted past, not wanting to hinder a mistress in a hurry to find the warleader. She darted through the aftstation, into the engineering hull and stopped on the main pathway barely panting.

She did not have long to wait.

"You should study and learn about us," the Mistress of Sails admonished him.

"I am, Anailiatha. I am, but I need some time to get familiar with the rainforest too don't you think?"

Anailiatha huffed, annoyed. Delwyn had a point. For all the jungle skill he had shown while on the moon in the Nikkiolo star system, it was not equal to what he needed to know for survival even in Elleio's northern temperate rainforests. Delwyn had told her about Earth's green forests, how much they resembled the sick-looking green plants on the Nikkiolo moon. He described Earth trees as even *smaller* than the ones on the moon. It was true. He had told her so.

Anailiatha thought Elleio's comforting, warm-colored canopies would tower far above any trees Delwyn had ever seen before. But she knew from her experiences on other forested worlds, bigger, taller trees did not increase or decrease the dangers found in a forest so much as did the colors dominating the flora.

She remembered the uncertainty that had filled her while stalking through the nauseating green forest on Nikkiolo's moon. Grasses were grasses, bushes were bushes, vines were vines, trees were trees, true enough. Even the strange shapes and tinier leaves different from Elleio plant life had not taken much time to get used to, but the dramatic difference between all alien forests and northern La'huaset forests came down to ambient light.

The moon's dark green and green-blue foliage blocked sunlight, making the forest floor shady, darker than any rainforest back home. Anailiatha's natural skin pigments mimicked her home forest's leaf colors, but they had made her stand out amid all the alien dark trunks and green branches. But even more unnerving was when the dark green leaves veiling the ground level in darkness had been lanced with bright shafts of unexpected sunlight, as the wind created gaps in the canopy, exposing her within her chosen hiding places!

It had not been a friendly forest. Green shades heralded death or dying on Elleio. The moon's spring temperatures, not uncomfortable, combined with the cold greens called to mind teaching songs about the north forest die-off caused by wastes during her people's short stint with the unfettered industrial development that had stricken the La'huaset Tribal continent.

Anailiatha shuddered. Would Delwyn view her world's rainforests in a similar light?

Delwyn watched Anailiatha's eyes glaze over. Her tail stood out behind her, its pons, the ringleted tail tuft, twitched. Her ears had swiveled out in a posture he knew as one reflecting deep thought.

Delwyn glanced at his Warrior escort.

They watched her, too. They seemed amused, and he wondered whether they thought he had stumped the Mistress of Sails.

"Mistress Anailiatha? Why are you worried Delwyn will not find our trees comforting?" one of his escorts blurted out.

Where did that come from? Delwyn wondered.

"What?" Anailiatha asked, blinking huge amber eyes, trying to focus on them and remember where she was and what she had been doing.

"Why are you wor…," Aheila began.

"I heard you the first time! I can smell your thoughts on your scent, too!" Anailiatha snapped, flushing furious crimson and vermilion shades under red and orange patterned skin.

Aheila backed down at once. Eyloni females observed rank and status always, and Anailiatha held mistress rank. The military rank hoop in her earring was packed with webs much more intricate than the three young Warriors could muster combined. That the Mistress of Sails also held high hierarchical standing in Elleio female-dominated society was obvious by their subordinate attitudes.

Aheila had embarrassed the older, higher ranking female while in the warleader's presence, and Delwyn wondered what disciplinary action she risked.

"You three, get back to your prowling! The Mistress of Sails can get along well enough without your foolishness!" he ordered.

The three Warriors spun on him, pitched their ears forward and tails up, their gulps loud to his ears. They met Anailiatha's eyes in respectful acknowledgment, turned back on him once again and raised hands to brush their left breasts, touching the adulthood knives hanging there, and fled down the trail and out of sight.

Delwyn faced a frustrated Anailiatha and raised an eyebrow at her.

"You can smell my thoughts too?" she asked, surprised.

"Yes, but I don't always get a clear picture."

That wasn't a lie, exactly. He smelled the change in the chief engineer's body odor, but his sense of smell cut short the Eyloni norm. Humans hadn't needed pheromonal signaling for millennia. His sensitive nose worked alongside an inherent situational awareness, giving him a sixth-sense impression about things. Eyloni signaling odors summoned feelings in him that not only rang true but also gave him an emotional window into whatever they happened to think about at the time. He didn't catch whole scent-sentences like they did, but he did at times snag a hint or two as if he was an eavesdropper overhearing whispers. He always failed to place a scent with its owner in a crowd, and those limits gave the crew pause. They exercised care in making sure that he understood them, but sometimes Delwyn wondered if his weak nose allowed them to evade issues impossible to hide from other Eyloni.

Anailiatha sighed. "I meant no disrespect, Delwyn."

"I know you didn't, and neither did they," Delwyn said, waving a hand after the vanished trio. "Why do you think I won't like your forests?"

"I was uncomfortable in the green forests on the Nikkiolo moon," she admitted.

"On Ibeetu? I know. It crawled with leeches. Did Phelindra tell you about the time she got herself covered with them and I…," Delwyn trailed off as Anailiatha began shaking her head, her tail twitching with agitated impatience.

"It is not just that. Elleio's jungles have their own dangerous animal life. I am sure the forests you are familiar with have them too, but Elleio jungles are filled with pastel ocher colors. There are no dark shades there, no grays there, not in daytime. Sunlight passing through the emergent and understory layers filters through orange-red, and yellow variegated semiopaque or diaphanous leaves. The ground layer receives blended, faded soft orange light. Even in heavy jungle cover a dim pale orange light penetrates all the way to the ground. There is never the dark shade of the Nikkiolo moon forest in our forests," she explained.

"I can see that being an asset or at least a convenience. I won't have to worry about things hidden in shadows if there are no shadows to conceal them," Delwyn assured her, thinking about the bright late fall forests of North America.

"No! Try to understand what I am saying. I had to learn not to assume my skin hid me in the foliage patterns. I had no problems because the green and dark shades were constant reminders. The hardest lesson I learned showed me how utterly useless my past experiences served me in the Nikkiolo forest. I relied on my night sight to see into deeply shaded areas, but the sunlight above and behind me ruined my night sight. My incomplete knowledge failed me, and what skills I knew had been dulled by the simple difference green leaves made. You have never prowled through a red and orange forest, and you cannot count the projected images in this warship as a forest. What you think you know here is not the whole truth of the matter there!" Anailiatha said.

"I don't think the difference will matter as much for me as it did for you. I don't think I'll be wandering around in your forests alone and I don't use my skin for camouflage. Besides, my tan hide matches close to a brownish orange. I don't have natural nightvision, although I do see well in the dark if there are enough stars, or if the Moon is out. The added light will help me avoid hazards hidden in overgrown areas."

Anailiatha shook her head as they walked further into the engineering hull. "Not all that light, all the time. I come from La'huaset's most northern region. I belong to the A'leki'ao Clan, the name means…"

"Something about ice, right?" Delwyn interrupted. His vocabulary grew as he picked up more words, or at the least he caught the root meanings.

"Yes," Anailiatha said, smiling with pride. Her warleader had learned much in his brief time with them. "It means the Land of Ice and Snow Clan. When I came into my season for the first time, the elders of my clan sent me into the frosty north to endure my adulthood survival ordeal there. Kidahin told you about the survival ordeals, yes?"

"She did," Delwyn nodded. "She told me she had to survive in the jungles around Om'tu Lake."

"Yes, I withstood the cold, ice, and spitting snow for three months. My elders started me out on the north polar ice. I had to make an ice boat and sail the north barrier sea eating nothing but the stray seaweed I could snag hoping against hope the ice floe did not melt. I made landfall and crossed the narrow northern grasslands and entered the polar sub-temperate forests. I thought I had never been so happy to see trees in the whole life."

"I understand. You make your home in a tree, and you could find food and shelter in the forest," Delwyn nodded.

"That is not the reason why I was so happy to reach the trees. The bright sun reflecting off the snow, the constant blinding glare made it hard to see, hard to gauge distances, hard to judge dangers," Anailiatha explained.

"You're talking about being snowblinded. I know. Earth has much larger polar ice caps, and it snows long and often there well into the middle northern latitudes. You don't have much ice, and snow doesn't accumulate much even in the far north. I learned even the La'huaset barrier mountain range sees only frost, no snow, and never more than a pons or two thick of it even in winter. But I'm not going to the north pole, Anailiatha!"

"It is not the cold, but the blindness of which I speak. You are accustomed to darkness and dark patterns varying with the daytime landscapes you prowl through. The dark gray shades, the green and black leaves and bark absorb backscattering glare and shades your eyes from reflected ambient yellow sunlight. You could find your eyes suffering the same blindness in Elleio's rainforests as mine did from looking across frost and snow-covered ground. That blindness will affect how you perceive the forest, will hide its hazards just as shaded darkness does in your Earth's green forests. Your depth perception and judgment will fail you unless you can adapt to it."

Anailiatha led Delwyn through the dense forest and into heavy undergrowth, an artistic rendering of the pathways and compartments filling the Power Systems and Propulsion engineering spaces. Here mechanical utility overrode the seeming random forest trails. Machinery had requirements incompatible with Eyloni aesthetics, and the ship's designers had done their best at blending the jungle into the utilitarian straight lines and sharp angles technology demanded.

They approached a wide blast door. It opened for Anailiatha, and they stepped into an engineering division unlike that of any starship he had ever seen before.

Everywhere Delwyn looked had been painted in Ellieo's primary jungle colors.

The decks had Elleio's daytime sky overhead masking even a hint of a ceiling.

Females manned their stations wearing their usual skimpy waistwear and neckwear, but a few of them wore full skintight body suits as well. Engineering spaces housed equipment, used volatile chemicals, and contained radiation hazards, which made the suits a necessary inconvenience.

The engineering crew, a few at a time, paused to acknowledge Anailiatha with eye contact and a pose, a posture reserved for formal respect, and then they gave Delwyn long pleased looks: the warleader had come with Anailiatha to inspect Power Systems and Propulsion engineering.

Delwyn noticed right off how the engineering crew had become busy and, oddly flirtatious. They posed as they worked. They gave the hierarchical stance, a salute not for their military rank but for their status in the various female hierarchies in Eyloni social life. They wanted him to caress them in hierarchical rank order, Anailiatha first of course.

By the time he finished petting the lowest-ranked female, Anailiatha had glided over and now stood next to a long narrow housing. She palmed a hatch control and the door opened into the port side gravity lensing system. She stepped inside, turned, and invited Delwyn to follow.

He stepped into a piston and gear driven factory scene pulled from the late Nineteenth Century. The lensing mechanism couldn't look any more primitive on first impression. An armature like something right out of an electric motor some one hundred meters long and ten meters wide spun around and oscillated in and out of a cylindrical housing the way a piston did in an internal combustion engine. Field windings covered the armature with cores of pencil-thick laminated plates wound with square wire as thick as a man's wrist. Detail faded into blur as the armature spun around and pumped in and out. Coils within resembled the fixed windings of the same motor assembly. Anailiatha explained how this retrograde-looking mechanical device and its twin in the adjacent housing generated fields used to form a gravitational fresnal lens. The lensing field extracted gravatons from quantum gravity and focused them at the point where hypergravity collapsed to form the quantum black hole used for teleporting the ship's entangled particle set.

Delwyn thought he felt a muted shimmying vibration but he didn't know if it was just a feeling he had or if he just heard it as another noise among the sounds of the equipment and the armature motion itself.

He caught Anailiatha frowning at the mechanism.

"Problem?" he asked.

She glanced at him and shook her head but did not follow up with the usual tail flick signifying his concern was no big deal.

"No, not if we remain at our current recharge rate. The jump drive under normal conditions spools up much faster. The spin is logarithmic scaled to the power build up, meaning the armature spins and oscillates much faster. You saw how we repaired the armatures back on the moon's surface. We had to replace the core laminates and install new windings manually by hammering them around the new core. It took back-breaking work to wind and balance the assembly. Balancing the assembly required spooling up the armature and monitoring the out-of-balance offset. We then adjusted the assembly by hammering and drilling the core or the wire. Had we not balanced the armature, it would have shaken its mounting in the field cylinder to pieces. My technicians carried out a delicate procedure in a crude manner using crude tools. If they had drilled out or filed away too much material, then they could have altered the core's field characteristics. If they had hammered the winding wrong, then the field geometry could have misaligned, making it useless as a graviton-focusing instrument."

Delwyn nodded. The armature was moving through a clearance gap in its cylindrical housing with less than a pencil width of tolerance. The slightest misalignment or balance error would have caused the moving armature to strike the stationary coils and either jam or rip apart whole sections of coil assemblies.

"So it's always been thrumming? Since you made the repairs?" he pressed.

The Mistress of Sails gave him a pained look as if she had bitten into a bitter fruit. Delwyn was perceptive and caring, a warleader and a male quality.

"Somewhat," she admitted. "There have been some steadily increasing vibrations, but they have been slow in building."

"What do you think is wrong?" he asked, all businesslike as the sight-seeing tour became a warleader's damage assessment.

Catching Delwyn's change in demeanor, Anailiatha nodded. "The field coils are wound at an assembly plant by heavy equipment. They are drawn around core assemblies so tight no slack remains in the wire and no gaps exist between windings. We had to manually unwind a complete core assembly, replace thirty-one laminated core plates, and then manually rewind the field coil using jackhammers, sledgehammers, and crowbars. The wire no longer fits snug around the core, and there are gaps between windings in the cores.

The angular momentum generates centrifugal forces that take up the slack and causes minor balance changes."

"Will the mechanism last until we arrive in homespace?" Delwyn asked.

"Yes, the plates and windings will hold, but the continued imbalance shakes and stresses the armature mounts. If the imbalance shifts too far out of tolerance, it will cause the armature to strike the stationary field coils in the cylinder mounting and at spooling velocities they will superheat, fragment, and fill the clearance space with fragments as the impact tears out another laminate assembly"

"Would reducing the jump rate any further help?" he asked.

Anailiatha hesitated an instant before flicking her ears in negation. "No. Reducing angular velocity by half will increase recharge time by just over what we have now. At rates necessary to reduce the angular velocity enough to make a difference, the recharge rates will increase to the point where we cannot complete the journey within several hundred years."

Delwyn swore aloud and then grimaced as he recalled how his outbursts tended to summon Phelindra's security detail.

Ha! He had no doubt Phelindra was hiding somewhere nearby, watching everything from the cover of crimson and pumpkin, gold-trimmed undergrowth. It wasn't in her nature to allow him the luxury of wandering off for long without her company. If not her, then at least one of her green-webbed Hunters was likely stalking him from the brush.

He'd know for sure in another minute or two.

Delwyn considered Anailiatha's report. Too bad Warleader Phalalin couldn't tow them back. If *Hunter's Moon* had been a Coalition ship, then a second Coalition ship could have locked tractor fields onto them and towed them through hyperspace. Compact FTL propulsion jumped a ship from point to point. A Compact ship's ability to jump both himself and another ship depended on the total mass to translate, and an assault battlecruiser's jump drive was pushing its theoretical maximum teleporting *Hunter's Moon's* mass. Phalalin's smaller *Fearless* might jump himself and maybe a small proxy vessel, but he couldn't jump Delwyn's ship along with him anywhere.

"Very well. Maintain current recharge rates, Anailiatha."

"By your command."

Anailiatha's ritual response to his order filled Delwyn with foreboding. The crew reserved the formal response for the warleader's commands alone. No female ever replied to another female using the word "command" even when an order had been given. They acknowledged orders among themselves with "affirm" or "affirm, acting." Those responses roughly paralleled Delwyn's more familiar "aye-aye" and "aye, executing" naval tradition.

A relieved Mistress of Sails snapped her tail and pointed her ears where he should go and walked with him the length of the armature and out the aft housing hatch.

Phelindra glided into the propulsion command center the moment Delwyn left the armature housing and glared at every female present.

"Inform Mistress Anailiatha that I will have words with her on this matter!"

Phelindra barely gave them time to flick their ears in response before she stepped into the armature housing and closed the hatch behind her.

Engineers and technicians twitched their ears and looped their tails smiling to one another. The Mistress of the Watch stalked Delwyn. Out of sight, out of mind so he thought, but they all knew better. The Eldest Huntress loomed dangerous when provoked and always had some thinly veiled threat for anyone foolish enough to place the warleader in any danger. No doubt Phelindra had overheard Anailiatha talking about the possibility of the armature shredding itself in its housing, a low probability threat too great for her to ignore. She was going to sing a loud complaint to Delwyn, all the pheromones blowing through the propulsion command center agreed.

Delwyn and Anailiatha entered the sublight drive command center, a round blister on the aft dorsal engineering hull a bare fifty meters from the ship's stern. They sat above two octagonal sublight engine ports. Operating at full power, their droning hum filled the center. The drive plasma did not exit from the ports below them. Instead, it began about a hundred meters beyond the stern, the thrust commuted to the ship through force field gimbals. Compact sublight propulsion impressed him with its efficiency. In theory it worked on the same principles as Coalition sublight engines did. But the Compact fuel transfer system quantum teleported reaction mass in to force field containment chambers aft of the ship. The force chamber contained and directed annihilating hydrogen and antihydrogen in pulse mode, reminding Delwyn of early Twentieth Century pulse jet engines. Helm fields could adjust trim and steer the thrust like a rudder diverting propeller thrust.

Delwyn had an idea, probably not an original one.

"Anailiatha, has anyone ever tried aiming the sublight drive plasma at a target?"

The Mistress of Sails brushed his face with her pons, a chiding gesture, and chirped a negative.

"Not as a beam weapon. Not efficient, Offsetting thrust is unwelcome in a weapon system. It necessarily requires counterthrust to maintain ship's attitude relative to target during firing. Better to quantum translate a hydrogen-antihydrogen magnetic bottle into an enemy ship."

"You can do that?" Delwyn asked.

Anailiatha snapped her tail in disgust. "In theory yes, but not in practice. All quantum translations require stable vectors and acceleration values. It is the same for the jump drive as it is for the quantum fuel feed. Closure and evasion maneuvers complicate quantum translation calculations and firing solutions. In practical combat scenarios, firing solutions would never become available in real time."

Her report made sense, which surprised Delwyn. The FTL drive on ships of *Hunter's Moon's* class needed about fifteen hours to recharge because it took the system time to build up the necessary power and make the calculations for a jump over any distance, even for a quantum computer. Teleporting personnel took no time at all because it was a local displacement, the mass was negligible, and the ship maintained constant vectors. Drive feed teleportation had even simpler parameters to calculate. However, an attacking or evasive ship undergoing combat maneuvers complicated vector parameters and increased both power requirements and computer time.

Delwyn glanced at the brooding Warrior female. She'd gone unusually quiet all of a sudden and by now Delwyn knew the expression of an Eyloni in deep thought. Anailiatha had curled her tail around her waist a few times and brushed her face with her pons like a woman folding arms under her breasts and tapping her face.

Delwyn followed her gaze out the aft ports, watched the red-shifted star patterns a moment and then looked back at her. He loved watching her . . . them. Strong and beautiful, their delicate rhythmic movements disguised a strength and endurance that far surpassed human norms.

"Anailiatha?" Melkorka's voice sang over the comm.

"Hmm? Yes, Mistress?" Anailiatha said, unwinding her tail and blinking her eyes.

"Is Delwyn still with you?"

Anailiatha glanced at him and pricked her ears in silent inquiry.

Delwyn smiled. He hadn't said a word in minutes, and now a question of uncertainty hung in the air. Anailiatha would never tell an outright lie, but the look on her face hinted that if he left the blister now, then she could honestly report in the negative. He entertained no doubts about Melkorka's ability to wheedle him into another lesson. His Mistress of the Ship was persistent, hard to divert and mercurial. Better to just meet her head on and get it over with.

"Yes, Melkorka?" he said.

"Delwyn, Phalalin has asked to speak with you."

It's not about the lessons again. Good.

"Patch him through. I can speak to him from here."

"No. He wants to speak to you on the warleader secure channel. You must come to the command center and access the secure channel from the Warleader's Watch," Melkorka explained.

Delwyn tensed, "Has something happened, Melkorka?"

"Nothing I am aware of," she growled.

"I'm coming."

"Affirm," Melkorka said.

"I wonder what Phalalin wants," he muttered.

"Nothing good," Anailiatha said.

Her flat voice alerted him. "What do you know that I don't?"

"I know a great many things you do not," she snapped.

"Anailiatha, what's wrong?" Delwyn asked, concerned by her growing discomfort.

"Warleader to warleader private channel requests signal one or two unpleasant events," she muttered.

"Which are?" he prompted.

"A discussion about Warpact precedence."

"Which I understand has already been resolved. Phalalin remained in Ibeetu orbit and Melkorka declared me warleader while we were in the Kuiper belt. Phalalin and Anlann both agreed I retained Warpact command until we reach homespace."

"Yes, Delwyn," she murmured, unhappier still.

"You said two reasons. What's the other one?"

Anailiatha ground her teeth, folded her arms beneath her breasts, and watched her bare toes clenching the uneven forest floor.

"A warleader wishes a face-to-face meeting," she said in her most resentful voice.

"Where? We're nowhere near neutral ground. If he wants a meeting, we'd have to conduct it on his ship or ours, and I… Oh, yeah!"

Delwyn remembered. Eyloni females didn't tolerate any male but their warleaders aboard their warships. A second male presence messed with their minds and caused them to worry over two different males. They needed one male with them. The real or hypothetical danger he faced increased their fighting potential, their endurance, and their savagery. The male in turn protected them by not walking himself or them into hopeless endeavors. That made him their focus and only one focus must exist on a warship, while combat ensues, or whenever they were engaged in any task where their single male focus needed female single-minded fortitude and strength.

A second male presence on a ship destroyed that harmony. Absent special circumstances, a female society always killed an interloper male; if they didn't or couldn't, then his own female occupational association killed him on his return for abandoning them in the first place. Even when accompanied by ritual, a visiting male upset the females of both ships.

"Well, if I decide we must, then we will allow Phalalin to come aboard. I won't keep him here any longer than is necessary for him to have his say," he reassured her.

Delwyn saw how his words failed to comfort Anailiatha one bit. She shook her head and keened to herself. It didn't take long for her to make the others in the blister upset.

"Anailiatha? What is wrong with you?"

"Phalalin will not come here. You are Warpact leader. You must go to *Fearless*," she wailed.

"Me? I'm going to Phalalin's ship? Aren't you being a bit premature? I don't even know what he wants. It's probably nothing. I'll go see Melkorka and find out."

Delwyn left the visibly upset Mistress of Sails behind and retraced the path out of the engineering hull. He passed a succession of upset females as he picked his way through jungle trails on his way to the command center.

He brushed leaves and grasses as he wound his way around trees and low hanging branches, watching for the forks meant to take him from the pathways and trails to wide logs that became branches at simulated height above ground. He stepped onto a bough and climbed toward a massive trunk with a fused aerial root bole. The simulated elleiu tree became a walkway not unlike a hollow log before branching into the command center.

Today the command center resembled an open treehouse hundreds of meters above the ground. Elleiu tree leaves filtered sunlight onto the command crew, and Delwyn hesitated as he adapted to the latest change of view. Sometimes the command center filled the base of a huge hollow tree, sometimes like now it was high in a tree, and sometimes it sprawled across the forest floor.

Melkorka turned in her command chair and gave him a tense smile. His grandfather's old cavalry saber still rested across her thighs, just above her knees, her tail wound around the blade. The sword laid there in full view as the outward sign of his preference. Melkorka, lower in rank than Phelindra as well as several others aboard, was Mistress of the Ship by his choice alone.

And right now she seemed none too happy.

"Delwyn," she acknowledged in a tight, flat voice.

"Any idea what Phalalin wants?" he asked.

"He did not say, but I can guess," she barked at him as though he was at fault for her worry.

Males dream up excuses just to annoy females, Melkorka thought to herself. Her pheromones reflexively sent the universal female maxim to the others around her: males are strange.

"Well, there's no reason for maintaining the suspense. Hlindredreda, hail *Fearless* and inquire whether or not Phalalin is available."

"By your command," the Mistress of Communications said unhappily. "Channel open. Mistress of the ship Verikaralee says Phalalin is already at his Watch awaiting your signal."

Now what? Delwyn wondered.

"Come," Hlindredreda said. She stood and led him to the Warleader's Watch, her tail swaying behind her. There she showed him how to access the warleader's channel before returning to her station.

"Phalalin? This is Delwyn," he said, wincing at the sound the name made in his ears. He preferred Del, but his crew considered a single syllable name a baby name, a nickname. They hadn't tolerated its use since he became warleader.

"Delwyn? Phalalin. Greetings. Are you well?"

"Well enough, Phalalin. My strength has bounced back. I'm much stronger than when I left Health Center. I'm taking long hikes through the ship."

"That is well indeed. Delwyn, as you know, my warship belongs to the females of clans belonging to the La'huaset Tribe. Many of the females here and on board your ship belong to the same clans."

"Yes, Hervorallin told me your ship has females of the La'huaset Tribe aboard. You said yourself that you belonged to the O'un Tu Clan, so I figured you had to have several O'un Tu Clan females aboard. I'd think that our crews share females who belong to our clan, and that we also share females from other clans that built our warships."

Phalalin nodded, pleased that Delwyn grasped that essential concept. "Yes, I do, and yes many of them share in mutual clan alliances. The La'huaset Tribe is steeped in a rich naval history. The La'huaset Tribal continent is the largest. Only Myat'ti'deep is a close second. Our tribal continent spans the nearside hemisphere and wraps slightly into farside. It also spans a diagonal line from the southern polar region through the equator and on into the northern polar region, giving access to diverse seas."

Delwyn nodded. If the west coast of North America from Alaska to northern Colombia had been ripped away along, say, Arizona and rotated about ninety degrees, it would closely match the La'huaset Tribal continent in shape and orientation, if not size, with Bogota at the south pole and Fairbanks at the north pole.

"That gives you a long coastline sheltering a lot of seaports over a wide variety of harbors."

Phalalin nodded and smiled at the thoughtful look on Delwyn's face.

"Our tribal continent has exclusive wet navy rights to Elleio's oceans. Most other tribal continents have poor harbors, are too remote, or those clans are disinclined to pursue a life on the water."

Delwyn understood. The Eyloni preferred dwelling in their mammoth elleiu trees. Sea level put them as low to the ground as you could get.

"And the La'huaset clans figure a space navy ship and a surface navy ship are one and the same?" Delwyn asked.

"That too, but many of La'huaset's clans operate what little industry is permitted on Elleio. We have the infrastructure, limited by edict, and we hold the largest technological base relative to the other tribal continents."

"Yes," Delwyn said. "Hervorallin gave me a lesson about that today."

"Good, good," Phalalin said, lost in thought.

"Phalalin just come out and say it, will you? You want something, and you're stalling. What is it?"

Phalalin nodded, his tail snapping as he made a decision.

"I want you to come aboard *Fearless* and meet with me face to face."

"My Mistress of Sails suspected you'd ask. She's not happy about it. Well, nobody's happy about it. Do you think it's that important?"

"It is, yes. We have talked from time to time over the comm these past several days, but I feel we must meet."

"Do you think it helps matters if our crews belong to many of the same clans?"

"No," Phalalin denied. "The ships belong to the females on them and territory is territory. Believe me, I do not ask this thing of you lightly. Since I invited you, the blame for your presence aboard my warship is accounted to me, not to you. I will have to put up with my association's wounded sensibilities for many long hours after you leave. It will probably involve much singing on my part. Your association will feel abandoned and that is not good for them so soon after losing Kalinn and claiming you, but I do not think we can put this meeting off until after our arrival in homespace."

"I already frustrate them. I'm not sure I want to aggravate them even more."

"I know, but what I have to say is important and better said now, while we are well beyond the noses and ears of the Compact Counsel."

The Be'atika Senge. "Can't you give me a hint? What do you know that my crew doesn't?"

"Been around many Eyloni males, have you?" Phalalin asked, rather dryly considering he had picked up the nuances of Coalition standard only a few days ago.

Uh-oh. Phalalin wanted to speak on male issues. Delwyn knew exactly two Eyloni males. Phalalin, of course, and Anlann, the Compact co-ambassador. Anlann had given Delwyn a "male talk" back on Ibeetu when he needed advice on how to sing the Death Songs for his crew's battle dead. Phalalin wanted a male talk away from prying ears and noses. Understandable, Eyloni females acted on a preemptive protective nosiness when it came to males.

"Okay, Phalalin. When?"

"As soon possible."

"All right, I know I can't step onto another male's ship. Anlann made that very clear."

"What he told you was correct, but there are ritual forms for allowing a male to visit another male's ship. I will ask my association for permission to allow you and your Protectress to come here. They will grudgingly permit it because they know I would not upset them so without good cause. You must ask your association for permission to leave them and take your Protectress with you aboard my warship. They will accept your word of honor assuring them the visit is necessary. Understand?"

"Yep," Delwyn said. "Go on."

Phalalin paused, wondering what "yep" meant, but he did understand "go on". He looped his tail in agreement.

"You and your Protectress will translate aboard my ship. You will be taken to my Counsel room, a place reserved for such visits. Delwyn, do not speak at all until I tell you otherwise. Your Protectress will know the ritual forms and will sing for you. If you utter a sound, my association will kill you. They will regret it, it will cause them anguish and grief, but this ship is their territory, as am I. Do you understand?"

Delwyn swallowed and nodded. His crew, his occupational association, always assumed a frightfully protective posture wherever they happened to find him, even in this closed environment where no outsider could evade their constant prowling for long. He tried to imagine how another female society might feel about their warleader.

The look on Phalalin's face, his ears, the set of his tail told Delwyn they were both in for some days of resentful female company.

"Give me a minute or two to brief Melkorka and Phelindra. How much time do you need?"

Phalalin shrugged with all the enthusiasm Delwyn had for drinking buttermilk.

"One hour."

About twenty-five standard minutes.

Delwyn closed down the privacy channel, stood, and walked with a stride that he hoped exuded confidence to his waiting command crew.

"Phelindra? Guess where we're going!" he tried to sound cheerful.

Her glare of abject outrage neatly froze him to the deck.

"You are going to *Fearless*!" Melkorka accused.

"Yes. Phalalin says he has something he must tell me in person."

"Do not speak to me!" Melkorka snarled. The unknown infuriated her, and she was in no mood for casual banter, not even her warleader's banter.

A spluttering Phelindra tried and failed at forming words.

The command crew gave Delwyn the silent treatment as Melkorka began tabulating incoming calls. The combat address system had already relayed his predicament to the crew. They knew, and he knew he couldn't leave them if even one of them said no.

"Come on Phelindra. We've about an hour to get ready. We can't keep Phalalin waiting."

A shrieking growl sang out behind him as they left the command center.

3
ABOARD THE COMPACT WARSHIP FEARLESS

The saying about time flying became a reality as twenty-five minutes rapidly approached zero, and Delwyn wondered why Phalalin had suggested the short TST hour. Maybe he likened it to ripping a bandage off a scab, because by the time he'd gotten his crew's leave to visit *Fearless* only a few minutes remained. As Phalalin had predicted, the entire crew accepted his word that the visit was necessary.

But permission wasn't approval, and they resented him for asking.

Delwyn and Phelindra met more than the usual prowling few on their way to the translation center. Crew members brushed him, insisting he caress them even as they gave him reproachful stares. They let him know just how much they hated his decision. They understood he was not leaving them for a trivial reason, but understanding didn't banish their annoyance. They were reacting to his pending departure in the same way they had whenever Kalinn had need to visit another Compact ship. The crew considered the warleader their territory, and Delwyn remembered when, while aboard their captured Ni'zakhonii Light Attack Craft, Zalzadrin had quipped a comment about him being their pet.

That wasn't the relationship, but sometimes they made him feel like something they all owned in common.

Delwyn couldn't have missed the serious warning stares they gave Phelindra even if he had been a stone. Her high military rank, her age, and her high social and hierarchical station did not prevent everyone they met from glaring daggers at her. Their accusatory stares rolled off her like water, but hers he felt boring into his back.

Phelindra walked an ell behind her warleader and ignored those they met on the way to the translation center, preferring to rehearse tactics and alternatives in her mind. Their pheromones told her the obvious: they had concerns. Delwyn had never visited another Compact warship before. The only male he had met face to face had been co-Ambassador Anlann, and he likely had not explained the intricacies of Eyloni male society to Delwyn in the short time they had spent together.

Delwyn's scent carried an upbeat swagger with it. That was a bad sign. It implied he felt he had a firm grip on this slippery tail.

He did not, and Phelindra knew it. He did not know the dangers he faced. Oh, Phalalin did not intend any harm against Delwyn. Clan males sometimes, and closely-related clan males often, formed unshakable alliances. As a clan male, Phalalin might consider helping Delwyn settle into the male aspects of clan life as an honor issue.

No, Phalalin did not worry her. The females aboard his warship now that was another matter. They would resent Delwyn's presence just as much as Phelindra and her society would have resented Phalalin's presence aboard *Hunter's Moon.*

Delwyn ducked under low-hanging branches and stepped into the clearing surrounding a greenhouse structure quite out of place amid all the orange and red foliage. The translation center struck him as so undeniably practical that it assaulted the ship's jungle aesthetics.

A bulky Warrior blocked the entrance, arms and legs outstretched, tail thrashing behind her: Akenallin, the Mistress of Conveyance, the chief teleport officer. She glared at him and then at Phelindra before letting them enter.

"Do not say a word from the time you arrive aboard until you are inside the honor suite. Wait until Mistress of the Ship Verikaralee seals you inside with Phalalin and Amindaldra his protectress. When Phalalin greets you, then you may speak at your ease," Akenallin sang.

"Yes. Do not speak and quench all song from you. No deep cough, no high sneeze, no mournful sighs, no inadvertent rhythmic whistles or whispers," Phelindra added.

"I know. Phalalin told me as much already," Delwyn said.

"He told you from his side of things, the male side of things," Akenallin snarled.

"We tell you from our side of the matter, the female side. We tell you what we listen for if Phalalin came here. Any sound from a male not the warleader is considered a dire challenge. If Phalalin's nose so much as whistled as he exhaled, we could not help but hear it and assume he tries to sing comfort to us because male music affects us so. We assume his song is meant to drive a wedge between us and you, and we would kill him, sadly, male though he is, for that," Phelindra said.

"Oh come on you two. You can smell his intent in his body odor. You're always telling me the body doesn't lie. Besides, I'd order you to ignore him."

Phelindra's incredulous look loomed as a solid wall over him.

"You do not see the danger! We always act on your behalf in such cases," Phelindra assured him.

"Yes!" Akenallin affirmed. "In close quarters we will act against his song before his pheromones have time to register in our minds. Over any distance his song carries to our ears before his scent reaches our noses, obliging us to fight for you."

True. Delwyn remembered how they had fought on the captured Lizard ship. The slightest risk anywhere near him flipped a male defense switch in them, an instinct impossible for them to ignore. His assault team had been furious with him for leaving the LAC's bridge to help Hervorallin give birth to Princess.

"I understand. Anything else? It's time."

Phelindra and Akenallin locked eyes and sang the same phrase at the same time: "Leave as quietly as you came."

"Got it. Let's go, Phelindra."

Akenallin stepped aside, and they entered the translation alcove.

No pads, Delwyn noted. "Where do I stand?" he asked Phelindra.

The Eldest frowned, mystified.

"Stand anywhere close to me. Ready, Mistress of Conveyance?"

"System ready, Mistress of the Watch," Akenallin replied.

"Remember Delwyn, silence!" She flicked her ears at Akenallin, "Establish translation lock on arrival. Translate!"

"Recall lock set and translate. Affirm, acting!"

Delwyn had never experienced Compact teleportation before. Unlike a Coalition mobius teleporter, this device scanned objects and quantum jumped an entangled set to a destination. It literally remade him. A Coalition teleporter flipped origin and destination volumes without altering the object teleported. Compact translation collapsed the object into an entanglement set that created a perfect replica on arrival. It worked like the jump drive but on a much smaller scale. He wouldn't be the same physically when he arrived on Phalalin's ship. So what? He'd been teleporting along with the ship and crew with each succeeding FTL jump.

His transportation concerns faded as he abruptly found himself in the middle of a forest. They stood in a jungle clearing with Warriors on both sides of them, forming a trail leading to Phalalin and his protectress. Behind him stood a large bole in a broad aerial root structure.

Between him and them stood the Huntress Verikaralee, Phalalin's mistress of the ship.

She started walking toward them. Stopping an ell from Phelindra she gave Delwyn a wan smile and a cautionary twitch of ear.

The patterns and colors on Verikaralee's waistwear bore a strong resemblance to those worn by Phelindra and Hervorallin, she apparently belonged to the O'un Tu Clan but to an extended family and not to either female's immediate families.

She greeted Phelindra in reserved ritual manner because her territorial instincts considered the Eldest a trespasser. These females held this ship as their exclusive home territory. Delwyn understood. A man never wanted to receive guests while in bed with his partner where prying eyes didn't belong.

Verikaralee gestured with her tail and turned, a signal for them to follow.

The Warriors lining the simulated trail fell in behind them, curiosity and resentment visible on their serious, tolerant faces.

Delwyn remembered to make eye contact so as to reassure them he harbored no nefarious intent against them or their warleader.

His scent should tell them so but being no empath himself he had no way of gauging how his scent affected them.

Verikaralee presented them to Phalalin. He twitched his ears, thanking her, and gestured with a tail flick for them to follow through the bole and into the massive fused aerial root structure.

Delwyn and Phelindra marched between a backward-walking protectress and the Warriors surrounding them. When they stepped inside and away from the bole, Phalalin looped his tail around the protectress and sealed the bole. Once it had closed, he nodded, relieved.

"Well done, Delwyn. Welcome to *Fearless*."

"Thank you, Phalalin. I am well come," he sang the ritual phrase in the scale Phelindra had taught.

"Warleader Delwyn, this is Amindaldra, my Protectress."

Delwyn caught the Hunter's eyes and nodded. "Well met, Amindaldra."

Amindaldra stood straight, ears perked forward, tail sticking out behind her, pons twitching.

"Met. You. Well. I. Am," she stammered, struggling with the unfamiliar words.

Delwyn's eyes lingered on her, trying to place the odd familiarity surrounding her. She had bright fluorescent orange hair styled like a close-cropped Raggity Anne doll.

She reminded him of a tall Zalzadrin.

"Zalzadrin?" Amindaldra asked in a clear voice, her eyes bright gleaming amber pools.

Phalalin raised his ears in shocked surprise. "What about her, Amindaldra?"

"Del-wyn think Zalzadrin," she whispered.

Her halting words told him in no uncertain terms just how much his scent told on him, if Amindaldra could smell an identity from his scent alone.

"Zalzadrin, yes. She's on my ship. She helped us capture the Ni'zakhonii ship. She got herself sliced up, and I had to staple the wound closed. She's going to have a terrible scar, at least until she has it removed and regenerated."

"That will never happen," Phalalin said. "She won it in battle, and it speaks volumes about her bravery. Amindaldra and Zalzadrin belong to the same extended family. They have the same mother. Verikaralee, you, and I belong to a different group of extended families."

"Tell her Zalzadrin fought with honor. That she helped us capture the enemy ship."

Phalalin sang a short statement, and Amindaldra nodded. Her polite manner at odds with a territorial watchfulness provoked by his intrusion into her most personal of homes.

"Come. Come, Delwyn. Walk with me. The females can look after themselves for a time," Phalalin assured him.

Yeah, right. Delwyn remembered Kidahin's posturing when he and Anlann told her and co-Ambassador Seralin to leave so Anlann could give him a similar talk. But Anlann's talk had been on Ibeetu and not on his ship. Indeed, the two Hunters were eying each other, wary, and Delwyn did not doubt their pheromones were doing all the talking for them.

"Are you sure?" he asked Phalalin.

The Eyloni male twitched his ears, rolled his eyes, and nodded at them. "Yes, they are fine."

Phalalin paused, thinking. He and Delwyn had spoken several times over the comm, but this face to face meeting gave him his first opportunity to sort out the images Delwyn's scent drew in his empathic mind. Those images revealed a calm male presence, one constantly weighing and adapting to new experiences. It reminded him of an Eyloni using her tail to maintain her balance. He approved. Delwyn did not drift through self-absorbed tailchasing, nor did he run leafchasing after daydreams, either. Phalalin smelled an open mind. Good. Delwyn's scent proclaimed his readiness to learn, and learning topped the reasons why Phalalin had asked him to come despite the visit upsetting the females on both ships.

Phalalin thought he smelled a prescient odor that gave him a feeling he and Delwyn must become close in the near future. Where that had come from he did not know, but the spirits must have plans for them.

Delwyn walked alongside Phalalin as they moved down the irregular hollowed-out tree trunk. Wide as a redwood's base and covered with fused roots grown gnarled around and through the massive trunk, the path glowed with dim simulated fungi bioluminescence. Soon enough the two males had drifted far ahead of the two Hunters.

"Delwyn? Just what makes a human male an adult in your culture?"

Delwyn shrugged, surprised.

"Age, why?"

"Age? What do you mean?" Phalalin asked.

Delwyn hesitated. The question sounded trivial, but Phalalin wouldn't have risked upsetting his crew to ask something trivial and easily answerable over the comm.

"Well, on Coalition worlds the law establishes an adult age for all humans. Below this age we cannot consent to contractual obligations or participate in activities legally considered adult-specific. For all people under the adult age limit, there is a legal right to shelter and security."

"Nothing is required of an individual to gain the benefits associated with this universal adulthood age?" Phalalin asked, perplexed.

"No. Adulthood is presumed upon attaining this age. Juveniles can petition for a waiver declaring them an adult if they meet certain legal criteria. Also, on rare occasions an adult can have the right suspended for his own safety."

"But you have no ritual prerequisites to complete before you are considered an adult?"

"We have birthday parties," Delwyn shrugged.

Phalalin frowned, and Delwyn knew from the warleader's pose that the flip answer made Phalalin uncomfortable. He tried to explain.

"A birthday party is given at the annual recurrence of the date of birth. That birthday has special significance when the year of adulthood age is reached."

Phalalin sighed, relieved.

"So you do participate in some ritual before you may claim your adulthood."

"No, not really. I remember having a piece of cake and eating a meal with my family. They gave me a few sentimental gifts and it was a done deal," Delwyn said.

Phalalin stared, and Delwyn sensed confusion mounting.

"You did nothing to prove your worthiness for being accorded adulthood status?" Phalalin demanded.

Insight struck, and Delwyn cursed his thick head. Kidahin had told him about her three-month survival ordeal and subsequent vision quest. She had been vague about the adulthood visions, but she described the three EST month, thirty-seven Earth day long survival ordeal, in the jungle naked and alone in detail. The adventure sounded abusive and extreme for a thirteen-year-old to have to endure. Nix that! In Earth time, Kidahin had barely reached seven years of age.

"How did you become a warrior?" Phalalin asked, interrupting Delwyn's reverie.

"Hmm? Oh, my family had a rich military history. The day after my eighteenth birthday I enlisted in the Coalition Fleet. I left Buenos Aires spaceport and did my induction training at Utopia Planitia on Mars. Much later I spent time on the Coprates Chasma canyon in the Valles Marineris canyon system, also on Mars. That's where I qualified for Special Operations Group duty, why?"

Phalalin ignored the question and asked one of his own.

"Did you engage in an adulthood ritual at your in-duk-shun?" he asked, struggling over the unfamiliar word.

"No. No, belay that. Let's just say intake separated the men from the boys. If you couldn't hack it, they kicked you out. Same with Special Ops training, and yes Special Ops had its own ritualistic elements."

Phalalin remained silent, lost in thought, humming to himself, an Eyloni musical muttering.

"Will that satisfy …will that be enough for the Be'atika Senge, the Clan and the Tribal Elders …?"

"Phalalin?"

"Did they give you a knife, an obsidian knife? Did you compose a song for them describing what you had learned from the spirits during the survival ordeal?"

"What? No. They gave me a medal to commemorate my accomplishment. I didn't sing for them…well, I did sing with them, but those songs had nothing to do with training!"

Delwyn caught Phalalin glancing at his left thigh again. Come to think of it, he'd been doing that off and on since he and Phelindra had arrived.

Phalalin snapped his ears and tried a different twist of tail. "You are a sire cairn, a battle leader. The society on your warship so name you. That means you have knives and can fight with them, yes?"

"Of course," Delwyn replied. "I handle knives quite well. I used them to my advantage on the Ni'zakhonii ship, killing about twenty or so with eleven knives in about a minute or so."

"Indeed?" Phalalin said, impressed. Delwyn's scent betrayed no falsehood, no boast.

Maybe it is enough, Phalalin thought. "Come with me. Are you willing to take part in an unarmed combat session?"

"With you?" Would doing so get himself killed here? Delwyn wondered. "What about Amindaldra? She's not going to like it."

"I told her we might test one another. This is no fight to the death, and in any event males seldom kill one another. The females would never allow it for matters of honor. If we get carried away, then our protectresses will intervene. On this they would be united."

"Oh? Sure, I feel great. Let's go."

Delwyn thought about what he was getting himself into. He'd sparred several times with Kidahin, an inexperienced young Hunter. Hand-to-hand combat tested the uses of body mass and skill. Kidahin looked petite standing next to him, and she looked sylvan and willowy compared to a Warrior female of Melkorka's build. Phalalin outmassed Melkorka by half again, was as tall as he was, and was just as muscular if not quite as broad in the shoulders as he was, too.

Delwyn recalled a certain Coalition intelligence summary: Eyloni had much denser muscle mass than a human and were double-jointed. They lived in skyscraper tall semi-hollow trees and had the long four-jointed fingers and toes and the muscle strength that made climbing and leaping through trees as natural for them as prowling jungle trails.

Phalalin was warleader here, and this ship's society wouldn't have chosen him if he had been weak or incapable. He'd also been warleader for some few years now and had more combat experience than a youthful Kidahin's skill could match.

Phalalin stepped through a folded crease in the aerial roots and into a long and narrow room with an uneven surface that gave like thick spongy dry moss.

Not an exercise mat, but it ought to cushion a hard fall. Good. This match would have a seriousness to it that his simple tussle with Kidahin had lacked.

"Ready?" the Eyloni male asked.

"Whenever you are."

"Begin," Phalalin said and jumped.

Delwyn spun and ducked just in time, grabbing for, and missing Phalalin's tail as the Eyloni twisted aside at the last instant.

Delwyn's combat awareness warned him not to use a standard follow up, so he stepped back and waited.

Phalalin spun, at once aware his ruse had failed to goad Delwyn into a foolish attack. He considered his adversary. Delwyn's human physiology should make a difference. He was heavier than an Eyloni male in both mass and in bulk. Phalalin knew Warriors used their heavier bodies to overbear and take down opponents. When those females hit, they hit hard and could take a punch without faltering. Hunters, lithe and light, relied on dancing feet and acrobatic ability to avoid all but glancing blows.

Delwyn should adopt a Warrior female strategy.

Phalalin decided on attacking and defending like a Hunter female.

Delwyn watched Phalalin's feet. Like Kidahin's had, they'd give away his next move but Phalalin had far more experience than Kidahin.

He'd have to watch for a feint.

Phalalin charged.

Delwyn watched bare feet. If Phalalin thought to feint, then his intended swing should go …

Phalalin jumped aside.

… there! Delwyn rabbit-punched Phalalin three times in the gut, drew back, and landed a solid punch to the Eyloni's jaw, jumped aside to avoid the tail, and twisted around to grab Phalalin's middle, lifted him off the deck and slammed him onto his back.

Phalalin rolled prone and sprang to his feet, crouching low, dancing on the balls of his feet, and watching for an opening.

Delwyn's fists had landed solid hammer blows. Phalalin guessed he had the edge in overall strength, but Delwyn had mass behind those huge human fists.

And he fought like a Warrior and a Hunter.

Phalalin charged Delwyn in what first looked like an overbearing maneuver, but at the last second he flattened his palms and slammed them into Delwyn's chest, knocking him off his feet and flat on his back.

Delwyn drifted, absentminded for a moment, wondering how he had gotten there. His chest hurt, and it hurt to breathe.

Bruised ribs?

Phalalin landed on Delwyn's chest and began pummeling him. He kept his tail whipping high in the air, balancing his body by countering the inertia of his strikes.

He knew better than to use his tail as a bola and entangle the heavier male's legs.

Delwyn pulled his thighs up, slamming his knees into Phalalin's back and used the momentum to pitch the Eyloni forward.

Unbalanced, Phalalin's arms shot out to arrest his fall, giving Delwyn the opportunity he needed.

Flat on his back, he punched the Eyloni's sensitive ears.

Phalalin rolled off Delwyn, angry now. This fight would decide the better male in hand to hand combat, and he did not intend to lose. He regained his feet and circled Delwyn, seeking an opening.

Delwyn eyed the Eyloni through a swollen left eye and noted with fleeting pleasure the oddly canted left ear and bruising along his opponent's left jaw.

Kidahin's voice echoed in the back of his mind, warning him Eyloni males fought without fear. Slow to anger by nature, males fought with methodical frightful cunning once aroused to combativeness.

Had Phalalin reached the limit of his restraint?

Phalalin was reassessing his opponent as well. They had traded blows, and Delwyn had regained the high ground and held it for now, but in a protracted fight they came out about even: at least on the ground.

That gave him an idea.

Delwyn's focus narrowed and sharpened as natural insight drew his gaze to the Eyloni's tail. It whipped about, an agitated cat's tail exactly 1.778 meters long. Phalalin shifted his stance, his long four-jointed toes splayed, opposable big toes gripping into the ground.

What am I missing? Does he expect me to rush and overbear him? Why give himself away? He's trying to draw me in. I'm not stupid enough to rush a set opponent!

Delwyn watched those knees bend, too late in realizing what Phalalin's stance had telegraphed.

Eyloni lived in trees. That meant they jumped, often down but occasionally up as well. Natural born high jumpers, they'd use that ability to their advantage. He'd been warned.

Phalalin launched himself straight up, his feet reaching a height just above Delwyn's head before powerful narrow heel strikes slammed down into his collarbone, snapping bones between neck and shoulders like dry twigs.

Delwyn had felt the impact microseconds before the bones broke and dropped to reduce the strike's fury. He folded under Phalalin and pulled his legs up as he hit the ground, driving his knees into the backward-falling Eyloni's kidneys and snapping the ribs along his diaphragm.

The impact pitched Phalalin forward hard, and he fell on top of him. Delwyn took the Eyloni's solid chest full in the face, pectoral muscles smashing into his nose. He drank blood, and the pain told him it was broken. He swore and turned his head aside, his left ear suction-cupping to Phalalin's chest. He laid there listening to Phalalin's rapid heartbeat and labored breathing and smiled.

Phalalin wasn't moving and Delwyn found it wise to remain where he was, too.

Outraged shouts from Phelindra and Amindaldra reached his ears, and he grunted.

"I told you they wouldn't like this," Delwyn muttered.

"I am surprised they let us carry on as long as they did," Phalalin wheezed above him.

"You've got broken ribs Phalalin. How long will you have to stay in Health Center?"

"For this? This is nothing but a simple bone repair. Amindaldra, help me stand," he groaned.

Delwyn felt Phalalin's weight lift away from him, and he tried to sit up.

Tried, at least until shifting broken collarbones changed his mind.

"Uh, Phelindra? A little help?"

The Eldest came at once, mulled over where best to grab onto him for a moment, and with little effort lifted him to his feet.

The two Hunters fought against conflicting emotions: pride and fury.

Phalalin smelled their emotional battle and smiled. The Hunters were pleased. Their charges had acquitted themselves in honorable, ritual combat. Their fury awoke because he and Delwyn had taken some minor injuries yet their disgust and humiliation would have been more evident had neither male been blooded.

"Females are strange," Phalalin sighed under his breath. "Amindaldra? Ask Tathilatha to come and bring a bone regenerator," Phalalin said.

Amindaldra glared at her warleader, but her eyes wandered back to Delwyn.

"Anu ana turadek, ar ahoun Unahaillaea *Tyreniioroneo*," she said.

You fought well, Warleader of Hunter's Moon.

Phelindra pricked her ears at Phalalin. "Anu ana turadek, ar ahoun Unahaillaea Alaho," she said.

You fought well, Warleader of Fearless.

Phelindra glided back to Delwyn and gave him a good looking over, a scrutiny as embarrassing as it was thorough while she reassured herself he had taken no serious hurt. She muttered under her breath, curses no doubt, as she inspected every bit of him with a tenderness at odds with the Eldest Huntress's imposing presence.

Phelindra, hard, muscular, and wiry, bumped and rubbed against him. Her warmer-than-human velour skin and scent soon became a soothing balm. The tail caresses and occasional tender expressions she gave were for him alone, as were her not so mock-serious scoldings.

"You did not anticipate Phalalin's leap!" she admonished.

"I didn't expect it from him. From a Hunter maybe but not from him."

"You think only Hunters leap?" she demanded. "I leap better than any Warrior or male, but all Warriors and males can leap. If they cannot leap then they die."

"Yes, I know. But I thought you leaped down trees from limb to limb," Delwyn countered.

"We do. Is quick way down. That or leaping onto a leaf and riding multiple leaf strikes down but sometimes you must leap up. You leap up one branch if you do not want to walk through a bole into the interior hollow and climb the central path filled with fused aerial roots shrouding the central trunk. Most upward leaping or sideways leaping happens when a weak branch you were foolish enough not to notice breaks under your weight, or if your grip fails. If you find nothing but air below, then you leap up, or you leap across, or you fall and die."

"Phalalin, Tathilatha arrives," Amindaldra stammered.

Phalalin nodded. "Admit her. Delwyn, once the door is closed, you may speak again but do not speak to the Mistress of Healers. Medical questions she will ask through me, and I will repeat your replies to her. Understand?"

"I do."

Phalalin nodded to Amindaldra, and the protectress stalked off.

"We need to do this more often," Phalalin said to no one in particular.

Phelindra growled what sounded like a mild curse, a tempered rebuke without the sting of a true insult, aimed at him and Phalalin.

Phalalin grinned for Delwyn's sake.

"She thinks we are strange," he said.

"I hear a lot of that, too," Delwyn nodded.

"Yes, but I am serious. You need to learn Eyloni personal combat techniques."

"I know, but I don't think combat exercises involving us are a good idea on your ship. Constant visits will drive both our crews insane."

"Oh, I agree. I mean when we arrive home. While your warship is under repair, I shall command a local space assignment, giving me broad options in making visits to the La'huaset Tribal continent. There we can request time at the training center."

Delwyn nodded as Amindaldra returned with the Mistress of Healers.

Tathilatha, a Warrior female, stood next to her warleader already waving a medical scanner over his body, growling to herself as she plied the instrument over his back. She glanced at Delwyn before frowning at Phalalin and Amindaldra. Tathilatha pulled another instrument from her medical kit, one resembling a large rubber-handled tuning fork. She dialed settings on its base and watched the small screen set in its base change. Satisfied, she placed the tuning fork end over Phalalin's left kidney and snarled an order.

Fearless's warleader drew in a deep breath, stood, and held it.

Tathilatha jabbed a control with her long four-jointed thumb and waited.

After a long minute, she thumbed the control off, snatched the medical scanner with her free hand and waved it over the treatment area, read the results, and scowled at him.

"A'pea!" she sang.

Phalalin gave her a sheepish grin and drew another deep breath, wincing as he straightened to hold it.

The Mistress of Healers repeated the procedure, scanned his back once again, and nodded.

"Better. Much better," Phalalin said. "My thanks, Tathilatha."

The Mistress of Healers, although visibly relieved, scowled at him a moment before turning her gaze on Delwyn.

Tathilatha glanced at Phelindra and snapped at her.

Whatever she said piqued the Eldest, and she snapped a blistering comment back at her.

They closed to within a tail length, an ell, and traded nasty-sounding trills.

"Phalalin?" Delwyn asked.

"This is nothing. They are arguing over our practice fighting."

His voice drew Phelindra's notice. She gave them a withering, indignant look and switched to the elusive sign language all females used.

"Battle language," Delwyn muttered.

"Yes," Phalalin agreed, his hearing keen as ever despite the blow Delwyn had landed to his ear. "They make sure we cannot hear how much they complain about us."

Delwyn winced, impatient for some Compact bone mending technology himself, but the opportunity to ask a question overcame his discomfort.

"Anlann told me only females know battle language. Hasn't a male ever tried to learn it or tried to talk a female into teaching it to him?"

"As if that will ever happen," Phelindra sang as she signed.

Phalalin nodded. "She is correct. Female hierarchies guard battle language usage. Teaching it to a male is a death penalty offense in all female hierarchies. It is also a death penalty offense for any male caught using battle language," he added.

"Wow," Delwyn muttered.

"Yes. Wow." Phalalin agreed. "It is an honor and privacy matter. We have a close contact culture, always touching, always together. Battle language allows them privacy while surrounded by others."

"I thought all females understood the same sign language," Delwyn interrupted.

"Yes. Of course. I meant privacy from male ears."

"Oh."

"Yes. Oh," Phalalin agreed. "Battle language allows them to say things we never like hearing aboard a warship."

Wait, what? Delwyn stumbled over the mental doubletake before jumping on Phalalin's words. "What do you mean?"

"Nothing much, just if they think you are in danger, they will concoct extravagant strategies to make sure you do not come to harm, and they will blatantly discuss those strategies in your presence using battle language."

Phelindra halted her silent argument with Tathilatha, growled a complaint at Amindaldra, and she sang a frustrated chord at Phalalin.

Phelindra glided to Delwyn, calling Tathilatha to her side.

Delwyn's eyes measured the Mistress of Healers. Like Amindaldra she gave him the wide-eyed best courtesy possible under the circumstances and scanned his nose and collarbones.

She healed the two collarbone breaks first.

His nose, bigger than an Eyloni's, presented a problem. She held the scanner, considered its report, and reached a decision. Lightning quick, she shoved two long fingers up his nostrils, braced her thumb against his bridge, and pulled.

The pain made Delwyn's eyes water. He'd had broken noses set before with sticks but never with someone's fingers.

He felt warmth flow underneath the skin, just as it had near his collarbone breaks as the bone underwent accelerated healing.

The Mistress of Healers tore a sanitary wipe from a pouch in her kit and wiped the blood from his face.

Delwyn nodded in gratitude.

"Do you feel better?" Phelindra asked.

"Much better. How about you, Phalalin?"

"Good as new," he said before gingerly rubbing his bruised jaw.

Phalalin stepped over to Delwyn, wrapped his tail around his waist, leaned into him, and *snuggled* him.

The embrace surprised Delwyn, but not as much as the first time Anlann had hugged him.

Eyloni male mannerisms came off as somewhat effete, and all Eyloni carried routine affection to extremes. They displayed fondness in the same manner male and female with males or females.

And, unlike Anlann, Phalalin and Delwyn belonged to the same clan.

The sudden unexpected realization that Delwyn once again had living relatives threatened to overcome him.

All three females hummed pleased rhythms. That made sense, too. They all belonged to the La'huaset tribe.

"We have much more to discuss. Tathilatha, you may return to Health Center," Phalalin said.

Delwyn knew the Warrior Mistress of Healers didn't want to leave, but her presence technically violated the rules governing warleader visits. Once she left Phalalin again chased the two protectresses off, assuring them they had no interest in further combat today.

Phalalin gestured Delwyn to follow, and they strolled through a bole and onto a wooded path under orange leaf filtered light.

"We males all together make up a society. Do you understand what this means?"

"Some. I know all Hunters belong to a society. Helmsmistresses have their own society. A Warship's crew is a society in itself."

"Correct. There are thousands of societies in our culture. A person belongs to more than one society, and often belongs to a great many of them. This belonging represents a physical Oyya Web of the spirits in our lives. When Hervorallin's daughter Princess…," Phalalin stumbled on the odd name, "… became your near-daughter, you became a member of several societies yourself. You are Eyloni, one of the People, the broadest of all societies. You are male so you belong to the society of males; you are a warleader, so you belong to the society of warleaders; you are an O'un Tu Clan male, thus you belong to the society of O'un Tu Clan males. I also know from viewing the Death Song record, you are a singing male. That makes you a singing male society member, and the singing male society is a very exclusive one too."

"I thought all males could sing," Delwyn interrupted, confused.

"Of course all males can sing. All Eyloni can sing. Our culture apotheosizes music, and it certainly encourages vocal talents. It is vanishingly rare for anyone not to sing. But singing males are different. They compose music for ritual occasions. Many warleaders are also singing males."

"Oh. What about you?"

Phalalin nodded. "I am, but my talents lie elsewhere."

His admission drew a soft hiss from the surrounding jungle thicket, and Delwyn knew the two busybody Hunters had been stalking them from faux forest cover.

Delwyn glanced at Phalalin, but he was ignoring them, pretending he heard nothing, and a thought came to him. Watching Phalalin might give him essential clues on the fine points of warleadership, or at least enough to know what his crew expected of him.

Phalalin continued blithely, "Males have special privileges in our society. We may go anywhere. We have autonomy, and our autonomy extends into everything except where courtesy and privacy prohibit. We, the society of males, will help you learn things an Eyloni male infant learns before he reaches the time of his survival ordeal."

Phalalin hesitated for a long minute wondering how much he should tell Delwyn about what could be asked of him once he met with the Be'atika Senge and the Clan Elders. Delwyn thought he smelled a change in the Eyloni's body odor.

"You anticipate them having a problem with me, don't you," Delwyn said.

"No, I do not think it will be anything serious. The females aboard *Hunter's Moon* chose you, you sing, and you held your own in unarmed combat with an experienced warleader. That you belong to the O'un Tu Clan is beyond dispute." He paused. "What was I talking about?"

"The society of males," Delwyn reminded him.

"Oh, yes. Males share a special bond. Our freedom of movement allows us to receive and dispense public news throughout the clans. We look out for one another. Our presence draws females because they think we cannot do anything without them. When they fight amongst themselves, and they do from time to time, we arrive and mix with them. They will never permit the risking of a male's safety and will relent. Our presence in counsels, whether they be clan, tribal, or the Compact Counsel, moderates tempers and impulsive reactionary decisions. We are the proactive elements of our society."

Delwyn's stomach sank. Bad enough he knew next to nothing about commanding a battlecruiser, but now Phalalin implied that he also had a say in both Eyloni society and Compact governmental affairs.

"I think I'm going to need a thorough briefing by someone in the male society so I can figure out just how I'm supposed to do that."

Phalalin beamed pure pleasure. "And I can help you now, while we have the time. I will give you a briefing on the workings of the Compact Counsel. But first, before I forget, I think we must work on a key element of Eyloni male life."

"Which is?" Delwyn asked doubtfully.

"The concept of first male on-scene precedence. That custom is the pons governing all male crisis management interplay. You understand some of it already, yes?"

He nodded. "Melkorka explained the basics to me. She said something about the first male arrival in a conflict zone commands all subsequent male arrivals. If he cannot handle the responsibility, he hands off Warpact command to another arrival."

Phalalin twitched his ears. "Well yes, you have the essential point. You hold Warpact command now because you arrived with an association and a combat vessel during a time when the potential for conflict existed. That means you had a better chance of dealing with the conflict issue than Anlann did. He knew the females with you intended to declare you warleader of the enemy ship, and his honor required him to yield because he had no warship and no females to support him. Once Melkorka declared you warleader, you became the first warleader with his warship and females in a conflict zone. That is why I elected to orbit the moon while you remained in the star's heliopause. Otherwise, if I had taken *Fearless* into the ice dwarf belt, you would have been honor-bound to recognize my ability and relinquish Warpact leader status."

"Then why am I Warpact leader now? There's no longer a continuing conflict crisis. Actually, I don't see how the events in the Iota Horologii system …" Delwyn hesitated. "…sorry, the Nikkiolo star system, amounted to an event serious enough given what Melkorka implied in her lessons about Warpacts."

"Technically, conflict existed from the moment your warship had been attacked and Kalinn killed. Concerning you, conflict existed the moment you ordered a female surface assault force into action as their sire cairn. The conflict zone grew as it included the light attack craft you captured. It expanded again when Melkorka, well technically Kidahin as huluhar, chose you. Further, the messages I received from the fireside taleteller Harrison warned me of conflict in the form of an attempt to remove you from the safety of those females. Finally, your warship has suffered severe battle damage, and so I am at the honor point escorting you back to Elleio. The conflict zone exists until we arrive in homespace."

"That's why I've been the Warpact leader from the time I arrived in the Nikkiolo system commanding the captured enemy ship while accompanied by a female association?" Delwyn concluded.

"Yes!" Phalalin said, nodding vigorously.

"Harrison," Delwyn mused aloud. "I wonder if Captain Winters ever found him."

"The Coalition counsel-speaker? The taleteller? Where could he hide on a warship?"

"I don't know. Winters told me that both Harrison and his aide had been missing at least since my Mistress of Healers confined me to Health Center."

"Missing? The male who threatened to have you removed from your ship? The male who threatened to arrest you for piracy against the Ni'zakhonii?" Phalalin demanded, his natural fierce anger rising in spite of his self-control.

"He's the one," Delwyn affirmed.

Amindaldra, as a protectress was wont to do, took her responsibilities quite seriously, and so she constantly sniffed the air around her warleader. A habit really, she knew this visiting warleader had no designs on Phalalin or their warship, yet her curiosity drove her to discretely spy on Delwyn. He smelled so open and accepting of Phalalin, and she knew the scent of a forming male alliance. The scent was tinged with an empathic image of a betrayer gone missing. The scent mingled with her warleader's, an indignant fury concerning the same tailcutter. Amindaldra's own anger started simmering when she caught a whiff of Phelindra's pheromones, and the images they made sent Amindaldra into convulsive laughter.

Waves of Eyloni mirth sang out from tall amber grasses off the trail near the two warleaders, and Delwyn turned on Phalalin.

"Does this happen to you a lot?" Delwyn asked.

Phalalin nodded absently, "Always."

He addressed the yellow-trimmed orange thicket, "What have you found so funny, Amindaldra?"

The singing laughter grew, as did sharp hissing sounds.

"Phelindra. Make. Tailcutter. Dead!" Amindaldra sang before whistling out another measure of musical laughter.

An outraged rhythmic challenge shrieked over the laughter.

Thwak!

Amindaldra flew out of the grasses and across the trail. Just missing Delwyn, an enraged Phelindra followed intent on beating the other female into the simulated jungle floor.

The two Hunters thrashed one another in the tall jungles grasses.

Delwyn moved to intervene but a laughing Phalalin yanked him back.

"Shouldn't we do something, Phalalin?"

"Do what? This is not our business. This is, properly speaking, female hierarchy business. Phelindra is defending her society's business, your ship's business. Amindaldra's outburst confirmed aloud actions taken by your protectress, and that is a serious breach of privacy."

"About what?" Delwyn asked.

Phalalin shrugged the question off and watched the two females wrestle.

Delwyn thought about it. They had been talking about Coalition Ambassador Harrison. Phelindra had been quite pleased when Winters had reported Harrison and his aide missing. She had even barked the most insolent laugh he'd ever heard out of an Eyloni. He remembered asking her if she had anything to say about the matter … and she had turned as sweet and innocent as a baby!

"She killed him, them!" Delwyn cried.

"Yes, undoubtedly," Phalalin agreed. "Maybe not herself, but most likely she sent warleader special security after him."

"I didn't order him killed, Phalalin!" Delwyn thundered.

Fearless's warleader turned and met Delwyn's eyes.

"You should have. I would have done so in your place. No Eyloni male has ever seriously thought of doing what Harrison attempted. Remember, your occupational association considers your safety before their own or even the safety of their ship. They will always take steps to protect you, and you will never even know about it. No order you give can prevent them from protecting you as they see fit. Phelindra saw fit to remove the tailcutter from the universe, least his continued plotting and taletelling bring you to harm or tarnish your honor. You carry their honor, and they reflect yours. If your honor is sullied, then theirs is sullied. We know the depth of a male's character by the scent of his female associates."

"Oh," Delwyn said. "It sounds complicated."

"It is not. Remain honorable and everything else will take care of itself."

Both males stood there, arms folded across their chests, watching the spectacle of two Hunters fighting. Five minutes later Delwyn wondered how much longer they would go at it when he finally noticed something odd.

"Phalalin are they trying to undress one another?"

"Yes," he said, nodding at them "The first to lose her waistwear loses."

Delwyn watched, fascinated as fall leaf patterns rolled in the holographic jungle undergrowth. Their skins blending into the leaves and grasses so completely that he might never have seen them but for their tussling. They barely made noise and what noise he did hear was the sound of force field sculpted grasses bending and brushing.

"Not going for the neckwear are they, not even for a good hand-hold?" Delwyn asked.

"Of course not. Nobody touches a female's adulthood knife either. That always gets you killed, unless she ritually gives it to you. Touching a female's rank web earring is deadly too, unless you are her current warleader."

Delwyn grunted, watching muscles flex, tails whip, and ears bend down and back.

They weren't playing, either. They backhanded, punched, threw, and kicked each other in a flurry of blows.

Phelindra held the upper hand at the moment. She had already yanked Amindaldra's short loincloth off, but the hip-riding underthong remained tightly tied against her skin at the hips.

They thrashed in the tall grasses for another five minutes before Amindaldra made a grab for Phelindra's loincloth and missed. Twisting her body almost in half, Amindaldra pulled back but she remained close enough for Phelindra to snag a hold of her tail.

Phelindra pulled Amindaldra to her as if hauling in an anchor. Then she slipped one hand along Amindaldra's bare skin and under the thong where Amindaldra's tail poked through and yanked, snapping the ties and pulling the underthong down the length of her tail. She jumped back and stood, waving the undergarment in the air.

Both Hunters sported minor bruises and cuts.

Delwyn stared at them and shook his head. "Females are strange!"

Phalalin spun on him, surprised.

"You know this saying?"

"What saying, Phalalin?"

If Phalalin had a ready answer, it died as a victorious Phelindra raced up to Delwyn and wrapped her tail around him, expecting touches and caresses for her success in defending her ship's honor.

She preened as Delwyn looked her over, making sure she hadn't taken injuries beyond minor scrapes.

"We," he stressed, "are going to have a talk about Harrison when we get back you know," he told her.

"Of course, Delwyn, when we get back!"

Phalalin gave Amindaldra the notice she demanded. He chided her, too. By custom she had been in the wrong for speaking on another society's business.

Amindaldra disengaged from her warleader's embrace and stalked up to Delwyn, ignoring Phelindra, and made eye contact with him. Ears perked forward, tail held high, she struggled for the right words.

"Sorry. I. You," she said.

He smiled at her, unsure just how far he could directly address this female even while in the honor suite.

Phelindra made her pleasure loud and clear with renewed snuggles. She saw the apology to her warleader as a concession to her as well.

"That's it?" Delwyn asked.

"Of course," Phalalin said. "Amindaldra will now dress again. They are not rivals, not enemies. They ritually settled a point of honor witnessed by us. They will not speak of it again, not even to other females. We will not speak of it either, because to remind them about it keeps the offense alive as if it had never been resolved.

"Remember one thing well, Delwyn. Male opinion carries far in our culture. A thing you do not forgive, they do not forgive."

Delwyn admired this custom. This spat was over, forgiven, and forgotten because it had been ritually resolved. No past ghosts would haunt them in Eyloni social life.

They started back down the trail again, and Delwyn thought about Warpacts.

"You said something about Warpacts and first male on-scene precedence. This custom recurs often in social life, I imagine."

"Yes it does," Phalalin agreed. "Conflict does not always imply physical or warlike violence. All subsequent male arrivals at a crime scene, rare but it happens from time to time; rescue missions, law enforcement and outlawry management all look to the first-arriving male because females gather around him to guarantee his safety. If he is involved in settling conflict, then they intervene and resolve the conflict before it can harm him somehow. When, say, rescue services arrive, they always bring a male competent enough to lead others in rescue procedures. The first on-scene male—usually an incidental passerby—then surrenders Warpact command but remains under the Warpact leader's command until the conflict is resolved."

"Melkorka's lessons mentioned that, too. She told me females associating with the first arrival would not appreciate being ordered about by any subsequent arriving male."

"Not appreciate?" Phalalin smirked. "They would bite their own tails in apoplexy. You cannot even suggest an alternative to another male's association. In Warpact you order the male, and he carries out your orders within the honorable best of his ability and the abilities of his association, but he has autonomy in pursuing your objective. A male telling a female belonging to a society in voluntary association with another male what to do is almost as bad as stepping onto another warship without the warleader's permission."

"Is Warpact granted and relinquished through ritual?" Delwyn asked.

Phalalin smiled, looking downright effete, and Delwyn thought about lemurs again. Evolution had made lemurs female-dominant, and Eyloni male behavior seemed a natural refinement of lemur male attitude.

"Yes, very much so. I think we ought to practice the rituals used to receive and transfer Warpact command back and forth between us."

Delwyn nodded. His initial notions had been prescient after all. Watching Phalalin, working with him, would help him become the warleader his crew expected.

"When?"

"As soon as you return to your warship."

"How?" Delwyn asked.

"I will tell you. First …"

It took Delwyn about an hour to learn the ritual forms of Warpact protocol. Warpacts by their nature regulated emergency chains-of-command, and long rituals would never suffice while your tree was burning down. In Warpact you made snap decisions and relied on experience, the experience of the females with you, and your judgement regarding the abilities of any subsequent arriving males.

The stance and words used signified the ritual difference. It presumed mandatory obedience as a matter of form and perceived issues of dishonor had to wait until conflict was at an end and the Warpact dissolved.

"When you return to *Hunter's Moon* we will begin practicing Warpact procedures," Phalalin concluded.

"I'm looking forward to it," Delwyn said.

They walked several long minutes along wooded paths listening to jungle sounds before Phalalin snapped his tail. "Delwyn, now is the time to tell you something about our governing system so you do not face them without knowledge. You must meet with the Compact Counsel and the females that make it up, the Be'atika Senge," he sang, "soon after we arrive. The Be'atika Senge will want to hear your report on the combat effectiveness of the LAC you captured and ask you questions. Then courtesy requires you to meet our Clan and Elders as well and a few days later you will also meet the Tribal Elders.

"While you are with the Be'atika Senge you do, as the warleader of a ship fighting for the Honor of the Ten Tribes, have a say in Compact affairs as your occupational association's representative. Even in Counsel you retain your autonomy and freedom of action. Honor and courtesy rule behavior in Counsel. The male counsel advisors will speak to you first. They will invite you to sing with them, a high honor indeed. The Be'atika Senge will listen. You do not speak the language, but a few people on the Counsel know your Earth tongue from speaking with the humans from the warship *Alexandra Witze*. Others will learn it soon enough in the same manner all of us pick up odd dialects, as Phelindra and the others on your ship have done. They will empathize with the images your pheromones plant in their minds and connect them with your words."

Delwyn remembered. Kidahin had understood no Coalition standard. She picked it up bit by bit until he sang for hours with her. The others had picked up pidgin standard when they sang with him during the Death Song ritual on Ibeetu.

"Maybe I should spend a day singing with them," he offered.

"Yes!" Phalalin nodded, perking his ears forward. "You are a singing male. A ritual performance would do them great honor."

"So, what do the counsel males decide?" Delwyn asked.

"Decide? Nothing. Governing power on Elleio is the exclusive domain of females, but the Be'atika Senge does not twitch a tail without first listening to the advice any male having an interest or concern offers. We advise, and they carry out policy on behalf of the Ten Tribes. Our advice, all male advice, is granted great weight, more weight than the concern of any single Be'atika Senge female. If a male holds a contrary opinion, and if he presents it to the Counsel, then the Counsel will argue and debate until consensus is reached. Sometimes compromises are made, but in general females are reluctant to ignore a male's reasoned concern."

"What if they decide he's arguing about nothing?" Delwyn asked, thinking about United Earth politicians and Coalition Government interagency rivalries.

"You mean stalling?" Phalalin stammered. The idea sounded dishonorable, and he said as much. "No one, male or female, ever makes a disingenuous argument before the Counsel. A person's honor never permitted it. Remember, your pheromones give away your belief in the merits of the argument at hand, and they will always find you out."

Delwyn wanted to smack himself on the forehead. He kept forgetting about Eyloni pheromonal empathy and its role in augmenting close communication. Evading a truthful point of fact was allowed, as was keeping one's own honorable counsel as an exercise of personal autonomy, but never let them catch you in an outright lie, not even a white lie. Lying created a social debt. The guilt associated with the social debt altered pheromones that always let them find you out, and they would hold your honesty and integrity suspect. The presumed late Ambassador Harrison had practiced diplomacy as an exercise in plausible deniability. That was why Anlann and Seralin had so despised him. He really did need to talk with Phelindra about Harrison when they returned to the ship.

Delwyn hesitated, chagrined that he hadn't asked Phalalin an obvious question.

"What does the Compact Counsel do?"

Phalalin stopped walking, looked down at his bare feet, wiggled his toes and watched his pons twitch in and out between his legs. Then his features turned deadly serious.

"The Be'atika Senge is the world government of the Ten Tribes of Elleio. The Compact Counsel guarantees the peace among the Ten Tribes and their clans. The Be'atika Senge is a female hierarchy and is the Compact Counsel. They are the only female hierarchy that consults with male advisors. The Be'atika Senge weaves all social societies and everyone in them into an interconnected whole within the Oyya Web. This interconnection discourages warfare among tribes and clans. The Compact Counsel preserves the environment and regulates industry. It also moderates the A'tayotan, the female hierarchy charged with exercising military power. The Be'atika Senge sets war policy and the A'tayotan carries it out, but the Be'atika Senge legislates worldwide policy, and we must all sing in full accompaniment to their will. The Counsel is also the guardian of male safety."

"The guardian of male safety?" Delwyn echoed. "I thought males had autonomy."

"We do. You misunderstand. The Counsel enforces honor codes among males to prevent us from killing one another without cause. Also, females loathe the idea of harming a male, let alone killing one. If a male violates a female hierarchy principle, such as the one governing battle language usage, the Counsel finds the truth of the matter before sentences can be carried out."

"Don't females have the same appellate standing?"

Phalalin frowned, testing the unfamiliar word before shaking his head. "No appeal for them. Judicial power wielded by females against females comes from their respective hierarchies. The Compact Counsel acts as our trail into the female hierarchy responsible for governing the world, which includes us of course. Females have thousands of hierarchies, and all of them weave together just as societies do. We males have just the one path into female judicial power, the path through the Compact Counsel. Males may have wide autonomy, but our infringement upon a hierarchy's privacy or honor will bring us before their justice. Females hold themselves to higher standards on hierarchy matters. In any case, the Territorial Boundaries of Rage and Forgiveness deal with all social debt except for assaults on hierarchy honor."

Phalalin paused, certain he had not answered his clan male's curiosity.

"History plays a part in Compact affairs. The Compact is an agreement among those many female hierarchies. It has existed for thousands of years. Its need came in response to the wars and skirmishes our ancestors fought. You are acquainted with the concept of males in danger inducing combat fervor in females, yes?"

Delwyn nodded, remembering Kidahin's abrupt violent change in response to one of his martial beats.

"Clans gather their males within their defense forces. When a clan suffered a defeat, the victorious clan either offered the surviving males amnesty and shelter or killed them if they refused. Without males, the surviving females have a dead clan. Most average clan families have females by the thousands, but they have only about thirty males."

Delwyn did some mental math. Fifteen males among some three hundred females in an average family elleiu tree added up in base-five numbers to thirty males among some twenty-two hundred females.

Phalalin continued. "Warfare killed off males, destroying entire clans and decimating the people. The Tribal Elder females in all Ten Tribes held a conclave under treaty in the name of male safety. They formed the Be'atika Senge hierarchy, and the Be'atika Senge created the Compact, an honor-bound agreement not to raise arms against other tribes or clans. They then set an Oyya pattern weaving the hierarchies and societies together."

Delwyn drifted off in thought about what he had learned from Phalalin. He had to reason it all out, and he had another lesson later in the day.

"Delwyn, it has been a true pleasure having you aboard," Phalalin said.

Delwyn relaxed as Phalalin wrapped his tail around him embracing him, rubbing his tail up and down his bare back, scent marking him with the heady pheromones in his pons. He broke the embrace, feeling guilty knowing how much of a toll the extended visit was taking on the females aboard both warships.

They would annoy them both with testing and testy quips for quite some time.

"Come, Delwyn, it is time for you to return to your warship. If I must suffer the ill humor of my association, then I am comforted knowing you will suffer along with me."

Delwyn sighed, wondering what Melkorka and the others had in store for him as signs of their frustrated annoyance.

They wandered back through the aerial root structure and soon found themselves at the exit bole.

"Remember, no noise from you whatsoever until you are safely returned to your ship," Phalalin admonished.

"Understood. When do you want to start the Warpact exercise?"

"I shall contact you with a simulated conflict soon."

"Very well. I'll be waiting."

"No Delwyn. I think your association will keep you busy."

"Probably true. Let's go, Phelindra."

The Eldest wrapped her tail snug about him and growled, "Let us leave."

Delwyn nodded, and Phalalin signaled for the door to open.

The much unhappier Warriors waited just outside the door.

They parted for Verikaralee. She nodded to Phelindra and walked Delwyn and Phelindra back to their arrival point.

When they reached the proper place, Phelindra twitched her ear, activating the comm unit there, and sang a string of rushed tonal notes.

And before he knew it, they reappeared in the translation alcove facing a glaring Akenallin.

Delwyn barely had time to exit the translation alcove before both females laid into him with outraged shouts.

4
A MATTER OF HONOR

Delwyn and Phelindra exchanged verbal barbs back and forth all the way to the command center. Phelindra refused to budge. Evasive and offended, her replies revolved around a central theme: she considered the matter private, none of his business.

Their raised, tense voices heralded their arrival. Melkorka, seated in her command chair, twisted around with supple grace and pricked her ears at them in greeting, but folded them back against her hair instead, concerned.

Had Delwyn bungled the visit to Fearless?

No, their pheromones told her otherwise. They argued over a personal matter.

Heated arguments, just as excitement or alarm did, ramped up pheromone output. An efficient signaling method, it notified those nearby that they should take care.

Delwyn's scent spoke of a deep displeasure over being left out of an important decision, but Phelindra's brought with it mental images of necessity, duty, and an unshakable overprotective zeal.

The command crew picked up on it, too. The Eldest's conduct and Delwyn's disapproval: the Protectress had somehow eliminated the human counsel-speaker, a threat to him in her mind, without his consent.

She should have known. Had Phelindra done it herself, or had she put her Hunters up to it?

Melkorka twitched her ears, a shrug directed more at the command center itself, and focused on him alone. Welts and light yellow and purple stains covered his solid tan skin. Outrage surged through her even as the others noticed their warleader's bruised appearance.

Delwyn and Phelindra froze in mid-argument as they both felt, and smelled, the tension rising around them.

Melkorka bolted from her chair with her warleader's odd curved sword in her left hand and stood face to face with him, her nose touching his.

She stood there trembling, furious, and Delwyn glanced out of the corner of his eye at Kidahin seated at her helm and remembered a warning she had once given about the Mistress of the Ship.

Melkorka was quick to anger; she did not suffer fools gladly.

"What happened to you?" she demanded.

"Nothing much, just broke my nose and collarbone. It's nothing serious, and they fixed everything," he deflected.

Melkorka's large amber eyes narrowed as she spun on the Eldest Huntress.

"And where, Mistress of the Watch, were you while this was happening?"

"Watching. Delwyn fought well. He broke Phalalin's ribs just above his gonads."

"Wait," Delwyn interrupted, "What?"

Phelindra curled her tail around his shoulders and pulled him into her, a sly look on her face. "Where you struck Phalalin is the place ovaries are in Hunters and Warriors, the same place testes are in males."

Melkorka stared flabbergasted at the snuggling pair, mouthing Phelindra's words, tasting the flavor of her reply.

Delwyn groaned. What he thought of as a mere kidney punch had been a dirty blow. That explained why Phalalin had fallen on him and why he couldn't get up without help.

"I thought I cracked Phalalin in the kidneys not his balls!"

Sibilant sing-song sighs filled the command center, Eyloni mirth. Their moods improved after his admission.

Melkorka's eyes drifted back to Delwyn and she spat-grimaced; she yielded, although still unhappy about his bruises. It took his touching shoulder rubs to calm her down.

The command center crew, watching him caress Melkorka, twitched their ears and tails in coy poses, a not so subtle hint they wanted reassuring touches, too. Delwyn spent the next several minutes jumping from console to console caressing each female according to her hierarchical rank. Kidahin, the last in line, was holding him in a fierce tail embrace when the Mistress of Communications interrupted the happy moment.

"Mistress, Phalalin calls on alert comm!"

"Accept!" Melkorka said.

The main panoramic holodisplay forward of the Warleader's Watch filled with Phalalin's image. Covering the entire bulkhead, it gave Phalalin a magnificent presence. "Mistress Melkorka, a conflict alert is now in effect. I must speak with Delwyn."

"Affirm, Phalalin. Delwyn?" she prompted, gesturing her warleader to his Watch with a snap of her tail, her eyes flashing daggers at him as he passed.

Delwyn grinned to cover a fleeting doubt. Maybe he should have warned her about the upcoming Warpact exercises.

Well, he shrugged to himself, maybe not. If Phelindra could keep secrets, then he could too.

"I'm here, Phalalin. Report."

"We have detected an energy pulse artifact of a Ni'zakhonii railgun discharge. I am sending tactical data to your Mistress of Tactics now.

"The nature of this artifact suggests a Ni'zakhonii destroyer has jumped into normal space at high sublight velocity some few light-hours from a fixed orbital target and fired a large kinetic mass. This offensive strategy is ineffective against targets mounting heavy shields, sublight velocity intercept capability, or targets having even minimal evasive maneuverability. Tracking solutions plot an approach cone with an apex intersecting Elleio orbit. We have not located the ship firing the mass, but to be effective, he must jump into normal space, fire, and jump back into FTL while remaining outside of our threat assessment scanning range. We have no enemy firing solution update scans, so this object is passive and is following a precalculated trajectory based on hyperaccurate targeting data."

Delwyn nodded. Phalalin had come up with this obvious wargame scenario. They were cruising in normal space well beyond light-hour range of Elle's heliopause, let alone Elleio herself. Analysis of this "artifact" must have confirmed a power signature matching a heavy- mass kinetic attack, some kind of small ferrous asteroid and not ordnance. High sublight velocity impacts using even low metric kiloton masses could trigger worldwide extinction-level events. Earth's dinosaurs had found out the hard way 65 million years ago what a "slow" asteroid impact could do. With no drive or active sensors, an accelerated asteroid gave itself away only by the energy signatures of space debris, dust, and hydrogen atoms hitting its leading edge at high sublight velocity, creating a shock wave.

"How do you wish to proceed, Phalalin?"

Phalalin pricked his ears forward in frank seriousness. "You are Warpact leader. How do you wish to proceed?"

Delwyn had his own ideas, but the search parameters he knew best dealt with terrestrial ground or air searches. Space had an unlimited z-axis component not bounded by solid ground or atmospheric ceiling. As he'd told his stubborn crew several times already, he was no starship captain. Certainly Melkorka knew how to proceed, and if they had been alone, then her orders would have governed the intercept strategy unless he intervened. But two ships, with two warleaders, raised Warpact issues and Melkorka couldn't issue orders to Phalalin without offending Verikaralee and her society.

"I yield Warpact command to you. How do you want to proceed?"

Melkorka and Verikaralee both sang a phrase at the same time.

Phalalin nodded. "Null point reference data predicts a ferrous object located at semi-major axis 1.043 AU, period 3 TST years, eccentricity 0.320, perihelion 0.141 AU, inclination 1,223.44 degrees."

"Melkorka?" Delwyn asked, struggling with the base-five numbers and a 10,120-degree circle.

"Phalalin's encounter analysis suggests an estimated Elleio orbital intercept in 32,342 seconds. Projected intercept distance is 32.34 light-minutes; encounter velocity is 0.22 cee. Impact probability is 44.4 percent. Atmospheric breakup probability is nil. Impact error ellipse is 10,010 kalells times 1,113 kalells. Projected impact trajectory plots an ellipse centered at 33 degrees north, 121 degrees nearside, bearing 312 degrees."

Mistress of Tactics Hlinlodyn interrupted. "Impactor projected summary: final impact velocity, 0.14 cee; estimated asteroid volume based on firing signature artifact profile is 4.342 kalells times 2.421 kalells times 3.302 kalells ellipsoid. Estimated volume is 144.414 kal^{2}ells^3. Average density is 0.12 oro/ell^3 with a total mass of 32 kaloros. Explosive equivalent is 144.3 kal^{2}oros. Most probable impact adjusted to 210 degrees north, 130 degrees nearside longitude, Eastern Gyre Ocean 41,300 kalells north of the Mawe'allea Tribal continent."

That was a twenty-seven gigatonne impact 600 kilometers off the coast in 37 minutes.

Phalalin nodded his agreement with her estimates. "Delwyn, with all respect, commence sensor sweeps of the mass's projected approach cone. Tie your sensors into mine in interleaved scanning mode. Given the mass's presumed velocity, scan for high-speed particle impact energy signatures."

"Acknowledged. Melkorka, tie our sensors into *Fearless* sensor tracking solutions and begin sweep maneuvers once we synchronize helm maneuvering. Scan for hydrogen atom impact bow shock signatures."

"By your command," Melkorka replied. "Mistress of Tactics, Mistress of Pathwalking, program for close-order combined search maneuvering with *Fearless*, interlace search and destroy scanning with Phalalin as point. Target is a small ferrous asteroid traveling at point one-four-cee within the most probable launch trajectories bounded by an approach cone radius 241 AU with a length of 1,422 AU and apex terminating at Elleio equator."

"Affirm, acting," both mistresses sang.

Delwyn stood near Melkorka's command chair or paced uselessly around the Warleader's Watch when he wasn't squinting at the three-dimensional tactical display.

They searched for a fast moving rock in a solution set plot of possible inbound trajectories forming a long narrow funnel with "Elleio" at its narrow end. They scanned conic sections, individual transverse slices through the trajectory cone, looking for the telltale energy spikes atomic hydrogen and other particles made when they smashed into a rock moving at relativistic velocities. Interlaced scanning gave the two ships more than double the scanning resolution of a single ship, a good strategy. They needed all the sensor resolution they could get to find an 800-meter rock moving at one-third cee somewhere in a 1,482,553 AU^3 volume in under half an hour.

Phalalin sent constant updates requiring Delwyn to retask his sensors to new search parameters. Some of them even made sense, but others mystified him.

"Delwyn, Phalalin's latest scan data requires the Mistress of Tactics to program for conic sections that exceed the volume defined by his initial encounter data," Melkorka reported.

"Any reason offered for the change in scan parameters?"

"None."

"Hlinlodyn?" Delwyn asked his Mistress of Tactics.

"I have received no updated trajectory plotting data that justifies this loss of sensor resolution and the waste of time scanning outside the impactor's predicted solution set, Delwyn."

He nodded. "Comply with the revised scan parameters, maybe he knows something we don't."

"By your command."

Phalalin contacted them nine more times with additional changes and updates in as many minutes. Minutes later, another update sent them scanning beyond the bounds of the predicted approach volume. Delwyn ground his teeth. Then Hlinlodyn reported more scan parameter updates falling far beyond the predicted approach volume. Delwyn visualized the geometry as a flattening approach cone. Their scans were missing volume beyond the flattened edges, and they were also scanning areas beyond the edge of the original circular cone.

"Hlindredreda, contact *Fearless*. I want to speak to Phalalin."

"By your command," the Mistress of Communications said.

"Yes, Delwyn? Is there a problem?" Phalalin asked.

"I'm not sure. My Mistress of Tactics tells me we are scanning well beyond the approach vector cone predicted by your original encounter data. Have you received updated data?"

"One moment, Delwyn," Phalalin said. He turned to ask someone off-screen a question. Seconds later he turned back, nodding. "Sensor fault detected, correcting now and sending you revised scan data. Well done."

Delwyn nodded. This exercise tested his willingness to surrender Warpact command. To be effective, a wargames exercise had to include possible faults programmed in for them—or at least for him—to discover.

Another four minutes passed before Hlinlodyn detected the bow shock signature of an unnaturally fast object on her tactical scanners.

"Mistress, sensors are registering charged particle emissions consistent with atomic mass impacts on an object moving at high sublight velocity."

Melkorka glanced at Delwyn, and he nodded in unspoken agreement: the iron asteroid. It couldn't be anything else.

"Contact Phalalin and relay the data," Melkorka said.

"Affirm, acting. *Fearless* acknowledges."

Since no target existed for them to destroy, the exercise ended when the asteroid had been "acquired" and firing solutions locked into Hlinlodyn's fire control system. Delwyn wondered aloud whether they should have reported the first discrepancy, but Melkorka flipped her ears back, a no gesture. "The first two errors fell outside the projected range of possible trajectories, but they also fell within calculated error range of possible trajectories. The data we did question had us scanning a cone with a base ellipse half-again as wide as the circular original."

"Mistress, message from Phalalin for the Warleader," Hlindredreda announced.

Delwyn smiled to himself and waited for Melkorka to prick an inquiring ear at him. When she did, he nodded. She commanded here, but warleader status and male autonomy gave him the freedom of choice.

"Accept," she ordered.

"Affirm, channel open," Hlindredreda said.

"Delwyn?" Phalalin asked.

"Yes, Phalalin. Standing by."

"I yield Warpact command back to you."

"Accepted," Delwyn said.

Melkorka and Verikaralee sang the same phrase they had sung when he had relinquished Warpact command to Phalalin.

"What did you two just sing to each other?" he asked Melkorka.

"*Heard and witnessed.* It means that both Verikaralee and I have witnessed a Warpact command exchange between you and Phalalin. We make this oath upon our honor. It signifies our reluctant acceptance of the necessity of having one of you being dictated to by the other."

"So you two authenticate Warpact command transfers?"

"Yes! A Mistress of the Ship warrants to her society that she has witnessed the change in Warpact status. If I were to vow a change in Warpact status when no such change has occurred and any female discovers my deception, then she will declare me guilty of a hierarchy honor crime and recruit every female to kill me for betraying you," she said.

"Oh," Delwyn muttered, wondering just how many excuses his beloved crew had for killing each other in his name.

Phalalin interrupted the lengthening dead air. "We will continue exchanging Warpact command under different scenarios, if it pleases you."

"Okay, fine. What sort of task should I give you?"

"Surprise me. Farewell!"

"Contact terminated at the source," Hlindredreda reported.

Delwyn nodded. "Let's give Phalalin something thankless and annoying to do. Let's have him jump ahead to his maxium FTL displacement, 3.043 TST light-years, and have him sit there and wait for us. His jump drive is already spooled up for the next scheduled jump. I'm warleader, so he'll have no choice but to leave immediately."

Hlinlodyn hesitated, and Melkorka had doubts of her own. Delwyn's idea sounded like the breeze that blew the leaf of discourtesy. No doubt he wanted to avenge his bruises but having Phalalin leave the honor escort point could be read as an unintended slap on his honor.

"I do not think that asking Phalalin to vacate the honor escort point for no reason at all is a good idea. Besides, you do understand that if Phalalin jumps into a conflict zone…," Melkorka began.

"No, this is a great idea. We have several hours remaining before our jump drive can generate enough gravitational field strength to jump us to Phalalin's jump terminus. He'll be stuck there doing nothing but waiting until we get there ourselves. I had to put up with things like this all the time in the Coalition Navy. Hlindredreda, open a ship-to-ship channel to Phalalin."

"By your command. Channel open. Mistress Verikaralee is standing by."

"Mistress Verikaralee, please ask Phalalin to jump immediately to our next jump terminus."

"Affirm!" Verikaralee replied. Her startled expression surprised Delwyn. Then he grimaced at what he thought she had in mind. If Anailiatha's jump drive armatures failed now they'd be fifteen hours from any help Phalalin could give.

Delwyn paced a slow circle from the Warleader's Watch to Melkorka's command chair and back again and considered strategy. Phalalin had acknowledged his request and jumped 3.043 light-years away, and he did so without offering any 'buts' or asking any 'whys', too. He paced and wondered, recalling the momentary shocked expression on Phalalin's face.

"I'm surprised he left us without so much as asking to what purpose," he muttered to Melkorka.

"You are Warpact leader. You asked Phalalin to go and he went. Obviously," Melkorka snarked.

Now what was biting her?

"Are you worried about Anailiatha's repairs failing?"

"No, I am worried about Phalalin having something untoward planned for you when we arrive at his jump terminus," she grumbled.

"Yes Delwyn, you have tugged on Phalalin's pons and he is going to respond in kind," Hlinlodyn added.

"How? Make us jump backwards?"

Trebithia looked up from navigation and shook her head. "No, of course not. He would not want to delay our arrival, but there are thorny vines he can lay about our feet and try to catch you unaware."

Delwyn considered the Mistress of Pathwalking's insight. Just what thorny vines could a devious Phalalin lay about for them? Something in line with teaching him about Warpact protocol? "What more is there? We've been trading command back and forth already. What can he do now he couldn't do before?"

Kidahin hummed an obscenity from her helm. "He is no longer here. He is light-years distant. He is there with his warship and his association. When we jump back to him, you will no longer be the first on-scene male!" she explained, glancing at her supervising mistress for confirmation.

The Mistress of Pathwalking's ears perked forward as she considered the helm trainee's logic, but Melkorka spoke up before Trebithia could reply. "That is his plan. You two males have been playing Warpact leader and surrendering command back and forth. But *Fearless* is well beyond honor escort point position now. In theory he could have jumped into a Conflict Zone. There is no way of knowing whether or not he gives you a test, or if there truly is a conflict issue upon our arrival. You will have no alternative then but to accept Phalalin as Warpact leader."

"No choice? I'm still Warpact leader, aren't I?" he asked her, mystified.

"Do you see any other warships about you?" Melkorka demanded. "A Warpact exists only to accommodate more than one male within a Conflict Zone. You are the only male in this vicinity. Phalalin is light-years away, also the only male in his vicinity. When we arrive at his jump terminus and no conflict exists, then no Warpact is necessary. By sending him on ahead, you have dissolved the Warpact you held since the conflict-specific event occurring within the Nikkiolo star system."

He shook his head. "No, that can't be right, Melkorka. I retain Warpact command because theoretical conflict exists with respect to our battle damage. The jump drive repairs among other things could fail at any time," he added, thinking about all the local force fields operating just in the combat hull alone.

Melkorka jerked her head, flattened her ears against her brilliant orange ringleted head, and snapped her tail behind her. "You are wrong. You asked Phalalin to vacate the honor escort point off our bow, which he accepted as meaning you believe our situation has improved beyond which further conflict is doubtful."

"He is planning something crafty," Kidahin blurted.

"Why thank you for stating the obvious, Kidahin!" Melkorka snapped.

"I am certain no actual emergency exists at his location. That means he must assert a pretense or a task for me to solve, but what?" Delwyn asked.

Hlinlodyn had been thinking the same thing ever since they suspected Phalalin of planning his own tail-yanking nastiness for sending him on ahead to leafchase the time away.

"He will demand Warpact command when we arrive," Kidahin offered.

"That has already been established!" Melkorka sang. Her fury over things unknown raged through her melody, drawing alarm.

"She is only working through the problem aloud, Mistress. We know Phalalin will demand Warpact leader status. He does not have to tell you why a Warpact exists Delwyn, but only that it does. He makes the claim on his honor. You may call him to task after Warpact ends on whether he asserted the right with honorable intent. Prepare yourself," Trebithia said.

Prepare yourself? Delwyn wondered what he could do in preparation for an unknown event several hours in the future.

He could eat some food?

He could get some sleep?

He could learn another lesson other than the one he was learning now?

"Phelindra, what can you tell me about Compact combat doctrine? The Coalition has use-of-force doctrines and rules of engagement restrictions."

"I can teach you everything you need to know," Phelindra sang over Melkorka's vehement objection.

"I know both use-of-force doctrines and combat rationales!" Melkorka snapped as she shot a resentful glare at the Eldest Huntress.

Delwyn pressed palms into his forehead, trying to forestall the headache already building there. They vied for his attention, a form of testing they did often. They seemed to enjoy his discomfort when he had to choose between or among them. It wasn't just a game in their eyes, either. Ranking made all the difference. He could choose anyone he wanted for any task, but when it came down to it he had to watch for the telltale signs of deference among them. Outward appearances mattered to female hierarchies, and he had to take care and choose the one most capable for the job and never choose solely as a sign of favor.

"You will both instruct me on this matter, Melkorka first. I have some lingering questions I must ask Phelindra afterwards. But first, I need to eat something and then get some rest while there's time."

His words satisfied them, and he thought he knew why. As his Protectress, Phelindra went everywhere with him, including the nutrition center, before accompanying him to their quarters.

There, she always slept next to him.

Delwyn left the command center Phelindra close behind him. Food was first on his mind, or at least it was on his growling stomach's mind. Strict vegetarians, Eyloni ate no meat products whatsoever. Kidahin had all but gagged on smelling cooked meat in the Coalition mess hall on Ibeetu.

As the crews of Coalition ships did, his crew also ate meals in the galley.

The warship's nutrition center served food around the clock. No set schedule seemed to apply: no breakfast, lunch, or dinner times. Although the crew ate three meals a day, they did not congregate at set times for those meals. A day in Tyreniioroneo Standard Time was 10.2592 Earth hours long, and his crew divided the day into equal awake-active and asleep-inactive periods, so they ate three meals in about five hours, or six meals in under an Earth day. Although they ate less than he did in any one sitting, they tended to snack throughout the five-hour active period.

Delwyn and Phelindra prowled through jungle cover together, admiring the view as they pushed golden fronds aside. Phelindra must have looked upon and touched the bushes and trees often over her years aboard, and yet she still paused from time to time to gaze and touch. Why? No dangerous, wild animals hid under the simulated cover. Maybe she was memorizing them or longing for the real thing he couldn't tell. His crew shared an affinity for this forest, fake as it was. They read signs on the trail, smelled the air, looked at the plants. Delwyn decided to ask her. "Why do you touch things so often?"

"We leave scent along the pathways and trails," Phelindra admitted.

"I thought so. You have to mark your territory."

"Yes. You mark the ship too, do you not? We can smell where you have touched a tree, a bole frame, a wall, or other fixture."

Delwyn sighed. He hadn't done so on purpose, but his scent-empathic female crew believed he did so to lay a claim on them.

"I didn't mean to suggest that the ship was mine, Phelindra, I know he belongs to your society."

"I know you leave your scent throughout the ship for our comfort!" She sang.

They stepped up and around a stout tree and onto a branch leading through a bole and into the nutrition center.

Delwyn smelled his favorite food waiting and his mouth watered.

Phelindra stepped into the warleader's abode ahead of Delwyn and glanced about.

All clear.

She prowled deeper into the large room, sweeping through several out-of-sight side spaces.

A stuffed, tired Delwyn followed the cautious Eldest Hunter into their quarters—the warleader and protectress abode—a treehouse built inside a large hollow tree. The walls followed an irregular outline of the trunk along its inside circumference. The central hollow space was a spacious roughly round room with several side rooms formed from cavernous bends that followed the trunk's outline.

He wandered through the spacious central room and out onto a terrace looking through huge leaves hanging in the open sky.

Over a hundred meters below, the Om'tu River spilled over a cliff. The sun's rays shining through the cascades made them glow with liquid fire.

Phelindra glided up beside him and wrapped her tail possessively around his waist.

"You must sleep. You are full with food and tired. I can smell it on you. You worry about what Phalalin has planned?"

Delwyn shook his head. "No, although I'm sure he'll do something we won't care for."

Phelindra twitched her ears, unraveled her tail, and pointed her pons at the nest they shared. "Come. Time for you to sleep."

Delwyn resisted her pulling halfheartedly, like a kid fighting sleep while yawning his head off.

Phelindra gave him a gentle shove onto the multicushioned round mattress and rolled up alongside him, snuggling into him with arms, legs, and tail.

"What do you think about today?" she asked.

"Overwhelming. Fighting Phalalin surprised me. I didn't expect him to get so physical."

"Phalalin exercised restraint," Phelindra growled. "Eyloni males are strong, crafty fighters."

"Yeah, well. I kept up with him, too," he said, yawning.

"Indeed you did. We are so proud of you."

She meant the comment as a comfort, a complement, but it made him feel like a kid being praised by his mother for going in the potty and not the diaper.

"What?" Phelindra demanded, smelling the mental comparison on his scent.

"It's nothing, Phe. I just don't feel like I did anything spectacular."

The Eldest perked her ears on hearing her natal syllable, the first half-chord in her infant name, *Phelin.* In private, it passed for a nickname. Its use between them implied a deep sharing, a personal connection. Calling her Phe in public signified in her culture that he must think of her as an infant. He called her that only here. She had warned him how humiliating it was for an Eyloni adult to be called by her infant name in public.

"You showed us you had no fear while facing another Eyloni male," she said.

"Yeah, but Phalalin is from my clan."

"That makes no difference. If anything, he fought harder so as not to show favoritism."

"Mmm-hmm," Delwyn murmured. Enthralled by her altering body odor, he fell asleep in seconds.

Phelindra held him in a gentle, warm embrace. She was determined to watch over him, content. In this special way, he was hers in a way he was not for the others. She listened to his breathing, smelled him, and relaxed.

Although her eyes never stopped roving the room.

If Delwyn only knew the depths of Phelindra's love, he would be shocked. She loved him with a fierce dedication matching the bond between mother and child and between spouses in human relationships.

They all did, but Phelindra was the oldest female, the Eldest Huntress of the Ship. Just over 104 EST years old, or about 23 Earth years old, she was the physical age of a 48-year-old human, the same age as Delwyn.

He slept on, and she planned his upcoming schedule. He would soon meet with Melkorka and discuss Compact combat doctrine. The Mistress would give him lessons on war theory, just war doctrine, and military organization. Melkorka had better give him a tactical briefing on the Ni'zakhonii from the A'tayotan's perspective. Once she was done, Phelindra would chase Melkorka off and teach him use of force rationales and female aggression and male caution in Eyloni society, since Phalalin probably had not bothered, seeing Delwyn as another Eyloni male. Had Hervorallin instructed Delwyn on the concepts of Social Debt yet? Honor formed its core, and right now honor was a sticking point with Phalalin.

Hours later, Delwyn awoke to huge amber eyes looking down on him.

"Why didn't you get some sleep?" he demanded.

"I did rest, yes, short naps here and there," she said, flipping her ears about.

Eyloni evasiveness, Delwyn knew her well. "Uh-huh. Sure. Well, let me get ready. Call Melkorka down here. I want briefings from you both before we jump into Phalalin's conflict zone."

Phelindra nodded but did not move a muscle.

He frowned up at her for the short time it took him to remember the combat address system. Melkorka had no doubt left the command center the moment she heard him voice his need for her.

Phelindra stood, stretched, and began doing calisthenics.

Minutes later, a whispering breezy sound filled the room, an announcement from the Mistress of the Ship's presence.

"Come!" Phelindra sang out without so much as bothering to ask Delwyn.

Like it mattered. Melkorka, like all Eyloni, had an odd sense of privacy. Even before Phelindra sang out, Melkorka had palmed the door sensor, poked her head inside for a look around, her body flowing like water after her into the room.

Phelindra glared at the Mistress of the Ship's droll expression, watching her eyes.

Melkorka's eyes coveted their nesting place.

Phelindra sighed. There was time enough later for her to sleep with Delwyn.

Sleep, meaning being in each other's company and resting, not mating. That scent came up often enough from Delwyn, and she wondered again why he always had thoughts about mating on his scent. The scent on the air said humans were always in season but she did not believe it for an instant. If you mated all the time, then how did you ever have time to get any real work done?

5

WHAT HONOR REQUIRED

Phalalin sulked. With nothing to do but wait, he spent hours pacing the Warleader's Watch, stalking command center stations and prowling the ship's jungle trails.

Why was he impatient? Males were the epitome of patience.

Delwyn must have had extreme confidence in his Mistress of Sails when he ordered them to leave the honor escort point.

Certainly Delwyn had not intended on rescinding the honor, which had to mean he wanted Phalalin to leave and spend the time tailchasing while his jump drive recharged. How would Delwyn decide his jump entry velocity? He could maintain the same sublight velocity he had before the jump, or he could jump back into normal space at zero velocity. Phalalin twitched his pons, a shrug. Melkorka would warn Delwyn about the energy expenditure a full stop entailed and advise him to maintain standard sublight velocity on jump exit, just as *Fearless* had done.

Separated by 3.043 light-years, two autonomous males aboard two autonomous warships now cruised independently of one another. Phalalin curled his tail in thoughtful humor. They cruised at Battle Status, and whether a conflict existed fell within the discretion of the male declaring it.

Hours from now Delwyn would arrive and find himself in a conflict zone.

Phalalin stalked off the command center to wander trails. For the fun of it, he stepped off the trail and pushed through the heavy forest cover that became impassible near the bulkheads it hid from sight. When he finally returned to the command center hours later, a discrete Amindaldra closed the gap between them and broke cover to stand beside him.

Phalalin brushed tails with everyone, his huluhar last. He glanced at Verikaralee and twitched a curious ear.

"They should arrive any moment now Phalalin."

He rested a hand on her shoulder and nodded.

Verikaralee arched her back in response and dusted his face with her pheromone-scented pons.

"Mistress! Delwyn has jumped behind us at standard maneuvering spacing and maintains matching velocity," the Mistress of Tactics reported.

Verikaralee glanced at him under lidded eyes, a veiled warning. "Have a care, he is our clan male."

"I know that. Delwyn knows that," Phalalin sang. He paused a moment for his soft melody to sink in before straightening and turning to face his Mistress of Communications.

"Hail them."

"By your command."

The fatigue on Delwyn's face bloomed in realistic clarity on the main screen, and Phalalin looped his tail in a gleeful twitch: he is as bored as I am.

"Delwyn, I declare a conflict existing and assume Warpact command until such time as I am satisfied conflict no longer exists. With respect, take your warship to Battle Status at once and resume jump drive maximum recharge rates."

Delwyn groaned. Anailiatha would love that. He'd been anticipating a tail pull, but he hadn't been expecting to come to Battle Status or to resume maximum apparent FTL velocities.

"I yield to the Warpact leader," he said.

What else could he say?

"Heard and witnessed," Melkorka and Verikaralee sang on the heels of his surrender.

"Battle Status! Resume maximum jump rate velocity."

"By your command," Melkorka replied. "Mistress of Tactics sing Battle Status. Mistress of Sails resume normal recharge rate and spool up the jump drive for maximum velocity."

###

"Mistress of Pathwalking, synchronize jump clock countdown with *Hunter's Moon* and prepare to jump."

"By your command."

Phalalin gave Verikaralee a reassuring smile. Delwyn had performed well so far. He understood the seriousness of the matter and complied without pause or complaint. If he performed as well throughout this exercise, then perhaps Phalalin could relax and the O'un Tu Clan females aboard *Fearless* could relax as well.

Phalalin drifted off, leafchasing, staring at the obsidian knife strapped to his left hip remembering what his adulthood ordeal had been like and thinking some adolescents did not come back.

###

A day and a half later *Hunter's Moon* finally achieved sufficient threshold power for an FTL jump. Phalalin loomed over his Mistress of Tactics's shoulder, watching for signs of stress as the elite warship maintained the complicated energy pattern and awaited the command to initiate the jump.

"I can read my instrumentation well enough without you breathing up my tail!" his Mistress of Tactics said.

"I know that," Phalalin sang. His counterpoint reply to her discordant harmony signaling his confidence in the Warrior and in her abilities.

A few beats ticked by before he added, "Well?"

Annoyed, the Mistress of Tactics flicked her tail across the scan summary.

"Delwyn's warship is ready to jump. Energy signature variations in his gravity lensing fields suggest several out-of-tolerance eddies resulting from increasingly misaligned or out-of-balance armature windings."

"Transfer your scan summaries to the Mistress of Sails for analysis."

"By your command."

While they waited for the primary engineer's report, Verikaralee transferred Phalalin's sword from her knees to her left hand. She stood up and glided without a sound behind her warleader and entwined her tail around his.

"You are worried," she hummed.

"A little. I do not want to cause the destruction of an elite warship."

"You will not allow that to happen," she reassured him. "But you do enjoy exercising Warpact command over Delwyn, do you not?" she teased.

Phalalin felt the intensity of the moment drain away. "I will admit to some pleasure, but I would rather yank Kalinn by the tail than Delwyn."

Verikaralee sobered. "I agree. Yanking a clan male around by the tail is no fun." She sighed, "I like Delwyn. Phelindra's scent gave me a strong impression, savagely strong."

"Personal association strong?" Phalalin asked, leaping to a vine he had no business climbing.

"Are you asking about Phelindra or me?" Verikaralee demanded.

Uh-oh, this vine was slippery.

"Phelindra, of course."

Eyes glaring, she nodded. "I think Phelindra is Delwyn's first personal association female."

Phalalin twitched his ears in what passed for a nod. He took Verikaralee's point, but something about Phelindra's presence here, something about Melkorka's on-screen demeanor, warned him that Delwyn's occupational association would soon be his personal association as well. Nothing unusual about that in itself. Most of Phalalin's occupational association was also his personal female association. Females reflected the character of the males they associated with.

He shook his head, tempted to stall but had no justifiable reason to delay.

"Mistress of Communications open a channel to Delwyn."

"By your command."

Delwyn's tan-faced, black-haired image filled the main screen.

"Phalalin, we are ready to jump."

"Jump as soon as jump clocks are synchronized, Delwyn."

"Affirm, Delwyn out," he said.

Delwyn faded from the holodisplay, replaced by an image of his warship floating in a black star field. Phalalin slapped a control on the Warleader's Watch console, and the warship expanded toward him, engulfing the Watch station itself and continuing until it stopped a tail length from Verikaralee's command console.

Phalalin walked into the display volume and examined the warship a moment before touching a point on the displayed ship.

The combat hull grew as it spread across the entire forward bulkhead and stretched out to Verikaralee's command console, swallowing Phalalin in the process. He stepped out of the image volume and studied the forward left quarter sections. The bow and left side hull showed signs of heavy damage: pitted hull plating, metal reduced to slag, and breaches open to space wide enough to pilot a hovertank through. Critical areas showed the scars of minimal patching necessary to maintain hull integrity.

Hull integrity mattered for successful FTL jump translations.

Delwyn's ship had rammed an enemy and penetrated deep. Exterior plating had been scored and ripped away from the outer hull. Visible torqueing along several breach points indicated that Kalinn had rammed after taking massive breaching fire to the left forward quarter. Only the spirts knew what had kept the hulled compartments from buckling and deforming the ship's symmetry.

Asymmetrical hull alignment affected quantum translation outcomes. A jump drive quantum singularity formed around a precise balance point. Just as an aircraft had a center of gravity point, so did an FTL-capable ship have a singularity origin point tied to ship geometry and mass.

Reprogramming for mass meant first finding a new total mass number and then recalculating. How many dead bodies? How much ship's structure had been vaporized by enemy fire? Revising total mass was tedious and time-consuming. Reprogramming for mass was complicated but possible.

Reprogramming for a new origin point, the point where the quantum singularity collapsed the ship, was impossible in practice.

Mismatched geometry jumps risked critical structural failure: mass either fell into the quantum black hole, or mass outside the origin radius remained behind when the bulk of the ship jumped. A nominal jump entangled ship mass into a quantum state, reduced that mass to component particles, and flung it around an accretion disk. At the jump destination the entanglement set 'played back' as the singularity evaporated, reassembling the ship.

Missing mass causes random losses in ship structure, in crew complement, in critical instrumentation, or even in individual body parts. Critical failure tended to be widespread and, thank the spirits, caused the destruction of the ship on jump completion.

"Phalalin? *Hunter's Moon* has synchronized to our jump clock and awaits your signal," Verikaralee said.

She knew he was worried, and not just about the jump either. His scent said it had something to do with Delwyn.

The jump clock counted down to zero.

"Jump!" he sang.

"By your command. Mistress of Pathwalking, jump the ship," Verikaralee said.

"Affirm, acting."

***

By the end of the second jump Anailiatha had established herself as a frequent visitor to the command center.

"This running fast to nowhere to no purpose must stop!" She trilled. Her bare feet whispered across the forest floor, Eyloni stomping. She drilled her withering Warrior's stare at the source of all her frustrations: Melkorka and Delwyn.

A silent voice in the back of Delwyn's mind agreed with her. For hours now he'd been feeling a subtle harmonic rhythm vibrating through the deck. If he could feel it here, then he could well imagine what machine shop bangs and shimmies were shaking Anailiatha's propulsion command center.

"How bad?" Melkorka demanded.

"Left armature failure is imminent!" Anailiatha spluttered.

"Can Phalalin pick up our drive transients on his scanners?" Delwyn asked.

"What?" Anailiatha snarled. "They can detect the field imbalance signatures from Elleio!"

Her reply surprised him. Eyloni rarely employed hyperbole outside of humor. Even then, hyperbole was a highlight of Hunter thinking. Gross overstatement was not a Warrior failing.

Yet, for some reason her report had a calming effect on him. His feelings about it must have been strong enough to reach the sensitive noses around him. Both Warriors spun on him, mouths agape, Melkorka in astonishment and Anailiatha in suppressed fury.

"You think I exaggerate?" Anailiatha demanded.

"Never. I think Phalalin knows full well the state of our drive. No doubt his Mistress of Tactics is monitoring our jump drive emissions. I'm certain this jump is the last one at normal recharge rates, and I'm also certain he'll soon ask us to resume a jump rate more acceptable to you."

###

An ominous signal spiked on a certain screen.

"Mistress? I show an out-of-tolerance spike in *Hunter's Moon's* gravity lensing system," the Mistress of Tactics reported.

Verikaralee spun in her chair, smacked at the combat address system intraship toggle, and sang a five-note warning.

"Phalalin, drive failure on Delwyn's ship is imminent!"

Phalalin's whereabouts never mattered. The combat address system tracked his movements and relayed Verikaralee's call to him and the waterfall plunging around him.

"Open a channel to Delwyn," he said.

"By your command. Channel open. Delwyn is waiting."

"Greetings, Delwyn. Reduce drive recharge rate to previous settings. Maintain course and speed and set for synchronized jump."

"Affirm," Delwyn said.

Phalalin sighed in relief. Delwyn had performed as expected. No doubt by now his Mistress of Sails wanted to pull the hair out of his pons.

Phalalin paused, his nose catching questioning pheromones. He looked down to the pool below and the glaring eyes ringing the bathing pool.

"Delwyn did well today," He announced. "I am satisfied. I will transfer Warpact command to him, and he will lead us into homespace."

Those bathing stood up in the shallow pool. Their tense scents revealed a need for closeness and reassurance. Drying himself first, Phalalin started rubbing skin oil into his legs, singing as he moved up his thigh. He groomed, and they watched and listened. When done, he put the oil back into its pouch, met their eyes with his and pricked his ears first forward and then wide apart, an embracing gesture inviting them to sing along with him. He changed tempo, letting everyone listening know they had permission to sing along with him.

In the command center, Verikaralee noted the change in beat and keyed the combat address system to omnidirectional mode so all females might hear and join in the shipwide singing.

***

"Trebithia, how long until our next jump?" Delwyn asked.

"Three hours," she said.

Three hours in Tyreniioroneo Standard added up to some seventy-five minutes Earth time. The dual time standard was a pain. He forced himself to think in both Tyreniioroneo Standard and Elleio Standard at the same time. If he didn't then things got confusing real quick. If Melkorka said she wanted him in the command center in an hour, then she meant a female time hour. If he told her to meet him in his quarters an hour later, then she would arrive a male hour later.

"Very well. Melkorka, unless Phalalin changes his mind, jump the ship in close-order maneuvering with *Fearless* when the jump clock reaches zero."

"By your command. Are you leaving?"

Delwyn nodded. "Notify me when the jump has completed. Kidahin come with me."

Melkorka acknowledged the order in the traditional manner, her eyes following Kidahin and Phelindra as they hurried out the bole after him.

Hopefully all this male posturing and ritual tail yanking was over by now, and things could get back to normal.

Males were strange.

Delwyn sat on a plump, plushy, pellet-filled bag and watched the two Hunters laying tails entwined on the bed, his nest they called it, and half-listened as they double-teamed him.

"There are things you must know before we jump into homespace," Phelindra began.

"How hard can it be? Knock on the door, ask if we may come in, they open the door, and in we go."

"It might sound that easy to you, but it is not," Kidahin warned.

He concentrated, trying to send a simple comment through his body odor.

So easy for them, a near impossibility for him.

"Arrival and leave-taking have a ritual importance you must respect," Phelindra said, ignoring his pheromonal tail tugging.

"Yes, I know." He stood and stretched. "I need a minute to clear my head and get my bearings. I'm going for a walk. I'll be back soon," he reassured them over their objections.

***

Melkorka paced the uneven forest floor between her command chair and the Warleader's Watch.

What was taking Delwyn so long? Entry requests hinged on formal rituals.

The Home Fleet never denied a Compact warship entry into homespace. Making a formal request bespoke courtesy: one did not barge in on another without notice, not even on fellow clan members. The welcoming reply from the Be'atika Senge had more ritual importance than simple permission to enter did. In his case the Be'atika Senge's welcome would ritually acknowledge they had survived battle, that they had suffered many casualties, that they had suffered the humiliating loss of Kalinn who had been the crew's to protect, that they brought with them an intact Ni'zakhonii light attack craft, and that they had chosen Delwyn, as warleader.

The ritual request and welcome would set the tone for Delwyn, and them for choosing him. First impressions mattered. More so for him, and them.

Melkorka swore: *what was taking him so long?*

Delwyn stepped through the bole into the command center and met a tense Melkorka standing next to her command chair, his saber in her left hand.

"Jump drive status?" he asked.

"Anailiatha's drive technicians are performing a complete systems check. She disliked the readings on her diagnostic screen after the last jump."

"We have one more jump to go and then we're home."

Melkorka brightened. He called Elleio *home*, which indeed she was.

Delwyn grimaced at the obvious relief on Melkorka's face. He didn't exactly share her relief. Soon he would have to deal with people he didn't know and had customs he didn't understand. He jogged up into the Warleader's Watch, wondering what tone he should take. He was a human commanding an Eyloni warship soon to dock at his home port. Just what would all those people make of that?

Home. Soon Elleio would become his home but what home would he find among pheromone-linked empaths? They had him at a disadvantage, and he counted himself lucky whenever he picked up rare insights from their scents. He had helped Hervorallin give birth to Princess, his near-daughter. What parental duties did he owe her? Because of his link with her they didn't consider him human. He was Eyloni. He was Delwyn La'huaset O'un Tu Eyloni: Delwyn, a Land of the Mountains Fire River Person.

Their estimated jump into homespace was less than 20 hours away.

Soon he—not Melkorka—must contact Elleio approach control for permission to enter the Elle star system. Failure to do so meant you didn't care if the Home Fleet shot at you. They never took risks when it came to Elleio or her male population.

Delwyn hadn't worked out how to make a meaningful request. According to his lessons on Eyloni culture, music formed the core of all ritual. His teachers kept at him until he finally had enough and took off for the solitude only the jungle could provide.

The request for entry sounded simple enough, just sing a formal greeting. But he just didn't have a voice capable of matching their vocal range. He couldn't sing multiple melodies at the same time through simple human vocal cords. They couldn't reproduce the notes an Eyloni's pan pipe voice box could make. But at least his baritone range came close enough to the male norm.

While his crew easily picked up his language through their pheromonal empathy, he had no such cheat sheet and had to learn their language by rote. To make matters worse, hyperlink couldn't send them his scent. Those hearing him for the first time wouldn't even have a means of establishing context.

Would Kidahin sign a battle language translation like she had for the Death Song ritual?

"Delwyn …?" Melkorka prompted. What was he doing up there anyway? Had he forgotten? He needed to make the request to enter homespace early enough for their reply to reach them by the time the drive recharged. She wanted him to make a good impression when they arrived. *Hunter's Moon* enjoyed elite warship status. The crew, Warriors and Hunters, held elite status. Established etiquette gave the warleader belonging to an elite society elite status himself. Delwyn's presence must reflect their standing, just as they reflected his.

First impressions mattered.

First impressions were very important!

She watched him, stalking him with her eyes. He sat at the Warleader's Watch command monitor. From it, he could override any command center console.

Melkorka stood and glided up behind him, her stride and her feet deliberate as she silently stalked him.

The command crew watched her, bemused. They often played this game trying to see how close they could get before he noticed.

Delwyn had an acute situational awareness, a shocking surprise for anyone thinking his blind nose left him unaware. Melkorka leaned over his shoulder and read the words marching down the command screen.

She frowned and flipped her ears back, reinforcing her scowl.

Reading? Now?

Pictographs in precise rows scrolled right as he read down and left at an infant's pace. The Eyloni written language was limited to a small set of pictographs that represented the key chords of the language syllabary. Each idealized picture represented basic syllables made up of two chords each.

In the beginning Delwyn had flubbed word ordering. Her people used a common worldwide spoken language having as many individual dialects as there were clans. The same common language had only two written forms, say'ta've and e'va'a. Neither one preserved dialectal usages. E'va'a, Spirit Language, was not pictographic but rendered in artistic looping lines: written music. E'va'a conveyed ritual ideas, and custom prohibited its use outside of ritual matters. Say'ta've, the word meant "things made from music", documented all matters not related to ritual.

Word order changes in both written languages produced different meanings in both languages. Sentences in subject, verb, object order did not mean the same thing when the same words appeared in subject, object, verb order. Rearranging the same words into other object, subject, verb orders also changed sentence meaning. Meaning also changed with musical notation. Delwyn understood the words, but grammatical order and punctuation always bit him on the tail.

Melkorka smiled at the memory. He had expected only three sentences with end marks, but words and sentence end marks used musical notation: marks for sharps, flats, rests, beats, and several others.

Her eyes narrowed. He was reading from Anailiatha's engineering summary. Anailiatha had given her some choice words over the abuse her repairs had been put through by the two males.

"I can hear you breathing in my ear you know," Delwyn told the console.

Melkorka flinched and then scolded herself. He was guessing, trying to trick her into betraying herself.

"Melkorka, if you want to read Anailiatha's engineering report, sit down and we can read it together."

Flummoxed, she huffed. "How did you know I was standing behind you?"

"Kidahin flashed me a note from her console," he lied.

"I did not!" Kidahin yelped.

Melkorka looped her tail in idle curls, knowing full well Delwyn only meant to pull the huluhar's tail.

"What does a'pea mean?" he asked her.

"What?" Melkorka leaned into him and read the jump drive status report. The physical contact reassured her, and she wrapped her tail around them both as she scanned several vertical sentences to find the context.

She trilled in his ear, a snicker, the kind of involuntary laughter that arose when exposed to something unexpectedly funny.

"The word has several meanings depending on punctuation and word order in the sentence."

"Yeah, yeah, I get that. It's used as an object here. I know the root meaning is 'to exit', but I don't get its use here. The way I read this, Anailiatha is saying Phalalin and I left together, and the tempo changes the meaning from 'left' to 'fled'. If she means an earlier synchronized jump, then why is she using present imperative tense for a passive near past event?"

Melkorka trilled again much louder this time, loud enough so even the privacy-minded command center crew could not ignore their Mistress of the Ship and their Warleader sharing physical contact and joy.

Melkorka turned to face them before they felt left out of the group companionship they all shared.

She read the sentence verbatim from the Mistress of Sails's report, and they joined her in lyrical trilling laughter.

Delwyn leaned back in the chair, arms folded across his chest. So it was funny, was it? Did Anailiatha mean he and Phalalin had exited early? Fled?

No, they wouldn't take allegations of cowardice as funny.

Melkorka reached out to him then extended a long, curved index finger and touched it to the tip of her thumb.

"We have a saying," she began as she moved her hand towards her loincloth. "When someone is being annoying, then we say she is being an …"

"Yes," Delwyn interrupted her, "I know a similar saying."

Anailiatha apparently favored the word. She had written several paragraphs laced with inventive variations on the a'pea theme.

Delwyn clicked on the report distribution header again, looking for a privacy seal he'd somehow missed.

Nope, the report was marked for general viewing. It was available to anyone wanting to read the primary engineer jump drive performance summary.

Delwyn rolled his eyes. Any chief engineer filing this report on a Coalition ship would soon found herself charged with rank insubordination and facing an Article 101a hearing. Here, on the other hand, Anailiatha only had to avoid making honor insults.

Calling warleaders assholes didn't qualify as an insult to honor, apparently.

Melkorka wrapped her arms and tail around him and giggled, a sound like rapid lyrical squeaking to his ear.

"You should spend some time tail twining with Anailiatha. Your concern for her will make her feel better, but say nothing about this report. Your scent will tell her all she needs to know."

Delwyn turned and gently twisted out of the loose embrace to gaze at expectant faces. He didn't want the command center crew feeling left out of the social moment, so he visited with them. They brushed and touched him, and he caressed them in return. The contact deposited their scents on him and his scent on them.

The ritual touching also reminded him of the rounds he had to make. He had a standing duty to give some twenty-five hundred females a chance to encounter him. The prowlers and stalkers would find him in the forested trails soon enough. Others would meet him when he passed their duty stations, or when he visited their living quarters.

A man prowling near a woman's quarters aboard a Coalition vessel would raise stalking suspicions, but here females had no thought of or interest in romance when not in their season. They expected him to visit them, talk with them, touch them, and reinforce social ties.

Phelindra slept beside him, her prerogative as his protectress. Her status among the other females made her a possible target of territorial jealousy if he failed to spend some time with all the others. He learned that lesson one morning when he awoke to fifteen of them sleeping on or around him. At the time he wondered if they expected some kind of Roman orgy. The obscene thought had carried on his scent, and several of them awoke, peered at him through sleepy eyes, and politely told him they were not in their season, and promptly fell back asleep.

Shaking his head at the memory, Delwyn strolled up behind Kidahin and hugged her. While holding the ecstatic young Hunter, he read the helm console time-to-jump countdown. He was wasting time. Sighing with regret he pushed back from the luxuriant warmth of a humming Kidahin and headed for the exit bole, an attentive Phelindra rising from her console in pursuit.

"Delwyn," Melkorka's voice stopped him in his tracks. "You should sing the arrival greeting for us. We will assess your performance and offer encouragement."

"Noted," he said. "I'll be back sometime …before the notice deadline expires."

Melkorka growled to herself. Delwyn should sing the welcome with them now and let them critique the song before he contacted home. He could visit while they waited for the hyperlink transmission to reach Elleio and for the reply to return.

Typical, Melkorka snorted. Males tended to put off matters until the last minute.

Females got things done when they needed getting done and hated chafing delays.

Males, rarely ever late, preferred waiting until the last minute. Males prioritized matters in ways that drove females insane. Males preferred letting things unfold in their own due time. Males tended toward living in the now, but females were more concerned about the future. Females leapt into action, but males took the time to look before leaping.

Only males sang the sane song females would hear while they raged in battle fury.

Disgusted, Melkorka sat back into her command chair and laid Delwyn's curved sword across her thighs, balancing it on her knees, and wrapped her tail around the blade. Minutes later, deep in absent-minded thought, she started beating a rhythm against the shiny blade with her deep red fingernails singing *a'pea* under her breath over and over again.

6
FIRST IMPRESSIONS

Thelindrallin curled her tail up her back and above her head, well above her perked ears, and danced on the balls of her feet in excitement over the prospect of welcoming the new warleader. Everything must go according to plan. As the Be'atika Senge High Speaker, a Council Mistress of the Compact Counsel, and the Eldest Warrioress in both the Be'atika Senge and the A'tayotan hierarchies, Thelindrallin had a duty to make sure this session followed the prescribed ritual songs down to the final note.

First impressions made for lasting impressions.

Despite her age, Thelindrallin bounced about like a female coming into season for the first time, although her first mating had been 330 years ago.

"Move everything from the Hall of Voices and bring it up here. He will contact us soon! When he does, I want him to feel welcome!" she snapped.

"You have several hours yet before he calls upon the Counsel," Mrallin sang from across the Open Venue.

Thelindrallin swiveled her ears on the old male, pinning him to the spot with a pained expression. "I know that, just as I know that all males tend to do things in their own good time. But he is different. He might even be punctual for a male. I would consider that a welcome change in this Counsel."

"Maybe not so much," Mrallin sang. "All females leap before they look. It takes a male's restraining tail to stop them from ill-advised leaping."

"That is not the issue, Old One. Why, I remember when you once advanced a plan for immediate action, and we had to …"

"Old One?" Mrallin interrupted. "Now who is calling the red leaf orange? Why again are we moving the Counsel Seat from the Hall of Voices to the

Open Venue? And why are you in such a hurry? Days will pass before he comes to Na'di Island."

"I want him to see the time and effort we have taken to welcome him. When he comes here, I want him to see a familiar place," she said.

"No, I mean why move the Counsel Seat at all?"

"You know how those northern La'huaset clans go on about the heat when they come here."

"Oh yes, I know. They cannot take it."

"No," Thelindrallin admonished. "They do not like it, and he is used to temperatures much cooler than ours."

"So the Counsel defers to him now? A new warleader?"

"New, yes, but he is not young. His medical records say he is 231 years old, much older than Kalinn when he died, and yet he looks half his age. Imagine that!"

Thelindrallin remained in high spirits in spite of Mrallin's swipes and looked forward to meeting the new warleader. His name was Delwyn, a wonderful-sounding odd male name.

Delwyn would swelter if the Counsel met in the Hall of Voices. The Hall sat at ground level within a fused aerial root structure several hundred ells across. It surrounded the oldest aerial roots that wrapped down and around the main trunk of the Elleiu Na'aheilu, the Tree of the Counsel, which served as the governmental center and a home for the Compact Counsel and the thousands residing and working within it.

The daytime air on Na'di Island tended to settle into layers. The forest floor retained the most heat, but the air cooled as it rose up into the rainforest shrub, understory, canopy, and emergent layers. The emergent layer leaves caught light swirling breezes and deflected cool air down through open boles and into the tree.

People acclimated to the far northern and southern temperate rainforests found the equatorial ground temperature stifling. It took those visitors days to adjust to the tropical Myat'ti'deep Tribal continental heat. Na'di Island, just off the northwestern coast of Myat'ti'deep, enjoyed an occasional relatively cool breeze tumbling off the island's northeastern mountain range. Those mountains, covered with cloud rainforests and not snow, could produce breezes that dropped over one hundred degrees below the average sea level temperatures, triggering rainstorms across the island.

Delwyn will contact us soon, Thelindrallin sang to herself.

Normally the Counsel did not concern itself with routinely arriving ships. Returning warships announced their intent to jump into homespace, and an alert warship waiting in some strategic orbit cleared the entry. *Fearless* had occupied an alert station when Melkorka's distress call came in. But this situation was unique, and so the alert warship receiving Delwyn's entry request had been ordered to transfer entry protocol to the Counsel-in-session.

Delwyn's fame had spread across Elleio in a short time. A mighty warleader, he had with a double-handful of females captured an intact enemy vessel and gave it to his occupational society. Phalalin's report describing Delwyn's command of Warpact conventions had impressed the population as well.

That, Thelindrallin smirked, ought to have piqued the Society of Warleaders' interest.

She wrapped her tail around her waist, absently stroked her pons, and planned.

She assigned herself to the role of Gracious Mistress of the Singing People for this ritual. She had not assigned the other necessary roles yet. Who should she pick as the Mistress of Names, the Mistress of Legends, and the Mistress of Songs? She chose Mrallin as the Male Guiding Presence, of course.

What songs should they sing? Delwyn would sing the Opening Greeting, but how could she prepare a return accompaniment for an unknown song? Delwyn certainly intended them to sing along with him. A singing male always did. The problem for her was hyperlink delay. They could not sing together. He would sing the Opening Greeting, the entry request, and the ritual songs solo. Their responding Greeting, welcome, and ritual accompaniment would reach him hours later. He would hear their songs, see the effort they had made, and know he was wanted home before his arrival. Thinking about her plan excited her, and Thelindrallin took to bouncing on her feet again. She wanted so much for everything to go well, and she began singing her heartfelt joy.

Mrallin smiled at the sound of the Eldest Warrioress's melody as it echoed throughout the Open Venue. She wanted everything perfect. He did, too. Delwyn must be quite some male to impress all the females aboard an elite warship.

He had to admit it: Delwyn fulfilling Kalinn's mission said much considering many in Counsel had thought at the time Kalinn was unlikely to succeed. He had died with honor fighting the Compact's enemies.

Delwyn had no reason to interfere with Melkorka's mission beyond what the fosterage oath he had given to Phelindra required of him: train Kidahin for forty-four TST days and keep her safe. The fosterage oath applied only to Kidahin and not every female he came into contact with.

Mrallin had much to think about and much more to consider. No matter how old Delwyn might be, he did not have enough experience to advise the Counsel. And unless the O'un Tu Clan Elders officially adopted Delwyn into their clan, there were some doubts in Mrallin's mind as to what that would mean to *Hunter's Moon.* Welcoming Delwyn to Elleio for bringing in an enemy ship was one thing and even though the welcoming songs called him a warleader, accepting him as one was another. Time would tell.

"Mistress Thelindrallin, an alert warship has intercepted Delwyn's hyperlink signal. He has ordered his Mistress of Communications to send a ten minute notice before he sings his first song."

Thelindrallin wasted no time in addressing the tree-wide intercom. "The Counsel will convene in the Open Venue. Warleader Delwyn of *Hunter's Moon* calls the Counsel-in-Session!"

All counsel members pricked their ears at the Eldest's announcement and dropped whatever they had been doing and ran for the Open Venue. Each tribal continent had chosen ten Hunters, ten Warriors, and one Comari from each tribal counsel: a total of 210 females. Male advisors also headed up into the elleiu tree canopy. They had been chosen from their tribal elders in the same numbers as the Hunters and Warriors, but each Comari brought her own male, the male she had chosen to protect throughout her life for reasons known only to her.

Comara bonded to adult males ranging in age from soon after adulthood ceremonies to the elderly. They preferred the lower middle age males because Comara lived longer than most Eyloni. Sometimes their choices, younger than the average counsel males, brought their own insight into wedge issues and tore apart hidebound thinking common among the older male advisors.

Some counsel members had to climb a great distance to reach the Open Venue. Some routes took them down through aerial roots fused around the central trunk. Others climbed up from the forest ground level along the outer, newer fused roots buttressing the tree. A few people climbed through hollow branches up onto wide boughs or walked in from narrow branches down into the crown.

The Open Venue sat atop the central trunk and around the first level canopy layer main branches. Branches tens of ells thick towered around them, their aerial roots growing from below them, twisting downward into bundled wooden knots that grew into hollow maze structures of fused and braided wood. Its central space resembled an uneven polished wooden floor. Walls of polished intertwined aerial roots grew to a height of only two or three ells. There was no ceiling but leaves twice as tall as a male's tail overlapped above, forming red, orange, and yellow parasols. The patchwork pastel umbrella shielded the open chamber from the direct sunlight beating down onto the equatorial rainforest below.

Breezes whispered through gaps in the twisted wood, some came off the southern coast visible on the horizon from this height, while other breezes swirled down from the distant northeastern slopes.

Counsel members filed into the Open Venue and formed a pattern with Thelindrallin at its center and the other females swirling in rank order around her into a branching crescent. Each female brushed her tail tip, her pons, against a neighboring thigh. Mrallin stood on the left and behind

Thelindrallin. Other male advisors danced among the Be'atika Senge hierarchy females before taking their places in the choreographed Oyya Web.

As with warleaders and their Warpact traditions Mrallin assumed Warpact leadership over the male advisors because Counsel sessions were rife with potential conflict issues. He assigned duties to the males according to their abilities. Custom presumed the eldest male present in counsel held Warpact rank. If some catastrophic event were to happen during a session, then the Counsel females would move to protect them. The males would surrender their autonomy to the Warpact leader, but unlike a warleader aboard his ship, Mrallin had limited power here and lacked absolute autonomy. He could never exercise supervisory command over the Compact Counsel.

Thelindrallin commanded here because the Compact Counsel remained an adjunct function of the Be'atika Senge hierarchy.

Yet, even here, in the seat of female ruling power, the Be'atika Senge celebrated and honored gender interdependence. Females ruled because males were rare, yet equality among Warriors, Hunters, males, and Comara remained carefully attended to. Four hundred and twenty people gracefully assumed their places in the Web growing out from the Eldest Warrioress, the Eldest Huntress, and the Eldest Male. Thelindrallin knew the pattern, the Oyya Web, had been completed when the most junior male and female began to sing.

The Mistress of Songs picked up the simple melody, took the lead, and opened the Counsel session with a song praising the trees and the leaves, the sun and the sky, the jungle and the sea, and males and females.

Thelindrallin followed the melody, listened to the whispering rhythms of all ten Comara. Although mute, they murmured soft sighs in time with the others. Joining into the ritualized Oyya Web placed a hardship on the Comara. Naturally standoffish and preferring their own chosen males or other Comara company almost exclusively, they tolerated this closeness because they too, in whatever thought processes the mysterious Comara had, had a say in the world they lived in and shared with others.

That they tolerated anyone near their males while in Counsel always mystified Thelindrallin. Comara were drawn to males they smelled an affinity for, to the males they felt needed them. Comara were deadly and killed without warning. Their victims died never knowing one of the permanently preadolescent females had killed them. Tribal custom excused every killing a Comari committed and had done so for millennia. If a Comari considered you a threat to her chosen male, then you died and every hierarchy in the world considered the death honorably justified.

Dealing with crowds so close to their chosen males stressed them, made them more impassive and even more deadly. Comara almost never actively participated in Counsel, either. When something captured their fleeting interest, they spoke their needs through pheromones. Of all Eyloni, Comara had the strongest empathic pheromonal signaling and often argued using scent alone. Comara lacked tails, yet they had tails of a sort: tails made from pheromones. People said those pheromonal tails dipped halfway into the Oyya Web of the spirits, as though the Comara were always off on some adulthood vision quest. They would sign in battle language to make a point, if the mood suited them. Whenever a Comari breathed an audible whisper your way, you either felt honored to receive her notice or you had just been warned: you never knew with Comara

Clear force fields shimmered in the air, shifted opaque, and then turned flat black. The field darkened the chamber and blocked sound, sealing the Open Venue from poking tails and making the open chamber suitable for visual hyperlink transmissions.

"Mistress of the Counsel Thelindrallin, greetings. I am Varellan of the Compact warship *Leaper*. I have intercepted an incoming message from Delwyn of the Compact warship *Hunter's Moon*."

"Accept and relay," Thelindrallin ordered.

"Affirm."

A solid panoramic wedge lit up around them, filling with identity patterns and pictographs that named the signal source and the sender: Delwyn ar ahoun Unahaillaea *Tyreniioroneo*. The dancing patterns resolved into a view into the warship's command center. The Warleader's Watch held the foreground with Delwyn standing next to the warleader's console. He seemed to look into her eyes, and Thelindrallin felt a rush of excitement, her heart quickened, and she sighed.

Phelindra his Protectress and Eldest Huntress of the Ship stood behind and to one side, her tail curving out and up behind him in both a warning and an endorsement. Offset to his left and farther behind waited his chosen Mistress of the Ship. Melkorka sat, her back rigid, her pons visible and twitching against her thigh. Delwyn's sword resting across her knees, held there wrapped in her tail.

The command crew had eyes for him alone. Among them, the young Hunter Kidahin was having trouble keeping her seat at the helm.

She, as their huluhar, had validated Delwyn as a legitimate choice for her society. Thelindrallin's eyes narrowed. She would have to speak to Kidahin. What about Delwyn had appealed to her juvenile instincts?

The infant Hunter clinging to Delwyn's shoulder stood out, and Thelindrallin brightened. Hervorallin, the infant's mother, stood beside Phelindra. The infant, Princess, now there was an odd chord series for a name, warded Delwyn with tail snaps or glaring eyes.

The territorial display uplifted the Compact Counsel. A near-daughter's first territorial imperative compelled her to declare her male her absolute personal possession. Delwyn was hers in ways no association …

Delwyn began to sing in a deep voice. "I sing greetings to the Compact Counsel, to the Be'atika Senge, and to each counsel member. I am Delwyn of the Compact warship *Hunter's Moon*. I bring my occupational association home, from Eldest Huntress Phelindra to huluhar Kidahin. We have suffered immeasurable losses, but we have been victorious. I bring war contraband taken from the enemy by female fighting prowess and valor.

"With your permission, I intend to enter homespace.

"I ask your leave to bring my warship into Wrathsee'a Anchorage and off-load the captured Ni'zakhonii vessel for analysis and then to present my warship to the dockmistress for repair.

"I ask the Counsel's leave to freely prowl the rainforests of Elleio, to visit the O'un Tu La'huaset Eyloni, and to introduce my near-daughter to our family."

Sighs arose around Thelindrallin. A bit formally sung, but then again this was Delwyn's first time addressing the Counsel.

Ears suddenly pointed up as Delwyn began to sing the ritual solo.

Thelindrallin watched the command crew. That they wanted to sing along with him was a simple understatement: they all but bit their tongues. No female sang with any male without his permission, but they also wanted the Counsel to hear him without the embellishments their accompaniment would give a poor singer.

The Counsel knew Delwyn was a singing male, had known since his Mistress of Saga had sent the Death Song record to the archives. Singing without female accompaniment hammered his singer status home. All males sang, and both males and females possessed perfect pitch. But some singers needed accompaniment or else they sounded neither original nor moving. Some males and females needed accompaniment to give their voices a sound that appealed to the attentive ear. Without accompaniment they could not effectively move an audience or their fellow singers.

Delwyn did not need accompaniment. Although he lacked the vocal range of other males, he sounded quite adept at making good use of the range he had. Thelindrallin knew if his association sang him an accompaniment then he could make the leaves rustle.

Delwyn sang how he won his near-daughter. He sang about his association and their valor. He sang about the events leading to the capture of the enemy ship. He sang about the Oyya Web and the essential connectedness of the Eyloni.

While Delwyn sang, Thelindrallin polled Counsel opinion by smell. The body never lied. Pheromones in the air told her Delwyn had almost all of them smelling interested and accepting. Why, even the Comara…

A sharp involuntary gasp escaped her.

The Comara smelled enthralled. Thelindrallin could not remember the Comara ever expressing such intent interest in Captain Lahiri when the warship *Alexandra Witze* had visited Elleio. Even when the human Ambassador Harrison addressed the Counsel before leaving with Anlann and Seralin the Comara had not reacted with such emotion.

The Comara had heard humans before, so why did they smell so interested in Delwyn? Was it because Delwyn was the first human they had heard singing?

Before the Death Song performance, the Be'atika Senge had all but concluded humans did not sing and might harbor psychotic tendencies—Eyloni suffering amusia always suffered psychotic episodes.

Why did the Comara smell so interested in him?

Delwyn sang a final song in salute to the Counsel and vanished. The screen filled with the warship's identity patterns and held them a moment before they too faded.

"Transmission terminated, Mistress," Mrallin reported.

Thelindrallin faced the Counsel-in-Session.

"What say you?" she asked them.

After she put the question forward the session turned anticlimactic. Without objection the Counsel sang several songs in greeting and well-wishing on behalf of the Be'atika Senge, ritually welcoming Delwyn and his occupational association home. Thelindrallin, thrilled but knowing all along formal permission had been a forgone conclusion, took to dancing on the balls of her feet again. They had initiated the welcome home ritual and gave him a good impression.

First impressions were important.

A smiling Thelindrallin caught up with Mrallin.

"Well, what do you think about Delwyn?" she asked, breathless.

"A strong male, he has elite standing at least by reputation. His association will not tolerate him apart from them for long. Maybe they should take turns traveling with him as he meets the people. He must meet with the La'huaset Tribal Elders. Capturing an enemy vessel intact has made him popular, which means he must visit all ten tribes and meet their elders. But there are still questions to be asked and answers to be listened to.

"Do not forget that repairs to *Hunter's Moon* will take months to complete. He ought to take the time and learn about us, which means he must sing with the clans."

"So are you pleased?" she asked in afterthought.

"I am, but did you get a look at the knife he wears at his hip? Do you think he meant that?"

"What about it? You cannot expect humans to award the same adulthood knives that we do. Volcanic glass for males and flint for females is our tradition. So humans award metal blades. Does it matter?"

"I suppose not. Adulthood is adulthood, but curiosity might drive people to ask, though."

***

Delwyn sighed. That had been easier than his command center crew had implied the whole time they critiqued him in practice.

"How long do they need to decide?" he asked Melkorka.

"Not long, a few minutes at most. Their return hyperlink should have reached us by now. Any more time we wait depends on how long it took the Counsel to order the alert warship to approve your request."

"Yeah, well…"

"Mistress? The jump drive has spooled up. We are ready to jump," Trebithia reported.

"Finally," Delwyn muttered.

"We cannot jump into homespace before receiving permission," Melkorka reminded him.

"Mistress? The Compact warship *Leaper* sends the Counsel's greetings. The Counsel sings welcome to Delwyn and asks him to return to Elleio and set the affairs of his warship and clan in order," Hlindredreda said.

Melkorka smiled. "That means we can go home now."

Delwyn nodded. He'd been ready. "Contact *Fearless* and tell Phalalin it's time. Synchronize the jump as soon as he reports ready and take us home."

"By your command. Mistress of Pathwalking, plot a jump for Tyreniioroneo equilibrium point four parking orbit at zero velocity relative on arrival. Set jump clock and relay jump parameters to Phalalin for a simultaneous jump."

"Affirm, jump plot entered for zero velocity emergence. Phalalin signals ready to jump. Jump clocks are synchronized. We are ready to jump," Trebithia said.

Melkorka looked at Delwyn. When their eyes met, she pricked her ears at him in quizzical inquiry.

"Take us home Trebithia," he said to the Mistress of Pathwalking.

"By your command. Kidahin, initiate jump."

"Affirm, acting," Kidahin said and slapped the jump initiator control.

Out- of- tolerance armatures protested as they released focused graviton waves into the jump origin point, creating a quantum singularity, tearing the ship into entangled particles.

With the gravity lensing system now destroyed, the quantum black hole melted away, and the ship's entangled set played back the particle stream at their destination in reverse, reforming the ship.

"Jump completed. *Fearless* jump completed. We have arrived in homespace in trans-Tyreniioroneo equilibrium point four parking orbital approach for Wrathsee'a Anchorage naval shipyards," the Mistress of Pathwalking said.

"Well done Trebithia," Delwyn said. He nodded to Melkorka, and she pricked her ears back at him, expectantly.

He took her cue and welcomed the crew home. His voice, as usual, carried to everyone. "We have returned home!" he sang. "Hlindredreda open a channel to Phalalin."

"By your command, hailing, ship-to-ship channel open."

Phalalin's inquisitive expression flashed on the forward screen.

"Phalalin, I see no further conflict and so I dissolve the Warpact. What will you do now?"

Phalalin gave a musical sigh. "Under normal circumstances I would resume my patrol assignment. These are not normal circumstances, so I have requested leave from my alert status assignment so I can help you settle into our clan. You might need me at the warleader's strategy briefings. The Counsel will ask you to give a report on Ni'zakhonii capabilities and ship operations."

Delwyn's heart rose at first on hearing he'd have a friend at homecoming, and then it fell as he thought, the navy was the navy, meaning hours of debriefing sessions lay ahead.

Great.

"For now we are returning to our patrol assignment. I shall meet you on A'lon'aloop station," Phalalin promised. He rippled his tail as his image faded from view.

Now what?

Simple: he'd let Melkorka handle everything. As Mistress of the Ship, she knew the ins and outs of shipyard operations.

"Melkorka, let's get that damned Ni'zakhonii ship out of the combat deployment bay first, and then get us moored into a repair slip."

"By your command," she rushed, leaping for Hlindredreda's console.

"Mistress of Communications open a channel to Wrathsee'a Anchorage."

"Affirm, acting. Mistress… Havalin himself answers."

Odd. Havalin almost always deferred matters to his Mistress of the Tower.

"Mistress Melkorka," Havalin said. He nodded a brief perfunctory greeting to her before shifting ears and eyes onto Delwyn.

"Warleader Delwyn! Welcome …Wrathsee'a Anchorage. I meet you well. Neutral territory. Be'atika Senge. Sings. Tow warship. Repair moorings. Extract Ni'zakhonii *d'la h'ne* Tyreniioroneo," Havalin stammered.

Delwyn gave the tall narrow-shouldered warleader a smile. Havalin looked so unlike Anlann and Phalalin. Delwyn paused a minute to place what other than his build was so different before it came to him: skin color. Both Anlann and Phalalin had predominant orange shades dappled with reds trimmed in yellows. The Anchorage warleader had much more red than orange skin and those reds were variegated with yellows. Orange splotches dappled his skin.

"Thank you," Delwyn said. Havalin was having difficulty with Coalition standard. He'd probably learned a few words the same way Anlann had once described as making him feel tone deaf. "As you see, we have heavy forward damage that needs repair."

Havalin nodded absently his ears perked at Delwyn, but his eye movement suggested he was reading from something below the screen.

"Yes. Much forward combat hull damage. One fusion plant offline. You are cleared for entry," Havalin said.

"Melkorka, take us into the Anchorage."

"By your command."

Finally. Melkorka had been wondering if the two males planned on talking all day. She wanted the alien thing removed from the combat deployment bay now, not after some long male fireside taletelling.

"Kidahin, plot for orbital maneuvering. Adjust from equilibrium point four to Tyreniioroneo approach into polar surveillance orbit for Wrathsee'a Anchorage intercept."

"Affirm, acting. Orbital maneuvering systems engaged. Leaving equilibrium point four parking orbit for Tyreniioroneo polar orbital entry and intercept. Intercept point acquired. Four hours forty-three minutes until Wrathsee'a Anchorage IP acquired," Kidahin reported.

About two hours, not bad considering Kidahin had to wrestle seven million metric tonnes out of the Tyreniioroneo-Elleio planet-moon system Lagrangian L4 point and into standard polar orbit around the gas giant, change orbits to intercept the Anchorage, and then null her rates.

Two hours. He had two hours!

"Melkorka, do you need me for anything?"

"I always need you, but no. I do not require your presence until they are ready to tow us into the shipyards."

Great!

"Why?" she asked.

"I need some exercise. I think I'll take a walk through the outrigger hulls."

Melkorka flicked her tail after him, a shooing gesture, and turned back to the screen and the light blue gas giant dominating it: Tyreniioroneo, the planet her warship had the honor of being named after.

Delwyn left the command center with Phelindra. He couldn't believe after all this time they were on approach for Tyreniioroneo orbit. They had jumped from 1.7 light-years outside the system into a L4 point well inside the sun's heavy mass hyperlimit and at the same time decelerated from 0.69 cee to zip in thirty billionths of a second. In contrast, a *Henri Edda* exiting hyperspace at the hyperlimit several hundreds million kilometers from Elleio would by now be spending long hours decelerating from 0.5 cee along a trajectory into Tyreniioroneo solar orbit before navigating into orbit around the gas giant, which was what they were doing right now.

Delwyn picked up his pace and jogged into the port outrigger hull, relieved he didn't have to wait those several long hours to get into the shipyards.

The port and starboard sides of the command hull sported outrigger hulls housing massive broadside weapon platforms, much heavier weapons than anything a Coalition vessel was capable of mounting outside of a battleship or orbital base. Ship design allowed for the heavier batteries. Compact ships were quite broad of beam compared to their rail-thin Coalition of Earth Colonies cousins.

The port outrigger contained few crew members. The weapon crews worked here alongside the occasional roving Hunters and the ever-present Warrior trios.

The jungle formed into heavy thickets, disguising the smaller compartments and reinforced heavy bulkheads needed to mount the weapons systems and give them added structural support.

Delwyn stopped often and visited with several fire control crews. He spent quite some time with them, to their joy. Phelindra reminded him again and again how much the rainforest altered the perception of time.

She was kidding, right? Time was relative. He'd make time. Besides, he wanted to see the starboard outrigger crews before returning to the command center.

Delwyn bid the port broadside fire control crews a final good-bye and hiked off through heavy undergrowth. Gnarled trees covered with vines and club mosses gave way to wide trails. The border between the two landscapes served as a reminder that they were leaving the outrigger hull and reentering the command hull. On human-built starships, logic and common sense demanded that a transversal corridor through the command hull should connect the two outrigger hulls.

The warship did have a path connecting the two outrigger hulls but not a direct one.

Looking ahead gave him the by now familiar jungle view. Open sky looked down on him, and trees sprung up around him. Grasses and underbrush filled out the landscape, hiding ship structures only an arm's length out of reach. Compact ships had wide passageways compared to a Coalition ship's narrow corridors and those wider spaces allowed for some drifting off a path. Thick jungle undergrowth barred departures more than a few steps off the jungle trails. Trails that led out onto tree limbs concealed physical bulkheads with treetop-high views. The vertigo he once felt when out on a narrow branch had felt real, and his swaying amused the females that happened to catch his missteps.

Phelindra knew where the pathways led, and she prowled ahead only as far as the length of her tail, expecting him to follow without complaint.

They passed the halfway landmark before it dawned on him that she'd been doing that a lot lately. She turned into a direction of his choice a half-second ahead of him.

He thought about the several alternate routes into the starboard outrigger hull he knew about. This transversal pathway wound through jungle terrain and had several branching trails that led off throughout the ship. Many did wind their way into the starboard outrigger.

Phelindra rounded a bend and came upon a fork in the trail. Delwyn lurched into the left path, and Phelindra stepped without hesitation into the same path before he had a chance to change direction.

"How did you do that?" he demanded.

"Do what?" came her innocent reply.

"You knew where I was going before I decided myself."

"Oh. That is easy. I smell it," She said.

Delwyn knew his crew gained more sensory input from smell than he ever hoped to, but her instantaneous change in footing sounded like mind reading.

"You smell it? How can you smell a change in direction?"

"Easy. You think about moving through the command hull, orienting yourself to jungle landmarks," she said, approval in her voice. "Your thoughts are about me," she added in pleased notes. "And you pace my prowling in your mind. Then you decide to change paths. Because you dwell so long on me, on the path and on my footwork, your scent changes to match the smell I know when you decide to bear left."

"And you know that smell means I'm going to turn left how?" he asked, confused.

Phelindra stopped and turned, her tail arching up behind her, her ears pointing at him, her eyes just for him. "I watch you always, so do the others. I am your Protectress, and my duty is to know where you are and where you are going. When you turn, your scent says 'I am turning here, Phelindra', and I know. Kidahin says you are unique among humans. You carry her in your mind when you are with her. You do it with us. You are doing it with me now. Kidahin told me every human she had met almost without exception thought about themselves going to and fro when walking with another. All Eyloni males think about their female associations and think about those associations accompanying them. You think about us with great fierceness, letting us know what you want and where you want to go with us."

Delwyn wrestled with the account while they continued down the path and into the starboard outrigger hull. Was she describing scent-based telepathy? Was that how Phalalin had anticipated his moves?

Chirping, trilling laughter burst from the Warrior trio escort scouting up ahead.

"You smelled that?" he asked them.

"Yes. You think strong, and your scent changes. Consider exercise. Body scent changes. It is the same with feelings. They change the pheromonal content in scent. Do you ever notice when you act without thought or on instinct you have more success evading us than if you consider your next move? Scent is not perfect. Distance and wind degrade it, instinctive training defeats it. You do so yourself, but somehow you are not conscious of it like we are," the lead Warrior said.

Was she quantifying situational awareness, the warning feeling he usually got during combat? But that feeling came and went without conscious control. Was she suggesting they could somehow call upon second sight at will?

The jungle cover grew thicker, a hint they neared their destination.

"I don't see how I could beat Kidahin during our first unarmed combat practice on Ibeetu if she could read my intent through scent."

Phelindra laughed, a throaty yapping song, and shook her head.

"Kidahin did not believe what she smelled. She told us your scent warned her about moves she believed you incapable of. She also complained about moves you made by reflex training or flashes of insight, and you distracted her with anger."

He grinned. He'd rubbed Kidahin's pons in her face, an insult meaning 'smell yourself and tell me if you truly are a female'.

The pathway narrowed and dipped into a small ravine. Above them, a fallen log bridged the gap. Orange moss and purple fungi covered the rusty old rotten bark.

Phelindra stood underneath it and waited while Delwyn stopped to eye the log, estimating its size and placement. Three or four meters above them and at least two meters thick, it sparked his curiosity. A huge log, but then again all trees on Elleio grew several diameters wider trunks than trees on Earth did. The log's declining angle looked wrong. If he climbed the ravine, he imagined he'd find the log rammed into the moss-covered rocky ground rather than laying atop it.

"This log hides a structure," he told her with certainty.

"Yes," Phelindra agreed, pleased. Delwyn knew how jungle terrain felt and knew when something seemed wrong. "The right outrigger main power transfer conduit runs through here. Environmental support did their best to blend structures like these into rainforest scenes."

As they walked, he thought about the explanation. Something wasn't right. In his mind the starboard outrigger hull ought to mirror the port outrigger hull. The outriggers served as weapon platforms for mounting broadside weaponry, ordnance bays, energy transfer banks, fire control stations and fire control support services. But the two hulls didn't mirror image one another as he had expected. They hadn't passed under a port power conduit on their way from the port outrigger hull. The rainforest landscape and trails, the foliage and the colors, even the setting looked different.

The outrigger hulls had been designed to avoid internal mirror image layouts. Compartments, decks, and bulkheads ran offset, producing wider or narrower trails and paths, longer or shorter paths, and left or right bearing paths. Environmental support programmers placed unique force field assisted holographic foliage all around the physical structures. Plants were selected and placed to give a pleasingly wild look. The flora in the two outrigger hulls looked so different. That made sense. This was supposed to be a rainforest environment. No doubt the crew would notice repetitive scenery, so the designers did their best to create a realistic fantasy given the physical constraints ship structure imposed. All this jungle scenery pulled power from environmental control, more so than just standard life support alone. Scenes looked lifelike, the air smelled alive and breezes animated the air. The power budget required to run all this beauty drew more power than a Coalition ship of equal class. Then again, having experienced it for himself, Delwyn wouldn't trade it for *Henri Edda's* doctor's-office-meets-gymnasium ambiance.

Phelindra's time sense told her two hours had almost passed, and she had to pry Delwyn away from the starboard fire control crews. "We should return to the command center. Melkorka is probably wondering where the spirits have taken us."

"Hold on a minute, will you? It's not like we're there yet," he mumbled.

Phelindra flicked her ears at the gun crew females and passed her pons across her eyes, a brief sign meaning that she had to strive for patience.

The fire control teams surrounded him, enjoying the familiar contact, turned on Phelindra and mocked her ear and tail stance.

They were giving her the finger, so to speak. He forgot. His scent gave his feelings away, and so the gun crews and fire control teams blamed Phelindra.

He sang another song for them, and they danced around him as they gave him parting coy brushes and touches. Finally, he bade them good-bye and headed back toward the command hull, wondering if they were on final approach for the Anchorage yet.

"Approach has been granted," Melkorka said, interrupting his musing.

Delwyn watched the screen, watched the ships close around them, honor escorts all. Wrathsee'a Anchorage brought up the rear as he grew behind them.

The Anchorage transformed from a wart on the blue background into a side view diamond popped from its setting. A faceted dome glittered in Elle's sunlight. Within, orange sparks bounced from facet to facet.

Delwyn paused beside Melkorka and read the changing patterns on her command console that summarized target attitude control.

It spun at a constant but slow rate, too slow for any meaningful artificial gravity. Odd, a people capable of producing true artificial gravity had no need for centrifugal force gravity.

Scans reported the Anchorage maintaining standard polar orbit around Tyreniioroneo. Delwyn watched a busy Kidahin pilot their approach. Trebithia, her supervising mistress, watched her with a more critical eye.

It took him a while to figure out the correspondences between Anchorage attitude and Elleio orbital mechanics. Both attitude and orbit changed to give the dome an accurate Elleio days-long daytime and nighttime. This close to Tyreniioroneo, the blue disk would dominate the faceted sky. Did it matter to those inside? Did the facets reduce the gas giant's image? The gas giant's name, Tyreniioroneo meant 'the Companion of the Hunters'. Had the namers meant he was the companion of all Hunter females, or had they meant he was the guiding companion of the hunters in foraging parties? Maybe he should ask someone.

"Mistress? Velocity zero. We are holding station and awaiting the Dock Mistress's pleasure," Kidahin reported.

"Mistress of Communications inform the Dock Mistress that we are awaiting her own good time," Melkorka said.

"Affirm. The Mistress of the Dock acknowledges and sings welcome to you and Delwyn. She is opening the outer doors."

Massive doors cycled open a kilometer below the faceted dome. Anchorage tractor fields locked onto the ship and started pulling them forward before the recessed inner doors had fully opened.

Delwyn thought of a slow-spinning top, hollow but for an inverted tower pointing down from the center of the faceted dome's base. The shipyards ran up the curved inside walls in tiers, with docks stacked all the way up and around the inside circumference.

Forward momentum stopped once they cleared the inner doors.

Delwyn stared at transparent encased platforms ringing the interior hull. People by the hundreds stood there, attentive and watching.

The Anchorage sparkled, cleaner than any naval station he'd ever seen. Every surface gleamed as though hand polished. Done in artistic glass, chrome, and pastel ochers, he saw no grays or blues or clunky outlines. Coalition orbital bases stood out as functional and utilitarian but Compact facilities carried an artistic flair. Wrathsee'a Anchorage possessed the subtle grace of an art exhibit.

Kidahin had her work cut out for her, maneuvering in here. Even using reaction control systems, a careless thrust could ram them right into moored warships.

Two small ships fast approached, each one having green trim along the blunt narrow bow and down along what passed for waterlines on oceangoing vessels. Green perimeter intrusion warnings flashed on Kidahin's console, and Delwyn opened his mouth to shout a warning when their purpose came to him.

"Why the tugboats? Can't they use tractor fields to shift us into the repair dock?"

Hlinlodyn shook her head. "Tractor fields at power ratings necessary to shift our mass stresses the damaged hull. We cannot risk tearing away the temporary repairs, underlying wreckage, and weakened bulkheads."

He agreed with that. He faced the Warleader's Watch and watched the tugs maneuver. Like wet navy tugs their essential work consumed time as they fought against the slippery inertial forces mass gained in a weightless environment.

"Contact!" Kidahin reported.

Delwyn didn't feel so much as a nudge. The warship's mass barely reacted to the tug's inertial fields as they locked onto hull surfaces, tug contact points where the hull could handle the torque transferred to the ship as he was pushed around.

The two tugs fired their thrusters, detached, moved, stopped, found new contact points, and fired their thrusters again.

The forward view slowly pitched down and to the right. Moving the warship into the waiting dock took some time, but soon the tugs would swing them around and tow them into a dock with an isolation slip built into the station wall. The slip, dock, and mooring support structure outgrew the warship by twice his length and was well lit. It looked like an aquarium for Leviathan.

"Quarantine dock?" Delwyn asked Melkorka.

"Yes, so they can remove the Ni'zakhonii ship from the combat deployment bay."

"Why the fancy doors and special seals? They look like airlock seals on a massive scale."

"They are," she agreed. "Once we are inside, they will seal the dock and pump in atmosphere."

"What? *Why?*" Oxygenated spaces made fertile ground for explosions and fires. "Why fill a cubic kilometer with air?"

"It lets us walk on the hull and see the damage done. The ship's artificial gravity generators then adjust field strength to give the hull surface Elleio-normal gravity. This makes repair work much easier. The AG field extends some four ells above the hull. Portable repair equipment, supplies, and assemblies are towed in zero-gee to the hull and then dropped where needed."

An eight-meter fall didn't sound to him like an insignificant drop for delicate materials or sensitive equipment, and he said so.

"Most massive or sensitive materials are quantum translated into the ship or where needed on the hull itself. Atmosphere and gravity keeps them there and work crews make repairs without having to deal with cumbersome EVA suits and thrusters."

Delwyn objected, thinking of bare Eyloni skin, dangling neckwear knots and hanging waistwear loincloths catching on torn metal and equipment. They needed safety suits to protect exposed skin. "You wear suits similar to Power Systems and Propulsion hazard suits."

"Of course. We wear neckwear and waistwear because they are comfortable in Elleio's climate and because they are traditional. They tell others things about us and declare our status. You can read the colored patterns on my waistwear, yes?"

"I can. They proclaim your tribe and clan, and your rank and status in both and that you are the mistress of an elite warship."

"Yes," she agreed, pleased.

"I'm not sure how well I can read the knots in your neckwear. They seem intermediate, showing neither high nor low status."

"That is all you need to know. Neckwear tells other females where I stand in the hierarchies. Males need know only high, medium, or low hierarchy status."

They told him long ago that what happened in the hierarchies remained the business of the hierarchies and not the business of males.

He turned back to the screen and saw more people gathering. They watched as the tugs towed *Hunter's Moon* but not dead-on to the dock, and Delwyn grew suspicious.

The tugs brought them parallel to the quarantine dock instead of into it. Then they towed the ship along the curving lookout decks about a hundred meters 'offshore'. Magnified on-screen images showed fingers pointing at his ship. People stared, ears pricked sideways and eyes wide in astonishment. Others perked their ears forward. Whether attentive or excited he couldn't tell, preferring not to think about his battered hull.

People waved at them as they drew past clear walls. An hour later the tugs brought them back around to the quarantine dock and lined the ship up for entry, one tug fore and the other aft.

"Approaching isolation dock," Kidahin reported. "One tug thrusting fore, the other tug thrusting aft. We are in trim. Correcting for microgravity. Moving ahead dead-slow."

Microgravity. That Delwyn did understand. Wrathsee'a Anchorage had enough mass to produce a gravity well matching Deimos, Mars's moon. Not much gravity, but enough to complicate precision weightless maneuvers when meters away from dense station structures.

They crept forward, now halfway inside the transparent dock.

The lead tug exited through the forward hatch but remained aligned to the warship's longitudinal axis.

They stopped moving minutes later.

They floated inside a glass box.

Mooring clamps extended from the sides.

"Holding station. Mooring clamps attaching," Kidahin reported.

"Message from the Mistress of the Dock, Mistress. She asks for Delwyn to order Power Systems and Propulsion to power down all internal power and stand by to accept external umbilical power and data feeds."

"Affirm," Melkorka said. She turned to Delwyn. "We must shut down all internal power and accept external power for the shipyards. This is standard procedure."

"I understand. Anailiatha, please shut down all power systems and transfer power distribution from internal power, auxiliary standby, and battery power sources to shipyard external power."

"By your command. Powering down from primary distribution to standby and transferring load sharing to external umbilical power … now!" Anailiatha replied over her discrete comm.

"We are operating on partial external power," the Mistress of Tactics reported.

Not so much as a flicker in the lights, he nodded in approval.

Docking clamps held them fast to the mooring station. Now what? To his task-oriented way of thinking, Delwyn did not consider the mission accomplished until they delivered the Ni'zakhonii LAC.

"What do you want to do now? I can take everyone who flew with me back to the LAC and pilot it from the bay," he offered in such a casual manner Melkorka gaped at him in shocked surprise.

"You want to pilot him out?" Phelindra asked. She sang a peculiar soft song under her breath. "It took the spirits' own luck for us to pilot him back to Nikkiolo, and the tractor pilot all but yanked her tail out of joint trying to fit him into the bay in the first place!"

"Yeah, but I know Kidahin can back him out better than the tugboats can lock onto him and pull him out, assuming they get a lock-on in the first place and don't need to physically attach some sort of relay system on his hull."

That comment brought heads up and started tails twitching.

Delwyn asked, "What's wrong?"

"The idea of others boarding our ship even to get a physical lock makes us uncomfortable. The ship belongs to us, and their presence raises territorial issues," Melkorka answered.

"Why?" he asked them. "People have to come aboard *Hunter's Moon* to make repairs."

"No," she said. "The Hunter societies responsible for designing and building *Hunter's Moon* gave him to us. Those builders along with a good third of the crew will repair him. The shipyard provides equipment and operators, but most work must be done by the clans themselves."

He let that pass as another thought occurred to him.

"Melkorka, I know Havalin is warleader here, so how do I or other warleaders enter the Anchorage without offending his society?"

Melkorka glanced at Delwyn a moment, surprised, and then nodded to herself. He did not know.

"You are right. Wrathsee'a Anchorage has a warleader and a society caring for him just as we do for you. But the Anchorage and shipyards themselves are considered neutral ground. The administrative center of the Tower is called the t'et. Think of it as a warship permanently moored within the Anchorage. Havalin's occupational association moves freely from the Tower to the yards or the Anchorage. So does he on rare occasions. But no female ever enters the Tower without the same permissions we give a strange female entering *Hunter's Moon*! The same warleader visitation protocols are in effect there, but with so much neutral territory, don't expect Havalin to invite you to the Tower."

That made sense.

"Well? What have you decided?" Melkorka demanded.

"About what?"

"Piloting the Ni'zakhonii ship from the staging bay."

"You really think they'd want us doing that in here?"

"You are our warleader. The decision is yours."

Delwyn turned to face the helm console. "What do you think, Kidahin? Can you pilot the LAC from the combat deployment bay?"

Kidahin blinked her large soulful amber eyes at him, nodding vigorously. "It is easy to pilot, not so easy to use the sublight or FTL drives."

"Maneuvering thruster piloting will suffice. Everyone who returned with me on the Ni'zakhonii ship report to the combat deployment bay immediately."

Phelindra flashed Melkorka a wicked grin and snapped her tail.

Melkorka advised Wrathsee'a Anchorage of their plan.

"Delwyn wants to do what?" the Dock Mistress demanded.

"Pilot the Ni'zakhoinii ship from our deployment bay and into a research lab," Melkorka said.

"He can do that?" the Dock Mistress asked.

"He piloted the enemy ship into the bay, so he can pilot him from the bay as well."

"One moment, Mistress Melkorka. I must advise Havalin about this development."

Melkorka nodded. The Mistress of the Dock had assumed the tugs would thrust into position outside the bay and tractor the vessel out. A tense, tricky task at best. The enemy ship barely fit into the bay in the first place. A tug would have to hold station outside the bay door and tractor the LAC out. The bay ceiling tractor pod pilot could always push him from the bay if she had to.

Come to think of it she should have done so in the first place, Melkorka thought. Eject the ship and let the tugs have at him.

Melkorka activated the combat address system, drew a deep breath, and hesitated. Everyone had heard Delwyn voice his notion about allowing Kidahin the honor of delivering the contraband vessel into Compact hands. To ask him to reconsider now would insult Kidahin's piloting ability. Since Melkorka told the Dock Mistress that Delwyn intended on piloting the ship, technically true because Kidahin would pilot under Delwyn's supervision, the custom of warleader autonomy had twitched its tail. For him to back down now risked appearances as if Melkorka had misstated his ability.

Of course, Havalin can always declare a Warpact and ask Delwyn to allow the yard tugs to extract the thing. By definition any conflict anywhere in or near Wrathsee'a Anchorage conferred first on-scene male precedence to Havalin. If he saw danger to his association or felt Delwyn represented a reckless danger to the Anchorage, then he would countermand the idea.

"Mistress? The Mistress of the Dock calls," Hlindredreda said.

"Accept."

The Dock Mistress loomed from the forward panoramic screen, nervous. Her ears flicked and twitched as if trying to listen to multiple arguing voices. Her tail swayed behind her, her pons snapping.

"Warleader Havalin has expressed an interest in observing Delwyn pilot the enemy vessel from your warship and into the research bay."

Dead air hung between them. No wonder the Dock Mistress wanted to bite her own tail!

"Affirm, Mistress of the Dock. I shall convey that information to Delwyn."

Melkorka glanced over at Trebithia. "Is Kidahin that good?" she asked the Mistress of Pathwalking.

"She is. Delwyn praised her piloting skill. She has impressed Phelindra as well."

Melkorka ignored the combat address system and commed the combat deployment bay on her discrete audio pickup and relayed the plan to the bay's Mistress of Combat.

7

WRATHSEE'A ANCHORAGE

Delwyn, Phelindra, and Kidahin stomped through tall, sparse, crimson and vermillion grasses and onto a yellow beach. A calm, cool-blue sea beat along a bright shoreline as far as the eye could see. The massive bay door at the far end of the bay was hidden behind a holographic horizon. It even sounded like a coastal beach. Funny, but he couldn't remember hearing waves breaking when he was here before.

Melkorka had declared him warleader on this beach.

Troop transports, gunships, landing craft, and support ships squatted on the sand that wasn't sand. Rows of Light Armored Vehicles, LAVs, the robotic ant ground force transports, hovertanks, light tanks and even a few heavy tanks sat in service alcoves waiting for their next mission.

Hunter's Moon supported heavy planetary surface combat and boarding action assault forces. The Warrior females aboard accounted for 2,308 of the 2,886 crew complement. The Hunter females made up the remaining 577. Out of the full strength 2,886 total, 1,250 females, two 625 female *bodies*, represented the ship's surface action full combat strength. Warriors formed four-fifths of each body, and Hunters filled in the remaining fifth. The remaining 1,635 performed strictly naval duties.

Delwyn watched Eyloni eyes narrow, and he followed their gaze out to the thing sitting in the middle of the pristine yellow deck. The damn enemy ship looked like two crystal pitcher plants welded side-by-side at their bulbous bases, down to the maroon-streaked green hull.

More people filed through hidden blast doors, and not just the original twenty-two he had taken with him on the Ibeetu recon mission either. These were Warriors, and they hadn't come here to see him on his way. This was their scheduled PT training. Some Warriors exercised in small groups, but the physical training session included others dueling in knife fights or engaging in one-on-one unarmed combat drills. One complete body packed the forward staging area.

Although occupied, the entire group of 625 watched as he led his twenty-two into the enemy's airlock.

"Delwyn? Mistress Melkorka says once you are clear to navigate, you are to follow the escort tug to the research bay. When you exit the LAC, contact Akenallin for retrieval," the Mistress of Combat said.

That's right, the Mistress of Conveyance couldn't teleport them off this ship. Something about its hull prevented a teleport lock.

"Understood. Remember, we cannot receive communications from you while we are inside the LAC. Open the bay door and prepare for vessel departure."

"By your command."

Delwyn stepped up into the LAC's airlock and examined its puckered edges. The iris hatch hadn't cycled shut. Good, he didn't know how to get it open from the outside.

They followed him inside.

"Ghaa!" Delwyn gagged. The stench of rotten flesh filled the outer lock.

Kidahin reached over dim glowing crystals in the airlock control matrix table. Her hand brushed a severed Ni'zakhonii hand and she recoiled. "Do we need it? We used it to open all the security hatches before we left," Kidahin said, her stomach rolling.

"I don't think so," Delwyn said, hoping his stomach would not embarrass him. He sympathized with her, and with them. Their noses beat his out every time, and he hated the smell of dead flesh. It tended to drive him into PTSD flashbacks of the carnage on Valhalla Colony, where his wife and daughters had been eaten alive by the Lizards.

"Take it to the disposal chute," Phelindra sang at imperative tempo.

Kidahin gulped, held her breath, grabbed the vile thing by one of its long claws, and ran out the iris hatch, into the bay and up to a small receptacle mounted between two hovertank alcoves. There, she dropped the hand into a transparent niche, slapped a seal closed, and palmed the control pad.

The activated touch screen displayed a vertical legend: 'Isolate', 'Decontaminate', 'Recycle', 'Incinerate,' and 'Power Eject'. Kidahin touched 'Incinerate' and hummed with pleasure as the horrid thing burned to nothing, not even an ash remaining.

"C'mon Kidahin," Delwyn yelled. "How long does it take you to dump that thing?"

She ignored him and ran into an adjacent emergency eyewash and shower stall, squeezed out a dollop of sanitary cleanser, and attacked her hands with a frenzy. She kicked the foot toggle to turn on the water and rinsed off. She kicked the toggle again, stepped clear and snapped her body, flinging droplets everywhere.

Her skin had not been in the water long enough to saturate. Velour-soft, almost fuzzy, water rolled off her skin rather than wetting it. The fine suedelike surface protected her from brief rainforests showers. It remained water resistant until the fuzz became saturated. She never had to worry about getting waterlogged or jungle rot unless she failed to take proper care of her skin.

Kidahin ran back through the outer iris hatch, through the inner airlock hatch, and palmed the glowing control crystal. Both the outer and inner hatches cycled shut.

"Even without the claw, I forgot how bad this ship stinks," Delwyn complained as they headed up to the bridge. The dim tunnels smelled like smashed earthworms, spoilt fruit, and a whiff of ripe roadkill.

The females hummed in sympathy. They knew their warleader's nose lacked a certain sensitivity, but spirits! If he smelled the cloying ripe fruit and dead flesh reeking down the tunnel, then it smelled awful indeed. Although not as strong as the rotting claw had been, it still discouraged any thoughts of eating. They had tolerated the smell over the days spent on their return to Ibeetu, but by now their tolerances had faded. Eyloni never became nose-blind to odor and they thanked the spirits this task would take little time.

Delwyn pulled the long throwing knife from the sheath strapped to his hip and passed it to the Eldest Huntress.

"Phelindra, you are Mistress of the Ship. Send the power systems team to engineering and give me power for the reaction control and attitude control systems and the maneuvering thrusters. We won't need the sublight or FTL drive systems."

"By your command."

He left Phelindra to her work and took Kidahin and the bridge crew up to the center blister atop the aft dorsal hull.

"Kidahin, take the helm as Mistress of Pathwalking. As soon as you get maneuvering power, hover us one ell above the deck and hold position."

"By your command." Kidahin scanned the glowing multicolored gems in the helm matrix table. "Power levels increasing," she reported. The helm systems matrix crystals grew brighter. "Thruster control online. Attitude control online. Reaction control online. Artificial gravity online. Adjusting inertial dampening for neutralizing gravity. Pitching up and maintaining trim. One ell above deck achieved. Thrusters at station keeping. Holding station and awaiting pilot pod tractor contact."

"Very well," Delwyn acknowledged.

The LAC shuddered as the ceiling pod locked piloting tractor fields onto them.

"Manual flight systems report full power available," Hervorallin reported from the engineering console.

Delwyn smiled at Hervorallin and wondered what Princess thought about their absence. If he could smell his near-daughter, no doubt the pheromonal empathy they shared would have conjured up feelings of outraged affront at being left behind.

"Open the emitter elements and tell Wrathsee'a Anchorage that we are ready to exit the ship," he said.

"By your command. Emitters open and broadcasting command center live feed on all comm and sensor frequencies."

He grimaced at the swearing he imagined was streaming at them from Anchorage communications. His LAC crew had never figured out how to open an isolated communications channel. They knew how to turn them all on or all off. This jaunt would necessarily swamp all local communication channels and short-range scan returns. They were now a security threat. If the Mistress of the Tower was anything like Melkorka, then by now she had probably ordered the Anchorage to Battle Status.

The forward staging area view receded as the ceiling pod pilot pushed them back toward the bay door.

Warriors stopped their PT routines and lined up along both sides of the bay. Waving hands and pumping fists, they yelled encouragements he couldn't hear, probably curses too. They had hated him for going to Phalalin's ship, and now he was leaving them again.

Kidahin trilled and Delwyn spun around. Two Warriors stood beside her, their expressions filled with wide-eyed awe. They alternated between staring at him and staring at the fishbowl viewscreen image and back again. Those two had taken serious injuries when their LAV had been fired upon. Their injuries, blast amputations, had prevented them from taking an active part in capturing the LAC and bringing him back into the Nikkiolo system. Allohindra had regenerated the lost limbs for them in Health Center, but getting them through physical therapy took time, and the Mistress of Healers had cleared them for duty only days ago.

They had been trapped in a food storage stasis chamber in the galley, and had nearly become Lizard food.

Reverse motion stopped. A moment later it resumed at a creeping pace. They crossed the bay door threshold and floated beneath the warship's aftstation, the interface decks between the command hull and the engineering hull.

The pod pilot disengaged her tractor field, and the LAC shook again as the warship's main tractor fields nudged them down and aft.

"Hold station, Kidahin."

"By your command. Thrusters at station keeping. Manual flight and piloting systems ready."

The warship's tractor field disengaged, and the heat shimmer effect vanished at the same time they received another shudder.

"Zero imparted velocity. Holding station. We are free to navigate," Kidahin reported.

"Very well. Where's that tug?"

Phelindra activated the passive proximity sensors. "Tug approaching ahead," she reported, approval in her voice. To approach an ally from behind was shameful.

Delwyn watched the tug roll, yaw, and pitch around, a showy maneuver, he thought.

The tug stopped dead-ahead. Lights flared in patterns from the tug's optical strobe.

"Drum Language, Delwyn. They ask us to follow," Phelindra said.

"No tractor fields?" he asked.

"No," she whispered. She cocked an ear at Kidahin. "Pursuit course. Match their maneuvers and maintain zero rate of closure. Let us not ram them."

"Affirm, maneuvering," Kidahin said.

Something felt wrong. Delwyn had conned this ship the last time they were here, but the intervening time aboard *Hunter's Moon* had taught him a lot about Compact command structure. Melkorka commanded, but he interjected command orders and decisions at will without assuming the conn or without having to issue them through Melkorka.

Melkorka commanded. Indeed, commanding a warship came naturally to her.

Which meant here Phelindra should conn the LAC with little input or interference from him, and here he'd been issuing more orders than usual since they arrived.

"Phelindra, do you want …"

"… to make a security sweep?" she finished for him. "I do not think you need to worry about security threats. Warleader special security prowled this ship for hours long before Allohindra released you from Health Center."

The look on her face told him to shut up.

"Okay then," he said. He was right, dammit. He knew when something felt off key.

"Delwyn, the tug has sent another message in Drum Language. They cannot tractor us into the research bay. The tug's tractor field can stray slightly from its lock-on point at any time. Our hull design makes a tractor lock tentative. A straying tractor field can sometimes gain a random lock. It could lock onto the research bay bulkheads and torque them right off the interior hull. Worse, if they locked onto laboratory equipment the attractive force could crush them. The tug is willing to use his tractor field if you prefer that to a manual approach. State your decision and the open comm will advise them."

He understood then what had been bothering him. Just as the combat address system blared his voice throughout his warship, the LAC's open comms transmitted his voice to Wrathsee'a Anchorage and to anyone else wanting to listen.

Phelindra wanted them to hear him conn the captured ship. She was showing him off.

Okay, he'd play along.

"Thank them for the offer, but I'm confident Kidahin can pilot us into the bay."

The young Hunter preened while sitting at her helm. "Destination ahead, Delwyn," she reported.

The tug veered off. Ahead, along the curving Anchorage hull, two large vertical tubes stood out like see-through mud dauber wasp nests, open at the bottom end.

"Have you ever piloted a ship this size into a bay that small?" he asked Kidahin.

"No, but this is no different than piloting out of the combat deployment bay."

True enough. The research bay door was narrower but taller than the bay door, a circle and not a rectangle. The bay itself was huge, resembling a university tiered classroom operating theater.

Or a morgue.

"On approach, decelerating to dead-slow, one ell per minute," Kidahin said.

"Continue at your discretion," Delwyn said.

The bay contained no independent slip guides, no mooring station, no dock, and no docking clamps. This was a soccer field-sized lab clean room plain and simple.

"Anticipate artificial gravity in the bay Kidahin."

"By your command. Ship is centered. Holding station. Adjusting trim. Thrusting forward. We are in the bay. Thrusters at station keeping. Holding station. Thrusting down."

The Light Attack Craft trembled as the ventral hull touched down onto the floor.

"Disengage piloting systems," Delwyn ordered.

"By your command. Anchorage gravity has us." Kidahin said as she pushed several crystals in the matrix table in a practiced sequence.

The crystal controls in the helm table dimmed to their standby settings.

"Report to engineering," he told them.

They hurried down into the vessel's engineering spaces, reset the reactor to stand-by, and then exited from the airlock into the analysis bay.

Victory songs erupted from at least a hundred spectators lining the edges of the bay.

Twenty-two females stood with him in solemn dignity and accepted the research staff's respect.

"Phelindra? Contact Melkorka. Let her know we are ready for retrieval."

She didn't reply, didn't otherwise respond. The old Hunter ignored him, a frequent habit of hers.

A fleeting memory of Melkorka's mercurial nature came to him, and he shook his head. It felt wrong not having her and the others around to enjoy this show of support.

Kidahin and several others were looking about, eyes wide open, tails motionless, and ears set apart on their heads, stunned.

He gave them all fond smiles and hoped Melkorka wouldn't jump down his throat later for the delay.

The research staff, along with everyone else on Wrathsee'a Anchorage, had watched the battered warship enter his repair dock. Their anticipatory interest and curiosity on seeing the new warleader had prowled along tails-entwined with their interest in seeing the enemy ship.

Delwyn scanned faces in the crowd. They didn't come rushing in although he bet they couldn't wait to get their hands on the Lizard ship.

"We're going to have to brief them on what we know about this thing. It can't be just a theoretical briefing, either. They'll need practical knowledge as well. We can't have a control crystal explode on them. Remember what happened with the drive shutdown?"

Phelindra wrapped her tail around him and cinched him up against her side with a showy possessiveness. "We can help you brief them, but not now. We must return to *Hunter's Moon.* We must prowl our warship and secure him for repair, routine maintenance, and resupply. There are many things we must do before we disembark. Formal greeting must soon take place. You must request repair, replenishment, and resupply services, and you must make a formal request for access to the repair dock facilities."

"Like I know how to do that!" Delwyn snapped. "None of your lessons talked about harbor customs."

"None are needed," Phelindra said. "Melkorka and the command center mistresses will accompany you. Mistress Anailiatha will come with us. Melkorka will make the proper requests and argue over scheduling. Your presence is required because she makes the request on your behalf. This is the custom and has nothing to do with you being a new warleader. The Mistress of the Ship works her tail off to coordinate these things for you, as other mistresses of the ship do for their warleaders."

"Makes sense, I guess," he conceded.

He looked around the research bay perimeter and saw more people gathering.

"They can't wait to get their hands on this thing, can they?"

"They want to meet you, but not now. We must return to our warship."

"Fine. Contact Melkorka and ask her to have Akenallin bring us back."

"By your command." Phelindra twitched her ear, pulling on fine whiskers embedded into a thumb-sized patch near her temple.

"Melkorka? Phelindra. Delwyn calls for retrieval."

One moment he was watching Kidahin staring into the crowd … and the next moment he was staring at Akenallin.

His inner ear complained for an instant before his zero-gee training told his brain to forget it. They weren't in a zero-gee environment, but conveyance translations shifted abruptly and gave a feeling of walking between funhouse mirrors.

Everyone except Phelindra and Kidahin returned to their duties. Delwyn had several obstacles in his way: females. Their warleader had left them for a time, and the many 'chance' encounters he met on the way up to the command center slowed him down. People stopped him often to reassure themselves of his good health.

By the time he reached the command center, Melkorka was already busy directing multiple activities at the same time. Disturbing her now guaranteed antagonizing her, but he wanted a progress report.

She gave him a harried look, growled an obscene phrase describing a novel a'pea usage, snapped at Hlinlodyn, and glided up to him.

"You want to know what happens next?"

"Yeah, I'd like not being surprised all the time at least once in a while, you know."

"Yes, I know. I keep forgetting all this activity is new to you."

Melkorka paused several minutes to organize her thoughts. It never occurred to her to tell Delwyn how repair and replenishment procedures worked. She had gone through harbor customs often enough with Kalinn. Like twitching her tail to convey a mood, prowling through the shipyard hierarchy followed a well-established pattern.

"As you know, we have been cleared for entry into the repair dock and the naval shipyards. Once our ship is moored, we can disembark. When all repair and replenishment issues have been addressed, we can request transport to A'lon'aloop, the primary naval base orbiting Elleio.

"First though, we—meaning you and the command mistresses—must accompany the Mistress of the Dock and survey the damage. Anailiatha heads the engineering surveys, which means she argues and complains the most during these assessments. The Mistress of the Tower is equal to a mistress of the ship here, and she must accompany us because by custom she takes an active interest in all warships moored in the Anchorage. She also certifies that the Ni'zakhonii ship represents no danger to Wrathsee'a Anchorage. The historical victory you won gives her another reason to meet us, meaning she will use the time to greet and assess you.

"She will bring Havalin with her. His interests are threefold. One, he will want to review our hull battle damage. Two, he will want to hear how we captured the enemy ship. Three, he will want to meet you in person. That means we treat them as though they are on Elleio. Male autonomy is preserved here under the same privacy and courtesy customs as on Elleio. Because the Anchorage and shipyard have so much neutral territory, no male ever visits the Tower. If a male wishes to meet with Havalin, then they meet on neutral territory."

"I knew other males had to work here outside of Havalin's Tower," he interrupted.

Melkorka's crimson and golden-highlighted tangerine face brightened. Delwyn understood them far better than she had hoped.

"Naturally, there are security and emergency forces throughout the Anchorage and shipyards. Maintenance and repair facilities, research and development centers like this one, and other support systems are run by occupational associations. They form societies just as warship crews do. Any occupation having a potential for conflict employs a male strategist with sufficient education and training to supervise them. He chooses a mistress, and she commands them."

"So he's the supervisor then? What is he called? Not warleader, that wouldn't make sense."

"No, he is not. He is called by name and his occupation. He is a sire cairn. If he supervises Anchorage security for example, then he is called *si're ki're' a'lux'e,* sire cairn of security, and his Mistress is called the Mistress of the Watch."

"He doesn't give her a sword, does he?"

Melkorka made a face at him. "Of course not. He gives her a large knife to wear at her hip."

"Oh," Delwyn muttered. So ritual played a part here, too.

"While we are here, my job is to arrange repair and replenishment services. Anailiatha and I will make formal requests for repair dock personnel and support facilities access. The mistresses who designed and built the ship must come here and review the damage control archive data and inspect the damage for themselves. Then they will summon the repair personnel from the Hunter societies that built him and supervise all repairs."

"Wait a minute! Repair dock personnel don't make the repairs?"

"Not directly," Melkorka replied. "They make portable equipment available. They operate the cranes and gantries. They also arrange for replacement bulkheads, hull plating, and modular assemblies transport. Some prefabrication must begin on Elleio. The prefabs are translated into orbit and then shipped here. All internal repairs and direct contact external repairs are always performed by the Hunter societies that financed and built our warship."

Delwyn recalled a story he had once read about a time when everyone on Earth owned a personal vehicle, called a car. People loved their cars and often refused to give them proper maintenance, preferring to make their own repairs. Some people rented repair bays stocked with the necessary equipment. The car owner supplied the replacement parts, manuals, and the dubious skill needed to make those amateur repairs.

"We have to repair our own warship?" he bellowed.

Several females converged on him at once, alert.

"Not us and calm down. You are sending combative signals and making everyone tense," Melkorka hissed.

Delwyn paused long enough to let them see for themselves he had taken no harm and that he hadn't perceived a threat.

"What do you mean by 'not us'?"

"I mean Anailiatha and her Power Systems and Propulsion crew, engineering maintenance, damage control, structural engineering, and fire control teams for the most part. Space frame technicians, hull repair teams, internal repair groups, and others will come from our clans' Hunter societies. They will enjoy helping us."

What the hell? Craft guilds? Coalition ship captains filed requests for maintenance and repairs and then waited until openings coincided with scheduled ships movement. Sometimes ships remained deployed with repairs long overdue because the repair docks had no openings. Compact ships returned to port and requested an open repair dock and then waited for the ship's original designers and builders to arrive in response to their mistresses of the ship's call for assistance.

Could it be that easy? He doubted it.

"Before we ship out for A'lon'aloop, we must first receive medical clearance because we have been exposed to the Nikkiolo moon's biosphere. We leave nothing to chance when it comes to male and environmental safety," Melkorka said.

"I'd be sick by now if I'd caught something from Ibeetu," Delwyn grumbled. Doctors, damn it. He hated doctor visits.

"We must clear medical screening, too. Oh, Allohindra has asked me to help her with some details in your medical file. She will come with us and explain to the Anchorage Mistress of Healers the details listed in your medical files."

"Mistress?" Hlindredreda interrupted. "The Mistress of the Dock reports all repair slip systems register nominal. All moorings and clamps are secured. The ship is drawing partial umbilical power. She says you may proceed at your discretion."

Melkorka thanked the Mistress of Communications and then palmed the combat address system open. "The Mistress of the Dock has cleared us for debarkation. Switch all systems to standby and commence reactor shutdown, beginning with …"

It took ten Earth hours to shut down the reactors and match the external power supply to the ship's load sharing systems without blowing out circuits and causing fires. Delwyn compared the load management problem to storm damaged city-wide power failures and how surges happened when short circuits or devices left on by the thousands made instantaneous demands on restored power supplies.

Some things couldn't be shut off on a starship.

The time had finally come for them to leave the ship. A warleader never left the ship last, and so Delwyn left first with Melkorka and Phelindra. The crew followed him out through the port docking clamp gangway in rank order, except for one.

Kidahin, the youngest, lowest ranked and newest crewmember had special duties: she alone certified the warleader gone, made sure the crew had evacuated the ship, and made sure all primary systems had been shut down. Kidahin had to give the repair crews permission to begin exterior staging operations. Why the most inexperienced person aboard had such high responsibilities mystified Delwyn.

He stood on the repair dock and gazed up at the slip guides and docking clamps. This was the third time in ninety days he'd been among the entire crew. The first time was when they had gathered before him for the Death Song ritual on Ibeetu. The second time was when they had gathered in the combat deployment bay to make him their warleader. And now they gathered around him again, paying close attention to him when they weren't looking their warship over.

He looked around the repair dock. Life support had filled the sealed clear structure with Elleio-normal atmosphere and gravity. The air felt quite warm and humid, but not so bad. After spending days slogging through simulated ocher forests, the narrow open dock and the people milling about made him think of passengers waiting to board an ocean cruise ship.

Delwyn's eyes returned to his warship. He hadn't been aboard when Kalinn had fought this ship in a naval battle against three Ni'zakhonii destroyers. No ship commander wanted to see ship damage. The females looked grim and at a loss. The scored and patched hull plating, the charred and twisted metal, and the gaping holes and peeled-back outer hull reminded them of Kalinn and the 314 casualties lost.

Delwyn, Melkorka, and Phelindra walked among them. As he understood matters, this wasn't a ritual event. Melkorka said he didn't need to worry about their ranking when in large groups like this. In small groups they always insisted he touch them according to their hierarchical ranking.

For some reason large groups excused the formality, unless rare ritual events demanded it.

From their lessons and his past experiences, he knew no female could stop another female from approaching her warleader. Small group touch interplay showed that he practiced no favoritism. But the entire crew took on an individuality: a society, an association. When so grouped, they expected him to show preference for them as a group, and it didn't matter which one of them he caressed first.

That made sense for a crew numbering over twenty-five hundred people.

"Delwyn? We must leave. Once we pass medical clearance, we can arrange repair schedules and transport to A'lon'aloop base."

He nodded, ready to go. They headed for the dock exit. There, the Anchorage Mistress of Healers and her medical retinue waited.

They picked Delwyn first as befitted his warleader status. Great! He'd been in enough waiting rooms in his lifetime and despised doctor's offices. No doctor appointment ever started on time. Waiting grew worse whenever a nurse came into the waiting room with a "The Doctor is OUT" sign.

Phelindra's abrupt musical laughter hit a nerve.

"What? You think this is funny? You want to trade places? I feel like they're going to dissect me!"

Phelindra's loud singing provoked the medical staff to growl at her disruptive behavior.

"The Mistress of Healers is asking Allohindra whether or not she ought to take measurements and have a guard made to protect you. Mating is important to us, and she thinks the lack of protection cannot go un …"

"Enough! I don't need a cup! I don't need a jock strap, either. Can't we get this over with?" he demanded. "Besides, who am I going mate with anyway?"

The offhanded remark shocked Phelindra. Speechless she gaped at him, her lips trembling.

"Why … why any Hunter or Warrior in season who wishes it."

Delwyn stared at her, aghast.

This was more Hunter humor. Surely they couldn't expect him to make love—mate—with them. He doubted it was even physically possible.

"Mating is always possible between males and females in season when consensual empathy ties are made during tail-twining."

He glared at her, a distraction, while the doctors demanded fluid samples, skin samples, hair samples, and every other sample he could imagine.

And then they exceeded his imagination.

Time passed at its usual doctor's office slowness. The Mistress of Healers finally cleared him for travel to Elleio, but her imprimatur, her approval, did nothing for his growing impatience. He had to wait for the others to receive their own individual clearances.

They passed one person every twenty minutes or so. The Anchorage medical staff gave them priority processing with assembly line efficiency. A staff healer grabbed a female, gave her a physical, compared her readings with stored baseline patterns, scanned for the usual bacterial, viral, and parasitic hitchhikers, updated her file, and NEXT!

Their best efforts still meant a good day-long wait for 2,571 females.

That meant waiting in temporary housing next to the medical wing. He spent the time visiting with those already cleared or playing with Princess.

The healers wasted no time clearing his near-daughter. When they cleared Hervorallin, the Mistress of Healers turned on the infant Hunter. The Mistress had concerns because Princess had been born on the filthy enemy ship. She didn't have to worry, though. Princess climbed Delwyn's leg to her perch, laid her head on top of his, wrapped her tail around his neck, and gave the medical staff a spat-grimace: mouth open, teeth showing, a sharp-nailed hand extended out to them. It was the expression of pure aggression they had expected from a male's healthy near-daughter.

To pass the time several females asked him out for walks around the Anchorage.

At first he demurred. He liked watching them interact with one another, but boredom and a desire not to hurt their feelings prompted him to jog after them. An alert Phelindra shot after him, and a curious Melkorka ran after her. The group exited the medical center and stepped into a long narrow transparent terrace.

Looking out across the Anchorage, the view reminded him of a canyon system. As it rolled in a panoramic circle around the terrace, Anchorage services and shipyard facilities hung in parallel cliffs and ridges rising and falling depending on where they were stacked around the tapered interior hull. The Tower, stretching down from the faceted dome like some shiny thick metallic icicle, dipped down far enough to partially block the view across the Anchorage from this level. It had its own docking facilities, reserved for Havalin and his occupational association.

Wrathsee'a Anchorage personnel spoke more wet navy terms than even the Coalition Fleet, and the Fleet borrowed heavily from Earth's wet navy tradition. He asked Melkorka about it as they walked.

"Most of the La'huaset Tribe's costal clans maintain Elleio's ocean fleets. We had ocean-going fleets long before we had starflight."

Delwyn tried to imagine the semi-arboreal Eyloni sailing schooners. That produced a chuckle until he had a sobering thought: they probably climbed the rigging better than the best able seaman.

Several ships were moored here, but none came close to *Hunter's Moon's* class. "When do we meet those ships' warleader, their crews?"

"Many remain aboard their ships. A few at a time rotate ashore to enjoy the forest scenery, the wandering paths and trails, and the shops under the dome above us," Phelindra said.

"Shops?" he echoed.

Phelindra nodded. "Many artisans make things for trade: furniture, waistwear, neckwear, wall hangings, and other things. Some shops serve exotic meals."

What she said surprised him. When he first met Anlann and Seralin, he'd compared them to First Nations people: Native Americans. Both co-ambassadors wore hardly any clothing, all of it apparently handmade. The flint and obsidian knives and other items had been handmade as well. Clans had cottage industries, and those industries made items for clan members.

He hadn't expected the Eyloni to have a market-based economy.

Of course they had a market-based economy. No national government developed naval shipping for nothing. Navies meant warships and logistical support for bases abroad. When the Compact Counsel outlawed outright military conflict among tribes and clans, the one remaining route to competition sailed through trade, and trade invited economic markets. Eyloni clans formed some social partnerships, so their economy likely relied on barter systems rather than money. Having no monetary system raised another perplexing question. How could multiclan partnerships or allied societies pay for the materials and technology necessary to build a warship like *Hunter's Moon*?

They walked through several transparent curving kilometers of observation decks until they returned to their starting point. They hadn't changed levels, content to gaze across the busy shipyards. Ships came and went with relaxed regularity. Accustomed to his ship's forest paths, the clear curving decks struck Delwyn as inconsistent. Why didn't Anchorage environmental systems project rainforest here with a cliff view rather than a terrace? What about the decks between the observation deck and the outer hull? It didn't make sense to restrict the jungle simulations to the dome above. The females must hate it, but he guessed aesthetics had to give way to function sometimes.

Kidahin waited for them, holding Princess. "Mistress Melkorka, the Mistress of Healers says we have been cleared for transport to A'lon'aloop Naval Station."

"What about the repair crews? Did you welcome them and clear them for access to the repair dock?" Melkorka asked.

"Yes, Mistress. The clans' elders told me to tell you all repair personnel are expected to arrive in earnest some four days from now. Right now they are taking scans to decide where quantum removal and replacement will be most effective. Other sections will need lift assist and manual refitting."

"Quantum removal and replacement?" Delwyn asked, mystified.

Kidahin twitched her tail at him playfully and nodded. "They can quantum translate out modular hull sections. New modules can then be translated into the cleared spaces. This method makes some structural repairs easy. Plumbing and power feeds cannot be joined together in such a manner, and so the repair teams must connect and test each module before powering them up."

Delwyn remembered an incident at the Daedalia Planum Naval Shipyards on Mars. CECS *Ruby Cole* had rammed a small asteroid. Orbiting above Daedalia P, repair teams hacked away at her hull like a demolition crew. Zero-gee jackhammers, laser torches, and even shaped charges had been used to blast wreckage from her bow. He thought at that time the hull technicians and their wholesale cutting had been no different than battlefield surgeons hacking off arms and legs.

Kidahin hummed a soft note, pulling him back from the memory.

"We may go," she repeated.

About time.

"Melkorka, you said we had to take troop transports to Elleio? Why not translate there?"

"Elleio is beyond conveyance translation range. The conveyance center is not a jump drive. Even if it were, arranging passage on transport ships is energy conservative, is easier, and is more efficient. Once a departure time is scheduled, we can be in Elleio orbit in about three hours."

Three TST hours! "Now that's the best news I've heard all day."

The navy was the navy, and Delwyn should have known better. It turned out not as easy as Melkorka had implied. As warleader, he had to wait for the Anchorage Mistress of Healers to report on his crew's health. Why she didn't report their status to Allohindra wasn't clear, but with her help the Mistress gave a comprehensive report.

She talked for over an hour and a half, but it turned out the time spent hadn't been a total loss. While he sat hostage with the doctors, Melkorka arranged their departure time and set up a meeting with Havalin, his Mistress of the Tower, his Protectress, and the Mistress of the Dock.

By the time the Mistress of Healers had finished, the Mistress of the Dock, a Warrior female, was waiting for him outside the entrance to the medical wing.

Delwyn doubted she just happened to show up at the right time. Pleased at finding him safe, healthy, and available, she launched into a complicated singsong monologue. Her bright orange eyes never left his face as she gushed her enthusiasm. Her pons wove abstract patterns that complemented her flitting ears. Her body movements seemed to follow a subtle choreographed dance.

The Dock Mistress stopped looping her tail and arched her back coyly. She edged forward to brush her tail against his face but withheld the gesture at the last second.

What in the world is going on now? Delwyn wondered.

Melkorka appeared by his side and ignored him, but she kept an appraising eye on the Mistress of the Dock, apparently lost in thought.

He glanced at Phelindra.

She too seemed deeply interested in the Mistress of the Dock.

Looks flashed among the three females, and Delwyn had a sudden uneasy feeling he'd stepped into something personal.

What happened? No one seemed angry. Angry Eyloni females let you know their anger by scent. Even his nose could sniff out an angry Eyloni. He couldn't describe the smell. An angry female didn't stink, but the hair on his neck would stand on end if they were angry.

The three smelled … well … like nutmeg and vanilla: amiable.

Then he decided that this must be a status thing. They did enjoy parading their social status to one another.

Delwyn focused on the Dock Mistress and tried to delve what Melkorka and Phelindra saw in her.

The Mistress looked about Melkorka's age and a bit lean for a Warrior female, but she was not willowy like Kidahin. She had beautiful orange-shaded skin splattered with yellow-trimmed reds, smaller patterns than Phelindra's. The spotting reminded him of those on a fawn, camouflage that concealed her in ground cover.

Her waistwear caught his eye, too. The hip-riding underthong ties, sky blue with different colored beads, ran from the undergarment's tail hoop to the knots and from the knots to under her loincloth. The short loincloth, embroidered with patterns and colors, told him she belonged to the La'huaset tribe. He had trouble grasping clan affiliation, but he thought he recognized a familiar pattern belonging to a wet navy clan.

Lindredha edged closer to the new warleader, lost in his scent. She was not poaching, not intentionally, but he liked her. Her nose told her so.

His Mistress of the Ship and his Protectress smelled noncommittal.

Lindredha stepped within his tail-length personal space and glanced again at Phelindra.

The old Hunter watched, but she did not discourage her.

"Warleader Havalin, Protectress Mawrandredha, and Mistress of the Tower Yolandraha come to meet you," the Mistress of the Dock sang to Phelindra. Phelindra forced down a grin, caught Melkorka's eyes, and stared into them.

Melkorka gave her a slight frown. She was not stupid. Of course the Dock Mistress could smell that Delwyn had no personal association.

Not yet, anyway. Not if she had anything to say about it.

Eyloni females working with a male associated with him. They chose him just as a warship's society chose a warleader. They spent time with him on a regular basis, and they focused on him. His presence triggered emotions and instincts, a blind protective savagery whenever they felt he faced a threat.

But Eyloni females also chose a male to associate with independent of occupational ties. Those personal associations formed extensive friendships not only with their male, but also with the females making up the association. A male could show a friendship interest in any female, but his association decided whether they would allow the new prospect to associate with them.

Females often belonged to both the same male's occupational and personal association, because by doing so they preserved continuity between personal and professional ties.

Association regulation, as with everything else strictly female on Elleio, came under multiple female hierarchies' interests. Female association served one purpose: to protect and cherish the male population.

Lindredha had found Delwyn interesting, and she had made overtures to two females in his occupational association through her pheromones. Her scent empathy connection to them asked a basic question: could she join Delwyn's personal association?

Delwyn, as usual, had no clue.

Lindredha gave him a tentative pons brush against a cheek, rubbing her scent on him, a preliminary scent mark.

Delwyn knew Eyloni craved casual physical contact, and so he brushed her cheek and cupped her right ear, felt it twitch in his hand.

Lindredha stepped into him, breathed his scent, and sighed. She wrapped her tail and arms around him, and Delwyn wondered if this kind of physical expression happened all the time on Elleio.

"She likes you," Phelindra said.

"Remember what I taught you about males and their female associations?" Melkorka asked.

"Yeah? She wants to join your society? I thought you decided that."

"We do, but that is not what I mean. Our society, the crew, is your occupational association. Lindredha wants to personally associate with you."

Delwyn knew males in Eyloni culture were granted sweeping autonomy, but he also knew in many cases males had few choices, or no choice at all. The female mind prioritized male safety. Safety for a male meant gaining female defenders. Females needed occasional casual physical contact with males to satisfy their mental well-being, and instinct drove the desire to associate. Association evolved both biologically and socially as a survival strategy and not as a reproductive strategy. Eyloni were social, so associations became friendship and companionship driven.

No male ever 'just said no' to an interested female desiring his company. His personal association decided her suitability. If they deemed her a bad fit for him, then they refused her. If he rejected her out of hand, then the female hierarchies ruling Elleio social life would have something dire or lethal to say about his disgraceful and criminal antisocial behavior. Rejecting social contact and companionship displayed intentional public cruelty and …

… Lindredha wasn't letting go.

"We like her too," Phelindra said.

"What about that Hunter and Warrior rivalry you two are always going on about?" he asked her.

"Not when it comes to this. Never this," she stressed. She hummed a haunting melody to the Dock Mistress.

Lindredha stepped back and gazed into his small brown eyes and waited, her nose a pons length from his.

Eyloni didn't kiss. They nuzzled rubbing noses and cheeks, stimulating oil glands and triggering pheromone activity, which in turn triggered deep empathic responses the most ardent kiss couldn't match.

Delwyn shrugged. What was the harm? She commanded the shipyards, and he commanded a warship. How often would he see her?

Lindredha inclined her head, and he rubbed his nose against her cheek and along her nose.

She returned his affection with open enthusiasm. He got a feeling of contentment from her.

Lindredha broke the contact and embraced the other two females.

Phelindra and Melkorka rubbed their noses where he had touched her face.

Were they sharing the scent? Sharing in a social bond?

"What's your name?" he asked the Mistress of the Dock when the threesome broke their embrace.

"She is Lindredha," Melkorka said, singing the name to give him its full meaning: a vine clinging to the ground forcefully.

Melkorka drew Lindredha aside and soon they turned businesslike.

"What's going on now?" he asked Phelindra.

"Lindredha commands all dock operations. Melkorka is telling her what needs doing and when. She needs dock workers to handle refit logistics and external equipment operations. You were wise to accept Lindredha's overtures. She will prefer you over all others when it comes to dock management issues. Only already in-progress operations, Anchorage, Fleet, or A'tayotan priority issues will override her preference."

"I didn't befriend her to get preferential treatment in the shipyards!" Delwyn bellowed.

Phelindra's knees turned watery in shock, but she shook the feeling off. *How could he even think that?* "I know that. She knows that. That does not stop her from helping you. We help the males we associate with as much as possible within the constraints imposed by rank and hierarchy status."

Privately she wondered just how much Delwyn's nose missed. Whatever he was thinking about floated on his scent, and she knew by smell he had no devious intent when he accepted Lindredha's interest. His scent drew an image of honesty in her mind, which meant his scent had done so for everyone. If he had harbored an ulterior motive for accepting Lindredha, then any female smelling the emotional abuse had a duty to tell Lindredha's hierarchy. Speechless with fury they would then seek revenge in such cases.

Phelindra leaned against Delwyn and watched the two Warriors sing counterpoint melodies about repair work and schedules. She listened so intently that she flinched at the sound of the Mistress of the Tower's impatient introductory chord.

Phelindra spun around and snapped her tail against his back, reminding him that they had company. "Delwyn?" Phelindra prompted using formal interrogative pitch.

"Hmm?" he murmured. His slow pivot away from the two haggling Warriors gave away his interest in Lindredha. New people standing nearby drew his attention away from her and to the waiting group.

"Delwyn, I present Havalin, Warleader of Wrathsee'a Anchorage. Accompanying him is Mawrandredha his Protectress and Yolandraha his Mistress of the Tower," Phelindra said.

Delwyn greeted Havalin first, met his eyes for a moment, and then he focused on the Warrior and Hunter and gave them each a formal greeting.

Havalin, taller, narrower in the shoulders and redder-shaded than Phalalin, stepped forward eagerly and impulsively, or so Mawrandredha seemed to think by the droll expression on her face.

"Delwyn! Pleased and honored. Meet you," he stumbled.

Mawrandredha waggled her fingers at Phelindra.

Phelindra waggled fingers back at Mawrandredha.

"She says not to laugh at him. He spent hours learning more Coalition words for this personal greeting. He struggled so much to learn them, so do not laugh!"

"I won't. Anlann said he and Seralin both had a terrible time learning Coalition standard without having a human scent reference to convey emotional context and meaning to the words."

Delwyn had a natural intensity and directness, what people referred to as being a straight shooter. Warleader Havalin smelled Delwyn's character on the air surrounding Melkorka and Phelindra. He smelled it reeking from Lindredha. His nose told him that she thought of Delwyn as the most wonderful male she had ever met.

Havalin glanced back and forth between Lindredha and Delwyn and fluted a low baritone snicker and received an impatient swipe from Mawrandredha's tail.

He returned the gesture by wrapping his tail around hers and giving a playful tug.

"Can you not be serious this once?" Yolandraha snapped at him. Males were strange.

"I am always serious. It just takes me time to order Delwyn's words in my mind," he sang.

She answered him with a frustrated musical sigh.

It didn't take long for Havalin to surprise Delwyn with his fluid use of the forty-odd words he did know. He commented on every passing thing. He carried off 'look here' and 'see that' phrases with keen excitement. Hospitality rated high in Eyloni social life, and Havalin intended to give Delwyn a memorable welcome.

Yolandraha hummed in rhythmic pleasure, proud of Havalin. He had studied himself to sleep preparing for this meeting, and now he carried on long chats with Delwyn in his native tongue. Pheromonal pride radiated from her.

Delwyn briefed Havalin on how they captured the enemy ship. His report attracted others, and Melkorka and Phelindra signed battle language supplements for the new arrivals. Havalin relied on the few words he knew, Delwyn's scent, and Mawrandredha's running translation to piece the story together.

Delwyn tried to use the same words Havalin had acquired some fluency in, and hoped he wasn't insulting his host with his simplistic vocabulary. His concern must have found its way into his body odor, for Havalin sang some comment to Yolandraha. She repeated it to Melkorka, and she repeated it to him.

"Havalin asks why you think you have insulted him. Havalin feels no insult. He is pleased. He wants you to repeat the fighting sequences in the enemy ship's security area. He wants to hear how you dispatched so many in so short a time."

"Oh. Okay, I'll start from when I jumped off the ledge into the brig bay but Phelindra can always supplement my story. She was in the brig and watched everything from her cell."

"I was not asked to add anything," Phelindra huffed. She crossed her arms beneath her breasts and gave him a you! look before returning to her signing.

"You're no help!" He bantered, tugging at her tail with his words.

Delwyn started the story over, his audience hanging on every word. He tried to convey feeling and specific detail through his voice pitch and posture and hoped Havalin smelled the details from the scent around him.

Words Havalin knew from self-taught drills made more sense once he had Delwyn's scent to draw mental pictures representing what the words meant in their proper context. With growing confidence, he fired questions whenever Delwyn paused. His answers, simple and imprecise due to the limited vocabulary, made better sense with the added pheromonal boost.

Delwyn found rhythm in Havalin's questions and answers. He preferred certain word orders and pitches, and his excitement threatened to overwhelm him at times.

Havalin danced on the balls of his feet, incredulous. The spirits had given him the opportunity to hear an initial after-action briefing before the Be'atika Senge and the A'tayotan! Why, the A'tayotan might even declare this report classified under Compact Seal. The idea of a crystal control system intrigued him. How could a chunk of crystal control anything? He wanted to see it for himself.

"Can I. See him?" Havalin sang in a soft lyrical sigh.

Him? Delwyn wondered. *Oh!* "Yes," Delwyn said. If Havalin wanted to see the LAC, then as warleader he could demand a tour aboard the stinky thing any time he wanted.

Havalin's excitement grew, and waggling female fingers signed rapid-fire conversations.

Melkorka, while signing, sighed irritably and gave Delwyn an impatient glare.

"You have just invited Havalin to a personal tour aboard the enemy ship."

"Yeah, what about it? The damn thing's in his yard. He can crawl through it anytime he wants."

"No, he can not!" she shook her head, ears cast wide apart. "That ship belongs to us until we formally give him to the Compact Counsel. An all-inclusive internal tour never happens on a ship having a warleader. We are no longer his society and so you are technically no longer his warleader, but he still belongs to us. We defer to you in this matter. You have offered to show him the ship yourself, and after all the time I spent arranging transport to A'lon'aloop!"

Oh, no! He just stomped all over Melkorka's transport scheduling.

Delwyn explained the difficulty. Havalin gave an order to Yolandraha. She twitched an ear to activate her comm and sang a string of orders.

She waited a moment and then reported back to Havalin.

He looped his tail as he spoke with Phelindra.

"Havalin says we have a priority travel authorization to A'lon'aloop anytime you need it," the Eldest Huntress told him.

Delwyn nodded and turned to Melkorka. "Do you want to come and see what we flew back to Nikkiolo in?"

Everyone watched Melkorka. Phelindra had been there before, but others had not and hoped for a glimpse inside.

Melkorka could not refuse without looking like a coward. She was not frightened, but she was not about to give anyone a chance to doubt her courage either.

"Yes, I will come, but we cannot stay long. There are many things we must do before you may come to Elleio, and those things await us on A'lon'aloop."

"I know, and I'm ready," Delwyn said. He missed the rainforest scenery aboard his ship and hoped A'lon'aloop had it. He was tired. Waiting for medical clearance turned out about as exhausting as doing nothing over long hours. Sleeping when not physically tired made him even more tired, more irritable.

"Let's go," he said.

Aboard the Ni'zakhonii ship, Havalin spent a lot of time in the brig. He paced off the distance from the brig hatch to the security pod, from the pod to the observation ledge. Then he climbed down the stairs into the bay and paced a diagonal across the compartment.

Delwyn walked Havalin through the knife fight from where he had jumped from the ledge onto a Lizard soldier and from there to where he threw the last knife.

Havalin stared at the heavy throwing knife tied to Delwyn's left thigh.

"Knife break?" he asked Delwyn as he pointed at the metal blade.

"This knife? No. This is a combat knife," he clarified.

Delwyn half listened to the comments passing between Yolandraha and Melkorka, distracted by the curious question.

Melkorka and Lindredha both bit back snarls. Phelindra willed herself to relax. Yolandraha had not been the first to comment about the missing adulthood volcanic glass knife. She had defended his honor aboard *Fearless*, and now she bragged to Yolandraha how Delwyn had fought with many knives during the battle and attested to his blade skill.

They walked through dim stinking tunnels to the bridge. There, Delwyn showed Havalin the crystal control matrix tables. He swapped crystals around in the bridge environmental console, bringing the lights up to full brilliance and then dimming then back down to normal.

Havalin smiled, nodded, and sang a complicated measure.

"He says you must give a thorough briefing before he can allow anyone into this ship. He thinks too much unknown lurks here to leave to guesswork and chance. Since we have learned so much already, we ought to help bring the research and analysis teams up to our level of competency," Phelindra translated.

"I'm okay with that, but we'll do it later. Right now we need to get over to A'lon'aloop, get some sleep, eat, and debrief them before I go to Elleio."

After three hours his guests had enough of breathing Lizard stink. Lindredha and Havalin managed quite well, but Melkorka, Yolandraha, and Mawrandredha all suffered from varying degrees of disorienting nausea.

They headed back through the airlock and into fresh air. Delwyn watched Yolandraha and Mawrandredha gasp at the fresh air in the research bay and wondered if they were going to fall and kiss the deck in relief.

Havalin conferred with his Mistress of the Tower, while Melkorka contacted Hlinlodyn and told her that Delwyn had ordered them to depart Wrathsee'a Anchorage for A'lon'aloop.

The females all managed dignified leave takings and tail brushings, but Havalin crushed Delwyn with affection. Mawrandredha sang a comment meant for Delwyn's ears alone. She turned and with Yolandraha's help hauled Havalin back into their territory.

"What did she sing under her breath to me?" he asked. "Something about time and him?"

"She said Havalin will spend hours talking about today," Phelindra said.

"Are you ready to leave?" he asked them.

"We have been ready to leave for hours!" Melkorka growled.

"Me too, let's go."

Thanks to Warleader Havalin's priority transport codes, Delwyn and his association soon found themselves aboard four bulk transports and heading for Elleio orbit and A'lon'aloop Naval Station.

8
A SONG OF WHISPERS

The A'lon'aloop Naval Station troop transport bay had no outer door or maybe the dock mistress had opened it long before the transports came into visual range. Lime-green light flickered as the ships passed through the transparent atmospheric force field seal and glided across an aquamarine ocean and over a bright yellow sandy beach. The bay looked like a sunny day at a seaside park.

The transports touched down onto rough-hewn slabs of rock and plugged into dockside service alcoves. Efficient heavy equipment silently moved cargo down a boulevard running between the seaside beach on one side and a heavy rainforest on the other.

"Go on, Delwyn," Melkorka urged. "Get out in front and rally the others to you."

Delwyn stepped out the troop transport hatch and walked to the edge of the uneven stone surface, turned, and stared down the transport's flank, past the beach, and out to sea.

Somewhere, on the horizon, the bay door hid behind the ocean view.

Activity ground to a halt in the busy bay.

Eyes turned on him, eyes everywhere, curious eyes belonging to people pausing what they were doing just to watch him. Melkorka preened. She was showing him off again.

Thoughts of Zalzadrin and her jokes came to mind. Melkorka's 'look at what I have' stance was vaguely insulting. He remembered when he brought Pixie, a childhood pet dog, to school show and tell. He wondered if Pixie had felt like he felt right now.

The bay's supervising mistress, a Warrior, joined them. She circled Delwyn with avid interest. Melkorka cleared her throat, a musical waa sound, and soon the two Warriors were jabbing fingers at each other.

Delwyn turned away from them and watched his occupational association disembark and make their slow way across the rough slabs to him.

Bay personnel resumed their work. Except for a few in skinsuit coveralls, they wore next to nothing. He was used to seeing Eyloni in their normal dress by now, and the maintenance coveralls worn by a passing Warrior brought straightjackets to mind.

Delwyn grinned at her. She stopped, sang a greeting, and circled around him just as the bay mistress had.

He'd sat through three hours on a 636,370-kilometer ride from Wrathsee'a Anchorage to A'lon'aloop without incident, and within ten minutes of arriving he already had two Warriors circling him. Oh, well. He was different, beyond their usual experience.

Delwyn eyed the shoreline. The bay easily held the volume of five warship combat deployment bays side-by-side. It wasn't a universal use bay, either. The landing slabs, service alcoves, and equipment were all designed to support this class of transport vessel.

Melkorka glided up to him. "Come on. We are distracting people."

"Where are we going?"

"Come," she said.

Melkorka led him across the boulevard and into the jungle. They walked through tall grass and brush. There was no heavy foliage in sight, which meant this area had a lot of open space with no inelegant station structures to hide.

Melkorka drifted off to her left. He followed her, and his association followed him. They were silent-stalking him. Bare feet brushed aside or stepped on golden and amber force field generated blades of grass as they prowled in silence. He was the noisy one, what little noise he did make. Like real grass, it caught between his toes like buckhorn did when walking through someone's overgrown lawn.

They walked under an elleiu tree, one leviathan of a tree. Shrouded with aerial roots, the thing towered above him eight hundred meters across and four hundred meters tall. Well over one hundred meters thick at the base, most of its width came from layers upon layers of cascading and overlapping fused aerial roots that grew from the lower branches down into the ground. Somewhere in the middle of all those root structures hid the tree's main trunk, itself fifty meters thick.

Melkorka led him through a cavernous tear in the root shroud that spanned ten people abreast and five times that high. Delwyn followed her through a short tunnel in the roots. Turning onto a gnarled, wooden, Swiss cheese looking passageway, she took everyone up through layers of twisted roots.

They emerged at last on the forest floor, where the dirt walkways were covered with flat river stones. Teal colored wood shavings covered the open ground between the stones. These shavings were real, not a holographic simulation. They smelled good, like new leather boots.

The Transport Bay Arrival and Departure Center had been designed to mimic ground level in an elleiu tree. Inside, polished apricot-colored wood marched up the insides of the immense semi-hollow space. The ceiling, walls, and floors grew out of countless polished woven roots that had an antique furniture quality to them. The branches and above-ground roots grew to form branching paths and enclosed caverns inside and up through the tree. The ground level was bigger than the environmental simulations aboard his ship.

"I didn't know elleiu trees grew so big."

"What? This?" Phelindra stepped up from behind him and gestured with her tail in a wide sweep around them. "Elleiu trees are mighty, and they have ground levels this size or greater. Everything here is accurate except for the exaggerated open space. If we were standing inside a living home tree right now, then you would see the trunk two hundred ells thick merging into the hanging roots above. The oldest aerial roots wrap around it, fusing to the trunk and to one another, before they too grow into the ground adding their support. Younger roots then grow down and around them, forming hollow chambers and paths allowing us to climb from the forest floor into the crown of the tree. All along the canopy branches roots grow down to make support columns and overhead structures. Much open space occurs between layers, but nothing quite as open as what you see here."

"What about the flat stones and wood shavings?"

"The ground within a tree is paved with stones everywhere foot traffic is heavy. The wood shavings cover exposed soil. The shavings are antiseptic and repel insects. The ground level is a common area, called the Hall of Voices in all inhabited elleiu trees. Meals are prepared there, people eat together there, and special meetings are held there," Phelindra said.

Melkorka led him up to a screen set into a knotty, wooden, polished, apricot colored, wall. The screen projected a three-dimensional view of A'lon'aloop, complete with a pointing arrow symbol, the classic 'you are here' sign.

A'lon'aloop Naval Station hovered in the screen like an ornamental candy dish on an antique tabletop. A tall spire grew out of the central hub, a disk-shaped hull. Five evenly spaced curved spokes sprouted around the central hub's mid-decks rim, each spoke connecting to its own, slightly smaller circular disk. Each secondary disk had its own five external mooring stations mounted equidistant around its mid-decks rim. The screen didn't display a stored image, either. It updated in real time. As he watched, a warship appeared on the screen's edge and crept toward a mooring station on this secondary hull.

The ship was a destroyer, the same class as Phalalin's ship.

Delwyn squinted at the tiny ship, unable to glimpse fine details. The ship might be Phalalin's, but even if it was he couldn't tell. The Coalition Fleet put ship names and designator numbers on port and starboard bows, but Compact ships had no numbers or letters marring their hulls, not even say'ta've pictographs. Instead, each ship displayed his own unique identity pattern made of antique gold leaflike panels. They climbed across the dorsal hull like vines growing up a brick building.

Phelindra watched the destroyer slide into a mooring station and frowned.

"Phalalin," she muttered.

"That's Phalalin's ship?" he asked.

"It is," she growled, a sibilant hiss.

Delwyn glanced at the old Hunter, alarmed. What grudge did she bear against Phalalin?

"You're unhappy. Why? We like Phalalin, don't we?"

Phelindra spun on her warleader and glared at him.

Her scent altered, even his nose could pick up the change. Had he never met Phelindra before, her intense stare would have made him flinch. He did know her though. She wasn't angry. She was frustrated, annoyed.

Delwyn sorted through the feelings her scent evoked in him until he found a childhood memory of Pixie standing between him and a stranger, growling.

"You think Phalalin and I are going to fight again? Put that notion out of your mind. My head isn't shoulder ballast, you know."

Phelindra's face brightened in relief as his words penetrated her instincts.

Kidahin's Uahua'asee'a Clan ran an oceanographic research fleet, and Phelindra had picked up a few words. She understood wet navy terminology. The idea of a male's head serving no other purpose but as ballast for his shoulders struck her as hysterically funny. She wrapped her tail around her waist and shook as haunting, rhythmic yapping rolled from her.

Delwyn shook his head in wonder. Hunters had an odd sense of humor, and they never laughed like this unless he was the butt of their jokes.

She was making quite a scene, too. Considering her age, the dignity she commanded, her behavior came off to him as unseemly.

For some reason he began to sweat.

"Have you taken leave of your senses?" Melkorka demanded.

"Don't glare at me like that. In case you haven't noticed, I'm not the one laughing herself into a fit. Why don't you ask Phelindra what's so damn funny!" he snapped.

Melkorka ground her brilliant white teeth, heaved a sigh, folded her arms under her breasts, and glared at him as though he was the cause of Phelindra's behavior.

Then it dawned on him, stupid and slow as he was, why Melkorka had spoken to him first and not Phelindra. *Hunter's Moon* was thousands of kilometers away, and Melkorka was no longer on ship's business. That meant Phelindra's senior military rank overshadowed everyone else in the transport bay. Outranked, they wouldn't think of interrupting the humorous moment she was sharing with her warleader without cause.

By the time he figured it out, Phelindra had recovered her wits, took in the faces around her, and knew she had made a spectacle of herself.

She needed to justify her behavior. She sang to them at length. When she stopped, silence hung on the air for all of five beats before her audience erupted with musical yapping.

People who didn't understand naval terms had the joke explained to them, and then they too joined in the laughter.

Delwyn felt the emotional thrust of their indulgent humor and let it wash over him.

Melkorka swallowed to moisten her dry throat and smiled. The common female maxim said that males were strange, but now they had another saying: a male's head served no purpose but as ballast for his shoulders.

"Come Delwyn, everyone is here. We must arrange quartering as soon as possible. Debriefing sessions scheduling comes next, and only those of us involved can participate. Everyone else may visit station facilities, the shops, the restaurants, and other sights. As with Wrathsee'a Anchorage, A'lon'aloop's ten outer disks are neutral territory, as are the outer levels of the central hub. The interior levels and the t'et are the territory of the station warleader and his occupational association. Nearly all A'lon'aloop is heavily forested. You will feel less exposed here than on Wrathsee'a Anchorage shipyard decks."

Melkorka turned and stalked off. People wandered off on their own into the forested secondary disk. Delwyn ran after Melkorka before she could leave him behind. When he caught up with her, she filled him in on station operations. A'lon'aloop Naval Station maintained geosynchronous orbit above Elleio. There were three identical stations in equidistant orbit but A'lon'aloop was the primary station. All three provided administrative services for the Compact Fleet, but they also tracked all orbital activity, observed all atmospheric aircraft traffic, and watched all oceangoing vessels. A'lon'aloop served as the Compact Fleet administrative center and admiralty. When a Compact survey mission had encountered humans for the first time mere months ago and escorted CECS *Alexandra Witze* into homespace, A'lon'aloop served as the counsellor station, the neutral meeting place where Captain Umma Lahiri received a formal ritual welcome on behalf of the Ten Tribes of Elleio.

A few months later, A'lon'aloop hosted the Coalition delegation and Ambassador Honorius Alphonse Harrison. Thank God Harrison wasn't here to screw things up. The man's provocative opinions had carried over into his body odor. His scent often brought Anlann and Seralin to a near furious boiling point. Delwyn knew just from their reactions how all Elleio would have reacted to the scent of the late Ambassador Harrison.

Delwyn missed Anlann and Seralin. They should be on Earth by now. Together they had told the Coalition Government they wouldn't talk with any human but Alan Dean Winters, Captain of CECS *Henri Edda*.

Delwyn had a hand in that, too. At Anlann's suggestion, Delwyn had Melkorka send a hyperlink green channel message to the Be'atika Senge, advising them to demand that the Coalition Government declare Captain Winters the acting Coalition ambassador. It turned out he needn't interfered. Harrison had already been rendered moot. But, then again, maybe Delwyn had been right. Who knew what idiot the Coalition Government might have sent in Harrison's stead.

Anlann's Earth assignment wasn't permanent. He was the warleader of *Surefooted*, and he had an occupational association of his own waiting for him to come home.

"Melkorka, is Anlann's warship moored here?"

She flipped an ear at him and nodded. "You wish to see *Surefooted*?"

"Sure if it's allowed."

"Of course it is. Come, he is moored at the fourth station in this hub."

Delwyn, his command mistresses, and several others drifted off down pastel red and orange trails. On the way, Delwyn noticed the heat climbing. "It's warm here," he complained to Phelindra.

"Yes," she said. "Our clan lives in the northern temperate rainforest of the La'huaset Tribal continent. Station temperatures follow the nearside tropical means. Had you gone into the rainforest preserve on Wrathsee'a Anchorage, you would have found it just as warm."

"Oh," he said.

The forest pathways were wider than those aboard ship. He looked around and back down the path. Several hundred people followed after him from a distance.

They hiked through open forests. Trails branched off, while others intersected the main path. From time to time people stepped off onto branching trails, while others popped out of forest cover and joined the main group. Other people joined them. The Eyloni territorial nature called to them first, but it was the female interest in anything male that triggered their interest in him.

The autonomy granted to the male gender by custom gave him free movement through the area. Station personnel approached him, brushed tails against him, encouraged his touch, and plagued Melkorka with questions.

More and more females pushed through the forest to see them as others drifted back into the bushes.

By the time they reached mooring station four, Delwyn had begun to notice members of his association coming and going in double fistfuls at a time.

"Why is everyone wandering around for? Tell them to take advantage of the free time while we have it," he complained to Phelindra.

The Eldest Huntress murmured a noncommittal series of notes. Delwyn did not have a need to know. Her society had important matters to attend to: reestablishing ties, reporting states of affairs, telling socially unattached females about Delwyn's availability, posting notices for replacement crew members from the northeastern La'huaset clans, and running other errands. All of them would play a part in proclaiming Delwyn's presence, character, and honor. They were making a showy display of support for him.

Trees thinned out and brush opened into a large meadow. A long, narrow, picture window running the length of the clearing hovered above the ground at shoulder level.

Delwyn stood back some distance from the huge portal and gazed into the star-filled blackness. The dock and mooring station stuck out from below the portal and off to the left. The destroyer's combat hull fit into the mooring cradle at least a third of the way, beginning from the bow and heading down the length of the ship.

Surefooted could be described as a stripped-down version of *Hunter's Moon.* He lacked the outrigger weapons platforms of an assault warship and had smaller combat and command hulls. A work crew stood on the dorsal engineering hull near the twin cylindrical gravity lensing armature housings. Delwyn watched the crews work for a while before an obvious question popped into his head.

"Why aren't they refitting the ship in the shipyard?"

"They do not need an enclosed repair dock, its life support, or its heavy equipment. He has no hull breaches and no extensive hull damage. They are completing a refit. By now they have installed new jump drive armatures. They are taking their time tuning the armatures. Once tuning is completed, they will spool up the armatures for testing. After testing, they will make several FTL jump trials, but they will prefer to have Anlann back before then."

"Why?"

"They do not like taking their warship anywhere without their warleader," Melkorka said. She met his eyes and made sure she had his full attention. "Neither do I."

By now they had stopped, and whenever people noticed a large group lingering for too long, they got defensive.

The females surrounding Delwyn heard the sounds before he did: feet dragging through the grass. Phelindra had done that once on Ibeetu, and Melkorka had taken it as an insult.

Delwyn followed their gazes to the forest edge, where a large group of females was pouring into the clearing.

The lead Hunter stomped up to Melkorka, jabbed a finger under her nose and opened her mouth to snap a challenge.

Phelindra stepped aside, giving the Hunter a clear view.

She froze in her challenge.

"Delwyn!" the Hunter's musical voice stammered.

"Ee matika ou sun su tek," he sang in a deep baritone.

The formal greeting, and he had delivered it flawlessly. The new arrivals sang questions on top of questions or they just introduced themselves to him.

The two groups mingled, reaffirming social and hierarchical ties with song for public matters and battle language for hiding hierarchy matters from a certain male.

Feeling left out of the reunion, Delwyn turned away from the observation portal and gazed wistfully back into the red-dominated, yellow-trimmed orange jungle.

Leaves moved.

The air was still.

He blinked, doubting his eyes. Hiding in this cover, an Eyloni would be invisible. Their skin colors blending them into the forest cover.

There it was again! Pale yellow in shape, a profile view of a person's head as seen from behind and to the side.

Delwyn's heart sank as he saw a towheaded blonde figure.

It was Valerie, his oldest daughter!

A *flashback*? He hadn't suffered a PTSD-related hallucination in weeks, not since a few days after meeting Anlann and Seralin for the first time.

Delwyn drifted farther away from the busy reunion and deeper into the heavy brush, his eyes riveted on the pale-yellow shape.

The girl's head wasn't moving, and he hesitated. She was either a figment resurrected by some PTSD trigger, or he was seeing coincidental shades and shapes on some jungle leaf. He couldn't be relapsing, not now. Determined to prove himself right, Delwyn closed on the pale ghost, intent on confronting it head on.

The *Surefooted* females wanted to hear about everything that had happened between Anlann and Delwyn. Starved for any first-hand accounts of their warleader and his protectress, they eagerly listened to what bits and pieces Kidahin and Melkorka could provide. When they turned to include Delwyn in the telling, he was already several hundred ells from them. Phelindra, far behind him, was busy keeping an eye on everyone and fielding the questions people kept firing at her.

Several pairs of large amber eyes watched Delwyn stalking the deep jungle cover.

"Delwyn, *stop*!" Phelindra yelled.

Her warning came far too late.

Delwyn rushed the small form, touching her shoulder as Phelindra's warning reached his ears.

The Comari spun on him, lightning quick.

She focused on the strange male.

Her eyes sought his. Who was he?

He was different. He smelled different.

He was a male, obviously. Females associated with him. Their scent markings reeked from him.

She opened her inward-focused mind to him. Giving him her undivided attention was hard, mentally trying. She rose from her low crouch and paced a slow, deliberate circle around him, careful to remain outside his one ell radius personal space.

He had no tail.

Curious.

He had no forest shades on his skin.

More curious.

She stepped up to him and touched his arm. His skin felt cool and smooth, not warm and textured like hers.

Most curious.

She stepped back, pricked her ears at him, and exhaled a soft whispering query.

She waited, but he did not sing a reply. Odd. His scent however, his pheromones, sang of stories both happy and sad. A gaping hole yawned from him. He needed her, yet he did not covet her. He had not sought her out because she was Comara. That was a relief. He did not smell opposed to her either, which she found strangely attractive.

He did not fear her, and he most certainly should have.

She would soon reach her full adolescence, but now was not the time. She did not yet feel the call to choose a male to protect and defend forever.

She smelled other females nearby. They watched from a respectful distance. Their scents filled the air with apologies for his behavior.

The male squatted down to her height, his eyes level with hers.

She stared back at him and weighed her options.

Delwyn waited, unsure what to do next. The resemblance between the Comari and a twelve-year-old human girl was uncanny. No wonder he had mistaken her for Valerie. The Comari's long blonde hair—not the fluorescent orange or fire engine red ringleted locks of other Eyloni—fell to her waist. Her ears, as flexible and expressive as any Eyloni's, pricked through the cornsilk strands. She had the face of a Warrior combined with some almost human features, but she also had the angular nose and jaw of a Hunter.

Delwyn quickly searched his memory for information about the Comara. They remained in an adolescent state throughout their long lives. They never participated in adulthood ordeals or ceremonies, yet custom considered them adults from birth. They couldn't speak. Kidahin had described them as savants, veritable geniuses within a narrow focal range. Oh, and custom excused any death they might cause.

Comforting that.

Comara courtesy was perfunctory, and they ignored cultural privacy standards. Other Eyloni saw Comara as the air. They came and went without giving offense because they kept their own counsel and rarely interacted with anyone not Comara, except for the males they chose.

Comara minds existed in their own reality. Kidahin had described them once as living partly in the Oyya Web of the spirits, their bodies merely ties to the physical world. They preferred to live in their own minds and experience the world around them as detached observers.

Comara wore the same neckwear and waistwear common to all females. This one was extremely fit, and her muscular development betrayed features of Hunter hard-body wiriness. She wore no knife, which made her appear naked in a culture of adult females and their adulthood knives.

The Comari shook herself, came to a decision, and stepped up to him again.

She rubbed her nose against his cheek and then sprang back into the forest cover.

Delwyn smelled a hint of the Comari's intense inquisitive nature as she darted away. As he watched her leave, she paused to glance back at him again before she disappeared into the heavy forest.

Phelindra, followed by Melkorka and several others, started shouting at him, their furious voices blending into a dissonant cacophony.

"Did I not warn you about the Comara?" Melkorka asked, less a rhetorical question and more a frightened demand.

"You were fortunate," Phelindra grumbled, "that she chose to see you."

"Chose to see me?" he echoed.

"Yes, chose. Comara are inward seeing. It takes an effort for them to interact with people. When they reach the same age as a Hunter or Warrior coming into her season for the first time, they seek out suitable males that need them."

"So she's not mature. I thought all Comara were considered adults from birth."

"No, she is not mature. Comara have adult status from birth by custom, but they still have to grow into physical maturity," Phelindra snapped. "Had she been with her chosen male, then she might have killed you for being threatening, and we cannot even challenge her actions through the hierarchies."

Phelindra grew more and more upset with each passing second. She had nearly failed him. As his Protectress, his safety belonged to her.

Everyone knew about the Comara. People learned early in life how to treat Comara and how to behave around them. Infants learned about Comara from the Comara themselves. Comara tolerated infants, even played with them. Something about the infant mind resonated with them. All clans had Comara members, and infants learned from scent what Comara liked and disliked and how to prowl alongside them without giving offense.

Delwyn did not know, having never been raised among them. No Comari prowled the trails of *Hunter's Moon*, and so he had no practical experience in dealing with the deadly females.

The *Surefooted* group stood around in an uncomfortable circle, horrified. Delwyn had not acted with reckless abandon. His scent told them so, but no male—*no one*—just walked up to and touched a Comari.

Melkorka breathed a sigh in relief and thanked the spirits. Delwyn's blissful ignorance had translated into his scent as guileless honesty, a mindset the Comara approved. Recovering from their surprise, the *Surefooted* females crowded around Delwyn and, through Melkorka, asked him to sing songs to them about Anlann and the adventures they shared aboard *Henri Edda* and on Ibeetu.

He really had no choice, and so he sang stories, musically accompanied by his occupational association. Not given permission, the *Surefooted* females did not join in but listened as tales fell from his lips. Delwyn sang about his first meeting with Anlann and Seralin, how he had almost ran them down on his way out of the amidships galley.

That provoked long spats of musical laughter.

He shared stories about Anlann and Seralin's visits to his quarters, and how they defended his decision to foster Kidahin. He wisely skipped Anlann's part in advising him how to proceed in singing the Death Song ritual for his association's battle dead. That story would insult them as it would reveal Anlann as poking his tail into the business of another warship.

The crowd grew as more *Hunter's Moon* females drifted in from the rainforest.

His deep voice swept over them, and everyone enjoyed the impromptu social sing-along. Anlann's females rocked from side to side, tails swaying, eyes closed, as they savored both the music and its subject matter.

Twenty ells away, still hidden in the forest, soft whispering sighs came from the preadolescent Comari as she hummed along with him.

Delwyn wound up the concert by recalling the good-byes he shared with Anlann and Seralin just before he ordered Melkorka to jump the ship out of Ibeetu orbit.

The *Surefooted* females reacted to his singing by sharing brushes and touches with his association. They danced in patterns. They closed around him but never quite touched him. After all the constant physical contact his crew share with him on a regular basis, Delwyn found it odd, almost a snub, for them not to share even one coy brush or two with him.

"Delwyn wants to meet with Phalalin and he has just arrived. He will soon complete docking procedures, so we must leave. We wish you well and hope to meet with you again, whether here on Elleio, or with the spirits. Farewell."

Delwyn rolled his eyes at Melkorka for making him the heavy, the excuse for their leaving. Her ritual departing farewell was the familiar one Anlann and Seralin had sung to him before he ordered his ship to jump out of the Nikkiolo star system.

By the time they had drifted away from the observation portal, almost everyone else had melted into the forest except for a core group of some two hundred and fifty people, including the supervising mistresses.

Melkorka knew where they were going, and she made sure Delwyn walked beside and about a half-step ahead of her. She looped her tail about his waist and gave him occasional subtle tugs or pushes to guide him down the right forest trails.

His curiosity finally got to him. "I hope I don't sound impolite, but why did Anlann's females brush and touch you and not me?"

Melkorka's bare feet rooted to the ground, her tail yanking him into her embrace so fast their close-quarters followers nearly slammed into them.

"You find them more appealing than us?" Melkorka demanded.

His nose filled with an acrid smell.

Jealousy.

The others picked up on the scent, and they added their own measure to the sour odor.

"No, I do not. Did I say I did? You're always telling me how important casual personal contact is, yet they left me out."

The honest confusion in his scent restrained Melkorka from lashing out. She swallowed the bile back down her throat and explained.

"We share physical contact with others, this is true. Nobody cares, within reason, who you want to tail twine with. You know about occupational and personal associations. Some or all of us can belong to your personal association. Lindredha associates with you, but she does not belong to our society, which by definition is also your occupational association. By custom females do not join into associations that have other warleaders as their focus."

"But Lindredha is Wrathsee'a Anchorage's Mistress of the Dock," he objected.

"Yes, but she does not associate with Havalin either personally, or professionally. The Mistress of the Tower does. There are males throughout the shipyard and Anchorage. They are here on A'lon'aloop, too. They serve as male focus points for their own occupational associations."

"You mean *sire cairns*, don't you?"

Melkorka nodded, impressed. "Yes, as you were sire cairn on the Nikkiolo moon before we made you our warleader."

"So that's how I could command an Eyloni strike force on Ibeetu."

"Correct," Melkorka said.

"Then how could you sit in the command center, before I was warleader, and obey my order to fire on the Ni'zakhonii spy probe?"

"On this matter we need never speak about again!" Melkorka snapped and stalked off into the forest.

Delwyn kept his mouth shut and followed her darting tail through the leafy jungle growth.

Melkorka's brooding silence felt out of place. He settled on a tune and started humming, trying to goad her into singing with him.

He didn't have to try very hard. Melkorka soon added her voice to his, and the others soon followed suit. They sang along with him until he broke out of the heavy forest and into a clearing. Across the orange and yellow grasses another rectangular portal, a flat black monolith measuring four ells tall and nine ells wide, floated in the air just like the one framing Anlann's ship. This one showed Phalalin's motionless ship from a starboard profile view. The mooring station had already extended docking clamps onto the ship's forestation, the section connecting the destroyer's combat hull to his command hull. Figures were steadily moving past the mooring tower windows as he watched.

"Hey, people are walking down a gateway and into the station on the deck below us. Why don't they just teleport aboard?" he asked Melkorka.

"They cannot. A'lon'aloop lacks the facilities and space to permit large scale translations. Ships rotate shore party translation schedules so everyone has an opportunity to visit the station without straining resources. Phalalin has not docked here for repairs or resupply. He came here to see you on neutral territory, to his association's great relief I might add. They will want to meet you, too."

Delwyn wondered if Amindaldra had forgiven him and Phalalin for fighting. Phelindra hadn't.

"Where *is* Phelindra?" he wondered aloud.

"She is probably gathering security reports from warleader special security. She is the Mistress of the Watch, after all."

"Yeah? We're not aboard ship, so what concerns can she have on a station that I'm sure has its own security services?"

Melkorka snugged her tail tight around him and pulled him into her, a sign of her true heartfelt affection. "The Mistress of the Watch supervises warship security, but her title implies she Watches. This means she watches you. Your station in the command center is called the Warleader's Watch not because you watch over us. We call it that because we Watch you there. Where

Phelindra Watches you. Had she not become your Protectress, she would still be the Mistress of the Watch."

"She wasn't Kalinn's Protectress, was she?" Delwyn asked.

Melkorka shook her head, her ears flattening at the sad memory. "No. Had she been, she would have died at his side. By becoming your Protectress, she doubles her duties and responsibilities."

"How? It's still me whether I'm in the command center or somewhere else on the ship."

"A protectress's duties require her near you for all but brief times. If she cannot, then she places females who have given blood oaths assuring her they will keep you safe."

"Oh, you mean the ones with the green strands in their rank earrings?"

Melkorka politely ignored him, wondering herself just where Phelindra had wandered off to.

Phelindra stood with her back to the group, looking back down the trail they had just been on.

"Something is amiss, Mistress?" a green-webbed Hunter asked, alert.

Phelindra tested the air and frowned. "I do not know. I do not think so. All these people, and Delwyn so new to them, makes me feel as if my tail drags on the ground for them to stomp on. It bothers me."

Phalalin, stepping off a side trail and onto the main path, spotted Phelindra, smelled her jumbled feelings, and cocked his ears at her in jest. "Do not tell me you have misplaced Delwyn somewhere in this jungle."

Phalalin meant his flip comment as a slight tail yank to smooth over any lingering resentment she might have over her visit to his ship, but he didn't expect her explosive reply.

"So you think you are a funny male, do you? Take your funny male self out of my sight!"

Phalalin flinched and stared at her in stupefied wonder. What was twisting her tail? Was she still nursing a grudge over the fighting exercise? Delwyn's injuries had not been serious and easily healed.

Phelindra's scent alerted him to her distress. Caution and tact were needed now. Females protected males, and Phelindra's worry made her dangerous.

"What about Delwyn?" he prompted her.

"I am sorry, Phalalin. I cannot shake the feeling I am being stalked. I cannot rid myself of it," she confessed.

He was about to ask her who would stalk Delwyn here, but that was a nonsensical question. Every female on this station would stalk him. He was a male and new to them. "He has not violated someone's privacy has he? Committed some discourtesy? Intruded into hierarchy business?"

"That depends. Delwyn forced direct contact onto an immature Comari!"

"What? Is he well?" he asked shocked.

"Yes, but he should have known better. She could have claimed an insult to her privacy."

Uh-oh. "What did Delwyn have to say about that?"

"Nothing! What could he say? He has no experience with the Comara," Phelindra snarled.

"Yes, yes, I know. He did not try to attract her, did he?"

"No, he did not. She resembles one of his near-daughters the Ni'zakhonii ate."

"Oh? And her scent? How did she smell after he approached her?" Phalalin pressed.

Phelindra twisted his question into knots, looping her tail in slow circles. "Curious," she conceded.

"There, you see? Delwyn is different, and his difference caught her notice, nothing more."

Phelindra and Phalalin turned together and headed back to the group.

Watching them from under deep forest cover, a lone Comari sang breathless whispers to herself.

Phelindra and Amindaldra fell into a sophisticated and interminable battle language exchange about the Comari incident. Comara did not journey off-world often, even rarer for a preadolescent to go off world. They speculated. Comara went anywhere they pleased and this one had come here. No one dared to stop her, either. Battle language gave Comara a voice, and their pheromones made their intentions clear. If she went to a conveyance station demanding translation, then only a fool mistress of conveyance refused her. The mistress might wonder about it but would send the Comari swiftly on her way. It was not her business.

Comara knew what they were doing. They always had some purpose in mind, even if to the casual observer they seemed to tailchase their lives away.

Comara had their own hierarchy, only one, and it sat between the Be'atika Senge and the A'tayotan. The Be'atika Senge had Comara members, but the A'tayotan did not. Called *Ti'ratni*, the Comara hierarchy exercised absolute veto power over both the A'tayotan and the Be'atika Senge. They did not exercise that power often, preferring to listen, watch, and wait.

Phalalin and Phelindra found Delwyn surrounded by Phalalin's occupational association. They were brushing against and exchanging touches with the *Hunter's Moon* females.

Delwyn, never one for crowds, felt like a man trying to push his way out a stadium exit at the end of a soccer match. His one break came in how people moved about. For all their need to touch, Eyloni had odd personal space issues. They danced around him. As they danced, they drifted aside as he headed for Phalalin and the large rectangular observation portal he was leaning against.

"Greetings, Delwyn. I am happy to see you again, and not under so stressful terms this time. I heard you had some excitement earlier," he deadpanned.

"Yeah, a curiosity that resolved itself." *And that is an understatement you can't possibly miss smelling.* Delwyn recognized his error the moment he touched the Comari. After everyone had calmed down, he replayed the encounter again in his head.

He'd seen pictures of Comara during the lessons Hervorallin had given him about the three female phenotypic genders. The physical combat skills Comara possessed were legendary. A Comari retained an infant's deep red, almost black, sharp fingernails and toenails. She could punch between ribs and pull out organs, or she could rake with her centimeter long, sharp beveled nails. Comara could climb near vertical uneven surfaces, trees and cliffs, with ease. He hadn't expected to see one of the rare females on a naval station.

But the Comari he met didn't seem to be the killing machine Hervorallin had described. She was curious, and her curiosity reminded him of Princess.

Kidahin had said a Comari formed a bond with her chosen male similar to the ones males shared with their near-daughters. His bond with Princess would mellow out as she got older but never fade away. A Comari bond remained fierce and strong throughout life. The bond drew on the mind of a willful adolescent, and not an infant's instinctive needs.

Delwyn sighed, relieved. His bond with Princess was palpable. He felt it now, and it reinforced itself whenever he came within nose range of her. But he had felt no second emotional surge, not even an inkling that the Comari had established a pheromonal-empathy link with him. He put the matter aside and walked with Phalalin through the crowd, stopping at times to hear courteous introductions. They led a parade, and Delwyn began wondering where they would end up when all at once he found himself all but abandoned.

So did Phalalin.

"Where did they go?" Delwyn asked.

"Hmm? Oh, them? They have wandered off together. They are reaffirming hierarchy standings and probably gossiping about us. Females love to gossip about males."

"Yeah, Anlann said something about that," Delwyn said. Only his command center mistresses remained behind, and a similar number hovered near Phalalin, his command mistresses had stayed behind, too.

"We," Phalalin said, sweeping his tail to include his group, "are headed for a sleep-tree. You must join us. In fourteen hours, you and I must brief the Be'atika Senge. You will have Warpact status over the meeting. I will give personal testimony concerning the hyperlink contact I had with the taleteller

Harrison, my arrival in Nikkiolo star system, Melkorka's sahagan warning not to interrupt, jumping into honorable escort point off your warship's bow, informing the other males they were no longer needed …"

Delwyn had forgotten about them. Phalalin's original mission had been to bring a group of qualified males from which Kidahin was supposed to choose a new warleader. One of them should have been *Hunter's Moon's* warleader, not him. Harrison had tried to convince Phalalin to *order* Melkorka to arrest Delwyn, and in the process displayed his ignorance of both male and warship autonomy. Once Phalalin and Verikaralee realized Harrison meant to assault the honor of a clan male, they had been furious.

Thinking about Verikaralee summoned her presence. Phalalin's Mistress of the Ship whipped an insolent pons under Phalalin's nose as she embraced Delwyn, wrapping her tail around him and hugging him with overflowing joy.

"Delwyn, I meet you! I am Verikaralee O'un Tu La'huaset Eyloni. We are family!" she sang, crushing him.

He chinned around the Hunter's neck and shoulder to make eye contact with Melkorka and smiled. "I thought you said warleaders …"

"… must have time to renew family ties?" she finished. "Of course you will have time to meet your clan. Immediate and extended family contacts are important, and you cannot expect warleader ties to interrupt family matters," Melkorka said.

"No, you're right," he agreed, hugging a persistent Verikaralee.

Three other hopefuls, all Warriors, drew up to him as Verikaralee broke the embrace and invited them to continue where she had left off.

Unlike Verikaralee, they didn't understand a word of Coalition standard, but they were just as enthusiastic and accepting of Delwyn as Verikaralee had been. After introductions had been made, Phalalin picked up where he had left off.

"There are several people from our clan you must meet soon enough. As to the briefing, you will control the rhythm of the discussion. You accomplished Kalinn's mission. You have Warpact command over the briefing session because you won the victory and have information that nobody may challenge."

Odd, Delwyn frowned. Since when did the subordinate briefing the government also hold command over it?

"Begin the briefing however you want, but do not say anything about you becoming warleader of the captured ship or your warship. That is never their business."

"What if they ask?"

"They will not. To do so is bad manners, dishonorable. If they did, your occupational association would raise a point of honor with their hierarchies, and those hierarchies would object to the Be'atika Senge."

Phalalin's words greatly relieved Delwyn's mind. He had been living with the false assumption that the government had a final veto over the crew's choice of warleader.

"Okay, then what?"

"You will explain how you gained control over the ship's engine and navigation systems. That means sooner or later you have to take them to the analysis bay on Wrathsee'a Anchorage and explain ship operations to them. You cannot do so until the ship is decommissioned, of course."

"Decommissioned? That thing was never commissioned in the first place," Delwyn shrugged.

Phalalin glanced at Delwyn, confused. "They made you warleader of the ship, yes?" He looked at Phelindra for confirmation.

"Yes, we named Delwyn warleader. He gave me one of his long throwing knives as a sign of his choice as Mistress of the Ship." She scowled at Delwyn. He was making things unnecessarily difficult again.

"That's true, but how does that make an enemy ship commissioned in the Compact Fleet?" Delwyn asked.

"Ships are first commissioned when a female society receives the warleader of their choosing because no warship fights for the Compact without a warleader. You captured the ship and gave it to the forty-two in your surface action assault force. They made you their warleader. Then you chose Phelindra as Mistress of the Ship. That makes the ship commissioned in the Compact Fleet. When you became warleader of *Hunter's Moon*, you ceased being the captured ship's warleader because a male cannot be warleader of more than one ship. Female territorial nature would never permit it."

"So what do I do, ritually relinquish the ship?"

"Yes, you may, if you have not done so. The assault force must then relinquish their ownership to the Compact Counsel before analysis may begin."

"I did that already. I'm sure of it," he said, giving Phelindra a befuddled look.

"You gave the ship to us, and not to the Compact Counsel. You hold him in our name, which means you can return to Wrathsee'a, demand him back, and pilot him back into our warship if you wanted and they could not stop you. That is why Havalin broke no custom by visiting the ship without the proper rituals. You hold him for us, but you are no longer his warleader."

That was insane. No private person could own a global military asset. Had they flown the LAC to *Henri Edda*, it would have been cordoned off on the flight deck by security, taken to Daedalia Planum Naval Shipyards, and if Delwyn Marsch ever got within a thousand klicks of it, security would have him gunned down like a dog no questions asked.

"Okay, how long does it take to decommission a ship?"

"Not long. You take your assault force back to him. You sing your reasons for decommissioning him. They agree with you, which is necessary if you do not want them to kill you. Then they renounce ownership and give it to the Be'atika Senge. Once completed, he ceases being a ship and becomes an it, mere equipment. Equipment may be dismantled, but a ship is considered a male person, and no research team will remove so much as a screw so long as the ship remains a he," Phalalin said.

"Wait, what was that about killing me?" Delwyn asked.

"Hmm? Oh, I understand. This is no joke. You are warleader of a ship until his society says you are not. No male resigns his warleader status. To walk away from your occupational association, your ship's society, without their leave is a slander against them. A warleader who walks away from an active warship also declares his society unworthy to fight alongside of. They would kill a male for the mortal slaying of their honor, a wound so deep no other male would accept them into their own associations, personal or occupational. Always remember that we males are a small minority, but what we say or do is given great weight and sometimes lasting and binding effect," Phalalin said.

"About this sleep-tree, Phalalin? I'm getting tired myself."

Phalalin, nodded, hesitated a moment, and sang a short measure to the forest.

"I told my association to arrange a place for us. There may be some crowding. A sleep-tree does not receive an entire ship's complement often, but if you do not mind sharing?"

Delwyn grunted a negative. "Not me, but I'd better ask." He turned to Melkorka. "What do you think?"

Melkorka sang a short beat to her command mistresses. They in turn sang to one another until they came to a consensus.

"Sleep will do you some good," she said.

Delwyn shrugged an affirmative. "Lead on, Phalalin. I am at your disposal."

The group pushed through the rainforest until they intersected a pathway. Phalalin led them through brush, around trees, and under low branches and hanging vines until the path narrowed into a series of branching trails.

The females half escorted, half followed the two males. They prowled by themselves or in small groups, depending on whether they were Hunters or Warriors.

Delwyn loved watching them. They disliked large gatherings. For all their communal touching and greeting, they preferred to break up into smaller groups and swirl in and out of a common focal point: him and Phalalin. The solitary Hunters always returned to the group before heading off into the forest again, reminding Delwyn of a flock of black birds swooping above wheat fields.

Phelindra explained the behavior. When together, they greeted one another in large groups. When they worked the forest, they preferred much smaller numbers.

Jungle survival, Delwyn guessed. Crowds distracted, made noise, and muddled sign and scent.

Up ahead, a soccer field wide tree trunk stood in the midst of jungle cover. Several open boles surrounded its base, and the group broke up and entered through some of them. They climbed through vaulting aerial root chambers until they stepped into a hollow wooden area.

"Come, Delwyn," Phalalin said. "We must arrange sleeping space and wake up time. You will want to eat before we leave for the briefing session."

Hell, I want to eat now. Maybe I can order room service?

Phelindra wrinkled her nose at him. "Food? I do not smell food here, and if I cannot then I know you cannot."

Damn her nose! He had to learn somehow to control strong feelings. His scent made his mind an open book for them.

"I'm hungry. That tapioca pudding stuff didn't stick to my ribs."

"Stick to …? Of course *e'bato* does not stay inside you for long. That dish provides calories but not much in the way of protein or fiber. You always choose quick energy foods, just like an infant."

Delwyn grumbled at her kid-and-candy shot and pushed thoughts of food aside. Eyloni needed between three and four Earth hours sleep out of an average eleven hour day. Would they eat first, or sleep first?

"Come. We have made sleeping arrangements. Come," Melkorka teased.

Delwyn and Phalalin exchanged glances, shrugged, and followed. Verikaralee and Melkorka waggled fingers as they drifted deeper into the tree.

"What are they going on about now?" Delwyn asked.

"I have no idea," Phalalin replied. "Sharing secrets, probably."

Phelindra whistled in Delwyn's ear, a giggle.

"What's so funny?"

Phelindra ignored him and signed to Amindaldra instead.

They shared whispering musical snickers as they climbed through the cathedral-like root shrouds.

"And you called me funny?" Phalalin asked Phelindra.

Both protectresses glared at him, flipped ears to include Delwyn in their assessment, and then went back to their signing.

Folded and twisted roots opened out into split-leveled multi-tiered lofts. They were long, narrow and they curved up through the tree.

The knotted wood walls glowed with the familiar mellow candle-in-the-pumpkin golden light. Wall art made from braided vines and flowers hung from the walls everywhere. They reminded Delwyn of hanging spiral remnant rugs and woven pine needle baskets. Sleeping cushions covered the smooth, uneven floors of each side niche and cubbyhole. Some sleeping spaces were larger than others. Staking out sleep territory, Phalalin and his command mistresses took over a small area, while Melkorka, her command mistresses, and the remainder of the crew took over the sleep-tree.

The place was huge, a large hotel, but how did this area sleep so many? His questing mind must have caused his body odor to change, because Melkorka offered an explanation.

"Remember, we are not in a real elleiu tree. Elleiu trees are much larger, much more varied than this structure. Here, each level and tier branches off into its own necessary and skyscape view. An elleiu tree holds thousands, but not in cramped spaces like these."

He followed as she led him through adjoining levels that branched off into more lofts and tiers.

"We have all but filled this sleep-tree to capacity. Because *Fearless* suffers no damage, it would be impolite for Phalalin to waste the sleep-tree spaces here. Except for his command mistresses, his association will rotate back to their warship. We will remain here until all meetings and briefings have been completed. Then we will go with you and meet with the Compact Counsel."

Delwyn tried to listen but kept nodding off to her soothing rhythmic voice. He slumped onto a cushion, spread eagle, and drifted off into deep sleep.

"Finally," Phelindra sang. "You should have let him lay down. He would have fallen asleep long ago."

"I was talking him to sleep," Melkorka objected. "He would have kept going if I had not dulled his senses with the obvious."

Phelindra smiled. "No, you have only to lay with him, wrap your tail around him and he will talk for a few minutes before falling asleep."

Melkorka glared at her. Phelindra would know. She slept with him all the time. They had been too busy to arrange communal sleeping with him.

Melkorka eyed her, speculating.

"You want to join us?" Phelindra asked "We have plenty of room. Invite a few others. Kidahin, Hervorallin and Princess, and …"

"Where is Hervorallin?" Melkorka wondered aloud.

"Here!" Hervorallin sang out as she climbed through the entrance and crawled up through the root-shrouded passageway, a sleeping Princess clamped to her back.

"Where have you been?" Melkorka asked.

"Making arrangements back home. As you know, I am responsible for giving the clan formal notice that Princess and Delwyn are coming. You cannot believe the competition raging down there, how many clans want to meet Delwyn. We will have to beat them off with our tails."

"When are they expecting you?" Phelindra asked.

"In a few days. The clan elders have been having go at the Tribal Elders since our arrival. The Elders are pressing the Be'atika Senge and the A'tayotan for details, which is like trying to sing up the tail of the Compact Counsel itself."

They listened with avid interest to the news Hervorallin brought from the O'un Tu Clan as they laid together, tails twined in friendship. Some already fast asleep.

Kidahin, Melkorka, Hervorallin, and Phelindra laid together around Delwyn. His scent woke Princess, and she jumped from her mother's back to the floor and crawled across his chest grumbling to herself over having to share him with so many others.

They smiled at her grumbling, snuggled together, and fell asleep.

Four Tyreniioroneo Standard hours asleep felt like no hours asleep for Delwyn. He needed a good six to eight Earth hours sleep, not an hour and forty minutes.

Energetic females frolicking about with ample energy didn't help matters. At least he always woke up instantly, a soldier's habit. To survive the Eyloni workday, he had to take naps on and off during the day.

"Melkorka has received a summons from the A'tayotan. They have called for a status inquiry in four hours. We should get something to eat, while we have a chance," Phelindra said.

Eyloni snacked throughout the day, and so finding food wasn't hard. Some visited the mess halls in this part of the station, while many others including Delwyn tried the various restaurants. No matter where they ate, the shops were not noisy or crowded, and they were accorded the courtesy of a quiet meal.

Delwyn chose from the dishes he knew and liked, but Kidahin tried to ply him with other suggestions.

Melkorka wasn't as subtle. "Eat that!" she snapped. "It has fiber and protein and will keep you full when you are briefing the A'tayotan."

She sounded just like his mother. Funny, but Kidahin and Melkorka fussed over his eating choices, but Phelindra let him eat whatever he wanted.

The meal didn't last long. On the ship people served their own meals from a smorgasbord of choices. So it was here as well. They were expected to serve themselves and clean up afterwards when they finished.

Personal responsibility counted as a constant virtue among them, as did courtesy to others. An Eyloni eating a meal on Earth would have been scandalized to find someone serving meals to her. Leaving the table dirty after a meal would have horrified her.

They ate with little small talk. This Delwyn understood as well. Eyloni maintained communal ties, always together, always sharing. Dining, among Eyloni, meant eating and not talking. The joy of being together negated a need to talk through meals, and but for table courtesies, they said nothing.

Besides, smacking lips and spitting food ran high on the list of disgusting table manners among them, higher than a finicky mother telling her children to chew with their mouths closed.

After eating, Phalalin, Amindaldra, and Verikaralee led Delwyn, Melkorka, Phelindra, Hervorallin and Princess, and Kidahin off on a walk through a shopping center.

Stores and shops were scattered throughout the vaulting maze of fused roots. A curving irregular spread of shops branched out like individual grapes on an inverted bunch, some above, others below. Shoppers got to them by taking twisting paths up, down, or sideways. Just like aboard ship, no escalators or lifts hid in jungle cover ready to take people elsewhere. Eyloni enjoyed walking.

They met more people going about their business, but people shopping here acted nothing like people shopping on Earth.

No one minded her own business. They greeted each other, went out of their way to do so, even if only for a few minutes. Eyloni didn't say common human social pleasantries such as 'good morning' or 'hi'. The encounter itself made such greetings unnecessary. Instead, people exchanged stories or information.

Delwyn wondered if the social pleasantries came over body odor or posturing. Maybe they weren't absent, just not a part of verbal conversation.

Watchful eyes and animated voices washed over him and Phalalin. To a great extent the dual male presence, although not trumping female social conventions, triggered more primitive social instincts. Eager for any chance to speak with the two males, people asked Verikaralee and Melkorka if they minded the intrusion before mixing with them or speaking with the males directly.

A lot of people surrounded Melkorka.

"I stick out like a sore thumb," Delwyn complained.

Phalalin glanced at Delwyn's hand at the same time Phelindra snatched it to her.

"Are you hurt?" she demanded.

"No, dammit! I was thinking about a saying that compares standing out in the open to being as obvious as having a sore thumb." He had to watch his thoughts. If he dwelled long enough or strong enough on a matter, then his body odor changed. Eyloni smelled the change, empathized with it, and knew what he was thinking, or was feeling anyway.

The newcomers did not understand him except through their scent-linked empathy, so Melkorka interpreted.

Phelindra pulled Delwyn aside and gave him a strong warning. Ignoring females, depriving them of male attention, raised social etiquette issues bordering on the hurtful and criminal.

Delwyn and Melkorka fielded what felt like hundreds of questions before Phalalin rescued him by drawing their notice and questions. Delwyn ducked into a shop stocked with cloth, thread, beads, furniture, wall hangings, eating utensils and even a few technology items.

Handmade items, many of them, it seemed to him: knickknacks. Some were quite beautiful and intricate. Frozen in a wide-eyed stare, he barely moved before Melkorka grabbed him and yanked him out of the shop.

"Come with me," she said. She wrapped her tail around his waist and pulled him into an adjacent clothing shop.

Melkorka wanted to shop for clothing?

The shop's proprietress and her staff came out to meet them. The waistwear they wore identified them as La'huaset tribal members. The proprietress, a Warrior, wore colors in her loincloth matching Hervorallin's except for the border designs.

That meant she was an O'un Tu Clan female.

The sales staff surrounded Delwyn, delighted to see him. Melkorka drew the Warrior aside and spoke with her. The clerks danced and sang around Delwyn, brushing and touching him with their tails, hips, shoulders, and hands, all the time singing scores of melodies.

The proprietress darted through an opening in the back of the shop. Melkorka stood watch as the O'un Tu Clan females gave Delwyn a welcome.

The clothing store catered to anyone wanting their wares, but it was in itself O'un Tu Clan land in the same way an embassy on foreign soil was designated the territory of the people it represented.

Delwyn, swamped with questions he barely understood, by happenstance saw the proprietress returning with a handful of waistwear.

Male waistwear.

"Delwyn, come here and show me the ones you like best," Melkorka said.

"Now wait a minute, I can't wear those. I need more, ah, support than what those things can provide."

Melkorka frowned, and Phelindra jumped into the discussion.

Feeling ignored, Delwyn watched the two haggle with the proprietress.

The storekeeper's ears flipped up in surprise, pointed them at him, and then twitched them back at Melkorka and Phelindra. She paused, her tail swaying side to side in a shallow arc, weighing options.

Then she fired off a question, and Phelindra held out cupped hands.

The astonished look on the proprietress's face made him chuckle. She glanced at him, looked back at Phelindra, and nodded, glided up to him, wrapped her tail around his arm, and pulled him into the fitting room.

"What does she want?"

"She will measure you for custom-fitted waistwear."

"Custom fitted…?" The image of cupped hands flashed across his eyes. "No thanks. That's not necessary. I can keep wearing these for now."

Melkorka eyed the solid tan shorts with loathing and snapped her tail at them. "Those things? Ugh! You need more than one pair, and they will not serve you well on Elleio. You must wear traditional clothing for a male. That means, for you, the colors of the La'huaset Tribe and the O'un Tu Clan along with the patterns identifying you as a singing male and warleader. Let Bedilin measure you, and do not act like such an infant!" she added.

He let Bedilin pull him on, and her clutch of females followed them.

This wouldn't be a private fitting. Her measuring felt like the doctor's office visit all over again.

Eyloni had no nudity taboos. Their shock came more out of a concern for his size and the seemingly herniated sack of internal organs his scrotum must have looked like to them.

The measurement process took some few minutes, and then they led him back to a smirking Melkorka.

"Now what?" he asked her.

"We come back here before we leave and pick them up."

"But I don't have any money. How do I pay for them, or is this a credit transaction?"

The simple question baffled her. What did he mean? His scent implied a universal trade item. "I do not understand. Money? You do not need to trade anything. You are a La'huaset tribal male. We take care of our males."

"You're not suggesting they just give males things, are you?" he stammered, feeling insulted, as if he was a charity case.

"Not in the way your scent implies," Melkorka growled. "You are a La'huaset male. La'huaset females generally, and O'un Tu Clan females specifically, will give you clothing and other basic necessities. Other tribes and clans will give to you in the measure your clan gives to them. Clans trade to a balance agreement. If Bedilin had been born a Zi'mondi tribal female, then she would report your transaction to her clan, and they would tally the inventory loss against items they receive from La'huaset or perhaps from O'un Tu directly. If her clan receives little or nothing from your clan, and the difference is not matched by your tribe, then you may take the items on your word that you will perform a service or give her a personal item in trade."

"Oh." *A society without money?* "How can you work out a balance for the cost of scientific research, industrial output, and technological advance? No one person, a small group, or even a clan can possibly trade a quantity of clan cottage industry items equal to the development and production value of, say a jump drive."

"All tribal, social alliance, or clan large scale industrial and technological developments are deemed worldwide social goods by the Be'atika Senge, as well as are all medical science and power distribution networks. The jump drive is a global social good, and any social partnership requesting it for a ship they are building never has to match its value in agreed upon trade."

"Why not?" he asked.

Melkorka smiled. "Females developed sciences, technologies, and industries to extend the lives of and protect males. The ultimate purpose of technological advances, medical sciences, or jump drive units is for your benefit. As a worldwide social good, you and all males return in trade yourselves."

To that, Delwyn had no reply.

9
A POINT OF HONOR

Delwyn found himself stuck doing the worst leisure time activity he could think of: shopping. The Eyloni loved to shop.

Large groups of them broke up into twos and threes and roamed down narrow trails to the stores. On Earth, people window-shopped. Human crowds ignored each other for the most part. Shoppers rarely engaged in social discourse with strangers.

That kind of social disregard came off as cold and disrespectful to the Eyloni. They didn't window-shop, and stores had no windows. People chatted or exchanged social touches as they walked down trails from shop to shop, through shop bole thresholds, and inside shops. The touching and greetings seemed to have an informality to them. They lacked the choreographed ritual meetings Delwyn had come to expect. People entered shops to meet just as much as to shop, hence the reason why shops didn't have windows. Why look into a shop when shopping also meant meeting the shopkeeper, her staff, and her patrons? The social interaction was as important as browsing for and purchasing needed items.

People from all tribal continents visited here when they came to A'lon'aloop Naval Station. They mingled, told stories, exchanged news of interest, or passed informal reports on to their respective hierarchies.

Everyone rushed to meet Delwyn. Their desire to visit with him brought a crowd everywhere he went. Individuals always waited outside the tail-length personal space radius for him to give the cue to make contact. Then they glided up to him, their eyes meeting his, their tails brushing him with fleeting caresses. They sang greetings and waited for him to respond in kind and give them brief touches in return. Then they danced aside to give others a chance to enjoy social contact with a male.

That made Delwyn feel like the celebrity he knew he wasn't.

Phelindra and Melkorka led him through intersecting random trails as they met more people and visited more shops, until they crossed the path leading back to Bedilin's clothing shop.

Bedilin politely but firmly shooed a few dozen people out and then brushed Delwyn with her tail. She sang a comment to Melkorka.

"She says your waistwear are ready. Try one on and tell her whether or not it fits," Melkorka said.

He sighed. Melkorka never gave up until he gave in to her wishes. The orangeheaded Warrior had a stubborn streak, and at times like these he remembered Anlann's truism: females thought males couldn't do anything without them.

He gave up, nodded his acceptance, and surrendered with dignity.

Bedilin laid her work out on the countertop. Her ears pricking at him, eyes expectant, tail drifting aimlessly behind her, she waited for his assessment of her skill.

All of them watched, patiently waiting for him to try one on. Nudity wasn't an issue for Eyloni, but Delwyn found it hard to banish human public nudity taboos.

With sudden vigor he yanked off his tan shorts, folded them, and laid them aside.

Melkorka snatched them off the countertop and effortlessly ripped them to shreds. Delwyn always marveled at how strong the Eyloni were. From personal observation, the Warriors had the edge in muscle over the other females. Warriors and males were evenly matched, but males had greater endurance and an inherent restrained strength of their own. Hunters could easily match the strength of the average human bodybuilder. He had been told that even though the Comara couldn't throw kilos of mass across a room, their wiry strength made them formidable.

"Pretty sure they'll fit aren't you?" he asked.

"If they do not Bedilin can fit them to you," Melkorka said.

Delwyn picked up the waistwear, looked it over, and crossed his fingers.

After putting it on, he hated to admit it, but the thing felt comfortable. It was soft, as if Bedilin had woven the outfit from pussy willow fuzz. His bare butt cheeks stuck out like everyone else's did. He felt exposed, vulnerable now that he didn't have the rear cover the shorts had provided.

Bedilin sang a query, pleased with his scent and tentative smile.

"She asks if it fits well. No discomfort? No binding or pinching?"

Delwyn walked a small circle around them, did a few deep knee bends, rotated his hips, and shook his head. "Feels fine. In fact, it feels better than I thought it would."

Bedilin's face beamed with pleasure as she unfolded one of the loincloths.

She had dyed and braided it with violets, blues, and purples of the La'huaset Tribe and O'un Tu Clan. Spirit Language designs in the cloth identified him as a singing male and as a warleader. Some areas along the borders had been left blank he noticed. Female loincloths had more colors and more e'va'a patterns along their loincloth borders.

"Are these border areas empty because I'm a male?" He doubted it. Phalalin belonged to the same clan and his loincloth borders had intricate patterns filling them all in.

"No," Melkorka replied. "Those areas are reserved for markings that will be added later by your clan elders and our Tribal Elders."

She stared at his left hip for a brief moment before nodding to herself.

"Thank her. We must leave," Melkorka said.

"Thank you, Bedilin. It fits well, looks beautiful, and feels comfortable."

Bedilin canted her ears and brushed Delwyn's exposed buttocks with her pons, pleased she had taken care of her newest clan male. She pressed her nose and cheek against his and rubbed, singing soft chords under her breath.

Her staff wove a pattern around them, and one by one they followed her example.

He remembered Verikaralee's greeting. Bedilin and her staff were his fellow clan members, his family members.

Delwyn held Bedilin, felt her tremble against him …

"Delwyn, seldom does anything yank the tail of family matters, but our appointment with the A'tayotan representatives is one of them. We cannot arrive late. Your good impression depends on it," Melkorka interrupted.

"What's everyone else going to do while we're at the briefing?"

"Probably prowl the length and breadth of A'lon'aloop," she shrugged.

"I thought we were restricted to this area."

"Here? No, why? We can prowl in any of the other four secondary sectors or anywhere in the central hub except for the t'et and its support decks."

"Where are we going?"

"Into the central hub on the inner administrative complex decks adjacent to the t'et."

"Let's go then," Delwyn said. He was ready for a change.

"Mistress of the Watch Phelindra, Mistress of Tactics Hlinlodyn, Mistress of Pathwalking Trebithia, Mistress of Communications Hlindredreda, Mistress of Sails Anailiatha, Mistress of Saga Mirrahindrallin, Mistress Hervorallin, and Kidahin come with me," Melkorka sang at command tempo.

"Who else?" she asked.

Now that was a good question. He wanted to take them all, but he couldn't take them all, as much as he wanted to. All of them had fought to secure the enemy ship, and half of them had contributed to figuring out key control systems. A combat briefing needed people able to report on enemy fighting skill and technology, which meant bringing the few who had fought the Lizards or had figured out key systems and could relate their findings and conclusions.

"Zalzadrin, Raelindra, Gruntilha, Rathrinda, Gaundellin, and Herallin come with me," Delwyn said.

Zalzadrin popped up behind him, having anticipated him. She stood there bouncing on her feet, eager and pleased.

Delwyn grinned at her exuberance. The older Hunter had every reason in the world to resent him, hate him even. The long puckered scar stretching from her left breast to her hip had been healed, but too late to lose the scar without getting cosmetic treatment. Mistress of Healers Allohindra had tactfully offered Zalzadrin the choice, and Zalzadrin had emphatically refused to consider it. She had received the scar defending him, and she didn't hate him for it. Her fondness for him was unbound, and she often swamped him with her enthusiasm and sharp strange wit.

She had called him their pet once.

The healed scar still showed the puncture holes from the wound stapler he had used to draw the wound closed. If he'd had Tathilatha's accelerated healing device when Zalzadrin had been injured, then she wouldn't have that horrible scar now.

Zalzadrin stopped bouncing and cocked her ears at him.

"The scar dozant … dossent … does not hurt, see?" She bounced again, and her beaded neckwear flew up into her face and over her shoulders. Her breasts jiggled free of the flimsy garment and in counterpoint with it.

The sudden stimulus coupled with a nearby Princess caused Zalzadrin's deep red nipples to weep milk. Like all Hunters and Warriors, Zalzadrin was a natural wet nurse whenever she came near a newborn.

"Yes, I see that. Are you ready to brief everyone on your combat experiences with the Ni'zakhonii?"

Zalzadrin nodded, but her expression soured.

"Not my best performance," she said, brushing her pons along the obvious scar.

Delwyn shook his head and pointed at it. "You and the other Hunters used your heads and killed those Lizards before they could sound the alert. Their best defense would have been to pop a pressure seal and vent the atmosphere into space, killing us outright if you hadn't."

He eyed her ripped abdomen. Zalzadrin, a Hunter phenotype female, had a lean build and muscles that gave her body a sharp, cut look. Her abdominal muscles bunched into four knotted pairs, into what everyone in

SOG-444 called 'eight packs'. Her sharp pectoral muscles made her large breasts seem even larger.

Delwyn's eyes wandered back to her scar. It wasn't a uniform human pink. It snaked across orange, red, and yellow-trimmed red skin, disrupting the natural camouflage meant to break up her body's outline against Elleio rainforest backgrounds.

Zalzadrin's scar stood out black and not pink. The red blood flowing under the scar tissue combined with the red and orange skin pigments. Together they turned the scar the same color as her lips and tongue. To him, the scar looked as if someone had drawn it on her with clumpy black mascara.

Zalzadrin nodded as she bounced on her feet. She couldn't sit still for long. Short for a Hunter, Zalzadrin tended to grind her teeth whenever surrounded by tall Warrior females. Hunter body types tended toward the tall and willowy. Warriors had more muscle and tended to be shorter than the Hunter norm, but most Warriors had at least a finger of height advantage over Zalzadrin.

The LAC crew stood with her and waited, their excitement revealing itself in more calm and dignified ways than Zalzadrin could manage.

After Phelindra, Zalzadrin was the next oldest Hunter in Delwyn's association. To his reckoning, Zalzadrin also held the second highest social rank, but not the second highest military rank. Did that mean she had high hierarchical rank? Then again, Zalzadrin should technically come in third if he included Melkorka, but her rank came from his decision to retain her as Mistress of the Ship. Female ranking drove Delwyn nuts. Military rank depended on a male's recognition of a female's combat ability and was revealed by the complexity of the dreamcatcher earrings they wore. Social rank could be guessed by how they behaved in social situations, but hierarchy rank was subtle and not obvious to male observers. Delwyn knew that Eirmilla, Kalinn's protectress, had been the Eldest Warrioress. Brelioranda followed Eirmilla in rank. Emendredaha had been third in line.

They had all died with Kalinn.

"We are ready," Zalzadrin deadpanned, trying to lift her warleader's thoughts from the melancholy drift she smelled on his scent.

Delwyn glanced up at an impatient, tail-stabbing Melkorka and nodded. "Lead the way, Melkorka."

They left the sleep-tree and headed down a trail to the curving spoke connecting this sector to the naval station's central hub.

The vast ersatz forest impressed him just as much as those on his ship had. Did they project the same images on both ship and station? He didn't know.

Curious, he asked.

"The holographic projectors do not replay the same forest over and over," Phelindra confirmed. "Tribal rainforests are scanned from time to time and added to the environmental database. Selected landscapes are programmed into the environmental system. Some detail is lost because the finite volume inside the station restricts things like the natural lay of the land. We notice these abrupt changes in scenery."

"You mean things like climbing inside a tree a short distance only to find yourself stepping out onto a branch several thousand ells off the ground?"

"Everybody notices that! Even you notice that. I am talking about discontinuities in the forest, abrupt changes in the flora. We know our territory. The treeline images are imprinted in our memories. I know this forest view runs much longer than the actual distance to the central hub. When we exit this sector, you will see how the change in trees, grasses, and landscape informs us that we have entered different compartments in the station."

"So the unnatural changes in scenery let you know when you've entered or exited areas like the curved spokes connecting this sector with the central hub?" he asked.

"Indeed," Phelindra said.

As if summoned, the landscape changed from open paths into dense jungle undergrowth and narrowing trails with no side branches.

"We are in the connecting spoke now, aren't we?"

Phelindra nodded. "As you can see, the change in the jungle is too abrupt. This unnaturalness tells us we are in a narrow space with no left or right avenues of retreat."

Delwyn remembered the holographic map displaying the connecting spoke as curved, like a sickle blade. But, the trail ahead seemed to continue in a straight line. Yet, the more he looked at the trail and the surrounding scenery, the more he thought he saw a gradual bearing to the left.

The trail broke into a clearing thinly veiled with golden jungle grasses. Immense crimson trees, much smaller than elleiu trees, seemed to block the way forward. But the blockage was only an illusion.

The narrow trail through the trees widened into paths that took them into a projected mountain scene so stunning it took his breath away. They were heading toward a cliff, a stone glacier. Its off-white shades looked even more brilliant because of the crimson trees and burnt orange brush growing around it. The cliff face loomed above the rainforest, imposing and awe-inspiring. From his ground level perspective, it towered well over a kilometer above the ground.

"Is that the t'et, the Warleader's Tower?" he asked.

Melkorka shook her head. "The t'et is the tall stone spire reaching into the clouds behind it. We are not far from the t'et, but the cloud rainforest and the cliff hide it from view. This cliff is in La'huaset Tribal land."

As they hiked closer Delwyn could see holes in the massive limestone cliff that looked as though they had been formed by drizzling acid over it, creating jagged openings where the limestone had eroded away. He saw a giant's shattered teeth or a stump of splintered bone, depending on how he tried to cope with the magnificent ancient edifice. He could not tell if the trail wound around the cliff or if it entered some hidden opening in the rock face.

Melkorka led the group into the formation. For all its imposing exterior stony battlements, once past the projected façade, the interior, surprisingly enough, was filled with twisted wooden mazes that seemed to go on forever.

It was beautiful and a more complex structure than anything Delwyn had yet seen. He ran his hand along a wall of continuous woven aged wood.

"This is real wood," he said.

"It is," Zalzadrin agreed. "This *Males' Safe* was once part of a dead elleiu tree. The wood is several hundred-thousand years old. We do not cut living elleiu trees other than to prune for artistic growth or to thin overgrown snarls."

Delwyn thought she meant they teased their redwood dwarfing home trees into growing into aesthetic shapes using topiary pruning methods. Interesting.

"Males' Safe?" he echoed.

Zalzadrin bounced up and down on her feet, pleased she had told Delwyn something new about them and their homes. "Every elleiu tree has on average ten Males' Safes between the understory and the emergent layers. They begin growing just off the oldest main branches in the crown. Sometimes the aerial roots sprouting from underneath the branches are pruned and shaped so they coil back up and around the branch and fuse together, creating thick wooden mazes, like this one. Other times they are allowed to grow down to the ground and become supports or pathways around the main trunk. We also shape them so they make large meeting rooms.

"If they are pruned to make a Males' Safe, those average 400 ells in diameter and 130 ells tall."

A 180-meter by 25-meter maze of petrified Swiss cheese. "But why call them Males' Safes?"

"Males' Safes are places for a clan's males to take refuge. The aerial roots are ells thick in places with limited access into or out of the mazes. The chambers are spacious enough to hold males, their defenders, and supplies for months. In ancient times when an enemy clan overran another clan, the defending clan put their males in these Males' Safes and defended them until they either repulsed the invading clan or died fighting."

Zalzadrin paused to caress the wall. "This tree is old enough to have sheltered males during an attack by a rival clan," she murmured.

"That long ago?" Delwyn whistled, impressed.

Zalzadrin nodded as they continued walking, "Elleiu trees have long lives. The living ones are hundreds of thousands of years old."

Delwyn did some quick mental math. One hundred-thousand in base-five counting translated into 3,125. Three thousand EST years came to about 2,500 Earth years.

"But many elleiu trees are much older, aren't they?"

Zalzadrin nodded, pressing her face against his neck. "Some are well over two hundred-thousand years old."

"Wow, trees over five thousand Earth years old," he whistled. To the short-lived Eyloni, an elleiu tree life span would seem like forever.

"Five?" Zalzadrin pulled her cheek away from his neck and frowned. "How you count continues to perplex me. There are ten appendages on a body: two arms, two legs, one tail. Two plus two plus one is ten, simple and plain. You have no tail. If anything, you ought to base your counting on four," she hummed in annoyance, "Why not base your counting on your fingers and toes? Yes? Can you answer me that, Delwyn? Why do you not count in base forty?"

"Twenty. Five, ten, fifteen, twenty," he demonstrated.

Zalzadrin disengaged her hold on him, and Melkorka wedged herself between them.

"That is enough, you two. This is no time for leafchasing," she snapped.

Delwyn winked at Zalzadrin, an act that always endeared her to him. His ability to wink fascinated and intrigued the others as well. Eyloni couldn't wink. They had to concentrate just to blink one eye. Something about their facial muscle attachments made squinting out of one eye about as difficult as opening a door with a doorknob only a few centimeters away from the center hinge.

"We are here. Try to act dignified," Melkorka growled at Zalzadrin.

Act your age, Delwyn translated.

Delwyn had long been expecting to run into guards. This area was important, a secure area, so where were the guards he knew had to be here? They hadn't met anyone yet. No guards and no challenges jumped out to impede their progress.

Melkorka stopped and sang what the Eyloni called a 'contact call' and was rewarded with an immediate reply followed by a hand of Warriors. The five greeted Melkorka first in some ritual made evident by their postures and musical phrasing. They started waggling fingers in battle language, which effectively excluded him from their plans.

Delwyn turned back to an expanse of wall and touched the grown wooden sculpture. It felt warm and smooth. The wood resembled a dense mahogany but stained in light burnt oranges. The wood had a fine grain and was obviously heavy. He doubted it could even float in water.

"This wood is hard and heavy. I could hammer nails with it. Hell, I could make nails out of it," he muttered.

Zalzadrin, irrepressible as always, leaned against him. "The wood is hard indeed, harder than steel. At one time we used it to make airplanes, sounding rockets, and the first artificial satellites."

"Really?" he asked. He doubted it. Zalzadrin was such a kidder after all.

"No, it is true. Our early rockets were made from casings and capsules carved from dead elleiu heartwood. Its density and structure also made it a natural ablative surface for reentry shields," Kidahin added.

Several minutes passed, and Delwyn hadn't decided if the two Hunters were pulling his leg or not. He wondered about that possibility until a Warrior came and told them the A'tayotan representatives were ready for them.

The Warrior ushered them into a large oval room. Seats of gnarled root filled the center, forming a gallery of sorts. A curved dais sprawled across the far end, a curved log tall as a man and long enough to seat ten people and yet preserve the tail-length personal space radius of each person.

Delwyn Marsch, no stranger to naval brawls in his career, knew a courtroom when he saw one. Ten females stood together between the dais and the gallery. Off to their left stood a lone male and female, Warleader Einlann of A'lon'aloop Naval Station and his Protectress.

Delwyn considered. These ten Warriors formed some kind of A'tayotan inquiry panel. They were all middle-aged, near Zalzadrin's age, maybe a bit older but not quite as old as Phelindra. Einlann and his Protectress, oddly, were both only two to three years older than Kidahin.

Einlann stepped forward and welcomed Delwyn with passible Coalition standard. Einlann gushed an enthusiasm hard for him to contain. Five minutes later and without a hint of stopping he would have continued to monopolize the hearing had the assembly's presiding female not politely told him to save his personal inquiries until after A'tayotan business.

The ritual greetings stalled when an awake and disapproving Princess growled at the new females. She considered any strange female a competitor ready to poach on her exclusive territory. Delwyn had to introduce her to the board members, one Warrior at a time.

Surprisingly, the serious-looking females eagerly took time out to play with Princess and ask Hervorallin all about her. Eyloni loved infants, other females' infants as much as their own.

Which made what happened next seem odd, out of place.

The presiding female invited Princess to climb onto her. They smelled noses. Then the presiding female held Princess away from her, frowned, and seemed to focus inward.

Princess shrieked in outrage and swiped at the presiding female with her sharp black infant fingernails. Princess then sang an imperious demand. All females in the room turned and lunged at the presiding female with combative fury on their faces before they had a chance to check the natural reflex.

The presiding female cautiously returned a trilling Princess back to an angry Hervorallin, stepped well away from everyone and held her hands up in surrender, asking their forgiveness.

"What was that all about?" Delwyn demanded. He was shaking uncontrollably. The empathic link tying him to Princess had telegraphed the infant Hunter's indignant fury. She was outraged by the presiding female's directed-threat scent.

"I was threatened?"

"Oddrilna tested the empathy link between you and Princess," Zalzadrin snapped, biting back her own anger that had been triggered by the infant's recruiting pheromones, the scent Princess used to summon females to help her defend Delwyn.

It took several more minutes before everyone could regain their composures and take their seats. The A'tayotan Warriors, shaken as well, returned behind the dais.

The presiding female, Oddrilna, announced for the record that the order of testimony would begin with Kidahin.

"Why would they call the most junior female first?" Delwyn asked Phelindra.

"To acknowledge rank and responsibility. Everyone's honor is at stake, and no female wants to yank on the tail of a higher ranked female or her warleader. The lowest ranked female must go first. This is so Kidahin cannot gainsay a higher ranked female or you. You will speak last. If you were to speak first, then every female would give her testimony in a way that best reflects your honor. No one would ever lie for you, but testimony would skew in your favor, as it would for Melkorka if she happened to speak first."

"I don't understand. How can Kidahin's testimony bolster my honor?"

"The way she relates the events at issue from the time she first met you until now will reflect your character, and the panel can hear, see and smell it. By speaking first, Kidahin can report her actions and give her impressions without worrying about trying to support the testimony already given by a higher ranked female or yourself. Nor will she be tempted to fail to report any contrary view she might have just to maintain consensus with what has already been stated on the record."

"So by not hearing a higher ranked female's testimony first, Kidahin is freed from assaulting someone's honor, and no higher ranked female has a problem with honorably contradicting Kidahin's view of events."

Phelindra nodded. "Indeed. This method gives Kidahin the freedom to speak her facts and opinions without risking hierarchical censure."

"But I don't belong to your hierarchies, so why do I still go last?"

Phelindra wrapped her tail around him, slipped her arm around his back, turned into him, pressed her bare muscular stomach into his, and stared into his small brown eyes. "We will always support you in all things to the extent our individual and collective honor allows and your honorable conduct permits. If one of us disagreed with your honorable actions, then we would achieve consensus on how best our society could address the issue either among ourselves, or with you. You carry our honor, and we reflect yours."

"So if I spoke first, then this A'tayotan panel would assume you'd all follow my lead, making your testimony redundant?"

"Yes. Your voice is our voice, and consensus with your view of the matter in question is implied. That happens because of how males are regarded in our culture. You might miss or ignore some crucial fact, some issue, and an implied consensus would ignore it. We established this order of precedence so individuals can relate their factual experiences and impressions without assaulting a declared or implied consensus or without causing harm to one's own honor or the social or hierarchical honor of others."

"It sounds complicated," Delwyn admitted.

"It is not. Watch and listen. They are about to begin."

Oddrilna, the presiding female, opened the session with a song. When she finished the refrain, the remaining board members sang a second verse and refrain.

Oddrilna introduced Einlann. He was present as a courtesy. Males almost never appeared in A'tayotan functions, unless they were the reason behind that function. Einlann stood and sang a verse, accompanied by everyone but Delwyn.

Delwyn felt small, like the only one in church not singing.

Einlann paused a moment, as though caught forgetting what came next, perked his ears at Delwyn and sang a five-note inquiry.

The simple inquisitive melody caught Oddrilna off guard, but Delwyn knew what que no nah qui neh meant: hold, or claim, your traditional seat.

The change in octave altered the root chord meanings, but Delwyn had heard this phrase several times by now. Einlann had asked him to assume the social role of a singing male and sing.

Sing what?

"Sing the same as when you sing with us," Melkorka hissed under her breath. "We will accompany you when you give us permission to join you."

Delwyn chose a song they knew, one he could shorten to about the same length as the one Einlann had just sung. He sang the opening verse in a deep rich baritone before spreading his arms wide to include the group.

His association added their musical accompaniment to his voice, sounding so much like musical instruments. Their voices still amazed him. When they finished the second refrain he gave the A'tayotan Warriors permission to join him and add their own a cappella voices.

Einlann's protectress joined the accompaniment as well.

Delwyn, not wanting to hog the time, tried to stay under the length of Einlann's opening song. He ended the song early, but his females knew he had ended early and sang discordant raspberries to admonish him.

Apparently the board members were just as annoyed at him for taking them out of the rhythm so soon, but then again Eyloni lived for music.

"I'm surprised Einlann's Protectress joined us," he said.

Zalzadrin gave him her best who are you singing to? look. "Of course she sings with us. If you think we are the only females you can sing with, then you are wrong. Singing along with males is pleasurable activity for us. Males do not sing in public often because they are too busy. If you tied my tail to the ground, then I would cut it off so I could go and sing with a male."

There she goes again, Delwyn smiled. Zalzadrin was such a kidder.

Her amber eyes locked with his, and he cringed. She wasn't kidding. She really would maim herself to sing with another male.

"Kidahin," Oddrilna called.

The session began, and Delwyn sat back and listened to Kidahin give her testimony.

She sang it in the same way she had when she reported to Melkorka how Delwyn had demanded her adulthood knife from her while on Ibeetu. Just as her society hadn't interrupted her then, the board members didn't interrupt her now.

When Kidahin finished, each A'tayotan Warrior asked her five questions.

Throughout the questioning there were no interruptions. A board member sang a question, and Kidahin sang an answer to it. No one cut her off or asked for clarifications. The Warriors never ambushed Kidahin with meaningless or loaded inquiries. Panel members didn't bother to cross-examine her answers, either.

Delwyn craned his neck around the room. Not a single hand twitched. No fingers jabbed. He dug Phelindra in the ribs with an elbow and whispered into her soft elegant, twitching elfish ear. "I'm surprised. With the courtesy silence rule in effect, why doesn't anyone sign battle language?"

"It is not allowed," she murmured. "Its use would give the impression that an attempt is being made to steer testimony toward a consensus."

That made sense. If everyone waggled their fingers, then Kidahin would know how the others felt about the subject and adjust her testimony accordingly.

Once underway, the session picked up steam as female after female added her testimony to the record. Just as Melkorka and her repair crew had done on Ibeetu after Kidahin reported her stalking failures, the A'tayotan Warriors nailed Delwyn with looks that ranged from respect and esteem to shocked incredulity, depending on the female giving testimony at the time and the Warrior appraising him.

Zalzadrin's turn came. Her voice was filled with sharp chords that made her sound testy, as though she was baiting the panel. The soft dissonant sighs passing between Melkorka and Phelindra put Delwyn up on how much Zalzadrin was exceeding what passed for respectful discourse in formal Eyloni rituals.

"What's going on with Zalzadrin? Is she trying to provoke somebody?" he whispered.

"She had been down-playing her role during the fighting aboard the enemy ship. She has not even mentioned the clawing attack that laid her side open. She is stressing how you stapled her wounds and how she insisted the others give you medical aid after you captured the enemy ship's command center," Phelindra said.

"Why is she being so snotty about it?"

"The board members are all Warriors."

"Yeah? So? I know there's some sort of rivalry between Hunters and Warriors. What does that have to do with giving testimony at a hearing?"

"It is not so much a rivalry as it is the territorial interests between the Society of Hunters and the Society of Warriors. No territorial dispute exists here, however. Zalzadrin's natural antagonism snaps its tail at them because the board members are all taller than the Warrior norm, taller than Zalzadrin. She sees them as a constant reminder of her short stature, and it infuriates her."

Phelindra paused and shook, not in anger but with amusement. To laugh outright would insult the dignity of the hearing and the honor of a seething Zalzadrin. By now she probably thought the spirits had conspired to put her before the tall A'tayotan Warriors.

Delwyn wondered if Zalzadrin could smell female annoyance mounting around her. He did his best to not dwell on the florescent orangeheaded female's fury and her snotty demeanor.

According to rank, Phelindra should be stepping into the dock next. He'd have his hands full with Zalzadrin then.

Oddrilna called Phelindra, right on cue. Zalzadrin sat down next to Delwyn, folded her arms under her breasts, wrapped her tail around his waist, and glared daggers at the Warriors seated behind the dais.

Some forty-five minutes later Melkorka and Phelindra swapped places. By now Delwyn had a good idea about how the proceeding ran and couldn't wait to give his account.

That plan got scuttled when problems became all too apparent well into Melkorka's testimony.

Clipped voices sang discordant questions to Melkorka.

The panel Warriors had all turned deadly serious. What had Melkorka told them?

"I think they're upset about Melkorka's conduct. Something about her leaving Ibeetu orbit and coming after us? I'm not sure. What do you think?" Delwyn asked.

No reply.

"Phelindra?"

The Eldest Huntress clamped her hand over his mouth.

"Listen!"

Phelindra frowned as she listened to the questions pouring forth from the Warriors. They had deep concerns, serious concerns.

"Oh no," Phelindra muttered under her breath, "I never considered this!"

"What?" Delwyn asked.

"The A'tayotan has raised an honor issue against Melkorka."

"For what?" Delwyn demanded.

"For firing on the Coalition fighters sent to destroy us," she sang. Her musical voice fell flat.

"She didn't kill anyone. In fact, she took great pains to avoid killing anyone."

"That does not matter. *Henri Edda* was in Compact territory under Anlann's Warpact. Since Anlann had already exercised his first on-scene precedence, the Coalition warship was a Compact guest and under Anlann's Warpact.

"In the A'tayotan's eyes, what Melkorka did was the same as if she had fired on another Compact warship."

Delwyn shook his head. "No. That's wrong. Anlann wouldn't have sanctioned Blue Squadron's attack run on us knowing we were in control of the Lizard ship."

"That is precisely the problem. Anlann brought Captain Winters into Warpact, and Captain Winters ordered an interception of what he considered at the time to be an incoming Ni'zakhonii attack."

"But Melkorka knew it was us!" he objected.

"No, she did not. Melkorka guessed it was us based on our poor course corrections into the Nikkiolo star system. She substituted her guess over Captain Winters's tactical judgment. Remember, by then a Ni'zakhonii demolition probe had already destroyed at least two Coalition fighters. Captain Winters had a rational, justifiable belief from his human point of view that Melkorka was deluded by grief."

Delwyn knew from experience that the Navy, or any navy for that matter, detested a commander who took the initiative. For all the Navy's praise of individual initiative when an exercise of discretion worked out, it almost never did. Disobeying orders or rules of engagement landed a commander in the crapper. Even worse, disobeying a direct order buried that commander in crap. Acting on initiative often turned into the same thing as disobeying direct orders.

Melkorka seemed to have violated a point of Warpact etiquette, the equivalent of a skipper sailing his ship up a creek of sh …

"Wait a minute, Phelindra. Anlann said I became Warpact leader the moment we reentered the Nikkiolo star system. He had already transferred Warpact command to me because he, like Melkorka, understood that our unfamiliarity with the ship's systems explained our erratic course changes."

"Melkorka cannot guess, cannot act on insight and cannot take independent action during a Warpact. To her best available knowledge an enemy ship was inbound and Anlann held Warpact command over Captain Winters. She threatened to fire on his assets if they fired on us, except in self-defense, without her permission."

Einlann listened to Melkorka, yet he watched as Delwyn reacted to her words. He held the high ground. The Warriors wanted to settle the question here and now. But no matter what they or the A'tayotan hierarchy had to say about it, the matter rested on how Delwyn and the Society of Warleaders felt about the incident.

Listening, Einlann made a covert grab for his 'minder and accessed Anlann's report. The *Surefooted* warleader's report described the issue at hand with exacting detail, almost as if he had anticipated the problem the A'tayotan might have had with Melkorka's behavior during a Warpact.

Oddrilna wanted to exonerate Melkorka, but Warpacts were steeped in tradition. Warpacts regulated how different warship societies under different males could coordinate combat and tactics without violating female territorial imperatives or male autonomy. Warpact etiquette was a creature of male interests, but the A'tayotan backed those interests with a fanatical tenacity, and it was the A'tayotan that had the practical final say in military policy among the Ten Tribes. Only the Comara hierarchy could veto an A'tayotan decree, but when it came to male prerogatives the Comara always sided with male interests.

Einlann read co-Ambassador Anlann's report. Using keyword searches, he found a log entry that addressed the facts at issue.

Einlann paged through several columns of text. Somewhere Anlann's log must mention something showing Melkorka knew with some certainty that Delwyn commanded before she had fired on the Coalition fighters.

He scrolled, scrolled, scrolled, and … Ah!

He backed up the file and reread it again just to make sure.

Captain Winters had been told long before Melkorka fired on his combat assets that Delwyn's presumed Warpact leader status would become active once he arrived in the Nikkiolo star system. She had told Captain Winters that Delwyn would command the LAC as warleader long before she fired her EMP torpedoes on the Coalition fighters.

Anlann's report was convincing. By the time Melkorka fired, Warpact had already transferred to Delwyn. When Warpact leadership is not contested, its change is seamless and automatic. Melkorka told Captain Winters after the engagement that, "*'Delwyn does not assume Warpact … He holds it because he is the first on-scene male with a combat asset. He does not declare a Warpact; we presume it.'*"

Satisfied with his efforts, Einlann waited with impatient glee. He wanted to speak with Delwyn. Delwyn was new to the subtleties of the protected status all males enjoyed in Elleio's female-dominated culture. The A'tayotan had nothing but honorable reasons for making sure Warpact protocol had not been tailchased away by an incompetent or willfully defiant Melkorka.

Delwyn sat and listened. He folded his arms across his chest, gripped his biceps, and did his best not to show his disapproval.

The Warriors kept grilling Melkorka. She remained steadfast and calm, a miracle considering her fiery disposition. The questions the A'tayotan Warriors threw at her had the sound of claims bordering on slaps to her honor. Those questions suggested to the point of accusation that her actions had been disgraceful. The intense barrage would have driven a weaker person to tears. But not Melkorka, she was a Warrior and had a healthy measure of a Warrior's aggression. From her point of view, she held the high ground and intended to keep on holding the high ground.

Einlann's youthful exuberance had tapered off. His expression had first turned serious and then thoughtful. Now he was reading from a personal electronic device, something like a Coalition omnipad. *Lucky him*, Delwyn grumbled. If this hearing hadn't concerned him and his, then he'd be reading a book on his 'pad too.

Einlann looked up into Delwyn's eyes and smiled.

At what? Delwyn wondered. Melkorka's plight? How her answers reflected on him?

Melkorka answered the last abrasive query raised by the lowest ranking Warrior on the panel. Physically and mentally exhausted, Melkorka began to rise but Einlann stood first and addressed the panel.

"I submit the following extracts from Warleader Anlann's co-ambassadorial log entries regarding this matter. I see no interference with Anlann's Warpact. It ceased to exist the moment Captain Winters and Anlann both knew Delwyn had arrived in-system in command of the Ni'zakhonii vessel. Captain Winters had already known that he was subject to Delwyn's command and should have ordered the fighters withdrawn. Melkorka is correct. The presumption that Anlann had yielded Warpact to Delwyn is valid. That she acted before receiving formal notice that Warpact had changed is immaterial. Anlann did not raise a challenge to her actions through Delwyn.

The sole purpose served by the Warpact between Anlann and Captain Winters was limited to permitting *Henri Edda's* entry into Compact territory to render assistance to *Hunter's Moon.* I find this matter resolved as to impinging the Warpact as it existed between Anlann and Captain Winters. The Society of Warleaders advances no Warpact protocol challenge against Melkorka."

The A'tayotan Warriors spent quite some time reading through Anlann's log entries before gathering together to reach a consensus. It wasn't easy for them to reach the major consensus, though. The minor consensus came easily enough, but they had to negotiate to get all members to agree to the major consensus. The holdouts agreed in the end only because Einlann had given them true counsel on matters pertaining to Warpacts as males saw them.

The A'tayotan Warriors were not vindictive. They wanted to absolve Melkorka, but when it came down to Warpact conventions, they always erred on the far conservative side. Their difficulty in reaching a major consensus served to put Melkorka on notice. The A'tayotan hierarchy would have stern and unhappy words for her when they gathered at the next hierarchy meeting, and in that meeting no male was allowed. No male voice would absolve her from the displeasure of the A'tayotan hierarchy.

"Delwyn ar ahoun Unahaillaea *Tyreniioroneo* is called," Oddrilna announced.

Delwyn took the warm seat vacated by Melkorka. Phelindra stood by his side, and at first he thought she was only performing her usual protectress role. That is, until Oddrilna spoke.

"Agree you Phelindra speak plain for us and you?" she asked him.

"Oddrilna asks if you mind if I stand with you as interpreter for both you and them," Phelindra said.

"I got what she said. No, I don't mind at all."

Phelindra sang a short, complicated score.

Oddrilna nodded. She drew herself to her full height, as did the other panel members, and they filed out from behind the dais and down into the gallery and surrounded him. They introduced themselves, Oddrilna first followed by her compatriots in rank order. That they hadn't done so before now emphasized the seriousness of the issues at hand, but now they postured around him. Oddrilna preened, her signal for seeking casual physical contact.

Delwyn reached for her shoulder and rubbed the soft velour skin around her collarbone, across her shoulder blades, down her spine, and trailed off just past her hip.

She coiled her long tail around his arm in loose hanging loops and brushed her pons against his face with a playful twitch.

He breathed in her scent, a slight vanilla and pumpkin pie with a touch of beagle smell.

Oddrilna leaned into the strange new warleader, pressed her cheek against his, and smelled him even as she caressed his muscular back. The soothing male scent filled her nose, and its exotic alien strangeness tugged at her. Delwyn's association got to smell this all the time?

Oddrilna took another whiff of male and snuggled into him.

Delwyn couldn't help having the natural reflex, which sometimes happened whenever a man found himself being held tightly by a scantily-clad woman.

Oddrilna, not in her season, took the subtle change in his scent and the mental image it conjured as an overture, an interest in having her associated with him.

She was flattered and intrigued.

Impatient sighs washed over her, hints from the other panel members waiting to greet Delwyn. She let him go, resentful of the idea of having to do so. Delwyn found her large amber eyes giving him playful looks, while the other panel members danced around him and brushed him with their tails.

They returned to their places behind the dais.

"What is it with you and Warriors?" Phelindra hissed.

Delwyn shrugged.

Oddrilna, resuming her role as presiding female, fixed her gaze on him and sang a single word.

"Begin."

Delwyn gave them a more extensive report, one that gave flesh to the outline he'd given Havalin. That outline had been brief and informal, a courtesy, but now he added the dispassionate formality of a tactical analysis and the panoply of details, rationales, and inferences that went with it. This briefing would have serious strategy and policy implications, implications the A'tayotan hierarchy would bury itself in, as was its purpose as far as he understood the hierarchy's purpose in Eyloni society.

The panel asked him respectful but penetrating questions. They didn't grill him like they had Melkorka or others. Delwyn did the best under the circumstance to explain his actions. Phelindra signed his words so the panel knew exactly what he said. Battle language was allowed now that only his testimony remained. No one remained to testify, no one who could be influenced by his words.

Einlann listened with avid interest. He pointed one ear at Delwyn and cocked the other one at his Protectress as she interpreted the battle language for him.

The Warriors asked questions about his experiences with Anlann and Seralin. Oddrilna grilled him on his reasons for including the Compact Forward Operating Base in his security sweeps through Ibeetu's forests.

Delwyn's taking of Kidahin's adulthood knife drew grave concerns. Oddrilna demanded he justify the taking to each panel Warrior until she was satisfied in her own mind that the taking was warranted. Asking a female to surrender her adulthood knife was serious business. If trivially done the female's hierarchy would demand the death of the one making the demand, even if the one demanding it was a male.

After hearing the facts, Oddrilna delivered the panel's ruling. Delwyn's actions had been well taken. She paused and gave Kidahin the a'pea sign for her stalking lapses and for not taking into account the possibility Delwyn might be able to climb a tree.

"As for your adulthood knife," Oddrilna added, "its replacement is a matter you must attend to as soon as possible."

"What knife? Phelindra? Kidahin still has hers."

"She means your adulthood knife. The metal blade you are wearing does not prowl alongside tradition. Your ceramic blades are even less traditional. The O'un Tu Clan will award you a replacement, so you may look like a proper adult in our culture."

Oddrilna cut Phelindra off and asked for a blow-by-blow account of the unarmed combat test Delwyn had given Kidahin the moment he brought her into the Coalition Surface Operations Base on Ibeetu.

Then Oddrilna asked Delwyn about his assuming responsibility for the females on board *Hunter's Moon* while the repair party fabricated replacement parts on the moon's surface.

He had no idea how to explain something he hadn't even known he'd done at the time.

"They needed my help," he said.

Oddrilna asked him about the clan lineage song he had sung at the conclusion of the Death Song ritual. Why had he wanted to form familial ties with the *Hunter's Moon* females?

Delwyn hadn't known he'd done that, either. He didn't dare mention Anlann's involvement in advising him how to perform that last Death Song ritual song. "I wanted to link them to me."

Oddrilna asked him about his decision to sever his naval service obligation to the Coalition before rescuing the forty-two females in his assault force. The panel wanted to know beyond any doubt whether Delwyn had honorably removed himself from Coalition Fleet obligation. He certainly could *not* extract himself from the layers upon layers of obligation he had woven himself into now. He was honor-bound to his occupational association, which effectively blocked all trails of retreat from that obligation.

No panel Warriors said a thing about him becoming warleader. Phalalin had been right. They avoided the subject. It didn't matter. Hlindredreda had transmitted the four-day long ritual to Elleio via hyperlink weeks ago. It was over, well beyond their control and censure.

Einlann wanted to hear more about the decisions Delwyn had made as warleader on the light attack craft and then later as warleader on his warship.

"Delwyn, why did you choose Phelindra as the captured vessel's mistress of the ship?"

What answer could he give? He had given her a long heavy throwing knife, and she wrapped her tail around its length and it was a done deal. "I felt she needed a knife, and I gave one to her," he said.

"And Melkorka? Why did you choose her as your warship's Mistress of the Ship?" Einlann pressed.

A tougher question for him. The warleader ritual in the warship's combat bay had been going on for over sixty hours straight. Somehow the Eyloni pheromonal chemistry around him had driven him like a stimulant. He was suffering from fatigue and shock at the time. By the time he'd tied the last adulthood knife below the left breast of the last female aboard he was feeling feverish and melancholy. He had been thinking about his wife and daughters. He had no living family, no one to bequeath the heirloom American Civil War saber to. In his confused mind he regarded the warship's crew as his daughters. He thought of Melkorka as his eldest, and he gave the cavalry officer saber to her in honor of the elder daughter role she filled so well.

"I saw her as my oldest near-daughter, well grown and able to take care of all my near-daughters."

Einlann dropped his 'minder, shocked.

The A'tayotan Warriors froze, suddenly wary.

"You. See. Your …," Oddrilna stammered.

Einlann's deep voice rolled over her dramatic soprano spluttering, cutting her off. "You consider your occupational association your near-daughters?" he asked.

"Well, yeah. After a fashion."

Einlann stared at his twitching pons, thinking. No wonder Delwyn's association postured so much aggression when … He let that thought drop. It was rare for a male to extend kinship over adult females from different clans because it was hard for adult females to accept near-daughter ties from a second male. All Hunters and Warriors were the near-daughters of the male present at their births. The male birth bonding empathic link was critical for infant female survival and persisted throughout life. Though it paled compared to its original strength by middle age, birth bonding was the most intimate empathy link in Eyloni life. A parallel empathic link of that nature shared by even a few females was very rare. For an occupational association, adult females all, to consent to share near-daughter status with one male was, well, all but unprecedented. The last time it had happened with more than a *fist* of females had been with Hlorrithin, the last Hero of Home.

Kidahin and Princess had somehow caused this to happen. Einlann knew. They were the youngest females aboard Delwyn's warship, and both had been linked to him during a crisis, a crisis shared by everyone else aboard their warship. That made them more likely to embrace a familial tie, even more so since Delwyn had already offered to sacrifice himself to save his assault force. They had given him the title of sire cairn, battle leader, because co-Ambassador Seralin had specifically referred to him by that title. She had told Melkorka that Delwyn was an unattached male, one having no female association, a near impossibility in Eyloni culture. And dangerous. So when he took an interest in them so soon after arriving on the Nikkiolo moon, as any male …

"Empathically weaved," Einlann sang to his Protectress.

Her ears flattened for half a beat and then flicked forward again. She stepped between Einlann and Delwyn. His occupational association would never allow challenges to go unanswered. They would fight for him. She glanced at Oddrilna. By the expression on her face, the Warrior had come to the same conclusion. Had Oddrilna spoken ill against Delwyn then his association would have fought the panel members to the death. His association's good opinion, evident by their pheromonal activity, put forth an empathic aura around him.

Well? So what? The Protectress shrugged. It was normal for females to reflect the character of the males they associated with, but this aura felt too strong for an association so recently formed.

Einlann shook his head, changed his tack, and asked Delwyn about the technical issues he had to solve aboard the captured ship.

Delwyn heaved a sigh of relief. It was about time someone got around to the more familiar waters of an after-action briefing. He'd given hundreds of such briefings to the high-styles in his career. As SOG-444 commander, his input in special operations strategy had been sought after by captains, commodores, fleet captains and admirals. This briefing should follow similar lines. Actually, this briefing should go even more smoothly because, while all the females had to thread the needle of rank among themselves, Einlann held Warpact because A'lon'aloop was his station. His was the only rank Delwyn had to worry about.

The briefing flew by. Delwyn credited the efficient briefing style to the incredible competence his LAC crew displayed as they reported their conclusions and analytical strategies.

Einlann interrupted to ask Delwyn if he minded if others could join the briefing. When Delwyn shook his head, he pressed a button and sang a short request.

Twelve people—six warleaders and their protectresses—entered the room and kindly but firmly asked Oddrilna and her Warriors to leave.

Oddrilna dallied, reluctant, looking at Delwyn as she left.

The warleaders, Phalalin and Havalin among them, watched Delwyn expectantly.

This briefing just became closed, he realized. "Melkorka, take everyone and go shopping or something. Phelindra and I will meet up with you back at the sleep-tree when we are done here."

Melkorka stood, palms pressed to her thighs, her long, four-jointed fingers clenching and unclenching, her tail darting behind her.

Not happening.

Melkorka's scent, an emphatic *no!*, caught Princess like a slap in the face. She jumped from her mother's back, darted to Delwyn, and crawled up his leg and around his back to his neck. From her perch there, she glared over his head at the newcomers.

It always surprised him how the doll-sized infant Hunter could crawl up his bare skin without clawing him. Her tiny hands held on to him with what felt like light thumb and forefinger pinches.

Princess's pea-sized eyes glared at the strangers. She smelled their pheromones and recognized the scent of males. They were no territorial threats as far as she was concerned, but they had females with them. Whether or not those females had designs on her male she did not know, and so her instincts warned her to remain alert.

Females took great pains to avoid harming a male and loathed harming one even in self-defense. In almost all cases his association intervened before he could come to harm. Princess's newborn mind toyed with the instinctive warning. She might have to save him from attack. She sang an inquisitive challenge to the protectresses and waited for their pheromonal empathy to reveal their purpose. An empathic species could not hide strong emotional intent.

The warleaders sang encouraging songs to the infant Hunter.

Instinct told Eyloni females of all ages that males were inherently safe, and so their songs reassured Princess. She surrendered her perch with some reluctance and jumped back to Hervorallin's shoulder.

Delwyn hailed Phalalin. "What are you doing here? I thought you were on Na'di Island waiting to brief the Compact Counsel."

Phalalin looped his tail, a shrug. "Plans have changed. We are here representing the Society of Warleaders, which has a priority interest in your analysis of the Ni'zakhonii light attack craft and its systems."

"I'm no engineer, Phalalin. I had experts working around the clock to figure out how to cut power from the reactor to the FTL drive. The ship is a quasi-organic crystal. The crystal structure changes as new active systems are needed. Think about veins of ore running through solid rock. Okay? Now think of the veins changing from iron to gold into diamond or into silicon, creating new circuits on demand. Power is fed into the bridge from engineering through what reminds me of cracks running through broken glass. That's how wiring is run throughout the ship. Every control is a separate crystal. When a matrix of smaller crystals is plugged into a control console, they control energy flow by the patterns they make in the matrix table. Touching one without removing it activates or deactivates it. Remove them and put them elsewhere in the matrix repurposes the crystals in the matrix somehow.

"If you pull a crystal from its matrix table and fail to put it back, or if you replace it with an incompatible crystal, then it will emit a warning drone and get blazing hot. I think, from the experiences we had, that a crystal left too long removed from its socket could explode with the force of an antipersonnel grenade.

"The best scans I could make with my battlefield scanner registered incompatible energy signatures among certain crystals. From what Hervorallin and Gaundellin tell me, I think certain crystals will catalyze an instantaneous energy transfer between them if they touch. I think the contact shorts them out."

Many nodded, understanding both Delwyn's account and agreeing with his conclusions.

"We must examine this ship. Delwyn, if you do not mind, can you demonstrate how the ship's crystal control systems work? Show us how you scanned the crystal assemblies and describe the deductive processes and methods you used to interpret those scans," Phalalin said.

Amindaldra signed in battle language her warleader's request to the remaining protectresses so they could advise their respective warleaders. The warleaders agreed with Phalalin as though he had invited them out for a night on the town.

"Wait a minute, Phalalin. I said I wasn't an engineer. There isn't much I can tell you about the ship's systems. You're better off listening to Gaundellin, Rathrinda, Hervorallin, or anyone else but me."

"You performed the scans and watched them operate the equipment," Phalalin countered.

"Yeah, but they told me where to scan, and they understood the results better than I ever did."

Phalalin nodded. "Indeed. I am no engineer either. I am a tactician. That does not mean I cannot demonstrate what my Mistress of Sails has already shown me."

True enough. Delwyn still remembered most of the crystal control sequences, among those including those sequences Kidahin had used for manual flight RCS, ACS, and OMS systems. Hell, he could even engage the sublight and FTL drive. Then again, plotting a course through normal space or through subspace would supersede even his limited knowledge and he said so.

Phalalin conferred with Einlann, Havalin and the other warleaders. They all agreed that Delwyn's experience made him more than qualified to face the task regardless of his protests of inadequacy. Einlann agreed to adjourn the meeting and reconvene it in the research bay on Wrathsee'a Anchorage, where Havalin would continue the Warpact.

They were leaving the ancient Males' Safe when a warleader raised a cautious ritual matter: had Delwyn decommissioned the ship?

Phalalin swore. "You have not had time to address this yet, have you?"

"Not yet. But if Einlann can put out a call to have my LAC crew recalled to the transport bay, we can return to the shipyard and decommission him. Then we may proceed."

By the time Delwyn reached the transport bay center, his entire LAC crew had already arrived. They seemed pleased to have him to themselves again. He knew he was going to have hell to pay from the remainder of his association for leaving them stranded on A'lon'aloop Naval Station.

###

Three hours later they arrived on Wrathsee'a Anchorage. While they were walking to the analysis bay, Delwyn reviewed what he wanted to do and how he wanted it done. Decommissioning a ship here was couched in musical ritual. Eyloni considered ships males, and the gender identity could not be trivially discarded. Decommissioning a ship stripped the male gender from him and reduced him to an 'it'. He tried to imagine the Eyloni female point of view and failed. The Coalition Fleet called ships by the female pronoun she or her. The tradition probably arose from the time when all crews were men who saw their ships as mother, mistress, or Madonna figures. No crewman actually saw his ship as a woman. Eyloni females did see a ship of war as a male personality, and that meant things could get complicated.

Properly speaking, the LAC belonged to the twenty-two Delwyn had rescued from the LAC's brig. He held the ship in trust for them up to now.

Delwyn and his LAC crew stepped through the crystalline puckered iris opening that made the stern look so much like a giant bending over and mooning him and into the aft airlock.

None of the warleaders or their protectresses followed, of course. Then again, the decommissioning ritual did not involve outsiders.

The custom preventing a male from boarding no longer applied now that Delwyn was no longer the vessel's warleader. While he held the ship in trust, as a courtesy he could fly the thing out of here and land in his warship's combat deployment bay if he wanted to. The twenty-two with him would not oppose him so long as he convinced them he had need of him. Properly speaking, the ship belonged to them because only female societies owned warships.

Delwyn stepped into the center of the bridge, and his crew formed a circle around him. He sang to them, a war song about a fighter pilot. In his head he could hear antiaircraft batteries firing and fighters dive-bombing as bagpipes played through the song's long bridge. His crew added their own haunting notes as they accompanied him.

By his singing, Delwyn set the proper mood for the solemn occasion. This ship was a he, presumed to have a male gender. Stripping the gender from the ship came, to the females with him, uncomfortably close to killing a male. The LAC was an enemy vessel, yet he remained a male in the Eyloni worldview. He had been redeemed when the twenty-two had captured him for Delwyn's sake. He had given the ship to them, and now he must give substantial and compelling reasons before they would consider inflicting the harm of revoking the male gender.

The trouble for them was that they had served with their warleader aboard this ship. Had they captured the ship and towed him into their warship, they would have stripped the gender from him immediately as a form of emasculation. A strange difference from Delwyn's perspective given that Eyloni males acted somewhat effete by human standards. In the present case however, a surface action assault force of twenty-two females and their sire cairn had taken possession of him, and that had made all the ritual difference.

Delwyn sang his reasons to his assault team rationalizing the need for having the LAC decommissioned. The Compact needed to learn his defenses and weaknesses. The research teams needed free access to the ship as a piece of equipment so they could take him apart, perhaps damaging him irreparably. Delwyn sang to them how much the greater good would be served by them consenting to separate the ship from the male gender.

In the end it was not a difficult decision for them, but it was stressful for them.

He asked them to declare their will.

They sang a reply in a morbid melody that gave him the creeps.

One by one they declared him dead, beginning with Phelindra and ending with Kidahin, a youthful Kidahin who not so many days ago had glared at the helm matrix table with murderous fury, shaking with a single-minded desire to smash the crystal matrix tables to pieces.

"He is dead," Phelindra whispered. "He no longer needs a society and its chosen warleader. You remain our chosen warleader of *Hunter's Moon*, and we accede to your judgement in this matter."

"So be it," Delwyn sang. Then he sang a song of comfort as they filed out of the bridge. He continued singing until Kidahin stepped through the airlock.

The warleaders and their protectresses stood in a circle around the airlock.

Delwyn swore they hadn't moved since he went into the ship.

Phalalin nodded. He began to sing, and the other males joined him.

Surprisingly their protectresses withheld their voices.

The warleaders sang their gratitude for the sacrifice the erstwhile LAC crew had made for the Compact, the La'huaset Tribe, and their allied clans.

Cheered by the overwhelming male response, Phelindra and the others relaxed from the tension, which had been building since the moment Delwyn had asked them to kill the ship.

"Are you sure everyone feels up to going back aboard and briefing them on equipment operation?" Delwyn asked, careful to avoid the words 'ship' and 'he' as if they smelled like rotting Lizard hands.

"Of course we do, Delwyn. We are not infants!" Phelindra admonished.

"I can show them myself, you know. I watched you activate systems as I scanned them."

Hervorallin and Rathrinda exchanged rhythmic sibilant snickers and snapped their tails playfully at him.

"You are no engineer. You can demonstrate, but you cannot tell them how, or why, the crystals do what they do," Rathrinda said.

"Can you?" he retorted.

"I can give theories of operation based on engineering principles I know and understand. You cannot. An engineering briefing is necessary for the analysis teams. We ought to do it now, otherwise we invite a later recall from Elleio to do then what we should be doing now," Rathrinda shot back.

Delwyn agreed and invited Phalalin and the others into the Ni'zakhonii captured equipment.

Phalalin shook his head. They had waited for this moment. This sacrifice proved again Delwyn's honor was unassailable. The males brushed and touched Delwyn, their tails wrapping him and their bodies pressing against him. Their warm velourlike skin felt comforting. In his mind, Delwyn thanked heaven his prior experiences with Anlann had prepared him for male touching.

Unlike humans, Eyloni culture did not view physical contact a sexual expression. Delwyn had to misdirect his mind away from human stereotypes, else he might hurt their feelings. They craved intermittent casual contact.

Delwyn remembered his lessons: withholding social contact was disrespectful. Withholding it signaled to others a belief the person excluded was unworthy of receiving basic Eyloni emotional needs. More often it signaled mental illness, and mental illness occurred rarely among Eyloni.

Delwyn felt like a new recruit at a hazing party about to go off on some dare as he invited the warleaders and their protectresses into the airlock and proceeded with the technical debriefing.

Two hours into the debriefing a frustrated and resentful Melkorka called from A'lon'aloop to update him on repair scheduling.

Repairs will begin within the next EST day.

18

ELLEIO, ON NA'DI ISLAND, HOME OF THE COMPACT COUNSEL

Delwyn sat at a graphics station in the analysis bay and reviewed the battle-damage assessment scans of the structural damage inflicted on his warship by the Ni'zakhonii attack. Mistress of Sails Anailiatha had already sent copies down to the naval construction center located within *Kem Basinga* Clan territory.

The center's fabrication equipment would compare the scans to those taken while *Hunter's Moon* was being built, extract damage data, and 'print' replacement structural components and entire modular sections. Kem Basinga Clan would then have the completed assemblies translated into transports in Elleio orbit, and the transports would deliver them to Wrathsee'a Anchorage. There, repair crews would install them into the warship once all the twisted scrap had been removed.

Delwyn commed Melkorka and asked her an obvious question. "Why don't you teleport all of the wreckage out? I'd think it'd save time."

"In some cases, whole sections can be translated away, but it is unwise to yank whole compartments out like a dentist carelessly pulling teeth. Go too fast and you might pull out a healthy tooth." Melkorka snapped.

"I thought you had bad teeth regenerated during a Health Center visit," Delwyn said. He couldn't resist the jab.

"Indeed I would, if I had bad teeth. I do not and never have. I am using a figure of speech to help your limited male mind understand a simple concept!"

Yep. She's mad as hell because I'm here on Wrathsee'a while she's stuck on A'lon'aloop. "Okay. My limited male mind understands. You don't go ripping out damaged sections indiscriminately."

"No you do not! You must survey the damage, make battle damage assessments, remove structures spanning multiple compartments and seal off conduits. Quantum translation is not a fixes-all gift from the spirits!" Melkorka spat.

"I guess not but it'd be nice to build up the damaged compartments from scratch, teleport the damaged ones out, and then teleport the replacement ones in. Your quantum translation technology can join them together better than any weld."

"Yes," Melkorka agreed. "And if your arm is cut off in battle, I will have Allohindra regenerate a replacement in Health Center and have Akenallin translate it onto the stump!"

Melkorka's testy retort brought Delwyn up short. Just thinking about the damaged cells, the severed nerves, blood vessels and bones, even the alignment of the stump relative to the teleported arm alone made Melkorka's point.

No thanks. As Delwyn understood it, quantum translation constructed an identical copy of an original object. That might be fine for whole objects. Using translation to join a teleported object to an independent one made him wonder just how close the joining alignment could be managed. Joining metal to metal probably wouldn't matter much if tolerances weren't an issue. Blood vessel and nerve connections now, that was something else entirely.

Melkorka's testy analogy was meant to remind him of all the wiring and plumbing systems running through the bulkheads. "I've figured it out for myself using only my tiny male mind. You know, it's different being over here with the guys."

"When are you returning?" Melkorka asked.

She missed him, the others too. He could hear it in her voice.

"Soon, I hope. About another …," Delwyn paused to consider the appropriate time standard. Males had to warrant the time periods they experienced from a gender point of view, which meant using the male standard time. He had about another hour to go plus the travel time back to Elleio orbit. That came out to about six TST hours, but as the Eyloni counted, "… eleven hours."

"Ten hours? That is almost half a day. By the time you return, you will need to rest before we leave for Elleio."

Delwyn ignored Melkorka's seamless conversion of his estimate into the female standard and smiled at what she considered a 'day'.

The female day was less than half of an Earth day in duration. Melkorka needed about three and a half hours of sleep to carry her through the remaining eight. His body had so far resisted all attempts to adapt with a vengeance. He still slept eight hours and stayed awake for sixteen hours, which drove Phelindra crazy.

"I'll try to get the briefing over with as soon as I can and have everyone back in time for a good night's sleep."

"See that you do. I am adrift without you and the others," Melkorka husked.

Delwyn stood his watch as fifth wheel, yawned, sighed, and watched Rathrinda demonstrate another crystal control setting.

Three hours had passed so far, three Earth hours.

Melkorka was probably having a fit.

They had started with a demonstration of the airlock control crystals. Then they went down into the engineering spaces, and Gaundellin showed the warleaders how to put the hydrogen-antihydrogen reactor online and feed power to critical ship systems.

Now they were crowded into the bridge. Phelindra, Kidahin, Gaundellin, Hervorallin, and Rathrinda displayed their skills in swapping crystals in matrix tables to activate the engineering, helm, and navigation stations.

Gaundellin engaged the artificial gravity and inertial dampening systems. Kidahin assumed the helmsmistress's station, chose a handful of manual flight crystals, and put the LAC through a series of programmed roll, yaw, and pitch maneuvers.

All the maneuvers were done inside the confines of the analysis bay.

Delwyn ground his teeth the whole time and hoped she wouldn't overcorrect and plunge the ship through the clearsteel bay windows and into the shipyard.

"Kidahin? Can you jump us from here to some point outside the Anchorage and then jump us back into this bay?" Havalin asked.

The request caught Kidahin by surprise, and she repeated it to Delwyn to buy more time than anything else.

"*Can* you do it?" Delwyn asked.

Kidahin turned to the Eldest. No female considered this equipment a ship now. Delwyn no longer had a controlling say in what happened to it or what to do with it, but social hierarchy did.

"Can you do it?" Phelindra asked. "There is no shame in saying you cannot."

"I can jump us outside the Anchorage. Of that I have no doubt. I am more concerned about our return plot accuracy. Delwyn did pose an interesting question when we first began experimenting with the FTL drive."

"Which was?" Phelindra prompted.

"Whether it would jump adjacent to a massive object or jump into it."

"Are you wondering if the navigation computer will let us jump back inside the analysis bay?"

Kidahin nodded. "I am not even sure if it will allow us to jump into the open shipyard volume inside the Anchorage."

"Inform Havalin of your concerns. Wrathsee'a Anchorage is his and shipyard safety is his responsibility," Phelindra said.

Kidahin briefed Havalin and he discussed the matter with the other warleaders.

They looked to Delwyn for counsel.

"Is it your judgment that Kidahin can do this?" Phalalin asked.

"I think so. Ni'zakhonii FTL technology drops a ship through a subspace manifold filled with an infinity of arcs. Kidahin can plot a minimal displacement arc and jump us outside the Anchorage. She only has to reverse the arc end points to jump us back inside the bay."

Phalalin sang a short statement to Havalin.

"Proceed at your convenience Kidahin," Havalin said.

Kidahin nodded but looked to Phelindra for permission.

Phelindra pointed her ears and snapped her tail.

Kidahin activated the FTL engine and navigation systems.

A crystal in the navigation matrix table began buzzing and flashing immediately.

Everyone flinched as they recalled what had been said about buzzing crystals in Delwyn's technical briefing.

"What did you do?" Phelindra demanded.

"Nothing! I initiated a jump command and the commit crystal buzzed when I touched it."

"Power," Delwyn interrupted. "We shut down the two-stage reactor and FTL drive feed after the tractor pilot towed us into *Hunter's Moon's* combat deployment bay. Someone has to go down to engineering and bring the FTL power systems online."

"I can do that," Gaundellin said and ran from the bridge.

Ten minutes later the crystal stopped its buzzing and flashing alert and settled into a silent, white diamond glitter.

"Power available. Course set for a 300,000 ell jump from Wrathsee'a Anchorage in a flat arc extending along our longitudinal axis and through the Anchorage hull," Kidahin reported.

"One moment," Phalalin said. He turned to Havalin and hummed a singsong statement.

Havalin twitched a left ear, activating the personal comm at his temple. He sang an order, waited for a reply, and then sang a status update to Phalalin.

"Our arrival point has been declared restricted space and cleared of traffic. The Mistress of the Tower will not blow us out of space the moment we violate Anchorage perimeter integrity," Phalalin said.

"You may proceed when you are ready, Kidahin," Havalin said.

Kidahin turned to Delwyn, her eyes meeting his. He reached around her, held her, and brushed his nose against her right ear.

"I am with you Kidahin. Let's get it done. I'm ready to go find Melkorka, get some sleep, and then go down to Elleio."

Delwyn's breathy baritone voice tickled Kidahin's sensitive ear, and she twitched it several times against his nose. She touched the commit crystal and it flashed a black light strobe. Then she pulled the null crystal from the initiation slot and popped in the violet velocity band crystal, the only crystal out of the twelve she knew for certain worked, the crystal that selected maximum FTL velocity.

"Jump …

…ing," she said as the ship jumped into subspace and then jumped back out of subspace five kilometers from Wrathsee'a Anchorage in the blink of an eye.

"Impressive," Havalin sang.

Kidahin immediately swapped the V-band velocity crystal with its null counterpart.

The warleaders waited a few minutes while their protectresses gave them a thorough visual examination. When satisfied their charges had suffered no harm, they turned on Kidahin and gave her a collective glare.

Nobody had told them what to expect. They had assumed Kidahin meant only to pilot the LAC around the shipyard volume inside Wrathsee'a Anchorage.

The warleaders, busy taking notes and talking among themselves, paused to give their protectresses apologetic tail brushes.

Phalalin and Amindaldra glided over to a Kidahin-hugging Delwyn.

"Havalin wants to lock combat scanners onto us and tie them into the sensors in the analysis bay so he can record our return jump. It will take several minutes before Combat Analysis is ready to proceed," Phalalin said.

"Fine by me. Kidahin, are you ready to initiate the return jump?"

"I am but jumping back worries me more than jumping here did," she snapped.

Delwyn felt for her. She had to plot a return for an alien ship using controls she had a guessing understanding of at best to jump them into a one-hundred-meter cube inside of a shielded naval station.

"Do you think the computer will register Wrathsee'a Anchorage's mass and reenter normal space outside the station?" he asked Kidahin.

She shook her head, her twitching ear flitting against his lips. She squeezed his waist with her tail and pulled him into the helmsman's chair between them. "I think it will find the internal shipyard volume adequate to accommodate the return jump. Whether we arrive inside the analysis bay or out in the shipyard is another matter."

"Delwyn?" Phelindra called from the LAC's tactical station. "I am detecting an energy signature emanating from Wrathsee'a Anchorage's outer hull. They have raised their primary defense shields."

"Phalalin? Wrathsee'a Anchorage's shields just came up. What's Havalin planning?" Delwyn asked.

"He wants to know if we can jump through the Anchorage shields," Phalalin said as he fended off Amindaldra's vehement objections to that plan.

"Ready to engage now?" Havalin asked Delwyn.

The other protectresses caught onto Amindaldra's concerns and objected as well. The males sang apologies. Havalin had Warpact command and the warleaders, Delwyn included, were honor-bound to respect his wishes.

"All right Kidahin, let's do this," Delwyn said.

"Affirm. Return arc jump plotted for zero relative velocity normal space entry on arrival."

"Jump," Delwyn said.

"Affirm," Kidahin said. She grabbed his hand and squeezed at the same time she used the other hand to swap the V-band and null crystals. "Jump …

…ing," she said as the LAC reappeared in the transparent-walled analysis bay, too close to the clearsteel windows for comfort.

"Did we drift a bit before jumping back?" he asked Kidahin.

"No! The ACS held us relative to the Anchorage," she replied, mystified.

"Phalalin, an effect of the shields maybe?"

Phalalin shook his head, still trying to recover from the shock of translating blind through Wrathsee'a Anchorage shields. A Compact warship could not do that. Interstellar travel did not take into consideration trivial notions like where exactly within a light-minute a warship reentered normal space. Pinpoint combat jumps not only took up a lot of computational time but needed FTL scans of the arrival site to lock the jump point into specific normal space coordinates. Wrathsee'a Anchorage's shields prevented a ship from getting an FTL sensor scan of the naval base's interior volume.

"I do not think so. I can think of no force carrier emanating from the shields capable of shoving us aside. It must have been a navigation error in our return plot."

Phalalin's remark provoked a snarl from Kidahin, and she gave her tail a violent snap. "Not possible. The FTL navigation system and drive worked perfectly."

"Microgravity?" Delwyn speculated aloud. "Mass in proximity?"

Everyone turned to Phelindra.

"I see a proximity warning symbol on the threat-assessment screen," Phelindra announced. "I think it means we have jumped too close to a large mass. Wrathsee'a Anchorage has the mass of a small moon, and I believe we have just found out how close the ship can jump to a mass."

The warleaders talked while typing notes into their personal electronic gear.

"Delwyn, please write a technical report summarizing all of the systems demonstrated to us today. Include any and all theories and conjectures on how the drive reacts to an adjacent mass and how, for the spirits' sake, can this thing jump blind into a shielded volume," Havalin said.

"Affirm," Delwyn said, using the Eyloni word meaning he willingly accepted a task. What Havalin really meant was, "Have your expert females write the reports, scan them, add your own comments, and pass them on to me."

"Phelindra, tell everyone it's time to get back to A'lon'aloop before Melkorka claws a hole through the hull," Delwyn said.

Phelindra agreed, but she did not look forward to returning. The moment they got back she would have to brief Melkorka, the command center mistresses, and select few others.

The three-hour trip back to A'lon'aloop Naval Station passed with the usual boredom of dull routine. As soon as they cleared the transport bay Delwyn ran down the orange and red rainforest trails until he reached the sleep-tree. He spent over two hours filling everybody in on the events that happened in the shipyard and then submitted himself to their careful scrutiny before falling asleep. The last thing he heard was Melkorka demanding to hear Phelindra's version of events and what the warleaders were planning.

Delwyn awoke several hours later surrounded by his association. They bustled about, wide awake, and completely refreshed. They had already showered, oiled their skin, and were waiting patiently for him to bestir his lazy self.

"The conveyance center can disperse our society onto the surface in another three hours. This leaves you little time to clean up," Melkorka said making hurry-up motions with her ears, hands, and tail.

He nodded in surrender.

"Phelindra, take me to the bathing falls. Fast."

Phelindra dropped what she was doing, leapt from the sleeping tier, and ran through the overgrown polished apricot beaver lodge, heading for the exit bole.

Delwyn had to hurry just to keep her in sight. A quick jog through crimson trees with bright orange catkins brought them to the sound of falling water. A few people were bathing below the gentle waterfall. Most of them, Anchorage personnel, paused as he stepped into the cascading stream.

They watched Phelindra scrub him.

"I can wash myself, thank you," he told her.

Phelindra ignored him and stepped back into the waist-deep pool to scoop up another handful of scrubbing sand from the bottom and attacked his armpits.

"You smell of work and stress from yesterday's technical briefing. You cannot smell ungroomed when you meet with the Be'atika Senge and the A'tayotan."

"Yeah, yeah, I know. Hey, what did Melkorka mean by dispersing the crew?"

"Not everyone is invited to Na'di Island. The command center mistresses, Anailiatha, some of my Hunters, a few others and you are invited. Everyone else will visit their clans. Phalalin and Verikaralee will come because they have been invited to sit in the Open Venue with us. Soon you, Hervorallin, Princess, and other O'un Tu Clan females will leave from Na'di Island and go home too, but for now you must hurry up. We cannot be late. Everyone will want to meet you before they …"

Phelindra froze.

Someone was stalking her.

Not the bathers. Oh, they watched all right, but this felt different, almost a calculating intent.

Someone was lurking out there under rainforest cover.

She smelled no one, but that meant nothing if the stalker was aware of her body and the air circulation patterns of this volume. Phelindra found a certain spot among the leaves, a pale-yellow spot. Was she leafchasing? Many plain light-yellow leaves covered the area around the bathing glade.

But this pale-yellow leaf was out of place.

Phelindra's eyes narrowed.

Delwyn stood among the females of his occupational association, all twenty-five hundred or so. They crowded into and around the conveyance center. He wanted to stay behind and watch them return to their clans, but they refused. Melkorka and the command mistresses had translated down to Na'di Island as an advance guard earlier to prepare the Compact Counsel for his arrival. Before they left, they all insisted he wait until they returned to the reception site, so his eyes would meet theirs when he arrived.

When the time came, Delwyn entered the A'lon'aloop translation center with hundreds of eyes on him as his association waited. Instinct and custom forced the females associating with a male to keep watch over him.

Delwyn waited and seconds later appeared in the Na'di Island conveyance center. The air was a bit warmer than it had been on A'lon'aloop, more humid too, but not as bad as he'd been led to expect.

The Mistress of Conveyance and her support crew greeted him with songs and touches. He sang a few words before doggedly following after

Melkorka's impatiently twitching tail across a lime green line on the ground and through the wide bole into open jungle.

The instant he cleared the force field threshold the steaming equatorial heat hit him. Pores opened, and his skin turned tacky. The air was hot, much hotter than anywhere he'd been since leaving Ibeetu orbit. The humidity was somewhere near eighty percent and the temperature was pushing forty degrees Celsius.

He squinted at the sky overhead, trying to get used to the sun. Elle was half again as bright as Earth's sun but lacking the coronal glare it appeared cooler and crisper. As if the sunlight had been put through an antiglare filter.

Elleio's atmosphere reduced the amount of long wave radiation hitting the surface, which meant Elleio received less light of the proper wavelength necessary for Earth chlorophyll photosynthesis. Elleio chlorophyll evolved to use the cooler colors, which explained why plants here reflected the reds, oranges, and yellows rather than greens like Earth plants did.

Melkorka led him up to the waiting group.

They in turn led him out into a vehicle parking area.

No roads marred the grounds around the conveyance center. Eyloni resisted the idea of roads at every turn, because building them ruined the delicate balance of the rainforest. The Eyloni preferred walking through the forest. Sometimes they rode inside vehicles resembling giant carpenter ants when they had to cross areas harboring dangerous animal life.

Eyloni sailed the seas and rivers and flew across the skies, but Melkorka had said once that point to point quantum translation was rarely used but for large-scale priority transport or in dire emergencies.

Phalalin poked his head out of a vehicle's hatch, pleased to see Delwyn again.

"Come and sit with us," he said, waving to a seat next to him and Amindaldra.

Delwyn saw only one other *Fearless* female with him: Verikaralee.

"Where is the rest of your crew?" he asked Phalalin.

"Off visiting with their clans, the same as yours are doing. I told them to enjoy themselves while they had the chance."

Delwyn sat down between Phalalin and Phelindra. Melkorka and the others claimed the seats behind him.

"First, please allow me to give you an aerial tour of Na'di Island," Phalalin said. He told the pilot to take off, and the VTOL aircraft lifted with a soft hum from the amber field and circled out over the coast and followed the shoreline toward the mountain range some 150 kilometers in the distance.

The aircraft leveled out at fifteen hundred meters above sea level and cruised along at three hundred klicks per hour, about 440 kanells per EST hour. The female time standard applied to airspeed because the velocity described a rate of speed over Elleio.

The fuselage windows followed the shape of the cabin beginning at the ceiling and curved down the sides to just under the passenger's feet. The glass-bottomed boat concept made the flight more immediate and personal than the bus experience a utility transport gave. Below, whitecaps lapped at baby chick yellow beaches. The rainforest grew right up to them, but as the forest marched inland the trees grew bigger. Here and there half a kilometer tall elleiu trees poked through the forest understory. At their current cruising altitude, the understory looked like a sea of rough orangy-red uncut grass with a few scattered orange, red, and yellow-variegated red leaved trees growing there. It was the leaves of the hundred-meter-tall trees that looked like grass from this altitude. The scattered elleiu trees were what looked like scattered trees towering above the 'grass.'

"Are all the elleiu trees populated?" Delwyn asked.

"Most of them are," Phalalin replied. "Na'di is home to the *A'way Senge* Clan of the Myat'ti'deep Tribe."

"I thought Na'di Island belonged to the Be'atika Senge," he whispered to Phelindra.

She shook her head. "Properly speaking, the Be'atika Senge is the female hierarchy sitting as the Compact Counsel. The A'way Senge clan hosts the Compact Counsel and has done so for centuries."

"Oh," Delwyn said.

Na'di Island covered 257,000 square kilometers, about a third of it was mountainous terrain. Elleiu trees branched out over half to almost three-quarters of a kilometer and grew in clusters some four hundred klicks apart. Each cluster had between three and five trees with an average of eight kicks between each tree. If Na'di Island had four hundred groups of elleiu trees, and each group had an average of four trees, then there were sixteen hundred elleiu trees, here alone.

If each tree housed an average of three hundred Eyloni, then about half a million Eyloni lived on the island.

Well, maybe not. Delwyn had assumed a maximum tree growth and a maximum number of people per tree. The actual number of residents probably fell somewhere between 280,000 and 380,000.

They cruised over a seaport where carved stone piers extended out into the sea. The piers reminded Delwyn of the few old limestone railroad bridges still standing on Earth. Made from quarried stone, they had survived the passage of time. Now historical societies maintained them as monuments to a bygone age.

Delwyn saw no roads leading into or out of the port.

The overhead view of sailing vessels moored there made Delwyn forget all about bridges and roads.

The ships' design threw him. His eyes narrowed as he considered the sails. Each ship had five masts. Each mast supported a vertical wing instead of a sail. The wings didn't look all that different from those on late Twenty-first Century jumbo jetliners. Well, close enough to get the idea anyway.

One of the ships must have just made port. As he watched, turbulent white water churned near its stern. That meant maneuvering thrusters were nudging the ship into the docking cradle. The thrusters were screws and not hydrodynamic jets. The white-water turbulence gave away the signs of propeller cavitation.

How quaint.

Stacks of cargo containers covered the deck, containers not much different than those used to ship cargo on Earth two hundred years ago.

"I don't see any cranes, but the dock workers have to shift the cargo off the deck somehow. What do they use? Quantum translation?"

"If they did, then why not just translate cargo here and forget the ships?" Phalalin asked rhetorically and then answered himself. "Heat pollution is a concern on Elleio. Quantum translation wastes energy, and energy expenditures increase with the amount of mass translated. We would need several coastal fusion plants to support constant commercial translations. The cooling systems would pull sea water into the heat exchangers and the warm water discharge would heat the shoreline and radiate waste heat into the atmosphere. Carbon fuels and their associated problems caused an ecological disaster during the … fifty-seven? Fifty-eight? … of your standard years we allowed such foolishness to continue.

"Hydrogen-antihydrogen fusion power systems are restricted to essential systems on Elleio. Standard boron fusion is permitted in small amounts. Most power comes from farside sea current and wind farms. See the purple vine growing up the side of the elleiu tree passing below? That is no parasitic vine, but a solar collector."

Delwyn stared down through the clear floor to admire the beautiful creeping structure with its mattress-sized triangular leaves. They swayed in the breezes like real leaves, too. Elleio's slow rotation gave them just over six Earth days of charge time so the tree's inhabitants could have electrical power during the six days of night common here.

"If they don't teleport cargo containers, then they must shift them using tractor fields."

"That they do," Phalalin agreed. "Fields move containers from the ship to the dock, and a second field pulls the containers into the warehouses. Once inside, good old-fashioned pallet management systems, automated carts, or manual labor unloads them and moves the contents to storage. When clans order items in bulk, the orders are pulled from warehouse storage and packaged. The packages—depending on the quantity shipped—are loaded into VTOL atmospheric aircraft, lighter-than-air craft, or smaller sailing vessels."

"How are bills paid for?" Delwyn asked.

"Paid?" Phalalin replied, confused by Delwyn's scent image of the context he meant.

"Delwyn means traded, Phalalin. How the trade balance between the requesting clan and the sending clan is managed," Melkorka interrupted from the seats behind them.

"Ah, that is easy. When O'un Tu Clan orders items supplied through this port, a balance sheet is generated. That balance sheet lists the items ordered and the clans that made them. The port mistress then calls up the current balance of trade status between our clan and all the clans providing the items in the order. If our balance of trade sits at the mean reciprocal level, we receive the goods. If the balance mean shows a deficit in our trading relative to any of the sending clans, our clan elders must pledge return items in trade to restore the balance. If we cannot make up the deficit in trade goods, we must reach an agreement with the clan on an equitable service to restore the balance mean."

"Oh," Delwyn said. "So just like Bedilin's clothing shop, trade among clans doesn't depend on a monetary economy. Balance sheets don't track monetary debt or credit. It doesn't even matter whether the items have similar values. As long as clans trade among themselves, they receive needed items for what items they give in return. Everyone's needs are satisfied. Nobody ever goes without."

"Wants," Phalalin continued, "now, those are different. In the past a collective desire to sacrifice for what they wanted drove groups of clans into alliances for building industries, research centers, and warships. Medicine and health care were social goods meant to benefit all clans. They pooled resources. Some clans specialized in hospitals maintained by medical societies. Nobody lacked care. Even today clans cooperate for things they want.

"Elleio's female population sacrificed clan time and labor to advance technology, raise armies, and build warships. They did so to make sure nothing would ever cause harm to the male population. Only after male welfare was addressed did they work for their own mutual benefit."

So, Delwyn thought, Eyloni 'wants' tended toward the socially conscious: they didn't want the latest fashion in shoes or clothing, didn't want the latest electronic gizmo, didn't want the latest vehicle or a fancier house. No consumerism and no commercialism existed here.

Delwyn laughed. He couldn't help himself.

"Care to let us in on the joke?" Zalzadrin quipped from the back seats. She waited, expectantly. Delwyn had a good sense of humor, better than most males.

Delwyn shook his head. "Remind me to tell you about it later. It'd take too long to explain it to you right now."

How could he explain? Part of Ambassador Harrison's dream had been to establish economic ties with the Compact of the Ten Tribes of Elleio, which meant he had hoped to find someone to sell Coalition of Earth Colonies junk to.

Ha!

No doubt by now Anlann and Seralin had taken a trip through a shopping center on Earth, rejected the rampant commercialism there, and settled for browsing through the native art of Earth's indigenous First Nations and their tribal art and knickknacks. Aesthetic crafts interested the Eyloni, not disposable commercial crap. Yes, he could imagine a cargo container stuffed with Native American dreamcatchers arriving here, but Bedilin would never order blue jeans and try to push them onto her customers.

The aircraft climbed to a new flight level so the passengers could look down over the mountain range passing below. The mountains stretched out below them, worn and ancient. They had no sharp peaks. No snow covered them. Na'di Island's equatorial heat encouraged the growth of cloud rainforest coverage so heavy it overwhelmed the gentle summits.

The aircraft banked above overgrown peaks and flew over a long deep valley, an ancient scar so rocky in places it prevented the tall trees from finding deep root support.

Lesser trees grew down through the rift, trees barely twice as tall as those in old growth forests on Earth. Crimson vines similar to kudzu vines draped bright orange trees. The vines had small leaves for an Elleio plant, at least the smallest of those he'd seen so far. They were tiny next to the tree's car-sized orange leaves. Vines covered the exposed bark and draped the orange leaves like bloody wraiths.

And yet they avoided the tree's leaves themselves. Delwyn asked why.

"Chemical defenses," Melkorka said, glancing down at the sight. "The vines draw sap from the trees, stunting their growth. The trees evolved a natural herbicide they release from their leaves' stomas, a toxin the vines abhor. They have fought this war to a stalemate. The trees cannot grow to their natural size, and the vines cannot envelop the trees. The vines never reach maturity, never flower, and never reproduce. They are ancient, reproducing only when a tree dies."

"The entire area seems well cared for from this height, almost as if manicured. I can even see trails through the vines covering the ground. Don't tell me the trees grow leaves down to ground level."

"The vines are not hacked away. They belong to the cloud rainforest and cannot grow in the warmer lowlands. The keepers of the Valley of the Heroes of Home pick a few tree leaves and steep them in hot water. The tea brewed from them is then sprayed down the trails every ten days or so. The oily herbicide is strong, and it discourages the vines from crossing the paths."

"Isn't it easier to synthesize the chemical and spray that?"

Faint disgust shadowed Melkorka's features a moment before passing. "We do not pour chemicals all over our forests. We do not employ even natural compounds often, preferring nature take its course as the spirits intended. Besides, why waste the energy and resource to make a product the forest produces every day?"

"Makes sense I suppose, but isn't it a lot of work to pick all those leaves, brew them, and spray the stuff down all those paths?"

"What work?" Melkorka demanded. "The keepers do it gladly. Brewing it takes little solar energy and the leavings are left to dry and are then scattered over the mountain range to join the leaf litter already covering the ground."

Delwyn saw an obelisk a third shorter than the old Washington Monument had been on Earth, but it had a base twice as thick. He couldn't tell from the viewing angle, but he thought it rested upon an inverted obelisk buried two-thirds deep into the valley floor. Even from this altitude he could tell it had been carved from solid granite.

"I see an object rising from the ground up ahead. I think it's a monument."

"The burial site of the Heroes of Home," Phelindra murmured with hushed reverence

A niche had been cut into the rocky granite mountain side near the obelisk.

Like national parks on Earth, this memorial also attracted visitors.

Here the six Heroes of Home had been laid to rest. In the past ten-thousand years, Earth years at that, whenever some worldwide crisis or calamity threatened, a male was chosen as a warleader who then declared the entire world population under his Warpact command. There had been only six Heroes in all of recorded history.

And just as the male chosen by a Comari had no choice, the Hero had no choice either. If he possessed some essential qualifying gift or some innate ability sought by the Compact Counsel, the obligation of Hero attached to him. A male was forbidden to seek or actively desire the honor, however. The Hero concept warped the Eyloni mindset by the very nature of the worldwide Warpact obligation it fostered on the people. The seriousness of the matter was so great that every female in the world would kill a male for so much as hinting he wanted the job. To actively seek it gave the appearance of unseemly covetousness behavior during a time of great need or sorrow.

Or that was how he understood Melkorka's description of the concept.

A Hero of Home came as close to an absolute monarch as the Eyloni ever had.

The VTOL aircraft circled the sight, giving Delwyn ample time to view from above what all Eyloni considered a sacred site.

"Can we arrange a visit sometime?" Delwyn asked.

"Let me check and see," Phalalin said. He jumped to his feet and bounded though the open flight deck hatch.

Delwyn squinted. Phalalin had borrowed the copilot's headset and appeared to be talking to someone.

Oh, no! Phalalin was asking for permission to divert from the flight plan.

"They're gonna hate me even before they meet me."

"Who will hate you?" Melkorka and Phelindra demanded at the same time. Both females radiated an aura-like combative ire at the thought of anyone hating any male, let alone him.

"The Compact Counsel. I just got us diverted from meeting them."

Melkorka shook her head. "You are a guest of the Counsel. The aerial tour above Na'di Island is included in the invitation extended to you. You may go anywhere and do anything within the bounds of courtesy and privacy."

The aircraft glided north for two klicks and descended to land on a flat stone pad. Delwyn counted thirty similar VTOL aircraft parked on scattered natural stone slabs surrounded by straw-colored grasses. The natural native stones had been a part of the local landscape for untold ages.

The plane touched down feather-light, the pilot taking extreme care not to mar the stone surface.

The best way into the memorial site was by air. If people wanted to walk, then they hiked the vine-bordered trails up from the foothills.

For a worldwide landmark, the obelisk wasn't attracting the patronage Delwyn expected, but then again Elleio was two-thirds the size of Earth and had a total surface area 2.6 times South America. Elleio had nowhere near the population a crowded Earth had.

Delwyn exited the aircraft and walked with the group down a narrow trail that joined other trails before they finally encountered a broad path approaching the memorial site and its central obelisk.

On the way into the memorial grounds they met other visitors. Those visitors had brought their infants and children with them, and when Hervorallin crossed another vine-bordered path, she met females with their infants.

When Princess saw them, she sang out to them.

They, much older than her, sang back a greeting.

Princess jumped from her mother's back and rushed to meet them.

The infants listened with mounting interest as Princess sang intricate melodies to them.

That is, they listened until they noticed Delwyn and Phalalin. Then they rushed the two males as if their tails had caught fire.

They walked in circling patterns around the two males, eager for notice, until they caught the difference in Delwyn's scent.

They withdrew from Phalalin and surrounded Delwyn. Princess rushed up behind them, singing with ecstatic joy.

Their arrival took Delwyn back to memories of grade school class field trips. He wondered what, if anything, they would remember of their visit here today.

Right now they were more interested in him than they were in the memorial site or Phalalin.

"They will follow us the whole time we are here. You will need to get used to that," Phalalin said.

Delwyn watched the infants watching him and Phalalin. They gazed at him with the single-minded intensity of possessed children in a horror movie.

"What are they so intent on?" he asked.

"Us," Phalalin said. "They are obsessively attracted to males. Their instinct to protect us is strong. They would be inseparable from us if we had an infant male with us."

Delwyn remembered Captain Lahiri's toddler and the story Kidahin had told him about how infant females had prowled through kilometers of jungle looking for him after his mother returned him to her ship.

"At least you have your near-daughter to mediate for you," Phalalin said with a mock-serious sigh.

"What about Princess? She's too young to interact with these older infants."

Zalzadrin chirped a laugh. "You are her male. She has exclusive territorial rights over you, and the other infants know her claim by the pheromones she has scent-marked you with. Infant females will consider themselves ranked by her in all matters concerning you. If a jungle animal attacked you now, Princess would call on them, and us, to help her protect you. They, and we, would respond to her call without a moment's care for their, or our, own safety. Even after we had the fighting under control, we would not call the infants back. That is one reason why males carry such a great obligation in our culture. They must watch where they are going and what they are doing, for even infant females will come to the defense of a male."

"But you wouldn't really let them fight though, right?"

Zalzadrin laughed. "We could not stop them. They fit into the female hierarchies but are too young to understand rational choices. They have an instinctive ranking system all their own within their own hierarchy. They will listen to higher ranked females. But if a male is in danger, they will act against that threat. We would never discourage them. Protecting you is too important for us to worry about them. That is why you are honor-bound by custom to exercise some care when you are out and about, least your self-endangerment summons females—even infant females—to your defense."

Delwyn didn't know what to say. The whole idea was alien to his understanding, beyond anything in human experience: babies coming to the defense of a grown man.

Zalzadrin led him into the small courtyard surrounding the obelisk. Warriors stood rigid in staggered posts around them and at various elevated posts surrounding what hadn't been a niche after all, but an entrance into at least ten caves scattered along a cleft in the rock. Six showed signs of extensive foot travel from centuries of people passing through the individual burial sites and shrines to the Heroes of Home interred there.

The memorial gave Delwyn a familiar feeling, as if he'd stepped onto the hallowed ground of the tomb of an unknown soldier.

None of the honor guard Warriors so much as budged a hairsbreadth. They didn't even acknowledge Phalalin. They wanted to though. Delwyn felt their eyes on him too. They wanted to meet him, but honor and obligation kept them silent and at their posts for however long their shift kept them there.

"You cannot enter the tombs themselves at this time, but you can read the platinum plaques that names the Hero and lists his accomplishments."

Delwyn stepped up to the closest gleaming plate and scanned the pictographic legend.

He read and learned the history of the six Heroes of Home, one at a time. Delwyn could read the inscriptions easily enough. Once he had the musical notation straight in his head, he was good with words.

Later, as their VTOL aircraft lifted into the sky, Melkorka leaned on Delwyn. "What are your thoughts about the Heroes of Home?"

"Interesting. I'm still thinking about them. Princess seemed to enjoy meeting infants for the first time."

Zalzadrin trilled a giggle. "Yes, Delwyn, just you wait until we get home!"

Delwyn let her comment pass. He watched the mountains give way to jungle as they flew across the island, heading toward a group of five tall elleiu trees rising into the sky on the horizon.

The home of the Be'atika Senge.

The aircraft landed in a large white clearing bordered by burnt orange grasses and crimson brush some 1.5 klicks from the nearest elleiu tree. Up close the five trees didn't look like a cluster at all. They were tens of kilometers apart, but from a distance they made a lightning bolt streak pattern among the lesser trees. They had landed a third of the way down the length of the zig-zag pattern made by the trees.

Delwyn stepped through the hatch and onto the white surface.

It wasn't concrete. It wasn't a stone slab either. It felt like packed crushed limestone. As hard as it was, it gave—a bit—when compressed by the VTOL's heavy landing jacks.

He thought he knew the reason for the material used. Making concrete produced heat and carbon waste and used a lot of energy. Why make more waste when a natural solution presented itself?

"The Compact Counsel occupies all these trees?" Delwyn asked.

"No," Kidahin replied. "The tree we walk under is called the *Elleiu Na'aheilu*, the Tree of Counsel. This tree shelters the Compact Counsel and the place where it meets. Support mistresses live here with the Be'atika Senge and their immediate families. The other trees provide living space for the A'tayotan hierarchy, Fleet Operations, world defenses, and intertribal relations."

This was the seat of the government for Elleio and its interstellar colonies?

"Kidahin just how many colony worlds does the Compact have?" Delwyn asked.

"We claim twenty-two systems including Elle. Of those, four can support Elleio lifeforms. Three have inhabitable moons orbiting gas giants, like Elleio and the Nikkiolo moon you name Ibeetu. One system has a marginally habitable planet."

"How many Eyloni live on the colony worlds?"

"Not many. What do you think Melkorka, about two billion?"

Melkorka nodded, "Two billion sounds right."

Two *billion*? Thirty times the populace of Elleio? Still, for four planets, even two billion sounded slim.

"I can't believe you have so many more people off-world. I don't see how it's even possible."

"What are you talking about? Our colonies represent but a fraction of Elleio's population. We have about as many off-world colonists as there are males on the homeworld," Melkorka said.

"What? How is … Oh. I get it."

Delwyn sighed. Whenever the Eyloni counted two billion of anything, he counted four million of them.

That was it? Earth supported a population of 14.7 billion people alone. Even the Moon had over sixty million. Mars had four hundred million. The population of all Coalition colony worlds far exceeded that of Mars and the Moon combined. The Compact had been lucky to find a habitable planet. Coalition planet hunters had found habitable moons, but no habitable planets so far. In fact, discoveries to date suggested the galaxy preferred evolving habitable moons over habitable planets.

Elleio's population hovered somewhere around sixty-seven million. Three million of those sixty-seven million were males. The Comara carved out a mere 660,000. The Hunters and Warriors split the remaining sixty-three million, with the Warriors ahead of the Hunters by some thirteen million.

Then the numbers hit Delwyn without warning.

Seventy million people! That's all? Only seventy million Eyloni lived?

"What alarms you?" Phelindra demanded.

"I didn't realize there were so few of you."

She frowned at him, flipped her ears aside and back and held her tail motionless.

"There are as many of us as there are. Do you think there should be more?"

"Well, there are many more humans than Eyloni."

"How many more?" Phalalin asked.

"Elleio's population comes close to Earth's airless Moon. Earth itself has orders of magnitude more."

"How do you have room to prowl through your jungles?" Kidahin asked.

"Earth is a much bigger world, a planet and not a moon," Phalalin said.

"And there's not a lot of jungle there," Delwyn added. "Earth is not a rainforest world. Tropical rainforests grow in a limited number of latitude zones above and below the equator. Industrial activity wiped most of them out long ago to make way for land development, lumbering, and strip mining."

Phalalin gave him a sorrowful look. "Earth sounds like a horrible place to live. Anlann and Seralin must be heartsick. It is no wonder you chose us."

Delwyn smiled at Phalalin's occasional odd turns of phrase. He was still having trouble with Coalition words and context.

They hiked under the elleiu tree's wide branches. Progress slowed to a crawl every time Delwyn stopped and gazed up two hundred meters into the main branches. Those branches, covered with pastel red and orange leaves trimmed in yellows, rivaled California redwoods.

A solar energy collector wound up around the tree's outer network of fused aerial roots and out of sight in the leaves.

Delwyn felt a … a presence …from the tree. It wasn't an awareness of the people he knew lived within it that he felt, but something about the tree itself. A sense of overwhelming awe floored him. He hadn't felt that moved by the Valley of the Heroes of Home. The tree radiated antiquity and sacredness. The spooky thrill he had when he once visited Stonehenge came to mind, and he couldn't decide if he faced a cathedral or an ancient sage.

People lived in this mighty relic, had lived here for centuries.

Melkorka stood next to Delwyn and watched him leafchase his thoughts through the branches of the tree. She understood how he felt, smelled his deep respect for the tree, for the forest. That she lived in a tree like this one did not breed familiarity with her. Tied as her people were to the forest, they always felt the same way he did all the time. That Delwyn also felt the presence of the tree reinforced her belief in him: he truly belonged to them.

Delwyn found the island heat and humidity exhausting, and he began to drip sweat while doing nothing but standing there looking up into the tree. He glanced down at the ground. The co-operative colonial farmer in him tugged at his curiosity. He stooped to grab a handful of the rust-colored soil and spread it around his damp palm with his thumb.

He let the dirt sift through his fingers, leaving behind a dull orange, perfectly round stone.

He rolled it back and forth in his hand.

"I think someone lost a marble."

Zalzadrin glanced at the stone in his palm and shook her head.

"He is not going to like it if you keep doing that."

"Who? The marble's owner?"

"No. *Him*," she said, pointing her tail at the stone.

Delwyn held his palm up to his eyes and stared at the stone.

He rolled it around his palm.

He blew on it, feeling absurd as he did so.

Zalzadrin and her jokes.

Delwyn stepped into a shaft of sunlight beaming down from the canopy far above and let it fall on the stone.

The sun warmed his hand, and the ke'nah decided enough was enough. As Delwyn watched, the marble unfolded like a large sow bug and waited.

The thing looked like a small trilobite.

It waited.

"If you do not put him down soon, he will bite you," Kidahin advised.

"Poisonous?" he asked.

"No, but he can give you a painful pinch."

Delwyn put his hand down on the ground and waited as the ke'nah scurried off, vibrated its eight legs to burrow into the soil, and rolled back into its marble shape.

"Inactive in the day, I suppose?"

"Yes, they aerate the soil. He is a small one. They get bigger," Kidahin said, demonstrating with her hands as she made a circle as big as a croquet ball.

Delwyn slapped the dust from his hands and followed Melkorka toward a large opening in the imposing tree's outer aerial root shroud. The tree had a wide central bole big enough to fly a betafortress through. He froze on seeing the dark green line marking the bole threshold.

Dark green meant a barrier force field was in operation here.

"They don't want unexpected visitors," he said.

"They do not want jungle animals visiting," Phelindra corrected.

Two Warriors stood just inside the bole threshold, one on each side.

One of them touched a switch and the green line vanished.

The two Warriors gave every female a personal ritual welcome before turning on Delwyn. Flanking him, they wrapped their tails around his waist and escorted him deeper into the tree.

Unlike the simulations he'd seen before now, he stood in a place that evoked such a strong awareness of life that no force field overlaid holographic image could match. Aerial roots dropped down from above and burrowed into the ground, forming pillars and soaring arches with their own side boles and more layers of fused roots leading around and up through the outer tree structures.

The escorting Warriors led Delwyn between thick root mazes, around buttressing growths and across smooth flat river stones placed along wandering paths around the main trunk. A second aerial root layer grew around the first some three meters apart. It too was covered with multiple openings giving access to the central spiral growth the inhabitants used as a living stairway into the canopy.

Wood shavings covered the ground everywhere there wasn't a flagstone path. The large, dull orange shavings felt feathery and soft.

Delwyn glanced up. Galleries of fused roots closed in around the tree well above him.

If a tree could house three hundred people, then this chamber alone could hold them with ease. The distance from the heart trunk to the entrance bole was at least forty meters. The heart trunk and its supporting root structures together measured at least another twenty meters. If the tree was symmetrical along its ground cross-section, then it had to have a ground-level diameter near one hundred meters.

"This place is called the Hall of Voices. Counsel sessions and other communal matters are addressed here. Because the warm forest level is uncomfortable even for those among us from the northern La'huaset Tribal continent, the Counsel has agreed to hold today's session in the Open Venue."

Another Warrior waited for them next to the opening between the heart trunk's inner and outer root drapes. She sang a query to Delwyn and waited.

"She asks if you will follow her," Phelindra said.

"I know what she said," he snapped.

"You speak as if you do not. You need to practice understanding different tribal dialects," she said.

The Warrior turned as the two escorting Delwyn let their tails drop, but both gave him shy pons brushes before surrendering him to the third Warrior.

The complexity of the tree didn't quite mesh with what Delwyn had come to expect. The projections aboard ship had been beautifully executed, but now he understood what Phelindra had said about the simulation having abrupt changes in scenery.

They climbed up a staggering spiral central shaft. Aerial roots threaded across the twisting inclined path, forming uneven but serviceable steps. The original trunk, the heart trunk, towered above Delwyn on his right, growing up through the aerial root ceiling and beyond. His left ascending view alternated between fused apricot colored wood walls and hollow spaces meandering off into the living maze. Gnarled roots wound around the heart trunk like jungle vines, forming natural orange and apricot colored handrails polished by centuries of hands.

The younger roots in the Hall of Voices gave it a pumpkin flesh yellow-orange color. The older apricot colored roots turned the wood around the heart trunk a dark orange. But there was also a dim phosphorescence that gave the living central spiral silvery highlights.

Delwyn traced the glow to shelf fungi. Finger-thick, they had the outline of a football-shaped pancake. They looked like the flat shelf growths found on tree trunks back on Earth.

They glowed across their entire surface area, like white objects bathed in a black light.

They had no odor. He had expected a musty smell.

"Can I touch one?" he asked.

Melkorka nodded. "They are sturdy. You could not kick them loose if you wanted to."

Delwyn reached out and grabbed a growth. It felt neither slimy nor sticky, but more like a piece of polished wood. It didn't seem to mind his touch, either. It kept on glowing, growing neither dimmer nor brighter.

The growths grew in clusters every three to five steps apart along the ascending central spiral walkway.

"I didn't see these things in the Hall of Voices," Delwyn said.

"They like it in the dark, and they prefer the slight breezes that prevail here. These aerial roots are among the oldest, and they penetrate deep below the ground. The fungi grow in the dark places in an elleiu tree, but many more colonize the central spiral than they do the outer chambers."

Delwyn smelled his hand. A vague earthy smell remained there, a faint mushroom odor.

"They negate the need for light fixtures," he said.

"They do at that. Ambient light hurts them, so we do not install artificial lighting in a tree's central pathways. Rooms, chambers, and side-trails are different. The wood varies in both texture and moisture content there. The growths do not like those areas because the temperature and humidity changes too much for them to grow well," Melkorka said.

Now that she had mentioned it, Delwyn noticed both the heat and the humidity had dropped. Not much, but enough to feel the difference.

"I remember something about air currents in elleiu trees. Wasn't there something said about the breezes changing directions at night?" he asked.

"They do," Melkorka agreed. "The nights are cooler relative to the ambient temperature inside the tree. Hot air escapes from the crown boles and the central chimney bole."

"Chimney bole?"

Melkorka nodded. "On the opposite side of the heart trunk is a large opening in the fused roots that ventilates the Hall of Voices. All elleiu trees form them to keep internal temperatures stable. In ancient times we kindled fires in a hearth made from river stones below the vent. The exhausting heat and smoke rises into the crown and out of the tree. Fires are kindled there even now for major ritual gatherings, but a fire's main purpose in ancient times was to drive back jungle animals during the night."

"I'd be more afraid of setting the tree on fire," Delwyn said.

"Not if care is taken when preparing the hearth. Living elleiu tree wood is difficult to set on fire. When it does burn, it slow burns, smolders, and tends to self-extinguish. The hearth is two or three ells from the vent, and the exhausting air is not even hot enough to singe the bark let alone ignite it. Even if the vent roots were to catch fire it would never get far. Water from frequent rains is caught by the leaves and directed more or less onto the branches. Most water tends to flow downward along grooves in the bark until it finds an opening into the understory fused root system. The system serves as natural plumbing that diverts water into natural cisterns, and they overflow and run down into the lower tree. There, water distributes into the central root system and flushes the necessaries. Any fire burning through is immediately put out by the water draining around the chimney bole and vent."

So now he knew what made the muffled running water sounds he thought he had been imagining all along.

"May the spirits spare you from a burn through into the necessary's drainage paths," Delwyn said.

"The necessary channels were mapped out long ago. They empty into the oldest aerial root growths near the heart trunk far below the ground. The potable water system is isolated. The hearth vent and chimney bole has been surveyed. It is a naturally sealed passage that avoided both systems."

"That's some drainage system if it's large enough for a person to crawl through. I don't see how you can guarantee the necessary drainage and the potable water systems haven't merged somewhere within a living and growing tree."

Zalzadrin tickled him under the chin with her pons, and Delwyn grabbed playfully at her tail. "Yes, people long ago surveyed the vent to make sure potable water did not drain in from the exhaust bole," she said.

"Yes," Phelindra added, "Someone as small as yourself for example. It is a solitary job, one a Hunter like yourself might enjoy, I am sure."

Phelindra's comment sent Zalzadrin off on a long but halfhearted series of complaints about tall Warriors. Halfhearted because Phelindra, a Hunter herself, had been the one calling notice to Zalzadrin's short stature.

Melkorka looked Delwyn in the eye and traced a circle in the air with her pons, a sign meaning the same as rolling one's eyes.

The winding natural staircase leveled out. Several boles opened off to his left below rafters of fused roots. Some grew outward, some continued up an incline as if heading out onto a branch, and some wound up and around like a Males' Safe area.

"Is this a Males' Safe?" Delwyn asked.

"No. The Males' Safes are well above us, but the Open Venue grows just as dense. The lower part resembles a Males' Safe in that the defenders of the tree can hold the access to the levels above it from there. Like a Males' Safe, it has mazes and bottlenecks, and they make defending the upper tree from an invading force much easier. The Open Venue is where the Compact Counsel—the Be'atika Senge and the A'tayotan representatives—await us."

Delwyn climbed on up, around, and through the dense wood maze until his Warrior escort pulled him into a large open space.

The Open Venue was an open-roofed treehouse with twisting branches for sides. Awning-sized red and orange leaves filled the crown overhead.

A Warrior older than Phelindra came to him on prancing feet to wrap her tail around his waist and trilled a welcome.

"I am Thelindrallin," she sang. "Be welcome to the Be'atika Senge."

Thelindrallin turned and sang the Compact Counsel into session.

Unlike the military briefings aboard the two stations this meeting had been arranged for Delwyn. They wanted to know all about him, how he knew Anlann and Seralin, and how he had met Melkorka and Phelindra.

They too questioned his taking of Kidahin's adulthood knife.

They also spoke with Phalalin, asking him about his conduct once his warship had arrived in the Nikkiolo star system.

Delwyn didn't expect briefings here, either. This ritual meeting satisfied Eyloni social graces.

"Have you and Delwyn practiced exchanging Warpact leadership?" Thelindrallin asked Phalalin.

"Yes, many times. He understands the custom and adhered to it even when doing so stressed the temporary repairs on his warship," Phalalin said.

"Perhaps he has some ideas about the tactical error Kalinn committed when he jumped into the Nikkiolo system in the first place?" Thelindrallin asked.

Melkorka growled in dissonant scale at the implied slander suggesting Kalinn had been reckless, bit her tongue, and shook her head.

"Delwyn was not aboard at the time, how can he comment on Kalinn's actions?" she trilled.

"Surely," Thelindrallin snapped, "he has had time to dwell on the attack and make conclusions?"

That started another lyrical argument.

"What are they arguing about?" Delwyn asked Phelindra.

"Thelindrallin asked Melkorka whether or not you have shared any theories on how Kalinn could have been so easily duped into jumping into an ambush," she hissed.

"Oh, I see. Melkorka's offended at the implied insult to Kalinn's memory."

"Yes."

"It wasn't his fault. Those Ni'zakhonii destroyers weren't waiting for him. They waited there for some other purpose. It was just his bad luck to have jumped into them."

"What?" Phelindra squealed.

Her musical shout drew everyone's notice. Thelindrallin, not in the habit of tolerating interruptions, glared at the Eldest Huntress.

"What Phelindra? Did Delwyn twist your tail to calm you down? Tell him to do that to Melkorka!"

"No, Mistress. Delwyn says the three destroyers were in Nikkiolo's heliopause for their own purposes, and we just happened to jump into proximity with them."

Thelindrallin, a Mistress of the Counsel and counsel-speaker, had a command of Coalition standard as good as co-Ambassador Seralin's had been before she left with Anlann and Ambassador Harrison on *Henri Edda.* She fixed Delwyn with a direct gaze and frowned.

"How did you come to that conclusion, Delwyn? Melkorka's after-action report mentioned they had detected a Ni'zakhonii faster-than-light drive artifact crossing their course and heading for Nikkiolo. The ship had to come from Surutia to give Kalinn an obvious ship to ambush, and he got himself ambushed instead."

"No, Thelindrallin. With respect, that's wrong. The Ni'zakhonii would have had to know in advance Kalinn's decision to head into the Nikkiolo Expanse. Melkorka told me Kalinn hadn't yet decided which star system he wanted to prowl in. He had the choice of Iota Horologii, which you name Nikkiolo. He could have gone to Chi Eridani, the star you call Surutia. Q-1 Eridani, Alpha Mensae, even Epsilon Reticuli were all viable possibilities. Of those, he thought neither Surutia nor Nikkiolo held sufficient prospects and decided to head for Alpha Mensae. That system held the best chance if he wanted to fulfil his original mission since the Compact fleet had stopped a Lizard incursion there once before.

"The Ni'zakhonii lack hyperlink communications technology and cannot comm intelligence at multiple FTL speeds. There is no way they knew enough, soon enough, to run an assessment through their admiralty and then dispatch three destroyers to Nikkiolo ahead of Kalinn. You can't coordinate ships' movement that fast, so how could the light attack craft we captured have plotted its maneuvering from Chi Eridani into Nikkiolo at the same time?

"No, those ships were stationed there for some other reason and the LAC had likely been sent there to support courier operations for the destroyer task force. We killed everyone on the bridge before they had the chance to alter any control settings. I'm certain the LAC's computer contains copies of orders meant for those three ships."

Everyone in the Open Venue stared at him, speechless.

Phalalin recovered his wits first.

"Are you suggesting those ships were staging there? In the star's heliopause? Why there, of all places? If they wanted the system, why not secure a bridgehead on the moon's surface and put the destroyers in high garrison orbit above it?"

"I don't know, but they tried their damnedest to destroy *Hunter's Moon.* I reviewed the intel you have on Lizard destroyers and based on careful observations and summaries of the warleaders who have engaged those ships and based on the damage they did to my warship, I'd say three Ni'zakhonii destroyers might have achieved parity against *Hunter's Moon* if they had achieved total surprise when they fired their first volleys. They were not successful, and for that you can thank Kalinn and the combat operations team of Melkorka, Trebithia, and Hlinlodyn. Once Kalinn destroyed the first ship, he had tactical superiority. Then all rational combat analysis should have told the two remaining Lizard commanders to engage their FTL drives and jump to safety before a vengeful Kalinn ripped them to pieces.

"What we need to know is: why didn't they cut and run? They must have wanted Compact eyes out of the system."

A shocked Thelindrallin waggled her fingers madly as she listened to Delwyn's summary. When he finished, she turned and addressed the Be'atika Senge. "I ask the A'tayotan to call for a closed session."

Thelindrallin turned on Delwyn. "Your analysis of this event smells like fact, and I agree the Ni'zakhonii could not have set a trap for Kalinn if he was uncertain where in the Nikkiolo Expanse he was heading. I am certain no intelligence was sent on a courier probe from homespace ahead of Kalinn in time for a light attack craft to arrive on-station at the perfect time. What do you think they were doing in Nikkiolo's heliopause?"

"I haven't puzzled that out yet," Delwyn admitted.

"Think harder. You are a warleader. I clear you for all classified briefings, subject to the will of the A'tayotan hierarchy. Your analysis must go before them immediately. You will brief them and advise them of the same conclusions you have just made here. Be prepared to speculate about the enemy's purpose."

Thelindrallin addressed the Counsel. "The Be'atika Senge is in recess pending a seating of the A'tayotan," Thelindrallin sang.

Phalalin rushed to Delwyn's side. Verikaralee and Amindaldra followed on his tail.

"You will need your Mistress of Tactics, Melkorka, and Phelindra," he said.

"What about data? That's back on the ship," Delwyn protested.

Phalalin shook his head. "No, your Mistress of Saga has already downloaded your warship's chronicles via hyperlink by now. The Counsel can pull all operational data from the Archives."

"Wait a minute Phalalin. How can I brief the military command of a world government? That's a job for an admiral, someone of Phelindra's rank."

Phalalin shook his head. "You were involved. You are involved now. You are the warleader. Your warship is involved. You are a male. While you speak, you are under Mrallin's Warpact because he is the Eldest Male of the Counsel. But when he surrenders Warpact to you, you will speak as the highest ranking Eyloni male present."

Delwyn wondered if they'd ever let him see the O'un Tu Clan.

11

THE A'TAYOTAN HIERARCHY

Seventy minutes later Delwyn found himself standing inside the hot but breezy ground level of another elleiu tree. Holographic panoramic screens hovered throughout the central meeting area filled with patterns, diagrams, and scrolling pictographs. People stood on flat river stones and watched data patterns drift down floating displays.

Delwyn felt the mood in the room bristling around him. This was a busy place where serious decisions were made. People didn't come here to hang out or make frivolous statements. These Warriors, Hunters, and Comara represented the core leadership and the core membership of the A'tayotan hierarchy. This society set military policy, rules of engagement, and strategy for the Eyloni people as a whole. He was standing in what served as the defense directorate for the Tribal Compact of the Ten Tribes of Elleio.

The A'tayotan directed three primary missions: protect the male population, protect Compact territorial interests, and protect the female population, in that order of priority. Other males had been invited here besides Delwyn: advisors to the Be'atika Senge and seven males wearing the same gold earring he wore himself.

Seven warleaders and all the Be'atika Senge male advisors stood in front of a wide, floating display. More males filled the large cavernous void in the living wood maze than he could recall ever seeing in one place since his arrival. That explained all the serious, heavily armed Warriors standing in half-circles next to curving walls, watching all male movement.

Verikaralee stood next to Delwyn. Never in her lifetime did she expect to find herself in the Hall of Consensus within the A'tayotan home tree. She did not belong to this peculiar and exclusive hierarchy. A few A'tayotan members belonged to *Fearless*'s society. A'tayotan membership remained exclusive and select because it held a sacred duty. Every female hierarchy in Eyloni society dealt with various female issues, but the A'tayotan dealt exclusively with keeping the male population safe: the A'tayotan was the binding fetter restraining open warfare among clans or tribes, thus preventing male deaths; the A'tayotan was the sword prohibiting industrial activity from sickening the world, thus ensuring continued male health; the A'tayotan was the shield protecting Elleio, thus preserving the home of all males.

Verikaralee nodded to Zalzadrin, and they dropped behind Delwyn to exchange battle language snippets.

She trilled softly, and Verikaralee pricked curious ears at her.

Delwyn spun on hearing Zalzadrin laugh, certain she'd found something about him to make a joke about. Eyloni humor tended toward the odd, and often they made him the butt of their humor when he ignored their good advice. Zalzadrin took humor to an extreme: she told jokes at whim, and he wondered if she did so out of habit as a defense mechanism because she saw herself as short in stature.

Zalzadrin didn't look that short to him.

Oddly, the more she seemed to like someone, the more she cracked jokes on them. She had taken a liking to him even before he'd stapled her wound closed back on Ibeetu.

Zalzadrin shifted her feet and stood against him. He felt her twitching ear brushing his, heard her breathing. Verikaralee stood a patient pace behind him.

Delwyn glanced at Zalzadrin. Her eyes narrowed and she frowned, an expression at odds with her usual irrepressible nature.

Three tails snapped around his waist so fast he thought about blanket parties, the hazing ritual in the Fleet where a squad wrapped a member in a blanket and took turns punching away. Then he remembered where he was. No female would allow that rule-breaking naval tradition here.

"What is wrong with you three?" he demanded.

"Nothing. Stand still!" Phelindra said. "A Comari and her male have arrived. Until you learn how to behave around Comara, we must keep watch."

Delwyn spied the long-haired, towheaded female walking with her chosen male, a warleader.

"I thought Comara didn't go in for warship duty."

"Comara go where they wish, but they do not care for military life. That said, if a Comari chooses a male, and he later becomes a warleader, then she is content to go where he does."

"That must make an interesting trio: warleader, protectress, and Comari."

"The Comari and his protectress collaborate and devise methods to keep him safe. She will tolerate the protectress because she has the same mission the Comari does."

Delwyn sighed. Having Phelindra underfoot all the time made having meaningful alone time rare. Having another constant presence would make alone time nonexistent. Phelindra wrinkled her nose and snapped her tail at him. "You would miss me if I stayed away for too long."

The warleader and Comari pair crossed his path, and Delwyn smiled at the memory of the Comari he'd met on A'lon'aloop.

The Comari froze mid-step, and her male slammed into her back.

Delicate twitching ears brushed her long blonde hair as she paused a moment to scan the faces around her before turning back on Delwyn.

Curious and exhibiting care for one having a reputation for deadliness, she glided up to him, ignoring the three Hunters with him as she did so.

The Comari leaned toward Delwyn and drew a deep breath in through her nose.

She nodded to herself, gave him a coy smile, and darted back to the side of the warleader she had abandoned for far too long.

Movement had stopped throughout the busy complex. Everyone, whisper-quiet, had been holding their breath throughout the rare spectacle.

A delighted smile played across the warleader's face as he tried to decide whether he wanted to continue on his way or remain near Delwyn.

Delwyn grunted, expecting the warleader to feel jealous or something. Instead he was getting a real kick out of it. "What's he all happy about? Did you set me up for some gag of yours, Zalzadrin?"

"I would never place you on a trail that intercepted a Comari. Comara never joke, do not play, and hate being manipulated. If she even suspected I intended actual harm to a male, especially her male, then she would have killed me before I could even get my adulthood knife out of its sheath."

"Well, something drew her to me."

Phelindra thought about the encounter and realized Delwyn was right. The Comari had been scenting the air. Her sensitive nose drew her to him. The Eldest Huntress turned and buried her face in his neck, smelled his cheek, his nose, and rubbed her nose in his wonderful oily scent.

"Phelindra, what?" Delwyn asked. The public display drew curious eyes. Her behavior fell within normal Eyloni public displays, but to him it felt as though he was a freak show spectacle.

Phelindra swore. "She has scent marked you!"

"Who? Her? She didn't even touch me," Delwyn said.

"Not her! The Comari you met on A'lon'aloop. You should have warned me."

"And you're just now noticing it? I thought your sense of smell was better than that," Delwyn said.

"Not for this! Most pheromones broadcast olfactory signals meant for notice by others. They leave emotional tags that describe health status, attachment, dislike, anger, mating choices, among other things. Other pheromones are subtle. I can mark a trail with scent so I can find my way back. Others cannot smell those pheromone unless they invest the time to smell the right scent layer at the right place. It does not take long to find the scent, but it does delay pursuit.

"Other pheromonal odors are used as tags so we can find people we have scent marked. You have several thousand such tags on you right now, so we can find you in a hurry if necessary.

"The Comari on A'lon'aloop has tagged you with her scent mark so she can find you again."

"You told me she was immature. Why bother to tag me?"

Melkorka and Hlinlodyn chose then to march up to Delwyn. They wore the harried expressions of Warriors thinking he had conspired to yank their tails for no particular reason.

"What have you done? Everyone is singing about it!" Melkorka said.

"About what?" Delwyn asked.

Melkorka gave him a pained look. "Is this some joke of yours, Zalzadrin? *Zalzadrin?* Why are you here? The summons included only mistresses of the ship and mistresses of tactics."

"The A'tayotan did not explicitly exclude others, and I am Delwyn's clan female."

"We," Verikaralee amended, "are Delwyn's clan females."

"That is not the issue. Did *you* play a part in this stupid stunt?" Melkorka demanded.

"*I* would never expose my clan male to the wrath of an offended Comari!" Verikaralee retorted.

The hair on Delwyn's neck stood on end as he found himself in the midst of rising female ire. Verikaralee and Zalzadrin locked eyes with Melkorka, their ears flat against their bright red and orange ringleted heads, tails whipping as they checked footing and balance.

Melkorka had all but accused Verikaralee and Zalzadrin of being incautious with the safety of a male, a slap to their honor and a criminal offense. Such a charge would also have assaulted their obligatory responsibilities because both Hunters belonged to the O'un Tu Clan and should have had an even greater interest in his safety.

"Phelindra, explain it to them before they do something stupid," he told her.

"That Comari on A'lon'aloop has scent marked him. Behave yourselves, I demand it!" Phelindra sang at imperative scale.

As Phelindra held high social rank in the Society of Hunters, both Zalzadrin and Verikaralee obeyed at once. Although she ranked females in the society of *Hunter's Moon*, Melkorka still had to yield to Phelindra when not aboard ship or not on ship's business. It did not matter that she carried her warleader's sword.

Melkorka scowled at Delwyn a moment before issuing orders to them. "Keep a watch out for her and keep Delwyn far from her."

"I'm here remember?" Delwyn retorted. "Talk to me, not around me dammit." One particular thing Delwyn found annoying about Eyloni culture was the tendency for the overwhelmingly female population to talk among themselves about a male while in his presence as if he wasn't even there. Oh, he was free to join their chat because they enjoyed male company, but they tended to talk about him. It made him feel like he was with parents who held to the notion that kids should be seen and not heard.

Except Eyloni females didn't act that way even with their own infants, and they bent over backwards to cater to males. It wasn't as if Eyloni males were frail. They weren't. His tussle with Phalalin had proven that. Eyloni males had a gregarious streak and, by Earth standards, had some rather effete mannerisms but that didn't mean they couldn't or wouldn't fight. They exhibited reckless violence if they thought their associations faced danger. In fact, from what he had learned during his lessons, an Eyloni male separated from female company suffered from a range of symptoms similar to PTSD.

Phelindra gave Delwyn a fond frown. She forgot how much he enjoyed interacting with them even when they discussed trivial matters. "That Comari, the one who nosed you on A'lon'aloop, has marked you so she can find you again when she reaches her adolescence."

"That's when a Comari seeks a male to protect forever," he said.

"Correct."

"What about it? What's that got to do with me?"

Phelindra stared at Delwyn, bewildered. As brilliant a warleader as he had showed himself to be, she found it hard to understand how he could be so dense at times.

"She found you acceptable as a bondmate."

"No thanks," he said. "Now that I know about it, I can honestly say no. She'll smell the disinterest on my scent and go away. Right?"

Melkorka, her staring match with Verikaralee and Zalzadrin coming out a draw, shook her head. "Stay away from her. She will interpret your disinterest as not coveting the relationship. Comara need to bond with males, but they are also put off by any desire to have or attempt to attract the bond. Your feigned disinterest will draw her to you."

"But it's not feigned!" Delwyn objected.

"But it is! Do you not see it? She reminds you of your dead near-daughters. She can sense it because it comes through on your scent. Your disinterest clings to your scent as a genuine lack of interest telling her you do not covet the bond for gain." Melkorka said.

"What gain could I get from a Comari?" Delwyn demanded.

Thelindrallin interrupted. "The A'tayotan have called the strategy counsel into session. Delwyn ar ahoun Unahaillaea *Tyreniioroneo*, the A'tayotan yields to the Male Voice. Stand and assume Warpact leadership over the Society of Warleaders."

What?

Mrallin came to his side, perked ears at him, and said, "I yield Warpact command to Delwyn ar ahoun Unahaillaea *Tyreniioroneo*."

Thelindrallin bounded to Delwyn and slipped her tail around his waist and tugged him to the Speaker's Place. "All data from your warship's chronicles has been called up from the archives. I have had the entries indexed by date, by event, and by the names of those making official or personal log entries. As successor warleader, you and you alone have the authority to break the seal on Kalinn's personal logs if you should wish to consult them. You have no time limit, no one will rush you, and no one will ask anything or interrupt in any way unless you give permission.

"As counsel-speaker for the Be'atika Senge, I am at your disposal if you need any assistance with the equipment, the records, or if you need anything we have not anticipated for this briefing."

Thelindrallin turned and addressed the A'tayotan assembly. "I remind everyone that the Be'atika Senge considers this session classified under Compact Seal." She paused a moment before addressing Delwyn. "You have the eyes, ears, and noses of the A'tayotan."

Delwyn looked out into a sea of curious and expectant female faces. Oddrilna's inqury panel had given him a court-martial hearing feel. Now he faced the equivalent of the Coalition Defense Directorate as a chief of staff and not as a witness giving testimony.

At least this felt more familiar from a briefings routine point of view. It shouldn't be all that different from giving mission briefings to his special operations group action response teams or to Captain Winters and the command staff aboard *Henri Edda*. In those briefings he held the floor for as long as he had something mission-critical to say.

Warriors and Hunters stood with tails idly waving behind them. Some had their arms folded beneath their breasts. They watched him fumble with the archive interlink system. The communications and data management menus mirrored those at his station on the Warleader's Watch. In no time he was calling up the necessary data and displaying it on the large, floating central panoramic display.

"The data on the screen," Delwyn began as Thelindrallin began signing battle language translations, "is from Kalinn's personal log. In summary, at the request of the Be'atika Senge, Kalinn left homespace and headed for the Nikkiolo Expanse. Kalinn's entries indicate he expected to find Ni'zakhonii activity in one or more systems within the Expanse because the Compact had stopped a Ni'zakhonii incursion there once before. He thought maybe they had put reconnaissance vessels in systems bordering the Compact edge of the Expanse. Finding nothing during the first leg of his cruise, he jumped to a point almost midway between the Surutia and Nikkiolo systems. Surutia made more sense to him because it lies just outside Compact territory and would serve as a likely staging area for any assault force raiding into Compact star systems.

"It is here where sensor logs reported a Ni'zakhonii FTL wake skimming the frontier between Ni'zakhonii and Compact space. Kalinn had to decide if the ship was heading into the Surutia or Nikkiolo systems or if it was heading on into Coalition space.

"I agree with Kalinn's assessment: he doubted they would send a single short-range scout or frigate class ship into Coalition space. He deduced, correctly I think, that the ship cruised toward the Surutia or Nikkiolo systems. It surprised him when Hlinlodyn reported Nikkiolo as a possible target, and I agree. The two stars are fourteen and a half light-years apart, so why skip securing Surutia and go on to Nikkiolo?

"The Ni'zakhonii could not have known Kalinn jumped to Nikkiolo. Even if the Be'atika Senge had ordered him to that system, the Ni'zakhonii could not have known about it until he came into sensor range because they don't have hyperlink FTL communications technology."

"I can state for the record that neither the Be'atika Senge nor the A'tayotan told Kalinn to investigate a specific system. We did not even suggest one. He commanded an elite warship, and we knew he would use his experience and the resources aboard his warship when choosing where to prowl," Thelindrallin interrupted.

Delwyn nodded. "So we know the enemy ship was cruising a course decided long before Kalinn received his mission briefing. That means the three destroyers held their formation in the heliopause for other reasons. From the FTL course vectors detected by Mistress of Pathwalking Trebithia and cross-checked with Kidahin's after-action report on the light attack craft we captured, it now seems certain the LAC did not travel from Surutia to Nikkiolo. Isn't that right, Hlinlodyn?"

His Mistress of Tactics flinched in surprise, narrowed her eyes, stretched her ears out wide and pulled them flat against her head, and swatted her tail at the air as she considered the data patterns on the screen.

"No, he—*it*—does not…" She trailed off into a musical grumble. "Melkorka, what do you think about this vector here?" Hlinlodyn asked as she pointed.

Melkorka stood and glided next to Hlinlodyn, curious, and watched as the Mistress of Tactics traced an arc along the navigation plot.

"What about it? Wait a minute. Thelindrallin, magnify the chart and superimpose the heliopause and enemy ship plots, and then project the captured equipment's intended course from Trebithia and Kidahin's navigation analysis," Melkorka said.

"Affirm. Accessing. Data ready. Projecting."

Delwyn watched as the LAC's projected FTL course neatly slashed through the destroyer's position instead of intersecting Ibeetu orbit.

"So the LAC," Thelindrallin grimaced in distaste at the thought of referencing a thing by any term that hinted it was male, "course plot intercepts the three destroyers?"

Delwyn nodded. "Those destroyers were expecting the LAC. Kalinn took Mistress of Tactics Hlinlodyn's analysis and concluded he'd jump ahead and catch the ship jumping into normal space. His plan made sense because the FTL displacement fell within his jump radius. He'd arrive in the heliopause in an instant and have hours remaining to consider combat options. Remember, he wanted to capture it intact.

"The sad fact is that with his ship within one jump radius he could have used his FTL scans to sweep the arrival point. Had he scanned the heliopause first, he might have picked up the destroyers lying in wait there. I say might because the scanning frame is so narrow at long range he would have to sacrifice resolution for frame size. The Mistress of Tactics had no tactical reason to scan the area cubic ell by cubic ell. She scanned in wide field, the mode suitable for pinpointing astronomical bodies but not for finding half-kilometer long starships and would miss them."

Delwyn paused to take in his audience. They watched him, attentive. If they had doubts, then they kept them to themselves. They glanced from time to time at the data screens, but their ears followed his voice. All briefings he had ever attended had been recorded. Surely the A'tayotan did so, too. They could pull upon archive data at need. Besides, they viewed him through an Eyloni female lens and concluded he wouldn't make up wild fantasies when describing serious matters to them.

His scent told them of his seriousness.

"Now," Delwyn continued, "this scan data comes from Mistress of Tactics Hlinlodyn's threat assessment scanners. Upon arrival, *Hunter's Moon's* hull plating absorbed coordinated massed pinpoint fire on his combat hull followed by multiple fire patterns and torpedo spreads before the destroyers broke off into independent attack runs. That makes sense for them because three Ni'zakhonii destroyers are no match for my warship, and they knew it. They didn't anticipate an elite class Compact warship, yet they did expect a live-fire engagement. Otherwise why have preset firing solutions for coordinated precision firing?"

"Delwyn," Mrallin called, stumbled over his tongue, wanting Delwyn so much to understand him that he gave up and sang a query to Phelindra.

"Mrallin asks if you are saying the destroyers were waiting to fire upon their own equipment?"

"Yep. Once they got over their surprise, they couldn't believe their luck. They wanted *Hunter's Moon* dead. They didn't want Compact scanners recording anything there, or anything about to arrive there in the near future. I read Kalinn's assault boarding team telemetry. He translated aboard the destroyer with no difficulty, and yet neither Captain Winters nor Melkorka could teleport me off the LAC."

"An experimental design?" Thelindrallin wondered.

"I think so. I think they were running acceptance trials, one of which included a wargame scenario. If the LAC can take coordinated pinpoint firing equal to the first barrage thrown at my warship, then that's *some* LAC."

"The equipment did look like new, for all its horrible stench," Phelindra admitted. "But the Ni'zakhonii were starving. No live food in the nutrition center meant the LAC no longer had a source of supplies."

"I know. They exhausted their food and had to live on water and the blood pudding mixture we found in the galley. They would have eaten all of you while still on Ibeetu had I not ordered Melkorka to fire on their spy probe. I'll bet those destroyers had replenishment-on-mission orders to resupply the LAC once the wargames had completed. A light attack craft is not a long-haul ship. It needs regular resupply from a nearby base, from its carrier mother ship, or from a rendezvous with a replenishment-on-mission vessel."

"But why the probes?" Thelindrallin asked.

"The LAC arrived in the heliopause in stealth mode expecting to engage those ships as a finale to the wargames exercise. When it jumped into normal space and found nothing but debris, the crew used passive sensors to scan the wreckage and the star system for enemy ships. It tasked one probe as a sentinel in the wreckage and made a few stealth passes at Ibeetu and our ships with the other probe. When Allinha began digging into the surface to make the Place of Mourning for the Death Song ritual, it must have looked to them like a joint Compact-Coalition military venture. They landed the LAC on Ibeetu and from there sent the probe out to scan preselected sites."

"Delwyn?" Phalalin queried.

"Yeah?"

"Why put an experimental design through trials near enemy territory? Research and development is done under a canopy of secrecy and in secure territory."

"I know. I thought about it for some time and couldn't come up with a really good answer. I can guess but guessing is a poor substitute for intelligence. I can eliminate certain key points, however.

"First, it makes no sense to take an experimental ship off into the frontier where an enemy might get a glimpse of the latest secrets. Traveling with three destroyers over a cruise from home to the frontier means the LAC had to take supplies from those ships three or four times on their way to Nikkiolo. We know the Lizards lack teleport technology, and their destroyers lack shuttle bays large enough to accommodate the LAC, which means it either hard docked with a destroyer, or a destroyer ferried supplies to it using shuttles or transfer drones. Gaundellin told me subspace resembles a manifold of soap bubbles and the LAC is like a drop of water traveling along bubble membranes. Each Lizard ship creates its own path of least resistance as it falls through the manifold, which means they can't transfer material between ships while in FTL flight. They have to reenter normal space to do so."

"We have to do the same thing," Thelindrallin said. "An FTL jump is instantaneous, so Compact ships cannot meet during a jump."

Delwyn shrugged and continued. "Second, three destroyers don't make a task force, and if I sent my new prototype out for trials near enemy space, I'd have sent a task force at least, if not a full battle group. If I detected enemy ships, I'd have sent my task force after them and made sure they couldn't report on my technical advancement.

"Third, three destroyers against one LAC is no wargame. Three destroyers are overkill against an LAC. They went there for one or two reasons. They either served as a screening force escorting the LAC from its research shipyard to Nikkiolo's heliopause, or they served as a low-profile force trying to detect the LAC and lock targeting solutions onto it. That suggests the LAC's original wargame mission had been to see how close it could get to the three ships while in stealth mode and then acquire a firing solution. The destroyers must have been briefed on the prototype's hardened hull, programmed a one-time coordinated barrage, and waited. That says something about the prototype's new hull shielding technology."

Mrallin sang a protest that Thelindrallin translated. "Mrallin says your analysis might be faulty because the coordinated combined assault caused massive damage to your warship. That kind of concentrated firepower would destroy a light attack craft no matter how augmented its shields."

"And I would agree with Mrallin had *Hunter's Moon's* shields been up. But Kalinn did not anticipate an immediate threat, and the record shows he ordered a jump into what he rightly thought of as a low-threat action zone. The destroyers fired on unshielded hull plating, which leads me to guess the LAC could have withstood at least one massed coordinated attack if not two or three before the power reserves of its modest reactor dropped below the minimum required to maintain its shields and still retain its FTL capability. My guess is the destroyers were ordered to try and lock their firing solution onto the LAC while it was in stealth mode. The incoming fire would have smacked the LAC hard, once, to let the crew know they had failed the stealth requirement of the assessment trials.

"Fourth, with no task force escort the proximity of the trial site to Compact territory can mean only one thing. There must be a research facility somewhere in the outer Nikkiolo system. Why they'd put it there I can't imagine. Research and development requires laboratory facilities, research personnel, and drydock in this case, supply logistics to manage, support personnel, a garrison, shipyard equipment, and a supply of raw materials. You'd have known it by now if the Lizards were sending convoys into the Nikkiolo Expanse.

"The only reason I can think of for why they are forced to conduct acceptance trials in the Nikkiolo Expanse is because they built the LAC there. The only reason I can imagine for building it in the system is because a supply of some crucial raw material is there."

Delwyn looked down at the faces watching him and waited.

"Is that all?" Thelindrallin asked.

Is that all? Delwyn wondered. Aloud he said, "That's about it."

Thelindrallin flicked her ears, stood next to him, looped her tail around his waist, and addressed the gathering. "The Hall of Consensus is open for discussion."

Females rose and danced around one another like fall leaves blowing across the grass. Some people read the holodisplays and read the excerpts from the archives. Others studied the star charts. It astonished Delwyn to see a running transcript playing on several floating screens. Groups stood before them, their tails entwined as they reviewed his analysis or read from a transcript of the briefing running down the right side like ticker tape messages ran across the bottom of Coalition display screens. Two Warriors were pointing at the words while a third Warrior traced a line through a plot on a neighboring screen.

People came up to Delwyn in small groups to brush him with their tails and exchange greetings before asking him to clarify some issue. Others intercepted him and carried on quite heated arguments with those with him, but no one yelled. Females detached from a group to glide up to him, make a polite inquiry, and then head back to whichever group they belonged to at the time and conveyed his reply.

They milled about the Hall of Consensus, and his mind began to drift when Verikaralee sang in a delighted tone. "Phalalin comes with the males."

The warleaders surrounded Delwyn, and Phalalin gave Verikaralee a slight frown before greeting Delwyn. "Have you given thought to a strategy?"

"I haven't. I know what I'd do from a special operations commander's point of view though, why?"

Phalalin gave Delwyn's female entourage a bland stare while stretching his ears wide and making showy gestures with his tail.

They returned his gestures to leave with defiant glares. Delwyn thought about Anlann's quarters on Ibeetu. There Anlann had told Seralin and Kidahin to leave so he and Delwyn could have a chance to talk away from female ears. Phelindra and the others were giving Phalalin the same rebellious looks that Seralin and Kidahin had given him and Anlann.

All except the Comari. She ignored Phalalin, preferring to stare at Delwyn with veiled amusement.

Delwyn wondered if she cared if he got himself bonded with her sister.

A ghostly, delighted smile flitted across the Comari's face.

She moved to just within a tail-length of him.

All talk in the Hall stopped. Ears perked forward in shock.

The males surrounded him. As they did so, the Comari stepped back and behind her bondmale rather than between him and Delwyn.

The Comari's male embraced Delwyn with aggressive gregarious enthusiasm, followed by Mrallin, and on around to the others, with Phalalin last.

"It is your place to present a strategy to address this threat," Phalalin said.

"You're kidding. I thought the A'tayotan did that."

"They do, but they take male advice seriously. You they will take even more seriously because you witnessed events, you defended Kalinn's conduct, and you command an elite warship. As the Male Voice of the A'tayotan, your song will carry great weight."

"A song? When I sing, I see relationships. When I walk and listen to music, I see things, how they fit together." He looked back at them. "I can't explain it, but I wish I had an hour or so to listen to some music and think this one through."

Phalalin pricked his ears forward and shrugged. "You state the obvious. This is how all Eyloni approach a problem."

Phalalin sang a comment to the other males.

They looked at Delwyn as if he'd just grown a tail.

Phalalin sang a summons to Thelindrallin.

Dignified, the old female took measured steps to them and canted her ears in inquiry.

Counsel Mistress of the Be'atika Senge that she was, here she was just another guest of the A'tayotan.

Phalalin hummed a short tune, and she whipped around on Delwyn, bouncing on her feet like Zalzadrin often did when she was excited.

Or being funny.

Thelindrallin sang a note for notice and made an announcement. "Delwyn wishes to sing a Song of Contemplation!"

"A song of what?" he asked Phalalin.

"A Song of Contemplation. Thelindrallin says you want music to help you think about strategy. Of course the A'tayotan will sing with you. Can you not see how much they want to sing with you?"

Phalalin was correct. The A'tayotan hierarchy began to gather into a branching pattern, tails lashed against neighboring thighs, reflecting in some symbolic way their hierarchical ranking. They seemed more excited about singing with him than they did the serious matter he had just outlined. It made him feel uncomfortable.

"How can I do this?" Delwyn objected. "They don't know the music."

"As if that has ever stopped us before," Melkorka snapped.

Hlinlodyn nodded. "You have many contemplative songs. Sing those we know, and we will sing with you while they find their places in the song. It is not as if you are offering first songs."

"These songs are first songs for them," he pointed out.

"True, but we learned them from you first, and we consent to the sharing," Hlinlodyn said.

Delwyn gave in. Females fussed over new songs. A singing male sang his songs to whomever he liked, but his associated females gave him reproachful glares if he didn't share any new music with them first.

"What about you?" Delwyn asked Phalalin.

"We," Phalalin swiped at the other males with his tail, "do not sing along with other males while in the company of females. Males sing together, apart, in our own rituals. We will listen and enjoy the music. We will not sing your songs unless you give permission. If you do not know it by now, I say to you a male's music is his mental property."

"Phalalin, I think I'd better decline. The songs I sing to focus my thoughts on matters like these are martial in nature, combat songs. I sang one to Kidahin, and she turned vicious and combative, as if hypnotized. I sang her out of it, but she said it was good for me to sing battle songs so I could calm or incite her."

Phalalin shared Delwyn's concerns with the warleaders.

Mrallin made a comment that Phalalin passed on. "He says if you can incite females with battle songs and dampen their responses, then he sees no problem. We do things like this all the time before a battle."

"Will my songs affect you the same way they affect females?"

"No," Phalalin said. Then he smiled a goofy grin. "They will move us, but males do not respond to a male's song in the same way females do."

Delwyn shrugged. "Okay. I have the songs I need in mind. I'm ready."

"Then proceed," Phalalin urged.

Delwyn began with the song foremost on his mind, beginning with the refrain. It told the story about a soldier laying on his bunk in a field tent, looking up into the folds in the canvas and thinking about how the campfire shadows made it look like a night sky. The soldier saw sand castles in the fire's reflecting light, but in the end he always woke up wondering just what it was that he stood for.

As he sang the refrain the second time, he cued his females to join the song. The A'tayotan followed the music with their ears and tails, waiting for the all-important signal, the permission custom demanded, permission they must have before joining in song with a singing male.

They waited, impatient and excited. Delwyn watched their ears track the melody as they listened to the song, his voice, and the females accompanying him.

The refrain neared its end. As they reached it, he began singing the first verse.

Delwyn sang with his female accompaniment, allowing the A'tayotan the opportunity to listen to the changes in melody between verse and refrain.

His intimate group continued singing through the third verse, and then Delwyn stretched his arms wide and embraced the Hall of Consensus, the ritual signal permitting others to join with him in song.

The assembly joined in with the force and joy that only people who sang together as a social necessity could. The music augmented their natural pheromonal empathy. And as Delwyn had feared, the martial beat and the song's subject matter began to affect them. Like bagpipes playing beside a marching infantry unit, his music sent their minds into single-minded combativeness. He mellowed the percussive beat before all the females succumbed to a male's combat-imminent call to battle readiness.

Delwyn noticed nine A'tayotan females, three Hunters and six Warriors, had drifted into his group and taken to singing the counterpoint. Their movement forced the assembly's tail-to- thigh rank pattern to shift, making some placements in the pattern quite difficult to maintain. They lingered in the pattern a few more beats before separate groups broke into the choreographed prancing dances females performed often.

The small group sang before him as they formed up into a smaller version of the rank pattern.

The remaining females danced around them.

Some danced and sang by themselves.

Others formed up into groups of four and twisted their tails together and danced in ballet.

Some paired up, twisted tails, and stood together raising their cupped hands and vibrating them as they sang.

Others danced in rhythmic gymnastics routines as they sang, passing hands and tails in a rippling pattern, an athletic but graceful promenade around and around him.

Delwyn's eyes drifted to the warleaders and the male advisors of the Be'atika Senge.

Their ears followed his voice, but their eyes followed the dancing and singing females.

Someone's whispered humming caught his ear, complex and sweet. Delwyn frowned. Phalalin had said something about males not singing, but he heard whispered singing.

Delwyn pivoted, curious, and caught her.

The Comari sang along with the other females but didn't dance with them.

Comara had no voice box, could not speak aloud, and Delwyn wondered if the others heard her whispered melody. Was she trying to sing just to join with them somehow in the communal event? Delwyn twisted around, searching for the other Comara.

He saw none.

He remembered. They had been with the Be'atika Senge, but not everyone in the Compact Counsel had been invited here. Hadn't there been more than one Comari here, though?

Delwyn finished a fourth song and remembered his purpose for singing. He did not sing to provide social singing opportunities. His females pressed him for this kind of social singing every chance they got. While these people enjoyed the sharing, they had a job to do, and so did he.

He wrapped his head around the problem, saw himself in the Nikkiolo Expanse, and pretended he was the LAC.

He swooped through the cosmos, falling through subspace in ways he couldn't imagine.

He had the same FTL drive other Lizard ships had.

He felt different.

He remembered the land trilobite he had held, the ke'nah.

It had unfolded into the creature similar to one long extinct on Earth.

It had clear crystals for eyes.

Well, it had clear exoskeleton over its eye pits.

The crystal eye spots and the creature itself drew him away from the musical fantasy that told them he had been a solid crystal flying free in space away from the singing females.

Delwyn's scent changed, following his mood as he sang.

The females singing along with him smelled the subtle change. Delwyn had enthralled himself into a contemplative state.

They smelled his delight in them.

They smelled his joy in discovering a ke'nah.

They smelled his oneness with the Ni'zakhonii equipment.

They smelled his mind trying to resolve a thread tying the animal, its crystal eye spots, its resting form, and a flying ball of crystal into an Oyya Web's strand.

They focused on him and sang strength to him.

Delwyn smelled them. Eyloni didn't sweat, but they sometimes panted in rapid shallow breaths. This was the first time he recalled seeing them panting, which didn't surprise him considering Na'di Island's equatorial climate.

No doubt the pheromones they sent his way conveyed more details than his pitiful nose could interpret.

Delwyn kept thinking about round rocks and trilobites with crystal eye spots.

The A'tayotan took their lead from the example given by Delwyn's females. They had signed for the exotic dance measures, but now it dawned on the A'tayotan females why.

Delwyn's inferior nose needed the increased pheromonal activity to help him grasp the ideas coming from them through the empathic link.

Delwyn imagined himself flying through space inside a geode, a round rock with a crystal interior. He became the LAC, shooting around Nikkiolo's gas giant and heading for its habitable moon, Ibeetu. He entered the atmosphere and the outer rocky surface turned red hot, but his crystal pilot's seat remained cool.

A geode?

Delwyn suddenly knew he needed to reread Kalinn's boarding party talkback telemetry data.

The singers smelled the change in the singing male's pheromones. He had found what he had been seeking.

Seconds later, the changing tempo signaled his desire to finish the song.

They in turn sang a reluctant, sorrowful agreement.

Delwyn had guidance to give them.

He built up to a crescendo and finished the refrain before releasing the singers.

Attentive eyes watched him and waited.

He returned to the data center and called up the scan data from Brelioranda's assault team. She had led them through the crippled destroyer's broadway deck, the main deck running the length of the ship, interrupted only by emergency breach doors. The scans had showed the ship as a crystal construct, but the workmanship had more of a glassblower's quality to it.

Brelioranda's scan showed shattered crystal partially blocking the deck as her party worked their way aft. The Lizards had mastered crystal fabrication technology, but this glassy stuff didn't look like the crystal structure on his LAC.

Delwyn ignored an inquisitive Thelindrallin and accessed Hlinlodyn's tactical scans taken during combat.

She had no trouble scanning the destroyer. She had pinpointed damage and even found where the enemy had concentrated their repair efforts.

They say that hindsight was 20/20. Given what he now knew and what he had guessed, he knew the truth. The Ni'zakhonii had tricked Kalinn into teleporting aboard. Brelioranda's attack in the engineering spaces hadn't pressed a desperate crew into suicide.

They had intended all along to draw as many Eyloni into the destroyer as they could before they blew the reactor control system.

Delwyn panned the scan, stopping when he reached the destroyer's power systems command center. The place reminded him of building site scaffolds made from durable blown glass

The LAC's engineering spaces didn't have smooth blown glass structures like these.

"Look at Brelioranda's scans. The engineering crew blew up their ship with Kalinn and his assault forces still aboard. This crystal technology is inferior to what we found on the LAC. I think they grow this material in a manner similar to our additive manufacturing technology."

Delwyn called up the scans he had taken of the LAC himself. "I took these scans using my battlefield scanner. Notice how the LAC's tunnels look like crystallized slag and not blown glass. These hatches grow from a crystal root in the frame toward the middle, like a closing iris. Hatches on the destroyer look like standard hatches made from sheets that look like layers of melted icicles. The visual differences between the destroyer and the LAC represents a radical change in their crystal technology!

"The hull reminds me of a ke'nah.

"I think the Ni'zakhonii have found a cache of geode asteroids or have found a planet they're mining them from. They can't haul them into their home system without committing even more ships, so they've built a research facility near all that mass, mass prohibitively energy expensive to haul home especially if they turned out non-viable for their designs.

"Had the LAC completed its acceptance trials, the enemy would have hauled it, the research, and as many geodes as they could carry back to their home system.

"For all the Ni'zakhonii know by now, the LAC and those destroyers blew up in some containment catastrophe."

"There surely is no element of surprise by now," Phalalin mused. "If they had time to launch two probes and land on the moon, then they had more than sufficient time to launch a courier probe to signal their military."

"Yeah," Delwyn agreed. "A courier traveling to the closest star, over fourteen light-years away, is a probe running at G-band velocity. By now it has been recovered."

Phalalin shook his head. "There is no fleet base at Surutia. The probes the equipment carried must have long range cruise capability to reach relay stations."

"I wonder if anything remained behind to retrieve it?"

"You mean a reserve force or maybe an outpost? That is a good question. All an outpost or research base could do is send the alert on using their own courier drone. Why bother?" Phalalin said.

"Thelindrallin? How do you wish to proceed?" Delwyn asked.

"I call the question of Delwyn and seek a consensus," she announced.

"Propose the question," an A'tayotan female sang out from the group.

Bewildered, Delwyn wondered what had happened. Thelindrallin must have decided he knew enough specifics to propose a strategy for them to debate. Not his rhetorical musing as a basis for deliberation, surely. Either a frigate had remained on-station in the event a courier probe arrived, or it hadn't. If they hid a research base somewhere in the system's Kuiper belt, then a probe might have gone there. But as Phalalin has pointed out, what good is that to a research base lacking hyperlink communications?

The probe Melkorka destroyed massed fifty metric tonnes, and a probe capable of traveling at greater than R-band FTL packed some mass, too. The probe that returned to the LAC under Blue Squadron fire was heavier: eighty or ninety metric tonnes total displacement. A Dart fighter massed just over ninety-two metric tonnes. Delwyn doubted a courier probe could exceed G-band FTL velocity for very long, but could it maintain G-band for fuel economy? A drone's mass added up: it had a hydrogen-antihydrogen fusion plant, FTL drive, sublight drive, maneuvering systems, sensors, spy gear, and oh yeah, the fuel itself.

The LAC massed what? Twenty-thousand metric tonnes? Not much room for cargo, but it had four torpedo launchers and four antitorpedo launchers. They barely had room for a full load of ordnance inventory. It had small living quarters and tunnels for decks. The airlock took up the volume of two freight lifts.

It hit him then. An LAC didn't have the space for a rack of probes. While they had been running from Blue Squadron fighters, Phelindra had reported the sentinel probe initiating autodocking protocol and lining up with an aft hatch.

"I pose the following: Melkorka destroyed one probe. Another probe docked with the LAC while the Coalition fighters closed on us. Two probes combined mass plus a full load of ordnance suggests the LAC can't carry any more probes. Therefore, I ask the A'tayotan to request a priority assessment of the LAC's probe launcher system and determine if a third probe might have been launched. If not, then it's possible the Ni'zakhonii don't know what happened to their ships."

"I propose a counter-question, Delwyn," Thelindrallin said.

"Go ahead."

"Would the enemy not have launched a probe when the prototype arrived in Nikkiolo's heliopause and found the debris field?"

"I don't think so. If their probe inventory is as light as I think it must be, then the crew couldn't afford to squander its remaining FTL courier without first reconnoitering the Nikkiolo system. They sought intelligence, so they left an armed probe in the debris field to kill any Compact snoopers arriving and sent the second probe on spy runs into Ibeetu orbit. They must have been overly cautious when making scanning passes near *Hunter's Moon*, because no neutrino emissions had been detected until days after *Henri Edda* arrived. Once the Coalition carrier assumed orbit, they had to chance closer scans. I think they waited too long, taking passive scans from a distance before they jumped the probe into Ibeetu local space for a series of close scans. When the probe became compromised on Ibeetu, it transmitted surveillance data out to the probe in the heliopause. Melkorka's swift response and Hlinlodyn's targeting destroyed the probe before it could transmit data.

"I think the sentinel probe in the prototype now is the long-haul courier probe. There should be no more probes in inventory."

"The counter-question has been well answered," Thelindrallin said, "I renew my call of the question of Delwyn and seek a consensus."

Phalalin whispered in Delwyn's ear. "I should have thought of probe mass and fuel economy myself."

"Don't jump up and down just yet. I might be wrong," Delwyn whispered back as he watched the activity around him.

The A'tayotan females formed into groups of two, three, five, and seven and wandered through the Hall of Consensus. People paired up and walked off after other groups. Those groups then broke up and reformed into new groups.

They murmured, hummed, and harmonized in rhythms far exceeding the best sounds a musician could wring from an instrument. Delwyn had played the saxophone in high school. The band director once called him 'magic fingers Marsch' because he made his sax produce evocative music that spoke to his listeners. They made him sound like a kid playing candy-wax pan pipes.

The Eyloni stopped singing.

"Mistress, we have reached a consensus," an A'tayotan Hunter said to Thelindrallin.

"What is the consensus?"

"That we must determine whether or not the captured equipment can hold more than two FTL-capable probes and have their findings reported back to the A'tayotan. Further, we do not allow the Hall of Consensus to adjourn until Delwyn ar ahoun Unahaillaea *Tyreniioroneo* proposes strategies for dealing with this threat."

"Now, wait just a min … Ugh!" Delwyn grunted as three sharp elbows caught him under the ribs.

"Quiet," Melkorka sang in his ear. "You have no place in this matter. Forming a consensus is a matter for the A'tayotan hierarchy. Your presence here reflects our honor."

"But I can't …"

Thelindrallin curled her tail around her waist and sang. "All those of the A'tayotan will now sing for the Major Consensus."

Delwyn listened as they sang as a group in a lighthearted melody meant to evoke serious feelings.

They sang for five minutes before the A'tayotan Hunter reported again.

"The A'tayotan, having achieved a Major Consensus, adopt the question as a statement of policy. We ask Warleader Havalin to confirm our wishes and instruct the Wrathsee'a Anchorage research teams to take immediate action."

Delwyn felt he'd missed something. If he understood the procedure, then there had been a majority, but the Hunter hadn't proclaimed a major consensus. That meant there had been holdouts, those not agreeing either with his analysis or with his suggested response. After a consensus had been announced there hadn't been a second round of mingling and discussing. Thelindrallin had called them to sing, and they had come to a major consensus. That meant, as he understood matters, there had been no remaining majority or minority opinion holders. If only the majority had sided with him, then the proposal would have failed. Majorities didn't carry decisions here. So how had the acceptance of a major consensus been made known to the A'tayotan Hunter?

Ignorant, he asked.

It turned out to be no veiled A'tayotan secret. Thelindrallin told him Eyloni sing the notes they are best at. Delwyn knew from experience they sang the notes musical instruments made. Their voices, just like drums or any other instrument, didn't all sing the same notes at the same time in any given song. If there had been disagreement in reaching a major consensus, then the Hunter would have noticed the missing voices in their song. She would have missed them like he would have missed the base guitar he knew should be playing in a favorite song.

"So you know a major consensus had been reached because nobody's voice was missing?"

Thelindrallin beamed at him. "Yes, of course. If someone disagrees, then she will not sing."

"It must be hard for them to disagree if disagreeing forces them not to sing."

"You understand," Thelindrallin said. She gave him a playful twitch of her tail. "Singing in accord is natural for us, but withholding music is not. Only a female's strong certitude will force her to withhold her voice. Such refusals are heart-wrenching, but we hold your safety and the safety of all males in our hands. We will refuse to sing forever before we will agree to a decision that places even one male in harm's way without honorable justification."

"How long do you think it will take them to inspect the probe launcher?" Phalalin asked Delwyn.

He shrugged. "It depends. The probe hatch is in the stern next to the airlock and exit bay. They should be able to access it from the airlock itself. That's where I'd put a maintenance hatch. That way, if I had to repair a probe or its launcher it is already isolated from the rest of the ship. An access hatch in the airlock should be large enough for a Lizard technician to make repairs. The launcher can't be loaded through a maintenance hatch, either. They must load the probes in through the launch port.

"Give them enough time to enter the airlock and search the port and starboard bay walls for a crystal iris hatch. It shouldn't take long for a quick look, too, once they figure out how to open the maintenance hatch. They get a good look and report back to us." Delwyn shrugged again. "Maybe two hours?"

Phalalin nodded and spread the word to the warleaders. Thelindrallin likewise passed his estimate on to the A'tayotan.

Converting from his TST estimate to the female standard gave the same result: about fifty minutes Earth time.

Thelindrallin returned. "Do you wish to present an action plan to the A'tayotan at this time?" she asked.

Delwyn nodded. He knew the analysis teams would confirm his guesstimate once they found the LAC garage. A light attack craft had no need for more than two FTL probes. The crew needed a means to convey intelligence at FTL speeds. Two couriers made sense, one a backup for the other. Courier probes didn't usually return to their launch vessels. A probe from the destination inventory took any reply back to the ship launching the courier. Probes couldn't meet while under FTL, which meant the courier had to run to preselected message points. At most, the LAC crew operated the two probes in tandem.

They used one as a spy asset, while the other had been hidden away in battlefield debris. There it remained ensconced and ready to either receive data from the LAC and courier it back home, or to scan for arriving Compact vessels and courier that intelligence back to base. Either possibility left him with the same result: that probe now sat in its launch tube aboard the LAC.

"Delwyn?" Thelindrallin pressed.

"I do," he said.

Thelindrallin sang five notes.

Everyone in the Hall of Consensus perked their ears at her.

"You have the complete and full hearing of the A'tayotan," she sang.

"I'm sure the research teams on Wrathsee'a Anchorage will find a probe launcher with a capacity for two probes. One probe remains, the one we picked up when we reentered Nikkiolo's heliopause. This leads me to think no courier probe came from the LAC.

"*Hunter's Moon's* point defense tracking data shows no courier launched from the two ships they destroyed. The only ship capable of launching a courier was the third ship, the one Kalinn boarded. It might have been possible to not raise an alert on Mistress of Tactics Hlinlodyn's threat assessment screen if they launched during Kalinn's ram attack. Even then it was launched without triggering a perimeter alert as the probe pulled away from the engagement. That can only happen if the probe was fired through the destroyer's baffles, his drive emissions, at dead-slow reaction control thruster speed, otherwise Mistress Hlinlodyn would have detected neutrino flux from an FTL jump so close to her sensors.

"What this means is, assuming the enemy isn't unnaturally stupid, that the third ship probably launched a courier probe after the ram attack and before they blew up their ship.

"Further, I think those destroyers served as a screening force for a research shipyard and its small-footprint support base. That means those destroyers had to have been based somewhere deeper in enemy territory. If the destroyer launched a courier probe, then it's well on its way by now. For efficiency's sake, a courier probe must travel at a decent velocity while exercising fuel economy …" As new thoughts came to mind, Delwyn's voice trailed off as polite listeners waited for him to continue.

Thinking quickly, Delwyn reordered his thoughts and began writing on his pad as he resumed speaking. "A V-band-capable probe would have to manage its antihydrogen fuel over a long haul. The only effective way of doing this is to throttle back to a midpoint velocity, say the G-band. The green band manages about 168 cee. Lizards can't throttle their FTL propulsion systems. Their ships run at constant velocities, and they have to drop back into normal space and recalculate new courses if they want to change FTL velocities mid-flight, so we can assume they would be unable to change velocities on a probe midway through the trip. Their probe speed would have to be constant from launch.

"Considering theoretical probe range and velocity constraints and the archive data from past Ni'zakhonii incursions into the Nikkiolo Expanse, the destroyers' home port can't be more than sixty light-years from Nikkiolo. A courier probe traveling at G-band velocity would take 133 days to reach home base. When it arrives, most likely the Lizards would sortie a force under V-band velocity, at 1,340 cee, and arrive in the Nikkiolo system seventeen days later."

Seeing that Delwyn was using human math numerals, Melkorka quickly started inserting Eyloni equivalents on the screen so everyone present could follow his reasoning.

"Fleet deployments are large-scale planning events. No fleet operations command sends battle groups out in a rush or on a whim. If they had the ships available, then they could sortie a battle group in forty-eight to seventy-two hours. It will take longer if they have to recall ships from their patrol sectors or call them in from deeper in their territory. A task force could launch quicker, but it lacks a strong show of force. Besides, they'd need firepower to escort transports taking research materials and maybe even incomplete ships back home.

"Ninety-four days have already passed since Kalinn's death. That means the Compact force has to arrive in the Nikkiolo system no later than sixty-four days from today.

"Assuming a Compact force sortied from Elleio, it will take about nineteen days for it to arrive on-station. Add what, another three days looking for the research facility.

"If the last destroyer launched a courier probe at G-band velocity to conserve fuel, and it reached the destroyers' base, then the Ni'zakhonii can send either a task force or a battle group to the Nikkiolo heliopause in 150…ah 1,100…days. We will have to send a battle group no later than 410 days from now."

That grabbed everyone's attention, and every female in the Hall of Consensus drifted off into roving subgroups for discussion. They glided from group to group, some racing about from one side of the Hall to the other. Many consulted the timetable he had suggested, while others read the accompanying transcribed testimony.

"Delwyn?" Phalalin said.

"Yes?"

"It cannot be said you did not make an impression on the A'tayotan."

"I might be wrong you know. Too much of my analysis relies on experience-driven guessing, and guessing is a poor substitute for actual intelligence and analysis," he complained, disturbed his word alone carried so much weight. "Don't you have anything to offer?" he asked Phalalin. He turned to include the other males. "Don't you have anything to add?"

"Granting the possibility of a third destroyer launching a courier probe, then we agree with your assessment," Phalalin replied. "That is a long 'if' however. If I were a Ni'zakhonii, I would start wondering what happened to my prototype once acceptance trial reports became past due. They have to investigate, and they will not send three destroyers this time. They will plan for a combat contingency, or at least they will send screening elements to support the cargo transports they are sure to send to evacuate raw materials and hulls in various stages of completion."

"Either one will require them to send at least a battle group," Delwyn said.

"Even better if we send our own forces as soon as possible," Phalalin said and then added, "My Mistress of Tactics scanned the thing. I do not want the Ni'zakhonii making warships from that crystalline material."

"I don't think they can. I'm betting they made the LAC from the biggest geode they found. Even so, an LAC carrier loaded to capacity with them would make them bad enough."

Mrallin sang a query, "What ships can we send?"

Delwyn understood what the Eldest Male had asked even without Phalalin translating for him. "Well, the research shipyard is either on an asteroid or a planetoid. Ground assault forces will be needed to take the research facility and evacuate all the data and materiel. If we have to, we can bombard it from orbit, but I'd hate to lose that research. We can't take the risk. They have research reports in their home system R&D department. If the Lizard government works anything like the Coalition Government does, then someone high up in the chain of command must be getting regular briefings on the new research progress. Far from their home territory, this secret project has to cost them in materials that could otherwise be put to use for more pressing needs.

"That means we will need one or two assault battlecruisers, a command battleship, and screening elements in some mix of destroyers and heavy battlecruisers. It comes down to what's available in the short run. Ships that aren't ready for deployment in the next 320 days will arrive too late to depart on time."

Phalalin did a humanlike thing: he pursed his lips. "An assault battlecruiser you say? Your warship is a planetary assault battlecruiser class warship."

"Yes, he is," Delwyn grinned back at him and sighed, "but *Hunter's Moon* is stuck in a repair slip for some time to come. There isn't enough time."

Phalalin shrugged and spoke to the other males.

They all seemed to share in a joke.

Bad enough he was briefing the A'tayotan on the action they should take, but worse if they adopted his guesswork as defense policy and others got killed because of his omissions or mistakes.

Delwyn and Phalalin were joined by their respective mistresses. Melkorka, Hlinlodyn, Phelindra, and Zalzadrin wrapped their tails firmly around their warleader. That they looked pleased was an understatement.

"You did well," Melkorka said. "Everyone is impressed."

"You think so? I think they're still debating options."

"Of course they are. They will yank their tails over the smallest of details while waiting for the report from Wrathsee'a Anchorage."

"They should get back to us anytime now. It doesn't take that long to look into a probe launcher," Delwyn said. "Speaking of which, I …"

"Warleader Havalin, Wrathsee'a Anchorage calls," Thelindrallin called.

Havalin glided to the hyperlink console, listened for a moment, and turned to the assembly. "The analysis teams have confirmed the launcher barely has the space for two probes. The one remaining shows signs of moderate battle damage. These findings support Delwyn's theory that no courier probe was fired from the captured equipment. The Ni'zakhonii will know that their prototype is missing only if a courier from either the third destroyer or from the research facility itself relayed that information. Either scenario works out to the same result. A courier probe traveling at G-band velocity should reach the destroyers' base."

Thelindrallin turned to the A'tayotan and sang. "Delwyn's analysis has proven correct. At this time I call the question of Delwyn and seek a consensus."

"Propose the question," an A'tayotan Warrior sang from the audience.

Ready this time, Delwyn replied with a confidence he didn't quite feel.

"I propose the following: a battle group consisting of a command battleship, one or two planetary assault battlecruisers, and screening elements in some grouping of destroyers and heavy battlecruisers must arrive within the next 1,100 days in the Nikkiolo star system. This mission is a search and destroy operation; however, planetary surface assault forces are necessary to guarantee partial or total recovery of captured research data and materials. In the alternative, they must ensure the destruction of all materials not captured or otherwise recovered. This battle group must depart Elleio orbit within the next 410 days."

This time the rotating discussion groups became even more involved. They examined data to exhaustion. Several times they asked the opinions of the warleaders. It was clear to Delwyn that they had been invited just for that purpose.

No question remained on whether to search for the enemy research facility. Even if Delwyn had been wrong about everything else, they knew ship trials so close to Compact territory had to have some rationale, and rare raw materials found in the Nikkiolo system answered the question better than idle speculation.

Discussion finally turned to the proposed response. Battle group makeup became the forefront issue. Here, the warleaders again answered queries and gave their opinions.

Some spoke with surprising intensity. The sight made him wonder if they argued for their own ships' inclusion but when he watched them accessing warship tactical data he knew better. They compared ship statistics and probable availability within the time limits he had imposed.

"Go with them," Melkorka urged.

"What can I add? I can barely read the technical specifications. Besides, they know how to fight those ships much better than I ever could."

"Go with them," Melkorka demanded, livid, "Reserve our place in the battle group!"

"Reserve *our* place? You're kidding. Anailiatha estimated repair time at four Coalition months. The deadline is better than two times less than her repair estimate. We aren't going anywhere."

Melkorka threw a fit. He couldn't describe it in any other way. She ground her teeth, sang a low rolling rhythmic growl, and tried her best to restrain her fury. Delwyn wondered if she restrained her anger for him or because of their guest status here.

"If we are considered for ship deployment, repair dock priority will shift. I know Anailiatha pads her repair estimates. She treats our warship like her infants. She would have given herself a margin of error, maybe as much as one hundred days," Melkorka patiently explained.

"That still puts us two months behind," he told her.

"If it cannot be done, then it cannot be done, but not for want of trying. Go!"

While they argued, Phalalin stood sideways to watch and grinned. He could not help himself and chuckled under his breath.

The exhaled mirth drew the other males from their heated discussion.

"You think my analysis is amusing, Phalalin?" Calalin demanded.

Calalin's Comari escort turned her pale amber eyes on Phalalin.

"Never. Look," Phalalin gestured with his tail.

Calalin's eyes followed his pointing pons to Delwyn, and then he laughed. Melkorka was furious with Delwyn. Her annoyance was obvious by her stance, although she kept a masterful control over her scent.

Delwyn now, Calalin read him much easier. His scent told them he was exasperated with his Mistress of the Ship and frustrated because he felt he had nothing more to contribute.

He needed them. Delwyn held Warpact command for the time being.

"Delwyn!" Calalin sang, beckoning him with a raised hand.

Delwyn turned away from a tongue-tied Melkorka to return the warleader's wave.

"Go!" Melkorka demanded, giving him a not so gentle shove.

Phelindra wrapped her tail around Delwyn's stomach as she put an arm around his back and dragged him over to Calalin and the others. "Melkorka is not angry with you. Well, not much angry with you. She wants you to support our honor by offering to participate in the battle group. It is not your fault that you did not know this."

"I'd want to go with them because they go based on my analysis. But I don't see how repairs can be made in time to join the battle group."

"Even if repairs are not completed in time, you will have preserved our honor by offering," Phelindra said. She stepped back to sign a battle language greeting to the Comari.

"It is about time you rejoined us, Delwyn. We are reviewing the combat statistics of the warships available for redeployment. The planetary assault battlecruiser is a new class warship. There are three in service, and a fourth is being built as we speak. *Hunter's Moon* is one, and one is well beyond recall within your time estimate. The third, *Pathfinder*, is within recall range, but barely. Refueling and minimal replenishment can be completed by the departure date, but mission briefings will probably have to wait until after the first jump to Nikkiolo has been completed."

Delwyn nodded, relieved. "I saw no chance of *Hunter's Moon* being permitted to join the battle group."

"You wish to join us in battle?" Phalalin asked, a delighted expression filled his face. "Are you asking, or did Melkorka put you up to it?"

"I want to come along because I'm responsible for sending those ships out there. Melkorka seems to think repairs can be accelerated to make the departure deadline, but I just don't see how it can be done."

"It depends on how complete the repairs are made. Hull plating and bulkhead modules can be fabricated in a month or two. The repair teams have that much time to remove wreckage and seal plumbing and conduits. They can install new gravity lensing armatures at the same time and begin spool-up testing. Ordnance, fueling, and resupply can happen at the same time. If all goes well, they can have bulkheads, compartments, and hull plating installed enough to return the hull and spaceframe to the integrity necessary for FTL travel. Critical systems and internal repairs sufficient to bring the warship to fighting capacity can finish mid-journey; however, the destroyed torpedo bay and the damaged reactor installation and restart might take much longer, but the other reactors can pick up the load. You can manage missing one torpedo bay."

"I still don't see how it's possible," Delwyn repeated.

"Well, it might not be. It is in the hands of the spirits," Phalalin flicked his pons in a 'what will be, will be' shrug.

Calalin wrapped his tail around Delwyn and pulled him over to the wall-spanning panoramic screen and together they scrolled through ship capabilities and their return-to-base timelines.

Calalin took a risk, and he knew it. The Comari who had adopted him mere months after he had completed his adulthood ritual became annoyed if he made abrupt physical contact with unfamiliar people. She had been unusually tolerant of Delwyn. He could feel her eyes burning into his back, but her scent drifted between admonishing him and conveying her amusement over Melkorka twisting Delwyn's tail.

The Comari glared at Melkorka. The chosen was in her care, and the chooser's pheromones lingered on him, very strong pheromones warning other Comara not to bond with him.

"It will take some time to recall these ships," Calalin said. "The warship *Green Ivy* will serve as the command battleship. The warships *Pathfinder* and *Hunter's Moon*—I hope—will provide planetary assault forces and screening elements. We plan to recall Anlann. He had been scheduled to return with Coalition Ambassador Winters anyway. That gives us *Surefooted*. *Fearless* is taking on fuel and supplies now. *Stone Knife* and *Night Shadow* are a few weeks away. That gives us four destroyers to work with. The heavy cruisers *Padfoot* and *Steep Trails* are about a week out and can arrive within hours of each other."

Delwyn shook his head. "Anlann can't make it from Earth to Elleio in time. The hyperlink recall to Earth plus the hyperdrive journey to Elleio takes forty-eight days even if he left immediately, and the Coalition Fleet never dispatches ships immediately. The only way you're gonna get Anlann into this fight is if he can rendezvous with the battle group in the Nikkiolo system. Would Anlann's mistress of the ship take her warship into a potential combat zone without Anlann aboard?"

Phalalin smirked a knowing smile. "If Anlann orders her to do so, she might. His endorsement order to his mistress of the ship would arrive before we have to leave homespace. She would have to begin readiness tasking and attend the briefings before his order reaches her ears."

Discussions continued around them. With nothing more to add, Delwyn nodded to them and headed back to Melkorka.

"Well?" she demanded.

"We are paired with *Pathfinder*, assuming repairs have been made sufficient to permit us to join the battle group without becoming a liability."

Melkorka said nothing, but the delighted smile on her face told him she had something in mind. She fled, running to the A'tayotan mistress of communications.

"Now what's she up to?" he asked Phelindra.

"She is going to pester Anailiatha. Staging for ship's movement gives priority to our repair scheduling."

Delwyn felt sudden relief that he wasn't anywhere near Anailiatha right now.

The warleaders, after asking Delwyn's leave, informed the A'tayotan of their recommendations for the mission.

Thelindrallin bounded over to Delwyn, and he wondered again where the old female got the energy to bounce on the balls of her feet.

Zalzadrin bounced along beside her.

Thelindrallin caught the Hunter mocking her and frowned.

"Why are you here Zalzadrin?" she demanded.

"Did I not answer that question …" she began as a Warrior's singing voice echoed across the Hall.

"Mistress, we have reached a consensus."

"What is the consensus?" Thelindrallin demanded.

"A task force consisting of *Pathfinder, Green Ivy, Steep Trails, Padfoot, Fearless*, and *Stone Knife* shall go and investigate the Nikkiolo star system. The warships *Surefooted* and *Night Shadow* are held in reserve pending the updated repair status of *Hunter's Moon*.

"We will send a request asking Warleader Anlann to return. In the meantime, *Hunter's Moon* is granted extraordinary accommodation."

"All those of the A'tayotan will now sing for the Major Consensus," Thelindrallin announced.

This time the singing lasted much longer, half an Earth hour before the music faded away.

"The A'tayotan, having achieved a Major Consensus, adopt the question as a statement of policy."

Delwyn listened as Thelindrallin instructed the Hall. That in itself took twenty minutes. "I wonder why it took so long for them to reach a major consensus this time."

"A few A'tayotan females held out for our inclusion in the battle group. Others have the same doubts as you do about our warship not being fully repaired within the time remaining," Phelindra said.

"I think they're right to keep that in mind. What do you think?"

Phelindra paused. So much depended on how extensive the damage had been and how long repairs would take. Translating all the damaged structures out at once rather than piecemeal could accelerate repairs, but it also meant discarding a lot of intact bulkheads and substructure. Printing replacements for so much structure took time and was energy expensive let alone all the plumbing and wiring the new sections would require. She turned to Delwyn, put her arm around his back, and wrapped her tail around his waist.

"I do not know. It all comes down to the extent of the damage, what must work, and what the warship can do without or can be bypassed while the journey is underway."

"Where's Melkorka? Is she still having a go at Anailiatha?"

"Probably. I do not think ...," Phelindra began.

"Delwyn? What is the likelihood of a Coalition warship rendezvousing with the task force?" Thelindrallin interrupted.

"In interstellar space? None. Hyperdrive can jump a ship to coordinates adjacent to a target system. Hyperspace plotting is conservative so to avoid jumping inside of a star's heavy mass hyperlimit. That means navigators program for outer system or heliopause arrival points and then continue into the inner system at high sublight velocity, adjusting for orbital velocity by breaking on their way in. Coalition ships rendezvous at hyperspace beacon marker points. Since no Coalition hyperspace beacon is in the Nikkiolo system's hyperspace anomaly, Captain Rodgers will have to jump into Nikkiolo's heliopause and navigate to some rallying point and wait for the battle group to quantum jump there.

"Logistics plays a part in it too, because it depends on how long it takes to have orders cut for *Henri Edda's* departure. We also don't know how far she is into replenishment. The crew is probably on leave by now. Then the administrative paper-pushing always involved with a change of captain takes time. Commander Rodgers is in line to succeed Captain Winters as commanding officer, and I doubt a new Captain Rodgers is ready to jump into a command event so soon. Remember that I once said that the Coalition fleet is a more bureaucratic body than its equivalent here."

Thelindrallin shook her head in confusion. "I do not understand this hyperdrive propulsion system the Coalition employs. It sounds dangerous, like slippery bark to me."

"I don't know what I can tell you about it. It works."

Thelindrallin nodded absently and watched the A'tayotan plan the mission.

"You will go home to your clan, meet with your clan elders and your family. You can do nothing further here.

"The A'tayotan declares this session of the Hall of Consensus is in recess. Phalalin, take Delwyn home with you!"

12
HOMEWARD BOUND

Delwyn felt hot humid air slap his face the minute he stepped through the main entrance bole. By the time he reached the waiting VTOL aircraft, he had gotten used to it thanks to the light breezes swirling around the A'tayotan elleiu tree.

"Where are we going now?" he asked.

"Home to our immediate and extended families' elleiu trees within O'un Tu Clan territory. The females in your occupational association living there will have arrived by now, so we are taking a direct flight to meet them," Phalalin said.

Delwyn looked up at the sun. It hadn't moved much. His internal clock told him some three hours had passed since he entered the A'tayotan home tree, but the sun contradicted his time sense with its apparent fifteen minutes or so of movement across the sky.

"We are going home," Zalzadrin said, bouncing on her feet.

Melkorka and Hlinlodyn dragged their feet.

"What's wrong?" he asked them.

"We are going home to our clan," Melkorka said.

"We will miss you," Hlinlodyn added. "You will contact us and tell us you are well?"

"I will. I promise," Delwyn said.

"I will take care of him!" Zalzadrin said.

"*We* will take care of him," Phelindra corrected.

Delwyn smiled at Phelindra's emphatic correction and then hesitated as Melkorka's words registered.

He frowned. She had told him they often visited their clans when they returned to Elleio.

He understood. His crew maintained deep passionate ties to immediate and extended families, but she had also assured him that they would accompany him when he visited other clans. She had even said he would have to visit clans in other tribal continents and attend the regional gatherings they held from time to time—some kind of combined family reunion and county fair.

"I thought you were coming with me," he blurted, realizing how deeply attached to them he'd become.

Melkorka stared at the bare ground, clenching and relaxing her long four-jointed toes. Grabbing footfuls of dirt with her toes, she sprinkled the soil across an offending leaf.

Hlinlodyn stood watching Melkorka cover the unfortunate leaf with layer after layer of dirt until she completely buried it.

Phelindra shoved him toward them without saying a word.

"Well?" he asked Melkorka.

"We will all come to visit after you have had time to adjust to your immediate and extended family members. They will want you to themselves for a brief time before they show you off to the clan as a whole. We have our clans to visit and family ties, friendships, and loves to renew. We," Melkorka paused to sweep her tail in a gesture that included Phelindra, Hlinlodyn, and Zalzadrin "are deeply fond of you."

"What should I do? Come to your clans and pick you up?"

Melkorka flicked her tail in apparent indifference. "No. We will come for you in a few weeks. Not all at once. A warship society would swamp extended-family hospitality. When the time comes for you to visit the other clans, we will take you to them."

"That many people will require quite a few aircraft," Delwyn quipped.

"Do not be simple," Melkorka chided. "Mass-movement on such a scale will require quantum translation priority. A body of us will always be with you, and they will rotate with another body," Melkorka said, still studying the pile of dirt and its burial victim.

Delwyn smiled. A body was a group of 625 troops, an Eyloni ten-thousand. He turned to a quiet Hlinlodyn.

Her gaze never left the object of Melkorka's interest. Hlinlodyn's feet gripped the ground. She did not dig up footfuls of dirt. Instead, she clenched and relaxed her toes and then wiggled them over and over, burrowing them into the cool soil. She felt it mound over her feet until she had buried them up to her ankles.

Delwyn stepped between the two Warriors, put his arms around them, and pulled them against his chest. "Go and enjoy yourselves while you can.

You're going to have enough of me when we return to our warship. After all, what is that saying you're so fond of: Males are simple?"

"Males are strange," Hlinlodyn whispered, hushed. She looked up and met his eyes, flicked her ears at him and Melkorka, and then she scowled at him. "We are behaving like infants, like Kidahin does around you," Hlinlodyn pouted.

Melkorka's ears came up at that. She glared at Hlinlodyn but said nothing. The Mistress of Tactics was more correct than she knew. She had not been present when Delwyn first met Kidahin who had developed a clear preference for him because her juvenile instincts made her more sensitive to his temperament.

And Hlinlodyn had the right of it, too. They were acting like infants. Well, not infants exactly. More like how females did when they had associated with the same male for a long time. Their behavior certainly was not typical based on the few months they had been associating with Delwyn.

They loved him: They loved him because he was a male; they loved him because he was their warleader; they loved him because they had developed a deep attachment to him.

But that wasn't why Melkorka and Hlinlodyn were stalling. They were worried. Delwyn was new to their world. He did not know the range and breadth of Eyloni social life. Worse, he did not know the dangers lurking in the forests. Living with a warship's society in a warship forest simulation for thirteen months did not prepare him for the harshness of life in the real jungle.

"Are we ever going to leave?" Zalzadrin demanded. "We are not going to let Delwyn walk into a *pa'zur* or fall from a tree."

"I know that!" Melkorka trilled.

"I need you to give me regular status reports on warship repair progress. Don't forget that for us to join the battle group repairs must surpass the minimum necessary to resume combat ready status. Otherwise we aren't going anywhere. You must also bring the crew complement to full strength if we are to guarantee sufficient combat forces to muster surface assault and boarding action teams," Delwyn said.

Both Melkorka and Hlinlodyn brightened at his words.

"We are going to Wrathsee'a Anchorage for some time. I enjoy watching the work being done on our warship," Melkorka admitted.

"Like you enjoyed watching Anailiatha directing repair efforts in Ibeetu orbit?" Hlinlodyn asked, eyes wide and innocent, her ears pricked at him, her pons twitching.

Melkorka growled, a sibilant fluttering in her throat. "That was different!"

Hlinlodyn had a sense of humor? And she was aiming it at Melkorka? That took courage. Melkorka didn't put up with laughter at her expense, but Delwyn had to ask.

"What did she do to Anailiatha?"

"Nothing!" Melkorka shouted.

"She pestered her for days on end, asking her when the gravity lensing system would come online so she could go chasing after you. Anailiatha and her engineering teams came close to banning her from the engineering hull," Hlinlodyn said.

"She didn't," Delwyn gasped, mock-serious.

"Of course I was not banned!" Melkorka sang at defiance pitch. "Anailiatha merely said her engineers and technicians would work better if I did not ask them every … neh'me … or so."

Neh'me? That was what, an hour? She spoke the word, so she meant EST time. An EST hour was only twenty-eight minutes long. He could see it now: Melkorka and Anailiatha, both Warriors, had a lot in common. Tempers, for one.

"I wish I could've seen that," Delwyn said, grinning.

"If you had been there, I would not have been trying to thread a needle with Anailiatha's tail!" Melkorka yelled.

Hlinlodyn's nose translated Melkorka's scent into a mental image. The words and the empathic reinforcement caused Hlinlodyn to snort hard enough to almost swallow her tongue as she trilled in laughter.

Melkorka's towering rage, the rage that came upon her when she felt helpless, melted as Hlinlodyn's scent painted pictures showing Melkorka darting in and out of Power Systems and Propulsion screaming at a harassed Anailiatha.

They clung to him, singing in laughter.

Delwyn looked over at Phalalin standing with his arms crossed over his chest. The expression plain on his face asking: *can we leave now?*

Delwyn chased the two worrywarts to an idling aircraft, grabbed their pons between his thumbs and forefingers and tugged. If Eyloni had an intimate body part, it was their ringlet-covered tail tips, their pons. They were sensual, sensitive, and emitted pheromones.

Melkorka and Hlinlodyn could have curled their tails around their waists and tucked their pons under their loincloths to stop him. Instead they played keep-away, daring him to grab and give them a gentle tug. And they made sure he grabbed their pons a few times each.

Stopping in front of the aircraft hatch, they said their good-byes, boarded, and then watched and waved at him as their flight lifted silently into the air and climbed into the northwestern sky.

Delwyn waved back to them until they were well out of sight before turning around. Lost in thought, dragging his feet on the way back, he returned to Zalzadrin, Phelindra, and Phalalin.

"If you take that long to say good-bye to them, then you will need a few hours to say good-bye to me," Zalzadrin said, bouncing on her feet as always.

Phalalin said nothing. He knew what Delwyn did not. Females knew males were not helpless and yet they always treated males as if they would die from neglect if they left them for any length of time.

"Well, they're gone. I guess we can go now," Delwyn said.

Phalalin nodded. "They will adjust. Once they rejoin their families, they will feel better."

Delwyn shook his head and stepped into another waiting aircraft and dropped into a seat.

"They think I can't do anything without them watching over me."

"No," Zalzadrin said. "They know you are new to the rainforest. They worry, but they worry for nothing. We are your family, and we will teach you all about the deadly and dangerous forest animals and other hazards."

They lifted off, and Delwyn looked down through the clear floor and watched the rainforest fall away.

The aircraft rocketed into the sky, pulling away from Na'di Island. It climbed high into the sky following a similar path taken by Melkorka's plane before turning to the northeast. Below them the ocean, which had been a harsh, intense, cold sapphire blue, turned turquoise as they climbed higher.

Soaring out over the ocean, Delwyn could see the shallow seas filling the basins in and around continents. Those seas let heavy storms form when cold farside air rushing in from both the eastern and the western terminators, collided with the warm humid nearside continental air. Frequent, violent, straight line wind storms were not uncommon.

Delwyn saw a red smear on the ocean below. Like a giant red amoeba groping through the light blue water, it stretched a pseudopod eastward toward the horizon.

"Is that an algal bloom down there? It's big, too. It'll kill the fish. Does this happen often?" he asked.

Cries of "what" and "where" erupted all around him. Shocked faces looked down on the flat sea and the bloodstained blob swimming through it.

To say they had a passing concern for the environment understated their intense reaction to his words. They fought their warship with the professionalism of naval combat veterans, and yet they showed a frantic worry about the ocean that would put twentieth century environmental activists to shame.

"I do not see anything, do you?" Verikaralee asked Phalalin.

Puzzled, he shook his head and continued scanning the water.

"I see nothing wrong," Zalzadrin said to Delwyn. "Where do you see anything harmful?"

"All the red stuff floating down there," he said, pointing and waving his finger around.

"*That?*" Zalzadrin and Verikaralee demanded in interrogative pitch.

"That is *a'ranyo a'turadek*, a bacterial colony that ages ago co-opted photosynthesizing plasmids. They are not toxic. Far from it, they filter the water, pull carbon dioxide from it, oxygenate the atmosphere, and provide food for sea life. They live in colonies and drift on ocean currents," Verikaralee said.

"What about when they are driven ashore by storms?" Delwyn asked.

"They ride the currents along the La'huaset southern coast far from shore. They come through the La'huaset archipelagoes as young and grow into massive colonies as they cross the warm nearside into the La'huaset northeast coastal currents. From there they enter the frigid farside oceans and reproduce. Then the colonies break up, and as they die, the wild storms scatter them throughout the hemisphere providing food for farside marine life. The young are drawn to the southwestern nearside ocean and the warm shallow seas around the archipelagoes. And the cycle repeats."

Delwyn endured disapproving stares all though Verikaralee's lecture. He'd given them a fright, and they weren't happy about it.

The aircraft continued its northeastern flight over the algae supercolony and on to the La'huaset tribal continental coast. Delwyn followed their progress on a global tracking screen mounted on the bulkhead separating them from the flight crew.

He spent some time studying the longitude legend superimposed on the map. The Eyloni divided the nearside hemisphere into four zones having forty-five degrees of longitude each. For want of better terminology, he labeled them from the eastern terminator to the western terminator, calling the first forty-five-degree wedge Zone-a, the next forty-five degrees as Zone-b, the third one Zone-c, and the fourth Zone-d. Wedges on the global positioning screen were labeled a'too're, which meant 'vertical slice', followed by a chord identifying longitudinal areas. Farside had its own zones labeled with the same notes sung at a lower octave. From west to east he called them Zone-A, Zone-B, Zone-C, and Zone-D.

It made him feel better knowing where he was relative to the ground. They flew north of the equator, in the nearside hemisphere and in Zone-d. The course plot on the heads-up display showed them shooting for the 135-degree longitude line, where it crossed the La'huaset shoreline some thirteen hundred kilometers away. Their airspeed was about eight hundred kilometers per hour, and they'd been in the air for fifty minutes. They had another fifty to go, he guessed.

Zalzadrin paced up and down the passenger cabin, while he sat mesmerized by the scenes unfolding around him. For all their familiarity with such views, everyone but Zalzadrin watched the sky and sea with the avid interest of a person watching an exciting in-flight movie.

Attracted by Zalzadrin's bouncy movement, Delwyn took a few minutes to glance around the passenger cabin. The décor called to mind a classic video series he had watched in an arts appreciation class that had featured two secret agents who worked for the old United States. Their base had been a steam locomotive luxury box car. The quaint woodwork inside that box car reminded him somewhat of those used in the cabin.

On the outside the plane looked no different than what he expected: a modern, silent, and emission-free aircraft.

"Zalzadrin's going to pace a groove in the deck," he muttered to Phelindra.

"She does not enjoy flying."

"You're kidding," he said.

"No, I am not kidding. She would have translated from our warship to her family if not for you."

"Is it because we are flying over water?"

Phelindra shook her head. "It is because the aircraft is not connected to the ground. She does not fear heights. No Eyloni fears heights, but an aircraft is nothing more than a branch falling through aerodynamic forces. Atmospheric air travel is like riding a broken branch through the air for some of us. Zalzadrin is not afraid, but she feels the air currents buffeting the fuselage and thinks about falling. She relieves herself by pacing. Do not say anything to her about it. For you to notice would both honor and humiliate her. You care for her, I can smell it on your scent. She can smell it, too."

He nodded and turned to watch a ship moving across the water with astonishing speed, trailing a comet's tail of mist a kilometer long.

"Phelindra, what is that? It must be traveling at least *two hundred kph*, a quarter of our airspeed." It cruised above the water but had struts connecting it to catamaran-like outriggers below the waterline.

"La'huaset wet navy patrol cruiser. He is making good time too," Phelindra said, glancing at the wall tracking system. "He is headed for one of the rivers, probably the T'anni River."

Delwyn half-listened, more interested in the ship's lines, and squinted.

"If you want a better view, use your console. Point at the cruiser and touch the screen."

Delwyn felt stupid but pointed at the racing vessel dropping behind them anyway and then touched the image.

The display came alive with the fast-moving ship framed in its center. At zero enhancement it looked like a toy boat racing across a pond.

"Now, with your finger, draw a box around him, touch the box with two fingers pressed together, and then spread them apart to expand the image," she said.

Delwyn did as he was told and watched as the ship expanded to the width he had spread his fingers. He repeated the gesture until it filled the screen.

The hull above the water had the lines matching a museum quality stealth jet fighter: a black and boxy hull built up from a collage of odd angles uncomfortable to look at for some reason. Below the waterline glided a manta ray shape with streamlined nacelles port and starboard. Struts connected the nacelles to the origami-folded hull.

"His propulsion systems take advantage of supercavitation, the engines travel underwater inside an air bubble," Phalalin said.

"What's his mission?" Delwyn asked.

"Environmental Interdiction."

"What? You need an environmental protection agency here? I thought everyone was a natural … well … naturalist."

"We are," Phalalin explained patiently. "No Eyloni means to harm the environment. Accidents do happen however, and we do have a limited industry on the surface. Waste disposal is clean and safe, but faulty equipment, accident, and negligence always stick their tails into the air, land, and sea. Environmental Interdiction also monitors sea life, the algae and seaweed farms, and the oceanic solar, wind, and sea current generating plants."

"I thought those power systems generated power without emissions by design." Delwyn said.

Zalzadrin shook her head, grateful for any topic that made her forget they fell through the air on a barely controlled leaf. "The water and air turbines can break down, throwing debris into the ocean. That debris can drift into sea life migration routes, hurting or killing them. Too many turbines in narrow channels can cause the current to lose some of its strength, which can affect the surrounding reefs and coastlines. Solar farms sometimes take direct hits from heavy tropical storms, wrecking their thermal receivers and photonic arrays. That wreckage must be retrieved before sea life can ingest small particles. Kelp and seaweed farms may not exceed harvest quotas."

Delwyn listened as Zalzadrin sang through a list of potential problems the ship could address.

"I wish I could take a ride on that ship," he said.

"Really?" Phalalin asked, doubtful. Eyloni lived in trees. Few people wanted to live so close to the hot humid ground. Even along the northern La'huaset coastline where certain clans worked for lengthy periods at or near sea level, they returned often to their inland elleiu trees.

"Well," he mused, "if you wish it, I can arrange a visit."

"I'd enjoy that. Thank you, Phalalin."

"Not at all," he said, nodding at the forward screen.

Delwyn looked up to see the La'huaset tribal continental coastline fast approaching. A mountain range marched along the horizon as far as the eye could see. The mountains felt wrong, different somehow, too uniform: a kilometers-tall continuous ridge covered with cloud rainforests in vermilions and scarlets. A few well-rounded bare ridges poked through the jungle, but they were too far away for him to tell if the bare areas were rock or snow. Kidahin had said that a few of the tallest far north peaks had frost or snow on them.

The heads-up display showed a large mountain lake up ahead, a volcanic crater some three hundred kilometers across filled with deep blue water that sparkled in the bright clear sunlight.

Delwyn looked back down through the cabin floor and watched the rainforest race past. Every so often he saw irregular straight lines cutting through the forest. He thought he knew what those strips were, and why the trees growing within the parallel lines were so much shorter than the trees to either side. His lessons covering Elleio's ecosystems stressed that because trees grew at glacial rates on Elleio, and even though they lived for ages, trees were to be protected from harm. The land below the aircraft had to have been abandoned long ago for there to be even short trees there.

He knew about land recovery from taking core conservancy classes for his agricultural degree. He'd seen examples on Earth, too. Over two hundred years of personal ground vehicles had required a lot of highways. Those highways had harmed the environment in numerous ways. The building materials had been energy-wasteful and released carbon dioxide. Particles from fossil fuels, catalytic converter by-products, inefficient combustion, lubricants, and tire rubber worn to dust had contaminated the roadsides and drainage areas. Road salts and heavy metals from ice abatement, rust, and corrosion products accumulated over time. By the 2100s the United Earth government had closed most highways and reclaimed the areas, but where hillsides had been cut for the roadbeds and sculpted for overpasses and underpasses, the scars remained.

"Phalalin? Is that a roadbed down there?"

Phalalin averted his eyes from the sight. So did the others. Even a somber Zalzadrin didn't crack a joke.

"Yes, only the La'huaset Tribal continent has them because La'huaset was the seat of our industrial awaking. We allowed it to continue for 240 years before we learned that the industrial toxins had been killing the environment."

"Killing *males*, you mean," Zalzadrin growled.

"And females too," Phalalin added.

"I remember a song Hervorallin taught me about the O'un Tu Clan fighting a great evil in another clan's territory—a civil war," Delwyn said.

Zalzadrin shook her head. "Not a war. The Compact Counsel exists to prevent open warfare between tribes or among clans. This was different, a criminal matter akin to declaring outlawry, ni'zakhon, and quarantining the areas. The Compact Counsel ordered power generation be scaled back to solar, wind, and limited nuclear sources and declared all power output be diverted to the development of clean manufacturing techniques and fusion power research. Spaceflight took on a new priority as it became clear to the Counsel that manufacturing had to move off-world. The Counsel implemented an industrial waste disposal protocol that required everything not recyclable or that could not be decontaminated be boosted into orbit and sent into the sun. Once hydrogen-antihydrogen fusion become a reality, quantum translation and faster-than-light propulsion followed."

"That's quite a commitment to the environment. It took 250 years on Earth for us to make any progress. Even so the environment still hasn't returned to pre-industrial conditions, especially in the equatorial rainforests and in the oceans."

"Delwyn, one third of all La'huaset infants died from environmental contamination. We never cut down or burn our forests. We did not spill chemicals into our waterways or spew them into the air. Subtle by-products and inadvertent releases altered our health. Male births are rare because gender is an inherited trait in us, a matter of dominance in a group of genes on a single chromosome. The same group of genes in both egg and sperm must be dominant to select the male gender. If a specific one is recessive, then a Comari is born. All other combinations produce Warriors or Hunters. Many health issues are associated with the gender selection genes and they became worse from accumulating industrial toxins," Verikaralee said.

"All the Comara and nearly all the males in the exclusion zones died," Zalzadrin added.

"That is why we put a stop to it," Verikaralee heaved, clearly upset from the somber tone their words had taken.

They watched the forest zoom by in silence for a time as the aircraft flew eastward. It gained altitude and jogged north a bit before turning back east again.

Delwyn saw another mountain lake in the distance, twice as wide as the first one and curving over the horizon. It stretched out over a thousand klicks.

"That is Om'tu Lake. Fire Lake," Verikaralee said, breaking the silence. "All the eastern shore belongs to the O'un Tu Eyloni. The Fire River People are our clan, our families, and this land is our territory."

The mountain range ran the entire length along the La'huaset Tribal continent, from the southern hemisphere down by the western terminator up through the northern hemisphere and the eastern terminator. Not a result of tectonic mountain building, the barrier range persisted as the ancient remains of a massive asteroid impact crater. The other side and most of the crater itself remained hidden beneath a thousand meters of water in farside's deep ocean. The impact had triggered volcanic activity in the deep ocean along the crater's edge even through the weaker crust on the opposite hemisphere, creating volcanic vents and craters tens to hundreds of kilometers across. Extinct, they had become freshwater lakes long ago.

Had the cataclysmic impact not occurred, the nearside ocean floor would not have been deformed upward to create the shallow seas and their five plateau 'continents'. Twenty percent of the surface was dry land. Had the impact not raised the ocean floor, Elleio would have remained a ninety-nine percent pelagic world, a living ocean. Limestone cliffs and marble peaks mixed here and there with basalt and granite proved Elleio had been such a world before the killing impact.

They flew over a structure built into the crater wall and above the lake. Delwyn pointed to it and tapped the screen, magnifying the image until it filled the heads-up display.

"What's this place for, Phelindra?"

She glanced at the image. "A pumping facility."

"I thought enough water fell on elleiu trees for everyone to have more than enough to drink."

"It does. This water is for industrial use. The amount withdrawn is strictly regulated because what cannot be decontaminated is launched into the sun. Water from ice bodies in the outer asteroid belts having the same mixture of hydrogen and oxygen isotopes are translated here to balance what is removed."

The aircraft vectored toward the volcanic crater surrounding the great lake. They flew above and along the crater boundary, giving them a good view of the lake, the sprawling eroded volcanic cone, and the valley between the supervolcano crater and the towering impact crater.

Far above the lake the ancient impact crater stretched to the horizon. Its ragged edges averaged four hundred klicks wide and included the crater's jagged inside edge, where the buckled ground heaved up along the deformation zone. The voids below them had filled with magma. Under pressure they had erupted, creating volcanic cones and vents. Over time they went extinct and filled with water. The view on the left made him wonder if the Grand Canyon would look somewhat like this if filled with water.

The aircraft arced across Om'tu Lake and flew over kilometers of southern forested mountains and rare industrial centers placed with care into their rocky niches in stony valleys and canyons. No blasting or bulldozing scars or rubble remained. Delwyn remembered Mistress of Fortifications Allinha fretting over Ibeetu's natural beauty as she directed her combat engineers to create the Place of Mourning. She had tailored the natural stone depression into a tiered outdoor amphitheater for twenty-five hundred people. Before they left and while he regenerated his wounds in Health

Center, Allinha had returned the cut stone pieces to their original places, along with the soil, the grasses, and the brush. She even replaced the sticks and dead leaves which had either blown or washed into the depression. Before they left, she and her work crews had sung to the spirits, thanking them for allowing their society to use the land and begging forgiveness for not replacing even one grain of sand in the exact same place they had found it.

The building below followed the contoured stone valley. No roads led in or out, but flight vehicles stood sentry in flat gravel areas along a wandering perimeter.

A huge parabolic dish antenna stood on a plateau above the site, pointing up into the sky. It wasn't an orbital communications station, not in this day and age. Nobody built planetary radio telescopes anymore, either. Modern astronomers put them in interstellar space, far away from a solar system's noisy influence.

"What's the dish antenna used for?" he asked.

"Microwave power receiving station. Power is beamed here from an orbital power plant. Industry needs uninterrupted power, and fusion generators beam energy to sites like this one," Phalalin said.

"What do they make here?" Delwyn asked.

"Wet navy hull plating and bulkheads using additive manufacturing techniques. Refined raw metals and carbon composites are flown here. The bulkhead or hull plate is printed layer by layer until completed. It is inspected and then flown to the shipyard that ordered it. Large or unwieldy modules are lighter-than-air airlifted to docks. Quantum translation is energy expensive, not economical, and its use is regulated. Besides, ships larger than coastal cutters are not translated because extending a translation field over so large an area is not feasible. If we could do that, then we would build warships on the surface and translate them into orbit instead of using a jump drive to move a completed warship into space."

"You can jump a warship 3.043 light-years. Why not jump larger oceangoing vessels to their home ports?"

"Because doing so requires operating a hydrogen-antihydrogen reactor on Elleio to provide the energy to translate so much mass. In practice, you need a jump drive, and we limit jump drive use on the surface," Phalalin said.

They cruised over two more manufacturing sites before crossing back over jungle- covered mountain peaks and Om'tu Lake again. This time they flew across the lake instead of along its length. The eastern shore on the horizon gleamed blue in the starboard window as they swept over more extinct volcanic ridges and down across the north-facing barrier mountain range.

The aircraft shook as it met turbulence.

"Rough air on this side," he commented.

"The north-facing ridge is a barrier to the cool north winds. They can be quite cold at times, but nothing like the frigid north polar winds of farside. The nearside north polar winds often bring frost and some snow during the nights, but sometimes polar vortices spin up from farside and blow over the north pole and across northern nearside. Those cold winds hit the crater lip and are pushed up into the warm moist air coming up from the interior. Cold rains follow, sometimes snow falls, but it melts before hitting the ground," Verikaralee said.

They flew over the north side of the mountain range. No foothills filled this side, and Delwyn watched the ancient impact crater wall pass below. Worn and eroded over time, it retained a near vertical semblance of a cliff that plunged down into the forests below.

Delwyn had visited Meteor Crater National Park in Arizona as a kid. That crater's inside edge multiplied by a thousand is what he saw here. The continuous cliff face curved a slight bit downward toward the jungle floor, and then the impact basin continued at a gentle grade toward the north polar sea some eight hundred kilometers to the north.

This side of the crater cut a diagonal running more or less across the nearside hemisphere. That had to have been some asteroid impact. Phalalin said Eyloni scientists believed Elleio had been a rogue planet that wandered into parabolic orbit around Elle, picking up water from Ceres-size ice asteroid impacts in the outer system before being captured by Tyreniioroneo. An ocean world before the impact, the life that had evolved here had been driven to exotic aquatic forms. After the impact, new life had evolved alongside the impact survivors. The older forms preferred the farside hemisphere ocean cool depths. The post-impact forms preferred the warmer, the shallower nearside climate.

The name Tyreniioroneo, the gas giant Elleio orbited, translated to "The Companion of the Hunter", but the emotional image evoked by pheromones gave a meaning closer to "The Hunters' tail-tied Companion". The word companion, sung at low-pitch and at a different beat, shifted the meaning to "heavenly male companion", a natural satellite: a moon, The *Hunter's Moon.* Although the gas giant wasn't a moon, without him there would have been no life. The Eyloni considered Tyreniioroneo a male. How they decided to name him the companion of only the Hunter females Delwyn had no clue and none had been offered, but he had a theory.

It made no evolutionary sense to him for a species to evolve two distinct fertile female genders and a third sterile one. What if the Hunters had been the original female template for the exquisite tree-dwellers, and as male births dwindled a heartier female, the Warriors, had evolved to protect them?

The aircraft banked right and began a slow and gentle descent, putting the lake to their right rear and drifting past the clear fuselage. They banked a few more degrees right, giving the passengers a view into the jungle below.

Forward movement stopped as they hovered high above the rainforest, listing to starboard. The pilots were probably waiting for landing clearance.

Zalzadrin shoved herself between seats, elbowing Phelindra aside. Verikaralee squeezed between the seats on his left between him and Phalalin and put her arm around him. Zalzadrin pointed with her right index finger and Verikaralee reaching under his left armpit and across his chest and aimed her own finger.

"From here you can see most of the O'un Tu Clan territory below us stretching out toward the horizon," Zalzadrin said.

He looked out across the jungle. "That's a lot of jungle."

"Our territory is larger than that," Verikaralee added. "We are not high enough to see the territory below the horizon."

That was what, a circle some six hundred klicks across? "How is it defined then? As a circle? A square?"

"Do you know how silly you sound?" Phelindra asked. "Who in their right mind would take a stick and draw a line in the dirt and say 'everything inside the line is ours, and everything outside the line is not'?"

"Then how is territory defined?" he asked.

"We walk it. We scent mark our trails and pathways. Clans do not arrange their territories so one clan's land marches against another clan's land. Free territory must remain available to allow others to pass through the forest. Travelers can take resources from there to have for obtaining food and water. They may also use materials to make personal weapons or other items as needed to pass safely through free territory."

Delwyn nodded, half interested, as he watched the golden rusty ocher forest rise to meet their slow descent.

The shoreline sported several stone piers, telling him that some O'un Tu Clan families traded with other clans along the twelve-hundred-kilometer-long, three-hundred-kilometer wide Om'tu Lake. The lake drained into the Om'tu River. Mightier than the Amazon it cut through the high plateau cloud rainforest some four hundred kilometers before dropping over the plateau edge and down into the lowland jungle below creating a waterfall so tall and wide that it put a hundred Horseshoe Falls to shame. There it continued along the inside edge of the ancient impact crater as it headed toward the northeastern polar sea.

He spotted intake ports along the river bank. "Are those hydroelectric intakes?"

Phalalin nodded. "They divert water through a generating station buried in the cliff. The water is channeled through the turbines and out through exit ports behind the Fire River Falls. It still operates, and power is beamed to a receiver, which then beams it to industrial sites throughout clan territory."

"I thought you used solar collectors on elleiu trees for power," Delwyn said.

"We do. This power is not for individual trees. It is reserved for supporting clan-wide industrial or cooperative ventures."

They spiraled down the east face of the plateau and toward rising clouds of mist and beheld the Fire River Falls. Like a tilted pitcher, it poured fresh clear mountain water into clouds of spray that dashed onto the rocks at the cliff base before fleeing the merciless impact and escaping down a river tens of soccerfield lengths wide. The essence of natural beauty, tranquil for all its driving fury, the majesty latent in the awesome power of falling water, seemed to enchant the rainforest with a mystical rush of eternal mists that echoed throughout the untouched virgin ocher paradise.

Delwyn knew the sight from the simulated view in his quarters aboard his warship: The Fire River Falls.

"Watch!" Verikaralee said as the aircraft banked to let them look out on the river as it plunged over the falls.

The sunlight struck the falling water, giving it the illusion of fire flowing over the edge of the high plateau. Opposite the falls, some five klicks away, an elleiu tree rose into the sky, its height passing the crest of the falls to tower another hundred meters above. The tree was magnificent, one of the closest ones to the mountain range by far. It looked forlorn there, abandoned. Others were scattered throughout the rainforest in the distance, but the next closest one was kilometers away.

They pulled away from the falls and continued down the river, overflying occasional river traffic. Small shipping vessels sailed the wide, deep river. Not the heavy cargo ships he'd seen earlier, but small shallow-draft ships. He doubted the environmentally minded Eyloni ever even considered dredging the riverbed.

"Do those ships sail the ocean or are they for river traffic only?" he asked Phalalin.

"Oceangoing vessels are permitted to sail up river beyond a certain point if they are local coasters. Ships from beyond La'huaset coastal waters are not permitted access to the river at all because there is always the chance they might have picked up an invasive species. Cargo is transferred at a port at the river estuary."

The aircraft angled off to the left and flew just above the emergent layer over more jungle. Crimson and tangerine branches passed below them. They looked like fall leaves scattered across a field of golden-brown wheat sprinkled here and there with small isolated groups of trees, the elleiu trees that grew far above the emergent layer of the lesser trees.

They headed toward an isolated group of elleiu trees off in the distance.

"Those trees ahead belong to our immediate and closely related extended families. One belongs to Hervorallin and your family," Zalzadrin said, pointing at the five elleiu trees on the horizon.

"Where is your family tree, Zalzadrin?"

"In the same group. Hervorallin and I are closely related."

"What about you, Phalalin?"

"The same tree as yours."

"Phelindra?" he asked.

"The same tree, very near Hervorallin's abode," she said.

"What about you, Verikaralee?"

"The tree closest to yours. We are extended family, you and I."

They drew closer to the trees, descending sharply now. The trees shared a power reception station mounted several kilometers away, dish pointing up, and Delwyn realized the hydroelectric plant didn't beam power to a ground storage site. It beamed power up into orbit, where it was collected and transmitted back down to receivers. This one was much smaller, maybe ten meters across.

They spiraled down into a straw-colored grass clearing. No stone landing pads covered the grasses here, which meant aircraft didn't land and take-off here often enough to harm the ground.

People came out to meet them, a lot of people. They streamed toward the VTOL from beneath tall grasses, under brush and smaller trees, along hidden pathways, and from a hundred side trails. Too many people too soon for them to have just climbed through a seven-hundred-meter canopy, down a four-hundred-meter trunk, and several kilometers from the distant local trees. The pilot must have called ahead and warned them they were on final approach.

"Come Delwyn! It is time for you to meet our family!" Zalzadrin said, smiling and bouncing on her feet. She dragged him through the open hatch and onto the grass-covered ground.

Delwyn took a tentative step into the high grass. Each one had a stalk with a head shaped like an upside-down strawberry. Each stalk had its own single blade of grass that grew alongside it and above the strawberry head.

Zalzadrin yanked him away from his stalling and turned him around to face the crowd that poured out to meet him.

"There is Hervorallin! See her? She is carrying Princess!" Zalzadrin sang.

Distant gentle mountain breezes gusted across the open grassy meadow. Much cooler than the air on Na'di Island, it felt like Florida in summer. The wind played at his back as he saw Hervorallin waving.

A delighted squeal echoed across the waving grass.

He knew that musical shriek.

Princess leapt from her mother's back and disappeared into the hip-high grass. Seconds later she found his leg and climbed up his side and clamped herself around his neck. Singing happily, she rubbed her face against his cheek and nose, complaining about his rough stubble.

A minute later Hervorallin stopped next to him, delighted. Behind her, the large group waited, curious and excited.

"I hope you have prepared them for me, Hervorallin."

"I have told them all about you. Be welcome to our family."

Hervorallin stood beside Delwyn and wrapped her tail possessively around his waist before addressing her immediate family.

"This is Delwyn of the O'un Tu Clan of the La'huaset Tribe and his near-daughter Princess, daughter of Hervorallin O'un Tu La'huaset Eyloni. He is a Singing Male and Warleader of the Compact warship *Hunter's Moon*."

13

THE O'UN TU CLAN

The males stepped forward, about seventy of them. They milled around Delwyn in a step-patterned dance with him at the center, touching him with their tail tips. Phalalin joined the male dance, and together they sang a soft, deep humming trill.

Delwyn hoped he wasn't supposed to join them. Male singing sounded much different than female singing did. Males filled a vocal void, which explained why Melkorka and several others sang with him at every opportunity. The females hadn't joined in yet, but by the looks on their yearning faces they wanted to.

The males sang, partners pairing up and then turning together into a circle. They came within a tail-length away from him. The sounds they made matched the whistling and moaning wind, leaves rustling, rain falling. Weaving through those sounds came deep mellow vocals alternating in and out of hearing.

The significance attached to the natural sounds was lost on Delwyn, but the words brought some understanding. He knew the root meanings, but timing and pitch altered word meaning. He relied on gut feeling and past lessons as he tried to make sense out of the smells that filled his nose as they sang:

"The male singer sits by the fire and thinks about what song he will sing. He stands at the edge of an abyss, raises his arms, and sings out. To sing means to use the Spirit Voice.

"The O'un Tu Clan says what lives shall die. What dies shall live in the Oyya Web. Strength comes from the spirits. Wisdom comes from experience.

"The power of song issues from an oyya. Songs are an expression of oyya. From songs come the threads of the Oyya Web. The spirits gave The People songs, telling The People that using them would call the spirits back at any time. Songs would bring to them the things they needed and transform or banish those things they did not want. The gift of music was a compassionate act that enables The People to call the spirits into Clan life. The song and the drum create a pattern of shared consciousness. The heart beats, and in both male and female, the heart is the drum of male identity, and as for a female, her heart is a he.

"The First Law of the Clan sings about finding one's clan."

They stopped dancing and singing and turned to face him, expectantly.

Now what?

"Sing from the Law of Homing," Phalalin's soft voice whispered from across the tail-long space between Delwyn and the waiting males.

Homing? Did he mean homing-in, as a missile does, or did he mean homing-in as in finding the way home? The words of the song "Homeward Bound" came to him, evoking memories of home, music, and love waiting. He hummed the tune first, giving them the chance to catch the rhythm. Then his deep baritone voice broke over them as he became their focus. Pheromones released while singing floated on the air with his scent, broadcasting his feelings. By singing about home and home's promise, his voice and scent told them how he felt and whether he wanted to live with them or not.

Delwyn saw it in the posture the males held as they waited: they were ready. Like band members readying to play their instruments, they tensed. They would not join his song without permission.

He ended the song, paused a beat, and then began to sing the same song as he stretched his arms out in a wide embrace.

The males sang with him. Their voices sounding nothing like the female accompaniment. They sang an accompanying rhythmic voice in the same way a person might mumble through forgotten words in a verse, yet their numbers didn't drown him out. When Delwyn finished, they collapsed their dancing circle and surrounded him, embracing him at first one at a time and then again in groups. They introduced themselves by name and by firm but gentle physical contact, including face rubbings and tail brushings. He returned the gestures as best he could using his hands.

Like the females, the males shared inclusion with a person or a group by shared physical contact. Embraces lasted for both short and long periods, and they came off as intimate from his perspective.

"You are not done, Delwyn. Now you must sing about homing to them," Phalalin said, sweeping his tail in a broad arc to include some fifteen hundred females.

"How do I do that?" Delwyn asked, distress tinting his tone.

"You invite them to you and allow them to sing along with you. We will withdraw to just behind them. They will not permit us to venture any farther," Phalalin said, making a small circle in the air with his pons.

Like rolling his eyes, Delwyn remembered, a visual sigh and an appeal for patience. The gesture made him think for some reason about something missing.

"Phalalin, aren't there any Comara here?"

His over-exaggerated ears pointing and the "Who, me?" face made Delwyn suddenly wary, and he froze. "They're behind me, aren't they?"

Phalalin smiled an Eyloni male's goofy grin and nodded. "They are between us, in a tight group half an ell behind you."

That close? He hadn't seen them, and his otherwise reliable instincts almost always warned him when things skulked about his stern.

"How many?" he asked.

"In your numbers or ours?" Phalalin asked, dragging out the suspense.

"What difference does it make?" Delwyn demanded.

"Well, their numbers are five or ten," he shrugged and then grinned again.

A five was an Eyloni ten, so he had five Comara crowded behind him.

Delwyn nodded and shooed Phalalin and the other practical jokers off, wondering if all males had the same joker tendencies as Zalzadrin.

He hoped not! One Zalzadrin was enough.

The males backed away from him toward the waiting females and Delwyn couldn't figure out for the life of him why.

When they had all moved out from behind him, the Comara followed.

The diminutive, long-haired, corn silk blonds gave him vague smiles as they whispered among themselves.

"They can smell her on you!" Phalalin sang as he turned and strode across the straw-colored grasses and through the wall of advancing Warriors and Hunters. Delwyn knew who the "her" was, and he wondered as he sang how long it took for a Comari's scent mark to dissipate.

The bulk of the extended families drew around him, not in a circle like the males, but in a choreographed weaving pattern. Individuals darted past him at random, playfully brushing him with their tails. Yet as a whole they seethed and surged, folding into themselves and then expanding out like a flock of black birds writhing in the air.

They came closer, prancing through the straw-colored buckhorn. The resilient grass sprang back up after bare feet glided over it. More of them surged out of the forest like dancers in a cornfield. The rainforest backdrop they trickled from, so much like Earth's autumn temperate forests drew him back to his childhood family farm and the woods surrounding it. The surrounding oranges and yellows laced with reds could conceal a fox next to him and he'd never see it.

The towering elleiu trees ahead and the others off in the distance gave away the fact he stood on another world; that, the gravity, and the deceptive, cool-looking sun creeping overhead. He'd have to watch the sun exposure. Less long-wave radiation fell here, but ultraviolet light came in with the cool colors just as it did on Earth. His skin would burn before he felt any heat. It would be just like getting a winter sunburn on Earth.

People waited, polite and patient. Most of them did anyway: Zalzadrin bounced on her feet while others danced in place.

Tails swayed as if blown by the wind.

They knew this song now, had committed it to memory as the males sang it.

He spread his arms in acceptance and began.

When he finished singing, they sang back to him. They sang vocals without musical accompaniment. That rarely happened, but he had heard his crew sing to themselves or in groups often enough to understand them better than the male singers. They too imparted the wisdom of the clan:

"The spirits come to us through sound, through music that vibrates the chest and excites the heart. They come through the drum and voice. They cause us to remember what substance we are made from and where we come from.

"The ancient songs say that the skin or body of a drum determines the person or thing called into being. Some drums are journeying drums transporting the drummer and his listeners to various places. Other drums are powerful in their own ways.

"The territorial boundaries of rage and forgiveness tells us rage teaches, calls for healing, belongs to the Spirit Male, and demands correct behavior. Personal rage and honor stand among withered trees. When it cannot find a resting place, it injures instinct. Clan rage and persistent rage summon the rite of forgiveness, which requires setting the matter aside for a time, withholding punishment, forgetting the offense, and abandoning the social debt."

The ritual song sung, people swarmed him in welcome. They had already chosen which elleiu tree he should visit first and led him to Hervorallin. A possessive Princess reclaimed him by jumping from her mother's back to the ground and then climbing up his side to his shoulders. A small crowd led him toward the nearest tree, while the three hundred or so of its residents danced on ahead of him.

Delwyn stared ahead into the grasses and brush. Here the ground lacked the impassible jungle tangles he'd come to expect. In fact, it could pass for a temperate rainforest of the northern Pacific coast. He walked through the heavy brush—no trails marred the ground here—that grew under the outer elleiu tree branches. Lesser trees some sixty to ninety meters tall rose up around him in naturally spaced intervals like those in deciduous forests on Earth. Only the incredible heights and the size and shape of the leaves pushed any semblance of Earth forests from the otherwise hauntingly familiar fall landscape.

Delwyn and his escorts passed under trees having leaves as big as field tents. They bent out and down, resembling orange palm fronds. Their trunks gleamed smooth as bamboo fishing poles. They even had segmented growth like bamboo, too. Each one had a notch on the same side of the trunk, as if someone had cut wedges in them with an axe.

A few non-photosynthesizing green parasitic vines grew on the trees above them. They grew corkscrew roots that bored into the trees. Some of the vines bridged neighboring trees until they ran out of trees and then hung down almost to the ground. Delwyn had to brush them aside like beaded curtains to walk through them. When he touched them, their leaves folded against the vine, just as sensitivity plants did when touched.

The grass changed in texture as they walked from a stiff, supple yellow straw to thin-bladed light orange grass similar to Earth meadow grasses. Mixed among the grasses grew strands of brick red plants towering well overhead. They looked like giant tulip leaves to him.

He looked past the looming elleiu tree into a background of mountains stretching across the horizon from west to east in the distance. The local forest remained relatively flat. The trees were scattered enough to afford a breathtaking panorama of alien flora scenes. In the distance rolling hills and highlands sloped abruptly into the rocks and large limestone deposits jutting out from the forest floor like marble ruins long overgrown.

Limestone dissolved in water over time, he knew, at rates dependent on rainfall acidity creating massive cave systems. Over the ages the ejecta from the cataclysmic impact had regained the open air either from constant erosion from the torrential rains and wind, or from deep root systems breaking up the ground. Delwyn knew how rocks seemed to migrate to the surface. Every year he plowed his fields he found more large rocks. What didn't come up one year eventually worked their way toward the surface where they got jammed in his plow. He had filled a small ravine with rocks he'd carried to it and pitched over the edge. The limestone plateau cliffs on the horizon had stood sentinel duty since time immemorial; massive and pitted, they loomed over the forest.

Delwyn gazed at the ground under the elleiu tree. Dense yellow and orange grasses, tall shrubs, and Earth-sized trees grew everywhere. With the first elleiu tree branches so far above the grasses, more than enough sunlight made it to the ground over six Earth days to allow them to grow here. Around the tree's soccer field wide base had been laid thick sheets of split shale in a checkerboard pattern. It began a meter or so from the outer fused aerial roots. The ground between it and the stones had been filled with course sawdust or chipped bark.

Beyond the crowd waited the ground-level opening, a bole in the fused roots and, like the Hall of Consensus within the Elleiu Na'aheilu, entering the bole allowed access into side passages and the main hall inside the tree.

The inhabitants put the central hall to multiple uses. Here the families held communal meetings, but it served other uses as well. It housed a kitchen and dining area and supported activity too involved for constant up and down climbing. Food and provisions were stored here, and property held in common waited use by anyone having need of it. Balconies and lofts filled spaces in the accumulated root dome overhead.

"You are O'ni'da O'un Tu La'huaset Eyloni now," an old Hunter told him in broken Coalition standard. "You may use anything stored here as fits your need. Come, we will show you your home."

Bracketed by Hervorallin, Zalzadrin, Phalalin, and Phelindra, the elder invited him up the central spiraling twisted roots that surrounded the original trunk of the ancient tree.

Delwyn climbed through the gnarled maze of polished apricot-colored roots until they met one of the ascending branches. The elder invited him into the hollow space.

Princess tensed, sniffed the air, and sang a complicated melody.

"Get ready," Zalzadrin warned.

"For what?"

"Just wait," she said.

Probably another joke, he thought.

They twisted around and climbed through a low passage and dropped a bit before leading out through a bole and onto a wide branch. The bark, rust orange and rough, formed parallel ruts running its length along the branch as it sloped into the sky.

"Looks like tire treads to me," he said.

Phelindra nodded. "These ridges gather water into natural channels. They also help us get a good grip," she added, demonstrating by grasping the bark with her long, four-jointed toes.

Delwyn had gone barefoot since leaving his warship's Health Center. The bark felt rough on his feet but not uncomfortable. Still, his short stubby toes wouldn't be gripping this surface no matter how rough the bark was.

"I wonder how slippery the bark gets when it rains," he complained, eyeing the reddish mosses and fungi growing here and there.

"He is not slippery when wet," Zalzadrin objected. "Molds are slimy, and they are harmful. We remove them from the tree whenever we find them."

They climbed a gentle incline on a branch as wide as a four-lane highway. Around them smaller but still monstrous branches twisted around fused roots to form Males' Safe fortresses or other less dense hollow growths. High above, layers of limbs and branches spread up and out, their awning-sized autumn-like leaves grew in bundles of hundreds of worn brooms that seemed to sweep the sky.

They entered the upper canopy, where the stout highway-wide branch began to narrow as the incline grew much steeper. They stepped through an open bole in its side and on into another hollow fused root growth large enough to swallow a gymnasium. It wasn't the heavy woodpile maze a Males' Safe was. It was open by comparison, filled with lofts and tiers and their niches, much like the layout of the sleep-tree lodgings on A'lon'aloop.

They looked the same, too. But knowing this place lived brought with it an awe no camouflaged construct could match.

"How many of these things are there here?" Delwyn asked.

"Eleven, not counting all the Males' Safes and the Vantage," Zalzadrin said.

"The Vantage?" he asked.

"The same area the Be'atika Senge calls the Open Venue. The place where you met with them for the first time."

"Oh. It is as open to the sky as theirs is?"

"It is, but they use their Open Venue for a secondary meeting place. We use our Vantage for a fortified lookout."

Delwyn was thinking about castle keeps when he heard a soft, amused trill escape from Zalzadrin.

"Here they come," she said, bouncing on the balls of her feet.

He didn't even get a chance to ask before darting infants poured from tiny passages around him. About thirty infants came at him, and Princess squealed at them from her perch around his neck. They crowded around him, all females, more of them Warriors rather than Hunters. He saw no infant Comara. Although older than Princess, they heeded her. How did she know they were here? A guess, or did she smell them hiding here?

Princess sang to them. When she stopped, they seemed to consider both her song and his presence. She jumped to the floor and walked up to them. They sang emotional baby talk to her. A Hunter and a Warrior, older than the other infants, did the—well—talking.

"Establishing family ties and hierarchy rank," Phelindra explained. "They smell Hervorallin on her, even the scent telling them she is Hervorallin's daughter. They are describing their hierarchy ranking to her."

"They have a hierarchy? Infants? What do they need a hierarchy for?"

Phelindra frowned. Had any other male asked that question, he would have sounded insulting. All females belonged to hierarchies. Delwyn's unfamiliarity with their culture came through on his scent as genuine curiosity.

"Infant females rank themselves by ability and experience. They look after one another, and they work together to further their own ends. There are several thousand cubic ells within this tree too small for us to crawl through, but they prowl those areas all the time."

Delwyn wondered who in their right minds would let babies crawl down paths and trails no adult could get more than an arm or head into. He let the momentary concern go. "Princess is the youngest one here, so she's the lowest ranked in their hierarchy?" he asked.

"Yes, for now," Zalzadrin said. "Age alone does not guarantee standing in any hierarchy. Rank changes as they change."

"Who determines that? The adult females?"

"No we do not," Phelindra stammered, shocked. Hierarchies worked together, but they remained autonomous, like males. More so in fact because hierarchies regulated societies, whereas an autonomous male regulated nothing. "They determine their own rank. When they come into season for the first time, they are no longer welcome and so they join other hierarchies."

Princess and the other two were singing up quite a tune.

"What do you think they're talking about?"

"Can you not smell them?" Zalzadrin asked, perplexed. "Their scent is subtle compared to adolescents, so you might not smell them as well as I can. Infants communicate emotion through pheromonal empathy and get caught up in exchanging feelings. They know Princess belongs to Hervorallin and to this family. Princess has convinced them you are family and," she smirked, "that you are her special charge."

"Because she's my near-daughter?"

"No," Phelindra said, "because your scent tells her you are apprehensive and wary about climbing the branches. She has asked them to help her take care of you," Phelindra said.

"Take care of me, huh?" Delwyn chuckled, amused.

Zalzadrin and Phelindra both growled at him, offended. "Do not mock them. The younger the female, the more inclined she is to protect a male. That instinctive drive increases when a clan male, particularly a family male, is concerned. Remember Kidahin? She is the youngest among our society. Her interest in you comes from her juvenile response to anything male."

Indeed, as Phelindra talked the infants had begun drawing closer to him, closing in on him, all except for one. "This one doesn't seem much interested in me," Delwyn said.

"The male infant will wait until the females have finished, then he will come to you. As you are an older male, he will look to you for guidance, as he does with the other males in our family."

"He's a male infant? The only one?" Surprised, Delwyn looked the infant over. He resembled the Warrior female infants in the face, but he had the more muscular body. Eyloni infants looked like scaled-down adults. He would look about the same fully grown as he did now.

"What do you mean 'the only one'?" Hervorallin asked. "One male in one hundred and two is within the statistical average birth rate."

Delwyn counted and indeed found a total of twenty-seven infants. One male in twenty-seven came out a bit low for Eyloni male-female gender ratios, but if they expected one male in twenty births then it came close.

The infants had apparently reached an accommodation. Princess and the older two infants separated. The older two chirped and squeaked notes to the others.

They came forward and surrounded Delwyn alone. He had a sudden urge to sit on the living, uneven, smooth tangerine-colored floor.

The infants crawled onto him, smelling him. They scrubbed their faces against his cheeks and found the stubble on his face both annoying and fascinating. Curious, they patted his face with doll-sized hands. They tried to rub the bristly stuff off, convinced he was dirty. Stymied, they consulted one another in the same 'we are all equal' sharing all females regardless of age did when discussing a problem.

The prickly roughness on the new male's skin confounded them. Worried, their instinctive minds assumed he had been hurt somehow. They squealed interrogative chords at Princess, and she sang back a vocal shrug: she had always known him to feel prickly from time to time.

The infant male watched the females. He sighed. Now was the time to greet the new male, while he was freed from their constant company. The new male would divert their interest away from him for a time. That was good. They ran him ragged with their well-intended care.

Now they had another male to chase after.

Delwyn watched the infant male approach, his ears posturing curiosity. The females trilled comments to him, and he murmured soft melodic answers back to them. His notes sounded deeper than theirs, but even so he still sang at a sharp treble.

He climbed into Delwyn's lap and rubbed his face against Delwyn's rough cheeks. Like the females, he rubbed his hands all over the bristly skin before singing a query to the others.

"He does not know what your facial hair stubs mean," Hervorallin said.

"You can understand him?" Delwyn asked.

Hervorallin nodded. "His scent paints an emotional picture in my mind, and his singing accents the empathy. He is pleased to have a new male to share the infant females with."

"Share them?" he asked, wondering what she meant. Princess was his near-daughter, and he didn't think Hervorallin meant he had gained more near-daughters.

Hervorallin started to explain when a laughing Zalzadrin interrupted.

"They want to share in your care with us. You will find them stalking you, following you to make sure you are safe. You will have to project a strong emotion to stop them from following you into the deep jungle."

The Hunter and Warrior infant leaders chirped to the others, and they vanished into the tiny hidden tunnels in the living cavernous woodpile.

Princess climbed up Delwyn's side, gave him a chin rub as she trilled, and then jumped off after the other infants.

"I guess it's play time," he said, feeling somewhat abandoned.

Hervorallin wrapped her tail around his waist and snuggled him up to her, laughing. "They are not playing, not now. They will spend some time showing her every small gap, crevasse, and passage they can prowl through. All elleiu trees have many such places that have been explored by succeeding generations over the centuries. The older infants know them inside and out, and they teach the newborns. I remember every path, every niche, and every tight squeeze in this tree," she said, her black pupils expanding until only narrow amber slivers remained of her irises. She trailed off and smiled at the distant memory.

"They do not always play," Zalzadrin chided. "They often find molds and pests. They scrub away what they can. If they cannot get rid of it by themselves, they make the problem known to an adult female."

"Do not worry about Princess," Phelindra added. "She will come back when she needs to nurse. Any female will nurse her and then send her on her way. She cannot get lost or trapped inside the tree. They will take her exploring.

"Do not forget. She is your near-daughter. She will stay close by and rarely leave you for long periods because her need to verify your safety will occupy her thoughts. Do not be surprised if she brings the infants to you every so often. They can move through home tree faster than we can. If she smells you alone, upset, or alarmed, she will summon them. When it comes to your welfare, Princess ranks them just as any other near-daughter sensing her male's alarm will rank the group when it comes to defending him."

Curious, he looked at the male infant nestled happily in his lap, tail curled around his wrist. "What if more than one male is in danger? I'd think it might cause conflicts within their hierarchy."

Phelindra shook her head. "They will divide their numbers."

"He doesn't seem in much of a hurry to leave," Delwyn said, nodding to the drowsing infant male.

"Keba is happy. He feels comfortable in your presence," Phelindra said.

Two adolescent females poked their heads out of a bole, looked around the passageway, and glided toward Hervorallin.

Delwyn smiled. Eyloni privacy standards still amused him. Although communal by nature, privacy tended to fall more toward relationships among people and not behind closed doors issues. Closed door privacy was declared when a visitor first poked her head in for a look. If she wasn't given the signal to leave, then she plowed right on in. The signal consisted of both pheromonal and physical signals, an odor and an expression.

The two Hunters were adolescents, meaning they would come into season for the first time soon. Eyloni saw people as infants, preadolescents, adolescents, or adults. These two could pass for tall willowy ten-year-old girls, but he had a tough time telling. Eyloni infants were born with a body style and proportions of adults and maintained them as they grew.

"This is Neenah, and this is Peital," Hervorallin said. "They are my daughters."

The two Hunters flipped their ears at Delwyn on hearing themselves introduced and greeted him before rushing to wrap their tails around their mother.

It never dawned on him that Hervorallin might have other children. What about others in his crew? Did anyone else have children? Females carried a fetus for one hundred Earth days. All fertile females came into season at the same time worldwide once every forty-seven days for a period lasting just over twelve days. That meant mothers could deliver infants over a twelve-day period every hundred days after the last season.

It took 596 days for the Tyreniioroneo-Elleio system to orbit the sun. That meant a female could have a baby what, four times in twenty months?

If three hundred females lived in this tree alone, and if they all gave birth within the same twelve-day period Hervorallin had, then why weren't there three hundred infants the same age as Princess here, let alone all the infants born from previous seasons in the past twenty Earth months? Hadn't Kidahin said something about females always mating, hoping to give birth to the rare male? A total infant population of twenty-seven didn't jibe with what he thought he knew about Eyloni childbirth. There should have been more of them.

"Hervorallin why aren't there more newborns? More infants?"

She looked up from her daughters' arms to answer.

"We mate according to a pattern set by the hierarchies so as not to strain family and clan resources."

"Oh, you practice birth control."

"Birth control?" Phelindra asked, puzzled. "You mean birthing control, as in control of the body when giving birth?"

"No, I mean artificial barriers to conception."

Everyone froze and then became agitated, upset.

"*Who,*" Zalzadrin whispered, "would want to prevent conception?"

"Hervorallin just said you rotate births through your population."

"Ah!" Zalzadrin brightened. They misunderstood. They thought he implied the ridiculous. "No. No. No. We just do not mate out of turn."

The Eyloni did not have sex any more than the birds and the bees had sex. They mated, and Eyloni biology had reduced mating to a purely mechanical act, one of making the proper contact. They received pleasure through empathic links when twining their tails together. For them abstinence didn't carry the same emotional overtones as it did for humans. They experienced pleasure without mating so long as they twined tails and established a mutual empathic link.

The infant male stood, alert. He cocked his ears after his departing fellow infants, trilled a good-bye to Delwyn, and scrambled off after them.

The two adolescents watched him leave with expressions kids got when the cat they wanted to play with so much scrambled behind the nearest couch.

They turned their gazes to Phalalin and sang to him.

He sang a greeting back and then prodded Delwyn in the back. "Keep going Delwyn."

"Where? More than one path leads away from here."

Hervorallin broke her daughters' embraces, stood next to Delwyn, and pointed. "That way, and upward."

They turned and headed toward the tree's center a short way and then climbed another twisting spiral root passageway lit by glowing shelf fungi. After a few minutes climbing they stepped into a squashed-down-looking hollowed out living area bigger than his quarters on *Hunter's Moon*, a hollowed-out wooden oval as large as a studio apartment. At the far end three boles opened off into twisting cavernous spaces.

A spiral rug stretching all the way to the curving walls completely covered the oval floor. A large remnant rug, it had been made from pieces of leftover dyed cloth twisted and braided together from the center out in strips as thick as his thumb. It looked new, and it felt soft.

Several items had been hung on the walls. Swords, spears, and bows adorned one curving side. Another wall had braided art hung all over it. Delwyn's grandmother had braided pine needles into baskets. Similar baskets of varying sizes and designs hung on the walls, woven from the golden yellow buckhorn grasses growing where his aircraft had landed. Box frames hung in random places on the walls. Necklaces made from shells or stones had been placed inside the frames.

A sleeping nest and its cushions filled a cubbyhole off to the side. Netting hung from the low ceiling.

They showed him the smaller side rooms one at a time. The first one contained a heating and cooling unit for food preparation. One room had enough space for ample supplies of drygoods and a sink or sorts: water drained into the living basin and from there it drained back out into the tree like a tap stuck on trickle.

The second room served as a storage unit the size of a spacious walk-in closet.

The third room contained the necessary—the bathroom. They kept the trickling sink, but they had installed a modern flash toilet over and around the natural outhouse bole.

The living area solar-powered lights filled the room with the now warm soft familiar orange-yellow jack o' lantern glow. The room also had video and comm terminals.

The abode had no door, not even curtained doorways, as usual.

"Well? What do you think? Do you like it?" Hervorallin asked, breathless.

Behind her, a substantial crowd had gathered, wanting to know what he thought.

Moved, Delwyn turned to her. "It's nice," was all he could say.

"Do not think you will use it much," Phalalin joked. "Soon you will return to your warship, as will I."

"Where do you stay, Phalalin?" Delwyn asked.

"Not far. Once you get a feel for where you are in the tree, you will notice all males have living spaces close to a Males' Safe."

"Why? There's no clan or tribal warfare anymore," Delwyn objected.

"That does not matter," Hervorallin said, and she refused to elaborate any further.

They led Delwyn from his abode and took him through all the trails, passageways, and living areas in the tree.

They told him he could visit anyone at any time. He only had to do what they did: poke his head into an abode, pause a half-second for a sign to leave, and walk on in. They did warn him to call from outside the bole to any abode housing a male bonded to a Comari. They finally climbed back down through the mazes of fused aerial roots surrounding the central trunk and stepped out into the Hall of Voices, where tables and chairs had been set out. During mealtimes his new family habitually ate together under the root entwined ceiling.

Phelindra and Phalalin escorted him to a table reserved for the clan elders. "You have been invited to sit with the elders. They have many questions for you, and I will stand with you and help translate as needed," Phalalin said.

Amindaldra, his Protectress, had been quiet throughout the tour. She had enough and snapped him hard with her tail. He turned in surprise, saw how she set her ears, and he looked into her eyes. His expression softened as he took in her stance.

She stood there, arms folded beneath her breasts, staring at him. A tired, pained expression covering her face. She pointed her tail behind him.

Phalalin followed the subtle gesture to an impatient group waiting there. They stood together, arms likewise folded beneath their breasts, looking grim-faced and forlorn without his company.

Phalalin trilled a musical sigh, and his heart melted at the sight. They belonged to both his occupational and his personal associations, called this tree home, and had held back while he helped make Delwyn feel welcome.

They had chosen to spend their time with him, and right now they felt left out of the homecoming gather.

Delwyn belonged to them, too.

"Phelindra? Zalzadrin? Perhaps you can continue with the introductions."

Zalzadrin's irrepressible humor surfaced as she followed his gaze.

"Yes, you should leave. They are not being patient for you. They want to associate with Delwyn."

Phelindra laughed despite herself. She spun in response to the flicker in her peripheral vision and saw Zalzadrin signing battle language to the group. She caught the tail's end comment and laughed again as they broke toward them, passing Phalalin as if he did not exist, and circled Delwyn.

When the females belonging to *Fearless's* society surrounded him, he turned wary. They stood, their backs to him, and glared at Phalalin. Delwyn knew females were overprotective of any male. From his past everyday experiences, they didn't seem protective now. They were making a scene, judging by the interest everyone else was showering on them.

Delwyn's reading of Eyloni body language had improved. They posed in what he termed their 'mock-serious tone' stance. They directed their posturing at Phalalin, but Phelindra's ease and Zalzadrin's bouncy good humor told him they weren't angry with him.

"You're responsible for this, aren't you?" he demanded.

"Who? Me?" Zalzadrin asked. "I merely suggested that if Phalalin was too busy to notice them, then you certainly had the time considering you only have a small personal association."

"*What?*" Delwyn was reminded yet again that this was not a lion's-pride culture. *Females* chose male friends to associate with. Nothing said a female or a group of them couldn't associate on a personal level with more than one male, but they tended to develop a preference for a specific few and in most cases just two: the male focus for their specific occupation, a warleader or sire cairn, and a male friend away from work, a personal friendship. Because of low male numbers, multiple females having the same temperament found themselves gravitating to like-tempered males. The male never chose, not directly. His association evaluated and invited females they felt both suited their male friend and themselves.

By custom, a female in an occupational association with a warleader never associated with another warleader on that level, and Delwyn understood what message they had been sending to Phalalin. He'd been, from their perspective, alone in a social sense for far too long, and their interest in all things male drove home how much they lacked close male company, and they felt Phalalin had deprived them of his company on purpose. Or so his premier joker Zalzadrin must have hinted with her insinuating wit.

Phalalin cast a bland eye on them, fluttered his tail, and gave himself an exaggerated shake and said, "Delwyn is our clan male. I think I will take a walk over to Lonadrin's tree," and then made as if to exit through the central bole. "Alone," He added.

The group surrounding Delwyn sang a defiant retort and hustled him to the clan elders' table.

Phalalin gave his best theatrical hurt-feelings expression to the dining crowd, and then it dawned on Delwyn that Phalalin had turned the event into a comedy routine as people sang in soft trilling laughter.

Everyone except for the six surrounding him. Delwyn didn't know what to do, but the feelings reeking around him suggested they had reached the end of their patience. He put his hands just above the tails on his left and right and then leaned into the Warrior staring at him.

They in turn pressed into his embrace. The three behind him dodged Phalalin to envelop Delwyn. They smelled his face and neck as they brushed their pons against him. One Hunter even tried to curl her tail around his nonexistent one.

That drew a low growl from Phalalin.

They broke away from Delwyn and turned to the now nearby Phalalin and rushed him.

Soft clapping and sibilant whispers filled the Hall, but expectant eyes followed Delwyn. Something significant had happened, but what? Delwyn was too tired to think about it. The heat, the effort, and the heartbeat-based EST and TST clocks kept him somewhat sleep-deprived. His body hated the slow planetary day and night cycle.

Zalzadrin, bouncing on her toes again, decided to sit down in a chair on his right. The long-puckered scar running down her left side drew the elders' eyes. They asked her about it, and she transformed from practical joker to serious Huntress in an instant.

Appreciative murmurs traveled around the tables as food was served. Zalzadrin ignored her plate to point out the staple marks running down the black puckered scar.

Thankful for the distraction, Delwyn turned and whispered into Phelindra's sensitive, curved ear. "I can't wait until I can get some rest."

She nodded. "My abode is above yours. I am happy to sleep with you tonight."

"That's not necessary, I'm sure you don't need to guard me in our home."

"If I do not sleep with you, then you will find yourself covered with infants," she said, smiling.

"What do you mean by that?"

"You are a male, and you are new to them. They will check in on you to make sure you are safe. If I am with you, then they will smell my presence, look in on you, and leave. The first few will pass on the news, and others will check in on you from time to time. If I am not with you, then most of them will crawl into the nest with you. A few others will remain awake to keep watch."

"You're kidding. They're babies. They'll sleep with their mothers."

Phelindra flipped her tail aside, a 'no' signal. "They are by instinct driven to care about a male's safety. If they think a male is in danger, then they will rouse the whole tree. If they keep watch over you, then they will nurse from the closest female rather than seek out their mothers. That in itself will tell the nursing females that something is awry.

"Even during the day they will stalk and shadow you. Sometimes they will let you catch them so they can enjoy your touch. Others will stalk, and you will never know they are about. We have a hard time catching them ourselves. Your weak nose will not find them unless they want you to."

Delwyn and Phelindra noticed how quiet it had become. Everybody had sat waiting patiently while they talked.

Phelindra mumbled an apology and Delwyn sang the same measure after her.

Eyloni didn't talk when they ate. Body language, signs, and scent mattered at the table. Eyloni considered smacking lips or spitting food disgusting, beyond bad manners. Their vocal apparatus followed a multi-pipe structure in which throat muscles constricted and relaxed to play notes: organic flutes. Speaking and singing came from a deep-throated whistle rather than from vibrating vocal cords. It was at least possible for Delwyn to talk with his mouth full, but an Eyloni trying to do so either blew the contents in her mouth across the table or choked because her speech came from notes made by both exhaling and inhaling.

They ate in the whisper-quiet of a monastery, like monks observing vows of silence. Eye contact, posture, and scent commanded at family communal meals.

Formal dining etiquette demanded people wait until the last person had eaten her fill before talking may begin at their table. Table talk never included a person from another table unless the entire Hall had finished eating.

Delwyn's human stomach and its unfamiliarity with many dishes made him the last eater not only at table, but also in the Hall as well. For some reason that seemed to please everyone.

A Hunter offered him a wet wash cloth and a soft dry towel. When another person finished eating, the Hunter offered her another pair as well. Each person wiped her face and then her hands, then her chest and breasts. It was socially unacceptable, a violation of group etiquette, to leave so much as a crumb on the body. Eyloni groomed often, fussy about their personal appearance.

He copied them. The wet cloth steamed in the warm air, hot to the touch. The water had a soapy feel to it. Eyloni didn't use tallow-based soaps, so it had to come from the local plant life, probably a saponin-containing root, something they could gather without harming the plant itself.

He finished and gave the washcloth and towel back to the Hunter and smiled his thanks. She in turn rewarded him with a tail brush across his neck. The table turned to a discussion on family business. They asked him many questions, questions he'd answered before. But soon the questions became more personal, more intimate.

They explained how a family member contributed to the immediate family, this tree and the extended families in the nearby elleiu trees, and then to the local and far-reaching families in all the elleiu trees within the O'un Tu Clan territory.

"We all contribute," a female elder said. "Some make tools and other items for us, our families, and our clan. Excesses are made for trade with other clans. Others perform tasks, build things, or develop science, technology, or industry. Still others teach, and they teach the young and the old alike."

That caught Delwyn's notice.

"I figured you taught the young here. We call it home-schooling where I come from."

She nodded, pleased again to see Delwyn was not as strange as they had feared he might be. "Some of us sing lessons to infants when they are old enough for their hormones to trigger accelerated growth. Only then have their brains developed enough to learn and assimilate knowledge beyond the instinctive programming the spirits gave them at birth. They learn the first songs, the oral histories about the local families and those concerning the O'un Tu Clan, the La'huaset Tribe, and the Compact of the Ten Tribes of Elleio.

"They learn to sing together, to find their place in the melody, and to share their emotions through pheromone signaling augmented with musical expression. They learn numbers and math, to hunt, to fight, and to craft survival items. They learn the jungle, what to eat, what not to eat, and where to find it. They learn medicinal fruits and plants, how to use them, how to find them, and how to prepare them. They learn the rainforest, its weather, its trails, and its hidden dangers. They learn about the animal life in the forest, how to avoid them, how to kill them if necessary. They also learn how to defend their home tree.

"Those showing an interest in the trades or the sciences are fostered to learning centers with other families in our clan or with other clans within the La'huaset Tribe, or sometimes even with clans living in other tribes."

"When do they start formal learning? The infants I mean," Delwyn asked.

"They learn their first songs at two years of age."

Delwyn thought about the number. Two years added up to about six hundred Earth days for females but just 553 days for males. Since she spoke, she meant the female standard. Six hundred days from birth, or fifty EST months. Eyloni aged a bit over twice as fast as a human. Even so, two years meant infants went to the equivalent of first grade at about the same time as four-year-old human toddlers entered nursery school, relatively speaking.

"I expect I'll have to get some training myself."

Another female elder nodded in agreement. "We can arrange this for you. You must travel through the forest, and the forest hides fearsome animals. Tell me, what fearsome creatures did you face during your survival ordeal?"

"None. Earth's rainforests are few and their animals are protected because many of them are near extinction. Only the First Nations are permitted to disturb forest animals, but even they limit contact with them."

"Who are these First Nation people, and why do they avoid the forest animals?" she asked.

"The First Nations are people who retain some semblance of their tribal lives and territory. They avoid making contact with the animals because they revere their spirits and want to preserve them for the future."

She nodded. "And you? Do you belong to these First Nations?"

"Not directly, no. I am Matsigenka, and their blood flows through my veins. I inherited my tan skin, dark brown eyes, and black hair from them, but I am far removed from their cultural and tribal ways."

"Is it because you do not keep the Matsigenka ways that you did not participate in their adulthood ritual?"

Delwyn shook his head. "By law every person on Earth reaching seventeen years of age is recognized as an adult. I chose to enlist in the Navy right from high school and went off into unknown space to explore and project a Coalition military presence."

The elders discussed his answer for some time before Phelindra whispered in his ear. "Remember what we said about the knife strapped to your hip?"

Delwyn nodded.

"They are trying to resolve a problem. A volcanic glass knife signifies adulthood status for a male in the same way a flint knife does for a female."

"I know that," Delwyn snapped, annoyed. Phelindra had a habit of belaboring the obvious.

"You do not wear the traditional adulthood knife, and yet your fame requires adults to consider you an adult, even preadolescents and adolescents must do so, too. To wear an adulthood knife without going through the adulthood ceremony is a crime against the clan punishable by death. The elders cannot just give you an adulthood knife because they did not witness you surviving a jungle ordeal, nor have they heard you sing your adulthood song describing what the spirits revealed to you during the ordeal.

"They know you are an adult by the customs of your people. You are well beyond the age when adolescent males take their survival quests. That you sang the Death Song and battled the Ni'zakhonii shows how much you are an adult. You can fight, and you can survive."

"So what's the problem?" Delwyn asked.

"They know you are an adult because they saw the Death Song record and the Warleader's Choice ritual. Intellectually they know you are an adult male. The problem, for them, is tradition. That, and being seen in public wearing a modern blade is … unseemly … like adults in adolescent company on equal footing."

"So what's the remedy?"

Phelindra listened to the elders talking and shook her head. "They want you to ask these Matsigenka people your blood runs through to declare you an adult according to their customs and give you an obsidian knife to declare your status. Then you need only sing to the elders about how the ceremony opened your mind to the spirits. Others are saying that since you killed so many Ni'zakhonii with your knives no one in your Matsigenka culture could mistake you for a child, and so you should sing about the battle you fought when you freed us from the Ni'zakhonii security holding area."

"The second choice sounds a lot easier because you witnessed it. Besides, I told you I was Matsigenka only by blood and not by tribal membership."

Phelindra froze, ears pricking, swiveling to her temples, and then she laid them flat against her head. That was never a good sign, and Delwyn caught his breath when she hissed. Clan and tribal identity mattered to Eyloni. Had he offended her sense of unity?

"A few are wondering whether or not you should just take the survival ordeal here since you are O'ni'da O'un Tu La'huaset Eyloni now."

"We don't have the time, what with all the task force planning and repair matters to attend to," he objected.

"A male's survival ordeal lasts for one TST month, not the three EST months a female has to endure."

Delwyn turned thoughtful. One male month lasted almost eleven Earth days. Three female months lasted almost thirty-six days. Male rarity saved them from the longer survival ordeal. "I can do eleven days. I've done longer wilderness training stints before."

Phelindra's tail wrapped around his mouth lightning quick. "You do not know what you are saying. Infants Princess's young age climb their home trees often. In a few more months they will prowl through the forest to visit infants in nearby trees. By the time they have learned their first songs they will have taken long jungle forays with adult females in attendance.

"We are born knowing how to prowl, how to stalk, and how to climb the forest. We are taught in those earliest songs about hostile jungle life. That life is celebrated in common songs worldwide. You are ill-prepared for survival alone in Elleio's jungles, even in our milder northern forests."

Telling Delwyn 'no' riled up his stubborn streak. However well-intended Phelindra meant her words, he took them to mean she considered him too weak and frail to survive what Kidahin had done three times as long.

"It can't be that bad," he objected.

"Oh? Imagine a ke'nah as tall as you!" she snarled.

"I thought they got no bigger than a fist."

"Ke'nah yes, but other creatures are similar but larger. Then there are the forest mammals, which are playful, annoying, or territorial. You do not have the time to learn the necessary survival skills in so short a time."

An elder overheard and asked Phelindra, "Delwyn does not object to taking a survival ordeal within our territory? This is the best of all possible answers."

"It is not!" Phelindra shouted. "He has no experience living in our jungles."

"I read Kidahin's reports. She says Delwyn stalked the forests on the Nikkiolo moon as if he had been born to it. I read your reports as well, and in them you said yourself Delwyn saved you from a massed leech attack."

Phelindra swore. "Kidahin is young and is infatuated with Delwyn. In my case, his blood made the leeches foam on contact with it. So much for Delwyn's jungle expertise."

"Ah, but you also reported how he stalked Melkorka in the forest and yanked her pons using Kidahin to distract her."

Phelindra swore again. "That is nothing. He had Kidahin's help. Survival ordeals are solitary events. Besides, Delwyn wore clothes, knives, and sensors."

"Melkorka wrote in her reports that he never carried the coward's weapon or used a scanner while working the forest with Kidahin or herself."

Phelindra trembled, wishing with all her might that she could go back in time and delete the archive records.

The elder watched both Phelindra and Delwyn. The body never lied. Delwyn felt he was up to the task, and Phelindra wanted to protect him.

The elder stood, excused herself, and wandered off to visit other tables. Seconds later the remaining elders also stood and drifted off to other tables as well.

Delwyn, Phelindra, and Zalzadrin had been abandoned.

Phalalin got up from his table. He and the six females with him asked Delwyn if they could join him.

"Of course, Phalalin, I wondered if I had offended the elders."

Zalzadrin shook her head, unusually phlegmatic. "They mingle with the others, wanting to hear what they think. They will pass along everything said here," she said in a flat voice.

"And just what did you talk about?" Phalalin asked.

"Oh, we talked about educating the young," Delwyn said.

"And then Apellia asked you about the creatures living in Earth's forests and how you faced them during your survival ordeal," Zalzadrin snarled.

Phalalin nodded. Of course, the adulthood knife issue. He had wondered when someone would poke their tail into that. "What did they have to say about it?"

"They are considering the idea of Delwyn asking his Matsigenka people on Earth to declare him an adult according to their traditions and present him with one of our volcanic glass adulthood knives."

Phalalin sighed, a trilling murmur deep in his throat. "That sounds best."

With mealtime over, people freely mingled. Delwyn and Phelindra visited each table. Sometimes Zalzadrin or Phalalin tagged along, but every so often they broke off to make their own rounds.

Delwyn visited with his new family. They drank water and fruit or vegetable juice. Some tasted sickeningly sweet. Others tasted tart and astringent. Some of those puckered his mouth and constricted his throat as if he'd drank cranberry juice spiked with alum.

He found no alcoholic beverages, not one. Eyloni abhorred meat, abstained from refined sugars, and couldn't tolerate alcohol. It didn't affect them like it did humans, didn't get them drunk. It killed them. Even tiny amounts made them deathly sick.

They didn't smoke tobacco, not even ritually. Even now the human race hadn't fully given up smoking. The habit persisted, and not just in tribal cultures either. Smoking wasn't lawful in public, but a sizeable number of people indulged in private. Medical advances over the past two centuries had made it not the health hazard it had once been.

People came up and asked if they could take the tables and chairs away.

"What's happening now?" he asked.

"They are clearing the Hall for tonight's singing. Come, I want to show you something first," Phelindra said, tugging at his waist with her tail.

She led him up through the outer spiral pathways until they came out on a main branch. Wider than a highway, it stretched out above the jungle floor and up through a gradual incline at first. The low sun cast parallel finger-long shadows on the rough bark. Delwyn looked around to see that the sun had begun to fall behind the distant treeline and would set in another hour or so.

The light blue gas giant hung overhead, a half moon five Earth full moons wide, a magical pale blue wraith that fought to overcome the sinking sun's burnt orange rays.

"This is your home now," Phelindra said. "You may sing with us tonight. Except for ritual events, males do not sing together. Those who feel like singing tonight gather in the Hall."

"I'll sing later. I need a break."

"Then watch the sun set. Smell the forest. Rest. Sleep now if you wish. I will watch over you." Phelindra murmured. She leaned back against the massive trunk and waved him down between her thighs.

Delwyn sat down between her knees, but she defeated him by twining her tail around his waist and drawing him into her chest. She put her arms around him and rested her chin on his shoulder.

Together they sat a quarter-kilometer above the forest and watched the sunset.

Lulled by the cooler evening breezes, Phelindra's warmer than human body heat, her soft velourlike skin, and her musky familiar-pillow smell, Delwyn fell asleep.

Phelindra remained watchful. Her duty to Delwyn did not keep her awake, although she took deep pleasure in having him all to herself. His lower body temperature made him feel like her personal enveloping cool breeze. She watched as the sun took its interminable time falling below the horizon.

The night approached. Elleio orbital phase-3 was ending, and phase-4 began at this latitude with the sunset. The sky would remain dark for the next twenty-three days, ten hours, forty-four minutes, and assorted seconds.

Delwyn had been born on a planet, not on a habitable moon like Elleio. There he experienced a constant 1.01 days in daylight followed by 1.01 days in darkness give or take a few hours depending on the seasonal changes caused by axial tilt. Elleio had a nearly vertical axial tilt, within one degree, and so seasons depended on where along the orbit around the sun she was at any given time.

Phelindra leafchased idle thoughts, lulled by Delwyn's sleep growls, when instinct alerted her. Curious, inquisitive little busybodies surrounded her. She cracked an eye open to find infants sitting in a half-circle around her.

Princess had already crawled into Delwyn's lap and fallen asleep.

The other female infants watched, content with one another and with Delwyn.

Phelindra lifted her chin from his shoulder and acknowledged them with a look and a flip of her ears, leaned back against the tree and looked up.

Above her, the solitary Keba clung upside-down from the bark, looking down at her. He was a quiet one, a sneaky one, this male was. Rather like a Hunter, she thought.

An odor of smug contentment wafted from him, and the infantile empathic image she received from him told her his smugness rode upon multiple levels. He had gotten this close to her without her noticing him. He had looked in on the new male. And for the moment he had evaded the notice of his constant female escort.

Phelindra sang soft reassurance to them.

The infants responded to the high ranked Hunter's song with counterpoints of their own, but they sang in muttered sibilant tones, and they directed their song to the sleeping male and to the infant male clinging above them.

Keba considered their song for a moment and then pricked his ears at Delwyn, flattened them, and then quickly reset them to their wide listening pose, declining their desire to sing with them. The feelings he smelled from the new male told him he was overwhelmed and needed rest.

Again, infantile instinct ruled. On a primal level, Keba knew the difference between male and female, knew he was in fact a male, and knew Delwyn was also a male. Males cultivated male friendships, and although the infant didn't know it, his instincts were preparing him for the eventual day when he and Delwyn would join in Warpact and need each other's help.

The infants complained, singing dire whispers at him.

Keba gave them an annoyed glare, shifted his yellow-amber eyes to the high ranked Hunter, made eye contact with her, and sang his own complaint.

Phelindra smiled. Keba wanted her to use her hierarchy rank to tell the others to leave off. She sang to them, promising that Delwyn would wake soon. Maybe if they wanted, he would sing with them then.

Princess cracked an eyelid open and sighed. She loved showing off her male to the little shes, but sometimes they went too far. The high ranked Hunter kept them on their best behavior. Princess had barely settled herself when the noisy-smelling female arrived.

"Where have you been?" Zalzadrin demanded. "They are about to start!"

"*We,* "Phelindra gestured to the infants, "have been here all along. Lower your voice."

Keba glared at the noisy-scented interloper and growled. His annoyed displeasure caught the instant notice of the other infants, and they turned to give Zalzadrin a pheromonal slap. Her rank did not matter much next to Phelindra's, and they were guarding a male—two males in fact.

"Zalzadrin, if you stir them up, I will throw you off this branch," Phelindra grumbled.

"I am sorry Phelindra, but it is time."

"I know."

Zalzadrin gazed out over the branch and down onto the lesser tree canopy below. Long viscous shadows oozed across the forest with infinite slowness.

"It is nice here," Zalzadrin murmured, giving Phelindra long wistful looks.

"You are welcome to join us if you wish."

Zalzadrin stared at her, at Delwyn, at the infants guarding him, at the orange afterglow of sunset, at the bole she had just came from, and back at Delwyn again. She flipped her tail and took a step toward Phelindra.

Soft infant squabbles argued with her as they moved aside enough to let her sit next to Phelindra.

Zalzadrin looped her tail around the sleeping Delwyn and twined it around Phelindra's tail, sharing intimate contact with her and their oblivious favorite male.

They spent another hour making small talk before Phalalin poked his head through the bole, looked at them, and shook his head.

"You cannot keep Delwyn to yourself tonight. Everyone wants to put on a good show for him, and I am sure they want to hear him sing."

Zalzadrin made a soft rude noise, echoed not so softly by the infants.

Keba knew Phalalin but decided to side with his infant female peers this time and sang a negative.

Phelindra sighed. Phalalin spoke the truth of the matter. Their immediate families wanted to make a lasting impression, and communal singing among an empathic people conjured up emotions shared by all. The music would carry across the jungle to the nearby elleiu trees and the extended families. They would hear the singing and eagerly mark the time until two days had passed, and then Delwyn would visit another tree and sing with them, too. *I had better teach him how to cross the forest at night,* she thought. "Delwyn? Wake up."

"Hmmm?"

"Wake up. Wake up. Wake up. Wake up. Wake up," Zalzadrin sang, her lips brushing his rigid, immobile ear.

Zalzadrin? was Delwyn's initial thought. He'd been dreaming about warm, soft, homey-smelling blankets floating on a sea of orange and red skies. Now a breast-bouncing Zalzadrin had come to unwind the blankets from him. Her idea of another gag, no doubt.

He opened his eyes and looked down.

Not a blanket, he realized: *tails.*

"What happened? I don't remember Zalzadrin …"

"You fell asleep," Phelindra interrupted.

"We are waiting in the Hall for singing," Phalalin added.

Delwyn loathed leaving. While he blinked sleep from his eyes, he got a face full of Princess. The baby chatter coming through her empathic link seemed all about telling him about others. He blinked again and stared at the group of infants surrounding them, twisted up against one another and Phelindra's legs.

Oddly enough, he felt better. A nap did wonders at times, and he felt as if this one had lasted an hour or so.

He glanced at the waning sunset. It had fallen below the horizon. Sharp, crisp orange and red light sparkled above the distant trees, another reminder of an alien world. Earth's sunsets tended to be, well, fuzzy with glare, a bit out of focus, a smear across the horizon.

Light flashed across the skies. He cocked his head and listened, expecting thunder.

He heard none: *heat lightning?*

Another rippling wave shimmered across the northern sky.

Auroras.

Delwyn remembered the mountains on Ibeetu. It had auroras visible during sunset, too. Since everyone on his ship came from the northern La'huaset clans, they saw the similarity between them and the ones beginning to race and flutter across the skies here, which had made the mountain background most fitting for a wake.

Elleio's atmosphere, like Ibeetu's, responded to charged particles diverted by their gas giant partner's magnetic fields into their own weaker fields. Both planets had fields extending far enough out to afford their living moons with just enough added shielding to save their atmospheres from being blown off by solar winds and to stop ionizing radiation from sterilizing the surface.

The magnificent light show put auroras on Earth to shame.

"I thought I saw cloud lightning at first," Delwyn confessed.

"If lightning had been flashing like that, then you would not be here," Zalzadrin said in her not-joking tone of voice.

"No, he would not, and neither would we," Phelindra added. "Lightning strikes elleiu trees often. We install strike abatement devices on them to channel the energy into static storage units, where static generators convert them into usable electricity. Lightning is not the only danger. Storms can churn up fierce winds, not enough to harm the tree, but air blowing over branches acts like an airfoil, and the resulting pressure differentials can yank a person off the bark."

Wide awake now, Delwyn thought he'd like to stay out and watch the auroras take over the night. Their greens, magentas, and pale yellows dominated what remained of the setting sun.

Riding high above, in his 11:38 AM vantage point, as big as a throwing disk held at arms-length, half of Tyreniioroneo gleamed in electric blue glory. Tyreniioroneo had an atmosphere, a mix of hydrogen, methane, and helium. Twenty-three percent larger than Neptune and hotter, the atmosphere generated its own lightning, auroras, and scattered lights that gave the dark half away in the night sky.

"Come Delwyn. They are waiting for us, and it is bad manners to keep them waiting."

Delwyn, sensitive to Phalalin's vocal pitch, knew right then these family meetings had more or less mandatory attendance duty for those in the tree or close enough to conveniently attend.

They headed inside and down through the great tree. Along the way Delwyn noticed the infants scattering off and melting into the shadows.

All except Princess, who sang a farewell to them.

"Going back to their mothers, I suppose?"

"Yes. They know faster ways to get down we could never get through," Zalzadrin said.

Delwyn stepped out of the central spiral and into a crowd gathered into small groups.

"They don't stand in those patterns you always stand in?" Delwyn asked.

"Family gathers are not rigorous ritual affairs. Here you will see friends, intimates, and associations together, with individuals taking turns visiting from one group to another. When the singing starts, people will tend to stay with a group and enjoy the shared feelings called up by the singing.

"When the music stops people will mill about until the next male is ready. When he signals, they will again gravitate to some group and sing with that group."

"Males?" Delwyn asked.

Phalalin turned. "A few male singers will lead everyone in song. After they have finished, the separate groups, the friends, intimates, and associations will sing."

It sounded to Delwyn like a night at an improvisation venue or karaoke night at a bar. Each male performed a lead singing role, but the female voices served as the band.

Two hours Delwyn time later the groups began to break up and trickle up the tree. Some of them went up through the outer spiral passageways, while most others headed up the central spiral.

Hervorallin with Princess clamped to her back and Phelindra guided Delwyn back up the tree to his abode. Zalzadrin came in a few minutes later and helped them take off his custom-made underthong and loincloth. Hervorallin bid them a good night and wended her way from the room.

"Are you staying?" Zalzadrin asked Phelindra.

She nodded. "I told him I would, else the little ones will come and sleep with, on, and around him."

Zalzadrin smiled at the image conjured in her mind. "They will without doubt keep him away from trouble."

"They would at that," Phelindra agreed. "Do you want to stay?"

Zalzadrin considered a moment before shaking her head. "No. Not tonight. Well, wait …" she paused to reconsider. "Maybe we should come up with a schedule?"

"A schedule?" Phelindra frowned. "What schedule?"

"Well, with the coming night, maybe we ought to take him out into the jungle between elleiu trees and let him get used to the nighttime jungle. He still has lessons to learn, and we should start him with the first songs."

Phelindra thought about it. Delwyn needed to learn how to prowl the forest, and maybe now was the time to teach him. Let him stalk them in the dark, and she told Zalzadrin so.

Delwyn woke hours later to find himself naked and in desperate need for the bathroom.

"Who took off my clothes?" he demanded on his way to the necessary.

"Zalzadrin and I did, why?" Phelindra asked.

"I don't think it takes the two of you to take that thing off me."

"Zalzadrin untied it, and I pulled it off. Sleeping with waistwear and neckwear is uncomfortable, and the ties can hamper blood flow if you get them bound up.

"You did notice I always remove my neckwear and waistwear before I go to sleep," Phelindra huffed.

"I'm always asleep before you are, and you are almost always awake before I am," Delwyn yelled from the modern toilet.

"That is so true!" she yelled back

Delwyn sat in privacy in his personal high-tech port-a-potty and looked around. A roll of soft paper sat in a spool on his left, and a control pad had been mounted near his right hand. He pressed a glowing red button, and it turned to a flashing green as a subdued hum began to moan beneath him.

Red to flashing green meant the unit had switched from safe to warning. For his adopted people red meant warmth, safety, and living; but green meant warning, danger, and death.

He stepped off the toilet and over to the dripping water bole, washed his hands with soaproot, washed the sleep from his eyes, and stared at the stubble-covered image in the mirror.

"Phelindra? Did we bring any hair remover from the ship?"

"How should I know? I am your Protectress, not your mother."

He grinned at the playful rejoinder, the falsetto notes in her tone telling him she had indeed packed everything.

"I need to use it. I look terrible."

"You look filthy, and the infants worry you are ill," she yelled back.

Delwyn cleaned up, put on a clean underthong and loincloth, and together they climbed down to the Hall for breakfast.

His personal effects had been brought into the Hall and stacked neatly against the outer root shroud of the central spiral. Nobody so much as brushed against them once left there, but curiosity garnered several volunteers to help carry them into his abode. There Phelindra, Zalzadrin, and Hervorallin unpacked and moved everything around—repeatedly—until satisfied.

To their liking and not his.

Every offer he made they pointedly ignored.

Seeing his meddling as useless and getting him nowhere, he left them to their work and headed back down to the Hall.

People out on their morning chores stopped and chatted with him in a mix of pidgin Coalition standard and informal Eyloni pitch.

It didn't take long before the resident infants found him all but alone and visited in their own way.

Princess came with them, and he got the impression from her that Hervorallin had given her an emotional hint that he felt lonely.

People took one look at him surrounded by infants and laughed in pleased relief, knowing if they watched Delwyn, then he could never step into any unknown dangers. They would not let him. They would die before letting him come to any harm.

Zalzadrin came in to tell him his abode had been made over to their liking, and he could come and see for himself.

Delwyn had to admit they did a respectable job with the moving and decorating. They found artistic, aesthetic placements and arrangements both functional and pleasing to the eye.

Without a sound they left him alone to enjoy his living area.

Alone! Delwyn didn't know what to do with himself. They didn't often leave him alone for long as it was.

Their absence felt wrong somehow. The feeling grew into an invisible looming presence. Inexplicably lonely, he stumbled to the personal comm station bole and put in a call to Melkorka.

14
SEEKING FEMALE COUNSEL

It took Delwyn three tries throughout the day to reach Melkorka by comm.

"Delwyn? Is something wrong?" she squealed, concerned.

"Other than missing you and the others? No, I had to fight for the few times I've had to myself. How are you?"

"I am well. I miss you too," she sang. "What are you doing?"

"Phelindra and Zalzadrin are teaching me about the large jungle animals. They won't let me walk a sweep through the jungle until I memorize them. I didn't know those infant females who followed Captain Lahiri's kid had wandered through the forest from the Be'atika Senge elleiu tree to the A'tayotan elleiu tree in the night."

Melkorka nodded. "Captain Lahiri had her infant male translated back aboard her warship. The infants could not find him anywhere in the Elleiu Na'aheilu and assumed he had wandered into the jungle alone. Captain Lahiri had gone to visit the A'tayotan at the time, and her scent drifted back to the infants. They assumed he went with her, and so they prowled the jungle and evaded the much more dangerous Na'di Island night hunters. What animals have you learned about so far?"

"Well," Delwyn paused, "they showed me the tame stuff first, the mammals. There aren't as many as I had expected. We talked about the four-legged grazers. They look like deer as big as draft horses. I think Kidahin mentioned them back on Ibeetu. They have yellow and red dappling on their otherwise tan hides. Their horns look like unicorn horns, one above the other, the bottom one is shorter than the top one. I don't know why they're arranged that way."

"Because," Melkorka said "they attack a predator head-on. They use the ell-long horn to spear it. If the thrust penetrates its armor, then the long horn goes on to impale the predator so that the second horn pierces its heart. What else did they teach you?"

"Well, we talked about the ke'nah …"

"Forget them," Melkorka snapped. "They do not bother anyone. They soften the soil and scavenge as they burrow. They will not touch you unless you are dead."

"We talked about the cute primates. They look like lemurs, a cross between Eyloni and a sifaka."

Melkorka nodded, her expression softening. "They are the little brothers and little sisters. We share an ancient common ancestor. They live in the lesser trees and have their own clans. They are cautious and may stalk you to see what you are up to. They have been known to help people in need find water, food, and shelter. They have on occasion even lead people to occupied elleiu trees.

"They make primitive tools, hammer rocks and sharp stone chips. Like us, they are obligate herbivores, but unlike us they have an even male-female gender split. Our scientists believed they did not evolve along with us because they did not have to think of ways to protect their males."

"So they'll help you in the forest?" he asked.

"Up to a point. But like us, they are territorial when it comes to their trees. They might throw their hammer stones at you, and from a height they can kill you with a lucky throw. What else did they teach you?" Melkorka demanded, wondering to herself if Zalzadrin and Phelindra had forgotten the dangerous animals.

"Well, they took turns showing me pictures of the most hideous creatures I've ever seen, things from a child's nightmares after looking through microscope slides."

Melkorka sighed in relief and nodded for him to continue.

"They're as big as rodeo bulls. The *zer'con* looks like a mushroom cap with crab legs. I thought the *alle'a* was a pig crossed with a cockroach."

Melkorka grimaced in frustration. She could not smell Delwyn, hence his reliance on Earth animal comparisons evaded her. She could not glean what he knew about the animals. "The zer'con emits an odorless gas that depletes oxygen within a few ells. Prey animals become paralyzed, then they pass out and die. It then buries the victim and eats it as it decomposes. The alle'a is an ambush predator, but they hunt only the four-footed herd mammals. Did they tell you anything about the *scut'ia?"*

"Yep. It looks like a horseshoe crab, is as big as a wolf, and eats fungi," Delwyn replied.

"Scut'ia will lead you to water and edible fungi. They have high animal intelligence. They release a slime that smells like *vfft'tang* when disturbed. If you smell the acrid spicy odor of vfft'tang and do not see its green leaves hanging from the trees around you, assume something has disturbed a scut'ia and watch out. The slime contains calcium oxalate. Do not touch it. It will burn you. Never kill a scut'ia; they are inoffensive animals," Melkorka warned.

"Phelindra described a *nei'la*, an eight-legged toad covered with pincers, claws, and hollow-tipped thorns."

Melkorka sat up straight in her chair and glared at him. "It is an eating machine. It eats living and dead animals. It moves fast on the ground but cannot climb, so run for the nearest tree. It is stupid and dangerous and will wait days for you to climb back down. It hunts by day or night. Always be on the lookout for this animal."

"The last one didn't sound so bad: a *rus'lus*. It looks like an eight-legged puff ball mushroom."

"They are unique," Melkorka interrupted, "because you can pull their long sensory quills off and make a neurotoxin to coat your weapons. Pulling them out does not hurt the *rus'lus*. Ask Phelindra or Zalzadrin to show you how to make the neurotoxin. It works in seconds if your weapon penetrates to a nerve. The toxin prevents synapses from clearing. Do not get it on you for it will kill you too and keep all coated weapons in their sheathes."

"Sounds like good advice."

"Is that all?" Melkorka demanded.

"Isn't that enough?" Delwyn asked. For all the warm-colored rainforest beauty surrounding him, its nights teemed with nightmarish horrors.

"Did they not tell you about the *eo'on?*"

Delwyn shook his head. "Can't say it sounds familiar."

Melkorka swore and busied herself tapping on her console. The image of a brown creature like a rhinoceros popped in a boxed window near Melkorka's head. "This is an eo'on. It eats wet mosses. The yellow and orange beads covering its legs are a wax it sweats to remain water resistant. We use this wax to make skin oil, but in its raw state it will burn."

"You kill them for their wax?" he asked, surprised Eyloni would kill any animal for some commercial use.

"No, we do not kill them!" she yelled. "They are inoffensive and will not harm you unless you let one trample you under its thirteen legs. They are helpful transport. All you need to do is find some club moss, climb onto its back, and hold the moss over its orange vertical beak. It will move forward to feed, but since you move with it, it can never reach the moss, but it is too stupid to know any different."

"So, I don't have to worry about it?" he asked.

"Not as long as you exercise care. Phelindra and Zalzadrin will take you into the forest between the elleiu trees and show you the jungle at night. When they do, remember we can see in the dark. Our night sight does not see into infrared, but the glare from any light source—artificial or natural—will night blind us. You should put some *hi'lah'il'ara* into a woven basket and take them with you. They will illuminate the immediate area without blinding anyone."

"Where can I find ones not growing into the tree?" Delwyn asked.

"There are usually several growing in baskets along the inside and outside spirals around the Hall. They are put there just for nighttime use."

"I'll remember," he promised. He paused and then recalled his official excuse for calling on her.

"Progress report?" he asked.

"Anailiatha has returned to Wrathsee'a and is directing the hull scanning teams. When they have completed their scans, she will use them to make pinpoint coordinate maps for the damaged sections and overlay them onto the final assembly scans from the archives. She will then use the composite image to generate targeting data for precision quantum translation damage removal.

"Anailiatha says she can have all the Forward Fusion-2 compartments and bulkheads replaced, but she doubts she will have a replacement reactor installed before the deadline. Forward Fire Control and Forward Torpedo Bay-2 hull repairs all come down to simple mechanical replacements and wiring and plumbing refits. Forward Torpedo Bay-1 can be rebuilt, and torpedo inventory can be translated into the bay magazine—violating safety edicts in doing so by the way. Forward Fuel Reserve-1 is fire-damaged beyond repair and must be gutted and rebuilt. Everything that was destroyed when the massed particle weapons fire tore through Environmental Control Central, the Forward Nutrition Center, the primary particle weapon mounts, and all the wreckage between there and Forward Fusion-2 will take time to repair. Anailiatha will not certify the ship if the life support systems are not rebuilt to her standards. I do not blame her. The repairs her teams made while in Nikkiolo moon orbit had been limited to bypassing and false-trailing the environmental systems.

"Our warship also took significant peripheral damage during Kalinn's ramming attack. The forward secondary weapon systems have been burned out from repeated pointblank firing. We have heavy forward dorsal hull plate loss and damage along with all the minor hull breaches on the forward decks. Hull plating and minor breach repair is simple in theory, but extensive damage takes time, materials, and energy, and she needs to address the damage affecting hull integrity and critical systems. You cannot believe how much time and materials will go into the power distribution networks and power systems failures that happened when the destroyer exploded in close proximity to our hull.

"Anailiatha insists I have the vine-and-leaf-patched jump drive gravity lensing armatures removed from her engineering hull, and on this she does not yield. She does not trust windings jackhammered, sledgehammered, and crowbarred back into place.

"The one easy trail she has prowled so far has led her to two new armatures made for another warship of the same class as ours. An alliance of La'huaset clans had intended to incorporate them into the ship they are building, but they will let us have them as long as we have a pair made for them."

"That's generous of them," Delwyn interrupted. "Can we get anything else from them?"

Melkorka shook her head. "Their engineering hull is nearing final assembly, but we do not need anything for our engineering hull but the armatures and a few random hull plates. They have bulkheads and hull plating, but we need all the forward section combat hull replaced. Hull plates follow the geometry of the ship in interlocking patterns. Anailiatha cannot force-fit hull plates designed for the engineering hull into the combat hull."

True enough, outer hull plating was a meter or so thick piece of complex machinery. It wasn't a simple duranium patch. It was a sandwich of emitters, electronics, and structural plates.

"When will they start translating the wrecked sections out?" he asked.

"In another two or three days. Once the work crews remove everything in bulk, Anailiatha will perform a walk-through inspection and certify that what remains passes Battle Status standards before the repair teams can begin their work. What does not pass standards must come out. All plumbing and power couplings are then capped and sealed. Some of those ducts, pipes, and wiring harnesses will no doubt need ripping out and replacing. Wiring repairs can take far longer than rebuilding the entire hull!"

Delwyn sighed. Coalition starships contained wiring harnesses thousands and thousands of kilometers in length. If even a small percentage of the critical systems conduits had burned out, then they could never complete minimal repairs in time. Melkorka's power distribution damage report reinforced his doubts, and he held his breath.

"What do you think? About the power distribution problem?" Delwyn asked her.

"Anailiatha's damage control teams cross-connected emergency battery power and most systems came back online. I do not think the problem lies in the optical cabling for the photonic systems. This comes down to an electrical power transmission problem. Electrical power runs through thousands of switching and stepdown transformers and load-sharing circuitry. Electrical systems are modular for the most part, so the teams can remove and replace them with little effort. They are wired into the distribution network, and Anailiatha will have to watch load sharing because there is a chance the transmission lines and wiring harnesses have damage lying in wait for the self-checking network to find. That, or they will pounce once some hidden short causes the load sharing safety crowbars to clamp off power before the wiring harnesses melt."

"What about the main kinetic weapons?" he asked, bracing for more bad news.

"The outrigger hull railguns are undamaged. The combat hull primary railgun and its mass driver ordnance delivery system is hopeless. The gun ports, the barrel, and both the automatic and the manual loading mechanisms are gone." Melkorka paused to glare at him. "I will tell you right now that just as Anailiatha will not certify the jump drive without new armatures, I will not certify the offensive capability of our warship without that main gun. That weapon is the primary orbit-to-surface kinetic battery. Its duranium projectiles can pierce bunkers several thousand ells below solid rock. If we must strike a hardened enemy emplacement on a planetary surface, we will need it."

Delwyn knew she was right. Particle weapons and force shielding made all the difference early in combat, but both of those technologies hogged power. Hydrogen-antihydrogen fusion wasn't perpetual motion. Antihydrogen cost the Coalition money and it cost the Compact in global public goods to make, so reserves ran dry rather quickly during offensive or defensive energy demand peaks. That meant combat tactics employed tactical and strategic kinetic assets regardless of the mass they added to a starship. He shrugged off the inevitable: they wouldn't be joining the battle group after all.

"Well, keep me posted. I want to know what's going on with my ship."

Melkorka smiled to herself in response to the possessive pronoun. He considered them and their warship his, which was wonderful to hear.

"What does Hlinlodyn think about our tactical response capability?" Delwyn carried on, happy to discuss things he had at least a feel for, if not knowledge of.

Melkorka told him Hlinlodyn had remained behind to help Anailiatha, as had the Mistress of Conveyance, the Mistress of Fortifications, the Mistress of Pathwalking, and all the command mistresses' teams.

"Is Kidahin with Trebithia?" he asked her.

Melkorka shook her head. "No, Trebithia will not need her until after the helm upgrades have been installed. Kidahin is with her clan."

"Would her clan consider it a bother if I called her?"

Melkorka gave him her best 'males are strange' look and shook her head. "Of course not. She associates with you and belongs to our society. She is no doubt biting her tail waiting for you to call her."

Delwyn smiled, followed up on a few more pressing issues, sat back, and relaxed. They talked for some time before he let Melkorka go. He wondered which of them hadn't wanted to ring off first the most. Melkorka sounded both tired and tail-biting mad, and she seemed to miss him as much as he missed her.

He missed her desperately. He hadn't felt quite himself since leaving A'lon'aloop. He felt antsy and hoped it didn't mean his PTSD symptoms had decided to return. He hoped not. He dreaded fighting flashback horrors.

He put a call through to the Uahua'asee'a Clan and soon had an ecstatic Kidahin beaming at him from the screen.

"Delwyn! How are you? I miss you! What are you doing? When are you coming to visit my clan?"

"Whoa, whoa, there Kidahin. So many questions. I miss you too. In fact, I miss everyone. I can't explain it. It's as if a piece of me has gone missing since leaving A'lon'aloop."

Kidahin stared hard at him, concerned. He needed her. Some males tended to get lost on the trails when separated from their associations over lengthy periods of time.

That was bad. An Eyloni male was normally patient, gregarious, and calm when safely ensconced in female company but reverted to a cunning killer when deprived of that contact if he thought a female associating with him had come under risk. A male alone endangered both himself and others, which was why females found even the idea of a male alone abhorrent and unnatural.

Kidahin knew a special bond had begun to form between them long before she had grown conscious of it. Back on the Nikkiolo moon he had called her a cute kid, which Melkorka had translated to mean a precocious infant or something like that. The comparison had infuriated Kidahin and goaded her into stalking him through the moon's ugly green forest. He had caught her at it when he should not have been able to do so and demanded she relinquish her adulthood knife for her sloppiness.

All the Hunters and Warriors aboard her warship also shared a special bond with Delwyn to varying degrees.

Kidahin listened to him talk, and as she listened she speculated. He had an intensity about him, a jumpiness, and she didn't think it came from describing the forest animals from his wildlife lessons.

"How are you enjoying time with your new family?" she asked.

"Oh fine, fine. Their tree is beautiful. You ought to see my abode. I'm supposed to go visiting at the other four trees over the next few days. Oh, and the clan elders want me to ask an Earth tribe to declare me an adult and give me an obsidian knife. They don't want me wearing a metal or ceramic throwing knife where an adulthood knife should hang."

Kidahin frowned. She knew Phelindra, Melkorka, and Phalalin had been nursing subtle worries about that knife. But if the clan elders had been satisfied with Delwyn's adult status, then those worries should no longer exist. But the La'huaset Tribal Elders now, they might make things difficult.

"Delwyn? Have you met with the La'huaset Tribal Elders yet?"

"No, not yet. They're giving me time to meet everyone in my extended family trees first."

Kidahin thought it over. She had been declared an adult thirteen months ago. Adulthood knives carried important cultural meanings.

"Delwyn, prepare yourself. I think they might ask you to submit to the O'un Tu Clan survival ordeal. That way, they can give you a volcanic glass knife themselves and have the honor of declaring you an adult in the eyes of the La'huaset Tribe."

"They already know I'm an adult, Kidahin."

"They know it, I know it; everyone knows it. Yet it is unseemly for an adult to appear in public without wearing an adulthood knife. You *should* feel embarrassed without it. Adults in your company *will* feel as embarrassed in not seeing that outward sign as if you habitually talked during formal meals with your mouth full and dribbled food on your breasts."

Her strident disgusted tone touched on a raw nerve, so much so that it made him sit up and take notice. Kidahin held a daughter's place in his heart in ways even Princess couldn't match. Even memories of his daughters couldn't compete with her. From her viewpoint he looked vulgarly naked to them without wearing the ritual adulthood blade.

They talked for hours before he rang off.

###

Kidahin looked down at her shaking hands. She panted rapidly, caught up in full-blown panic. The O'un Tu Clan elders would ask him to do it. Of course they would. If they did, then tradition demanded he have no help, no clothing, and no tools. She wracked her brain, asking herself how she might help him and yet remain within survival ordeal requirements.

In the end, only one exception presented itself.

Kidahin knew Delwyn's honor would drive him to take the survival ordeal if his family asked him to do so.

She stood and glided across the abode to her nest and pulled a carrysack from the heaped cushions, untied its drawstrings, and pulled out her spirit bag. She opened it and shook out the contents onto a cushion, unfolded a soft white fuzzy square and set her oyya web on it. Satisfied with its placement, she reached for the carefully folded cloth that had fallen from the spirit bag, unfolded it, wadded it up into a ball, and pressed it into her face.

She inhaled, allowing the wonderful male smell to fill her awareness.

Kidahin closed her eyes and concentrated on her oyya web and breathed deeply through her nose the scent that soaked the sweat-stained light blue Coalition tee-shirt.

Thinking about him, she let her left hand grope for a starting point on the oyya web.

Her fingernail slipped between two strands within the large circle of intricate woven webs. She inhaled once more through the dirty shirt in her right hand and then set is aside.

Kidahin glanced down to see where her finger had pierced the weave and sighed.

The strand her fingernail grazed led through multiple overlapping webs. That meant her plan would take her through a metaphorical jungle filled with thick twisting vines and dense undergrowth. The strand went into the heart of the overlapping webs, which meant a difficult and worrisome journey ahead. The longer she followed the strand, the more it wove in and out and though the webs, each time getting closer and closer to the circular wooden frame before heading back into the center of the web again.

Kidahin spent hours tracing the strand through the interlocking weaves. The oyya web resembled the female military rank weave she always wore hanging from her left earring. The oyya web covered thirteen times the area of her rank weave earring, and it contained more overlapping and interwoven webs than any rank weave could hold.

She had made the oyya web long ago, during a ritual she had attended as a preadolescent. It represented the Oyya Web of the spirits, the metaphysical underpinning of all existence. Through it she communed with the spirits of her people. If a positive result was forthcoming, then she had to trace the strand back to her starting point. Losing the strand among the other threads in the web, some having the same colors and others having different colors, meant defeat. Her path ran forward from her starting point. She could not double-back and could not start over. Time did not reverse, and life did not give do-overs.

Kidahin concentrated hard on her plan, on Delwyn's scent, and on the spirits as she followed the strand through the interwoven webs to the wooden frame and on around the bent polished branch, passing over a phrase of spirit writing, one of several engraved around the oyya web. Kidahin read the quote from the Cautions of the Oyya Web, a warning about "the naïve female as prey." She grimaced and traced the strand around the polished berry-stained rim again. This time she looped over a quote from one of Life's Lessons about "the feral female."

Kidahin traced the strand back through the webs to the opposite side and around the rim and read another engraved passage from the Cautions of the Oyya Web, the one dealing with "backtracking and looping."

She chased the strand through the entwined webs one last time, running her fingernail along it until she returned to her starting point.

Her plan should succeed but tracing the strand through the thick interlocking webs meant the journey would fight her through tripping vines and meshed brambles. The overlapping webs signified an overgrown and circuitous trail. The "naïve female as prey" had to mean she would expose herself in some foolish fashion. "Backtracking and looping" told her she must remember when and how to get behind a threat and remember when to shiver and run and when not to. In the most general sense, backtracking and looping warnings meant she should know when to hold her ground and when she should retreat. That "the feral female" felt appropriate to her quest, she had no doubt.

The circuitous trail warning caused her some worry. It and the tangled path both hinted her plan might take up more time than she had. The rush to sortie the battle group put an immutable limit on the time she did have. That and she knew the Tribal Elders would want Delwyn to complete the ordeal before the battle group left, assuming *Hunter's Moon* could meet Battle Status standards by then.

Time would defy her.

Kidahin gathered up her oyya web, its white mat, and Delwyn's sweat stained tee-shirt into her spirit bag along with her totem items. She tossed additional items into her carrysack and ran from her abode to the outer spiral path and climbed down through the youngest and outermost fused aerial root passageways to exit near the central bole. Two Warriors stood along the bole threshold inside edge. Another pair stood along the outside edge watching the forest.

"Is an aircar available this morning?" Kidahin asked the Warrior standing next to her.

"Yes," the Warrior replied. "Where are you going?"

"I must return to Na'di Island on warship business."

There. That should satisfy them. Warship autonomy extended to his society whenever they acted in the furtherance of ship's business. She told the truth, too. Anything concerning Delwyn came under ship's business.

"Are you traveling to the spaceport there?" the Warrior asked.

"Yes, I must go to A'lon'aloop."

"How long will you be gone?"

"I am not sure. I must speak with the Mistress of the Tower on Wrathsee'a Anchorage, and as busy as she is I will likely encounter delays."

The Warrior nodded, satisfied. "Safe journey, Kidahin. May the spirits go with you."

Kidahin repeated the ritual farewell and waited for the dark green line marking the bole threshold predator-repelling force field to vanish. When it did, she stepped through the broad natural arch and out into the night.

Kidahin prowled off under her home tree watching the auroras flash and ripple across the sky before picking up her pace and rushing through the cool night air to the waiting aircar.

She climbed into the driver seat, powered up the 'car's systems, and performed a preflight check.

Satisfied, she engaged the engine and punched in her destination as the 'car rose into the crisp aurora-filled night sky. Once clear of the trees, the autopilot took over and plotted a course for Na'di Island and the A'way Senge spaceport. The aircar was no VTOL aircraft and could not match its cruising ceiling and velocity but Kidahin had no choice. She could not justify taking a family aircraft; the flight would take hours.

###

After Delwyn rang off he remained seated at the comm terminal, lost in thought.

If the La'huaset Tribal Elders wanted him to take the adulthood survival test, they would have to defer to his clan elders and the family elders living in this tree. They would insist he live off clan land during the test, wouldn't they? Every adult here had done so at one time. He needed a few pointers. That meant talking to someone. He headed out the open bole and into the winding passageway. Phelindra lived above him. Zalzadrin lived halfway across the canopy. But Hervorallin's abode grew into the tree nearby.

Delwyn stumbled around fungi-lit knobby branches and through twisting fused root paths. From time to time he passed bole openings to other abodes, other living areas within the living family complex. He counted the bends and boles, relying on his memory to find Hervorallin's abode, musing as he walked how much easier time he'd have of it if he could only smell her scent marks.

Delwyn froze, a sudden wariness tickled in his head: a warning. He was being stalked. Inquisitive doubts followed the intuitive warning, and then a hailstorm of empathic exclamation points darted at him. A handful of infant females poked their heads out from irregular tiny openings in the living maze.

Those little imps, he thought with a smile. "Let's go see Princess," he told them.

They did not understand the new male's words, but his weak scent told them who he wanted. Two Hunters ranged on ahead, two more fell in behind and three Warriors remained with him until they arrived at Hervorallin's abode.

They stopped, and Delwyn poked his head through the bole, looked around, and hesitated as he stepped inside. The casual entry into the abode, without waiting for permission to enter, felt akin to home invasion. Custom said if a person wasn't challenged the instant her head broke the threshold, she could either enter and announce her presence, or she could just wait until she was recognized.

Hervorallin and at least two others slept together amid cushions and pillows. He didn't see Hervorallin's older daughters anywhere in the room.

Well, so much for this idea. Delwyn sighed and turned to leave, but Princess trilled a demand that shattered the silence.

Four figures sat up and looked at him.

"Delwyn?" Hervorallin asked.

"Yeah, it's me. Sorry. I'll come back later."

"Why?" Hervorallin asked. "We have more than enough room for ten."

In the dull fungal glow, he saw Hervorallin, another Hunter, and two Warriors. Four female friends enjoying tail-entwined company. For some reason they reminded him of warm blankets, and he yawned.

"Come here," Hervorallin demanded. "We will keep you company. You should know by now we often sleep with intimate friends. You will sleep much better if you sleep with us. Phelindra cannot keep you tail-tied to herself all the time."

"I just came over to ask you about your survival ordeal, but it can wait until later."

Hervorallin flattened her ears. Seconds later the other three females responded to her pheromonal signaling and flattened their ears as well.

"Why?" Hervorallin asked, wary and suspicious. "The clan elders are satisfied with your adult status."

"I talked to Kidahin. She seemed to think the Tribal Elders are going to ask the clan to ask me to take part in the survival ordeal."

Hervorallin cursed. Her bedmates flinched. The infants crooned vague sympathetic warnings.

"We are not aboard our warship. What Kidahin thinks has nothing to do with the O'un Tu Clan! She should keep her tail in Uahua'asee'a Clan where it belongs and out of O'un Tu Clan business."

Hervorallin shook, visibly upset. Delwyn ran to her, put his arms around her, and tried to calm her down before she woke the neighbors.

"She is thinking about ship's business, and I think she's right. Our clan and our immediate and extended families should not fight this. We should anticipate this, welcome it. I wanted to ask you about your own experiences. Your ordeal took place in clan territory, didn't it?"

Delwyn pulled her down into the nest, where the others surrounded them. He struggled to resist their combined warmth and scent and fought the urge to fall asleep.

"Tell me about your journey," he said.

Hervorallin relaxed in the company of her intimate friends, her favorite male, her infant daughter, and twelve infants. After a few minutes, she began.

"I told Phelindra when I first came into season that I was ready. She made the arrangements for my survival ordeal. When the day came, she plugged my ears and nose and blindfolded me. She led me into an aircar, and we flew for hours back and forth across the sky to scramble my orientation sense so I could not guess where I stood within clan territory.

"We landed. She stripped me naked, and she told me not to open my eyes until I had counted to ten-thousand. When I finished counting, I opened my eyes to at first unfamiliar jungle and …"

Hervorallin's tale ran over four hours. When she finished, Delwyn had forgotten that he wanted to ask her why she had gone to Phelindra. He laid among the four females and thought about her story until he fell asleep.

Princess watched him. He smelled weary. He needed refreshment. She trilled softly to the other infants. They trilled back.

Then every infant in the nest vanished.

Delwyn smelled the malutha berry under his nose even before he woke up.

Princess gave it to him. Huge in her tiny hands, it looked something like a kiwi fruit and felt as dense as an apple. It smelled and tasted like concentrated maraschino cherries. The clan used them for making the sickeningly sweet juice he had tried earlier. The fruit wasn't as bad as the juice made from them. In fact, he loved them. He'd eaten a handful earlier. Princess had picked up on his liking them.

"I wonder where she found this," he muttered.

"From the fruit cellar in the Hall," Hervorallin said, giving her daughter a stern look.

"She's not supposed to go there I take it."

Hervorallin shook her head, glaring at the troop of infants gathered around her.

"She had help," Phelindra added.

"What makes you say that?" he asked.

"The fruit cellar door uses a static seal to keep it closed." She waved her tail at the waiting infants. "They pulled the door open far enough for her to go in and back out again."

"Them?" Delwyn asked, impressed.

Phelindra nodded. "They work together."

He shook his head and gnawed on the berry, watching Princess watch him. He caught hints of her happy empathic sendings. When he finished chewing and swallowed, she crossed over to her mother and nursed. In less than a minute she fell asleep clamped to her mother's back.

Delwyn squinted at Phelindra. "When did you get here? You have the look of a Hunter on a mission," he remarked.

"You are correct. Zalzadrin and I will teach you how to prowl the night jungle this morning after breakfast."

"Good. I'll get ready and rejoin you in the Hall." He gave Hervorallin a hug, being careful not to awaken the sleeping Princess, and headed back to his abode. On the way he wondered when Hervorallin's bed mates had left. He doubted they left because of Phelindra. Did they have chores and duties to perform for the family? Did they have occupational assignments, jobs, and had to leave?

He returned to his abode to find Zalzadrin wandering aimlessly about.

"Did you have a good night's rest?" she asked.

"I did, brief as it was. I don't often sleep well during my first night in a strange place."

"But this is not a strange place. This is your place, your home. If you can sleep aboard our warship in deep space without difficulty, then you should feel at ease here."

Something in Zalzadrin's tone raised alerts. "Do you find it hard to sleep aboard ship?"

"No, not anymore. I used to. We all do at first. A warship might look and feel like a rainforest, but he izzant—issant—is not one. What helps us feel at home is that we recognize our ship as a male, that our warleader is with us, and that we have one another."

Delwyn gave her a polite nod, but if he'd've had ears like hers they would have pricked as she tried to pronounce the contracted word. This made it the second or third time he'd heard her attempt to say a contracted word.

Eyloni refused to speak the contractions common in Coalition standard. They knew what they meant because his scent gave them an empathic rendering, and that gave them a seamless swap for the non-contracted form.

The problem rested with usage rules in their language. An Eyloni hearing "isn't" or "is not" felt the same empathic construct for both words and interpreted them as having the same meaning. When they spoke however, they could not account for how "isn't" and "is not" did not use the same chords or beats and still have the same meaning. Pitch and timing changes between the two words had to correlate to subtle changes in meaning. But what were they, exactly? Status? Seriousness? Insult? They smelled a slight difference when Delwyn used one over the other: an apparent formal-informal nuance.

They understood Delwyn spoke his own dialect. Dialectical speech differences distinguished clan memberships by their changing regional pitch and beat. Dialects varied far and wide among the tribes, but even tribal dialects tended more toward differences in octave and beat than his slang speech did.

Whenever an Eyloni spoke in Coalition standard, she sang the words at the same pitch and beat she sang in her native tongue. She would never sing in another region's dialect. To do so was to steal another's regional identity.

Delwyn smiled at Zalzadrin's verbal flub and attributed it to disturbing memories she had from having to learn to sleep "on the ground" as it were, light-years away from home.

Zalzadrin paced as Delwyn got ready. Then they grabbed Phelindra and headed for the hall.

There, tables and chairs had been set up, but nothing like they had been for the evening meal. Eyloni ate at regular times but snacked often throughout the day. Eyloni conducted dinner as a formal family event, but they ran their breakfast as an informal small group affair. A few people ate by themselves and read from their 'minders. Others ate together in small groups. People in those small groups spoke one at a time in turns. Just like the night before, no one spoke while eating. When a person stopped talking, she passed a wooden object resembling an ornate pepper mill to another person. That person swallowed, wiped her face and breasts, patted herself dry, and then began speaking.

"What's the wood carving the Warrior passed to the Hunter now speaking for?" Delwyn asked.

Zalzadrin frowned. Looking in on others unless you intended to join them came close to poking a tail into courtesy. "That is a stafn'boi, a speaker's totem. If you wish to speak during informal meals, you must stop eating, make sure no food is in your mouth, clean yourself, and claim the speaker's totem."

"We never used one of those aboard ship," he said.

"We did when we ate together. You did not because you never ate with more than four at a time. A hand or less in close association, or associations eating informal meals, take turns talking and eating. You always ate one serving, drank to clean your mouth, wiped you face, and spoke before advancing to the next dish. You talk in-between dishes."

She was right. He ate helpings separately: salad first, then veggies, then meat, and then dessert last; well, not meat since meeting Kidahin. He remembered when he had taken her to a Coalition mess hall. She picked fruits, water, and the coffee she had since fallen in love with. She had eaten the fruit while he talked. She drank the water and then talked between sips of hot coffee. Table etiquette concerning beverages only was laxer.

Kidahin had been quite obsessive about her personal cleanliness. Self-conscious he squirmed, feeling grubby sitting next to Zalzadrin.

The three ate, while he worried about his table manners.

They dished him up a large portion of porridge made from creamed white roots with little translucent pagodas sprinkled on top. Inside them hid red pea-sized berries.

What should he do? Peel them?

No. Zalzadrin and Phelindra were eating them whole.

He picked up a polished spoon and scooped up a mouthful. The porridge had a vanilla cream of wheat flavor and was smooth in texture. The cherries puckered his mouth with a tart crab apple taste, but their parchment coverings tasted sweet.

They finished eating, stood, and walked through the Hall and out into the dark night. The setting sun had vanished below the horizon.

Tyreniioroneo's neon blue half-moon beamed from his fixed 11:38 AM overhead sky. Bright alien constellations filled the cloudless sky, and he stopped to marvel at the clear starry night. Night sky scenes like these were rare on Earth because lights blazed all the time day and night. Cheap, clean, safe electrical power meant everybody had it. No longer did cost issues plague the poor on Earth. Basic services had become public goods a century ago, but electrical service beyond basic amperage required a license. Since everybody used lights, light scattering through the atmosphere made views like these nearly impossible. A nighttime glimpse toward any horizon was met with the ever-present glow of modernity.

Standing in a dark jungle with no light surrendered the advantage to the hunter. Kidahin would say he stood on low ground now. Delwyn held the glowing basket in his left hand. An occasional twinkle glimmered from a bole above him. The ground level main bole gave away no hint of light but for the hard, green line across its threshold.

"They've polarized the field, haven't they?" he asked.

Phelindra bobbed her head in the pale blue glow. "Light attracts insects that feed on the glowing fungi."

Delwyn nodded. The insects he'd seen so far resembled dragonflies, mayflies, and damselflies. A few matched Earth dragonflies in size if not color, which varied from amber to deep tangerine or from scarlet to brick red. Their sizes ranged from those of fruit bats down to fruit flies.

Few insects roamed the night, and Elleio had no blood-sucking mosquitoes. Phelindra and Zalzadrin led him off into an Earthly forest writ large. Towering trees with orange and yellow-trimmed red parasol leaves glowed in the ethereal pale blue light from the gas giant. The light cast an eerie pall over the alien forest.

"We are heading for Verikaralee's tree," Phelindra said. "We will flank on the right and swing behind him. When we reach their aircraft landing area we will separate and take independent prowls back to this spot."

"That's it? I thought infants did more than this," he complained.

"You know less than an infant does," Zalzadrin said. "And even when an infant male forays into the forest, his infant female association never leaves him."

"Yeah, but infant females go without escort."

"True," Phelindra said. "They accompany one another, watching each other's tails. Come, you are wasting time for nothing."

Phelindra and Zalzadrin led him away from their home tree. After a time, the branches above began to thin out and the lesser trees beyond the canopy outline grew into the sky like perimeter sentinels.

Delwyn glanced into the night sky and tried to fix the stars against the canopy. He took a second bearings check and still found no change in the night sky, no central guiding star, and wondered why until it came to him.

Elleio's slow spin gave her long days and nights. It also gave her a static night sky compared to Earth skies. Nor did he find a pole star, but for the brief time they remained outside, any remarkable star would work for night reckoning.

In the darkness temperature differentials caused by uneven cooling brought steady breezes. Air soughed through leaves larger than any he'd ever seen before. They made the breezes sound different somehow. He heard a fwip-fwip-fwip sound, like kites caught in branches by their tails banging and rattling.

Delwyn and his two minders followed the perimeter set by the shade-retarded growth surrounding the neighbor tree.

"If they shoot me, I'll never speak to you two again," he whispered.

"Zalzadrin called ahead and told them we would be stalking and prowling around their tree," Phelindra said, keeping her voice low.

"I did not. I forgot!" Zalzadrin yelped.

Delwyn froze in his tracks. Eyloni disliked territorial intrusions and he bet that was true for unannounced family visitors, too.

"Stop that!" Phelindra snapped. "This is serious business."

"I am serious. I got the outdoor gear and told the sentinels we were going into the forest for about ten hours. You told me you were going to notify Hervorallin and the family," Zalzadrin objected.

Phelindra froze and pulled her 'minder from one of several loops hanging from her underthong ties. She tapped its screen, and it came alive. She thumbed the comm switch, called ahead, and told Verikaralee's immediate family they had visitors skirting their perimeter helping Delwyn get his bearings in the night jungle.

After a few minutes she stepped away from him and Zalzadrin.

"Private call?" he asked her. He didn't think so. But for special circumstances no such things happened among Eyloni unless an honor or privacy issue took precedence.

"I do not think so," Zalzadrin said, no trace of the joker now. "I think someone has decided to play 'seek-and-find' with us."

Night-ops security sweeps, he translated. "Teams or independent units?" he asked.

"Independent. We are in their territory. We cannot prowl beyond the tree's cover. Our objective is to meet where we walked in under the tree perimeter. If we are captured, they will 'hold' us until night ends."

"It isn't fair if they use perimeter monitors."

She shook her head. "Who comes after us will not have comms or scanners. Everyone inside will watch our progress on the perimeter scanners, but they will not report our progress to those outside."

"How many will come after us?"

"We belong to an elite warship society. They will send four times our number," Zalzadrin said as Phelindra rejoined them.

"They want to play seek-and-find with us," she growled, in no mood for play.

"You could have said no," Zalzadrin and Delwyn said together.

"Jinx!" he yelled.

The two Hunters gave him their best bewildered stares.

"Never mind," he said.

"This is not an unarmed combat drill. If you are touched, you are captured. This is individual goal seeking. The goal is the clearing below the outermost branches back the way we came."

"We are behind enemy lines," Delwyn translated.

Phelindra nodded. "You cannot travel beyond the canopy circumference. You ought to cover your glowbasket, Delwyn."

"No kidding. Do you know what forces are arrayed against us?"

"Half Hunters and half Warriors. They did not name them. This close to the extended family trees no dangerous animals should lurk. Be careful Delwyn. They hunt at night and one can always make a rare appearance."

"Thanks a lot."

"Anything to add?" Phelindra asked.

No one spoke, and she nodded. "Separate then, and may the spirits go with you."

Delwyn covered his basket, hid it where he could find it again and broke off into the cover growing beneath the broad sweeping branches. As a one-time special operations group commander, he excelled in night missions and security sweeps under night cover. He ran some thirty meters in silence, stopped, changed course and moved perpendicular to the others and began irregular creep movement.

He planned as he inched forward. He'd never seen the lay of the land in daylight, but maybe he could turn that to an advantage. He wouldn't consider heading into places they figured he might go.

Six Hunters and six Warriors. Hunters preferred solitary stalking, which explained why Phelindra and Zalzadrin wanted to scatter. Hunter combat style conflicted with Phelindra's protectress duty that demanded she stay with him.

He bet she was furious with Zalzadrin.

Without combat scanners, darkness was a great equalizer. He gained confidence as his innate situational awareness kicked in. Soon he had eyes on the Warriors moving in two groups of three.

They were the beaters trying to flush them out.

He found a Hunter. Too noisy. She was a decoy, which meant his bolt hole paths were no longer viable.

It was time to retreat.

He sidestepped, slow and quiet, thinking he had it made until an indignant squeal yammered on contact with his foot.

He looked down and saw several small creatures surrounding him: Princess and a slew of infants.

"It's not fair if you're helping," he whispered to her.

Happy baby-babble trills came in reply, followed by intuitive love and warm feelings.

The infants with Princess joined her humming.

"Wait! Wait! Wait! Wait! Wait!" Verikaralee sang from very close by. "Seek-and-find is not fair when infants are involved. Everyone come on in!"

"What do you think Princess? A trick?" he asked his near-daughter.

"Come on in Delwyn," Phelindra sang.

Zalzadrin sang on Phelindra's tail. "It is a trick! Let the infants lead you home!"

Only Zalzadrin's joker laughter convinced him it wasn't a trick.

He headed in, disappointed he didn't have a chance to sweep the area and return to the clearing.

They ushered them into the tree, and Delwyn began his first extended family visit much sooner than expected.

Over the next few days he met with the extended families living in the remaining three elleiu trees. When he returned to his home tree, he got a good night's sleep for once and woke to find himself, Phelindra, Hervorallin, and Zalzadrin smothered by infants. He got up and had just stepped into the necessary when someone called from the bole.

"Delwyn, the Tribal Elders are coming this morning."

A vacant knot formed in the pit of his stomach, a hint, a gut feeling, one that never steered him wrong: he was doomed.

15

KIDAHIN

"This is Na'di Island approach control calling Uahua'asee'a Clan tu'ri'me-four zero one traffic indent," a voice demanded from the open comm.

"Huntress Kidahin Uahua'asee'a La'huaset Eyloni inbound from Uahua'asee'a Clan to Na'di Island," Kidahin replied to the Na'di Island Mistress of Air's challenge.

"To what purpose do you visit Na'di Island, Kidahin?"

"I am the helmsmistress and the Mistress of Pathwalking's second aboard the warship *Hunter's Moon.* I seek conveyance to A'lon'aloop on ship's business."

Kidahin waited. Leaving the island was easy. Landing there was another matter. She continued inbound as the security systems verified her voice, her vehicle, and her status.

Minutes dragged by. That she should not be here at all made the wait interminable.

"Kidahin of Uahua'asee'a Clan, you are cleared for landing at the spaceport conveyance center. Mistress of Pathwalking Trebithia wants you to contact her upon landing. Be welcome to Na'di Island and go with the spirits."

"*Me na ti ka meh,*" Kidahin sang in ritual response.

Trebithia? Had the Mistress of Air contacted her, or had Trebithia asked for a tail tug if anyone decided to return to the warship early?

Kidahin ground her teeth and settled back into the seat, knowing other things besides the automated approach lurked beyond her control.

She arrived over Na'di Island an hour later. As the aircar approached the landing pad, traffic control tripped the 'car's manual flight override and commanded it to execute a one-ell stationary hover. Small flashing lights coalesced up ahead, a swarm blinking a tattered line for her to follow from the landing area into short term vehicle parking. Kidahin engaged the maneuvering fields and followed the blinking lights to an open meadow among scattered modest trees and parked in the spot where the blinking lights gathered.

She turned off the 'car, got out, closed the door, and pressed her palm against the window.

The long walk through the breezy warm air relaxed her. Prowling always made her feel better. Like all Hunters, she hated confinement and waiting. Although the aircar flew faster than she could ever walk, flying did not come close to walking.

Now she felt like things had finally begun to move a pace again.

Kidahin stepped into the spaceport and headed for the conveyance center. She met few people along the dim jungle paths, and by the time she exchanged greetings and walked into the conveyance center an hour had passed.

"Mistress of Conveyance? I am Kidahin of *Hunter's Moon.* With respect, I ask for conveyance to A'lon'aloop."

The Warrior gave Kidahin a swift appraisal and canted her ears in puzzlement.

"You need no intermediate clearance, Kidahin. You know that. Why not translate direct to a transport heading for Wrathsee'a Anchorage and your warship?"

Kidahin had to stalk this female with some care. Eyloni as a people or as individuals could not lie without their pheromones telling on them. It was permissible to evade comment as long as silence did not impose upon honor and courtesy. To refuse to speak on a matter did not make silence itself a lie by omission, nor did keeping the truth to oneself.

That said, honor and courtesy also demanded an answer to the direct question. "I have need to seek assistance in the furtherance of warship business."

There. Not a lie, but the absolute—if vague—truth. Further inquiries by the spaceport Mistress of Conveyance risked delving into the autonomy granted warships and their societies. On her word of honor Kidahin claimed autonomy as a defense against further inquiries. If her word proved false, then the hierarchies had ways of hearing about it. Discipline would follow swiftly on her like a leap from an elleiu tree: fatally.

The Mistress of Conveyance considered the young Hunter's scent. Her pheromones drew pictures hinting at worry and doubt. She saw images, the people uppermost in Kidahin's thoughts: a male and four females. The male was Delwyn, of course. The four females, from Kidahin's scent she saw two Warriors, a Hunter, … and a Comari?

"Very well. A'lon'aloop destination approved. I hope you know what you are doing Kidahin of *Hunter's Moon.* Go with the spirits."

Kidahin flicked her ears in acknowledgment and sang her thanks.

She stepped into the conveyance station and waited.

The Mistress of Conveyance nodded, smiled at Kidahin, and brushed her tail against her assistant.

Kidahin twitched in reflexive readiness as she abruptly arrived in the A'lon'aloop translation station. She glided from the station and palmed a touchplate to register her presence on the naval station. She sent a quick text message to Trebithia's message queue before darting off into the trails that filled the compartments, connecting the various station facilities and services scattered throughout the rainforest. As soon as she reached the overgrown side trails she pulled the stained T-shirt from her carrysack, wadded it up in her fist, and carried it so the occasional breezes broadcasted its scent.

Kidahin spent the next few days prowling every square ell of the station paths searching, Trebithia long forgotten.

***

Something nagged at Delwyn, had been nagging at him ever since they came back from the failed seek-and-find Verikaralee had instigated. Had she and Zalzadrin planned the whole thing as a ruse to get him into Verikaralee's immediate family tree?

But that wasn't what was nagging at him now.

The main entrance force field had been set to repel solid matter when they left.

"Zalzadrin? How did the infants get outside?"

"Do you not have more important things to worry about than that?" Zalzadrin demanded.

"No, not really. When we left, the forest level bole had been sealed. I remember asking about the polarized force field."

"They can climb, Delwyn. If they want to go outside, they just climb onto a branch and then down the trunk to the ground," Phelindra said, as if describing an everyday occurrence.

Delwyn looked askance at her. That meant they had all climbed down a two-hundred-meter tree trunk. He didn't believe her, and his scent told her he didn't believe her.

His outright disbelief assaulted her honor like a slap in the face. Growling and bearing her brilliant white teeth, which looked even whiter against her red-black lips, she snarled at him. "If you do not want to hear what I have to say, then do not ask me!" she fumed.

Implying an Eyloni had lied was a sure way to end up on her bad side. Delwyn knew right then that if he had been a female, Phelindra would have claimed an honor insult and jumped him by now. Only his gender saved him from what would have been a no-contest brawl. Phelindra was no inexperienced Kidahin. His crew called her Eldest Huntress for a reason. She was the oldest and most experienced Hunter aboard. She had the strength and skill to rip him in two.

"Phelindra, Delwyn's scent reveals his shocked doubt, not his disbelief," Zalzadrin said.

That comment bought Zalzadrin a share of Phelindra's bad temper.

Spirits, Zalzadrin thought, Phelindra wanted to bite something.

Hervorallin sat and watched Phelindra, considered her scent, and relaxed. Phelindra felt no honor insult. Her worry was showing.

Princess crawled down Hervorallin's back and into Phelindra's lap. There she took the Eldest Huntress's cheeks in her tiny hands, looked her in the eyes, and gave her a humming chirp.

"Oh! I forgot about that," she trilled softly to Princess.

"Forgot what?" Delwyn asked over Zalzadrin's loud trilling giggle.

"Sometimes the Comara let them out," Phelindra clarified.

"The Comara let them out? Why would they let infants out into the dark?" he demanded.

"Because they asked. Comara play with infants. They have a certain emotional resonance with them."

"Seems odd to me for a Comari to let them out and then abandon them," he growled.

Hervorallin flipped her ears back and forth, a negative gesture. "A Comari always accompanies infants on short prowls in the jungle once she is satisfied her male is safe. If a Comari did let them out, then the perimeter defenses may have picked her up shadowing them. Comara have fine pheromonal control and can dampen their scent, making them quite difficult to track. No doubt she prowled near you and you did not notice."

Hervorallin's causal mention of Comara abilities didn't trump the mental picture of seeing Princess climbing down an elleiu tree.

Princess smelled her male's pheromonal reference to her, climbed down Phelindra's chest, and jumped into his lap. She sang convoluted melodies filled with reassurances and comforts.

Delwyn felt a feeling of absolute certainty riding high on their shared empathy.

Zalzadrin laughed. Phelindra smiled, vindicated. Hervorallin squirmed in mild discomfort.

"What?" he asked. He missed so much of the detail carried on their scent-empathy links.

"She has climbed down the outside of home tree once before, but not this time. A Comari let them out to keep watch on you," Zalzadrin laughed again.

"How did a Comari know I went outside?"

"Their scent told her," Zalzadrin said smirking.

Zalzadrin sounded certain. He wasn't. He had doubts. Why should infant scents alert a Comari about him? Why did the infants want out anyway? Why would a Comari care when she was supposed to care only for her chosen male?

He changed the subject. "So, what's going to happen when the Tribal Elders get here?"

"They want to meet you, want to see how you are settling into your new home. They will explain what they expect from you as a La'huaset Tribe clan male," Phelindra said.

"And what do they expect?"

"That is for them to tell you, but at a minimum you are expected to visit La'huaset clans. Remember, La'huaset Tribal Elders are selected from the clan elders in each clan residing within the La'huaset Tribal continent."

"So, all Tribal Elders are also clan elders, but not all clan elders are Tribal Elders?"

Hervorallin nodded and picked up where Phelindra left off.

"We are expecting a hand of them here soon. Our clan is involved, so our Tribal Elder cannot take an active role as an elder. That does not mean she loses her clan elder standing. The tribal council chose ten of them from the thousands of La'huaset clans. They come to welcome you to the La'huaset Tribe in the same way we welcomed you to our clan."

"So, we just wait?" Delwyn asked.

"No, why wait? Watching your tail never gets it to do work for you. What do you want to do?" Hervorallin asked.

"Review damage reports and repair survey updates," he said, jumping from his seat and heading up the central spiral pathway.

Phelindra watched him leave.

Zalzadrin and Hervorallin watched her watch him.

"What are you so worried about?" Zalzadrin demanded.

"The Tribal Elders will ask Delwyn to submit to the survival ordeal. He has already resigned himself to it. I smell it on him. He is planning, and I can smell that too."

"That is just his mind working through our warship damage and repair estimates. You heard him. He is going to his abode to reread the reports Melkorka has been sending him," Zalzadrin said.

"No," Phelindra said. "Kidahin planted the thought in his mind, and it has stuck there. I think he wants to prove he can survive in our jungles."

"Tell Kidahin to change his mind. Delwyn is an adult from his birth clan's viewpoint. We never ask a male from another clan to submit to a second survival ordeal if he gains a near-daughter here!" Hervorallin said.

Zalzadrin looped her tail, a negative gesture. "That is because the Tribal Elders witness all clan adulthood ceremonies. This was impossible in Delwyn's case."

"I do not know if Kidahin did a good thing or not," Phelindra spat.

Delwyn sat at the comm terminal and scanned through Melkorka's notes. The Warrior wrote and dictated technical reports and summaries surpassing captains log quality. As he read and listened, he thought about her. Melkorka commanded the ship. She fulfilled a captain's role. He tagged along, a cross between a co-captain and a rear admiral. Melkorka carried the captain's share when it came to commanding officer responsibilities. Her reports read less formal than anything a Coalition of Earth Colonies captain might put into words, but her insights opened his mind to possibilities. She wrote nothing like a captain trying to avoid unfavorable notice from the high-styles.

Coalition ship captains kept an official log and a personal log. The Admiralty read the official log, but a captain kept his personal logs to himself. Then again, the Defense Directorate had subpoena power over them, so the career-minded captain exercised prudence when dictating them.

Melkorka reported facts, opinions, and conjectures. Facts for her amounted to empirical truths. Her theories explained how those facts came about and presented factual claims following from logical deductive chains. Her conjectures ranged from hypothesizing to running commentaries rising from an emotional well.

Those wells ran deep, and many of her emotional theories had a ring of truth to them. Both her written and her dictated analyses appealed to his instincts, felt right in his gut, and he wondered if being a pheromone-linked empath made her feelings more trustworthy than say, a captain's gut feelings.

Melkorka didn't hide that her feelings and instincts figured into her analyses. Formal Eyloni language usage required 'warranting' phraseology. A speaker had to state evidence for a proposition and declare its source as hearsay, deduced, inferred, or observed.

Delwyn read on and wondered what a fleet commander would think after reading Melkorka's intuitive report based in part on how the warship, a male personification, made her feel as she surveyed the battle damage.

They'd have taken her ship from her and locked her up in a loony bin.

Her structural damage assessment recommended repair teams use the shipyard bulk quantum translator to teleport all the damaged sections into a cargo ship. Have the cargo ship take them into Elleio orbit. Then teleport them to a naval repair center on the La'huaset continent. If they could 'port the sections onto a scaffold and cut out all the junk, then she had high hopes—and all the math—to prove that a section scaffold-to-translation-into-orbit procedure would cut repair time in half. Her idea might save even more time if the wiring and plumbing chases in the damaged sections still worked.

He read through her time and materials management comparisons and contrasts. She relied on her informed feelings as much as she did detailed manufacturing and wiring time estimates.

No Coalition captain ever quantified her feelings in an official report. Why bother? Whatever a captain might feel about her ship, she couldn't direct repair operations herself. A Coalition shipyard had its own command, and they filed repair requests in typical government efficiency and told a know-nothing captain where she could shove her feelings.

Melkorka not only forwarded her reports to him in his capacity as warleader, but she also sent copies to Havalin, to Lindredha, to the Kem Basinga Clan warship hull manufacturing center deep in the La'huaset Tribal continent interior, and to the Hunter societies that had designed, financed, and built *Hunter's Moon* in the first place. She hadn't sent so much as a word to the Compact Counsel, nor did she bother to send anything to Thelindrallin either.

Delwyn chuckled at the idea of a hypothetical Captain Winters transmitting a *Henri Edda* damage assessment to General Spaceframes. One based on his feeling concerning the potential failure rate in a hull plate. Yet Melkorka, fulfilling her duties as Mistress of the Ship, had looped her tail into everything.

Delwyn took his time paging through the Mistress's Assessment Summary. Melkorka had filed over three hundred reports in it herself thus far. Three hundred in his number system, not three hundred in her base-five figures.

She wasn't the only one either. The command mistresses had their own icons listed in the Summary. So did Anailiatha. He thought he knew what she would have to say and braced himself before opening the ledger next to her icon. Four hundred and fifty-four reports filled the engineering assessment ledger.

Curious, he scanned the report titles, shrugged, and picked one at random. He touched the screen at the "Forward Fusion-2" heading, dragged his finger across the screen to its center, boxed it and spread his fingers to open and expand the file.

The wreckage in the panning video resembled the explosive aftermath of a boiler room disaster in an old coal-burning plant. The reactor had slammed into emergency stop, but the containment fields had held. Fuel had been cut off and routed well away from the reactor. The power systems produced electricity by direct conversion, no turbines, and the momentary runaway surge had melted the converters to slag or blown them to ashes.

Anailiatha's scathing rants were in no way meant for admiral-eyes reading. She made it clear that the rebuilt Forward Fusion-2 reactor spaces wouldn't have a working Fusion-2 reactor. She planned to have Forward Fusion-1 run at maximum rated power through bypassed load sharing systems to maintain the combat hull at Battle Status readiness. She also recommended that Power Systems and Propulsion main power be rerouted into the combat hull forward power systems. The extra effort needed to patch into the load-sharing system had not made Anailiatha happy at all.

Delwyn learned as much about his all-female crew by reading their reports as he did by watching them. Their insights amazed him as much as the anger they gave expression to in their writing. They didn't swear, didn't curse, but they made liberal use of furious or snotty turns of phrase.

A'pea themes recurred often in those sentiments.

Yet their feelings came through in the competent, well-reasoned reports and analyses. He wondered if engineering physicists writing technical reports in satirical prose would sound something like Anailiatha's emotionally charged engineering assessments.

Delwyn closed the file and exited Anailiatha's ledger. He scanned more supervising mistress icons until he came upon Mirrahindrallin's icon. Why would the Mistress of Saga file a battle damage assessment? She was the ship's historian and chronicler. What battle damage had she assessed? He opened the file and wished he hadn't as a casualty list numbering three hundred and fourteen dead belched forth.

Mirrahindrallin had also listed the clans the dead belonged to and a tentative schedule for him to visit them. He paged through the list, reading each casualty's biographical summary and noting her rank, honors, missions, and accomplishments. Mirrahindrallin had listed Kalinn last.

Delwyn read for a long time surrounded by silent infants, while Princess watched from his lap.

"Delwyn! They are here," Phelindra sang from the bole leading into his abode.

"Huh? Already?"

"Already? You have been in there for hours. Gellin and his Comari have been blocking my passage! When I asked him why, he smiled at me and said his Comari felt like standing there, watching infants."

"Well, I didn't put them up to it. I've been reading some entertaining BDAs and repair assessments from Melkorka and Anailiatha."

The Eldest Huntress laughed. She knew from firsthand experience the fiery tempers both females could summon, and she did not have to guess what they had said in their reports.

"Never mind that now," she said. "The Tribal Elders are in the Hall. Do not keep them waiting."

"I'm coming, I'm coming."

Delwyn stepped into a Hall of Voices filled with people. Near the original trunk five stood quietly, four Hunters and one Warrior, all of them older than Phelindra. Was that good or bad? He got along with Hunters, but something drew Warriors to him. He wondered why. Warriors were, in general, more conservative than Hunters. Then again, maybe those conclusions came from his subjective familiarity with Melkorka and Anailiatha.

Formal greetings were sung. The Elders told him about themselves, their roles as elders, and their clans. The Warrior and a Hunter represented two southern archipelago clans. The central interior clan representative was also a Hunter. Another two Hunters represented a seaside clan each. They wanted Delwyn to tour their wet navy facilities. The archipelago Elders wanted to take him out on the ocean and show him their tidal energy power stations and sea farms. The central interior Elder wanted him to inspect their science and technology center. Their collective enthusiasm disarmed him, making it even more of a shock when they suddenly glared at the knife strapped to his left hip.

"Delwyn, you do know it is unseemly for a declared adult not to wear his or her adulthood knife?" Eindvridi, the interior clan Tribal Elder asked.

"I do."

"Do you have the adulthood knife given to you upon finishing an ordeal meant to signify your adult status?" she asked.

Delwyn shook his head. "People on Earth are presumed an adult when they reach a universally applied minimum age. What I do after attaining that age defines my adulthood to me."

Virviran, the Warrior Elder, shook her head. "What passed for adulthood status in your former life, before you came to us, is not sufficient to our customs and traditions. We all know you are an adult, but we cannot give you an adulthood knife because you have not completed the survival ordeal and have not composed a song about what you learned about yourself. For an adult male his adulthood knife is made by his home clan from volcanic glass during a ritual. It is the outward symbol of clan adulthood, and other people and their clans will look to that symbol when engaging in social discourse with you.

"On several levels anyone you speak to and anyone watching you speak with other adults about adult matters will feel uncomfortable with your involvement on an equal standing. You understand that an Eyloni can die in old age and never earn adult status?"

"I do. It became obvious to me not long after I took Kidahin's adulthood knife. Had I not tied the knife back onto the harness below her breast no one aboard *Hunter's Moon* or when we returned here would have recognized her as an adult."

"Correct. You understand why this matter is so difficult for us?"

"I do."

"Then what alternative do you propose we accept? Should we send a request to your birth clan asking them to declare you an adult and award you with an adulthood knife?"

"No. I agree to participate in the survival ordeal on your land," Delwyn said.

Approving rhythmic murmurs echoed throughout the vast Hall.

"Do you understand what the survival ordeal entails? You are dropped naked into clan territory far from this tree. You cannot take clothing, food, water, or supplies. You must remain away from the extended families for one month. You may always return late, but you may not return before month's end."

"I understand."

"Very well. The honor of your association reflects well from you. Your survival ordeal will begin mid-orbital phase-2."

Six days and nine hours Earth time from now.

With the potential adult status problem settled in family and Tribal Elder minds, the gathering proceeded on to the regular communal evening meal. Once everyone had finished eating, the Tribal Elders vied for his ear. They tried to wrangle a commitment from him, some sign telling them which clan he might visit first.

Delwyn had no idea how to decide. Did clans fall under some hierarchical preference? Did some protocol he knew nothing about come into play? No clan elder so much as gave him a hint.

He didn't know what to do. O'un Tu Clan was a northeastern interior mountain clan. The central interior clan would be more of the same without the hills. The archipelago and seaside clans maintained a wet navy tradition. He wanted to board a vertical airfoil sailing ship and cruise along the shallow seas in the nearside ocean. Farming was in his blood too, and the archipelago sea farms sounded like just the right compromise: farming and wet navy shipping.

Elder Virviran from one of the archipelago clans sang exciting adventure tales. She told him about raging storms and western terminator wild sea passages. Delwyn had once taken a cruise from South America to the west coast of Australia, and the seas four hundred klicks off Perth had writhed in storms from colliding warm and cold ocean currents and the warm and cold fronts they generated.

The archipelago Elder Olrunka stepped in to regale him with tales about the farside ocean. Not much land marred the farside ocean surface except for a few La'huaset archipelago islands and the northernmost tip of the continent stretching into the north pole. The Big Island of the Mawe'allea Tribal continent and a third of the Zi'mondi Tribal continent also straddled the eastern terminator into the farside abyssal ocean. That ocean she described in terms he related to a cool Atlantic Ocean. The farside hemisphere averaged about fifteen degrees cooler than the nearside hemisphere, and the difference made for some wild weather along the terminators. The farside north and south poles had no land at all. The sea froze into thick ice sheets. Those sheets fractured and reformed repeatedly to form multiple tall pressure ridges. Ice quakes split white monoliths off into the current, seeding the northern and southern farside oceans with lumbering ice floes. The Elder also helped her cause by describing research missions those supercavitation ships took part in. She had his complete enthralled attention.

Something warned him then. It started out as a subtle feeling, an ethereal nudge. Something felt wrong. Not threatening, but the emotion in the room made him twitch. He blinked to clear his head and focused on the other three Elders.

The two Hunters from the seaside clans seemed lost, as though cast adrift. Their ears perked wide apart, tips pointing perpendicular to their temples and dipping downward. A clear sign they felt left out and alone. Social relationships mattered in Eyloni life. The interior clan Tribal Elder Eindvridi had withdrawn into herself as well.

Delwyn stared at Virviran and Olrunka until they smelled his changing pheromones and shifted their attention to the other three Elders.

Virviran's sharp intake of breath told him she finally realized that she was hogging male attention. Olrunka came to the same conclusion seconds later. Horrified, they asked forgiveness for the social debt. Delwyn redirected the discussion to the southern coastal clan Tribal Elders and their shipping fleets. He asked about the challenges of sailing a wind-powered cargo ship across the terminators.

Competitive and seeking to outdo the archipelago clans, they double-teamed their stories about high seas and freezing sprays, the difficulty of navigating protected coral reefs in heavy storms, firing station thrusters to hold a course, or even dropping the sails when necessary and using the ship's hydrodynamic engine, an engine that generated thrust by squirting water like a jet engine exhausted hot air.

"Why not just use the engines to drive the ship and scrap the sail technology?" he asked them.

"Hydrodynamic propulsion consumes power and is unnecessary when so much wind power is available. Hydrodynamic and supercavitation engines are used when speed is needed, the ship is becalmed, or when storm winds do not cooperate," one of the seaside Elders explained.

"Many times transporting cargo by airship is the better solution," Eindvridi added.

"Airships?" Delwyn echoed. Hadn't someone mentioned lighter-than-air ships before?

She nodded. "Lighter-than-air airships haul cargo from naval stations to the interior clans and from them back to the naval stations. We also use them to deliver goods across a continent rather than sailing around it."

She meant zeppelins and dirigibles: early twentieth century technology. "Why use zeppelins?" he demanded. "You have quantum teleport technology and aircraft."

"Quantum translation is energy wasteful and is used to transport items not otherwise easily moved by other means. Aircraft make occasional point-to-point deliveries, but bulk shipment to, say southern Myat'ti'deep, Sa'ranja, or Zi'mondi Tribal continents are sometimes best done by airships. Once they navigate into the global air currents only thrusters are necessary to maintain course and trim."

Delwyn changed his mind as another choice filled his head with visions involving blimp cruises.

"Do they take passengers?" he asked.

Eindvridi smiled. She had him by the tail now. "Shipping airships have room enough to convey a hand or two, but they are cargo vessels. People fly on airships if they want transport to the delivery point."

"How much does it cost?" he asked.

"Cost?" Eindvridi asked, at a loss on how to interpret his scent against her poor Coalition language skills. "You mean trade? You help them fly their airship and they take you with them, simple and plain."

Delwyn had forgotten again. Eyloni had no money-based economy. They had a service-exchange barter system. He only had to perform a useful service during the flight and the crew would allow him to travel with them to their next stop.

"What about pleasure cruises?" Maybe they had travel agencies booking airship cruises, like those on Earth in the 1930s.

"Pleasure cruise? Cruising for enjoyment on an airship?" Olrunka interrupted, shuddering.

"Yes, flying above the trees for pleasure," Virviran said. Her lips, ears, and tail all twitching in humor at the Hunter's discomfort. "I find hanging above the forest quite stimulating. Really, I do not see how it can be much different from floating on the ocean."

The archipelago Hunter smiled a tight smile but shook her head. "It is not the same. The ocean is on the ground."

Phelindra whispered in his ear. "Remember what I said about Zalzadrin? In general we Hunters do not care for hanging in the middle of the air."

"I take it Warriors don't mind it as much?" he whispered back.

"No." She gave him an accusing glare. "And all males love air travel."

"Me too," he conceded. "I'd love to fly across the continents on a zeppelin."

Phelindra and Zalzadrin glared at him, muttering a shared phrase under their breath: *males are strange.*

The seaside coastal Hunters delighted in Delwyn's enthusiasm, even if they did not share his desire to ride atop a floating leaf, one ready to fall to the ground at any time.

"We should go together sometime!" Phalalin sang.

Phelindra gave him her best withering stare. "You say nothing the whole time you sit here, do not offer to defend Delwyn's adulthood status, and now when you do speak, you invite him on an airship ride?"

"Delwyn and I already talked about his adulthood knife problem. I stood ready to help if he needed advice. He has chosen the survival ordeal. I will brief him on how to prepare for it later.

"However, that reminds me Delwyn, over the next few days you should eat carbohydrates."

Delwyn gave Phalalin an offhanded shrug. He knew how to bulk up on carbs.

Phelindra listened to the two males, but something picked at the back of her mind. How should she approach talking Delwyn out of a trip on an airship? Oh, she was not afraid. She tolerated air travel by imagining looking down from a tall elleiu tree. A tree where your climbing skill mattered for naught, where a pilot's skill held you tail twined to any error in judgment she happened to make.

***

Days later Phalalin came to Delwyn's abode and asked Phelindra, Zalzadrin, Hervorallin, a few visitors, and all the infants to leave.

His request did not go over well.

"Go on everybody," Delwyn said, remembering how Anlann had shooed Kidahin and Seralin from his quarters on Ibeetu. "Phalalin and I must have a male-to-male talk."

Phelindra and Amindaldra appealed to him at first. Then they appealed to Phalalin. Without success, and they left grumbling and complaining.

But Hervorallin had the last word after all when she sang a melody to Princess.

The infant Hunter dropped from her mother's back and climbed up Delwyn's side.

Since Princess was not leaving, then the infants would not leave, either.

Phalalin sighed, resigned. In general no one told Eyloni infants what to do. They followed their own hierarchy, and they obeyed higher ranked females. For the most part, infants free-ranged until they were old enough to learn teaching songs. Until then, they learned by watching social exchanges among their extended family members. They showed the same fussy cleanliness as the adults did. They knew how to use the necessary. They went to females to nurse and for company and didn't need constant care.

Human babies were loud, squalling poop factories by comparison. Human toddlers suffered from 'the terrible twos', and Eyloni infants did have a stubborn streak. They didn't ask 'why', but they did watch and learn.

Delwyn glared at Phalalin and shrugged his shoulders.

Phalalin smiled and swept his tail to include the infants. "You will not lose them. Hervorallin asked Princess to stay and she signaled them to stay."

Delwyn nodded, and they got down to business.

"Think about this as an assault briefing," Phalalin began. "First, let us discuss the time period involved.

"A male remains in the forest for one TST month. You will begin the ordeal midway through orbital phase-2, when the sun reaches its mid-afternoon point in the sky. From that point you will have ten days and thirty hours of sunlight remaining before phase-4 brings the night.

"Night travel is always dangerous. The forest animals own the night. It also becomes quite cool after two days of darkness. You might not find it so uncomfortable. The night rains are cold, and your skin lacks the natural water repellant ours have. You need to find a waxy substitute before nightfall.

"While you can travel short distances in the night with caution, do not prowl over long stretches. Find a tree and stay there. Take several hours to find a good tree and provision it before sunset. You might find the smaller elleiu trees best, but remember the mature ones contain families and you are forbidden to approach them.

"In your place, I would make a knife and a spear first. Then take a *wol'ha* blossom, fill it with water, and tie its petals together. It will make a decent canteen if you are careful with it."

Phalalin had a lot to say, and Delwyn absorbed the briefing. As he did so he recognized how relieved he was to have met Phalalin. Males shared such knowledge with adolescents when they prepared them for their survival ordeals.

Phalalin mentioned at this latitude temperate rainforests dominated, covering the ground with broadleaf hardwoods some three-hundred ells tall.

Growing below them other trees some twenty to one hundred forty ells tall flourished. Above them was the emergent layer and at this latitude there were less dense scatterings of elleiu trees then those in the tropical rainforest. The forest floor was packed with dense shrubs, mosses, grasses, and bamboo-palm tree scrub.

It rained often and a hand below the surface soil stayed damp. Rains saturated the ground in no time at all, which soon gave way to runoff that drained into washes, gullies, and slot canyons.

Phalalin warned Delwyn to stay away from the slot canyons. Rains coming over the mountains or stationary storms overhead or upstream brought rushing water crashing down them. Rainforests had marginal seasonal change other than wet and dry seasons, and La'huaset was heading into the wet season.

Phalalin's final advice urged him to stockpile adequate food and water, rain cover, weapons, and sleeping bindings in a good tree before sundown.

16
NAKED AND ALONE

"Do not attempt to make a fire and camp on the ground during the night," Delwyn recited to himself as he rode in the VTOL aircraft with his ears plugged, his eyes covered, and his nose pinched shut.

They'd been flying for over an hour now, trying to confuse his direction sense and distance estimates.

A half hour later they landed, pulled him out the hatch, yanked off his custom loincloth and underthong, and left him counting down like a game of hide-and-seek before he could remove the eye, ear, and nose coverings.

When he reached 625, he removed his blinders and glanced at the sun in its 15h00 skyclock position.

Elleio had just passed midway through her orbital phase-2 sector around Tyreniioroneo. Three nearside longitudinal zones and one farside longitudinal zone experienced daylight as the sun crept across the western terminator. By the time phase-5 arrived, darkness would claim nearside. A day and a half later the sun would rise over the eastern terminator, renewing the seemingly endless day-night cycle.

The heavy jungle cover didn't hide the mountains now. They were much closer than when he had taken his bearings before leaving the O'ni'da families trees.

The mountain view told him he'd been dropped in the same fifty-five-degree north latitudes but a lot farther west.

He pivoted north. Nearby rolling hills flattened out in the distance toward the northern polar ocean. That meant he had been dropped on the north slope, along the crater rim mountains, at a higher elevation, and somewhere along a diagonal line between the hydroelectric plant at the end of Om'tu Lake and the O'ni'da elleiu trees. If he had to put a number to it, then he guessed he stood some thirty to fifty klicks west of home and no farther than sixty klicks.

The peaceful forest conjured restful scenes, and he fought the urge to regard it as a typical autumn deciduous Earth forest. It harbored deadly features and animals. For all its beauty, the rainforest was alien.

He saw elleiu trees clumped together in a line far to the east but didn't see the O'ni'da trees among them.

That explained the drop off in the middle of nowhere. He shrugged.

Survival training said to seek running water and follow it downstream. His best route should take him up and around the foothills to the Fire River Falls and follow the mighty Om'tu River downstream and then cut back into the forest when he paralleled his home tree.

He crossed a runoff ditch and paused for a few minutes to pry a middle finger-long sharp serrated stone from the damp ground before continuing through the rainforest. Every so often he paused to reacquire his bearings. He could lose his way surrounded by so much bracketing foliage.

Dense jungle greeted him from all sides. Trees and grasses matching Eyloni skin coloring—pumpkin, crimson, and yellow ocher—surrounded him. The hot humid air forced him to move with a deliberate slowness. Breaks in the heat came from rare mountain breezes or north winds. He walked on, reconnoitering the immediate area, searching for drinking water and some plants to eat. He peered up into the trees searching for the bright sun. It hovered in the afternoon sky somewhere around the 15h40 hour skyclock time. That was deceptive: nightfall was some thirty-six hours away.

He couldn't afford to drift off task. Food didn't worry him while the daylight remained, but the increasing temperatures building up over the past four and three-quarter Earth days made finding water a higher priority than food before water loss affected his ability to cope with the environment.

Delwyn searched for the vines Kidahin had described. She said many different vines grew in the forest. The parasitic green plants drew water and nutrients from the trees and held them in fleshy hollow vines under tough thin bark. Most of them contained drinkable water. "Take your time," she had advised. "Some tree saps contained water laced with tannic acid, toxins, poisons, and sugars." He had to find the right parasitic vines on the right trees.

He found a green vine hanging down from a tall broadleaf. He jumped high and cut the vine off as he pulled its corkscrew roots from the tree. Kidahin had warned him not to cut it near the ground and try to drink from the cut end. A cut vine sucked all its precious stolen nutrients and water up into itself. He cut the other end before putting it into his mouth like a straw and drank about two liters of the green tea-tasting water.

Delwyn used the same sharp stone he cut the vine with to saw off a thumb-sized piece, split it, and rolled it into a plug. He cut down a second vine and stuffed the cork halfway into one end, bent the vine into a hoop, and plugged it into the other end. Now he had a water-filled hoop to wear around his neck.

He gathered what dry kindling he could find. It was the most valuable resource after water. Smoke from fire would keep insects at bay while he slept. Fire and smoke frightened wild animals. Fire cooked food too, and some tubers and starchy plants needed cooking to make them more digestible.

Phalalin had told him before he left not to make daylight campsites. The successful strategy called for sleeping in trees. He'd never find enough wood for fires, and the night hunters wouldn't fear small fires in any event. Ground sleeping, if necessary, should be restricted to brief daytime naps. He'd have to brave the trees eventually.

He planned as he worked. He needed to get through the forest and arrive back in O'ni'da families territory in one TST month, and he had to do all the traveling in half a month, some three days four hours, first. Then he'd climb up into a tree for the six day and eight-hour night before he'd have another day to finish traveling if he arrived on time. He could use the last two days of orbital phase-1 to finish if he had to. That would keep him in the forest for almost thirteen Earth days, longer than a TST month.

Delwyn set about making a better knife, a spear, sandals, a hat, and clothing to shield him from occasional direct sunlight. One break so far had been the dense forest, but even under the trees the ground had an orange glow matching a cut acorn squash.

It took effort to find landmarks. He knew all about green Earth forests. He even had a feel for the dahlia-purple and aquamarine Ibeetu forests. Both had greenish cover scattered with brown trunks, brown sticks, brown twigs, dark shade, and sun-dappled dark umber patches of standing water.

This temperate rainforest pulsed with ocher and pastel vermilions, pumpkins, scarlets, and crimsons. Subtle and sometimes not so subtle yellowed orange, yellow ocher, goldenrod, and sunburst yellow trims broke up the reds but didn't make a difference. Tree trunk bark varied from white, French gray, beige sienna, and henna to burnt ochers. Shade lost all meaning to him as sunlight filtered through the colorful leaves. The forest, bright and shade sparse, teased his visual awareness. Evolution had programmed him to suspect the dark as a likely hiding place for hidden dangers. The relative brightness cast the forest in Earth fall color familiarity. It looked and felt safe.

Only a fool would think so.

Trees covered with yellow mosses backlit by the sun glowed as if they had auras. The relentless faded ocher glow would sun-blind him over the long planetary day. Reflected goldenrod light already gave him afterimages whenever he glanced down at the chestnut soil or closed his eyes.

The trees around him dwarfed redwoods. On the distant horizon, elleiu trees towered over them, home trees where other O'un Tu Clan family groups lived.

Mustard mosses growing on nearby trees sported black magnolia blossoms. Green color twisted through the mosses, reminding him again that green meant plants were dead or dying marked the presence of infrequently occurring parasitic vines.

He headed down a wandering trail. Up ahead ruts of standing water reflected pastel shades, making it hard for him to gauge how deep they went.

Hours ran together as Delwyn hiked through chest-high orange ferns. Vines ran pale yellow on the ground among the chest-high clumps. Every ten centimeters or so a thumb-sized black begonia blossom poked through burnt orange moss. The moss grew on the nearest trees, giving the rusty bark a long dead and rotted cast, yet they lived. They created niches for other plants. The mahogany soil had a peaty feel to it. It gave a bit under his weight, making occasional squishy sounds. Holes dug in it filled with water in less than fifteen minutes.

Delwyn followed soggy puddle after soggy puddle until he stumbled into a clearing at least a kilometer long and fifty narrow meters wide. Three rough granite boulders, an ancient landslide remnant unclaimed by the forest, stood as sentinels barring access to a curved small lake. Amber grasses and sable reeds grew from the water into the surrounding trees. Violet bladder plants floated on the water among pale yellow lily pads. Fall leaves raked from a hundred lawns paved the shallow lake bottom. Tall narrow tan trees, dead pines, stood on the far shore.

He walked along the trees around the silver lake to reach them.

The trees didn't smell piny when he bruised their leaves. An almost familiar resin scent floated on the air, but he couldn't remember what it reminded him of. The trees didn't have needles either. The amber and sand leaves looked like crocus flowers down to the white streak in a crocus leaf. Hervorallin called these trees permaleafs because they never shed their leaves.

Most rainforest trees dropped their leaves at some point, but they dropped off when they suffered irreparable damage, when hit by rare frost at this latitude, or when they simply wore out. Most trees had leaves as large as or larger than his body. The trees couldn't waste energy to replace them all at once, so they replaced them a few at a time. Some broadleaf trees had permanent leaves too, which they shed. But like the crocus pines, they kept their leaves unless new growth pinched old leaves off the branches.

Permaleaves healed when damaged. If the damage did not heal, then they fell off.

He stepped away from the trees into the straw grasses and sunk to his knees. Warned to watch for hidden water, he waded back to the trees and dry ground.

The creeping sun made it an unreliable means to gauge progress over time. It took the sun hours to creep through 15h50 skyclock time. It disheartened and disoriented him when his body told him he'd been in the field for hours, but the sky said he'd been out for a mere forty minutes total.

The crocus trees ran along a jagged line into the otherwise broadleaf forest. Softball-sized purple clinkers, like the stuff once used to protect railroad embankments from erosion, along with cobalt-blue stones littered the ground. Blue clinker paths ran in veins strewn through the forest where ground cover hadn't reburied them yet. Among the broadleafs grew even stranger trees. Brown trunks grew some fifteen to thirty meters and then stopped as if cut flat off. Around the flat top and spiraling inward at least thirty fernlike fronds grew. Each frond grew up to fifteen meters long and bowed downward, giving the trees a pleated umbrella look. The fronds, bright apricot, overlapped to give each tree a twenty-meter-wide spread. Here and there a frond had snapped at its midpoint and sagged down, turning light green as it hung there dying. Each frond had small leaves, and the light blue cloudless sky gleaming through them was stunning.

On the ground, more cobalt paths wandered through the forest. They felt like volcanic rock, broken up ancient lava fields long eroded down into soil and clinkers. To the farmer mind in Delwyn, the stuff felt insubstantial. It made the soil fertile but lacking the peaty prevailing soil, volcanic cinders and clinkers didn't hold much water for long. Yet, there was water everywhere. That fact alone told him it rained often. Prodding at the purple slag with his spear he found rubble beneath, fractured slag and pumice from what had once been a volcanic vent.

Small trees grew among the tall ones, some reaching only forty meters before the other trees blocked the direct sunlight. They stood out like stumpy burnt out match tops, missing leaves and covered with clubfoot mosses.

Water fell up ahead. The roar rose in volume as he walked. The air turned sultry, and the mosses dominated every surface. Rough blue clinkers broke through the ground and continued into a broken-up pavement. He'd been right. This had been a lava field in ages past. He saw the grain, how it had flowed. Moss covered it now, along with old soggy logs and long dead branches strewn across the ground.

Delwyn broke through the dense mossy undergrowth and stumbled onto slippery rocks and waterlogged wood.

Damn! Water plunged in torrents, cascading down rocks littering a wide deep pit, a flooded volcanic vent. The ground around him felt slick under his handmade sandals, and he couldn't see into the pit without risking a fall into watery oblivion. Creeping on hands and knees, he approached the stony edge and watched water spilling onto rubble and sluicing off into the pit, keeping it filled to a constant level forty meters below him. Around the edge the soil had lost its peaty nature in favor of soggy packed moss. A few maple leaf plants grew from stems stuck into the ground, as big as those on Canadian flags and painted pale yellow. The moss grew in the same patterns as reddish-yellow brain corals. Phalalin had called them o'ka'me and said they were edible. Thoughts about eating them evaporated at the sight around him. Other mosses grew among them, covering the ground and reminding him of scum from some drained pond.

Ugh!

He didn't dare try to circumnavigate the flooded vent. He'd have to go far around it. To the right eroded lava fields covered with more moss looked treacherous. On the left side a vague trail climbed a slow rise into the broadleaf trees.

He'd have to swing up and around through them until he reached the tall burlap bark trees behind them. Those trees grew crammed together. He walked among them and marveled on not seeing a single tree fused into its neighbor. The ground around them didn't have its usual fernlike plant coverage but did have more maple leaf plants. A meter across, they hung at thigh level. The farther from the waterfall they grew, the more yellow they turned.

He tore a strip off a leaf, put it in his mouth, and chewed. It tasted like spinach with a dandelion sap bite.

Delwyn looked for green vines, a guaranteed safe water source. He found none.

He climbed along the trail and ran into more fractured lava fields buried partway in the leaf litter and mosses. The ground dropped into a gentle decline and water seeped up from the ground to trickle across his path. Up ahead the trickles met at a large deep pool, an artesian well judging by its size, obvious depth, and motionless surface. Runoff was causing it to overflow and drain into the forest.

The trees thinned out into ferns and palms similar to Earth varieties in shape if not in color or size. One lone invader didn't seem to belong, some kind of weird radial fern tree. It sported what looked like a giant orange carnation instead of branches and leaves made from layered ferns. No other tree matched its beauty.

Delwyn followed the trickling ditch because the ground around him had become too rocky and slippery to walk on. Granite boulders barred his easy passage. Their scarlet moss coverings and orange fern trim hid crevices and shallow holes. The beautiful cover proved distracting as crimson four leaf clover leaves two handprints wide speckled the ground all around the granite barriers.

Seepage from the spongy soil swelled the spring overflow into a creek. Here and there it bubbled over stone slabs, sheared limestone crammed around the edges with moss-covered flood debris.

More permaleaf trees grew all around him. The tall trees seemed strangely denuded. They had knotty, gnarly trunks and branches pale yellow with vermilion leaves. The trees didn't have many leaves, and Delwyn wondered how the trees could survive with so few of them. Up ahead for kilometers on end stood rocky hills covered with them.

Crossing the creek proved no problem. He waded through water much warmer than he expected. He walked for some time before reaching burlap barked trees. There he found more clubfoot trees. The clubfoots had a different colored moss covering, a pale yellow and golden mix hanging from the branches like ones on weeping willows. Black flowers struggled through the moss, themselves surrounded by orange ferns.

###

"Why are you here Kidahin?" Trebithia demanded.

The Mistress of Pathwalking stood on the main trail just outside the Wrathsee'a Anchorage transport bay arrival center, arms crossed beneath her breasts, and glared at Kidahin.

The last person Kidahin expected, or wanted to see, was Trebithia.

She had been told to contact Trebithia. She had left her a text message two days ago and had not received a reply during her time on A'lon'aloop nor during her flight here.

"Well?" Trebithia demanded.

"I am here on ship's business," Kidahin sang stiffly.

"Oh you are, are you? That excuse works on others, but I am your supervising mistress. I did not send for you, and I am certain Melkorka did not, either."

"Nevertheless, I am on ship's business," Kidahin repeated.

"What business?" Trebithia persisted.

"For Delwyn."

"For Delwyn? What are you doing for the warleader that Melkorka, Hlinlodyn, or I cannot do?" Trebithia demanded. "And what are you doing carrying Delwyn's old chest covering? Do not tell me you are returning it to his quarters. He does not wear those things anymore."

"Delwyn has agreed to take the O'un Tu Clan adulthood survival ordeal!" Kidahin wailed.

Trebithia halted in mid-rant. No. Impossible. Everyone knew Delwyn was an adult, knew he had been an adult longer than anyone aboard their warship had been alive.

"When?" Trebithia demanded.

"He is already several hours into the ordeal!" Kidahin said.

Trebithia cursed. "Does Melkorka know?"

"I do not think so."

"What about Phelindra? She knows. Why did she not contact us?"

"How should I know?" Kidahin's voice rose. "I was not there. They are not my clan, remember?"

Trebithia bit her tongue to keep a disgraceful insult from passing her lips. Of course she knew Kidahin did not belong to the O'un Tu Clan, as if Trebithia ever forgot something as important as her helmsmistress's clan affiliation.

"What can you do about it? You look like an infant carrying that cloth around in your hand," Trebithia scolded.

"Delwyn has not had enough time to adjust to the rainforest. He has not been here for more than a few days. He needs help."

Trebithia froze in shock for a moment, shook it off, and glared at Kidahin.

"No one can help a person during a survival ordeal. They told you the same thing before you took yours, just as they told me the same thing before I took mine. It is the same for everyone going back ten-thousand centuries."

"There is a special case for males!" Kidahin insisted.

Trebithia shook her head. "The male ordeal lasts for one Tyreniioroneo month instead of the three Elleio months we must endure. That is the only exception granted a male!"

Kidahin snapped her head around, her anger rising. "There is another one, a rare one!"

"What? Tell me! The one true special case for males does not apply to him."

"But it could!" Kidahin objected.

"How? Tell me how!" Trebithia demanded. "How does he qualify? I know what you are thinking. It will not work. You are coming close to poking your tail into a private matter. You could get yourself killed!"

"I am going to ask the Mistress of the Dock to help me."

Trebithia glared at the young Hunter. "Lindredha will cut your tail off and hand it to you if you involve her in this insane idea of yours," Trebithia warned.

"She belongs to Delwyn's personal association."

Trebithia let that go for the moment and shook her head, snapping her tail for emphasis. "That gets you her attention. She has responsibilities here. She is not going to run down trails leafchasing fantasies with you."

"She can use her shipyard resources to help."

"Not if Havalin says no," Trebithia growled. "This is not their affair. It is, as you claim, warship's business. They are not going to interfere, even to preserve his life when the A'tayotan wants him included in the battle group. It is not even a certainty our warship will achieve Battle Status capability in time."

"I still want to talk to her," Kidahin said, her tail and ears assuming a stubborn set.

"As you wish," a frustrated Trebithia snapped.

Kidahin left the transport arrival center and hurried down the main jungle trail.

Privately, Trebithia hoped Kidahin would succeed. Maybe the scented chest covering she carried would help.

###

Delwyn squeezed between thick tree trunks and stood before a stone wall. Above him towered craggy limestone cliffs. Bone white to light gray, they had a drizzled-with-acid look about them.

Could that have happened? Elleio had more carbon dioxide in the atmosphere than Earth, so carbonic acid could rain out, couldn't it?

Delwyn didn't know much about climate science, but he thought the chemistry sounded right. The limestone had been etched as if hot water had been dribbled onto an ice cube. From a distance, the etchings had looked jagged and sharp, but up close they looked smooth, weathered. This mountain range had not been formed by uplifts from plate tectonic activity.

Elleio had minimal volcanic activity. The heat from ancient asteroid impacts had churned up its core; gravitational tidal forces from Tyreniioroneo squeezed and stretched the core just enough to keep it and the mantle molten to form a magnetic field-generating dynamo. Tyreniioroneo's magnetic field extended just far enough into space to envelop Elleio's orbit with a secondary magnetic field. Without the dual particle shield, solar winds would have made life impossible ages ago.

The crustal chemistry and mantle temperatures gave Elleio a plastic crust, one more resistant to fracture. While it did float on the mantle, and although it did have fractures left by the ancient cataclysmic asteroid impact, the crust remained cracked just as a cracked hard-boiled egg remained cracked. The shattered pieces stayed more or less in place kissing against one another, but the mantle lacked sufficient turbulence to drive them into one another. The ancient impactor had gouged out all the uplifted mountains from its crater walls and from all the disrupted and dislocated crust along the rim. Impact-spawned volcanos poured magma through the shattered crust, producing volcanic mountains as tall as Olympus Mons on Mars, stratospheric cones that dwarfed Mount Everest. Erosion over the centuries had worn them down to still impressive remnants. The same wearing had exposed this limestone and marble mountain, itself a fossil graveyard for shelled creatures living long ago in an abyssal sea. Limestone deposits so badly eroded meant pitfalls and caves littered the area.

He turned left and followed the narrow gravel path around the cliff face. Skirting around the limestone heap beat jungle slogging any day. He likened it to walking around a crumbling skyscraper several city-blocks wide. The limestone folded in on itself in places, forming columns fused to the massive edifice. Rubble covered the two-to-eight-meter-wide berm. The rubble leaned away from the cliffs too, in some spots quite steep. Marble slabs had separated from the limestone and tumbled down the steep slide to be lost in the concealing jungle. He had to hug the cliff to keep from causing a landslide that would take him down to a forest burial.

He made good time. The clear path let him maintain a pace he could only dream of while shouldering through the jungle. The smooth and weathered cliff had been split by cracks and hollowed out by running water over time. Some cracks he barely fit into but others were several meters wide. They didn't run straight either, and he had no idea how deep they ran into the mountain. Unlike the pastel orange forest, the dry fissures were dark and probable dead ends. He didn't know what beasties might lurk in them and didn't want to find out.

Delwyn glanced at the distant eroded limestone cliff edge above. The weathering gave the limestone a petrified coral reef texture, if the corals had polyps a meter across. The slow-moving bright pale-yellow sun gave the uniform impressions a spooky bleached bonepile pall.

The ghosts and goblins common to humanity's ghost stories had no place here.

Delwyn thought about those stories as he dodged sharp stones his crude bast sandals couldn't shield his feet from. Eyloni sang about and to their spirits, but those songs never ventured into macabre horror. They told no Grimm brothers fairy tales. They sang about artistic truths, metaphysical ideas, or empirical facts. They also sang to aid didactic learning or for simple entertainment, but they never told murder mysteries, no slash and gore. They didn't have ghost stories either, no undead. The jungles conjured enough fearsome horrors, and they didn't need supernatural terrors to quicken the heart. Their songs addressed nature's beauty, proper behavior, family ties, and social issues revolving around moral or point of honor themes.

He rounded a curve and ran into two limestone pillars that had eroded away from the cliff face. He imagined them as the middle and index fingers a stone giant might have held up in a V-for-victory sign. One towered above him, over a hundred meters, the other stood a bit shorter. Both ends, as flat as tabletops, would allow ten people to stand side by side hands outstretched.

He passed between them and continued around the pockmarked and blasted limestone wall and stumbled into a cave. Darkness made even darker by the surrounding washed out yellow-orange forest brightness filled the wide, short maw.

He stepped inside and walked a few meters into a limestone vault. Cautious, he waited for his eyes to adjust. Phosphorescent slime glowed in eerie ghostly beauty. Blues, blue-white, and pale green blobs and streaks filled the cavern as far as he could see. Walls alternated between uneven pale patterns and pitch blackness. Whether the black areas gave away rocks unappetizing to the slime or actual voids he couldn't even guess.

The cave sagged under the mountain and continued for several hundred meters or more. Like the bright pastel ochers outside, the cold dim light in the cave screwed up his depth perception. Blotchy patterns floated in his field of vision like retinal afterimages. It took him a few minutes to recall that afterimages would follow his gaze, and these glowing splotches stayed put.

Delwyn followed the cave into a level chamber. Above, the ceiling sloped upward into a long, narrow dome. An alphafortress troop transport could stand on its tail where he stood and not touch the ceiling.

This chamber covered an area at best fifty meters wide. Gravel, stones, and large rocks had been dropped into dips along the cave floor. Floodwater did this. Stalagmites and stalactites taller than he attested to the limestone formation's ancient origins.

Water dripped from the ceiling and down walls. The seepage produced runnels, and they trickled into clay deposits and sand bars filling the deeper depressions. Overflowing puddles dotted the floor as they wound deep into the cave. No glowing slime grew anywhere near the struggling tiny creek, giving Delwyn a not so subtle hint that when it rained sufficient seepage and cliff runoff from outside turned the hesitating trickle into a raging river half a meter deep and up to three meters wide in places.

Delwyn weighed his options. The cave offered him a possible shortcut. It might turn into a convenient way around both the cloud rainforest and the insurmountable stone cliffs. Then again, it could dive below the ground never to return to the surface, a fatal dead end. He shrugged. If nothing was ventured, then nothing was ever gained.

After more than an hour of cautious walking he found a ragged split in the floor. The echoing sound of flowing water made his hair stand on end as it betrayed the underground river rushing below. Maybe the underground river flowed below the cave. If so, then he stood in the middle of an upper tier in an at least two-level cavern system. The lower caverns were either partially or completely flooded.

This was an old cave system, at least six or seven hundred million years old for this much limestone and sediment to form, erode, and uplift.

Delwyn stopped for a closer look at the white pale light glowing off the walls. Up close the slime smelled like iron water mixed with wet lime. He touched it. It felt like a gob of snot laced with cobwebs. It stuck to his fingers as he pulled them away like spider webs, trailing a gleaming filament. It glowed with the constant light of a weak candle.

The glow gave him an idea. The ooze glowed just enough to outline peaks, depressions, arches, and spires. He needed a portable light source to probe the dark pits and crevasses dotting the floor. And having light—any light—gave reassurances.

He looked around for signs of former or current animal occupants. No Eyloni had ever lived here. They had always been tree-dwellers, unlike his human ancestors when they came down from the trees into drying savannas and much later sheltered in caves likes these. This cave alone dwarfed the Miao Room passage in China's Ziyun Getu He Chaundong National Park. He'd been there once and knew from seeing it for himself.

He avoided the damp clay deposits, trickling pools, and even the slippery edges. No telling how deep they went or what might live in them.

###

"I need your help," Kidahin said. "Delwyn is in danger. The Tribal Elders have suggested he complete the survival ordeal so they can award him the adulthood knife. But he is unprepared. As we speak, he prowls O'un Tu Clan territory. If you do nothing, he will die."

The female listened to the young Hunter, confusion warring with indignant affront. Who did this female think she was baiting? The Hunter carried a ball of cloth, a cloth having the most wonderful scent about it.

And here this young Hunter had baited her with it!

She scented Kidahin, sampling her pheromones for clues. Why had she come to the shipyard? To accost her like this made an unseemly public display. She had things to do, a male to find, and this Hunter stood before her waving the one male scent she wanted, filling her nose with it, teasing her.

Livid, the female switched to battle language.

<<You intrude, Kidahin Uahua'asee'a La'huaset Eyloni. You intrude, and you tease. His warship has priority repair status. I wait for him to return here. I will kill you should you interfere.>>

Kidahin smelled the irate female's scent. Kidahin's brain, like all Eyloni, had strong wiring between olfactory and language centers. Pheromones formed words in her mind, and right now this female's scent caused a flurry of words to fly through her head in one long run-on sentence.

That sentence screamed fury. The pale lithe female wanted an association with Delwyn, obviously. She also wanted it on her terms, not one arbitrated by Kidahin. Strictly speaking, this female stalked the most intimate of privacy interests in Eyloni society.

"You have to go. You must leave Wrathsee'a Anchorage and return to Elleio, to O'un Tu Clan territory," Kidahin said.

<<Why?>>

"Because Delwyn will die if you do not!"

<<Why?>>

"He has never prowled our jungles before. He knows nothing about them!"

<<You belong to his association. Why did you not teach him?>>

"I did not know he would agree to participate in the ordeal. He is an adult by the standards of his home clan."

<<I know he is an adult. I would not have shown an interest in him had he not been an adult.>>

Kidahin brightened. That thought had never occurred to her. Females did not scent mark adolescent males. The co-Ambassadors Anlann and Seralin had been the first Eyloni to scent mark Delwyn, followed by Phelindra, Melkorka, and herself, and later by her warship's society.

"You could tell them you would never scent mark an adolescent."

<<Why?>> she signed. <<If he participates in the ordeal, he does so to satisfy his honor and to uphold his associations' honor and the honor of those speaking with him in public.>>

"You can help him," Kidahin pleaded. "No dishonor would accrue to you or him should you go to him. By tradition your wishes supersede any argument the Elders could mount. They know we would never associate with an adolescent male, and they know you cannot bond with one."

<<No.>>

"Why not?" Kidahin cried. "Only you can save him!"

<<How do you know he needs saving? I might insult his honor just by my appearance.>>

"You cannot take the chance. Just days ago he did not even know what the jungle smelled like. Zalzadrin O'un Tu La'huaset Eyloni told me the first wildlife Delwyn met was a ke'nah only a few days ago, and now he prowls blindly through jungle only days before the long night!"

Kidahin's fear scent moved the seething female more than her emotional argument.

That and the constant reminder of his scent balled up in Kidahin's hand. She had smelled its intoxicating odor the moment Kidahin entered the shipyard. She had been waiting for this very scent to return to her, and she had been infuriated when she found that he had not come with Kidahin.

Kidahin's scent told her that she had not staged this meeting as a ploy to draw her to him.

That was good.

She perked her ears, felt them brush against her long pale hair. She regarded Kidahin with rabid fury tempered with a grudging respect. For Kidahin to impose upon her private mind impressed her as brave, although stupid. Kidahin had acted like his protectress in this matter. She was not, but her bravery revealed the character of the male she wanted. Kidahin reflected his honor.

Of course he was an adult. The idea he might not have been burned within her, kindling a fire, a raging inferno. Those elders risked his life! If he died in the forest, then he could not come to her, because he would never return to the shipyard.

<<He participates in the adulthood ritual to proclaim his honor. His honor is reflected in your scent. I find this attractive,>>she signed.

Kidahin smelled pride, pride and a single-minded possessiveness rolling off the angry female. And she was angry, furious at Kidahin for poking her tail into the female's interests. Doing such a thing to any female risked much. The risk increased when the female ranked you in hierarchical standings.

That risk turned to danger, a suicidal one, when it came to poking a tail into a Comari's interests.

A pale streak darted at Kidahin. Before she could react, the Comari snatched the tee-shirt, tore it from Kidahin's grasp, and fled the shipyard with it.

"I thought for sure she would kill you," Lindredha yelled from safe distant cover. "Only the foolish or the desperate would confront a Comari with demands. You have raised the stakes to a whole new level by making demands concerning the male she is interested in. I should like to think you have made history, but I prefer not to think about the mess she could have made of you in my shipyard."

Still talking, the Mistress of the Dock broke cover and strode up to Kidahin. "When you told me about your plan, I told Warleader Havalin you would likely fail. He thought otherwise. He likes Delwyn. That does not matter now.

"She was content to prowl the trails between the transport bays and the shipyard waiting to ambush Delwyn. Now she has fled.

"It might already be too late if you believe Delwyn's chances are as low as you seem to think they are. She has to reach Na'di Island, fly across the Hama'ellea sea and far into the La'huaset Tribal continent, land in or adjacent to O'un Tu Clan territory somewhere near the O'ni'da families trees, and then find him by instinct and his scent.

"The long night will have fallen upon him well before she has any chance to find him. If she does find him and gets hurt, then he must somehow pull her and himself through the survival ordeal. You might have complicated matters for him by putting a Comari into danger," Lindredha snarled.

Caught up in blinding fury, Lindredha took a menacing step toward Kidahin. She had not even had the time to solidify her association with Delwyn, an association approved by those females with him at the time. Now Kidahin's meddling might have decreased his survival chances.

The Warrior female stopped well within Kidahin's personal space. With an iron will Lindredha strove to restrain herself. Kidahin had acted from juvenile panic.

"I know Delwyn stole aboard a Ni'zakhonii ship. He killed most of them. He freed you and other females. He did so although wounded. I know he did it for you and others in association with him. I know you feel an honor debt is owed and you are trying to help. I know you risked your life provoking a Comari to act although doing so was foolhardy, stupid, and brave. But this smells to me like an emotional last resort and an impulsive one. You belong to an elite warship society, and you should know better than to react with rash abandon.

"I will have words sung about this to the hierarchies.

"I know Delwyn did not approve your actions. Who else knew what you were planning?"

Kidahin stood her ground and let the Warrior vent her anger.

"I might have said something about it to Trebithia," Kidahin replied.

"Trebithia? Your Mistress of Pathwalking? And she allowed you to continue your mad plan?"

"She had her doubts. She did not think I had a chance to succeed," Kidahin admitted.

Lindredha's anger abated then—a little—on hearing the Hunter's sheepish admission. Of course Trebithia did not. Lindredha would have thought so, too.

"Understand this, Kidahin. If Delwyn dies because you interfered, I will claim a point of honor against you."

Of that, Kidahin had no doubt.

Lindredha did have a point. A slim chance and the spirits own luck might let the Comari arrive in O'ni'da territory before the long night began. Assuming she could scent track Delwyn at all, she would have to do so after sundown, perhaps even several hours into the night. Kidahin knew her interference might well have put the Comari in danger. Delwyn too if he defended her from animal attacks.

But Comara were deadly. They had lightning-quick reflexes, zero reaction time, could smell an intent to attack, evade without thought, and follow through with a countermove or counterstrike before the attacker even began the strike. She could punch her fist through a rib cage and pull out the beating heart. Never mind what a Comari could do when she held a weapon.

But jungle animals had both armor and arms. A Comari could hurt them, make them angry, and distract them but not easily kill them.

"I will remember, Mistress. Perhaps things will turn out for the best."

"You had better hope so," Lindredha growled in warning.

***

Delwyn passed cave walls glistening with crystallized calcite. Although pale looking in the persistent gloom he bet they were white, but the blue-white ooze gave them the eerie semblance of a mausoleum in moonlight. Brownish stones and blue granite rubble peppered the chamber.

Muddy depressions spotted the uneven and slippery floor. The plip-plip-plip sounds reminded him that water flowed through the cave often. He was stuck underground in a rainforest, and for all he knew it was raining torrents above ground and he'd never know about it until the accumulating runoff overwhelmed the eroded pits in the cliff and rushed down into the cave entrance. The flood water would turn the floor into swift rapids swirling around a whirlpool before draining down the crevasse in the cave floor.

Assuming the cave didn't flood when the water table rose first.

Delwyn imagined cave drawings on the calcite walls. He knew the surrounding geology had formed ages ago, but after millions of years he could still feel the power the water exerted when it wore away the limestone. As he walked through the cavern, he heard his heavy breathing in his ears, the constant drip-drip of water echoing off walls and ceiling. Caught up in the rhythm he imagined ancient music and the beat of the dance as a storyteller stood against the pale wall covered with animal figures ready to lend substance to her song.

The romantic caveman scene, its caveman fire, and its caveman animal art all drew from Earth folklore and a human mind on an ancestral level harkening back to cave dwelling. No human racial memory stretched so far back in time to remember even on an instinctual level when trees had been the fortresses of safety.

No Eyloni had ever lived in this cave, had ever lived in any cave. For them the trees had always been home. As vast as elleiu trees grew, as slow as they grew, as long as they lived, they had served as above ground wooden cave systems. They never flooded and never caved in. So why would they ever consider living in a hole in the ground?

The glowing streaks and blotches narrowed up ahead and rose along a gentle incline. The air grew warmer. Breezes hinted at a nearby opening to the surface. That meant he should have passed under the limestone cliffs. The chamber closed in around him. Warm air competed with the cool cave air, drawing a sharp contrast between above and below ground air temperatures.

Delwyn felt his heel skid on wet clay, and his feet shot out from under him.

Scrabbling for balance, he tumbled backwards down the wet muddy center passage.

His back snagged on a dry patch a split-second before he started sliding again. The slick clay accelerated him just as wax paper accelerated a kid down a sliding board.

Delwyn twisted sideways and dug his fingernails and toenails into the slick mud and stretched to improve his grip along the slick sides.

His knees slid like greased bearings along the ground. He couldn't lever his body up to kick himself onto the stone floor.

He felt the void approaching more than he saw it. The warm air cooled and fell to the cave floor and sank into the fast-approaching fissure.

He flew over a long, narrow gaping maw. He had to stretch to reach both sides across the muddy gap.

He stopped sliding. His ankles and wrists the only things keeping him suspended across the crevasse.

He felt no solid ledge, nothing hard enough to push against and stop his muddy feet from slipping, nothing rough enough to give him traction, no surface he could shove against and launch himself from the slimy gash.

He stared down into darkness. No glowing ooze glimmered back. The air hovered around him, cool and damp. He didn't hear moving water but not hearing it didn't mean bone dry ground waited down there, either.

He spit into the darkness.

Twenty seconds later he heard a faint splat followed by whispering echoes.

His best guess was he was suspended over a flooded chamber either mere centimeters or several meters deep and filled with submerged rocks. He couldn't see down there and didn't know if he could safely dive into the water. Even if he could, he didn't know if he could find an exit even if he missed the rocks waiting to bash his brains out. Assuming, he amended, that the way out didn't involve being swept into a vast underground lake.

His only choice was to crawl sideways until he no longer hung over the flooded chamber.

But which way? If the clay pulled away from the stone ledge, he'd fall. If the gap grew wider the direction he had slid then he'd use up his strength going the wrong way and then have to reverse course.

He had to creep his way back up the incline.

He cursed. He'd already squandered valuable minutes assessing his predicament. Then again, impulsive action now would lead to death.

Advance! He ordered himself.

He slid his right foot over a bit, then he slid his right wrist along the wet, snot-slick clay, then he slid his left foot and then his left wrist. Right foot, right hand, left foot, left hand, repeated over and over, scrabbling like a lobster avoiding boiling water in a pot.

He took short incremental moves. Spread his arms too far and he'd lose the muscle tension keeping him from sagging. Sag too much and a foot or hand would lose hold and slip off.

Move too fast up the shallow incline and the inertia from the forward movement would rebound like a pendulum on its return swing. And like a pendulum his body would tend to slide back down farther than the forward movement he'd gain. Do it too often and like a pendulum out of gas he'd wind up suspended over the midpoint arc above the pit again.

The successful strategy called for creeping movement. Each ten-centimeter shuffle took about two minutes. It dropped below a minute as the crevasse began to narrow. Still, it took Delwyn an hour to crawl sideways up the incline and out of the muddy trench.

He stood. His muscles complained. His back, thighs, shoulders, arms, and wrists burned from supporting his suspended weight for so long.

He had just burned through calories he couldn't afford to lose over the past hour. He needed food and water.

But first he assessed his injuries. Released from crisis management, his fingers and toes began to hurt from torn fingernails and toenails. He saw he'd lost the nails from both big toes, both middle fingers, his left index finger and his right thumbnail. He had scrapes and bruises and had lost half the skin off his back, but the smooth cave floor had saved him from suffering cuts and broken bones.

He had lost the hooped water vines, his leaf hat, his bark sandals, his moss loincloth, and his bladder plant pouches and their starchy tuber contents. The sharp stone he'd been using for a blade and the spear had both tumbled into the abyss with the rest.

Losing the sharp stone was bad. Sharp stones turned up rarely in rainforests. Most stones he'd found had been limestone, sandstone, lava cinders, and some granite.

He had no choice. No matter how close to the surface he was now, he had to backtrack into the cavern to find clean water. Water dripping from a stalactite was best. The survival manual said the ground above filtered out any pathogenic critters from the water as it drained into the cave ceiling. Water superseded all other priorities. He found a dripping stalactite and drank his fill. He didn't have a container, not even dry moss to sop the water up and carry it for later use.

His thirst sated, Delwyn started picking through stones left by previous floods. He found a flint rock as big as a football. He grabbed a smooth gray hammer stone and struck the flint a glancing blow.

A chip the size and shape of a scallop shell flaked off in one piece, beautiful blue-gray. It contained no imperfections.

He shaved his forearm with its sharp edge.

The remaining flint was too valuable to toss back onto the ground. He didn't want to carry the hammer stone, but a source of sharp blades couldn't be overlooked. He struck off more pieces, including one long enough to serve as a crooked spear point.

Now he needed bone or wood to make handles. Bones and sticks stuck out of the rubble. Flood runoff washing into the caves had swept animal carcasses and battered branches deep inside.

Like the calcite walls kilometers behind him, the gloomy glow made bone appear spectral against the cave floor.

He yanked a long jointed bone from a rock pile, dragged the socket end along the cave wall to pick up glowing slime until it covered the ball with sticky ooze.

It glowed like a kid's birthday candle. He held the bone out and picked through a bone pile made from creatures he couldn't imagine.

He took time out to make a knife, a hatchet, and three spear points.

He affixed one spear point to a knotty but straight stick having the feel of a good quarterstaff. The spear, braced, could also serve as a pike, a much better one than his old spear now resting in its dark watery grave.

Keeping the flints attached proved quite a challenge until he discovered by accident that as the pale slime dried it turned tacky, like pine gum.

Over time it might even harden, although he bet the stuff lost adherence if it stayed wet for too long.

Still, it might work better than crossing his fingers and hoping the flint points didn't fall out and become lost in the forest or inside a stabbed animal.

Kidahin had said her people knapped flint, and not just to make female adulthood knives. Clan artisans made knives and everyday utensils because many people enjoyed the natural material craftsmanship over more modern substitutes. Tradition, Kidahin had called it. He called it nostalgia. Everyone knew how to knap flint into serviceable blades. When he asked why they bothered, her reply had been simple and direct; you never knew when you might have need for a weapon.

Indeed.

If she could teach him how to knap flint, he felt sure he could make quite an effective and beautiful weapon. He'd have to press her about it before they returned to space.

Ready to leave the cave, he hurried, wanting to see just how much the nearly fatal shortcut had shaved off his route.

Standing near the cave entrance, he blinked several times and waited for his eyes to adjust to the blinding sun and the blooming oranges and reds. When his daylight vision returned he walked out onto the ledge and surveyed the crimson and scarlet view spreading out before him.

He smiled.

Hunters hated air travel, but he wondered what they would make of walking through a six kilometers-long cavern. Somehow he doubted tree dwellers would ever consider a subterranean shortcut. Eyloni built starships, airplanes, and boats. They disdained highways. The only overland vehicle they used with any regularity—meaning rarely—was the six-legged crawling vehicle. They had never even domesticated a work animal, a horse equivalent.

The sea of crimson ivy opened up before him. Just like kudzu vine, this stuff grew up the steep slope from a modest valley and onto the ledge surrounding the cave entrance. Three stone pillars arose from the valley, surrounded and overgrown by the ivy. That made them as featureless as the ground itself. Each massive stone pillar pointed into the sky. He saw a stone giant's left hand missing its thumb, index finger pointing up, the tallest ivy-covered spire. Tall fused middle and ring fingers came next, followed by the smallest, a crooked pinky finger.

Behind them, dwarfing them, stood hectares of broadleafs three to four times taller than any Earth tree. The ones near the veiled pillars were also smothered in ivy. Although trees farther in the distance kept their orangey colors, many had obvious crimson highlights.

A bluish haze had settled above the ivy nightmare. Indeed, it hung above the canopy for as far as he could see. His agriculture classes had gone into some depth over the matter, too. It had something to do with natural rubber. A chemical some plants made. What was it? Latex?

No, what latex came from, a hydrocarbon: polyisoprene.

Plants made isoprene. What didn't become latex became a gas, but it wasn't a wasteful by-product. Isoprene gas protected plants from the damaging effects of high temperatures.

Delwyn glanced up at the eroded limestone mountain behind him. Ivy had heaped up along the cliff face in places, resembling leafy coiled crimson ropes that had tried to scale the cliff face on their own but fell back to the ground in little mounded heaps.

Odd. They seemed unable to climb the limestone but had no problems suffocating the stone pillars in the valley below. Curious, he walked to the stony ledge for a closer look.

The ivy felt like binder twine and had pads sprouting along the crimson vines instead of the burrowing corkscrews normal for the parasitic green vines. Unlike them, these red vines used sunlight to make their food.

He pulled a flint knife and tried to cut off a piece. It took some effort to loop the vine over the blade and saw through it. He stripped the leaves, wrapped it in a coil around his wrist, unwound it, and tied several knots along its length. It bent and made fine cordage. It braided well enough if he kept it pulled taut while braiding. The ivy had small leaves given the average leaf sizes the jungle produced. Tough, they flexed and took a puncture without tearing. He could sew them together as needed without ripping them.

He looked at his hands. Ivy sap had turned them yellow-orange. Testing his survival skills, he touched his tongue to the cut stem.

The mucus membranes in his mouth puckered in response to the bitter astringent and antiseptic sap.

He sat back a minute to think. The rice-sized dragonfly insects surrounded him, attracted to the salt in his sweat. They didn't bite, but their tongues lapped it up. Butterflies drank water from puddles for the same reason: to get salt. They found his skin a bonanza, but their constant crawling on him would drive him nuts.

They avoided his stained hands, although his palms gleamed with sweat. He bruised a leaf and smeared its juice on them.

No joy. The sweat dragonflies ignored the juice. Maybe the sap in the vine was more concentrated. He tried the cut stem and found it an efficient bug repellant, and he hoped he hadn't also discovered Elleio poison ivy.

It took an hour for him to cover his exposed skin with vine sap. Then he passed another hour stitching a pair of sandals, waistwear, a hat, and sheathes for his flint knives and hatchet.

He planned while he sewed. The cavern shortcut had paid off by giving him a six klick or better direct route, but it had also backed him up against a cliff surrounded by deep piles of red ivy that would give any sharp machete a real go at it. His flint knives and hatchet simply could not hack a path through the tough plants.

Now what? Backtracking through the caves was out. So was walking around the limestone cliffs. That meant going farther up into the mountains, and he needed to reach the Om'tu River flood plains. Lunging through ivy-covered ground would make him feel like a World War I infantryman stomping through barbed wire. Tripping every other step, he'd burn through too many calories for what gains he'd make.

First he needed to find some carbohydrate-rich tubers to roast and eat.

He decided on checking out the ivy draped stone sentinels below. Hopefully the ivy spent more energy growing up them and into the sun than creeping along the shady ground behind them. The downhill plunge from the cave ledge was steeper than it looked covered in vines. The rolling ivy disguised the land, hid its true rough rocky nature. Just what lived under all these vines? Images of eight-legged horrors haunted him.

At least they never came out until after the sun went down, he reassured himself.

His big toe snagged on a vine. The tough stuff didn't snap, and he fell. Ivy coils snagged him and halted his plunge down the steep side.

It took him twenty minutes to climb down over the ivy and reach the split between the index and the fused middle fingers. From there he pushed through hanging vines, disturbing the insects clinging underneath leaves and sending clouds of them into the air. The ivy grew up the granite spires, seemingly trying to climb into the air above them, before falling back down upon itself. Then, just above his head as if realizing it grew the wrong way, it started curving upwards again.

Delwyn shoved through the thick crimson shroud and came out the other side and saw more red ivy covering the ground into the distance, even part way up the nearby trees.

Delwyn remembered overflying places like this on Na'di Island. The ivy was environment selective. It didn't take over the entire jungle because it didn't like higher or much lower elevations. The limestone cliffs exceeded an altitude constraint, and just beyond his limited view no doubt the vines thinned out as the altitude dropped below their comfort zone.

Still, fighting for every decimeter of ground would take time and strength.

He paused to get his bearings, noting the sun shining in the 16h35 skyclock position.

About eighteen hours had passed since they had dropped him off. He needed sleep. The best place to sleep was on the cliff face in the cave entrance. It was cooler, defensible, and offered him a retreat option.

He heard water bubbling nearby. That meant running water, maybe food as well.

He slogged downhill through piles of snagging vines. After a half hour of crashing through the forest he reached a small sparkling tributary stream, not much more than a creek in a shallow ditch, but it moved at a steady clip. He glanced upstream and spied water spilling over a rocky ledge. Thirst overcame him.

He had to rehydrate. He stepped into the water and waded the ankle-deep stream towards the tiny falls.

Always choose aerated water if you can't boil or chemically process it. Air killed anaerobic bacteria, and Elle's high ultraviolet light zapped some too. Moving water also prevented stagnation toxins from accumulating.

The bluish haze above contrasted with the dampness in the air he felt near the water. The falls didn't even raise a mist. It was tiny, yet he felt damp, as if the ivy shielded the moisture from the sun above.

Delwyn glanced up and caught his breath on seeing the beauty surrounding him. Twigs, leaves, and grasses were highlighted by the sunlight bouncing off sparkling water.

The vines gave the bank around the runoff stream a wide berth. Why? The water should have turned the area into a swamp.

He drank from the sparkling waterfall again before he began to wash the dried clay and mud from his body. The ivy juice didn't wash off, but he doubted it retained enough potency to repel the tiny salt flies. He'd have to get more from the vines before he went to sleep.

He found more brain coral-looking moss and a few rhizomes resembling cattail roots. He grabbed all he could carry and started back up the short steep rise to the cliff face and its cave opening.

With sticks and dried moss found hanging from trees near the ditch and the cordage made from vines, he made a spindle for a hand drill, a bow from a bent stick and cordage, and drilled into a hearthboard until he got a good hot coal. He brushed the coal onto the moss kindling, blew on it until it caught fire, and put it into the meager stack of firewood.

It wouldn't last long, maybe an hour or so. He found few dry sticks in the rainforest, but the little caveman fire made him feel safe.

He stuck the white roots into the fire and turned them over every few minutes. Water sizzled and popped from them before they split open.

He set them aside to cool and ate the moss first. Then he chewed on the hot starchy roots. He toasted and ate several more until he was full. Phalalin had told him they had a lot of carbohydrates and a fair amount of protein.

Delwyn compared their nutrient value to a bagel. They made him feel full and sleepy.

He had to take a nap on the stone ledge. Ivy alone made a poor mattress, and he didn't have time to waste looking for materials.

He cut an ivy plant at the roots, one big enough to double as a tumbleweed, and piled it over him until it covered him, protecting him from the direct exposure to the sun's rays and sweat dragonflies.

He was asleep in minutes.

17
THE LITTLE SIBS

The Comari walked out of the Na'di Island spaceport and headed for the short-term parking area. Kidahin had told her repeatedly that she was welcome to use the clan aircar as if the young Hunter thought her unable to grasp the simple statement the first time.

The Comari's anger had faded. She came so close to killing Kidahin before she even had the chance to sing her concerns. Kidahin should have known better.

Of course the Comari saw Delwyn as an adult. She had planned so carefully. She waited for his return to the shipyard, had resigned herself to a wait lasting over the next few months. She planned to claim him before he returned to his warship. If Kidahin Uahua'asee'a La'huaset Eyloni had deceived her to impede her claim, then she would hunt her down and kill her anyway.

The Comari passed several people. They yielded to her presence without conscious thought. Comara had absolute autonomy, even more so than a male. Nobody wanted to cross tails with a Comari.

To her most people struck her as intangible objects. It took a conscious effort for her to pay them more than fleeting notice. Talking to Kidahin had been an exhausting chore.

She climbed into the aircar and engaged the piloting systems. She drew a finger across the map from Na'di Island to a point along the Om'tu River adjacent to O'un Tu O'ni'da territory. The O'ni'da families likely dropped him off somewhere opposite their families' trees, someplace where he had a reasonable chance to return home at the end of a Tyreniioroneo month.

Kidahin had said Delwyn did not know the rainforest. They had to have taken that into account and dropped him in the jungle near a challenging but not outright perilous route.

If he reached the Om'tu River and made a raft, he had only to float downstream until he spotted the O'ni'da trees. He could then beach the raft and strike out into the jungle and keep going until he reached his home tree.

That meant they had dropped him off somewhere near the eastern mountain ridge. Innumerable trails led over and around the marble tor. Once he crossed the eastern ridge and passed through the cloud rainforest, he had one clear path. The heavy jungle guaranteed no landing space. She would have to land north of the river and prowl that path until she found him.

###

Delwyn awoke to see the sun hadn't moved much.

The air had climbed well into its forty-degree Celsius day. Humidity hung in the air. It and the isoprene haze made the view look even gloomier.

He put his palm in the ashes.

Nothing. Not even a warm coal. At least two hours had passed.

He kicked the ivy screen aside, thankful its leaves had shielded him from the sun. Even now they hadn't wilted, which meant they could get by without water for some time.

He grabbed his gear, slipped his braided vine and bast slippers on, and headed down the steep ivy-covered slope.

Halfway down he felt a sudden surge of guilt. He looked back up the slope at the coiled vine. He sighed, turned around, and stomped back up the hill.

He grabbed the cut stem and pulled the mound behind him all the way down the slope. He passed between the crimson-draped stone sentinels and stopped where sun dappled the orange grassy clumps. He dropped the ivy, stepped into the babbling ditch and sopped up some water with a handful of moss. He returned to the ivy, poked a finger into the damp soil, and squeezed water into the hole. Then he cut the end off the vine and stuck it into the hole, packed soil around it, and squeezed more water around the stem. He gave the planted vine a curt nod before turning back to the trickling stream.

Water flowed downhill. If he lucked out, it flowed all the way to the river. He hoped it didn't end up feeding a marsh below the foothills.

It began to drizzle.

Delwyn revised his plans. He was still several kilometers north of the river, and he'd have to follow it down river for kilometers more before turning back into the forest and hike for even more kilometers. Between here and the river, farther down into the foothills, stood a broadleaf forest filled with trees that grew only as big as redwoods. He needed to find a suitable tree in time to set up for the long night.

Phalalin had said the long night got quite cool, and the night rains got cold and violent at times—hurricane strength. He had to get deeper into the foothills and into an adequate shelter tree and still have time to make equipment and forage for enough food and water to last over six days.

Walking for hours through the downhill forest proved about as easy as struggling through a vine-entangled cornfield. He had to step into and out of the ditch to avoid impassable tangles. He soon found himself in the water more than on the trail. More water flowed now from the drizzle and from the damp soil draining down the hills into the ankle-deep water.

The drizzle raised the specter of hypothermia. The warm rain would cool when the sun set. He'd take a chill. Eyloni could tolerate all this wetness. Their skin had a keratin outer covering resembling peach fuzz. It made their skin feel as soft as velour or fine suede. The fuzz kept water from coming into contact with their skin unless it became saturated. He wished he had skin like that. His skin lacked natural protection from frequent rains. He'd have to spend some time searching for oily plants so he could rub their sap into his skin.

He covered ground faster by wading the creek but walking through water in a humid rainforest put the health of his feet in danger. The special operations survival manual warned action response teams about trench foot and jungle rot. Skin waterlogged and peeled when submerged for long periods, and abrasions, holey socks, and soaked shoes would cause blisters or peel off swollen skin. That and damp creases in toes offered molds and funguses a beachhead for wrecking sound feet. Standard operating procedure dictated drying out the boots and feet and putting on dry socks. Easy to do when Type-II uniform boots were made from water-hating fibers that drove moisture out of them in minutes. He had no boots and no socks. Barefooted but for the plant fiber bast sandals, he'd have to build a fire to dry his feet. A soldier always cared for his feet. Rotten feet made a soldier useless, a liability. But for now he didn't want to lose the ready access the creek provided through the heavy cover.

He used his knotty spear as a walking stick. He stabbed at suspicious-looking legless eels and freshwater crablike creatures hiding in the rocks. So far the slime cementing the spear point to the stick held but had turned tacky. He'd have to keep a watch on it. The next time he went to stab a toothy or pinchy critter he might lose it and end up holding a blunt stick.

Water ran faster as the creek dropped into a shallow ravine that it had carved through the forest. The misting rain had stopped, and although soil drainage accounted for the rise in water level, the current had picked up because the hillside had grown steeper. The creek had eroded through muddy top soil to expose smooth light blue rocks and blue clay.

Delwyn grew cautious. Wet ground on slopes set the stage for muddy drop-offs. The humidity hung in the air so bad the leaves dripped warm water on his head. This was a violent environment cloaked in subtlety. The shortcut around jungle ivy led down the steep ravine and through stony scars in the eroded soil.

The farther down the hill he waded, the deeper the creek had eroded into the surrounding soil. Standing up straight and looking at the bank, Delwyn saw orange grass at eye-level. The ground had clay and subsoil mixed in with stones, some quite large. The subsoil had a rusty tint to it and walking through the water had turned it rusty as well. The ground had been washed out below and under the grassy banks with each passing storm, undermining the sod enough for it to roll into a crest that hung over and down into the bank.

The undercut soil gave him some idea about how high the water reached during storms, and Phalalin had warned him not to get trapped in these gullies during heavy rains.

Delwyn looked across the grasses and saw brush, tall plants, and more trees. None had red ivy growing on them. He must have left it all behind him an hour ago. That meant he'd dropped below the elevation the ivy found preferable. Now he stood in heavy forest that felt like an Earth forest but for the colors and taller trees. He felt relieved.

'Bout time, too. The creek bank had eroded deeper as the incline grew steeper. The water sang to him in warning as it rushed down the ravine.

Wading out of the water and climbing up to the bank's eroded edge he grabbed hold of a handful of orange plants. Jamming his left knee into the damp slope and pushing his right knee into the grassy crest Delwyn started pulling himself over the unsupported edge in order to lever himself out of the ravine and up onto the forest floor.

Held in place by grass roots alone, his sudden weight caused a ribbon of the undermined sod to split. Ripping free from the bank and falling down into the ravine, it took Delwyn along with it. Hitting the shallow water, he rolled downstream for three somersaults until his left foot wedged between two limestone rocks. His ankle, caught between the stones, abruptly stopped his downhill plunge. It twisted and rolled as he was suddenly suspended above the creek. A split-second later he dropped. He didn't even have time to cry out before his forehead smacked against the flat rock poking above the waterline.

Out cold, the same flat rock was the only thing keeping Delwyn from drowning in the tiny creek.

***

Delwyn came to hours later twisted and in agony.

Thunder rumbled over the mountains.

He passed out again.

***

Water. Ditch. Ravine? His ankle hurt.

Delwyn couldn't feel his left foot. His ankle twinged in sharp pain whenever he moved his leg.

He planted his fists in the creek bed and pushed his chest above the water and straightened his right leg, using a knee to lever himself up for a look.

His ankle bent at an unnatural angle above where the foot had wedged between two large rocks half buried in the wet ground.

The ankle had swollen.

He couldn't wiggle his toes.

Hell, he couldn't even feel his toes!

Thunder pealed through the humid air.

He had to get out of the ravine.

He bent his left knee and crawled backwards, gritting his teeth as the ankle tried to pry against the two rocks.

He pushed against the far rock, trying to open up a gap and free his foot.

It moved a grudging few millimeters in the hard wet mud.

No joy. The soil, compacted and water saturated, wouldn't give, at least not from simple pushing and shoving.

He tried the near stone. It wasn't as slippery and he got a decent hold on it.

It rocked a bit, but suction held it fast to the creek bed. His best efforts only made his ankle scream. The pain would come back with a vengeance once the blood started to flow again.

He needed a lever. The walking stick? Where had his knobby spear gone?

Delwyn looked downstream and saw the spear laying on the rocks under water.

He stretched and came up short.

Remain calm and look for alternatives, he told himself.

He needed the spear to help him force the flint point between the stones. Even if the flint snapped off, the stick might at least penetrate deep enough for him to pry the two rocks apart.

He needed a grappling hook.

The stripped ivy vine ball still hung from his waist. He had enough line, but what to use for a hook? He saw no sticks, no gnarled branches, nothing that might snag the heavy stick and not bend when he pulled on it.

What about a loop? Could he lasso it?

He tried, but the vine, thin and light, didn't throw well. Each time he threw it far enough, it floated downstream rather than sinking under the spear. He needed to snag it, and to do that the loop needed weight.

He thought about fishing. He needed a sinker.

Every rock in reach heavy enough to do the job was too smooth and too round for the ivy vine to bite into no matter how tight he pulled the knot.

Sinkers were crimped onto leaders. He couldn't crimp stone, but maybe all he needed was a groove for the twine to grip into.

He scooped up stones from the creek bottom until he found a large sandstone rock and ground it against the flat stone he had smacked his head against until he carved a fine grove into it. He untied the loop and wrapped the vine around the groove, tied it securely, and then tied a new loop.

He threw the weighted noose at the spear and took up the slack.

The vine slipped under the knotty shaft and like setting a hook in a fish, he jerked up and back on the line, flinging the shaft within easy reach.

The breezes had picked up a bit. He hadn't felt them down in the ravine, but the soughing leaves warned him the weather was changing.

It was raining somewhere, not far from here. Damp iron rode on the wind.

Thunder rumbled in the distance, but the concussive boom reverberating through the ground told him what was coming was no mid-summer shower.

Delwyn examined the spear point. The water had soaked into the dried slime, allowing the flint chip to wiggle like a loose tooth.

He couldn't dig into the clay with it without pulling the point free.

He tried digging around the near rock with the spear butt. The knobby wood had made a fine grip, but the round smooth end made a poor digging point. Still, he pushed the stick against the seam and gouged at the wet, packed earth.

Thunder struck the air with the force of a sonic boom and rumbled for several seconds across the clear blue sky. The seeming discontinuity confused his wavering awareness.

He dug against the rock down to some four centimeters before reaching a point where his efforts brought no further progress. He was pushing from the wrong angle, and the wet clay was acting as a lubricant bearing surface, causing the spear butt to slip more than dig.

Delwyn shifted forward, gripped the rock, and pulled back.

It rocked back half a centimeter, jostling his ankle with every millimeter of movement. He tried rocking it back and forth, crying out as the movement flexed his foot.

He had no choice. He had to shove the spear point between the rocks and pry them apart. He'd have to shove down hard and deep the first time, otherwise he risked breaking or losing the flint point. The flint point might also slice into his ankle or heel, maybe even sever the Achilles tendon if he wasn't careful. He still couldn't feel his foot.

He braced the shaft against his lower calf muscle and probed the stream bed for a soft spot in the mud near the far rock. He shoved down as though driving the spear into a wild animal and then pulled down using the first rock as a fulcrum, prying up the second rock.

He felt the spear point snap. Flint, hard but brittle, didn't take shearing forces well. He cringed and shoved the shaft deeper, hoping to push the broken spear point farther into the ground for the wooden shaft to follow.

Bottoming out against something hard, he pulled down again.

The stone erupted, straight up, his foot grinding and twisting against it as the stone rolled out onto the creek bed.

He tugged free gasping and laid his foot in the warm water.

He panted, sucking for breath, and rolled into a prone position on the flat rock, legs stretched upstream, and probed his ankle.

Creases in the swelling caused by the compressing rocks resembled bloodless bite marks.

Blood flow restored, his foot began to burn as it turned purple.

No compound fractures and no breaks, it looked like he'd rolled his ankle: a sprain. Torn ligaments bled into the surrounding tissues and settled in his foot. The sharp aching pain felt bad enough now. In a few hours walking on clear trails would become unbearable, let alone trying to walk through uneven and snagging jungle undergrowth.

He had to escape the ravine. Downstream the ravine would become a deathtrap, and climbing up unstable soil wouldn't work, either. That left retreating upstream. Using the spear as a cane, he limped up the creek until the bank dropped enough for him to lever himself up onto the smooth orange grass.

Delwyn looked up at the sky, saw the sun hanging in the 17h15 skyclock time. He had less than ten hours until sundown.

It would take him about that long running nonstop in his current hobbled state to reach the tall trees. He dared not sleep. He didn't even have time to stop and make tools or forage for food. The approaching six and a half days-long night put him in survival mode. It had been drilled into him that survival on the ground at night was impossible. The tall trees had become a must-achieve goal. Water would come with the rain. He'd need a container to catch what fell for later use. Food depended on the tree he settled into for the night.

First he had to bind the sprained ankle. He had to take care. The ivy twine could cut off blood flow if tied too tight. He needed to make a splint, pack his ankle with soft moss, and bind the splint around his leg to compress the ankle, immobilizing it and giving it some stability.

He had the twine; he had moss for packing around the ankle; he needed something flat and straight. He looked everywhere and found nothing.

His eyes settled on a sheet of bark peeling away from a nearby tree.

He hopped up to it, braced himself against the trunk, and gave it a good yank. The dead bark pulled away like a ripping burlap bag. It felt course and flexible. A stiff bast, it pulled apart in long vertical strips as if it had a grain. Cutting across the grain took work and more time.

He wrapped the cut pieces around his ankle, packed the inside with moss, wrapped another layer, and lashed it tight with the ivy. Then he pulled a flexible bark tip around his heel and stitched it to the woven sandal before packing the gaps with more moss. The makeshift cast would work better as a complete unit rather than as two pieces flexing above his heel.

Thunder hammered, closer this time.

He needed as much support as he could get and considered packing the splint with clay. No, clay meant climbing back into the creek. He couldn't afford the effort needed to climb in and back out. The coming storm would wash it all away anyway.

His ankle felt snug, and for now only sharp jolts and taking weight caused it pain.

That would change soon enough as blood seeped around the tissues and caused more swelling. At least he could elevate it over the next few days up in a tree a few hours from now.

Delwyn took a deep breath to clear his head and pushed the pain from his mind as he staggered away from the ravine and into the forest.

###

The Comari landed just beyond O'un Tu Clan territory, instructed the aircar to return to Na'di Island, and watched it lift off into the late afternoon sky.

A Comari's interest in a male superseded every law and custom but one: willfully placing a male in danger without honorable justification. Her presence in an adulthood ritual itself didn't invalidate it as long as she did not bring any food, water, clothing, weapons, or equipment with her.

She stood naked in the sun, ears flexing, listening to the wind.

Comara did not participate in adulthood rituals. They never left adolescence. For them, bonding those males who needed them was the ritual stepping stone into another life.

She scented the air and planned.

Delwyn must come this way to reach the river.

She turned around and mentally traced a path up through the foothills, the tall trees between her and the white eroded tor far in the distance.

He would not try to climb the marble-veined limestone cliffs. Nor would he go up over the ridge around it. The best route would take him on a trek around the northeastern exposure and down through the foothills, the smaller trees, and into the largest broadleafs where he could settle in for the long night.

The Comari ran for the distant foothills, her feet a blur.

***

He wasn't going to make it.

Hiking through this part of the temperate rainforest came in as a close second to hiking through a forest on Earth. The ground put forth myriad obstacles that alternated between clear paths, tall grasses, briars, brambles, and vines, all just lying in wait to snag his feet. He had to make up time here, because the forest grew thicker the farther down the foothills he went.

Time passed as Delwyn finally settled into a loping gait. He hustled at a decent clip with only one goal in mind: the nearest tall trees. He thought the problem through to keep his mind off the pain in his ankle.

Phalalin had said the ordeal prepared a male for adult responsibilities. It demonstrated a male's ability to live in the forest during the long day and night periods alone and without supplies or equipment. The participant did not need to go anywhere during the long night. He should make steady progress through the forest down into the foothills. Once he reached the tall trees he should remain in place close to a base tree and stock up one of its many semi-sheltered leafy dead-end boles with food and water and wait for the daylight to return.

He had gained time using the cavern short cut, but he lost all those gains and more while unconscious. He hobbled toward the trees as fast as he could without supplies or the time to find them.

He'd be lucky if he could lug himself up a tree.

Could he even lug himself up a tree?

Forget that! What about the ordeal?

Okay…strategy came down to the effective use of the long night. Sleep and predator avoidance ranked high on the nighttime activities list. The two-phase-long daylight period gave an initiate enough time to survive the hot long day and replenish the body with food. It also tested endurance and fortitude because all sane travel happened in daylight.

Delwyn started second-guessing himself. Maybe the best strategy would have been to find night shelter early on, stock up food and water, wait out the long night, and travel during the four Earth days in daylight. Maybe even plan on returning later than necessary to complete the ordeal.

It sounded like a good plan. He could return late, but he couldn't return before the end of the TST month.

Was the desire to explore the jungle affecting his judgment? Why hadn't he headed up a tree with supplies in the first place?

He had a strategy. He knew he did. Why did it sound wrong now?

Delwyn's head ached where his forehead had kissed the rock. The blinding headache and blurred vision had gotten worse. It began to affect his objectivity, filling him with doubts.

One reason—if not the only reason—females permitted rare males the chance to participate in the survival ordeals was to see if they could make sound decisions and survive far from females and their stabilizing pheromonal influence. Female scent had been inhibiting Delwyn's PTSD symptoms in the same way it grounded Eyloni male aggression. Injured and far from female pheromonal influences, the flashbacks and nightmares would surely find him again.

Where in the hell was the damned LZ? Delwyn wondered. He remembered something about an extraction point in the tall trees up ahead.

He'd taken a hit to his leg, an antipersonnel round of some kind. It slowed him down.

Ignore it!

Something had happened to his eyes. Flash grenade? The forest had taken on a riot of orange nightmares. *Where* was he? Not Valhalla, the colony world had plains, not forests. His wife, his daughters hid somewhere up ahead in the distant trees.

Why am I naked and wearing a grass skirt?

Images collided, from Valhalla Colony, from forest extractions, from Elleio forest trails and jungles all crashing together, warping, stretching, blending.

Delwyn ran for the distant trees, ignoring the blinding pain, using it to tap into energy reserves as he ran from a combat zone. He ran and ran. The trees had been designated a rallying point. Just exactly why there Delwyn didn't know, but a brother had told him to run for the tall trees.

It was hot. Sweat ran into his eyes. They stung. He blinked furiously, eyes tearing up. He didn't dare stop to rub them. That took too much effort. His running hops took all his attention. No matter how well he could ignore the sprain, he couldn't ignore the lost stability in the joint. Come down wrong and it would roll again. The pliable bark splint cinched tight gave the ankle some support, but it didn't replace a field splint. It didn't wrap tight enough around the ankle to immobilize it. It wasn't even plasticast. Packed tight with moss, it might have worked well enough on an immobile foot. It might even have done well enough for moderate walking, but his constant running had packed and ground the moss into powder, opened gaps, and reduced the compression necessary to keep the joint stable.

Delwyn's lungs burned. The high humidity seemed to rob him of the oxygen his body craved, but Elleio's three percent less oxygen caused it. Like running at high altitude, he had acclimated to the difference while on his warship. But the atmosphere also held more carbon dioxide than he was used to. It made his lungs burn as if he was rebreathing the air someone had blown into a balloon.

His gasping sucked in bugs as he ran. Iridescent bright orange dragonflies brushed by his face in clouds, some got caught in his clenched teeth.

He swallowed them, chewed and swallowed more of them. His parched throat couldn't even work up a spit, and he couldn't afford the water loss even if he tried. He remembered that insects were a protein source. He ran through more insect clouds, mouth open, crunching them between his teeth.

They tasted like juicy, salty ear wax.

Their legs and wings scratched and tickled his dry throat, and he doubled over with hacking coughs.

Every cloud he ran through he breathed in more bee-sized bugs to get a good mouthful.

And they swarmed to him, too. Some crawled up his nose, some poked his already teary eyes. He was a rich buffet for them, the salt in his sweat made his skin an overwhelming sight and drew them to him like moths to light.

The wind picked up, an escort for the persistent rumbling throughout the long late afternoon. The warm moist southern heat had collided with the cool northern mountain air. The storm fury lashed out against the barrier ridge. This time the mountain storm boiled over the peaks, towering above them and breaking free of the cold, circular wind patterns of the Northern Farside Gyre, and slamming into the hot humid Hama'ellea Gyre air.

The air cooled rapidly, allowing more oxygen in the same gulp to enter Delwyn's parched lungs. The air behind him, its moisture rained out, dried out his lungs and throat. Humidity drained resolve by impeding a body's effort to cool itself, but a runner preferred humid air. The cool dry air pulled moisture from his lungs and his mucus membranes.

The sky ahead had turned dark blue. Delwyn didn't notice. His peripheral vision had clouded from both the head injury and the single-minded tunnel vision that came from instinctive crisis management.

The storm overtook him, the first few splats hit him as though flung from cups across a dining table. They tasted cool, refreshing, and he hoped it would last. He counted to ten before the downpour cascaded onto him.

High storm clouds pulled far ahead, slate gray and black. Convoluted like brains, they rained on him. Lightning flashed all around him, a lot of lightning, an electrical storm.

Delwyn drank down the shot glass-sized drops while he had the chance.

The rain chilled him and cleared his head.

I'm on Elleio. I must reach those tall trees before nightfall.

The driving rain hit leaves and trees before falling on him, making the way clearer than if he'd been out in the open. Like any woods, it took some time for the giant trees to become saturated, and he received the full force of the rain whenever he ran out into the open.

His skin steamed. The strain and the hot air had warmed his body. The cold rain evaporated from his skin. That signaled rapid heat loss.

That's bad—hypothermia risk.

Lightning arced above him. The cloud-to-cloud rippling bolts made no sound, but the ground strikes smacked the air with thunder.

One-one thousand, two-one thousand, three-one thousand, four …

Wham! According to his count, the strike hit almost five klicks away.

The cold rain saturated his moss-packed splint. It also mixed up the powdered moss. The water and his body heat activated the poultice, and pain-relieving chemicals in the moss were soon absorbed into his waterlogged skin, making his swollen ankle feel better. Delwyn felt the skin warm and tingle, as if wrapped in mild stinging nettles. It didn't burn, didn't itch. It tingled like bee stings on numb skin.

The pain vanished, replaced by a cocoon of tingling warmth.

His mind cleared, and he lost the tunnel vision drive the pain had given him.

He wished it hadn't. The moss juice did not banish his PTSD along with the pain. Instead, it freed his mind from fighting the pain and let it roam through innumerable fantasies.

The rain howled. It beat against the ground, trees, and leaves. Gusts shoved branches aside.

The gray sky turned the forest surreal. He'd been here before.

We landed here.

This had been a special ops mission.

Or had it been a training mission?

God, his head hurt. He couldn't think straight.

Yeah, this mission had been to blow a command bunker in one of the Aquarii star systems. But which one, 53-A or HD210277-A?

Or was this a training mission aboard *Henri Edda*?

No. He remembered fog, not rain.

The Aquarii mission, there'd been no rain there, either.

This is no flashback?

This wasn't Valhalla. Storms are about right, but Valhalla had few trees and none over thirty meters tall.

"Tha's rhit, 'm on Ell'yo," he slurred.

Elleio.

Princess.

His near-daughter.

Delwyn's memory kept flashing Princess's face, one alternating between her and a long-haired blond girl with twitching pixie ears. *Comari?* He wasn't on *Henri Edda's* flight deck. He wasn't in either 53 Aquarii or HD210277 Aquarii. This didn't have the feel of a flashback.

He ran.

The storm raged for two hours overhead before pulling far to the northeast, racing for the coast.

The ground was covered in standing water, ankle deep in some places.

It would soon sink into the ground, but some of it would linger in shallow puddles for quite awhile. Those shallow kiddie pools had a name he couldn't remember. He'd caught tadpoles in similar ones every spring, to his mother's everlasting frustration. She had said not to get his feet wet. So he took his shoes and socks off, rolled up his pant legs, and waded into the pool after them. It had been late-March; one of those warm spring days when frogs croaked and chirped.

His skin no longer steamed. The air, not as humid, began to warm.

The deep puddles he avoided but splashing through water for so long had diluted the moss's natural analgesic qualities, and sharp throbbing pain began to stir awake.

Delwyn slowed. Endurance running called for periodic walks between runs, and he'd not slowed down that he could remember. Yet he resisted out of fear. The damning curse of injury brought with it insistent, insidious pain to force an injured person into immobility, into resting the injury, and into falling asleep. A downed animal was doomed in the wild. Immobility caused muscles to stiffen, and later attempts to rise became an agony. Injuries summoned sleep, a desire to remain still and escape to blissful unawareness.

He'd sleep when he reached the LZ in the trees up ahead.

Delwyn counted to himself during the time he spent walking. Bumps and snags against the splint transferred to his outraged ankle. It wouldn't take much longer before he was forced to stop. Whatever had been in the moss or the bark had let him get this far, but it was fading fast now. Without a cast or a decent splint he wouldn't have the support he needed to walk on the leg. Without pain meds, every step would only get shorter and slower.

Delwyn had a moment's clarity. If he had to spend over six days up a tree, then maybe over time with the foot elevated enough healing would let him walk back home. It wouldn't heal much. He knew sprains took a long time to heal.

The slow-moving sun, while not yet below the horizon, had fallen behind the trees and into the mountain side. Long shadows stretched out before him. Dark clear skies in the east rose above the trees and glittered as the brightest stars outshined the fading sunset.

He considered the tall trees around him. Up ahead half a klick grew one to give a redwood a run for its money. He stopped in his tracks, his heart sinking as he stared at it.

The tree was an easy twenty-meter climb to the outstretched lower limbs, but without a rope he couldn't do it. His ankle, now engulfed in pain, could no longer take the twisting pressure needed to climb unaided.

Darkness crept across the forest as lengthening shadows swallowed the low ground. He should have a good hour or better. Confused, he fought to understand. The sun told him he had only minutes remaining. He felt as though he was running out of time, and his skewed viewpoint didn't help. Time was fickle. It never passed at the rate you wanted it to: it surged forward when you wanted it to drag, and it dragged when you wanted it to zoom by.

A tree not fifty meters on the left caught his eye. It had light, yellowish-gray bark. It seemed out of place among the burnt orange, auburn, and rusty barked trees. The leaves, there was something about the leaves. He struggled to remember.

What about them?

Phalalin. What had he said about them? If they were bright orange with yellow streaks, then they belonged to the *arberi* tree. Arberi contained a stimulant: caffeine.

Yeah, he could use the caffeine. Caffeine relieved pain.

Each leaf could wrap around him like a valentine heart-shaped shower curtain. One hung from a low branch, just beyond reach.

He needed the stimulant. He'd just give it a good bash with his trusty knobby spear and …? Where'd it go? Hadn't he been holding it in his hand? When had he lost it? Time had run together over the past several hours. He must have dropped it while running in the rain.

Why'd he do that? It seemed like a stupid thing to do.

He made a quick self-exam. He had many pokes and scratches, some long and deep, covering his legs. His leaf and ivy waistwear had frayed and was missing pieces, but it still held together.

At least he had his trusty ivy twine ball and a small bone-handled flint knife stuck through it like a knitting needle thrust through a skein.

Delwyn jumped for the yellow-trimmed orange leaf and tore a piece off before landing on both feet.

His left ankle screamed at the jolting impact and threatened to roll under his weight. The splint pinched flesh as it rode up against the ankle bone. The warning pain triggered reflex training that pitched him into a tumbling roll to the ground rather than trying to support the sudden weight. He landed on soaking wet ground covered with puddles. Fresh water, he'd need to bag as much of it as possible.

He scanned trees glowing in the gas giant's pale blue twilight.

The sun had dropped well below the trees, behind the mountains, and beneath the horizon by now. He looked around and made a full circle assessment while chewing on the leaf.

It tasted dry, vaguely sweet, and bitter at the same time. He had to work at grinding the parchment leaf into mulch, and as his spit began breaking it down, a cinnamon flavor filled his mouth. It had a bite to it too, a hot pepper chaser.

He wondered if it might make a good tea.

Water containers, he had to find water containers.

Delwyn's heart slammed into full throttle, skipping beats along the way as his system reacted to the caffeine overdose. Wired now, he reconsidered the water problem. He saw none of the blossoms Phalalin had suggested for canteens. He wasn't near a lake and its gas bag aquatic plants, but he did find several large melon plants.

On a hunch, he cut the top off one to expose the watery flesh inside.

He bent down to taste it when the color registered: *green*. The insides were all green. Wary and suspicious, he dabbed a sticky finger to his lip and recoiled in pain, threw the melon down, and dove into the shallow water trying to wash his flaming lip and now burning hands.

The honeydew-like fruit contained a caustic agent. Lye? His wife had used lye as an ingredient in pretzels. She floated the dough in a crock filled with a weak water and lye mixture, grape leaves, and onion skins. She floated them for a minute before taking them out and baking them. The baking neutralized the lye and browned the pretzels without giving them a hard surface. He had been horrified the first time he saw her making them.

The next thing he knew, the shadows had vanished into darkness. The yellow and orange sunset flared, silhouetting the mountains. He couldn't find a container substitute now if it grew bare meters away.

That left digging. A last resort but if he dug out a hole deep enough, he'd have what water seeped in from the surrounding soil. It might last up to four or five days. It shouldn't evaporate during the long night, and a wide deep hole should make a fine catch basin for any rain that fell during the night.

It didn't take him long, and soon he felt water filling the hole.

Time to climb a tree, he sighed to himself.

The arberi branches hung down far enough for him to climb into them, if he could jump high enough to grab onto the wide branch. He grabbed all the moss he could find and soaked it in water. He couldn't climb up and down, and he couldn't risk coming down all the time if any night predators waited by the make-shift watering hole for him, either. He'd use his twine to tie up a moss ball and fish for water sips at a time.

Ready, he jumped. He missed the low branch and came down with a jarring impact.

He tried again.

The third time he caught a hold, heaved himself up, and pulled himself onto a wide, smooth limb that spread out beneath him wider than he was tall.

His ankle screaming death threats, Delwyn rolled onto his back, looked up into his savior's canopy, and watched auroras play across the night sky as they contended with Tyreniioroneo's aquamarine glow.

Exhausted and in pain, he prayed to the giver of victory not to let him roll off the branch in his sleep.

Delwyn woke some time later to the sound of nearby movement.

He felt footfalls transmitting pitter-patters through the limb.

Whatever it was, it stood near him.

Quiet, it looked him over.

He cracked an eye open.

Tyreniioroneo's soft blue light made the small creature's skin fluoresce a pale yellow. *Comari!* That Comari had come looking for him! Delwyn didn't know whether he should be happy or afraid. Had she tracked him here so she could bond with him? And by doing so would she invalidate the survival ordeal?

He sat up and looked into deep amber eyes. The pair of amber eyes became two pairs, then four pairs, then eight pairs.

The breath caught in his throat. In shock, he didn't notice the pulse throbbing in his ankle as the clan surrounded him, an animal clan the Eyloni called the little sisters and brothers.

They sniffed him and patted him, making soft musical squeaks as they did so. They seemed curious about him, and they seemed concerned. Concerned about him or for him he didn't know which. Each one the size of a Verreaux's sifaka, they had the same matte keratin fuzzy skin, the same velour skin, as an Eyloni except it was golden-yellow. Two little sibs stood quite close. The others held back, waiting.

The two squeaked to one another and at him. One had an infant clamped to her back.

This was the dominant female and male pair, and they seemed at a loss as to what to do about him.

They resembled sifakas all right but had the long tails of ring-tailed lemurs. They had muzzles like sifakas, too. More pronounced than even an Eyloni's vestigial remnant.

"What do you guys want?" he asked them.

They came up to him, squeaking in rhythms no lemur could match.

They wanted him off the branch. Everything about them, their demeanor, their insistence demanded he vacate the branch. It was their home after all. They waited in the branches above him. He could see their outlines, their eyes reflecting the dancing auroras above.

The gas giant had grown a bit. If its phases changed at the same rate the sun moved across the sky, then its waxing half moon shape told him he'd been asleep for several hours.

The night creatures would be out and hunting by now.

The little sibs had reached a communal decision. They grabbed him and tugged, insistent.

Delwyn could see nearby trees he could climb into, but he hated abandoning the water hole below.

He couldn't stay. They could always roll him off the branch as he slept.

How could he land and not injure his ankle lurked uppermost on his mind as he levered himself along the broad branch.

The little sibs grabbed for him and pulled him back onto the branch, urging him toward the trunk.

To climb down? Delwyn knew he had no chance. Better to drop and roll than try to climb down on a sprained ankle.

He reached the trunk bracketed by the little sibs.

They pushed him.

Up, toward waiting hands.

It wasn't so simple. The little sibs had real strength but were small, and they had to anchor themselves to the branch with their tails. That thought made him giggle hysterically. Eyloni used their tails for combat, striking certain poses, and for intimacy. Rarely did they use them as a third hand: to use it so bespoke unsocial behavior.

The little sibs squeaked and whistled to one another and at him, alternating between encouraging and cajoling sounds. He could smell their various scents. The Eyloni and the little sibs had evolved from a common ancestor. Both species possessed pheromonal empathy.

No doubt Phelindra could tell him what they were thinking, but even she had said making an empathic link with them was hard. Past encounters had mentioned the little sibs as all but exclusive pheromone communicators. Many emotions had common ground between the two species, but some did not. They ended up mystifying one another: a pheromonal "you can't get there from here."

The Eyloni didn't study animals in the same way humans had studied animals on Earth. Animals roamed free on Elleio. No zoos and no laboratories filled with caged animals had ever existed here. The Eyloni saw themselves as fellow animals, no different than the little sibs and other fauna. Animals had an equal right to live their lives in peace and freedom. Animals defended themselves, and so Eyloni killed jungle animals when they threatened their males. They didn't want to eradicate all dangerous and hideous jungle creatures.

The little sibs never seemed satisfied with his progress. They pushed, pulled, and prodded him into the double fork of the branch, each split as thick as a door was wide. Set into and around the forking base was the largest squirrel nest he'd ever seen.

Excited squeaks sounded all around him as they prodded him through a hole in its base. He groped through darkness, felt woven branches scrape his broad frame as he wiggled through the hole and into a pitch-black chamber. Soft plant matter covered the floor. He crawled on hands and knees and felt around. The nest had enough room to hold three men in cramped quarters.

Questioning squeaks came from outside, and Delwyn twisted around to look back through the faint, pale blue opening. He poked his head out and found himself face-to-face with the female. Her large amber eyes and huge black pupils gleamed in the darkness. She squeaked a demand, and he felt the obvious intuitive translation: *move!*

He backed up into the giant beaver lodge and let the female and her infant slip through the opening followed by her … what, exactly? On Earth he'd have assumed a mate, but Eyloni didn't form male-female pair bonds. They formed social ties regardless of gender. They mated when they came into season. The little sibs didn't have the three distinct female phenotypes the Eyloni did. Eyloni evolutionary scientists thought their differences pointed out that whatever had happened to cause male births to plummet had also caused the ancestral Eyloni female to undergo phenotypic evolution. The morphological differences among Hunters, Warriors, and Comara had to come from some originating impetus that caused selection pressures to prefer those specific phenotype traits, and they had remained stable to this day.

That meant ties between genotype and phenotype to biological fitness had coalesced around the survival of the Eyloni male. With modern technology prevalent in Eyloni society, Delwyn wondered if females in the far future might return to a common female phenotype.

Damn! He forgot. The water. He bet he had climbed too high to fish moss-soaked mouthfuls now. He wasn't even sure if he could find it again. He'd have to climb back down for water later, and no doubt his lodge hosts wouldn't want to waste energy prodding him back into the tree again.

One squeaked at him. Then they squeaked to one another for some time before one, the male left.

What was that all about?

The female curled up next to him. Her infant, smaller than Princess, chose then to climb from her mother's back and check him out.

The curious infant crawled all over him, sniffing. She smelled under his neck, around his face, and against his nose. She kept sniffing there. She squeaked notes and started purring like a barn cat.

Her mother twitched at her daughter's purring and crawled over to him. She sniffed where her daughter's nose rested.

The male came back twenty minutes later and laid three oblong things on Delwyn's stomach. Fruit! He could smell their ripeness. In the dark, they felt like butternut squash. He remembered the fleshy melons below, the caustic sap they held, and hesitated.

No, the little sibs couldn't eat them any more than he could.

He bit into one, and juices ran down his face as if he'd bit into an over-ripe pear. They tasted like pears. They even had the gritty texture of pears. He chewed into the center, where seeds grew in squash, to drink the nectar surrounding a large pit. The nectar tasted like fruit cocktail juice, maybe a quarter liter's worth.

Delwyn ate them all and fell asleep

18

SHADOWS OF THE MIND

Delwyn awoke alone in the dark. Above him a light aquamarine glow poured through a hole the size of his fist.

He knelt on his knees and pressed his forehead against a smooth branch and looked through the hole. It gave him an unobstructed view leading up into the foothills. They stood in shadows, but the limestone cliffs and the impact crater ridge behind them loomed above the shadows, a colossal phantom in Tyreniioroneo's blue light. Far above the brooding phantom stars rode upon a clear black sky rent by rippling auroras.

Breezes blew through the peephole. Cool and comfortable, he guessed the temperature at somewhere in the twenty-five to thirty-degree Celsius range. How far would the temperature drop? Farside temperatures at these latitudes compared well to those in central Canada in wintertime. Here on nearside the air was much warmer, but during the long nights temperatures fell another fifteen or twenty degrees. He had been dropped off well below the frost line, but breezy fifteen-degree air on wet skin might expose him to hypothermia.

Delwyn craned his neck around and down to glance through the exit hole. Below, the ground had blossomed with white flowers resembling tiny tulips. They didn't fluoresce, but they seemed to hover above the ground as though illuminated by a black light. They glowed pale in the gas giant's light. Was there some kind of night pollinator roaming the jungle? Why else would flowers open at night?

Delwyn shook his head in wonder and staggered as sudden shooting headaches dropped him to his knees.

He collapsed onto the fuzzy catkin floor coverings and passed out.

###

A female's high-pitched five note warning trill shredded the darkness. Delwyn flinched, banging his head on low-hanging aerial roots filling the maze in the Males' Safe. Whimpers of fear caught in his throat as he huddled in the dark, afraid.

People shrieked and wailed. Shouts of rage carried to his hidden niche. Feet padded through the safe zone. Items clattered. People cursed and panted in the dark. Delwyn heard the fires roar to life below long before he caught the first faint whiff of smoke. Within moments it settled around him, thick and choking. He could barely breathe.

"Run you filthy Mo'ti Ama'ke Clan! Run!" a harsh female voice cried out.

The hollow smack of a club striking a skull made him wince as if he had taken the blow instead of a nearby infant female. An adult female screamed so close she must have been next to him. Another infant began to keen.

With a sick smacking sound the infant's trilling warnings died. The adult female whimpered before being silenced by a second smacking impact.

"Filthy Mo'ti Ama'ke female," the harsh female cursed.

Delwyn's heart hammered like a singing male's drum.

He gasped for air and had to stifle the coughing that came with breathing in the smoke.

Another small group raced past. He heard the frantic whispers of adult females and infants. One told the others to take the infant male through the tree's tiny passages and flee into the jungle.

"Hurry! Hurry!" a second female voice urged.

A second storm of feet came rushing into the safe area. Heavy breathing and the twang of bowstrings followed. Another female screamed, and another infant shrieked. Something slapped flesh, and the shriek muted into a gurgling rattle.

A sob worked its way up into Delwyn's throat. He clamped a hand over his mouth. Too late.

"What was that?" the harsh female demanded.

"I did not hear anything," a second female said. "Where did it come from?"

Delwyn held his breath.

"Maybe I missed one," the harsh female said.

"It is as dark as the Dark Mistress's Abode in here," the second female complained.

"Mistress!" a third voice sang out. "We have killed all the remaining Mo'ti Ama'ke Clan females. We have found no males. They should have accepted our offer of home and safety by now. Is it possible this clan has no males, either? Is this a dead clan too?"

Delwyn raced into the dark jungle, fearless no matter what horrors lived there. He sang out a rallying cry to the infant females who had escaped along with him. They would come to him. They would protect him with their young lives.

And they fell under his guardianship. Any asylum granted to him by the attacking clan would naturally include all infant females associating with him. But first he had to wait for them to find him in the midst of the night battle.

And they came, too. They surrounded him in their hierarchical rank pattern and sang a query to him. What did he want them to do? Fight for him or accept asylum with him?

Delwyn sang a comforting reply to them first and then sang out a loud keening cry.

"Mistress! An infant male comes with his association!"

"Spirits! Sing welcome to him! Welcome him and his association into our clan," the harsh female demanded, sounding not as harsh as before.

Delwyn stalked up to the harsh female. His infant female association flanking him, all 313 of them growling with furious menace.

In the glow of the burning torches and the smudge pot bellows pumping smoke into the elleiu tree Delwyn stood his ground, ears flat against his head, his tail whipping side-to-side.

"What are you called?" she begged him.

Delwyn glared at her, but for the sake of his female association he deigned to reply.

"Fara," he snapped.

"Fara. May you bring joy to the O'un Tu Clan," the Warrior mistress sang.

###

"... Whadizit?"

What the hell? Delwyn wondered. He had dreamed he lived with the Mo'ti Ama'ke Clan during some time in the distant past, before the Compact Counsel had outlawed intertribal and interclan warfare.

Hervorallin! She had told him how the clans fought to protect their males from jungle creatures and from clan raids in those ancient times.

A clan without at least one male, even if only an infant male, was a dead clan.

Males had autonomy. They could live in whatever clan they wanted to.

Full membership came once they had bonded with their first near-daughter. If males didn't want to live with a certain clan, and if by leaving they left the clan without a single male member, then that clan went to war with another clan and killed all the adult females. Deprived of female protection, the surviving males had excellent reasons for accepting the victor's overtures.

"Simple and plain," Hervorallin had said.

At least he hadn't disturbed the little sibs or their infant by thrashing in his sleep.

He had to relieve his bladder. All the rainwater he'd drank had filled it to bursting.

Where was the latrine, anyway?

It was an ironclad cinch the little sibs didn't use necessary boles. The arberi tree was a more earthly looking tree than any elleiu tree, which meant no hollow boles. The little sibs were clean. They had to have a common spot in the tree where they eliminated.

Delwyn crept to the exit hole, and by doing so he woke the male next to him.

He squeaked softly, sounding concerned. He brushed Delwyn's face, gave a happy chirp, and slipped through the hole.

When Delwyn followed him out onto the wide branch, the little brother turned and walked along the branch away from the trunk until Delwyn lost him in the branches.

A minute later he heard a wet splat hit the ground.

The little brother came back and shoved Delwyn down the branch toward the leaves.

"When in Rome," Delwyn muttered. He limped-hopped into the leaves, aimed between them, and let fly.

The night wind blew, causing him to sway on his feet.

"Careful Del, that's a three-story drop to the ground."

Crystal clear white, blue, and yellow stars painted the pitch-black sky. Tyreniioroneo was well past his second quarter.

Delwyn climbed back into the lodge and fell asleep.

###

"So it's a test of character," Delwyn was saying.

Kidahin smiled but shook her head. "No, your character is reflected by the females associating with you. Me, Melkorka, Phelindra, Hervorallin, Zalzadrin, Hlinlodyn, Hlindredreda, our entire society, and any females choosing to associate with you on a personal level. We reflect your character, and you carry our honor.

"Becoming an adult is an important part of clan life. The First Law of the Clan requires us to find our own clan. Finding your clan invokes the First Caution in the Oyya Web: beware the natural predator of the mind. Only an adult can identify this predator. The first caution calls forth the steps to adulthood.

"During the survival ordeal you must know and demonstrate how to scent the facts, know when to let things die, expose the crude shadow, navigate the dark, face the Wild Mistress, survive the irrational, separate truth from fact, ask the spirits, stand on two legs, know what the tail is not, cast your shadow, and use the Spirit Voice.

"To succeed in the survival ordeal, you must make the unknown bargain, experience clan's dismemberment, wander naked and alone, tame the rainforest, work with endurance and fortitude, enter the realm of the Wild Mistress, and successfully argue with all things male."

"Argue with all things male? Isn't that a part of the female adulthood ceremony?" he asked.

Kidahin nodded. "We must learn to control our aggression for the protection and defense of males. Females must survive for three months in the jungle without male contact. This is upsetting and unnatural for us. We struggle to survive the ordeal absent male company, and the male part of us rages to rejoin other males, to quit the ordeal and run like an infant to the males we watch over and protect.

"A male struggles with himself as well. Deprived of female company he becomes uncertain, fears sleep, feels shame, and forms female figments in his mind to care for him. His clear thinking drops. His impatience increases. He becomes reckless and aggressive. A male must keep his head even when far from female pheromones and their stabilizing influence. By doing so he proves himself reliable enough to save females in return.

"As you did for us without female accompaniment at first aboard the Ni'zakhonii light attack craft," Kidahin added.

Delwyn mulled over her words. He had so many questions. "You say the steps to adulthood and the adulthood ceremony are interrelated?"

Kidahin nodded. "An Eyloni, male or female, must cross the trails, each trail signifies one step. Females are pulled into an Oyya Web, a spirit journey where her actions in the Web reflect both the steps and how she overcame them. A male returning from his ordeal has one day to compose a song and relate how he overcame the steps to adulthood in its verses."

"Sounds like females have it easy."

"We do not. A female can survive the ordeal and still become lost in the Oyya Web during the adulthood ceremony held after she returns from the ordeal. I almost lost my way myself when I went chasing after the spirits, something I had been warned not to do. A male only has to sing a song that moves the Tribal Elders in its coverage of how he overcame the steps to adulthood."

"Do the steps come to you in the order you listed them?" he asked.

Kidahin shook her head and took another sip of coffee before continuing. "No, the adulthood ceremony follows a unique order toward adulthood for each of us."

Delwyn's mind drifted. Where had Kidahin found coffee? They hadn't brought any with them from *Henri Edda.*

"Beware the realm of the Wild Mistress. That step is often paired with facing the Wild Mistress," she warned.

"Who is the Wild Mistress?"

"The female aspect of a male. Just as females have to contend with arguing with all things male, all males must face their inner Wild Mistress."

###

Whatthehell? What kind of crazy dreams was he having? Did those fruits he ate contain a narcotic? If they were medicinal in any way, then he'd have a hell of a time sleeping through the long night.

He wasn't sleepy now.

He felt his forehead and winced as even the slightest touch caused him to twinge.

Those twinges made him nauseous.

He wanted to go back to sleep, but something Kidahin had said in the dream kept him awake. *I've found my clan, or at least the La'huaset Clan found me through Princess. That means I've satisfied the First Law of the Clan.*

Kidahin also said males didn't have vision quests. They didn't travel along the Oyya Web, yet she had also said that finding one's own clan pulled everyone into the First Caution in the Oyya Web, and that they should beware of the natural predator of the mind. An adult was supposed to know what this predator was.

"Doubt," he muttered. He mouthed the word again. Doubt hid in the dark heart of uncertainty and second-guessing. Melkorka had once said doubt kills. He knew that from experience, too.

As to the adulthood ceremony, he'd made the unknown bargain by agreeing to the ordeal. That was the bargain every person must make before they could advance any further in Eyloni society. He hadn't known what might befall him in the jungle, yet he had agreed to participate.

"Unknown bargain. Check," he mumbled.

Experience clan dismembership had to mean his temporary exile from the immediate and extended O'ni'da families. He had been cut off from the body of the clan until the ordeal ran its course.

"Separated from the Clan. Check," he whispered.

Wander naked and alone. Hell, he'd been doing that from the start.

"Check. Duh," he grouched.

Tame the rainforest. Well, the jungle personified nature and you didn't mess with Mother Nature. You worked with her, took the path of least resistance. He'd tamed the rainforest by taking the cave system as a shortcut.

"I'll buy that."

It sounded obvious to him that he strove to test his endurance and fortitude. He was doing so now.

Kidahin said the next step in the adulthood ceremony meant entering the realm of the Wild Mistress. Then he had to successfully argue with all things male.

"So what's the realm of the Wild Mistress? The little brothers and sisters?"

But Kidahin had also said the steps to adulthood came during the ordeal. The first, scenting the facts, had to mean being able to see with clarity and to know. Knowing alleviated doubt.

"Done that so far," he grunted.

The next step, knowing when to let die, baffled him. Let what die? It couldn't mean himself, other people, or animals. It had to refer to plans, ideas, concepts …

Childish things?

Know when, or how, to let childhood die.

Easy enough for him, he'd lived an adult life for over thirty years.

What did Kidahin mean by exposing the crude shadow? You exposed a shadow by shining light on it. Did she mean a real shadow or a figment of the mind?

If the survival ordeal revolved around shamanistic initiation, then the loss of all social contact must have some adverse effect on the Eyloni. It played with their minds just as if he had taken a swig of a shaman's hypnotic joy juice.

That sounded like a figment to him.

"So what is a crude figment of the mind?" he asked the sleeping pair beside him.

Crude meant roughly done, but crude also meant vulgar.

What vulgar figment lurked in the mind?

It wasn't doubt, was it? That sent him back to the First Caution of the Oyya Web.

Circular reasoning?

Well, why not? A constant return to doubt led to what, paralysis and surrender?

His sprained ankle had raised a crude shadow in his mind, so had the knock on his noggin.

A concussion. That explained why his head felt like he'd been out on an all-night bender and getting his ass kicked. He hadn't surrendered. Somehow he'd gotten here as night fell.

Navigating the dark came next.

Wasn't he doing that right now, too? Certainly the aspiring adult had to navigate the forests during the long night in any longitudinal zone.

But did navigating the dark connect with exposing the crude shadow? If it did, then this step signified a mental one that made sense in a metaphysical, shamanistic way. Physical darkness could summon the darkness of the mind.

Fear. Wandering the dark corners of the mind meant confronting fear. For the Eyloni, this too must connect with the loss of social contact, the fear of being alone outside of the light of companionship. For an Eyloni male, he had to find his way through the figments his mind created to alleviate the symptoms caused by the loss of female companionship.

For Delwyn this would manifest as PTSD ghosts hovering on the brink of awareness.

Could the little sibs' pheromones hold them back?

Imperfectly, it seems. They were a different species than the Eyloni.

If he was navigating the darkness now, then in the next test he would face the Wild Mistress.

Did that mean he'd already entered the realm of the Wild Mistress but had yet to face her?

Kidahin had said all males must face their inner Wild Mistress.

Inner meant mental, right?

Delwyn's swimming head brought spots, retinal afterimages. They danced across his vision. Eyes open or closed it didn't matter. The floating green and yellow flashes led him back into a fitful sleep.

***

"Are you afraid?" she asks.

"No."

The Wild Mistress shifts as though that is the wrong answer, as though her body is a veil concealing what? *I should be afraid.*

"Fear is good, Delwyn. Do not shy away from it."

"Courage is better," I whisper.

I have fought in many battles, seen many of my ARTs team members lying prostrate on the battlefield dead, wounded, and dying. Some screaming in terror, crying for their mothers. Their wails terrifying everyone around them. Some of my men and women did not cry out, never made a sound. Soldiers in the truest sense, they defied death, letting it caress them like a lover. Their fortitude gave their comrades strength.

I yearn for their bravery now.

But they are not here, and I've had time to think. My injuries hinder me. My ankle's sprained. Walking on it will cause me unimaginable pain. My head rings like a gong, and I have tunnel vision.

"Do not crave courage so desperately," she says. "It is only when you are frightened that the spirits know you love them."

I doubt that. "Love out of fear has been the impetus of many religions."

"What is religion? I speak of the spirits. You should not fear them, but fear should make you seek their counsel."

I doubt that, too. "Fear walks with love, and love walks with fear?"

"Something like that."

"But," I object, "any spirit demanding I fear first wants me to suffer in fear first. How is that just?"

"Do they really?" she whispers. "If you fear for your life, should you hate the spirits for making you wail?"

"That depends on whether or not they show me a way out of my fear."

"Seeking the way out is good," the Wild Mistress trills.

"Like fear?"

"Yes."

"Why?"

"Because if you have no fear, you will never seek out the spirits."

"Which is why I said courage is better."

The Wild Mistress snaps her tail and shakes her head. "The journey to get there is long and hard. There are many touching points on the Oyya Web through which you must travel. The spirits living there have set traps and snares to try to catch you unaware."

"Kidahin told me that involved only females during their adulthood ceremonies," I object.

"For males it comes during the ordeal itself. I want to make sure you understand that."

"Understand what?"

"Quiet. Listen with care."

I nod, and the nodding makes my head swim as a loss of balance overwhelms me.

"The next three steps, surviving the irrational, separating truth from fact, and asking the spirits will come upon you all at once."

"I have courage. I am ready," I tell her.

"Against the irrational you do not. And no, you are not."

***

The dream dissolved, Delwyn sank deeper and it reformed.

***

Where am I?

Who am I?

I am Tellin.

I am a Warrior.

I am not yet an adult, but I will be one soon. I am ready to face my adulthood ceremony.

I came into season for the first time three months ago.

The drive to mate was strong, but only adults may mate.

I am in my immediate families' pheromone-induced Oyya Web of the spirits.

Inside my head is a cave made of darkness. Something lives there, screaming with many voices all at once. I have to wait for it to stop before I can think. I try not to look at it because it is everything at once. It will pull me in and consume me. I keep my eyes rooted to the ground. If I do not I will be pulled into the darkness and never be expelled from the Oyya Web.

There is no need to worry.

"Tellin."

Who said that?

"It is going to be all right."

Yes. I keep my feet planted on the trail.

No! It is coming again.

"Remember what you have learned. The clan females told you about prowling the Oyya Web. Breathe in slow. Hold. Exhale. Again."

I gasp.

I know this vision is a construct made by all the females' pheromones acting on my subconscious mind.

"Who says this is your adulthood ceremony?"

I listened to the clan elders. I know what to expect.

"That is the problem. You did listen to them."

I feel fingers tearing into me, reaching for my heart.

My head is ripping apart.

I cannot tell what is real.

Spirits come find me!

"We are who we are. Just as we follow our way, so must you follow yours."

Visions came, beginning with death.

Get away! Get away!

The spirits wove, conjuring images of battlefield carnage.

Bitter defeat and death increase.

Males dead.

Females dead.

Infants dead.

All dead.

Where are the Warriors? I do not see any dead Warriors. Wait! I see one, the only Warrior among thousands. She stands. She is alive! She is …

Oh, spirits! She is me. *She is me!* Older, but she is still me. What does it mean?

How can I be the only Warrior female remaining in the world?

***

Delwyn groaned. Somebody grabbed his ankle. He screamed and passed out.

***

"Think you are ready now?" the Wild Mistress demanded and faded to black.

No … What just happened?

I know who I am: Delwyn Wyrnette Marsch, Chief Petty Officer, Coalition of Earth Colonies Navy.

I hear … weapons fire … screams. The sounds of war.

A blast of pure white light envelops me.

Blackness.

The battlefield reappears out of the darkness.

I see only in shades of gray.

I'm lying on my back.

I smell corpses lying in pieces all around me.

I hear voices.

"We lie here dismembered, decaying and rotting. Our duty is done. This is our reward. No valkyries to take us, no warriors reward to sate us."

Karen Grabor… That's Apprentice Crewman Karen Grabor. I recognize her voice.

I try to look at her, but I can't move my head.

I can't move my eyes!

There's dirt and grit in my eyes. Why doesn't it hurt?

"Hey Chief? Chief Marsch? Looks like you ain't gonna retire to that farmer co-op like you said you was!" one of the shattered corpses mocked.

No! No! No!

***

Someone woke him, forced water and mashed fruit down his throat. He fought it, choked, and passed out again.

***

The Wild Mistress had returned.

"Not a true vision," I tell her. "I came back, had a family."

"You had a mate and three pre-adolescent near-daughters.

"You have another family now. You have a new near-daughter.

"So many have suffered before you.

"But what they learned can be shared.

"Their voices are your power.

"We are the Clan.

"We live.

"We die.

"We sacrifice everything for the Clan.

"You will reach across the ages and save your people.

"Kidahin knows who you are."

"Kidahin? Wait a minute. Kidahin isn't even an O'un Tu Hunter, so I know this is all wrong too."

"You have always been Eyloni," the Wild Mistress trills ominously.

***

Delwyn sighed. Content, he slept for several hours before sinking back into the maelstrom once again.

***

Dream images crashed and thundered in the form of the Wild Mistress.

Every time I saw through her tangled tales, she pulled me out of the Oyya Web, asked me a question or two, offered a comment or two, and sent me off into another spinning nightmare.

After what feels like days I find myself sitting on powdered dust near a river bank. Sweat trickles down my back. I'm back in my ivy and leaf waistwear. I feel better, more aware, more *here.*

I glance in disgust at my swollen ankle and purple foot.

The Wild Mistress stares at it as well, frowning.

"You are a good teacher," I tell her.

"I am no teacher, and I have taught you nothing you do not already know. I am an aspect of you. We share this moment of time and there are no accidental moments. A teacher sets an idea into stone, thereby constraining it. Have you ever noticed that Eyloni song is never written in say'ta've, the form of writing that documents all matters and makes them unchangeable? You sing verses, but female accompaniment varies according to the abstract spiritual nature of e'va'a, the spirit language used to express the music's freedom needed at that moment.

"Even you change words or add verses as your freedom leads you.

"A teacher offering a Truth does not give but takes away."

"Some things are facts that cannot be disputed," I tell her.

"Yes, yes, but only the facts that can be observed, facts that can be called empirical in nature. Everything else is an artistic truth. Truth that is free to follow the meaning the hearers give it until a teacher explains it in absolutes.

"Then it is dead. It cannot grow or evolve."

"Are you saying that the ultimate truth is that everything is in flux? Wouldn't that make even empirical facts aesthetic truths?" I ask her while watching a grimace play across her face.

"There are no ultimate truths. Ultimate implies a final breakdown—what a teacher does—to a point where all aesthetic truths become empirical truths."

"Aren't they? For the spirits, I mean?"

The Wild Mistress smiles at me in a most intimate, knowing way.

"Have you ever watched water?" she asks suddenly.

"Of course I have. I've seen it in a cup, in a river, in a lake, in an ocean, as rain … I remember rain. I was running through a cyclone, wasn't I?"

"Forget rain," the Wild Mistress snaps. "Our time together is nearing an end. I do not mean just looking at water. I mean have you studied it, its nature, how it moves?

"Do you know its nature?"

"Sure," I reply, "It's wet. Oh, it can exist as a solid, as a liquid, and as a gas."

She flicks her ears in a negative expression. "Water is the softest, most yielding thing in the world. It must work hard when it flows over or around an object. It splashes against something when it is being resisted and has no choice."

"I splash water when I swim. The water doesn't splash me," I point out.

She shakes her head at that. "No. Your body oppresses the water and it splashes against you, trying to push you above or pull you into its enveloping embrace.

"What does water seek?" she asks.

Easy question. "Its own level."

"Yes."

"What about it?" I demand.

"You think of spirits as zal'to'eyloni, sky-people. They are not. Spirits are ki'to'eyloni, water-people. In that way they rain from the sky, bathe the land, and sink below the ground to rise into the air again. Your human male self looks for them in the air, but your Eyloni Warrior self knows better.

"You must separate the truth from the fact."

Her advice, powerful and profound, sends me off into dreamless sleep.

***

"Squeak! Squeak-squeak-squeak! Squeak!"

"What the …," Delwyn muttered as a lemur face peered at him.

The little sister, her infant riding on her back, stared at him until she was sure he was awake.

His bladder was full to bursting again.

It was her turn to lead him out to the leafy latrine.

He nodded and rolled out after her.

His ankle felt wooden, as if Pinocchio had lent him his. He crawled on hands and knees out of the lodge and down onto the wide limb. He stood there and waited.

So far, so good.

He stepped gingerly forward. His ankle protested supporting his full weight, but if he stood straight and kept his full weight off it, it didn't feel so bad.

But when he lifted his right foot to complete the step, the joint threatened to roll under him, and he had to limp the rest of the way to the outhouse in the sky.

Pale light bathed the forest.

Too much blue in it he thought, and he glanced up at a nearly full Tyreniioroneo shining overhead in its frozen 11:38 AM spot.

The sign of a full Tyreniioroneo told him Elleio had arrived in her phase-5 orbital sector around him. Delwyn had been in the forest for five days. The survival ordeal was about half over.

He finished his business and headed back, passing the little sister on her way to the spot he'd just vacated.

Delwyn watched and wondered. Would she hold her infant out into the open air, or did she climb out onto the limb on her own?

He stood there a moment, felt the cool wind on his face, and braced himself against the occasional gust blowing through the tree.

The air felt close to room temperature, maybe as much as five degrees cooler.

Auroras flashed in the night sky.

Constellations blazed. No longer crystal clear, they had turned fuzzy. So had Tyreniioroneo's pale blue disk.

Something about the auroras bothered him, too. He waited for them to light up the sky again.

Then a band of green flashed across the northern sky.

No, not across. It vanished into clouds after crossing two-thirds of the sky: into broad, mean-looking, towering thunderheads.

"The fury of the long night," Kidahin had called them. Without the sun to heat the northern latitudes over the past three Earth days, the ground had cooled and the polar winds breaking over the mountains had spilled south, meeting the warm air driven north and east from the shallow seas. Like lake-effect snows common on the east sides of the North American Great Lakes, Elleio had ocean-effect storms raining out over much of nearside beginning partway through longitudinal zone-d and advancing through the zones to the eastern terminator where they dissipated over farside's oceans.

A noise on the ground distracted Delwyn from the coming storm. The sound of something bulky being pulled through the undergrowth.

The female returned, grabbed his arm, and frantically pulled, urging him to hurry.

Delwyn hesitated, trying to pinpoint the noise on the ground.

He found it soon enough, one of the giant mite-like horrors roving the night forest. He couldn't tell what kind it was, but he knew it wasn't the humble aquatic one or the tree climbing ambush predator.

A steady concussive drone, like the sound of a lifting alphafortress, came rumbling out of the night. Not from the forest hunter, but from the approaching clouds: a threatening continuous earth-shaking thunder that couldn't stop.

Flashes appeared on the southern horizon. Not impressive bolts, no waving arcs, just sky-filling flashes inside monstrous horizon-spanning clouds.

Yet the horror on the ground continued its determined straight line.

It wasn't hunting.

It was running for cover.

"*Squeak!*" the female demanded.

Delwyn nodded at her. "I'm with you, sister!"

He crawled into the lodge first, the female pushing from behind. What prompted her insistence, the approaching storm or the creature below, he had no idea.

Something had changed back in the lodge. The light had vanished. It couldn't be overhead clouds. They remained some distance away. He soon found the reason why. The peephole had been covered in his absence. The male, wide awake, must have plugged it. That meant he anticipated blowing horizontal rain.

Thinking about the male must have triggered a pheromonal label, an identity tag the little brother associated with himself—a name.

He came over to Delwyn and greeted him with lyrical squeaks and sniffed him all over, paying particular notice to his head and ankle.

He squeaked a query to the female.

She squeaked what Delwyn thought sounded like a grumble, dropped her infant onto his stomach, and vanished through the pale blue exit.

The male gave Delwyn six butternut pear fruits. They ate together while waiting for the female to return.

The infant female sniffed at him, sniffed at the fruit he ate, curled up against his neck and over his heart, and purred a deeper throatier purr than any house cat could match.

Unlike Princess, the infant did not curl her tail around his arm or neck. She let it hang behind her in a slight curve along his side.

The rumbling thunder drew closer, interspersed now with low concussive booms better felt through the tree than heard.

The female poked her head back into the lodge, looked everyone over, and climbed over him.

Thinking she reached for her infant, Delwyn pitched his shoulder up, propping the infant forward, and opened his mouth. "Here you go, safe and … Urf!"

She crammed something wet and slimy into his mouth, squeaking with authority as she held her palm over his mouth.

He tasted at least three distinct flavors. One he couldn't identify, the other two tasted something like parsley and cucumber.

It wasn't dirty. Was it food? He didn't want to spit it out in her lodge for fear she'd pitch him out the exit for being filthy.

He swallowed the mouthful.

Happy he'd cooperated, she reached for a fruit and ate with them.

The infant found Delwyn's eating an interesting diversion. She watched him like a dog watched a kid eating a cookie.

Delwyn offered her a small piece of the strange pear.

She sniffed at it, licked it, and squeaked like a kid being offered a healthy snack over the cookie.

Her mother chirped in what sounded almost like humor.

Delwyn laughed too, and tiny baby eyes glared at him from the darkness.

The rumbling grew louder. Flashes lit the floor exit hole. They didn't have the usual cracks and bangs that came with lightning and thunder. The flashes might have been heat lightning, but the concussive rumbling that seemed unrelated to them brought memories of heavy summer thunderstorms.

He staggered, dizzy. His tunnel vision warped as pale-yellow afterimages blossomed across his eyes. Strength drained from him, and he couldn't even manage to keep his eyes open. He spiraled around, weightless. Lacking an up or down reference, he fell back into the abyss.

###

You are falling through time and space.

Is that true? I mean is that a Truth?

Is your body falling through space, or is your mind falling through, what? Consciousness?

Are you conscious?

Are my questions about truth or fact?

Do you have a head injury? Is that a query answerable by a fact or a truth statement?

Where are you? Do not think about it, just answer me.

How do you know whether or not you are being held in a sensory deprivation chamber?

Without sensory input, what empirical fact can you use for substantiating an answer to the question *Where am I?*

"Here."

And where do you think *here* is?

"Where I am now."

Can you describe where you are now?

"It's dark. It goes on forever. It's warm. It feels like I'm floating."

You have just described an empty universe. That is not a where anymore than if you told your Mistress of the Ship you stood somewhere in the universe.

Try harder.

"I'm with me."

You have a split personality?

"No. I mean I'm with myself."

You imply you have an existence apart from yourself?

"Yes."

How do you know?

"I just know."

Do you know it through empirical fact, or do you know it through an aesthetic truth?

"I know it as an empirical truth."

How? You have no senses to tell you that. The darkness is nothingness, and since you feel neither heat nor cold you assume you are floating in warmth.

With no sensory input you have no access to empirical knowledge.

"I know my own mind. I am here."

Prove it. You cannot prove you exist through deductive reasoning that calls upon empirical knowledge.

"You're speaking to me. That is an empirical fact. I am hearing you. We are talking. I exist apart from you by definition."

Am I really here? Or are you talking to a figment in your mind?

"I didn't dream you up."

Prove that, too. See, you cannot. There is nothing you can grasp to tell me you exist.

"It is a true statement that I exist."

How do you know?

"I am that I am who knows that I am." *Wry humor.*

And We are who We are because We know who We are, too. But that is beside the point. What truth leads you to believe you exist as a matter of truth when you cannot prove you exist as a matter of fact?

"I have past experience memories that include other people."

Your memories are subjective. How many of them have you forgotten? Who is to say We have not filled your consciousness with imaginary experiences to comfort you?

What did the Wild Mistress tell you about truth?

"There is no ultimate truth. An ultimate truth implies that all aesthetic truths have been reduced to empirical truths."

Do you know what an aesthetic truth is?

A pause. "Something that evokes feelings or thoughts, like what happens when I look at a painting."

Yes! Good! An aesthetic truth is an artistic truth. Tell us what you know about artistic truth.

"Not much. I'm no artist."

No? Do you not compose music and songs? Do you not paint pictures?

"I do, but I'm no artist."

Why not?

Indifference. "I sing what I write, and I sing what others have written. Musicians and singers performing for a living have way more talent than I could ever hope to have."

That is wrong. You should know why, because the Wild Mistress spoke about this as well.

Remembering. "She said songs and stories had to vary. Once frozen into place they lose their aesthetic value."

Yes. The professional singers you refer to sing the same notes, the same words, in the same way. They are not singing but performing, mouthing the same notes. The music has lost all meaning to them.

"What does that have to do with proving to you that I exist?"

Think about it.

"Are you saying I'm an artistic truth?" *Incredulity.*

Yes. We are as well. Think about it. Without your senses, and for all you know without your body as well, you are not stuck in the same mental state you had when you first woke up here. You have been adapting, changing the melody, adding words to the verses describing your existence.

Understanding. "I'm a song?"

Yes. We sang you into existence.

Doubt. "How does that work?"

Neither brain nor body is necessary for consciousness as long as data storage exists and there is synthesis: a synergism. Integrated data is consciousness, whether they are networks in nervous systems, root systems, or storm systems. Anything that can move data and act on it raises a question: how conscious is it?

Consciousness is inherent in reality. It is a fundamental universal property. The Eyloni also create a conscious metamind through their pheromonal empathy. Music enhances it. The complexity music can achieve implies a relationship working in the same way excitor and inhibitor neurons process data in neural networks.

"That Oyya Web Kidahin and the others always talk about?"

Yes.

"It's a song?"

Yes. Your mind holds a concept: the music of the spheres.

Denial. "That's just an old reference I read about once, a philosophical reference to a genesis myth."

Yes. The Singers sang existence into existence.

"Kidahin told me about that during one of my lessons on *Hunter's Moon.*"

Yes. Melkorka, Phelindra, Hervorallin, even Zalzadrin told you about these things.

"Is that why I'm imagining that I'm talking to the spirits now?"

Perhaps. Maybe we are just figments floating in your fevered mind.

"Thanks to my blown ankle." *Betrayal.*

Not your ankle. Your head injury. The little sister smelled your emotional need and gave you what she could to help.

"The little sister knows what to do?" *Amazement.*

You occupy the low ground. Of course she helped you.

Wary. "Why must I separate the truth from fact?"

You must stand on your two legs and argue with all things male.

Doubt. "Okay. Why?"

So you will know what the tail is not.

Bafflement. "That doesn't make any sense."

It is not supposed to. It doesn't matter. What does matter is that you remember artistic truth does not belong to verses in a song or to their obvious figurative meaning. They show you the song's discursive material, extended thought weaves, moving from topic to topic, loose, rambling. The product of the song, the artistic phenomenon, is not discursive. It is implicit, hidden in the song as a totality. In this way, a song presents a concept to the mind beyond the totality of the words themselves and the artistic truth speaks to the heart and the soul.

This artistic truth has no inconsistency, and its truth-value cannot be reversed. It can express opposites at once without conflicting. It can show something present as an intuitive pattern of senses on a deeper level of insight and attitude.

Artistic truth and personal insight may be taken as equal to an empirical fact. But remember, unlike literal factual empirical truth artistic truth has degrees of structure. You know this when you judge music as good or bad, and yet another judges the music as bad or good.

The enemy of artistic judgement is literal judgement. The reason your Eyloni never had what you consider religion is because they never thought to project a literal judgement onto an artistic concept. The more you force a literal judgement onto an artistic concept, the more you miss the artistic impression that depends on artistic truth.

All ritual is artistic symbolism.

Do you understand?

"Uhh …" *Vagueness.*

We have forever to teach you this. So we will repeat it again, from the beginning.

You are falling through time and space …

###

Wham!

Delwyn cracked his eyes open at the sound of thunder rumbling above. Rain poured over the roof as if the lodge had been set under a waterfall.

Lightning arced and flashed all around them.

The infant remained curled around his neck. Her mother asleep against his back.

The male, wide awake, watched the flashing lightning, his mate, his infant, and Delwyn in roving order.

He saw Delwyn's eyes open and crawled over to greet him with low squeaks, pushing down on his chest.

"Don't worry. I'm not going outside in that!"

Delwyn noticed his tunnel vision had faded away, although his head still swam, causing green and yellow flashes and floaters to fill his vision at the lightest jerk.

Nausea threatened his heaving stomach. The striking lightning with its bright strobes and the crashing thunder with its deafening percussive blasts where bad enough without his inner ears doing their best to convince him he was rolling around in a barrel over the cascade drowning the arberi tree.

"I'll just close my eyes for a few minutes and relax."

It didn't take him long to fall into a normal, healthy, dreamless sleep.

###

The Comari crouched in a hollow trunk, trying to keep the night torrential rains from flooding the small space.

She had made it into the foothills and the towering trees growing there an hour before the southern storm broke. The spirits and luck had led her to this tree before an ocean fell on her. Two ells above the ground, tree rot had eaten away an ell into the wood and about an ell in height, making a small bole. She had to squeeze to fit.

It had been a challenge to get inside. She had to wiggle through a hole while having nothing to pull on or push against. At least the bole had been low to the ground, otherwise it would have filled with stagnant water from previous rains. As it was, she had to hold two large leaves against the opening to keep the wind-swept water from billowing into the tree.

No doubt Warleader Delwyn was doing the same.

How far had he gotten by now? The limestone tor? It was the obvious landmark to strive for. It held the high ground, and by simple orienteering around the cliffs to the southeastern exposure he should be able to hear the Om'tu Falls with ease. The rubble and scree should pave an excellent trail free from entangling jungle cover. It might take him time to circumnavigate the massive weathered heap, but it was a lot faster than prowling a direct route through the highland flank.

Her best guess put him at or just beyond the eastern cliffs.

Fortunate for him if so. This southern storm would rage against the limestone cliffs. Depending on where he was, he might not even feel more than mists and moderate rain. The rocky bulk would shield him from the gale force winds driving the rain northeast.

His way might be blocked by temporary cataracts cascading down the worn grooves in the cliffs. Rainwater falling on the weathered spires would accumulate as it drained into pockmarked stone before falling to the forest floor. The water would make small, fast-moving rapids and carve runoff ditches and ravines into the forest. He would certainly not try to cross them.

Besides, some cliffs had folds, shelves, and even small caves he could always shelter in and wait out the storm.

That made sense to her. Other bonuses came with traveling around the ancient fossil, too. It gleamed pale blue in Tyreniioroneo's light and could be seen for some distance. Most dangerous jungle animals avoided the rocky heights. By now he was surely enjoying a dry stone niche and a small fire.

The Comari sighed. She wished she had a fire. She preferred her equatorial home territory over the temperate north. The air felt cold and damp against her skin as mist and spray blew through the gaps in the wide leaves she held against the open bole.

She considered. A male did not become warleader by being stupid. Delwyn could certainly survive a month in the jungle. He was no infant. He was not an adolescent, either. He was an adult!

She had told Kidahin so.

Kidahin. That young Hunter had been hysterical. Well, Kidahin is young.

The Comari paused to recall Kidahin's scent. She had smelled young, impulsive, wildly protective of her warleader—not a bad thing—and juvenile. She had chosen him for her society. She had been the huluhar who chose him, after all.

Oh, for the spirits' sakes! Kidahin's emotional empathy had driven the Comari to this rash act. She stood in a hollow tree, in the wild jungle, surrounded by storms, cold and wet for the male she felt certain needed her protection more than any other male.

A male who probably did not even need her help right now.

She had gone leafchasing after him at Kidahin's insistence!

Her hand convulsed around the spear shaft she held against her side.

She would have words about this with Kidahin! She would take this matter up with the hierarchies.

No. She would not. She sighed. Kidahin had his safety in mind. *But she would teach her what it meant to interfere with the concerns of a Comari.*

Now what? Her best move now might be to break off the intercept course into the jungle foothills and head back to the hydroelectric plant. From there, she could call for transport back to Na'di Island.

Once the rain had stopped.

***

The storm, having vented its fury on the northern longitudinal zone-c, continued through zone-b and into zone-a.

Delwyn awoke to the assault of a pounding headache, but at least no yellow and green spots or tunnel vision marred his eyesight.

His ankle felt better. Tight and stiff, but he could wiggle his toes.

And he winced every time he did so, too.

He looked through the exit hole. The pale blue light had lost its intensity. He was alone. Where had the little sibs gone? Potty breaks?

Delwyn poked his head through the opening and saw the little sibs on the branches. They worked together, but he couldn't see what they were doing. He crawled out onto the wide branch and strolled over to watch them work.

At first he thought they were grooming one another, and yes they were taking part in that communal act. But that was not all. They drank from pools in depressions in the smooth bark. They scoured the branches for every last drop.

Why? The ground had its own supply of puddles.

He looked up at Tyreniioroneo and understanding struck. The gas giant had dimmed as he passed through his waning phases. That meant Elleio had entered orbital phase-6. This time of night was analogous to somewhere around 03h00 in the morning on Earth. The sun should rise in another thirty-eight hours. No doubt by then the absorbent soil would have sucked all the puddles below ground.

The little sibs got all the water they needed from the fruits they ate and the water they found in the hollows, nooks, and crannies in their tree.

The early morning air felt cool and calm, no breezes at all. His skin felt damp, clammy. It would get even more humid when the sun came up.

The little sibs came up to him, petted and touched him, and led him to a dip in the wide bough that glistened in the pale light as the water it held reflected the auroras flashing across the clear early morning sky.

About a liter remained in the dip, and they insisted he drink it—all of it.

He crouched on hands and knees, pursed his lips, and slurped the puddle dry. Water—he hadn't known how thirsty he'd been. He could drink liters more, but he didn't dare take excesses from his host.

He stood up and practiced walking up and down the branch.

His foot looked as if an eggplant had been grafted to his ankle. It twinged with every step. He'd have to bind it again before he could try any distance walking.

Getting down to the ground he preferred not to think about. Dropping onto his feet from any height would ruin the benefit the last five days had given him.

Then again, awake and well rested he felt much better.

The northeastern foothills compared well to an old dense mountain forest below the tree line on Earth. He had found rough patches impassible and places where he couldn't see the sky through the canopy, no matter how much the pastel fall ochers let more diffused light reach the ground than any earthly heavy forest. The rainforest had been quiet compared to Earth forests, too. Insects didn't chirp. No cricket or katydid sounds echoed here. No birds lived here either. Bugs grew larger than bats and smaller than sand grains. The heavy rains had interrupted normal night activity. But now, in the early morning, the forest creaked and groaned as night breezes soughed through parchment awning leaves. Glowing insects, fireflies that didn't flash, flew in globular swarms by the hundreds.

Every so often he heard a hard surface being pounded against wood, like woodpeckers but heavier and not repeating as fast. But what confused him the most was the slow, soft cracking sounds surrounding him, as if the tree had been invaded by clacking beetles by the millions.

Delwyn happened to be staring at a leafy branch when he noticed that it seemed to stretch in the dim light.

No wind blew to disturb it. The clacking grew louder.

Delwyn stood up and walked to the leaves surrounding the airborne necessary and watched the leaves stretch. Spellbound, he held the leaf in both hands. It flexed in his hand. He recoiled, almost pitching himself off the branch.

He reached out again and placed his palm under the giant leaf and pulled it to him. He watched it grow in his hand in the pale blue glow. It grew at night, like corn. The leaf felt more alive now than it had looked when hanging there in the daylight.

He watched, enchanted, as the leaf grew a millimeter a minute. What caused its flexing? Uneven growth? Yes! That was it. If it grew at a constant rate, it would tear.

The little sibs headed back into their lodges. He counted at least forty climbing up into the leafy heights.

His two hosts came up and sat down next to him. This was the first clear view he'd had of them, albeit in the gibbous pale blue light. They did look something like hairless lemurs after all. Their skin color patterns followed Eyloni patterning, but these patterns incorporated creamy pale yellows. They had no red or orange skin, not a bit, anywhere. They sat on their haunches like big fat tabbies or walked on all fours but often switched to a two-legged sideways skipping gait.

They did look like Eyloni Hunters in the face, but the little brother had the more humanlike Warrior female face. Their ears were as expressive as Eyloni ears were too, but their tails not so much—at least not as far as he could tell. He compared their body language to the Eyloni behavior he knew but had no idea what the little sibs were telling one another half the time.

They watched him, curious, almost expectantly.

They relied on eye contact signaling, too. Staring at them didn't challenge them in the way some animals on Earth would feel challenged. These animals, like their Eyloni cousins, sought eye contact and considered avoiding the eyes a sinister, evasive act. Such behavior wasn't tolerated. The eagle-eyed sneak got a good melodic squeaking scold. If scolding failed, then the offender got a cuff on the nose.

And they had a rank structure. Both males and females had some kind of gender ranking, but different groups had different standings, a social pecking order. It had to relate somehow to the lodge levels in the tree itself. It depended on the individual, but it also depended on the group the individual belonged to as well.

He couldn't find a pattern to explain it.

Several looked down at him from the different branches. Apricot and red amber eyes all blinking down at him, the flaring auroras often blinding him to their eyes' dim orange sparks.

The little sister's infant climbed into his hands and curled up into a ball.

"What am I supposed to do now?" Delwyn asked her mother.

The infant rumbled a deep rough purr.

They sat on the branch together, staring at the blue orb above.

Minutes later they started squeaking lyrical melodies.

They sang to Tyreniioroneo, like wolves howling at the Moon.

Other trees, far off in the distance, produced their own concert of rhythmic sibilant squeaks. The combined sounds blended in consonant harmony, but each family tree echoed a melody in counterpoint.

Delwyn caught the beat, felt the rhythm, and started to hum it when the female pressed her hand against his lips gently but firmly.

He was not welcome to sing with them.

He listened to them sing, the infant asleep against his stomach. Not tired, he fell asleep listening to their song anyway.

Sometime later Delwyn awoke, climbed into the lodge, and went back to sleep. Hours later he awoke again, looked outside to see Tyreniioroneo in his narrow crescent and the sun peaking over the eastern horizon. Elleio had entered orbital phase-7 while he slept, and the sun had slowly crept into his 06h00 sunrise skyclock.

Time for him to leave. He chewed a piece of caffeine, cinnamon, and hot pepper charged arberi leaves and repaired his sewn leaf shorts.

The little sibs gave him straight sticks from their lodges to splint his ankle. They also brought him a meter-long catkin. Its floral scent smelled strong, pleasant, and vaguely medicinal—like witch hazel. They chewed it into mush and packed his ankle with it.

Delwyn stared at the goldenrod spitwads, wondering what they used them for, and if they'd been doing so for the past six days or not.

The leaves felt smooth and strong. The upper side shined, glossy; but the underleaf felt fuzzy like a mullen leaf. The wide, heavy leaves had fibers running through them to reinforce them, which kept them from folding across their width from their own weight. They folded easily enough along their length.

He wrapped his ankle with them, squeezing little sib spit from the chewed catkin as he sewed them together as tight as an athletic bandage. Then he placed the smooth flat sticks around the joint and wrapped the remaining folded leaves, sewing them to the sticks and the inner wrap.

He used some ivy twine to make new sandals.

When he was ready, the little sibs gave him three more butternut shaped fruits and watched him eat them.

As he ate, others climbed down to enjoy a morning survey through their territory. The ground was damp but not so much as a puddle remained, not even where he'd dug the shallow pit.

He turned to the problem of getting down without tearing his half-healed ankle.

Eight little sibs squeaked from the ground and headed off into the jungle.

Delwyn paced the branch and decided the best strategy would be to walk out into the leaves and hang on as the branch bent to the ground, and hope it didn't snap.

It was bad enough he'd land in their outhouse.

About the same time he decided to chance it, excited squeaks echoed throughout the forest.

Minutes later the little sibs came back, each one helping to drag a long green vine. They climbed the tree with ease, pulling the vine after them. They dropped it at his feet, where it fell across the wide bough and dangled to the ground.

Delwyn knew then that these animals weren't stupid. Two demonstrated how he must climb. They had no idea what a knot was, but they knew enough to hold both ends of the vine, or else it would slip over the bough.

He grabbed one end, and a female handed him the other end. Holding both ends tight, he swung under the branch, hoping the vine could take his weight.

It did. The two-centimeter-thick vine was smooth, the little sib demonstrating the climb down had stripped the vine of its green leaves and black flowers.

Delwyn climbed down hand over hand, not wanting to risk losing a grip on either one of the dangling vines and falling.

His feet touched damp, almost soggy ground. His leg felt stable, at least for now.

How long would it last?

All the little sibs came down the tree and gathered around him. Fifty-three in total, all squeaking. They followed as he headed off toward the towering broadleaf trees in the distance.

The little sibs trailed him, tails arched up and walking on all fours like ring-tailed lemurs. They walked for over an hour before giving him a squeaking send-off, turned around, and headed back up the trail to their tree.

"Good-bye!" Delwyn yelled after them. "I'll never forget you!"

He turned back around and set a cautious but steady pace.

He had almost three daylight phases, almost four Earth days daylight to work with. It would get hot and humid before the next twenty-four hours were up.

19
A SHOW OF SOLIDARITY

Melkorka sat in the mission planning session taking notes as she listened. Seated next to her, Hlinlodyn typed nonstop on her own 'minder. On Melkorka's other side, Anailiatha was busy going over engineering repair and replacement reports.

The Mistress of the Hunt had just finished presenting her assessment of *Hunter's Moon's* repair status. She only grudgingly agreed that their part in the mission, while possible, remained doubtful.

Well, Melkorka did not blame her.

The repair crews had already scanned, mapped, and quantum translated whole compartments to the cargo tugs. The damaged compartments had then been ferried to A'lon'aloop for translation to the warship manufacturing center operated by the Kem Basinga Clan on the La'huaset Tribal continent. The compartments were being mounted into the assembly scaffolding for assessment. Hopefully those damaged compartments could be rebuilt even faster than Anailiatha's estimates.

Melkorka saw firsthand what they had done to her beautiful warship. He looked like a diced fruit with rectangular pieces cut out of him. The sight made her skin crawl. Before the damaged compartments had been translated away, he looked even worse. The blackened, twisted, broken hull reminded her of a male hit by antipersonnel rounds.

But now he looked like a male on an autopsy table.

Surgery, she corrected herself. Their warship lived.

But somehow the view looked far worse now. Compartments, some several decks deep, had been ripped out. Several compartments could not be removed intact. Power budgets rose with the amount of mass translated. Mass cost more in energy expenditure than distance moved, so the repair crews removed the damaged compartments piecemeal.

She shuddered, sought a diversion, and watched Hlinlodyn take notes.

This briefing included all mistresses of tactics because they commanded their warships' Combat Analysis Centers. A mistress of tactics fought the ship. She was the combat operations mistress, and she acted on data coming from Combat Analysis in a manner consistent with whatever overall strategy her mistress of the ship devised. Hlinlodyn found targets, plotted firing solutions, and commanded the gun crews and torpedo bays. She also assigned gun crew target priorities unless overruled by the mistress of the ship or the warleader.

As warleader during Battle Status and while engaged in combat, Delwyn could overrule any mistress at will. That mistress would then adapt her seamless response to his judgement. The warleader commanded missions and served as the strategist, but his presence served a more primitive need: a male in danger was both a focus and a rallying point for any female.

Hlinlodyn had to consider all variables, present alternatives, and then discuss them with Melkorka. She would then brief Delwyn about what had been discussed here.

Melkorka smiled expectantly.

Thinking about her favorite male brought nagging worry with it. *He is about two-thirds the way through the survival ordeal by now.*

"I am thinking about him too," Hlinlodyn sang under her breath.

"I worry about him," Melkorka murmured.

"Do not. Your scent is distracting me, and the others may take it to mean you do not consider him capable enough to survive it. If we can survive three months, Delwyn can survive one."

"I know. I know. But he knows so little about the rainforest."

Hlinlodyn heaved an exasperated sigh. "He knew nothing about the Nikkiolo moon and its ugly green forests, yet he persevered."

"Yes," Melkorka agreed, "but Phelindra or her Hunters always shadowed him."

"But they did not interfere," Hlinlodyn pointed out.

"There is no one shadowing him now," Melkorka said.

"I am not so sure," Hlinlodyn muttered offhandedly.

"What do you mean by that?" Melkorka demanded.

"Hmm? Oh, nothing. I heard Trebithia was complaining about Kidahin poking her tail into the matter."

"Kidahin? What can she do about it?" Melkorka asked. "She cannot interfere without invalidating the ordeal, an insult to Delwyn's honor and hers."

"Kidahin has been trying to find a certain Comari," Hlinlodyn trilled obliquely.

"What certain …?" *Oh.* "Why should she get involved?" Melkorka asked, suspecting she already knew the answer.

"I think Kidahin means to confront the Comari with Delwyn's ordeal and its possible danger to him."

"Why should she listen to Kidahin? If she had been near her time she could have claimed Delwyn when she scent marked him. She is just biding her time marking potential choices. The only thing Kidahin can do is get herself killed for interfering with a Comari's personal autonomy."

Melkorka thought about Kidahin's reckless, brazen, foolhardy, and courageous act for moment or two.

"Do you think Kidahin found her?" Melkorka added.

"I doubt it. Comara are secretive, sly, and unobtrusive for the most part. Her skin might be as pale as Delwyn's skin is beige, but a Comari can pass unseen when she wants to. Males and Warrior females find them hard to track, and even a Hunter's success at stalking them is low. Pity the Hunter caught stalking a Comari. They do not appreciate people snapping their tails at them."

"So there is no chance Kidahin will ever find her," Melkorka said, satisfied. Good. Nobody was going to be demanding Kidahin's life.

Melkorka returned to her waiting 'minder, sighed, and flicked her long, four-jointed index finger across the screen, resetting the display to the beginning of the briefing materials. She read again the mission preamble and toyed with the thoughts racing through her mind.

The Compact Counsel considered four aggression standards permissible by the Eyloni as a people to justify a purposeful end: instrumental violence, revenge, dominance, and ideology. The last standard, ideology, employed violence to advance tribal or clannish credos. The Compact Counsel had outlawed ideological violence centuries ago.

The battle group mission statement classified this operation as "A combat operation meant to administer instrumental violence for the removal of a danger to male health and safety embodied in the Ni'zakhonii technological breakthroughs illustrated by the equipment captured by Delwyn O'un Tu La'huaset Eyloni ar ahoun Unahaillaea *Tyreniioroneo.*" The quote satisfied the need for instrumental violence and invoked the natural aggression common to Eyloni culture and ethics.

The mission preamble also set forth the Compact Just War Doctrine. All mission operations planning included a statement asserting one of four rationales: territorial defense, protection of the innocent, the defense of males, or for punishing outlawry. To justify the use of force rationales, the A'tayotan hierarchy and the warleaders involved had to certify upon their respective honors that a just cause existed, that all Eyloni had a just interest, and that war was a last resort. They had to agree to this in a formal statement to the Be'atika Senge declaring that each one of the three requirements did in fact exist.

Melkorka read the particulars calling for the Nikkiolo Expanse operation.

The combat operation had been justified under the male defense and the safekeeping of innocents rationales. Safekeeping males always raised a just cause.

Females had a survival interest in defending males. The planned mission was a last resort. They could not allow the prototype light attack craft research materials to reach enemy home territory. The A'tayotan and the Be'atika Senge had then authenticated the mission.

The warleaders would do the same prior to battle group departure. Males wielded the final approval on war-making power. Autonomous males, warleaders commanding autonomous warships, could stymie the will of the Compact Counsel as a final check on war-making power—but they had better have an honorable reason for disregarding their obligations.

Melkorka scrolled through several columns until she found the war theory heading. Mission planning called for an engagement with enemy forces. War theory said indirect attacks led to victory. The mission operations plan called as much for stealth as it did for combat. They had been instructed to destroy all soft targets encountered as long as they held the high ground.

That was standard operating procedure, Melkorka knew. They would not slug it out in a battle of attrition unless victory could not be gained in any other way. Eyloni always fought territorial wars and never sought wars of attrition. Battles of attrition on the other hand could come about by happenstance or by design. If nothing could be gained by attrition, war theory called for the warleader to withdraw, saving his valuable male self and his warship society. But sometimes a ship could not withdraw, and sometimes victory demanded a warleader and society fight to the last measure.

Compact War Doctrine existed to keep males from dying needlessly.

"Simple and plain," Melkorka hummed under her breath.

"What was that?" Hlinlodyn asked.

"Nothing. I am reading through the force utilization plan."

True enough. That was the next subtitle. Melkorka skipped over ship utilization plans until she found the subsection highlighting the mission profiles for *Hunter's Moon* and *Pathfinder.*

Pathfinder's mission called for assaulting any natural body the enemy research shipyard might be built into. Operational planning said he was to lay off standard surveillance orbit and bombard the surface, softening up enemy defense forces before landing assault forces and combat vehicles moved in.

Melkorka read on until she reached the mission profile for her warship: *Hunter's Moon, assuming he is sufficiently repaired to sortie with the battle group, shall assume honor point escort off* Green Ivy *and stand ready to engage any capital ships such as the enemy might send against the battle group.* She swore an obscenity, something about where somebody could shove her tail.

"What?" Hlinlodyn blurted, shocked by the vile disgusting curse.

"We have been relegated only to honor escort duty, but we do have the freedom to engage any capital ships that happen to get in our way."

"*What?* What about the assault forces? There is a much greater likelihood for a defended base than a picket force of any strength. They have to know that."

"I am sure they do," Melkorka sighed. "*Pathfinder* has been given the planetary assault mission—if we find a planet to assault—because even now it is uncertain whether or not our warship can meet the departure deadline."

Hlinlodyn scowled. "If Delwyn's analysis is correct, then we should encounter nothing more than garrison strength ground forces and at most a few supply ships and their escorts. That means fleet support ships and a light cruiser or two, maybe even a few light attack craft. Certainly nothing able to withstand the punch of a Compact destroyer. What are we supposed to do Melkorka? Feel honored about our holding the honor escort point for the command warship?"

"Yes," Melkorka growled through clenched teeth. "It is an honor because the honor and its intended obligation has been accorded to Delwyn. The A'tayotan could have decided to have us following them instead. The honor point escort during ships movement places the welfare of *Green Ivy* in Delwyn's hands. The honor exists whether or not enemy capital warships are expected or encountered."

"That does not assuage my sense of honor one bit," Hlinlodyn retorted. "Could they have another reason?"

"Such as?" Melkorka asked.

Hlinlodyn whispered in a small voice. "Delwyn?"

"What about Delwyn?" Melkorka demanded, rage surging into her breasts.

"Not so loud," Hlinlodyn hissed. "And you know what I mean. The A'tayotan might have considered Delwyn … insufficient to the need."

Heat radiated from Melkorka's body as she fought to regain control over her violent anger. She had a temper hard to manage even over what others might deem 'minor' slights. Her body, reacting to her blistering rage, poured pheromones into the air, which alerted everyone in the room to her righteous fury and the reason behind it.

"Do you have something to add, Mistress Melkorka?" the Mistress of the Hunt, a much older Warrior than Melkorka, asked.

"No, Mistress Atridredha, I do not."

Hlinlodyn began to open her mouth when Melkorka silenced her with a glare of murderous fury.

"Oh, I think you do. Why not tell the other mistresses here what is really on your mind? Or you, Mistress Hlinlodyn? What insult burns in your Hunter's heart?" Atridredha trilled.

Melkorka shook her head, biting her tongue. While she had a vicious temper and once unleashed had a hard time controlling it, she could keep silent and let her pheromones raise the issue. By failing to follow up on it with a verbal indictment, everyone picking up on her empathic scent would politely let the matter drop. The life of any person living in a pheromone-linked empathic society turned on such customs.

"You doubt our Warleader's ability!" Hlinlodyn spat.

Oh, no! Melkorka mouthed and then mentally cringed. Her anger vanishing.

"What?" the Mistress of the Hunt demanded. "You dare accuse me of undermining your warleader's honor?" She pulled her adulthood knife from its curved sheath beneath her left breast.

"No! She does not!" Melkorka said and jumped between Hlinlodyn and Atridredha.

"I say she does, Melkorka. Let the Hunter affirm or deny the charge herself!"

Melkorka turned in time to see Hlinlodyn pulling her own adulthood knife.

The other females in the room stood and spread out into a wary circle, surrounded the three, and watched for treachery.

"I say you have relegated Delwyn's part in this mission to nothing!" Hlinlodyn sang in challenge.

Melkorka stepped aside and joined the circle with the others. Hlinlodyn had answered the Mistress of the Hunt's challenge. They had to argue it out to their mutual satisfaction, or else they would duel to the death over the perceived insult to their respective honors.

Atridredha could not let the insult to her honor go unanswered. She would never deliberately demean a male's honor. Had she done so by accident? She ticked off what she knew about Delwyn and shook her head. Better she fall on her own adulthood knife than what the mistresses here might do to her if they believed Hlinlodyn's charge was true. All hierarchies deemed insults to male honor a capital crime.

"The A'tayotan listened to Warleader Delwyn and is honored that he has offered his services in this mission. But mission planning cannot assume his warship will meet Battle Status readiness by the time the battle group reaches the Nikkiolo Expanse. Planning must therefore consider *Pathfinder* the primary assault warship. As a mistress of tactics, you must know this. Do you still accuse me of sullying the honor of Warleader Delwyn, Mistress Hlinlodyn A'to'ka Lena La'huaset Eyloni?"

Hlinlodyn gripped her knife, eyes narrowed, panting. A small voice in her mind screamed accusations at Delwyn for her violent instinctive reaction. It was all his fault! He affected her, Kidahin, and at least several hundred others like this, much more than any other male had ever affected them before. *Oh, Spirits!* If Delwyn had been standing here, she would have already sliced Atridredha's breasts off! "No Mistress, I do not. I ask forgiveness. I am not myself when the interests of my warleader are near my heart."

Melkorka had been squeezing the pommel of Delwyn's oddly curved sword so hard she wondered that it hadn't squashed like a ripe malutha berry.

Atridredha smelled the truth of Hlinlodyn's words. Both hers and Melkorka's scent reeked with protective intensity.

The females in the circle understood both the honor issue and the rage that came up on both sides. Each one of them would have felt the same way had her own warleader been slighted.

Atridredha sheathed her adulthood knife and nodded.

Hlinlodyn shoved hers into its sheath, nodded back, and rejoined Melkorka, glaring defiance at her. A defiance that soon turned into sibilant grumbling.

"Continuing," Atridredha said with wary caution, "if *Hunter's Moon* and his destroyer escorts are Battle Status ready on time, the battle group will jump from Wrathsee'a Anchorage staging orbit for Nikkiolo."

"Mistress Atridredha?" a mistress of the ship interrupted. "What about Warleader Anlann? How has Mistress Ahwroona decided to proceed?"

Melkorka held her breath. Now this should be interesting indeed, she thought to herself. She pricked her ears at the still seething Hlinlodyn until she noticed and looked up.

Ahwroona dipped her ears and absently reached for her own adulthood knife. She gave herself a slight shake and let her hand continue to her shoulder to scratch an imaginary itch. Her left hand throttled Anlann's sword pommel as she considered her reply.

"The A'tayotan and the Be'atika Senge sent inquiries to Anlann asking if he might consider returning home early. I know they sent him enough details for him to grasp the need. His communications avatar discussed options with me concerning plans for a Nikkiolo system rendezvous. I know he will meet us there because I know him better than I know my own tail.

"Anlann must secure transport to Nikkiolo. The Coalition warship that conveyed him to Earth should also bring him back because the Coalition has agreed to send a male counsel-speaker to the Be'atika Senge. One issue remains concerning departure times. I do not know how long it will take the Coalition warship to refuel and resupply before he can begin the journey to Nikkiolo. Delwyn O'un Tu La'huaset Eyloni of *Hunter's Moon* can answer this better than I."

"So you have agreed to sortie with the battle group?" Atridredha interrupted, thunderstruck.

"I know Delwyn asked for Anlann in this matter. If his warship is Battle Status ready by the departure deadline we will place our warship under the safekeeping of Delwyn O'un Tu La'huaset Eyloni as his honor escort destroyer. If his warship is not battle ready, then we will not participate in combat operations without our Warleader." Ahwroona said.

Shocked amazement flooded the room. People glanced back and forth between Ahwroona and Melkorka. Mistresses of the ship resisted taking their warships anywhere without their warleaders. To do so made everyone aboard feel lost and abandoned. They all but refused to do so over even short interplanetary distances, but Ahwroona seemed all too willing to do so across interstellar distances. That she agreed to do so put forests of credibility into Delwyn's hands.

Everyone turned their attention on Melkorka.

The stunned silence played at Anailiatha's ears as she read page after page of engineering assessments. Immersed in physics and mathematics—her existential pastime—she tended to miss events happening around her. Her ears began to twitch as she read, missing the droning voices her mind had long since relegated to the background. But the odor of heart-stopping surprise caused her to blink at her 'minder as she finally noticed the timeless silence. She glanced at the shocked group and then turned to Melkorka.

"What? Did I miss something?" she asked.

Melkorka brushed Anailiatha's tail with her own and shook her head. "No. Go back to your engineering analysis."

Atridredha found her voice. "But if *Hunter's Moon* cannot depart with the battle group, then Anlann will end up getting himself stranded in the Nikkiolo Expanse!"

Ahwroona flipped her tail in negation. "He will not be stranded anywhere. If he is aboard a Coalition heavy warship and we are not at the Nikkiolo rendezvous point, then he will continue on to Elleio with the Coalition counsel-speaker."

"You will not go there to meet Anlann?" Atridredha demanded.

"No. Anlann has been gone from us for months. We know he is returning to us. The Coalition warship will not join the battle group. As things stand now, he will either bring Anlann to us in the Nikkiolo Expanse, or he will bring him home to us much sooner than we expected had the request for his recall not been issued."

"And how does all this sit with your society?" Atridredha all but shouted.

"That is our affair, not yours. Do not intrude into our warship's business," Ahwroona sang at warning pitch.

"I think this issue has been adequately addressed," Verikaralee interrupted.

"This does not concern you, Mistress Verikaralee. Your warship has been integrated into the primary task force. *Hunter's Moon*, *Surefooted,* and *Night Shadow* make up the reserve task force."

"I want our warship reassigned to the reserve task force," Verikaralee demanded.

"Why?" Atridredha asked.

"Because I said so."

Startled into momentary helplessness, Atridredha turned to *Night Shadow's* mistress of the ship "What say you, Renaldra?"

The destroyer's mistress of the ship turned to Verikaralee, met her eyes, and perked her ears. "We have assumed the honor of remaining with Warleader Delwyn. Likewise, we would be honored to have a place in the primary task force. As honor accrues to us in either event, I have no quibble over Verikaralee's request."

Faolindra, *Green Ivy's* Mistress of the Ship, had the sudden feeling she was witness to a subtle power play in action. One mistress had agreed to sortie her warship without her warleader as long as they accompanied Warleader Delwyn. Another mistress had withdrawn her warship from guaranteed placement in the primary task force in preference of waiting in reserve for the same warship and warleader.

Anlann and Phalalin had excellent reputations. Faolindra knew them both, knew their warships' societies. Delwyn had spoken to the A'tayotan and recommended a strategy they had reached consensus on with little changes, but she knew him only through his character reflecting from Melkorka, Hlinlodyn, and Anailiatha.

"Excuse me, Mistress Atridredha, but if I may?"

"Yes, Mistress Faolindra?"

Faolindra turned to Melkorka. "Tell me, Mistress Melkorka, why did Delwyn not demand his place in the primary task force?"

"Delwyn thought the repairs could not proceed fast enough to guarantee full combat capability by the departure deadline. I told him to press our right to participate contingent upon ship's status."

"Delwyn did not ask this on his own?" Faolindra asked, frowning slightly.

"No, but only because he believed adequate repairs within the time allotted could not be made."

"Since then you have commenced repair operations. What is your assessment now?" Faolindra asked.

Melkorka's ire re-awakened in response to the nosey question, but she shoved on Anailiatha's shoulder. Melkorka had brought the Mistress of Sails for this reason in the first place, after all.

"Now what?" Anailiatha demanded.

"You have had your nose in those repair estimates for hours. Given what you know now, can you reassess your repair estimate and share with the group the latest projections?" Melkorka asked.

"Reassess?" Anailiatha echoed. "Replenishment has been completed. Aft refueling has been completed. The new gravity lensing armatures have been installed and are undergoing spool-up testing."

Anailiatha paused as she paged through her 'minder, speed-reading.

"All undamaged torpedo bay inventories have been restocked. Internal damage is well under repair. That is the good news.

"Now I will give you the bad news. We will not have one of our hydrogen-antihydrogen fusion reactors. We can get the plant equipment installed, but even if we can install the reactor itself, I will not have sufficient time necessary to begin cold start test runs before we must depart. I will have to tie load sharing into the Power Systems and Propulsion main reactor and reroute main power through the auxiliary power network.

"The damaged compartments sent to Kem Basinga have been mounted into the assembly grid. They have been inspected and the wiring and plumbing chases have been exposed, whole harnesses have been ripped out. Hull component manufacture has been proceeding nonstop but printing composite replacement hull components is time consuming and cannot be rushed. Reassembly is a straight-forward process, but it too is time consuming although not as much as replacing all the plumbing and wiring harnesses.

"When completed, the repaired compartments must be translated into Elleio orbit and tugged to Wrathsee'a Anchorage and then precision translated back into our warship. Once hull integrity standards have been met, our warship will meet spaceworthy FTL jump trials. But several dead compartments will remain offline until the couplings can be unsealed and reattached."

Faolindra frowned at her thoughts. Her tail unmoving, her eartips pointing to her sides.

Was she doodling on her 'minder? Melkorka wondered.

"Mistress Anailiatha," Faolindra said, "what do you think *Hunter's Moon's* status will rate by the time the battle group arrives in the Nikkiolo star system?"

Anailiatha's long fingers flew over her 'minder as she read real time replies to queries sent to Wrathsee'a Anchorage shipyard and to the Kem Basinga facility.

"By the time we arrive on-station in the Nikkiolo star system, I can certify *Hunter's Moon* Battle Status ready."

"You are joking." Atridredha interrupted. "You cannot guarantee your estimates because you cannot know how much wiring you need to replace. It could take you months to track down every short and every burned-out wire in the power network and load-sharing chases."

"Yes, if I had wanted to keep the main power bus and spend the time fixing individual faults, but I elected not to do so. Instead, I ordered all couplings disengaged and had the main power bus translated out in its entirety."

"You did what?" Melkorka cried. "You mean to tell me all power is off aboard our warship?"

"Of course," Anailiatha replied. "Not even umbilical power from the dock is in use. He rests in the docking clamps with all reactors operating in shutdown mode. He is moored in an environmental slip. All external hatches, vents, and airlocks, including the combat staging bay are open to drydock life support and artificial gravity."

Faolindra and her mistress of tactics huddled together and exchanged long intense musical whisperings before she came to a sudden, intuitive decision.

"Mistress Melkorka, we consider it an honor to remain in staging orbit until your warship can achieve Battle Status capability."

"You will not exclude us from the primary task force," *Pathfinder's* Mistress of the Ship trilled heatedly.

Melkorka gaped in astonishment at Faolindra. Was she serious? She was the mistress of the command battleship. Honor escort had already been offered to Delwyn, but the offer had been a technical courtesy contingent on a repair status Atridredha had deemed impossible to meet. If Faolindra held out for Delwyn, then further tactical planning had to include *Hunter's Moon* in a combat capacity.

"*Pathfinder* will remain in the primary task force. *Hunter's Moon* will assume planetary bombardment and landing force operations. I ask *Pathfinder* to assume a support role and back up Delwyn's surface assault forces and hold the high orbitals in case enemy ships arrive on the scene while *Hunter's Moon* is striking the surface from low orbit," Faolindra said.

Ahwroona exchanged perked ears with *Night Shadow's* Mistress of the Ship. They no longer held reserve status, were no longer considered theoretical participants in a theoretical secondary task force!

"No!" Atridredha sang. "Mission planning must take into account current-capable warships. You cannot know for certain whether *Hunter's Moon* can resume Battle Status in time. Mistress Melkorka, you do not even have a full complement."

"We have more than enough time to recruit females from our clans," Melkorka sang in discordant melody.

"And all of them new to warship duty!" Atridredha countered.

"That is true, but over half our losses came from combat forces, and we will ask for combat-trained females first."

That was easy enough. Everyone learned some combat in her life. They would drill the newcomers before departure and drill them over and over again on the combat staging and deployment bay during the voyage to Nikkiolo. They would scatter them among seasoned combatants. She would tolerate no deficit in female combat prowess aboard her warship. The new females would be watched, leaned on, coddled, and supported. Besides, females were not helpless. Eyloni females had been born to fight, otherwise how else could they defend males?

"Have you and Delwyn spoken about this?" Verikaralee asked Melkorka.

"No, he is otherwise occupied. His bitter disappointment clung to the air around him. He did not think we could join the mission he recommended to the A'tayotan. He takes pride and has confidence in us. If I say we are ready to then he is ready to serve as well."

"No," Atridredha objected. "I prefer probable success to possible success. You will not form a battle group when all evidence suggests your warship cannot meet the departure time."

All the mistresses in the room turned menacing eyes on the Mistress of the Hunt. Faolindra spoke the sentiment the others unanimously felt.

"With respect, Mistress Atridredha, warship autonomy does not bow to A'tayotan consensus. We are all going together on this mission as one battle group and not as one primary and one reserve task force in a hypothetical integrated battle group. We will follow A'tayotan war theory and use of force doctrine. We will carry out to the fullest the targeting, assessment, combat, and asset recovery efforts as the A'tayotan have decreed in their mission goals and engagement rules. We pledge our honor to advance Compact policy as decreed by the Be'atika Senge and the A'tayotan. But we are all going together as one battle group."

Atridredha scowled at them. As Mistress of the Hunt she ranked them all in social, military, and hierarchical status. She could and should be able to roll them under her fingers. They might snap their tails in protest, but they would all sing "Yes Mistress" as they complied.

Except they had her on the low ground over one immovable fact. Their warships were extensions of the males they had chosen as their warleaders. Custom declared warships male, and they had the same autonomy their warleaders had. Warleaders chose their mistresses of the ship. When they worked on behalf of their warleaders or in their warships' interest, mistresses of the ship wrapped themselves in a mantle of delegated male independence and they used it to their ships and warleaders best advantage.

When it came down to it, Atridredha did not care which warship went where, so long as they held to the operation plan and executed it as Delwyn O'un Tu La'huaset Eyloni had suggested, and that they agreed to adopt the refinements already approved by the Be'atika Senge and the A'tayotan long before this meeting had even begun.

No wonder Thelindrallin is who she is, Atridredha growled. Thelindrallin had advised the A'tayotan in a Compact Counsel closed joint session that these mistresses would conspire to bring Delwyn along with them.

How had she known that?

Atridredha knew Melkorka had not lobbied for inclusion into the primary task force. She agreed with Delwyn. Warship repair status would disqualify him.

Faolindra had twined her tail with Melkorka the moment Verikaralee and Ahwroona had stood up for her. *Pathfinder* held out until his mistress of the ship had been reassured that they would play an important role in the battle group. The other mistresses of the ship, never in danger of losing their places in the mission, had no further argument once Faolindra had demanded *Hunter's Moon* stand as the honor escort for her command battleship.

Why had Faolindra Uahua'asee'a La'huaset Eyloni demanded the change? Atridredha E'uka met ka Myat'ti'deep Eyloni wondered.

***

The Comari climbed with surefooted skill deeper into the foothills. The sun, already a finger width above the trees, warmed the forest, had been warming it for the past several hours now as she struggled through dense jungle on the shallow sloping incline toward the bare rocks marking another volcanic vent.

After several more winding and weaving hours of silent stalking through the heavy tangled undergrowth, she guessed herself about a third of the way there. The ground had begun to slowly steepen and gain in altitude over the last hour.

She headed for an apparent split in the rocks ahead, a narrow high-mountain pass. It should lead into a gorge, its far end a steep climb up to the flat plateau and the flooded eastern end of Om'tu Lake. From there she would follow the river to the Fire River Falls. There, the automated hydroelectric power plant had been carved into the rocky plateau centuries ago. Once she gained access to the subterranean tunnels and found the power network control center, she could summon transport.

But first she had to get there, which meant periodic climbs into the trees to confirm both her route and satisfy her need to survey the cover ahead. Sometimes it made more sense to walk around jungle thickets than try to muscle her way through them and it was easier to plan her course knowing what she was facing.

She chose a good tree and climbed well into the understory with ease and beheld her distant target. The sky overhead clear and bright blue made the western mountains glow in the sunrise. Her vantage point shielded her from the morning glare, giving her an exceptionally clear view.

She picked a fruit from a nearby leafy branch, leaned back against the trunk, and chewed while looking back the way she had come, a good prowling strategy. You always made sure nothing stalked you. The Comari munched on a second fruit and mentally retraced her path back to the river-facing trees she had left behind.

She panned left, following the trees up toward the foothills, the limestone mountain in the upper left corner of her view. She glanced to her right and caught movement in the distance, movement against the wind, constant steady movement.

The sun had risen in the east on her right and bathed the mountains. Every yellow leaf glittered back at her as they fluttered in the sunlight except for one yellowish spot. A pinpoint the size of a bright star in the night sky was moving among them toward a stand of dark red leaves.

She knew of only three possibilities that could maintain a constant speed and bearing and reflected yellowish light: a little sib, another Comari, or Delwyn O'un Tu La'huaset Eyloni.

A little brother or sister would never keep to a straight line. She knew no Comara prowled here. That left Delwyn, and a male alone was the most offensive idea any female could imagine.

And Kidahin, the spirits take her, had been right. Only a Comari could intrude into a male's survival ordeal and not invalidate it.

She would soon choose a male but confronted with a male alone she decided to stalk him through to the end of the ordeal after all. She could watch him prowl. She could stalk him close. She could admire him.

All three choices sounded so much better than climbing into the underground power plant and calling for transport.

The Comari bit into another fruit, held it in her clenched teeth, and climbed back down to the ground. There she turned back the way she had come, munching thoughtfully on the fruit as she retraced her steps.

***

Delwyn made slow and steady progress into the low foothills as the sun crawled into the sky. He'd been walking for eight hours, but the sun insisted it was around 07h40. It was time for him to make a temporary camp, build a fire, make a bed, eat some fruit, and sponge up some water from the ground.

Most of the standing water had soaked into the peaty soil. The sun was doing its best to dry the dead light green and brown grasses, but the rising humidity hampered its effort. It didn't feel too bad yet, but the increasing moisture would soon turn the air hazy, limit visibility, and make him feel that much worse.

The hottest part of the long day would come in another twenty-eight hours or so. The heat would be a like an amazonian summer over a few days without a sunset. He'd have to walk less and rest more as the long day progressed.

Water remained a first priority. He found a few water-filled vines—the wrong ones—and had to scavenge the puddles under the trees, finding a few holdouts that the soil hadn't sucked dry yet.

Soon he would be reduced to digging holes to reach any quantity worth the effort, at least until the mist turned into rain again.

Forty-five water-hustling minutes later he put damp grass and a few good-sized sticks aside in the sun and then set about making an elevated bed frame.

An hour after that Delwyn started a small fire and watched the smoke rise into the air. Fires here didn't smell like wood fires on Earth. The atmospheric differences altered his sense of smell, and to him the smoke from the burning wood smelled like scorched cloth.

Sheltering under a tree on a bed knee-high off the ground, he ate a handful of small round fruit that tasted like raw dough. He had to wait a bit for them to settle in his stomach before he could fall asleep.

***

The Comari smelled smoke.

It was too late after the storm to come from a lightning strike.

Only Delwyn's presence could explain it.

That meant he had stopped.

Just how long could he keep going? He had walked an entire day without stopping. He had made incredible time. How was that possible?

She closed the distance and homed in on the smell of smoke. She saw no smoke. The blue haze covering the forest hid it. The burning wood smell grew stronger, and so she changed her prowling strategy. Her solid pale-yellow skin would give her away up against the orange and red background. She stepped, barefoot of course, lightly over grass and small jungle plants, picking her way through ground vines. Plants matted the ground and sent off shoots—natural tripwires—rooted into the soil for support.

Foot placement demanded both some care and a natural feel for the ground. Stepping through the grass made a rushing sound and stepping on most ground plants made snapping sounds. A wrong step could pull on the tangle of ground vines and make a ripping sound heard by anything in the immediate area. Then forest litter, sticks, and some leaves conspired to advertise an errantly placed foot.

The Comari knew she could easily out-stalk a Warrior female, could stalk better than most Hunters, and almost always could out-stalk a male. But stupidity did not rule her thoughts, and she never followed a strategy built upon unfounded guesses.

The Comari continued on her indirect path through the heavy forest, avoiding the dark orange, ochers, and rust-tan tree trunks which would highlight her profile. She crawled under or through tall yellow grasses in the small clearings between tall trees, climbed through more yellow-, sand-, and sunburst-colored ground-hugging plants in silence.

She stopped several times to smell the air, to gauge its subtle breezes and assess the smoke carried on its breath.

She prowled over grassy trails, jumping from one to another at random. Eyloni instinct said never to prowl in straight lines and never prowl in the same stalking pattern. Stalking should take random patterns. But with the sun halfway to its zenith, her soft matte pale skin would reflect sunlight like a signal mirror. It forced her to seek and follow the yellow ground cover, which destroyed any true random stalking pattern.

She drew close. Smoke hung on the humid air, not much, but enough to distinguish it from the blue haze given off by the forest.

She crept under bushy plants, brush and small trees, saplings that had grown top-heavy and rolled over like a frozen ocean wave turned into foliage. The leafy wave cresting above her blocked out the sky and direct sunlight, but its waxy, shiny yellow leaves gave the dim passage below more than enough light.

She crawled through a tube-like path deeper into the thicket. A sound, like someone stepping on a brush pile followed by scampering feet, rustled through the thick cover.

She froze, smelling the air.

Some ground mammal had bolted from its hiding place. No doubt she had invaded its refuge from the jungle's thirteen-legged horrors.

She whispered apologies to the spirits for scaring the animal and continued ahead.

The hollow path opened into converging trails under an ample dome made from thick overgrowth. She crawled forward. The ground dipped, and she had to shimmy over a hard-deep rut tricking with water.

Never pass up water, her instinct whispered as she paused to drink her fill.

The branch-and-leaf shrouded trail wound around and down over branches long fallen from trees before the thicket and its yellow carpet had grown over them. Old branches as thick as her body and well rotted blocked her easy path. They crumbled as she crawled over them, sending ke'nah and worms fleeing from the dim light.

She came upon a small tree trunk, perhaps three times as thick as she was tall. The brushy cover had over the years assaulted the low branches. She could not tell which had won, the tree or the thicket. At the impact point of their frozen collision they grew upward in twisted tangles to form a hollow space an ell from the trunk and to just over her head.

She stood up, leaned against the tree, and massaged her body while peeking between leaves.

Delwyn!

She saw him easily. He was no more than a handful of ells away from her, resting on a raised platform made from sticks he found in the forest. A small fire burned, tiny flames visible in the partial shadow the tree above afforded.

Swarming insects hovered near him, frustrated by the smoke.

That they persisted in spite of the smoke made her wonder. Few insects bothered Eyloni. The moisture seekers dove for the eyes, mouth, nose, and exit; and the nipples if they happened to be weeping milk.

The biters, and there were few, did not want blood so much as they wanted the salts in the blood. They bit and licked the wound, and they always went for her sensitive ears. Thankfully, they never came out until high sun several days from now.

Why did the small insects buzz around Delwyn so much? Some hovered in clouds, while others darted around him in apparent determination.

She smelled umara in the smoke. Delwyn had used the epiphyte's air roots for kindling but its pseudobulb contained natural insect repellants. It would smoulder in the small fire for hours.

That in itself forced her to reconsider Delwyn's camp.

He had cleared a space under an *eenkdril* tree, itself a medicinal wonder of the rainforest. The plants surrounding him, *im'ahailee*, had razor-sharp leaves that could slash through skin with ease. He had knocked them down and used them as a perimeter defense. Their stiff leaves would deter most small thin-skinned animals, and they would rustle and rattle when something tried to shove through them.

He lay on an elevated framed nest cushioned with soft and fuzzy ell-tall *oneachizlen* grasses. He also used *buhnnie* tree fronds. Buhnnie fruit was poisonous. They looked edible, smelled edible, but the lime-green rinds warned animals to not take a bite.

The Comari narrowed her eyes and squinted. Delwyn looked wet to her.

Why was his skin wet? Had he poured water all over himself? What an unconscionable use of water during a survival ordeal!

Was he ill? Fever prompted a person to cool core body temperatures by immersing in water.

Had he eaten the poisonous fruit?

No. Buhnnie poisoning interfered with synapses and caused the body to contort into grotesque postures.

He just laid there, his skin glistening in the sunlight.

She had to check on Delwyn and reassure herself that he had not poisoned himself. Cautiously, she crept under the living brush mound above her to its edge, moving slow to reduce the brushing sounds as leaves and sticks rubbed against her body.

Was he sleeping? She did not want to wake him.

She poked her head out from under the thicket and twitched her ears. She listened to the forest noises as she grumbled silently at the fine branches snagging and catching in her long pale hair.

She focused on Delwyn's breathing. His chest rose and fell with the regularity of sleep.

The Comari pulled herself out from under the brush and crouched low, listening.

Satisfied he remained asleep, she broke cover and stalked him. Filled with caution and more careful than when she stalked Hunters, she crept forward.

The forest made sounds, could not help but make sounds. Almost always the sounds came from breezes blowing around and through the leaves blocking their way. Breezes moaned when they glanced across boles at just the right angle. Even the grasses made rustling sounds when the wind passed over them. Insects buzzed. Occasional animal sounds, running or prowling noises, caught her ears.

The wind sang life into the forest, and—as always—it produced constant low background noise waiting to lull the mind away from specific sounds. Background noise made listening harder if you wanted to pick up soft sounds, so she tried her best to keep what noise she did make consistent with the sound around her, so he would not hear her approach.

The Comari reached the campsite perimeter. Leaves from the sharp-edged plants lay scattered on the ground like caltrops. She had to walk with care to avoid stepping on them.

He had piled the cut plants around his sleeping platform, making a shallow ell-wide berm encircling him and his small fire. He had not knocked them flat, but their leaves had wilted and folded toward the stems, poking up along the ground like a two-edged pons.

She closed to within two tail-lengths and stopped. Any farther and she would have to brave the sharp leaves on her bare feet.

Her eyes drank him in. She smelled him. The desire to curl up with him hammered at her senses.

She was alone, far from the company of her people. Although Comara preferred their own kind, they did not enjoy being far from each other or even the other Eyloni genders. The Comara also felt the same outrage Hunters and Warriors felt upon seeing a male alone.

The Comari smelled her lingering scent mark on him, smelled the scent marks belonging to other females, too. Delwyn's association, his family females, and several male scents radiated from him. Included in those scents she found an infant female and Kidahin.

The Comari cursed, her mute voice a breathy whisper, "Kidahin …" She drew the name out into a sighing hiss. *Fine.* She would not kill the impudent Hunter. For Delwyn's sake.

She eyed the sleeping male and made plans.

The Comari jumped over the wilting im'ahailee leaves and landed on the grass next to the raised nest. She could reach out and touch him if she wanted to.

He moved!

She froze before dropping flat to the ground.

Body awareness made Eyloni wary of anything within a personal space extending from them to the length of their tails. Being Comara, she did not have a tail. Yet she had the same one-ell personal space awareness all the same. She stood well within his, and he had twitched in reflex.

She looked under the raised platform, saw the short orange grasses there. He was a short distance off the ground, maybe two splayed hands.

Wistful, she rolled onto her back and wiggled under him, her nose a finger width from rubbing the branches above her head that supported the buhnnie fronds making up his nest.

She inhaled deeply his scent, and the smell of male filled her. The scent of salt and sweat tickled her nose, mixed with his musky odors and pheromones. He rested, but he smelled of lingering pain, and she had seen the bruising on his forehead and the bound-up lower leg.

The Comari settled into the shade of his nest, listened to the breezes, and felt contented. The spirits had meant for Eyloni to enjoy each other's company.

Lulled by Delwyn's scent, she fell asleep beneath him.

***

Hervorallin jumped at the chance to answer the beeping comm signal. Princess had been in a bad mood for several days now. She missed Delwyn, felt his distance from her, and she could not understand his lingering absence. She had been venting her anger on the other infant females until their hierarchy had set her down hard on her tail, which made her even angrier.

Hervorallin smiled and tried, oh how she tried, to keep humor from reaching her scent. She smelled the reeking displeasure on her daughter. She had tried to bully the infants into venturing into the jungle to search for Delwyn. The spirits knew infants tended to their own affairs absent guidance from their mothers or the males they had bonded with. They were instinctive operators and headstrong, but they were not stupid. They sang their concerns to the adults females. The adults smelled their curious demand for the missing male and sent them pheromones telling them Delwyn was beyond the jungle. The emotional impression meant that he had gone beyond their ability to find since nothing existed beyond the jungle in their young minds.

The infants had then sought out Keba and sang complaints to him. They asked him to sing to them just where 'beyond the jungle' was, but he had no clue, either. His instinct told him that nothing bad had happened. Delwyn had gone beyond their reach.

Princess had found his lack of concern frustrating to say the least.

Keba convinced her not to worry about Delwyn. He liked Delwyn too, and he made sure Princess remained first among the others with him, always. The other infants watched Princess. She had influence over Keba, and Keba stood as an immovable force that their hierarchy could barely budge.

The comm beeped a second time just as Hervorallin reached the console.

Melkorka's face flashed on the screen: a tired and haggard Melkorka.

"What happened to you?" Hervorallin demanded.

"Work is what happened to me!" Melkorka snapped. "You should try it sometime."

"Me? I cannot do a thing until Anailiatha recalls the gravity systems engineering staff. That is not going to happen until the armatures pass spooling simulations," Hervorallin snapped back.

Melkorka sighed. "I know. I know. Count on returning soon. Spooling sims are completed. Power Systems and Propulsion is the only place that has power, damn Anailiatha. She is trying to build up power for a singularity simulation. If she can do that without the main power bus, then you should be able to tap in for inertial dampening and structural systems testing."

"She wants me on Wrathsee'a Anchorage now?" Hervorallin asked.

"No. I have news. Faolindra, Verikaralee, and Ahwroona have all insisted on Delwyn honor escorting the battle group."

"You are pulling my tail," Hervorallin cursed, in no mood for teasing.

"Seriously, I could not believe my ears. I thought Atridredha would chew through her tail."

Hervorallin turned suspicious. "What do you want me to do?"

"Recruit replacement combat teams from your clan. I have already sent Kidahin back to hers. Keeping her busy and out of the way might save her from running afoul of the Ti'ratni."

"How could Kidahin upset the Comara hierarchy?"

"She tried to bully the Comari who scent marked Delwyn into going after him during his survival ordeal."

Dead air whispered over the communications channel.

"Hervorallin? Did you hear me?" Melkorka demanded.

"Yes. I do not believe it. That takes courage!"

"No," Melkorka said, ears flattening against her head. "That takes stupidity. Even if Kidahin gains the victory, her victory will not guarantee that the Comari will not come back with Delwyn and kill her anyway for accosting her in the first place."

"You know, if Kidahin is successful, and she saves Delwyn from death, you ought to consider asking the hierarchies to advance her in rank for taking an extraordinarily hazardous and reckless action that resulted in keeping a male and a warleader safe."

Melkorka privately thought the same thing, although Trebithia had been furious beyond reason for the huluhar's interference.

"You know Kidahin is likely to lose her huluhar status with the new recruits coming," Hervorallin pointed out.

The gravametic engineer's comment blindsided Melkorka. It should not have. The huluhar aboard a warship was by custom the youngest female in her society, for Kidahin it meant she might lose her huluhar status.

"I know," Melkorka whispered.

"Where would you reassign Kidahin?" Hervorallin wondered aloud.

"I do not know. She could stay with Trebithia as helmsmistress. I know Phelindra wants her. The mistress of arms and the mistress of battle supervisory ranks have been vacant since Brelioranda and Emendredaha died with Kalinn."

"You should not make Kidahin the mistress of battle," Hervorallin protested. The mistress of battle served as the assault forces equivalent to a mistress of the ship, a demanding job. It made her the commanding mistress of all ground assault forces. She could even overrule Melkorka on a matter concerning surface tactics. Only Delwyn could overrule the mistress of battle, and she would argue with him about it to her last breath, and frankly the job needed a Warrior female, simple and plain.

"No I would not." Melkorka agreed. "But I might consider her for mistress of arms."

"No," Hervorallin said. "Not yet. Kidahin needs an intermediate combat assignment. Given her performance aboard the Ni'zakhonii equipment, she might do well as a boarding party assaultmistress or a surface action scoutmistress. If you make her a surface action assaultmistress, she will come under the supervision of the mistress of battle and Phelindra."

Melkorka thought about it. Hervorallin made a good case. "I will consider the wisdom in your words, Hervorallin," Melkorka trilled, pleased. "Now, about recruitment, we need combat-capable Warriors and Hunters. Try to find people to fill the mistress of inner strength, mistress of the decks, and the mistresses of arms and battle."

"I have ideas about the arms and battle mistresses," Hervorallin interrupted.

"Who?"

"Make Zalzadrin the Mistress of Arms and Nynava the Mistress of Battle."

"I'll think about Zalzadrin. She might make a good fit. Nynava? She serves with the surface action combat teams. She is pure infantry. I am thinking more of Nurrilldra, one of the senior boarding party assaultmistresses or Karadenlin, the senior surface assault scoutmistress. And

I keep thinking about Andrealea in covert scout surface operations for Mistress of Arms.

"Now bear in mind we need people trained in fire control, environmental, and auxiliary reactor control systems. Those priority appointments need to be filled."

"Affirm," Hervorallin acknowledged.

20
OBLIGATIONS CONTINUE

Kidahin stood on a high branch in her immediate family home tree and stared into the southeast. The sun, halfway to its zenith, blazed in the clear sky. Behind her, gray northern clouds heralded the coming of needle-fine cold rain. In the far north needle rain occurred often and not just during needle rain time. Needle rain brought icy cold wind-driven fine rain. Those fine drops stung when they hit, as though icy splinters were being driven under the skin.

The times, what Delwyn called 'months', would soon change.

Uahua'asee'a Clan territory extended from the north coast south to the northern rim of the ancient crater and the mountain chain it had created so long ago. Clan territory expanded west and east along what had once been the ancient impact crater's shallow sloping interior wall. Erosion over the ages had backfilled the crater floor as the stratospheric rim eroded down to its present-day relatively modest heights. The gentle slope ran out to the coast and continued underwater over the north pole before diving to the incredible depths on farside. There, through perforations in the thin crust, underwater volcanoes erupted often, releasing hot magma churned up by tidal force heating caused by Tyreniioroneo's gravitational influence kneading Elleio as she orbited him.

The Uahua'asee'a Clan held a vast industrial complex and polar ocean education and research center in common trust. In keeping with Compact environmental policy, the research center also policed the industry, monitoring even the waste heat radiated by the buildings. The industrial complex designed and built hydrogen-antihydrogen fusion plants. Kidahin's clan planned to contribute a reactor to replace her warship's destroyed one, a substantial investment.

Kidahin could not wait to show Delwyn her clan's lands and accomplishments. He had little interest in engineering physics, true enough. His occupational specialty concentrated on agriculture.

Land-based agriculture did not exist on Elleio. Clans lived off their lands. They traded foods, but agriculture on Elleio was confined to the sea farms managed by the La'huaset archipelago clans.

The Uahua'asee'a Clan research center lured people interested in pursuing any one of several marine specialities. Here they learned wet navy ship and submersible design, oceanography, oceanic power systems design, and oceanic farming. People completing their studies went on to fill marine occupations in ship design, ship building, ship operations, ocean exploration, ocean ecology, and ocean environmental interdiction. Kidahin's clan operated one of the four marine higher learning centers in the world and the only polar research center on Elleio. She could not wait to take him through the education and research center and surprise him.

Her thoughts returned to Delwyn. She squared her shoulders and stared at the easternmost peaks. O'un Tu Clan territory ran from the eastern crater lip to the interior volcanic mountains and Om'tu Lake eastern shores, cutting a wide swath north and south as it extended into the east.

Kidahin called to mind Delwyn's forest stalking techniques, the ones she had watched him use on Ibeetu. The ugly green world had forests similar in density to her native northern home range, except the trees grew somewhat stunted there. She stared south. If she stalked in a straight line through the temperate rainforest, up the crater wall, over the extinct volcanic chain, swam across Om'tu Lake, crossed the impact upheaval mountains, and climbed down hills formed from impact ejecta and more extinct volcanic cones, then she would reach the high-altitude cloud rainforests. Continuing farther south and down the mountain slopes, she would then reenter the temperate rainforest and soon encounter heavy jungle.

Delwyn had most likely been dropped into a tiny clearing somewhere around those dead volcanic vents. If he had been paying any mind to the ground as he flew over it from Na'di Island to O'un Tu Clan, then he should have noted the eastern ridge and the easier to navigate foothills temperate forest stretching toward the Om'tu flood plain.

She had said as much to the young Comari. Had she found him yet?

"Kidahin?" an old Hunter called.

"Yes, Elder?" Kidahin replied without turning.

"Mistress Melkorka sends greetings and asked me to tell you to return to your abode and contact her on Wrathsee'a Anchorage."

Kidahin turned, made eye contact, perked her ears forward in respect, and thanked the Elder for her time.

Yet she resisted leaving her solitary perch. She wished she could sing strength to him from here.

Fear gripped her heart. What if Melkorka had bad news? Kidahin knew it was far too soon for Delwyn to have completed the survival ordeal.

She stumbled along the several hundred ell long branch. Barely wider than a tail-length, it quickly thickened to several ells wide as it merged into the trunk. Kidahin scrabbled up and around into the open bole and climbed down and into the dense tangled living fortress, winding her way through aerial root mazes that had fused into massive passage-ridden galls, trails dead-ending into several individual abodes.

She charged into hers and stumbled over her three intimate friends coiled up together in her nest.

"Where have you been?" Méatika, a young Warrior, asked, yawning in greeting.

"Above the crown, in the upper canopy. Never mind that now. I have to speak to my Mistress of the Ship. The call will likely concern ship business. I am sorry, but you must all leave."

The Warrior yawned again and nodded. Females respected privacy to a fault. Males had a limited indulgence, more for female reassurances concerning their whereabouts than for giving them a break. Infants, well, they were something else. They learned about privacy issues as they matured. Even so, they had been plaguing her nonstop ever since her return home.

They smelled a different male scent on her, and their infant female interest in anything male drove Kidahin to seek refuge on the remote branch. That had not discouraged them for long. Her immediate family had two infant males. The spirits had blessed them. Kidahin had gone so far as to sing a complaint to them. The infant males in turn had given the infant females long discordant harangues about it.

And it had worked, too. Somewhat. A few infant females always snuck off and found her, innocently pretending to visit an adult family female. They sniffed all over her for signs of Delwyn.

They wanted to meet this new male, and they had become quite pushy about it, too. Kidahin had to sing comfort to them. She also reassured them with pheromones that they would soon see him for themselves.

Kidahin waited, snapping her tail in frustration as she watched the two sleeping Hunters get a tugging-on by a yawning Méatika.

Her yawning was catching, and soon Kidahin found herself yawning right along with them. Yawns triggered an empathic response. Why yawning of all things was anybody's guess.

The two Hunters and Méatika converged on Kidahin and wound their tails around hers and each other, sharing intimate contact as they group hugged. Pleasure tremored from the base of Kidahin's tail down to her pons.

The communications console message queue began to beep in soft insistence, shattering the tender moment.

"Time for you to go," she told them, reluctance and impatience warring within her.

"Come and find us if you need us," Méatika trilled.

"I will. Go now, before Melkorka becomes impatient enough to tear my ears off."

They sped together through the open bole, and Kidahin glided up to her personal comm system.

"Accept," Kidahin told the pattern-filled screen.

Melkorka's exasperated expression formed out of the identity pattern.

"I have not yanked your tail away from any minor importance, have I?" Melkorka asked, singing in pure sweet harmony.

Um-Oh. What did I do now? An ear-tearing angry Melkorka was immeasurably preferable to a sweet-sounding pleasant Melkorka.

"I was in the upper canopy, staring off into O'un Tu Clan territory," Kidahin told her truthfully.

Melkorka's features softened, and she breathed a musical sigh. "Before you ask, I have not received any word one way or the other about Delwyn, so relax. Honestly Kidahin, I do not know what to do with you. Trebithia is having a fit over you going off after that Comari. The Ti'ratni cannot decide whether you are brave or stupid. But know this: If Delwyn and the Comari both survive, they say an honor debt is owed to you. But if that Comari dies, they will cut you into tiny pieces starting with your pons!"

Kidahin squirmed in discomfort. "Something had to be done to tip the leaf in Delwyn's favor. A Comari may accompany a male during the survival ordeal, and she wants him so much I could taste it."

"But she is not bonded to him yet. She is not old enough, although her time is soon. Custom and tradition allow for a Comari having a rare interest in an adolescent male, but only if she is present when the ordeal begins, or if she finds him in the forest on her own.

"You interfered. You sent her after him. While I am sure she was seeking him, she should have found him on her own and without your help.

"If Delwyn gets himself killed protecting her, then you will have caused what you had hoped to prevent. If she dies while looking for him, the Ti'ratni will make you wish you had jumped from that high branch!"

"It was worth the risk Mistress," Kidahin sang, defiant.

Melkorka swore in lyrical curses and remembered. Kidahin's impulsive act fell well within normal adolescent and young adult female behavior when it came to males and the effect they had on young females.

Stalking infant females crept up behind Kidahin, and Melkorka clamped her teeth down on the smile threatening to split her face. Those infants, given the opportunity, would have followed Delwyn, or any male, off into the jungle in their instinctive desire to protect him.

That instinct, what remained of it, had made Kidahin an ideal huluhar. The empathic link she had forged with Delwyn satisfied her about his temperament as a leader.

"Kidahin, you do know you are not likely to remain huluhar," Melkorka blurted.

"I do. I no longer wish to remain huluhar. I could not bear to choose a male to replace Delwyn should he die."

Melkorka shuddered at the thought and mentally screamed at Kidahin for conjuring up the dread she feared most. Delwyn was a soldier, a fighter. He had more experience as a fighter than many living Eyloni thanks to his longer than normal life span. He had stalked through forests before. But people did die in forests on rare occasions. Experience in forest ways sometimes bowed to accident, misfortune, or mistake.

"I do not think you will ever have to worry about that. I wanted to speak to you about recruiting from your clan. We need people with knowledge and experience in fusion power systems. You might also ask the wet navy people if they would consider serving aboard a warship."

Kidahin nodded. "Several Warriors and a few Hunters from the territorial defense forces have already asked me when we might begin interviewing for new combat assignments. What specialties do you wish?"

"Initial combat prowlers and stalkers for both surface combat forces and boarding assault forces. Oh, by the way, try to find surface scouts you would feel comfortable stalking and prowling with," Melkorka added.

"That I would feel comfortable stalking with?" Kidahin echoed with suspicion.

"Yes. Unless you prefer boarding assaults."

"Given my choice, I prefer combat on the ground. Most Hunters do, you know. But if you are hinting that I cannot recruit Warriors for boarding parties, let me tell you that thirteen Warriors have come to me expressing an interest in joining our society and fighting with the boarding assault teams," Kidahin sniffed.

"I am not saying you cannot recruit boarding assault team members. I am telling you to take the time to pick Hunters you would want with you on a surface stalking mission, with you as their surface assault scoutmistress."

"Me? I never considered myself ready for leadership. What about Trebithia? The helm?"

"You are a most capable helmsmistress. Trebithia says so. But Trebithia will remain the Mistress of Pathwalking for some time to come. Besides, even she had to work up through leadership mistress duties before being considered for supervisory mistress duty. Even so, I did consider you for mistress of arms. After some time with the assault forces, you may find supervisory mistress duties open to you. As it stands, if you take on the leadership duties I am suggesting, you will come under the supervision of the Mistress of the Watch and the Mistress of Battle."

"Who are you going to present to our society as the mistress of battle?" Kidahin asked.

"I was thinking Nynava and maybe Zalzadrin as the mistress of arms."

"I think Delwyn would prefer Zalzadrin as the mistress of battle," Kidahin objected.

"Except for choosing the mistress of the ship, Delwyn does not dictate who may serve what duties and where she may serve them aboard our warship," Melkorka reminded her.

And that, Melkorka reflected, was something Delwyn both understood and approved. On his former warship supervisory duties had been divided up among rankings called officers and petty officers. Other duties had been carried out by nonsupervisory personnel. Some could advance into minor supervisory rankings, but for rare special cases they were barred from the primary supervisory ranks. Officers did not perform duties reserved for the minor supervisors and vice versa—a wasteful force-allotment scheme if she ever heard one.

Although a Compact warship belonged to his female society, military rank was given or taken by the warleader. The mistress title on the other hand was a warship society matter acknowledged by the female hierarchies. Simply put, a helmsmistress—not a mistress in the supervisory meaning of the title—could be shifted into a combat hand or into leading a combat fist, be sent to a duty station an apprentice crewman would fill aboard a Coalition vessel, and then return to the helm as helmsmistress again, or even the navigation console as the new mistress of pathwalking.

"I know that, Mistress," Kidahin prompted, breaking into Melkorka's leafchasing.

"I considered Zalzadrin," Melkorka confessed, "but in almost every case where it matters the job is made for a Warrior. The combat forces a mistress of battle leads are Warrior-heavy in composition. Besides, Zalzadrin's insulting humor and sensitivity to her short stature would soon have them all ready to kill her, and I will not have resentment in my combat forces. Zalzadrin will become the mistress of arms.

"I know Phelindra wants you in her prowling forces under her exclusive authority as Mistress of the Watch, but that would tie your tail to ship security or warleader special security."

"Warleader special security?" Kidahin mouthed, at a loss for words.

"Yes. If you want to stalk that path, let the Eldest know. I warn you against choosing this path, however."

"Why?" Kidahin gulped.

"Warship security is necessary, but security teams rarely see combat unless the ship is boarded. Your exemplary conduct aboard the Ni'zakhonii you-know-what has made it clear to me that a security posting now would not advance your status unless you chose warleader special security. Hunters serve exclusively as warleader special security and work with Phelindra alone. They are both free and honor-obligated to disregard any order, including mine, the warleader's, or even Phelindra's if it means protecting him. You do the dirty work that saves and protects him, and you never let him know what you have done for him. You may act on his behalf aboard ship, on any station or base, on Elleio, or even in his home tree. At this stage in your young life I strongly urge you not to choose this occupation until much later, if ever."

Kidahin thought about it. Security sounded dull after the adventures she had experienced on the Nikkiolo moon. But warleader special security? They were feared almost as much as Comara. They also tended toward a dour and ill-tempered lot, always so serious. She doubted she could cultivate the proper mental attitude. She was not the jokester Zalzadrin was, but she was not terminally phlegmatic, either.

"I am honored to accept a surface assault scoutmistress appointment."

"Good," Melkorka trilled, pleased her favorite Hunter had accepted the challenge. "Log your helm repair notes and recommendations and send them to Tulloraha."

"Tulloraha? The auxiliary command center helmsmistress? Why?"

Melkorka nodded. "She will rotate into the command helmsmistress seat. Our new huluhar, once we find her, will intern under Hlinlodyn."

"Really?" Kidahin asked. That poor female.

"Yes, really. If she does well as tacticalmistress, she will rotate into Combat Analysis Center. There she will learn how to fight our warship inside and out."

Kidahin nodded. That, she reflected, guaranteed Melkorka had a Warrior in mind as the next huluhar. Well, custom did call for alternating Hunters and Warriors as huluhar to maintain fairness.

"I have not made my mind up yet. Either Zalzadrin or Andrealea for Mistress of Arms and Nynava or Karadenlin for Mistress of Battle. You, bothersome one, I am certain of. Remember that although autonomy gives our society absolute say over approving mistresses, hierarchical matters come into consideration least we cause offense to someone's honor.

"As to your recruits, remember that our society must find them acceptable. You already know that in most cases this is just a snap of the tail anyway. Consider yourself a surface action assault scoutmistress. You will report to Zalzadrin or Andrealea. Your command paths will branch through Zalzadrin, Andrealea, Nynava, and Phelindra."

"Yes, Mistress. Is there anything else?"

"We have been moved into the primary task force by the Mistress of the Hunt is all," Melkorka said, and gave Kidahin an indifferent flip of tail.

"What? How did that happen?"

Melkorka smirked with unmistresslike joy. "The mistresses of the ship for *Green Ivy*, *Surefooted*, and *Fearless* demanded it."

"That means Delwyn can accompany his battle group."

"It does, assuming Anailiatha has not over-exaggerated her engineering estimates and the manufacturing and assembly teams can maintain their current speed and quality control."

"You will need those recruits soon then, I take it?" Kidahin asked, already knowing the answer.

"Yes, I will notify you when our society can meet in free-range territory on La'huaset for the initial interviews. Obviously it cannot happen until after Delwyn returns from his ordeal, composes his adulthood ceremony song, and sings it at a full gathering before his clan. Since we will travel with him as he meets with other La'huaset clans and the Tribal Elders from the other four tribes, we can use the opportunity for interviewing and selecting females."

"Melkorka? What if Delwyn has a Comari wrapped around him?"

Melkorka thought about it and shook her head. "She is close to her bonding age, but I am sure Delwyn will be halfway to Nikkiolo before she feels the need to bond with a male. She will not wait, either. By now she has several prospective males in mind. The only reason she went after him rather than kill you was that she prefers Delwyn over her current choices."

***

Delwyn rolled over in the hot sun and yawned, hovering in that place between awake and asleep.

The change in his pheromones tingled the Comari's nose. She jolted awake, remained quiet and tense, and waited.

His body odor told her he was waking swiftly.

She slid soundlessly across the grassy ground beneath him, rolled prone, leaped across the sharp wilting leaves, and sprinted back into the thicket and its concealed tunnel.

She did not look back, but her ears swiveled to listen as popping joints and rustling grasses told her he was awake but had not rolled over to see her fleeing form.

She turned and peeked at him through bright yellow undergrowth.

He sat up, stretched and stood. Then he looked around, wary. He knelt down and looked under the bed frame. She watched him rub a hand over the grass she had vacated just moments ago. He stood back up, turned and looked right where she was hiding!

Delwyn blinked. He swore someone or something had been watching him, was still watching him. His combat training and his natural awareness was giving him an intuitive nudge that told him something felt wrong.

An animal checking him out? A little sib maybe?

Uh-uh, not the little sibs. They'd come as a group. Besides, this felt more like an Eyloni female trying to catch him off-guard. Kidahin had pulled the same trick on him more than once in Ibeetu's forests, and Princess stalked him every chance she got.

Someone checking on his progress? Scratch that, too. Hervorallin had said the survival ordeal was a literal survival test. If you couldn't survive to adulthood, then tough noogies for you, male or not. Oh, they'd keen songs about your death, but in the Eyloni worldview the jungle had spoken.

Even in the dim past custom and tradition prohibited non-adults from mating. Since sexual pleasure had nothing to do with mating, this wasn't the horrific outrage it would be for humans. Eyloni mated when the female desired offspring, not for fun or pleasure. If she desired pleasure, she needed only to twine tails with any willing person or group of people, females or males. Eyloni females expressed no mating interest in males not declared adults. Something in their pheromone sensing ability toggled a mental state that weighed male biological fitness. They refused to mate with any male who hadn't gone through the survival ordeal, instinctively afraid that some peculiar defect in them would carry into their infants.

Phalalin had said a male could decide to abort the survival ordeal. No shame accrued to his character so long as the reason for quitting had been both dire and honorable. Males or females who quit had an obligation to try again within one Elleio Standard Time year. Both male and female adulthood ceremonies came under EST timing because all rituals followed female timing conventions. A male or female could try up to five times, and if he or she quit or failed on the fifth try, then he or she was considered a child in all social matters for life.

Phalalin had also said that perhaps only a few thousand people in the world fell into that category. The overwhelming reason for failure to complete the survival ritual came from physical or mental incapacities. Given that the custom required even a quitter to come out of the woods on his own, Delwyn doubted anyone could be shadowing him now.

Besides, if they wanted to monitor his progress they could have sent a drone out to spy on him. Hell, they could even have tracked him from orbit if they wanted to. But they wouldn't do that. Eyloni privacy and honor etiquette wouldn't permit it. Spying was tantamount to declaring him untrustworthy, as though they thought he had a cache hidden in the jungle.

He watched the coiled shiny yellow brush and chewed over the possibilities. It was probably some curious critter's hiding place. Rabbits made warrens in coiled thickets and briar patches. Back on the farm his dad had made an old brush pile from dead trees he had blasted to extend the fields into the woods. The splintered logs had been piled up against the field edge and into the woods. Over time briars and burdock had grown in and around them. Rabbits holed-up there to avoid wolves, foxes, and hawks.

Delwyn gave the large long mound another hard look, shook his head, and sat back down on his makeshift rack.

His foot looked better now that it had lost some of its purple bruising. The toes and the left side along the foot remained purple, but everywhere else the bruises had faded to yellow-blue. It twinged from time to time and didn't appreciate taking his full weight. He could walk better, but it would tire under exertion. He didn't dare stress it, which meant he had to keep it bound tight. The joint would have no stability the minute he exerted any twisting or shearing force on it. In his predicament foot placement, weight dispersal, and terrain awareness would carry the day. He had a good pain endurance rating, but if he blew the ankle he was crippled. "Simple and plain," as Kidahin would say.

Delwyn found some meter-long flaxen grass, which turned out to make a nice soft and strong string. He braided a few meters of it, grabbed a tough leaf, folded it around his ankle, filled it with tiny yellow ferns, and wrapped the whole affair with the flaxen string. When he finished, his foot from heel to lower calf looked like a mummy leg wrapped with binder twine. But it worked, and it felt better than the job he'd done with the leaf, stick, and moss wrap he had made before leaving the little sibs.

Ready to leave, Delwyn took his bearings and marched through the clearing and into the heavy rainforest. Now he had to find water and food.

The Comari held her breath. Could he smell her? How could he? She had extremely fine control over her pheromones and could remain nearly odorless. Only if a stalker came within an ell of her and actively searched for her scent could she be found. Delwyn should not be able to smell her from any distance, yet he knew something was hiding in the thicket.

She backtracked out of the undergrowth and circled wide to flank him, pulled ahead, and then waited until she heard him coming.

He prowled quietly, but not as quiet as even a Warrior could manage. His foot injury was spoiling his silent-prowling skills.

Good.

The Comari decided not to reveal herself to him. Instead, she continued on ahead to clear the way and then backtracked to his flank or dropped behind him and made sure no forest animals threatened him.

She found water, ground fruits, edible plants, and tubers. She paused to expose them just enough for him to notice and attribute the disturbances to feeding animals his approach had startled.

When not making food and water obvious, she also brushed aside plants and grasses in ways to give him a better trail. She did not alter the landscape much. Delwyn was a born forest tracker and combat fighter.

He was not stupid.

Delwyn wasn't stupid, and it didn't take him long to notice he had stumbled onto several game trails. One had been used so often it had turned-up dirt showing in the straw-colored grasses. Others looked recently used too, as if a larger animal had been prowling on one trail but then veered off onto other trails as it prowled farther into the lowland forest.

Sometimes the newer paths branched off into the brush. Irregular, they looked like ones a dog made when plowing through high grass only a short time ago.

There were inconsistencies.

No footprints marred the damp bare spots. The random breakout trails and their returns felt wrong. Animals moved with purpose whether foraging, hunting, or stalking. If his presence drove them forward, then they shouldn't change paths so consistently. If he wasn't driving them forward, the natural foraging behavior shouldn't swing about so wildly, leaving food behind.

That told him several animals, a whole pack maybe, worked the ground ahead. Either that or a single intelligence was at work.

The Comari withdrew to Delwyn's flank and crouched, hiding in plain sight watching him study the signs on the forest floor. She smiled her approval.

He certainly was not stupid. He was suspicious. It was time for her to prowl without leaving revealing signs.

Warriors had difficulty working a trail without leaving some trace, but Hunters did so with ease, and Comara did so by reflex. From her perspective, she had to remind herself to leave signs on the forest floor. Of the few daytime mammal predators crossing her path she killed bare-handed and hid the remains lest he find them and suspect her involvement.

The sun hit its 09h00 skyclock as Delwyn exited heavy undergrowth and looked out onto the narrow greenish-golden grassy Om'tu River flood plain. By his reckoning, he had forty-eight hours remaining before the TST month ended. If he stayed out for the entire 12.6813 Earth day long orbital period, then that gave him seventy-six more hours before the Elders would start worrying about him.

The river reflected the partly cloudy sky like a lake. It was deceptively calm, glassy smooth, and several hundred meters wide. It flowed at a good clip too, around ten KPH judging by the occasional debris floating by. That meant some seven to ten hours by raft should put him parallel to the O'ni'da families elleiu trees if his distance and river current guesses turned out accurate.

Delwyn searched the riverbank and within fifteen minutes found several small branches. Green vines remained clinging to them, enough to serve as cordage for binding the snapped branches together. He dragged them up from the shore onto the grassy ground and laid them out.

He had enough wood to make a three-meter-wide and four-meter-long raft and have one long pole left over for castoff and maybe for use as a rudder if he could tie something flat to it. He might even be able to use it for a paddle if nothing else.

The wood was strong and healthy, had all its bark, and wasn't waterlogged.

Where had it come from? The Om'tu River drained from Om'tu Lake, a long narrow overflowing series of volcanic calderas. No forests grew along its shores, and the cloud rainforest grew down the slopes on the other side.

So where had all the small branches come from? Delwyn looked up and down the river, gauging the distance from the trees to the shore upstream. Could the long-night storms have ripped up trees and blown branches into the river? That would take a good southern windstorm, and the night storms had blown northeast.

Tornado? Yeah. That made more sense. A northeast-moving twister might fling debris off in any direction.

Delwyn built the raft and before pushing off the river bank took time to braid more cordage from the greenish-golden grass and tie some around a river rock just in case he needed an anchor later. He jumped on and rocked the grounded raft as he pushed off. Even halfway into the water, he felt the current greedily sucking on the raft.

Cold mountain water splashed on his bare skin as he shoved on the pole and paddled out thirty meters to avoid any submerged rocks. This far out he shouldn't find any rocks or any snags for that matter.

I can't swim in this. The frigid water would get to me in minutes.

The raft picked up speed, and Delwyn settled into navigating the river on his sluggish barge.

The Comari watched from far downstream as Delwyn built a raft from the branches she had carried out of the upstream forest.

He was clever, resourceful, and strong.

Her greatest task lay ahead now. She had to run along the riverbank to keep up and keep him in sight until he grounded the raft. A possible but no easy task, not even for a Comari.

Delwyn floated down the river. He couldn't tell for sure as he glided over the water, but he thought the riverbanks seemed low, which explained the grassy flood plain. That made it easy to watch the forest and look for landmarks.

The raft tended to hold its course off the left bank. Delwyn felt little turbulence. The river flowed on a straight line with no narrow constricting riverbanks. What turbulence he did see came from slow water near the bank dragging against the faster flow farther out into the river. If he pushed his two-and-a-half-meter long oar straight down, he could feel occasional bumps as the pole skidded along the river bottom.

He didn't feel the thump-bump-thump of wood on stone. The bottom felt more like grassy silt. That meant the river had already crested and spilled into the grassy flood plain. And yet the straw-yellow grass grew at least a hundred meters from the forest to the current riverbank. That told Delwyn just how far the river really could rise. No trees grew in the grass, so those heavy floods happened often.

He pulled the oar from the water and wedged it between two crossmembers and pulled it to port or to starboard. Two knots roughly dead center let the pole ride amidships. Using some elbow grease, he could shove the inclined pole to the right or left to turn to starboard or to port.

'Turn' in this case came down to more of a euphemism than a literal fact. He could bear to the right or to the left. How well the raft turned depended on its speed and the current. Below the surface the water ran faster than on the surface in places. Sometimes the current welled up into a slow rotating water column, and if he wasn't careful it would tow him farther out into the river.

The makeshift rudder didn't do much to correct for drift. If he oversteered, the raft tended to turn on its vertical axis, sending him down the river in a slow spiral without taking him where he wanted to go.

Delwyn pulled the pole out from between its knotty bosses, poled against the river bottom, and shoved the raft back toward the river bank.

He poled for ten minutes every half hour to keep the raft from drifting back into the main current. He knew right then and there that if he ever lost the pole or the shallows he'd have to jump for it.

Better to swim thirty meters or so in the freezing water than to swim from midway across the river.

###

The Comari stalked Delwyn, moving fast enough to keep him in sight and yet slow enough to lag behind and out of sight against the forest.

For the next several hours he drifted and poled, and she ran after him, keeping him in her sight and herself hidden among orange and yellow riverbank brush bracketed by orange and red trees.

###

River travel lulled Delwyn's senses. Headache and double-vision strained his eyes. He came close to falling asleep only to jolt awake at the last minute to see himself drifting away from the riverbank. If he got stuck in the main current he'd remain there until the river discharged into the sea twenty-five hundred kilometers northeast in the polar sea.

Delwyn considered time and speed. He had a good feel for the current now and decided he'd better start watching the surrounding jungle. He saw O'un Tu Clan elleiu trees off in the distance. Because he had studied the elleiu tree groups when he overflew them on the way to the O'ni'da families trees, he had at least some idea of what their jagged spread would look like from ground level. He watched and waited for trees at the right height to intersect his northward gaze. Using the azimuth-elevation system for finding his bearings, he assumed all elleiu trees grew to a uniform 450-meter height. The upper canopy he sought was about ten kicks into the jungle. An easy trigonometry calculation told him he had to sight along a 2.5-degree plumb line. He tied a stick to a string, tied the other end to his anchor stone, held the stick to eye-level, sighted the distant elleiu trees, and watched the angle as he sailed past them.

Another hour passed before he found a familiar staggered pattern at the right general angle, but he would have a hard time spotting his family tree through the nearby intervening trees. It wasn't as if he could put the raft in reverse and back up to look again. They might be the O'ni'da families trees, or they might not. Their distance away meant that the tall trees near the riverbank blocked his view and made tree height guessing more difficult than he thought it would be …

Thock! Thock! Thock!

The wood-on-wood banging startled Delwyn. He dropped the plumb over the side, and the heavy stone carried it to the river bottom. That knocking had sounded like a night horror trying to scare a little sib out of a tree.

Thock! Thock! Thock!

Delwyn poled the raft toward shore, landing a hundred meters downriver from where he first heard the hammering sound.

He grounded the raft, not knowing whether he would have to sail farther downriver or not.

The sun hovered in its 09h40 skyclock point. Almost eight hours had passed since he launched the raft. He had nineteen hours to go before orbital phase-1 began, and he had the daylight heat coming in another ten hours to contend with. He ought to hike into the forest as far as his ankle allowed and then find a tree to hole up for a good eight to ten hours and sleep. His best guess put him ten klicks from the trees as the crow flies. All the weaving and backtracking he'd have to make around impassible obstacles would extend that trek well beyond ten klicks.

Yeah, it was time to find a place to duck the mid-day heat and sleep.

***

The Comari thanked the spirits. Now she had the chance to resume a dignified pace once again. She drank deeply from the river, her first water in several hours.

She barely had the strength to beat the drift wood cudgel against a hollow log. After all the running, walking made spots sparkle across her eyes. She stood, shaking, gulping air between drinks, and tried not to make herself sick drinking too much cold water so soon after her heated exertions.

She followed after Delwyn, occasionally flanking him on either side before falling back or scouting ahead as he made a campsite. He was wise not to stress the foot injury. He still had a ways to go, too. He shouldn't camp here for long on the ground. Daylight animals came to the river to drink.

The forest here didn't have as much tangling, oppressive, enclosing shrubbery, grasses, ground vines, and parasitic tree vines. Water posed a concern. He should get all he needed from eating fruit. That ought to be no problem. Fruit trees grew everywhere. She smelled them. Sleeping through the mid-day should be his immediate concern. He should have climbed into a good tree. Sleeping on the ground for more than short naps was ill-advised, but then she saw trees as hallmarks of safety. She considered Delwyn's upper body strength and weighed his ability to grasp the scarlet vines hanging from broadleaf trees and decided he would have no problems climbing into one of them.

Why did he insist on sleeping on the ground?

***

Delwyn woke an hour later, buried his fire pit, drank from the river, and headed off into the forest. Six hours of heavy slogging later put the sun at 10h15. The elleiu trees remained off in the distance, seven or eight klicks away. Well-rested and in better shape the ordeal wouldn't rate much more than routine jungle combat training.

But he wasn't in tip-top shape, he was tired, his head hurt, and his eyes blurred.

He spent fifteen minutes scouting until he found a tree suited to his plans. He had to take the time to make it comfortable for the several hours he'd be stuck up in it like a raccoon run down by dogs. He built a recliner into a forking branch and stuffed it with tangerine and cherry leaves and goldenrod moss. Then he pulled down vines and made a safety harness—just in case he rolled in his sleep. He'd try for eight hours, but the idea of sleeping in hot broad daylight drove him crazy with thoughts of all that time wasted. He knew he needed sleep and time to rest his ankle.

It took him another forty minutes to fall asleep.

***

The Comari sat in her own tree, not more than a stone throw away. She watched him for some time before she felt comfortable enough to sleep.

Satisfied he had finally climbed into a tree, she still woke often to check on him.

***

Delwyn panted and wiped his sweaty brow, shooing clouds of sweat dragonflies from his head. The sun hovered near the 11h20 skyclock. He had just completed the ten-day, sixteen-hour, and twenty-eight-minute Earth time Tyreniioroneo Standard month in the jungle. At his best guesstimate the ritual Elleio Standard month would come to an end when the sun reached its 12h55 skyclock position.

He had to remain in the jungle for twenty more hours and yet make steady progress through the tripping, snagging, and detour-laden undergrowth.

Time dragged by in the muggy heat. Delwyn had taken 10 one-hour long naps and hiked for at least ten more.

The afternoon was hot. Sweat dragonflies buzzed around him in the dense undergrowth as he pushed through it to the next landmark. Footprints marked the rusty dust on the path, not the crab-scrabble signature gait he associated with the giant mite animals. These were daytime mammals.

After an hour of pushing his way up through a crimson vine-strewn ravine he came upon a kill. Sweat dragonflies buzzed in and out of the hollows of her skull. Only a rim of flesh and matte velour skin remained around the spot where the delicate ears had been. Blood had soaked into the ditch, still red and damp under the few rare stones he found there. It had been a messy kill, made a bare few hours ago, sometime during his last short nap.

What a gruesome way for her to die.

Delwyn wondered if she had been the lingering presence he felt hovering nearby ever since saying good-bye to the little sibs.

The daylight mammal things hunted in packs. They served as Elleio's answer to a wolf. He didn't want to hang around anywhere near them when they got hungry again. With daylight lasting so many hours he had no doubt they held a large territory and ranged even farther.

***

The O'ni'da families waited patiently for Delwyn, just as they had when he had stepped out of the VTOL aircraft when they had first met him. Perimeter sensors had detected his approach, and they poured out of their trees. Phalalin and Phelindra stood out in front with Verikaralee and Hervorallin hovering nearby. Zalzadrin ran to her favorite male, getting only halfway to him before several small creatures pounced on him from the tall grass.

Princess and her infant female posse brought him tumbling to the ground, where they piled onto him singing pleased relief. He was no longer beyond the jungle!

The infant male held back, smelling the air, ears lowering, tail whipping.

He stared at Delwyn's head.

He sang out for an adult female.

Zalzadrin reached his side as Keba sang his distress. She hesitated, looked at Delwyn's bandaged ankle, saw his swelled forehead, and sang in imperative tempo. "Phalalin! Phelindra! Delwyn has a head injury!"

A sea of people surged across the jungle grasses as vicious and protective infants surrounded Delwyn, in no mood to leave him now.

"Are you all right?" Zalzadrin demanded.

"Of course I am. My eyes are a little out of focus sometimes is all. My ankle hurts like blazes, though. I sprained it," he added simply.

Zalzadrin unwrapped the makeshift bandage, grimaced at the purple-yellow bruising, and shook her head. "So your ankle hurts. It does not matter. Head injuries can turn serious. You are going to the healing center."

"Oh, no I'm not. I just need something for the headache and some rest. Phalalin, can you have Tathilatha wave her magic wand over my foot?"

"The healers can heal your ankle for you while they are examining your head injury," Phalalin said.

"I just got home. I'm not going anywhere."

"Yes you are," Hervorallin interrupted. "It is not a long trip by aircraft."

"I am not going," he told her.

"Everybody! Find a spot and lift," Zalzadrin sang from behind him.

Six female arms slid under Delwyn and hoisted him into the air and then onto their shoulders. They veered away from the foremost elleiu tree and headed out into the grassy meadow to the family aircraft.

"I am not going to the hospital!" he roared.

"You are not warleader here, and I am a clan elder," Phelindra said. "Who do you think will win this argument?"

"You cannot win, Delwyn," Phalalin added. "Relax and use the time to compose the song you will sing during your adulthood ceremony. Consider how you will sing to everyone on how you survived the ordeal alone."

"Not so much alone, Phalalin, I slept in a nest with a little brother and a little sister and her infant during the long night."

The infants had been smelling Delwyn nonstop. Clearly they had found the foreign scents marking him. They jabbered to one another about it as females carried Delwyn away from them and toward the waiting aircraft.

"You did? Delwyn, that is extraordinary!"

"I hope they didn't somehow invalidate the ordeal," Delwyn said.

"No, of course they do not. It gives you much to sing about. You did not happen to see anyone else, did you?"

"No, why? I thought something was following me a few times, but I never caught anyone at it. Then I thought maybe some nosey animal had caught my scent. Then up to about a day or so ago I thought it had been a persistent little sib."

"I am not so sure," Phelindra muttered.

Delwyn hesitated, about to ask what she meant when they carried him into the aircraft. The infants piled in after him.

"No! You do not go with him," Phelindra told them.

They looked to Princess and considered her singing complaints. Their pheromones pointed out to everyone that they were determined to go wherever Princess went.

"Hervorallin, perhaps you should remain behind with Princess. Then the others will calm down and wait until we return," Phelindra suggested.

Hervorallin, not pleased, nodded nonetheless and stepped out of the aircraft. At the last second an outraged Princess jumped to the grassy ground and darted back into the aircraft, jumped onto Delwyn and wound her tail around his arm, insistent. He had left her for so long, and she was determined never to allow that again for some time to come.

And the infants refused to leave her. They sang for help from Keba, and he jumped onto Delwyn's chest and wrapped his tail around Delwyn's other arm.

"Good. Problem solved. They don't want me to leave, either. Take me back now, please," Delwyn said.

Adult female and infant female eyes locked as scents flew back and forth.

Females cared for males to obsession, and in the end they all had the same goal.

Someone closed the hatch and banged on the fuselage.

Delwyn felt the VTOL aircraft lift and mentally agreed with Phalalin. He had no chance of winning this argument.

The Comari watched the aircraft lift as she broke into the grassy clearing. The crowd around the aircraft parking area made it clear they had concerns and wanted Delwyn away from here in a hurry. Why? Because of her? No, she had held back out of respect for the O'ni'da families. Then she remembered: the head injury. They would take him to the O'un Tu Clan healing center rather than risk his life.

She should have known. The moment they got a good look at his forehead they would force him to see a healer. Had she considered the possibility, she would have followed him right up to his family.

As it was, she decided to stay here and wait for his return.

The Comari ambled toward Delwyn's immediate and extended family members, conscious of their apprehension.

They turned as one to face her.

Two of the Comara making their home here stepped forward, their males several steps behind them.

The Comari studied them. Delwyn's immediate family members waited patiently.

She smelled their pheromones.

Why are you here? Their scents asked her, suspicion and pleasure mingling in her nose.

<<I have come to see Delwyn O'un Tu La'huaset Eyloni ar ahoun Unahaillaea *Tyreniioroneo,*>> she signed in battle language.

The two Comara took in her state of undress, breathed in her scent, and sighed.

<<You helped him survive the adulthood ordeal?>> they signed.

<<I intercepted him halfway through it. He never saw me,>> she signed back.

<<You helped our clan male?>> they signed, but their scent did not make it the question their signing had.

<<I might have left a trail here, and overturned tuber there, a stick or two scattered here and there. I might have killed twenty-four daylight predators he might have otherwise met.>>

<<You do not wear neckwear or waistwear. You must have intended to help him,>> they persisted.

<<If necessary, yes. But it turned out not to be so,>> she signed.

<<You wear no clan or tribal color patterns. Who are you?>> they asked.

<<I am A'pea Su'tayo Mah'heyo Myat'ti'deep Eyloni.>>

A'pea Lake families, Su'tayo Mah'heyo Clan, Myat'ti'deep Tribal continent People.

<<You are far from home,>> they signed.

<<Yes,>> the Comari agreed.

<<You have scent marked Delwyn.>>

The Comari bit back her shock. Comara did not often refer to any male but their own males by name. They signed the appropriate pronoun along with a change in their scent to identify any male but her own. It was significant that they referred to Delwyn by name.

<<I have,>> she signed, her pheromones leaking hints of annoyed aggression.

<<And yet you are not ready. Why do you come now?>> they persisted.

<<Huntress Kidahin Uahua'asee'a La'huaset Eyloni sought me out. She advised me to look after my interests.>>

Shocked surprise rode the scents on the air, generating sharp intakes of breath from the Comara standing behind them.

<<Do you think the Hunter's interference was warranted?>> they demanded.

The Comari thought about it for a long moment before replying through her pheromones.

Yes!

The Comari's admission caused intense sibilant breathy whispers to sigh from the other Comara as they conversed among themselves in sighs, signs, and body odors. They entertained the idea of bringing Kidahin's interference to the Ti'ratni's notice.

<<What will you do until your time comes?>> they asked.

<<Remain near Delwyn,>> she signed.

She had not signed it as a request.

The two Comara watched her. This fellow Comari had roamed far from home seeking a male compatible with her for when she reached the time her particular biology demanded she adopted a male to protect forever. Eyloni biology had selected the Comara phenotype as a last-ditch effort to preserve at least a few breeding males. Born sterile, the Comara had no reproductive drive to mate in the hopes of giving birth to the rare male, which freed up all their energy for protecting their one male continuously. Social custom recognized the Comara's valuable service and permitted them free rein, or free reign for that matter.

They would have hours and hours of signing in store for one Kidahin Uahua'asee'a La'huaset Eyloni.

<<Certainly, you have found others needing you and matching your temperament?>> they asked.

<<Not many,>> she admitted, <<and none like Delwyn,>> she insisted.

<<Delwyn is a warleader,>> they signed.

<<I know this,>> she shot back, irritated.

<<You would leave Elleio for him?>> they asked, interested.

Few Comara ventured into space true enough, but the very few Comara in space served as a second, one-female warleader special security force for their warleaders. She, the protectress, and warleader special security formed a protective cabal, and they would scheme nonstop over different strategies meant to keep him from harm.

I would, her pheromones sang in their minds.

"What is she doing here?" Verikaralee demanded.

"She is the one who scent marked Delwyn," Hervorallin growled.

"I know that! Did she accompany him throughout the survival ordeal?" Verikaralee asked.

"I do not know, but her nakedness implies she either did, or that she intended to go looking for him had he not returned today."

"She has not reached her time yet, otherwise she would have bonded a male already. What is she doing here now?"

"We can thank Kidahin for that," Hervorallin grumbled.

"Everyone, listen to me," an Elder sang. "This Comari has come from the Su'tayo Mah'heyo Clan of the Myat'ti'deep Tribe searching for Delwyn O'ni'da O'un Tu La'huaset Eyloni. She has not yet reached her bonding time, but she wants to wait for Delwyn above all other males she has found. She will wait for him in his abode until his return."

"Maybe we should call the healing center and ask Phelindra to take him somewhere else," Hervorallin suggested.

"Ha!" a Hunter trilled.

And she was right to laugh, too. Interfering with a Comari was never recommended. Hindering a Comari's bonding was a capital offense against the Ti'ratni, which tended to put the interloper on the wrong end of a knife.

Verikaralee shook her head. "Delwyn may not return for some time. The healing center might keep him under continuous monitoring just because his physiology is so different. They will need his records from your Mistress of Healers. Spirits, they might even call her in to hear her medical opinion. When he leaves the healing center, he will have to meet with the clan elders and Tribal Elders, sing his adulthood ceremony song, and receive his adulthood knife. Melkorka will want to see him just to reassure herself of his health and safety. Then she, Hlinlodyn, and Anailiatha can update him on their warship's repair status. She will certainly tell him about the status change in the battle group."

"Someone should tell Melkorka he is back right now," Hervorallin suggested.

"Someone from your society," Verikaralee amended quickly, "you, for instance."

"*Me?* No thank you. I will wait for Phelindra to do it. She is his Protectress, is the Eldest Huntress aboard our warship, and is a clan elder," Hervorallin objected.

"I would not wait very long if I were you," Verikaralee warned, knowing Melkorka's mercurial nature.

###

Delwyn wanted to leave. His ankle took much longer to regenerate than his broken bones had while aboard *Fearless*, but it felt fine now. In fact, it felt like a heating pad had been wrapped around it, an aftereffect of the accelerated healing.

But the Mistress of Head Trauma refused to let him leave. She admitted him to the medical facility and called Allohindra away from her clan to consult on the matter. They point-to-point quantum translated her to the medical center, and together they had taken eleven full body scans and twenty-two head scans on him.

It was only a smack on the forehead, for goodness sake.

"Just give me a couple of aspirin and send me home with orders for bed rest," he snapped.

The healers ignored him, except for Allohindra. She gave him her best intense frown.

A subtle worrying apprehension began nibbling at his thoughts.

"You have a head injury, a concussion, and you are staying here for a day under medical watch," Phelindra advised.

"You can observe me just as easily in my own abode. We're going. Now," Delwyn said.

Phelindra laughed in his face. "You are going nowhere. I cannot take you from here, and even if I wanted to, I would not. And I do not."

"I can refuse treatment!" he yelled.

Phelindra stared at him through large, slitted eyes. "No, you cannot. A female may refuse medical treatment once she demonstrates her sound mind and her understanding the consequences of her refusal.

"A male admitted to a healing center with evidence of serious injury does not have standing to refuse medical care," she said.

"You're joking! What about my inalienable rights? What if I don't want to stay here?" he demanded.

"What inalienable rights? You have honor and obligation that derive from male autonomy, which are restricted only by matters of courtesy and privacy."

"Now that's what I'm talking about," he nodded vigorously. "I have autonomy. I want to leave now," Delwyn added as his head swam and his vision doubled.

"You owe every female in the world the duty not to die needlessly. The Mistress of Head Trauma commands here. If you continue to resist, she will call upon the sire cairn of surgery. He will consider your failure to obey as a conflict issue and demand you yield to his Warpact command."

"*Warpact?*" Delwyn asked as his head swayed and his chin dipped to the left. "How can a sire cairn have Warpact over a warleader and how can Warpact apply to non-combat events?"

Phelindra's pheromones kicked into overdrive the moment she saw his head pitch left and heard his slurring voice. In the well-ventilated trauma center, her scent would summon aid faster than singing the ten-tone alert.

She had to keep him talking.

"You are a subsequent-arriving male. You belong to us, and you are a much-honored male. Nevertheless, the sire cairn of surgery commands his occupational association here in the same way you commanded us on the Nikkiolo moon and later when you rescued us. Warpact comes into being anytime a conflict exists and more than one male is present. The sire cairn of surgery is the first on-scene male during all medical matters in healing center by definition."

"What conflict?" Delwyn whispered.

"Your refusal of medical services," Phelindra growled with a frighteningly serious intensity.

Allohindra burst into the trauma room, the Mistress of Head Trauma all but climbing Allohindra's tail to get into the room first.

"What has happened?" Allohindra demanded.

"Nothing," Delwyn said. "Tired."

They ignored the muttering male and glared at Phelindra.

"His head is dipping to the left, and his voice carries a slight slur."

Allohindra nodded and exchanged a few words with the Mistress before returning "We think he has been having these episodes on and off since the head injury. A three-hour regeneration is indicated in these matters. Drugs can alleviate concussions like this one, but this injury happened about twenty-three days ago. Minor nerve damage has set in, and scans reveal minor swelling and bruised brain tissue. The only reason he is not worse off is because he ate adequate amounts of ahn'ahn during the long night. I am surprised he found any in the dark and in his condition."

"Delwyn told me he slept for some time with the little brothers and sisters," Phelindra said.

"Really? They probably saved his life," Allohindra said.

"At least now I do not have to call the sire cairn here," the Mistress of Head Trauma snarled. "Allohindra, do you grant consent for his treatment?"

"I do."

"Then let us get him into regeneration. You will have to alter the programming to account for his brain physiology."

"Affirm," Allohindra replied.

###

Hervorallin stood in the bole to Delwyn's abode and sang. "Mistress Comari? May I enter?"

The Comari, staring at Delwyn's sleeping nest, nodded absently before turning to face the Hunter.

<<Your daughter is Delwyn's near-daughter?>>the Comari waggled her fingers.

"Yes," Hervorallin said.

<<Where is your daughter now?>>

"She took the other infants with her and accompanied Delwyn to the healing center."

The Comari smiled a vacant smile, but her eyes remained thoughtful.

<<It is you I owe most dear,>> she signed.

"How do you owe me?" Hervorallin blurted, shocked.

<<Had you not given birth, Delwyn would not be prowling among us.>>

"I am not so sure," Hervorallin admitted. "We thought Kidahin had a mind to chose him regardless, and I think Melkorka might even have gotten a major consensus in accepting Delwyn even if he was ni'zakhon, outside the law."

<<Kidahin again. Spirits. Does she have her tail in everyone's business? No, I think the Be'atika Senge would have declared *Hunter's Moon* ni'zakhon. This way is much better, and I thank you. What have you heard about Delwyn?>> she signed plaintively.

"The O'un Tu Clan healing center has admitted him and has placed him in limited brain regeneration for a moderate concussion. If there are no adverse effects, the healing center should release him early tomorrow.

"He must complete the adulthood ceremony. His family and many of his immediate and extended families members will fly him to the clan gather site. There he will sing about his survival ordeal experiences and receive his adulthood knife from the Tribal Elders in attendance."

<<I will attend Delwyn's adulthood ceremony,>>the Comari signed simply.

Hervorallin perked her ears forward and nodded. "I will advise you as further events develop."

The Comari nodded. Delwyn would not be returning for several more hours. She crawled into his nest and went to sleep, exhausted.

Hours later, she awoke to find herself surrounded by watching infants.

They spoke to her through body odor, detailing their experiences with Delwyn in graphic pheromonal detail.

They told her Delwyn had been quite fierce about wanting to leave the place they kept him.

That made sense to her: *males were strange.*

Each infant contributed her emotional picture surrounding the events they had witnessed, the scents they had sampled. Their mental picture of Allohindra had them all in ugly moods, and they hinted she might have hurt Delwyn more than she helped him.

Dark emotions reeked from the Comari, igniting protective rage in the infants. If Delwyn died, then she planned to pay a visit to the persons the infants' pheromones drew scent pictures of.

Her satisfaction grew. She did not have long to wait now. Delwyn would sing and then receive his adulthood knife within hours of his return.

Thank the Spirits, she whispered.

Delwyn had much more yet to do.

About the Author

David Michael Martin graduated from the Ohio Institute of Technology in 1982 and designed PC-integrated laboratory analyzers until 1987. An avid science fiction and fantasy reader, Mr. Martin successfully wrote and told engaging and entertaining stories as a games master for several of the popular fantasy-roleplaying game systems appearing today.

Mr. Martin returned to college and pursued his interests in English and the humanities at Ohio University and Adams State University.

Mr. Martin has over twenty years' experience tutoring adult basic education classes for adult students seeking their G.E.D. diplomas. Mr. Martin currently lives in western Michigan and trains puppies using Karen Pryor Clicker Training techniques to become guide dogs for the blind.

Honor and Obligation is his second book in the Hunter's Universe saga.

www.ingramcontent.com/pod-product-compliance
Lightning Source LLC
Chambersburg PA
CBHW030419310726
48979CB00009B/1532/J

* 9 7 8 1 9 4 2 6 6 5 0 6 9 *